The Portable

IRISH READER

The Viking Portable Library

Each Portable Library volume is made up of representative works of a favorite modern or classic author, or is a comprehensive anthology on a special subject. The format is designed for compactness and for pleasurable reading. The books average about 700 pages in length. Each is intended to fill a need not hitherto met by any single book. Each is edited by an authority distinguished in his field, who adds a thoroughgoing introductory essay and other helpful material. Most "Portables" are available both in durable cloth and in stiff paper covers.

THE PORTABLE
IRISH READER

Selected and Edited by
DIARMUID RUSSELL

THE VIKING PRESS · NEW YORK

Copyright 1946 by The Viking Press, Inc.

Published by The Viking Press in June 1946

PUBLISHED ON THE SAME DAY IN THE DOMINION OF CANADA
BY THE MACMILLAN COMPANY OF CANADA LIMITED

EIGHTH PRINTING SEPTEMBER 1968

Much of the material in this book is included by special arrangement with the holders of copyright and publication rights, listed on the Acknowledgments pages, and may not be reproduced without their consent. Dramatic rights on the plays included (Dunsany, Gregory, Synge) are controlled by Samuel French, Inc., N. Y. C.

LIBRARY OF CONGRESS CATALOG CARD NUMBER: 46-25223

SET IN WEISS, ELECTRA, AND CALEDONIA TYPES AND
PRINTED IN U. S. A. BY THE COLONIAL PRESS INC.

CONTENTS

INTRODUCTION	*Diarmuid Russell*	xi
IRELAND	*Dora Sigerson Shorter*	1

LETTERS, ESSAYS, AND SPEECHES

LETTER TO ROBERT BRYANTON	*Oliver Goldsmith*	3
GOOD MANNERS: A LETTER	*Jonathan Swift*	7
ADVENTURES IN CONNEMARA: A LETTER	*Maria Edgeworth*	11
ON BICYCLES: A SPEECH	*T. M. Healy*	43
ON THE BOER WAR: A SPEECH	*T. M. Healy*	46
THE BEGINNINGS OF JOYCE	*John Eglinton*	49
ON NEVER GOING TO THE BRITISH MUSEUM	*Robert Lynd*	63

PLAYS

SPREADING THE NEWS	*Lady Gregory*	71
A NIGHT AT AN INN	*Lord Dunsany*	91
RIDERS TO THE SEA	*John M. Synge*	105

POLITICAL ECONOMY

QUESTIONS *from* THE QUERIST	*George Berkeley*	121
THE HOUSE AT WORK	*James Bryce*	123
THOUGHTS *from* THE NATIONAL BEING	*A.E.*	138

FICTION

ANOTHER TEMPLE GONE	*C. E. Montague*	159
TRINKET'S COLT	*E. Œ. Somerville and Martin Ross*	179
THE PRIEST'S SUPPER (*from* HARRY LORREQUER)	*Charles Lever*	196
THE TRAMP	*Liam O'Flaherty*	219
LILACS	*Mary Lavin*	234
A BORN GENIUS	*Seán O'Faoláin*	261
THE WEAVER'S GRAVE	*Seumas O'Kelly*	294
SONG WITHOUT WORDS	*Frank O'Connor*	356

CONTENTS

Mr. Bloom Takes a Walk (*from* Ulysses)	James Joyce	365
Mrs. Johnson	Norah Hoult	387
Schoolfellows	James Stephens	429
Look at All Those Roses	Elizabeth Bowen	437
Lord Arthur Savile's Crime	Oscar Wilde	451

AUTOBIOGRAPHY

Mount Venus (*from* Hail and Farewell)	George Moore	493

HISTORY

Bricriu's Feast	Anonymous (translated from the Irish by George Henderson)	502
The Cattle-Raid of Cooley	Anonymous (translated from the Irish by Dr. Joseph Dunn)	537
The Outlawed Chieftain	Standish O'Grady	594

POETRY

Dark Rosaleen	James Clarence Mangan (*from the Irish of* Costello)	617
Easter 1916	W. B. Yeats	620
By Memory Inspired	Anonymous	622
The Memory of the Dead	John Kells Ingram	624
Aghadoe	John Todhunter	626
O'Hussey's Ode to the Maguire	James Clarence Mangan (*from the Irish of* O'Hussey)	627
Lament of O'Sullivan Bear	Jeremiah Joseph Callanan (*from the Irish*)	630
Lament for the Death of Eoghan Ruadh O'Neill	Thomas Osborne Davis	633
Clonmacnoise	T. W. Rolleston (*from the Irish of* Angus O'Gillan)	635
The County Mayo	James Stephens (*from the Irish of* Raftery)	636
Adieu to Belashanny	William Allingham	637
Corrymeela	Moira O'Neill	641

CONTENTS

THE NAMELESS DOON	William Larminie	642
THE CRAB TREE	Oliver St. John Gogarty	643
PANGUR BÁN	Robin Flower (from the Irish)	645
A POOR SCHOLAR OF THE FORTIES	Padraic Colum	645
THE VILLAGE SCHOOLMASTER	Oliver Goldsmith	647
THE VILLAGE PREACHER	Oliver Goldsmith	648
ON A CURATE'S COMPLAINT OF HARD DUTY	Jonathan Swift	649
THE RAKES OF MALLOW	Anonymous	650
GALWAY RACES	Anonymous	651
A GLASS OF BEER	James Stephens	653
THE OUTLAW OF LOUGH LENE	Jeremiah Joseph Callanan (from the Irish)	653
I SHALL NOT DIE FOR THEE	Douglas Hyde (from the Irish)	654
SONG	William Congreve	655
FALSE THOUGH SHE BE	William Congreve	656
THE WOMAN OF THREE COWS	James Clarence Mangan (from the Irish)	657
"BALLYVOURNEY"	Thomas Boyd	659
MEETING	W. B. Yeats	660
MY GRIEF ON THE SEA	Douglas Hyde (from the Irish)	661
DEAR DARK HEAD	Sir Samuel Ferguson (from the Irish)	662
MY HOPE, MY LOVE	Edward Walsh (from the Irish)	663
THE SHEEP	Seumas O'Sullivan	663
FOUR DUCKS ON A POND	William Allingham	664
THE MEDITATION OF THE OLD FISHERMAN	W. B. Yeats	665
ODE	Arthur O'Shaughnessy	665
I SAW FROM THE BEACH	Thomas Moore	666
OUTCAST	A.E.	667
SHE COMES NOT WHEN NOON IS ON THE ROSES	Herbert Trench	668
THE OLD WOMAN	Joseph Campbell	668
PROMISE	A.E.	669
A CRADLE SONG	Padraic Colum	670

ACKNOWLEDGMENTS

Thanks are due to the following publishers and holders of copyright who have given me permission to include material in this book:

Alfred A. Knopf, Inc., New York, and Jonathan Cape, Ltd., London, for the story "Look at All Those Roses" taken from the short story collection of the same name by Elizabeth Bowen. Copyright 1941 by Elizabeth Bowen.

The Macmillan Company, New York, for the chapter "The House at Work" taken from *The American Commonwealth* by James Bryce.

S.D. Campbell for Joseph Campbell's "The Old Woman."

Padraic Colum for his poems "A Cradle Song" and "A Poor Scholar of the Forties."

Professor Tom Peete Cross for the right to use his shortened version of Dr. Dunn's translation of the *Táin bó Cúalnge*.

Dr. Joseph Dunn for *The Cattle-Raid of Cooley*, being a shortened version taken from his book *The ancient Irish epic tale Táin bó Cúalnge "The Cúalnge cattle-raid" now for the first time done entire into English out of the Irish of the book of Leinster and allied manuscripts* published by David Nutt (A.G. Berry), London 1914.

Lord Dunsany for his play *A Night at an Inn*.

Florence V. Barry and Jonathan Cape, Ltd., London, for the letter by Maria Edgeworth.

The Macmillan Company, New York, for the essay "The Beginnings of Joyce" taken from the book *Irish Literary Portraits* by John Eglinton.

Constable & Co., Ltd., London, for the poem "Pangur Bán."

Oliver St. John Gogarty for his poem "The Crab Tree."

G.P. Putnam's Sons, New York, and Putnam & Co., Ltd., London, for the play *Spreading the News* by Lady Gregory.

The Irish Texts Society for the translation of *Bricriu's Feast* by George Henderson.

Norah Hoult for the story "Mrs. Johnson" taken from the book *Poor Women* by that author.

Dr. Douglas Hyde for the poems "My Grief on the Sea" and "I Shall Not Die for Thee."

Random House, Inc., New York, and John Lane, The Bodley Head Ltd., London, for the chapter "Mr. Bloom Takes a Walk" taken from the book *Ulysses* by James Joyce. Copyright 1914, 1918, 1942, 1946 by Norah Joseph Joyce.

ACKNOWLEDGMENTS

Russell & Volkening, Inc., New York, for the story "Lilacs" taken from the book *Tales from Bective Bridge* by Mary Lavin.

Methuen & Co., Ltd., London, for the essay "On Never Going to the British Museum" taken from the book *The Blue Lion* by Robert Lynd.

Chatto & Windus, London, and Doubleday & Company, Inc., New York, for the story "Another Temple Gone" by C.E. Montague taken from the book *Fiery Particles* by that author. Copyright 1926 by Doubleday, Doran & Company, Inc.

Appleton-Century-Crofts, Inc., New York, for the excerpt "Mount Venus" taken from the book *Hail and Farewell* by George Moore. Copyright 1911 by D. Appleton & Company.

Alfred A. Knopf, Inc., New York, and Harold Matson for the story "Song Without Words" taken from the book *Crab Apple Jelly* by Frank O'Connor. Copyright 1944 by Alfred A. Knopf, Inc.

The Viking Press, Inc., New York, for the story "A Born Genius" taken from the book *A Purse of Coppers* by Seán O'Faoláin. Copyright 1938 by The Viking Press, Inc.

Harcourt, Brace & Company, Inc., New York, and Jonathan Cape, Ltd., London, for the story "The Tramp" taken from the book *Spring Sowing* by Liam O'Flaherty.

P. J. Kenedy & Sons, New York, and Ernest Benn, Ltd., London, for the story "The Outlawed Chieftain" taken from the book *The Bog of Stars* by Standish O'Grady.

Michael O'Kelly for the story "The Weaver's Grave" by Seumas O'Kelly.

Moira O'Neill for the poem "Corrymeela."

Seumas O'Sullivan for the poem "The Sheep."

Maud Rolleston for the poem "Clonmacnoise" by T.W. Rolleston.

Diarmuid Russell and Macmillan & Co., Ltd., London, for the poems "Promise" and "Outcast" by A.E. and for the chapters taken from the book *The National Being* by A.E. (G.W. Russell).

Doris Long for the poem "Ireland" by Dora Sigerson Shorter.

Dr. E. Œ. Somerville and Longmans, Green & Co., Ltd., London, for the story "Trinket's Colt" taken from the book *The Experiences of an Irish R.M.* by E. Œ. Somerville and Martin Ross.

The Macmillan Company, New York, and Macmillan & Co., Ltd., London, for the poems "The County Mayo" and "A Glass of Beer" and for the story "Schoolfellows" taken from the book *Etched in Moonlight* by James Stephens.

Random House, Inc., New York, and Denis Synge Stephens for the play *Riders to the Sea* by J.M. Synge.

ACKNOWLEDGMENTS

D.P. Trench for the poem "She Comes Not When Noon Is on the Roses" by Herbert Trench.

Vyvyan Holland for the story "Lord Arthur Savile's Crime" by Oscar Wilde.

The Macmillan Company, New York, The Macmillan Company of Canada, Ltd., Toronto, and A.P. Watt & Son, London, for the poems "Easter 1916," "Meeting," and "The Meditation of the Old Fisherman" by W.B. Yeats.

I would like here to express my gratitude to Miss Patience Ross, without whose assistance this work would have taken twice as long to complete. Many of the permissions, some not easy to trace, had to be sought for in England and Ireland and her aid was a considerable lightening of a task that often proved annoyingly tedious.

INTRODUCTION

WHEN the Roman legions swept out over Europe they brought more with them than arms. They brought a culture that obliterated the native customs and the native languages of the peoples they conquered. The Roman culture was almost as powerful as the armies that preceded it. Less than a century after Vercingetorix was killed, Romanized Gauls were excelling in the art of Roman oratory. By the sixth century all traces of the Gaulish language had disappeared. Only those countries on the periphery of the Continent, those outside the influence of the Roman Empire, were able to preserve their nationality and customs. Of these countries only three received the art of letters early enough to be able to leave some record of their life—the Irish, the Icelanders, and the Anglo-Saxons. Of these three primitive literatures the Irish, so most authorities believe, is the earliest.

It is difficult to find out how early the Irish had a written language. One Ethicus of Istria, a traveller in the fourth century, reports that he made a trip to Ireland to examine the books written by native Irish scholars. Nothing this old is in existence though it is known that occasional Irish scholars had learned the art of writing from Roman sources. It is generally held that the written language came into Ireland with St. Patrick and his companions in the fifth century and what manuscript documents that have survived the passage of time date from the fifth century on. These are in the Latin language. It was another two centuries before the Irish language appears, during which time the Roman letters were transformed into characteristic Irish script.

The entrance of St. Patrick into Ireland brought not only Christianity but also all the learned scholarship of the religious orders. The Irish received both the religion and the scholarship with eagerness so that by the time the sixth century had arrived Ireland was the great centre of learning in Europe, the island of saints and scholars, the land that Dr. Johnson in a memorable letter called "the quiet habitation of sanctity and literature." We have direct evidence in the words of Bede as to the lure of the island. He writes that "many of the nobles of the English nation and lesser men also had set out thither, forsaking their native island either for the grace of sacred learning or a more austere life. And some of them indeed soon dedicated themselves faithfully to the monastic life, others rejoiced rather to give themselves to learning, going about from one master's cell to another. All these the Irish willingly received, and saw to it to supply them with food day by day without cost, and books for their studies, and teaching, free of charge." For several centuries visitors came to the monastic schools from all over Europe—even from as far away as Egypt—and the monks in their turn went out to many lands, bringing with them the scholarship and religious zeal of which Ireland was the great European repository.

Many of the early manuscripts that have come down to us from this period are, like the celebrated *Book of Kells,* religious writings, copies of the Gospels, lives of the Saints; but a multitude of these early works deal with the pre-Christian era. Frequently these writings were gathered together in miscellaneous form to make a book, often the property of some well-known family. They were evidently regarded as objects of value for there are records that they were on occasions used to ransom some captured chieftain. While much of this literature is miscellaneous, being random annals, stories, or poems, many of the documents group themselves into classes. One group consists of accounts of early invasions and

INTRODUCTION

attempts to colonize Ireland. Another set of stories centre around Finn and his band of soldiers and a third group, most famous of all, deal with Cuchulain and the warriors of the Red Branch of Ulster.

It is estimated that the stories dealing with Finn relate to a period about A.D. 200 and that those dealing with Cuchulain refer to a period some two hundred years earlier, just about the time of the birth of Christ. How much is fact and how much fiction is a matter for historians. Douglas Hyde remarks that manuscripts dealing with events as far back as the middle of the fourth century have been proved accurate, even to the day and hour, when they refer to natural events such as comets and eclipses, and he infers the accuracy probably also extends to the other matters dealt with. In general the early recorders seemed to be honest and we must assume, even where checking is impossible, that there is a substantial body of fact in those documents that deal with events prior to the fourth century. Tighearnach, an annalist who died in 1088, who presumably had access to many documents now lost or destroyed, remarked that after investigation he believed records relating to events prior to 300 B.C. could not be regarded as true but that records relating to events after that date contained a fair body of truth.

One must also take into consideration the fact that these documents dealing with pre-Christian Ireland were written many centuries after, most of them between the eleventh and fourteenth centuries. It might be speculated that tales passed down orally from one generation to another would be subject to much distortion and it is true that in many cases several versions of the one story are in existence. The difference however seems to be more in detail than in essentials. Hyde puts forward some evidence to show that story-tellers, a special class, were taught stories in a highly condensed form and that each story-teller, in relating a story, embroidered the essential facts with detail of his own imagination.

The group of stories that centre around the Red Branch are by far the most fascinating of these early tales. These legends are little known and except for the story of Deirdre, told in novel form by James Stephens and used for several plays, almost the entire cycle remains an untouched field for the exploring writer. In this group there is a magnificent epic, the *Cattle-Raid of Cooley* (*Táin bó Cúalnge*), which might well be compared to the *Iliad*. It starts with Maeve, Queen of Connaught, talking in bed with her husband and discovering, to her great mortification, that they were equal in goods save that her husband had one bull, a famous bull, more than she had. To make things equal she sallies out to capture a famous bull in Ulster and so precipitates all the famous doings which end in the single-handed defence of Ulster by Cuchulain. The *Táin* is full of humour and heroism and has many resemblances in mood to the *Iliad*. As in that epic mysterious powers ally themselves with the warriors or else act against them, and like the *Iliad* the remarks of people on one side about those on the other are free from the venomous attacks of modern propaganda. Warriors in this ancient epic exalt their enemies and show a nobility that seems to have departed from modern battle. These early legends deserve more attention and need to be made more available for, just as ancient architecture provides inspiration for modern buildings, so might a study of these provide a new mood for contemporary Irish literature.

Ancient warfare being no less destructive than modern warfare to life and scholarship, the attacks of the

INTRODUCTION

Vikings that started in the eighth century and carried on intermittently until their final defeat in the eleventh century resulted in the loss by burning of many of the early writings. And no sooner were the Vikings defeated than a greater and more powerful enemy appeared on the scene, the English.

With the entrance of Strongbow into Ireland in 1170 there followed continuous and devastating battles for some 500 years so that, as Hyde laments, there was almost nothing original written in Ireland till the middle of the sixteenth century. How ruinous were the battles that swept over Ireland can be gathered from the historians of the time. One remarked on the multitudes of people dead in the ditches, their mouths stained with the green of nettles and docks, and the Four Masters reported towards the end of the sixteenth century that "the lowing of a cow or the voice of a ploughman could scarcely be heard from Dunqueen in the West of Kerry to Cashel." The customary practice of the time was to burn all buildings and crops in the fields and leave the people to starve. Under such circumstances nobody prospered, writers least of all.

St. Patrick and his comrades when they had come to Ireland had brought over the written word as well as Christianity. The English when they came over brought not only arms but a new language, English, and with the new language began a new era in Irish literature, the Anglo-Irish, the works of Irish writers who wrote in the English language.

This new era coincided almost exactly with the final battles which assured to the English government their victory over Ireland. By 1700 Ireland had been crushed and though there was from then on a continuous history of uprisings and rebellions these were more nuisances than threats to English domination. Physical force had triumphed but the battle merely moved into another sphere. In 1698 one of the earliest of Anglo-Irish works appeared, Molyneux's denunciation of the commercial injustice done to Ireland by English laws. The work was offensive to the English government and was ordered to be burnt by the common hangman.

History indeed is full of ironies; and English pressure to make Ireland conform to English standards, to replace Catholicism with the Protestant religion, to cause the use of the English language rather than the Irish, brought about unforeseen results. The religious pressure in the end turned Ireland into one of the most Catholic countries in the world, religious convictions being hard to eradicate. The Irish language, though not easy to root up, was not so resistant as religion. It might be said that in 1700 everyone in Ireland spoke Irish. In 1825 it was estimated about 500,000 used Irish exclusively and that about another 1,000,000 used it among themselves, though knowing enough English to carry on commercial transactions. By 1910 the use of the Irish language was confined to remote coastal regions and for practical purposes could be said to be extinct. Two centuries of pressure, aided by the pressure of commerce, had got rid of the native tongue.

If it had been hoped that the use of the English language would bring about an English habit of thinking, that there was a connection between the thought and the tongue, that hope was never realized. It was not only not realized but from Molyneux on a large part of Irish literature is the literature of oppression and complaint. The English had not only done injustice to Ireland but they also, and very conveniently, gave them the language in which they could cry their wrongs to the world. If they had left the Irish language alone the world, of necessity, would have heard less about Ireland.

Prior to the English domination of Ireland there was really no such thing as national feeling. Local feelings there were in quantity. Every Irish chieftain had his own little kingdom, was willing to fight to defend or enlarge it. None had been powerful enough to have welded the whole country into unity. The literature in the Irish language prior to English domination is a literature of nature, of battles, of histories—but not of conscious nationality. It was the English conquest that produced that sense of unity and it was in the English language that it was expressed to the world in the Drapier letters of Swift, the poems of Mangan and Moore, the speeches of Parnell and O'Connell. The early Irish writings are Irish by reason of character but the Anglo-Irish literature is flooded with the sense of nationality and race, of a proud past, of national heroes, of injustices done, of wrongs that would have to be righted. There was a sense of unity in the Irish mind that had never existed before.

From 1700 to 1900 the Anglo-Irish writers appeared about as sporadically as the rebellions and during this period appear Swift, Sterne, Berkeley, Congreve, Burke, Sheridan, Mangan, and many other poets, the novelists Lever and Lover. It might be conjectured that the uneven flow of writers was due to the still disturbed conditions of the country. Uprisings, famines, and commercial discrimination did away with serenity and though conditions were better than those which had existed prior to 1700 they were hardly good enough for writers. There seems good reason why many of those writers in this period were able to write. Berkeley and Swift had the security of the church. Burke, Sheridan, Congreve, and Goldsmith lived in England.

It was not until the beginning of the twentieth century that writers in quantity began to appear, and when they came, they came in such quantity that for a period of some twenty-five years Ireland produced more literary names of note than any other country in the world. Shaw in England, Joyce in France, Synge, Yeats, A.E., Lady Gregory, George Moore, James Stephens, all erupted into activity. The Abbey Theatre came into being and a host of dramatists arose, Lennox Robinson, St. John Ervine, Brinsley Macnamara, Seán O'Casey, and many others.

The reason for this outburst is hard to explain. Fifty years of comparative peace probably had something to do with it. Perhaps it was a kind of transmuted nationality. The last rebellion of any note had been that of 1798 though abortive outbreaks like that of Robert Emmet in 1800 were scattered through the first half of the nineteenth century. In addition the scholars had been at work delving into the Irish past. Douglas Hyde, Standish O'Grady, Kuno Meyer, Whitley Stokes, Eleanor Hull, and Richard Best were at work translating the ancient Irish literature. It may have been this sudden discovery of a heroic past allied to a nascent nationalism that lit a spark in Irish minds. Whatever the reason Ireland was once more, if only for a short period, the great literary centre of the world.

It is probably a useless speculation to wonder what political relations between the two countries would have been if the Irish language had been left alone. It is certain that literature in the English language would have been the loser. The long and splendid stream of English literature has been enriched by the contributions of Irish writers who, though they had been deprived of their language, had probably gained. Not only had a sense of national consciousness given dignity to their work but the new language had given them access to one of the most magnificent of literatures.

INTRODUCTION

I hesitate to say that Irish names in world literature would have been less important if they had not had the use of the English language. But there is no reason to suppose that more would have passed into world thought than has come from other small countries like Denmark and Holland. Translation is a screen through which not all writers can pass.

The complete failure of the English language to carry with it English thought is well testified to by Anglo-Irish literature—as it is indeed also testified to by American literature. The words written by the Irish carry not only a different national feeling but also distinctive habits of thought. English writings, from Shakespeare on, are filled with a curious sense of majesty and power and security, as if the English people by intuition were aware of their destiny in the world. There is also a faint sense of insolence and smugness in much English work. Is it the character of the comfortably-off man who is hardly aware of how other people struggle? England had not been invaded since 1066 and even in Shakespeare's time Englishmen could look back for centuries to security from external aggression and could look across the Channel to a Continent hardly ever free from wars. I can only surmise that England's geographical position played a part in the formation of national character. The sense of satisfaction with their own country, the good-humoured tolerant contempt for other countries often creeps into English writings and I think this feeling must have had some connection with the restless waters that parted them from their enemies in Europe.

The English proved more intelligent than the Irish and more adaptable. They soon perceived the advantages of the sea and turned into a sea-faring race, making of the waters around their island a barrier that to this day has not been penetrated by an invading force since the early Norman invasion. To the Irish the sea merely proved a source of invasion, a well-travelled path over which came the Viking ships and the English soldiers. Up to the beginning of the eighteenth century the country had been nothing but a battle-ground for almost a thousand years and from then on, for two hundred years, the country was poverty-stricken, racked with famine.

Perhaps it was just this severity of existence that brought into Irish writings that sense of comedy which seems to me its most marked characteristic. It seems to matter little whether the subject is one of sadness or marked for tragedy. Everywhere in Irish prose there twinkles and peers the merry eye and laugh of a people who had little to laugh about in real life. Swift's humour is savage, Synge's is tragic, Stephens's is impish, Wilde's sophisticated, and Lever has the schoolboy touch, but they all share the common characteristic of using humour to achieve their ends. The only offset to unhappiness is happiness and it was probably some divine law of compensation that gave to the Irish the ability to squeeze laughter out of an existence from which they could extract little else.

If humour seems a necessary ingredient of Irish writings it has missed, so far, dealing with a theme which has not failed to engross the writers of other countries. Love or passion is an elemental topic writers in all countries have dealt with. The Irish have not missed this subject but they have missed that small boy curiosity in sex, that prurience that produces the sniggering allusion in many English writers. One might suspect here the influence of religion on a strongly Catholic country if it were not that many, if not most, of the Anglo-Irish writers were Protestants. The literature of France, itself a Catholic country, would disprove the fact that religion was the factor. The only Irish writers who have been disposed to treat of sex in a sportive way were those who lived in England, Congreve and Sterne and Wilde, and I think we must assume that sex, treated in this manner, is either urban or cosmopolitan in character. Irish literature as a whole is remarkably chaste and I assume this has some connection with the fact that the country has never developed the highly sophisticated culture and manners of a great city.

Indeed, as a generalization, it might be said that the difference between English and Irish writings is, among other things, the difference between sophistication and the lack of it. England as a great power with a huge city had a ceaseless come and go, people with many trades and interests, an influx of foreigners; and all these tend to sharpen the wits, to burnish the intellect, to create a wider range for the mind. It would have been unlikely in the Ireland of the past for a Maugham or an Aldous Huxley to have arisen. These are the products of a great urban civilization dealing with the people and problems of that civilization—and these in most cases are several stages removed from the problems of the Irish people. Galsworthy might write of the Forsytes, a family preoccupied with the making of money, with their external prestige and their internal family quarrels. Irish writers could hardly have dealt with a subject like this. The people they wrote about existed in a state of poverty or near-poverty, preoccupied with food and the roof over their heads and the elementals of living. This is perhaps an exaggeration of affairs as they used to be for there were many people who got along comfortably. But there were enough of the other kind so that no one could be unaffected by their state. The tragedies of Irish writings are less likely to be those of the divorce court than of starvation or death itself.

For a country that has always had a strong sense of tradition it is astonishing how little Irish writers have delved into the past as a subject for books. Their work has almost always been contemporary and yet the history of the country is filled with extravagant deeds and strange characters. Standish O'Grady did one magnificent novel, *The Flight of the Eagle*, about the Elizabethan era in Ireland and a number of shorter tales, but with this exception the Irish past is an untouched field. Multitudes of historical novels and biographies of historical characters appear in America. The history of the country seems important to us and seems to bear some relation to the future. Yet Ireland has a history of at least equal richness, filled with political manœuvrings interlinked with European affairs, thronged with brave actions and wild battles, and through all these scenes moves a multitude of members of the ancient Irish clans, wild, proud, untamed, and fearless. Garrett, eleventh Earl of Kildare, from the time he was twelve, was harried all over the Continent for seventeen years by the far-reaching power of the English government until he was restored to his title. An earlier Earl of Kildare, the eighth, on trial in England before the King, was accused among other things of having burnt the church at Cashel. With the Archbishop of Cashel listening he bluntly replied he had burned it because he thought the archbishop was in it. These are suitable characters to rescue from the past.

So far, both in prose and plays, Irish writings have been mainly about the small farmer and the villager, and though this can be justified by the fact that these were indeed the bulk of the Irish people, I would like to see some of the odd characters of the past brought to life.

INTRODUCTION xxiii

What writer would not be attracted by the Lord of Leitrim, Brian of the Ramparts, called "the proudest man who walks upon the earth today." And with another, one O'Flaherty, who when asked by what title he held his lands, answered straightly, "By the sword, man. What shall I say else?" The conventionality and timidity of modern life was not in these people and their fearlessness is worth preserving.

Perhaps this historical gap will now be filled up. The strong mood of national consciousness caused by the domination of an alien power is now no longer necessary and without that external pressure I doubt that writers will have that internal flame of nationality that fired so many writers of the past. The most promising of the younger Irish writers, Mary Lavin, though possessed of a powerful and magnificent talent, resembles the Victorians in her work and in no way gives a clue as to what the mood of future Irish writing will be. It yet remains to be seen what the interacting forces of national government, of the attempt to revive the Irish language, and of the onrushing sweep of scientific progress will produce. From having been, in a sense, removed from the great struggles that have shaken the world twice in a generation Ireland will probably be, by the medium of the aeroplane and other inventions, moved into close contact with the rest of the world and its problems. It will be this participation in the world, I suspect, rather than what happens domestically, that will dictate the new mood of Irish writers to come.

I would like to make it clear that this collection of Irish writings is not all-inclusive, that it does not contain selections from all Irish writers of merit. Surprisingly large as is the space offered by this compact volume it is still not large enough to anthologize in any comprehensive fashion the literature of a country. The job of doing so, to bring the case closer home, would be exceedingly difficult with American literature, yet Ireland has as many famous men of letters as has this country and has, in addition, as I have earlier shown, a literary history that extends far back before the discovery of this continent.

What I have tried to do, since complete coverage was impossible, is to take a sampling of authors from different periods and of different talents—and to give each adequate space. I have tried not to be influenced in favour of poetry, or of plays, or of fiction as against other kinds of writing. All the works chosen, except those dear and familiar to me, have been read several times—and so have many works which were contenders. Many of the decisions were difficult to make but from the point of view of balance and readability these decisions had to be made. So, while I have no excuses to make for what is here contained, I do have apologies to tender to many eminent men of letters who have been left out and some explanations to give as to the reasons for selection and omission.

Primarily I was plagued by a plethora of playwrights and many of the absences belong to this group. The three short plays selected were ones I wished to have. Lord Dunsany's play and Synge's *Riders to the Sea* are so well known that no explanation is necessary for their inclusion. Lady Gregory's play could have been equalled, or even excelled, by many others but I could not conceive of any Irish anthology that would not be the worse by her absence. She was the warm-hearted friend of many Irish writers, the encourager of the Abbey Theatre and of all young talent, and it would have been impossible for me, having known of the part she

INTRODUCTION xxv

played, not to have included something by her in this collection. But, in spite of the fact that a better play could have been found, not much apology is needed for *Spreading the News*. It is an excellent example of her work, deftly planned, readable—and it must be remembered that not all plays are readable—and altogether representative of her contributions to the Abbey repertoire.

But observe what happens to the anthologist when once decisions are made. With three plays chosen I had all the plays this collection could stand if it was going to have any balance. So Seán O'Casey, Vincent Carroll, Lennox Robinson, Brinsley Macnamara, St. John Ervine, and a whole host of able Abbey dramatists had to be omitted. I have nothing but apologies to make to these writers. It would have been easy to have chosen three good plays from this group. It just happened that my choice fell elsewhere and was to some degree influenced by my desire for short plays. One other well known Irish playwright is missing—George Bernard Shaw. The explanation here is simple. He refused permission in a courteous letter on the grounds that he didn't think it was good business for authors to be represented in anthologies. He may well be right for authors as famous as himself.

It will be noted that Sterne is missing—for the reason that I could find nothing of suitable length that I liked. Admirers of Sterne must excuse me. Lover is absent but Lever is present. These two authors wrote in somewhat similar moods and with space a consideration one had to go. Banim, Carleton, and Griffin have also been omitted. They would have had their place in a more comprehensive work, if only to give a chronological perspective of Irish literature, but their writings are patchy and often dreary and make little claim to attention these days. Burke and Sheridan, it will be noticed, are not here. The speeches, though deservedly famous, are not only long but they also need a commentary to make the reader aware of the times and background. For the same reason many other famous Irish orators have been omitted—Parnell, O'Connell, and others who spoke up for Irish freedom.

It will be seen that I had far more than I could use and while it is unfortunate that I had to pick and choose, that no matter what I did some author was going to be slighted, there may be compensation in the fact that this automatically has made this selection more personal. When space is limited personal prejudices come into action, and this collection at least has the unity of my own likes and dislikes.

In the selection of material I found myself more than once confronted with dilemmas. Just as the plays chosen meant that other playwrights had to be left out, so it happened, more than once, that some story chosen meant that some other author's story had to be passed over. For example, the story of Seumas O'Kelly, *The Weaver's Grave,* was a must for me. I think it is one of the most engaging and skilful stories written in the last fifty years. The author, in my opinion, never equalled this work and though on the long side nothing else of his could have been chosen. This selection immediately knocked out my first choice for Mary Lavin. In her recent novel, *The House in Clewe Street,* there was a masterpiece of an incident, a race between two funerals, that I wished to use. But the O'Kelly story also dealt with graves and a funeral and it seemed to me one long story on this subject was enough. And as O'Kelly could not otherwise be adequately represented Miss Lavin has to have another story chosen, which, though

INTRODUCTION

not first choice, will, I hope, show with what talent she is endowed.

On most of the works here included I need to make no comment. The authors' names are mostly well known and their work will speak for itself. The only speeches selected are two oddities. Mr. Healy, late Governor General of Ireland, was at one time an Irish member of the English Parliament at a time when that minority group, supposedly spokesmen for Irish needs, were being brushed aside in most matters of Irish legislation. Not unnaturally this treatment irked them and some revenge was taken in gadfly attacks on English mentality and English problems. The worst gadfly unquestionably was Healy who had a legal mind of a high order and a tongue which few cared to face. Though these speeches have long been buried in Hansard they still carry their bite and humour with them over the years and are rightly well remembered by connoisseurs of Parliamentary orations.

The Maria Edgeworth letter I think better than any of her fiction and it gives a rather unusual picture of the West of Ireland in the middle of the last century. Implicit in that letter too is the picture of a courageous old lady, for Miss Edgeworth was in her sixties when she made the trip. The selections from A.E.'s *The National Being* and from Berkeley's *The Querist* seem to me to have more than merely Irish interest though both books were written about Irish problems. In both cases the authors' minds could not be constrained to think of national problems in a narrowly national manner. The chapter from Bryce's *The American Commonwealth* will, I hope, persuade many to read that work. Though published fifty years ago most of the comments still seem to me true and the facts which are now out of date are no obstacle to reading. The book is a masterpiece of shrewd, statesmanlike thinking with a most astonishing understanding of American political institutions as related to American character.

Robert Lynd is an essayist whose considerable merits have almost been overlooked because he has done his work so well. Week in, week out, for years he has been doing essays under the pseudonym Y.Y. for a weekly journal in England. They have all been on such a high level, the intelligence has been so masked by humour, that they have been taken for granted. Yet it seems to me that the best of Lynd's essays will stand comparison with the long line of English essayists.

The two Irish text translations should be of interest for they represent a picture of early Ireland in pre-Christian days. *The Cattle-Raid of Cooley* I have referred to earlier in this introduction. The version I use is the translation made by Dr. Joseph Dunn which has to some degree been condensed by Professor Tom Peete Cross. *Bricriu's Feast* seems to me a first-rate story, full of humour and character. It also illustrates a kind of archæological value that these old stories have. Posidonius, a friend of Cicero, coming back from a trip to Central Europe about 100 B.C., made a comment about the rites and ceremonies connected with "the heroes bit." Now the Celts of Ireland most probably came from Central Europe, carrying with them the old customs, and though Posidonius said little about "the heroes bit" *Bricriu's Feast* gives a full account of the old custom. It is a kind of peep-hole into Europe when it was under Roman domination.

The poems in this collection, like the prose selections, need no comments to make them enjoyable. However I would like to point out that many of them are translations from the Irish and are so marked. Some of them are from very early times and some date from much later periods. For example *Pangur Ban* is a translation by Robin Flower of a manuscript found in the monastery of St. Paul in Carinthia, dating approximately from the ninth century, reminding us how far afield the Irish monks travelled. All the Mangan poems are translations. The ode to the Maguire is a translation from the poem written by O'Hussey, bard to the Maguires of Fermanagh, in the sixteenth century. Raftery, whom Yeats has written about, was a blind musician living in Mayo in the eighteenth century. There are still many thousands of untranslated poems lying in the archives of libraries and other institutions that for the poet with a knowledge of Irish represent a wonderfully fertile field.

In regard to who was Irish and so eligible for this collection I have taken a rather broad point of view. In general I have merely required that the author be born in Ireland and have not taken the view of one purist who told me that no writer was Irish unless Catholic by religion, who did not speak and write in the Irish language, and was not Irish for uncounted generations. Such a definition or even any variant of it would have entailed the kind of research work of which I am not capable.

There are, however, two writers who do not even meet my modest qualifications. Mary Lavin was born in America of Irish emigrants and so is American. But she returned to Ireland at the age of ten, has lived there since, and has written almost entirely of the Irish scene. C. E. Montague's inclusion makes me blush slightly— but only slightly. I have long been accustomed to see Irish authors referred to in reference books as "English author of Irish birth" even though the author may never have left the country in which he was born. It was with considerable glee that I saw Montague, one of my favourite writers, referred to in a reference book as "Irish author born in England." That was enough for me and since the story chosen was about Ireland I took it with thanks, feeling I had a good case for his inclusion—even if it might not stand a legal test.

The arrangement follows a conventional pattern in the belief that no reader of anthologies reads through from page one to the end but dips and samples here and there. If there are such consistent readers I can point out to them that an attempt at arrangement by mood has been made in the case of the two longest sections—fiction and poetry—and that I have attempted to make the various groups follow one another in such a manner as to make continuous reading most varied. I hope, no matter what style of reading may be adopted, that there is enough here to amuse and entertain.

DIARMUID RUSSELL

DORA SIGERSON SHORTER

Ireland

'Twas the dream of a God,
    And the mould of His hand,
That you shook 'neath His stroke,
That you trembled and broke
    To this beautiful land.

Here He loosed from His hold
    A brown tumult of wings,
Till the wind on the sea
Bore the strange melody
    Of an island that sings.

He made you all fair,
    You in purple and gold,
You in silver and green,
Till no eye that has seen
    Without love can behold.

I have left you behind
    In the path of the past,
With the white breath of flowers,
With the best of God's hours,
    I have left you at last.

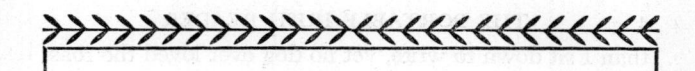

LETTERS, ESSAYS, AND SPEECHES

OLIVER GOLDSMITH

Letter to Robert Bryanton

Edinburgh, Sepr. ye 26th 1753

MY DEAR BOB

How many good excuses (and you know I was ever good at an excuse) might I call up to vindicate my past shamefull silence. I might tell how I wrote a long letter at my first comeing hither, and seem vastly angry at not receiveing an answer; or I might alledge that business, (with business, you know I was always pester'd) had never given me time to finger a pen; but I supress these and twenty more, equally plausible & as easily invented, since they might all be attended with a slight inconvenience of being known to be lies; let me then speak truth; An hereditary indolence (I have it from the Mothers side) has hitherto prevented my writing to you, and still prevents my writing at least twenty five letters more, due to my friends in Ireland—no turnspit gets up into his wheel with more reluctance, than I sit down to write, yet no dog ever loved the roast meat he turns, better than I do him I now address; yet what shall I say now I am enter'd? Shall I tire you with a description of this unfruitfull country? where I must lead you over their hills all brown with heath, or their valleys scarce able to feed a rabbet? Man alone seems to be the only creature who has arived to the naturall size in this poor soil; every part of the country presents the same dismall landscape, no grove nor brook lend their musick to cheer the stranger, or make the inhabitants forget their poverty; yet with all these disadvantages to call him down to humility, a scotchman is one of the proudest things alive. The poor have pride ever ready to releive them; if mankind shou'd happen to despise them, they are masters of their own admiration; and that they can plentifully bestow on themselves: from their pride and poverty as I take it results one advantage this country enjoys, namely the Gentlemen here are much better bred then among us; no such character here as our Fox-hunter; and they have expresed great surprize when I informed them that some men of a thousand pound a year in Ireland spend their whole lives in runing after a hare, drinking to be drunk, and geting every Girl with Child, that will let them; and truly if such a being, equiped in his hunting dress, came among a circle of scots Gentlemen, they wou'd behold him with the same astonishment that a Country man does King George on horseback; the men here have Gennerally high cheek bones, and are lean, and swarthy; fond of action; Danceing in particular: tho' now I have mention'd danceing, let me say something of their balls which are very frequent here; when a stranger enters the danceing-hall he sees one end of the room taken up by the Lady's, who sit dismally in a Groupe by themselves. On the other end stand their pensive partners,

LETTER TO ROBERT BRYANTON

that are to be, but no more intercourse between the sexes than there is between two Countrys at war, the Ladies indeed may ogle, and the Gentlemen sigh, but an embargo is laid on any closer commerce; at length, to interrupt hostility's, the Lady directeress or intendant, or what you will pitches on a Gentleman and Lady to walk a minuet, which they perform with a formality that aproaches despondence, after five or six couple have thus walked the Gauntlett, all stand up to country dance's, each gentleman furnished with a partner from the afforesaid Lady directress, so they dance much, say nothing, and thus concludes our assembly; I told a scotch Gentleman that such a profound silence resembled the ancient procession of the Roman Matrons in honour of Ceres and the scotch Gentleman told me, (and faith I beleive he was right) that I was a very great pedant for my pains: now I am come to the Lady's and to shew that I love scotland and every thing that belongs to so charming a Country Il insist on it and will give him leave to break my head that deny's it that the scotch ladys are ten thousand times finer and handsomer than the Irish. To be sure now I see y^r. Sisters Betty & Peggy vastly surprized at my Partiality but tell y^m flatly I don't value them or their fine skins or Eyes or good sense or—a potatoe for I say it and and will maintain it and as a convinceing proof of (I am in a very great passion) of what I assert the scotch Ladies say it themselves, but to be less serious where will you find a language so prettily become a pretty mouth as the broad scotch and the women here speak it in it's highest purity, for instance teach one of the Young Lady's at home to pronounce the Whoar wull I gong with a beccomeing wideness of mouth and I'll lay my life they'l wound every hearer. We have no such character here as a coquett but alass how many envious prudes. Some days ago I walk'd into My Lord Killcoubry's don't be surpriz'd my Lord is but a Glover, when the Dutchess of Hamilton (that fair who sacrificed her beauty to ambition and her inward peace to a title and Gilt equipage) pass'd by in her Chariot, her batter'd husband or more properly the Guardian of her charms sat beside her. Strait envy began in the shape of no less than three Lady's who sat with me to find fault's in her faultless form—for my part says the first I think that I always thought that the dutchess has too much of the red in her complexion, Madam I am of your oppinion says the seccond and I think her face has a palish cast too much on the delicate order, and let me tell you adds the third Lady whose mouth was puckerd up to the size of an Issue that the Dutchess has fine lips but she wants a mouth. At this every Lady drew up her mouth as If going to pronounce the letter P. But how ill my Bob does it become me to ridicule woman with whom I have scarce any correspondence. There are 'tis certain handsome women here and tis as certain they have handsome men to keep them company. An ugly and a poor man is society only for himself and such society the world lets me enjoy in great abundance. Fortune has given you circumstance's and Nature a person to look charming in the Eyes of the fair world nor do I envy my Dear Bob such blessings while I may sit down and [laugh at the wor]ld, and at myself—the most ridiculous object in it. But [you see I am grown downright] splenetick, and perhaps the fitt may continue till I [receive an answ]er to this. I know you cant send much news from [Ballymahon, but] such as it is send it all everything you write will be agre[eable and entertai]ning to me. Has George Conway put up a signe yet ha[s John Bin]ley left off drinking Drams; or Tom Allen g[ot a new wig?] But I leave to your own choice what to write but [while Noll Go]ldsmith lives know you have a Friend.

P.S. Give my sincerest regards not [merely my] compliments (do you mind) to your agreeable [family] and Give My service to My Mother if you [see her] for as you express it in Ireland I have a sneaking kindness for her still. Direct to me, Student of Physick in Edinburgh.

JONATHAN SWIFT

Good Manners

Those inferior duties of life which the French call *les petites morales,* or the smaller morals, are with us distinguished by the name of good manners, or breeding. This I look upon, in the general notion of it, to be a sort of artificial good sense, adapted to the meanest capacities, and introduced to make mankind easy in their commerce with each other. Low and little understandings, without some rules of this kind, would be perpetually wandering into a thousand indecencies and irregularities in behaviour, and in their ordinary conversation fall into the same boisterous familiarities that one observes amongst them, when a debauch has quite taken away the use of their reason. In other instances, it is odd to consider, that for want of common discretion the very end of good breeding is wholly perverted, and civility, intended to make us easy, is employed in laying chains and fetters upon us, in debarring us of our wishes, and in crossing our most reasonable desires and inclinations. This abuse reigns chiefly in the country, as I found to my vexation, when I was last there, in a visit I made to a neighbour about two miles from my cousin. As soon as I entered the parlour, they forced me into the great chair that stood close by a huge fire, and kept me there by force till I was almost stifled. Then a boy came in great hurry to pull off my boots, which I in vain opposed, urging that I must return soon after dinner. In the mean time the good lady whispered her eldest daughter, and slipped a key into her hand. She returned instantly with a beer glass half full of *aqua mirabilis* and syrup of gillyflowers. I took as much as I had a mind for; but Madam vowed I should drink it off, (for she was sure it would do me good after coming out of the cold air) and I was forced to obey, which absolutely took away my stomach. When dinner came in, I had a mind to sit at a distance from the fire; but they told me, it was as much as my life was worth, and set me with my back just against it. Though my appetite was quite gone, I resolved to force down as much as I could, and desired the leg of a pullet. "Indeed, Mr. Bickerstaff," says the lady, "you must eat a wing to oblige me," and so put a couple upon my plate. I was persecuted at this rate during the whole meal. As often as I called for small beer, the master tipped the wink, and the servant brought me a brimmer of October. Some time after dinner, I ordered my cousin's man who came with me to get ready the horses; but it was resolved I should not stir that night; and when I seemed pretty much bent upon going, they ordered the stable door to be locked, and the children hid away my cloak and boots. The next question was, what I would have for supper? I said I never eat anything at night, but was at last in my own defence obliged to name the first thing that came into my head. After three hours spent chiefly in apology for my entertainment, insinu-

GOOD MANNERS 9

ating to me, "That this was the worst time of the year for provisions, that they were at a great distance from any market, that they were afraid I should be starved, and they knew they kept me to my loss," the lady went, and left me to her husband (for they took special care I should never be alone). As soon as her back was turned, the little misses ran backwards and forwards every moment; and constantly as they came in or went out, made a curtsy directly at me, which in good manners I was forced to return with a bow, and "Your humble servant, pretty Miss." Exactly at eight the mother came up, and discovered by the redness of her face, that supper was not far off. It was twice as large as the dinner, and my persecution doubled in proportion. I desired at my usual hour to go to my repose, and was conducted to my chamber by the gentleman, his lady, and the whole train of children. They importuned me to drink something before I went to bed, and upon my refusing, at last left a bottle of stingo, as they called it, for fear I should wake and be thirsty in the night. I was forced in the morning to rise and dress myself in the dark, because they would not suffer my kinsman's servant to disturb me at the hour I had desired to be called. I was now resolved to break through all measures to get away, and after sitting down to a monstrous breakfast of cold beef, mutton, neats'-tongues, venison-pasty, and stale beer, took leave of the family; but the gentleman would needs see me part of my way, and carry me a short cut through his own grounds, which he told me would save half a mile's riding. This last piece of civility had like to have cost me dear, being once or twice in danger of my neck, by leaping over his ditches, and at last forced to alight in the dirt, when my horse, having slipped his bridle, ran away, and took us up more than an hour to recover him again.

It is evident that none of the absurdities I met with in this visit proceeded from an ill intention, but from a wrong judgment of complaisance, and a misapplication of the rules of it. I cannot so easily excuse the more refined critics upon behaviour, who having professed no other study, are yet infinitely defective in the most material parts of it. Ned Fashion has been bred all his life about Court, and understands to a tittle all the punctilios of a drawing-room. He visits most of the fine women near St. James's, and upon all occasions says the civilest and softest things to them of any man breathing. To Mr. Isaac he owes an easy slide in his bow, and a graceful manner of coming into a room. But in some other cases he is very far from being a well-bred person: He laughs at men of far superior understanding to his own, for not being as well dressed as himself, despises all his acquaintance that are not quality, and in public places has on that account often avoided taking notice of some of the best speakers in the House of Commons. He rails strenuously at both Universities before the members of either, and never is heard to swear an oath, or break in upon morality or religion, but in the company of divines. On the other hand, a man of right sense has all the essentials of good breeding, though he may be wanting in the forms of it. Horatio has spent most of his time at Oxford. He has a great deal of learning, an agreeable wit, and as much modesty as serves to adorn without concealing his other good qualities. In that retired way of living, he seems to have formed a notion of human nature, as he has found it described in the writings of the greatest men, not as he is like to meet with it in the common course of life. Hence it is, that he gives no offence, that he converses with great deference, candour, and humanity. His bow, I must confess, is somewhat awkward; but then he has an extensive, universal, and unaffected knowledge, which makes some amends for it. He would make no extraordinary figure at a ball; but I can assure the ladies in his behalf, and for their own consolation, that he has writ better verses on the sex than any man now living, and is preparing such a poem for the press as will transmit their praises and his own to many generations.

(From *The Tatler* No. 298.)

MARIA EDGEWORTH

Adventures in Connemara:
A Letter to Pakenham Edgeworth

BEGINNING OF THE JOURNEY.

March 8th, 1834

Ever since I finished my last to you I have had my head so immersed in accounts that I have never been able till this moment to fulfil my intention of giving you my travels in Connemara.

I travelled with Sir Culling and Lady Smith (Isabella Carr). Sir Culling, of old family, large fortune and great philanthropy, extending to poor little Ireland and her bogs, and her Connemara, and her penultimate barony of Erris and her ultimate Giants' Causeway, and her beautiful lake of Killarney. And all these things he determined to see. Infant and nurse, and lady's maid, and gentleman's gentleman, and Sir Culling and the fair Isabella all came over to Ireland last September, just as Fanny had left us, and she meeting them in Dublin, and conceiving that nurse and baby would not do for

Connemara, wrote confidentially to beg us to invite them to stay at Edgeworthstown, while father and mother, and maid, and man, were to proceed on their travels. They spent a pleasant week, I hope, at Edgeworthstown. I am sure Honora did everything that was possible to make it pleasant to them, and we regretted a million of times that your mother was not at home. Sir Culling expected to have had all manner of information as to roads, distances, and time, but Mrs. Edgeworth not being at home, and Miss Edgeworth's local knowledge being such as you know, you may guess how he was disappointed. Mr. Shaw and the Dean of Ardagh, who dined with him here, gave him directions as far as Ballinasloe and a letter to the clergyman there. The fair of Ballinasloe was just beginning, and Sir Culling was determined to see that, and from thence, after studying the map of Ireland and road-books one evening, he thought he should get easily to Connemara, Westport, and the Barony of Erris, see all that in a week, and come back to Edgeworthstown, take up Bambino and proceed on a northern or a southern tour.

You will be surprised that I should—seeing they knew so little what they were about—have chosen to travel with them; and I confess it was imprudent and very unlike my usual dislike to leave home without any of my own people with me. But upon this occasion I fancied I should see all I wanted to see of the wonderful ways of going on and manners of the natives better for not being with any of my own family, and especially for its not being suspected that I was an authoress and might put them in a book. In short, I thought it was the best opportunity I could ever have of seeing a part of Ireland which, from time immemorial, I had been curious to see. My curiosity had been raised even when I first came to Ireland fifty years ago, by hearing my

ADVENTURES IN CONNEMARA

father talk of the King of Connemara, and his immense territory, and his ways of ruling over his people with almost absolute power, with laws of his own, and setting all other laws at defiance. Smugglers and caves, and murders and mermaids, and duels, and banshees, and fairies, were all mingled together in my early associations with Connemara and Dick Martin—"Hair-trigger Dick," who cared so little for his own life or the life of man, and so much for the life of animals, who fought more duels than any man of even his "Blue-blaze-devil" day, and who brought the bill into Parliament for preventing cruelty to animals; thenceforward changing his cognomen from "Hair-trigger Dick" to "Humanity Martin." He was my father's contemporary, and he knew a number of anecdotes of him. *Too besides,* I once saw him, and remember that my blood crept slow and my breath was held when he first came into the room, a pale little insignificant looking mortal he was, but he still kept hold of my imagination, and his land of Connemara was always a land I longed to visit. Long afterwards, a book which I believe you read, *Letters from the Irish Highlands,* written by the family of Blakes of Renvyle, raised my curiosity still further, and wakened it for new reasons, in a new direction. Further and further and higher, Nimmo and William deepened my interest in that country, and, in short, and at length all these motives worked together. Add to them a book called *Wild Sports of the West,* of which Harriet read to me all the readable parts till I rolled with laughing. Add also that I had lately heard Mr. Rothwell give a most entertaining account of a tour he had taken in Erris, and to the house of a certain Major Bingham who must be the most diverting and extraordinary original upon earth—and shall I die without seeing him? thought I—now or never.

At the first suggestion I uttered that I should like to see him and Erris, and the wonders of Connemara, Lady Culling Smith and Sir Culling burst into delight at the thought of having me as their travelling companion, so it was all settled in a moment. Honora approved, Aunt Mary hoped it would all turn out to my satisfaction, and off we set with four horses mighty grand in their travelling carriage, which was a summer friend, open or half open. A half head stuck up immoveable with a window at each ear, an apron of wood, varnished to look like Japanned leather hinged at bottom, and having at top where it shuts a sort of fairy-board window* which lets down in desperately bad weather.

Our first day was all prosperous and sunshine, and what Captain Beaufort would call plain sailing. To Ballymahon the first stage. Do you remember Ballymahon, and the first sight of the gossamer in the hedges sparkling with dew, going there packed into the chaise with your four sisters and me to see the museum of a Mr. Smith, who had a Cellini cup and a Raphael plate, and miniatures of Madame de Maintenon, and wonders innumerable—but Sophy at this moment tells me that I am insisting upon your remembering things that happened before you were born, and that even Francis was only one year old at the time of this breakfast, and it was she herself who was so delighted with that first view of the gossamer in the glittering sunshine.

But I shall never get on to Athlone, much less to Connemara. Of Athlone I have nothing to say but what you may learn from the *Gazetteer*, except that, while we were waiting in the antiquated inn there, while horses were changing, I espied a print hanging smoked over the chimney-piece, which to my *connoisseur* eyes

---

* The original letter has a model of the "fairy-board window."

seemed marvellously good, and upon my own judgment I proposed for it to the landlady, and bought it for five shillings (frame excepted); and when I had it out of the frame, and turned it round, I found my taste and judgment gloriously justified. It was from a picture of Vandyke's—the death of Belisarius; and here it is now hanging up in the library, framed in satin wood, the admiration of all beholders, Barry Fox above all.

But to proceed. It was no easy matter to get out of Athlone, for at the entrance to the old-fashioned, narrowest of narrow bridges we found ourselves wedged and blocked by drays and sheep, reaching at least a mile; men cursing and swearing in Irish and English; sheep baaing, and so terrified, that the shepherds were in transports of fear brandishing their crooks at our postillions, and the postillions in turn brandishing their whips on the impassive backs of the sheep. . . .

BALLINASLOE.

. . . We did not reach Ballinasloe till it was almost dark. There goes a story, you know, that no woman must ever appear at Ballinasloe Fair; that she would be in imminent peril of her life from the mob. The daughters of Lord Clancarty, it was said, "had tried it once, and scarce were saved by fate." Be this as it may, we were suffered to drive very quietly through the town; and we went quite through it to the outskirts of scattered houses, and stopped at the door of the Vicarage. And well for us that we had a letter from the Dean of Ardagh to the Rev. Mr. Pounden, else we might have spent the night in the streets, or have paid guineas apiece for our beds, all five of us, for three nights. . . .

GALWAY.

. . . Next day to Galway, and still it was fine weather, and right for the open carriage, and we thought it would always be so. Galway, wet or dry, and it was dry when I saw it, is the dirtiest town I ever saw, and the most desolate and idle-looking. As I had heard much from Captain Beaufort and Louisa of the curious Spanish buildings in Galway, I was determined not to go through the town without seeing these; so, as soon as we got to the inn, I summoned landlord and landlady, and begged to know the names of the principal families in the town. I thought I might chance to light upon somebody who could help us. In an old history of Galway which Mr. Strickland picked up from a stall at Ballinasloe, I found prints of some of the old buildings and names of the old families; and the landlord having presented me with a list as long as an alderman's bill of fare of the names of the gentlemen and ladies of Galway, I pitched upon the name of a physician, a Dr. Veitch, of whom I had found a fine character in my book. He had been very good to the poor during a year of famine and fever. To him I wrote, and just as I had finished reading his panegyric to Lady Smith, in he walked; and he proved to be an old acquaintance. He was formerly a surgeon in the army, and was quartered at Longford at the time of the rebellion: remembered our all taking shelter there, how near my father was being killed by the mob, and how courageously he behaved. Dr. Veitch had received some kindness from him, and now he seemed anxious, thirty-five years afterwards, to return that kindness to me and my companions. He walked with us all over Galway, and showed us all that was worth seeing, from the new quay *projecting*, and the new green Connemara marble-cutters' workshop, to the old Spanish houses with projecting roofs and piazza walks beneath; and, wading through seas of yellow mud thick as stirabout, we went to see archways that had stood centuries, and above all to the old mayoralty house of that mayor of Galway who hung his own son; and we had the satisfaction of seeing the very window from which the father with his own hands hung his own son, and the black marble marrowbones and death's head, and inscription and date, 1493. I dare say you know the story; it formed the groundwork very lately of a tragedy. The son had—from jealousy as the tragedy has it, from avarice according to the vulgar version—killed a Spanish friend; and the father, a modern Brutus, condemns him, and then goes to comfort him. I really thought it worth while to wade through mud to see these awful old relics of other times and other manners. But, coming back again, at every turn it was rather disagreeable to have "fish" bawled into one's ears, and "fine flat fish" flapped in one's face. The fish-market was fresh supplied, and Galway is famous for *John Dorees*. "A John Doree, ma'am, for eighteen pence—a shilling—sixpence!" A John Doree could not be had for guineas in London. Quin, the famous actor, wished he was all throat when he was eating a John Doree. But still it was not pleasant, at every turn and every crossing, to have ever so fine John Dorees flapped in one's face. Sir Culling bought one for sixpence, and it was put into the carriage; and we took leave of Dr. Veitch, and left Galway. . . .

A LITTLE EPISODE.

. . . Next day, sun shining and a good breakfast, our spirit of travelling adventure up within us, we determined that, before proceeding on our main adventure into Connemara, we would make a little episode to see a wonderful cave in the neighbourhood. Our curiosity to see it had been excited by the story of the lady and the white trout in Lover's *Legends*. It is called the Pigeon-hole; not the least like a pigeon-hole, but it is a subterraneous passage, where a stream flows which joins the waters of Lough Corrib and Lough Mask. Outerard is on the borders of Lough Corrib, and we devoted this day to boating across Lough Corrib, to see this famous cavern, which is on the opposite side of the lake, and also to see a certain ruined monastery. We passed over the lake, admiring its beauty and its many islands—little bits of islands, of which the boatmen tell there are three hundred and sixty-five; be the same more or less, one for every day in the year at least. We saw the ruins, which are very fine; but I have not time to say more about them. We crossed the churchyard and a field or two, and all was as flat, and bare, and stony as can be imagined; and as we were going and going further from the shore of the lake, I wondered how and when we were to come to this cavern. The guide called me to stop, and I stopped; and well I did: I was on the brink of the Pigeon-hole—just like an unfenced entrance to a deep deep well. The guide went down before us, and was very welcome! Down and down and down steps almost perpendicular, and as much as my little legs could do to reach from one to the other; darker and darker, and there were forty of them I am sure, well counted—though certainly I never counted them, but was right glad when I felt my feet at the bottom, on *terra firma* again, even in darkness, and was told to look up, and that I had come down sixty feet and more. I looked up and saw glimmering light at the top, and as my eyes recovered, more and more light through the large fern leaves which hung over the opening at top, and the whole height above looked like the inside of a limekiln, magnified to gigantic dimensions, with lady-fern—it must be lady-fern, because of the fairies—and lichens, names unknown, hanging from its sides. The light of the sun now streaming in I saw plainly, and felt why the guide held me fast by the arm—I was on the brink of the very narrow dark stream of water, which flowed quite silently from one side of the cavern to the other! To that other side, my eye following the stream as it flowed, I now looked, and saw that the cavern opened under a high archway in the rock. How high that was, or how spacious, I had not yet light enough to discern. But now there appeared from the steps down which we had descended an old woman with a light in her hand. Our boy-guide hailed her by the name of Madgy Burke. She scrambled on a high jut of rock in the cavern; she had a bundle of straw under one arm, and a light flickering in the other hand, her grizzled locks streaming, her garments loose and tattered, all which became suddenly visible as she set fire to a great wisp of straw, and another and another she plucked from her bundle and lighted, and waved the light above and underneath. It was like a scene in a melodrama of Cavern and Witch—the best cavern scene I ever beheld. As she continued to throw down, from the height where she stood, the lighted bundles of straw, they fell on the surface of the dark stream below, and sailed down the current, under the arch of the cavern, lighting its roof at the vast opening, and looking like tiny fireships, one after another sailing on, and disappearing. We could not help watching each as it blazed, till it vanished. We looked till we were tired, then turned and clambered up the steps we had scrambled down, and found ourselves again in broad daylight, in upper air and on the flat field; and the illusion was over, and there stood, turned into a regular old Irish beggar-woman, the Witch of Outerard, and Madgy Burke stood confessed, and began to higgle with Sir Culling and to flatter the English quality for a sixpence more.

Meanwhile we were to cross Lough Corrib; and well

for us that we had the prudence to declare, early in the morning, that we would not take a sail-boat, for a sail-boat is dangerous in the sudden squalls which rise in these mountain regions and on these lakes, very like the Swiss lakes for that matter. For instance, on the Lake de Lucerne, I have seen sunshine and glassy surface change in five minutes to storm and cloud so black and thick, that Mont Pilate himself could not be discerned through it more than if he never stood there in all his sublimity.

Our day had changed, and very rough was the lake; and the boatmen, to comfort us and no doubt amuse themselves, as we rose up and down on the billows, told us stories of boats that had been lost in these storms, and of young Mr. Brown last year, that was drowned in a boat within view of his brother standing on that island, which we were just then to pass. "And when so near he could almost have reached him, you'd have thought."

"And why didn't he, then?" said I.

"Oh, bless you, ma'am, he couldn't; for," said the boatman, dropping his oar, which I did not like at all, "for, mind you, ma'am, it was all done in the clap of one's hand," and he clapped his hands.

"Well, take up your oar," cried I; which he did, and rowed amain, and we cleared Brown's Island, and I have no more dangers, fancied or other, to tell you; and after two hours' hard rowing, which may give you the measure of the width of Lough Corrib at this place, we landed, and were right glad to eat Mrs. O'Flaherty's ready dinner, Lough Corrib trout—not the White Lady trout. . . . .

THE MAIN ADVENTURE.

. . . So the morning came, and a fine morning still it was; and we set out, leaving Mrs. O'Flaherty curtseying

ADVENTURES IN CONNEMARA

and satisfied. I cannot make out any wonders, or anything like an adventure between Outerard and Corrib Lodge; only the road was rough and the country like the Isle of Anglesea, as if stones and fragments of rock had showered down on the earth and tracts of bog-heath such as England never saw and Scotland seldom sees, except in the Highlands. We were only about twice the time that Sir Culling had calculated on getting over this part of the road with our powerful Galway horses and steady drivers, and reaching Corrib Lodge Sir Culling said: "These roads are not so very bad, we shall get on, Miss Edgeworth, very well, you will see."

Corrib Lodge is a neat bleak-looking house, which Mr. Nimmo built for his own residence when he was overseer of the roads, now turned into an inn, kept by his Scotch servant, who used to come with him to Edgeworthstown, and he gave us bread and butter and milk, and moreover, hare-soup, such as the best London tavern might have envied, for observe, that hares abound in these parts, and there is no sin in killing them, and how the cook came to be so good I cannot tell you, but so it certainly was. Invigorated and sanguine, we were ready to get into the carriage again, purposing to reach Clifden this evening—it was now three o'clock; we had got through half our thirty-six miles; no doubt we could easily, Sir Culling argued, manage the other half before dark. But our wary Scotch host shook his head and observed, that if his late master Mr. Nimmo's road was but open so we might readily, but Mr. Nimmo's new road was not opened, and why, because it was not finished. Only one mile or so remained unfinished, and as that one mile of unmade unfinished road was impassable by man, boy, or Connemara pony, what availed the new road for our heavy carriage and four horses? There was no possibility of *going round,* as I proposed; we must go the old road, if road it could be called, all bog and bogholes, as our host explained to us: "It would be wonderful if we could get over it, for no carriage had ever passed, nor ever thought of attempting to pass, nothing but a common car these two years at least, except the Marquis of Anglesea and suite, *and* his Excellency was on horseback." As for such a carriage as Sir Culling's, the like, as men and boys at the door told us, had never been seen in these parts.

Sir Culling stood a little daunted. We inquired—I particularly, how far it was to Ballinahinch Castle, where the Martins live, and which I knew was some miles on this side of Clifden. I went into Corrib Lodge and wrote with ink on a visiting ticket with "Miss Edgeworth" on it, my compliments, and Sir Culling and Lady Smith's, a petition for a night's hospitality, to use in case of our utmost need.

The Scotchman could not describe exactly how many *bad steps* there were, but he forewarned us that they were bad enough, and as he sometimes changed the words *bad steps* into *sloughs,* our Galway postillions looked graver and graver, hoped they should get their horses over, but did not know; they had never been this road, never further than Outerard, but they would do all that men and beasts could do.

The first bad step we came to was indeed a slough, but only a couple of yards wide across the road. The horses, the moment they set their feet upon it, sank up to their knees, and were whipped and spurred, and they struggled and floundered, and the carriage, as we inside passengers felt, sank and sank. Sir Culling was very brave and got down to help. The postillions leaped off, and bridles in hand gained the shore, and by dint of tugging, and whipping, and hallooing, and dragging of men and boys, who followed from Corrib Lodge, we were got out and were on the other side.

Further on we might fare worse from what we could learn, so in some commotion we got out, and said we would rather walk. And when we came to the next bad step, the horses seeing it was a slough like the first, put back their ears and absolutely refused to set foot upon it, and they were, the postillions agreed, quite right; so they were taken off and left to look on, while by force of arms the carriage was to be got over by men and boys, who shouting, gathered from all sides, from mountain paths down which they poured, and from fields where they had been at work or loitering; at the sight of the strangers they flocked to help—such a carriage had never been seen before—to help common cars, or jaunting cars over these bad steps they had been used. "This heavy carriage! sure it was impossible, but sure they might do it." And they talked and screamed together in English and Irish equally unintelligible to us, and in spite of all remonstrance about breaking the pole— pole, and wheels, and axle, and body, they seized of the carriage, and standing and jumping from stone to stone, or any tuft of bog that could bear them, as their practised eyes saw; they, I cannot tell you how, dragged, pushed, and *screamed* the carriage over. And Sir Culling got over his way, and Lady Smith would not be carried, but leaping and assisted by men's arms and shouts, she got to the other side. And a great giant, of the name of Ulick Burke, took me up in his arms as he might a child or a doll, and proceeded to carry me over—while I, exceedingly frightened and exceedingly civil, and (as even in the moment of most danger I could not help thinking and laughing within me at the thought), very like Rory in his dream on the eagle's back, in his journey to the moon, I kept alternately flattering my giant, and praying—"Sir, sir, pray set me down; do let me down now, sir, pray."

"Be asy; be *quite*, can't you, dear, and I'll carry you over to the other side safely, all in good time," floundering as he went.

"Thank you, sir, thank you. Now, sir, now set me down, if you will be so very good, on the bank."

Just as we reached the bank he stumbled and sank knee-deep, but threw me, as he would a sack, to shore, and the moment I felt myself on *terra firma*, I got up and ran off, and never looked back, trusting that my giant knew his own business; and so he did, and all dirt and bog water, was beside me again in a trice. "Did not I carry you over well, my lady? Oh, it's I am used to it, and helped the Lord Anglesea when he was in it."

So as we walked on, while the horses were coming over, I don't know how, Ulick and a tribe of wild Connemara men and boys followed us, all talking at once, and telling us there were twenty or thirty such bad steps, one worse than another further and further on. It was clear that we could not walk all the twelve miles, and the men and Sir Culling assuring us that they would get us safe over, and that we had better get into the carriage again, and in short that we *must* get in; we submitted.

I confess, Pakenham, I was frightened nearly out of my wits. At the next trial Lady Culling Smith was wonderfully brave, and laughed when the carriage was hauled from side to side, so nearly upset, that how each time it escaped I could not tell; but at last, when down it sank, and all the men shouted and screamed, her courage fell, and she confessed afterwards she thought it was all over with us, and that we should never be got out of this bog-hole. Yet out we were got;

but how? What with the noise, and what with the fright, far be it from me to tell you. But I know I was very angry with a boy for laughing in the midst of it: a little dare-devil of a fellow, as my giant Ulick called him; I could with pleasure have seen him ducked in bog-water! but forgot my anger in the pleasure of safe landing, and now I vowed I could and would walk the whole ten miles further, and would a thousand times rather.

My scattered senses and common sense returning, it now occurred to me that it would be desirable to avail myself of the card I had in my bag, and beg a night's lodging at our utmost need. It was still broad daylight to be sure, and Sir Culling still hoped we should get on to Clifden before dark. But I did request he would despatch one of these gossoons to Ballinahinch Castle with my card immediately. It could do no harm I argued, and Lady Smith seconded me with, "Yes, dear Culling, *do*," and my dear giant Ulick backed me with, "Troth, you're right enough, ma'am. Troth, sir, it will be dark enough soon, and long enough before you're clean over them sloughs farthest on beyant where we can engage to see you over. Sure, here's my own boy will run with the speed of light with the lady's card."

I put it into his hand with the promise of half a crown, and how he did take to his heels!

We walked on, and Ulick, who was a professional wit as well as a giant, told us the long ago tale of Lord Anglesea's visit to Connemara, and how as he walked beside his horse this gentleman-lord, as he was, had axed him which of his legs he liked best.

Now Ulick knew right well that one was a cork leg, but he never let on, as he told us, and pretended the one leg was just the same as t'other, and he saw no differ in life, "which pleased my lord-liftenant greatly, and then his lordship fell to explaining to me why it was cork, and how he lost it in battle, which I knew before as well as he did, for I had larned all about it from our Mr. Martin, who was expecting him at the castle, but still I never let on, and handled the legs one side of the horse and t'other and asy found out, and tould him, touching the cork, sure this is the more *honourable!*"

Which observation surely deserved, and I hope obtained half a crown. Our way thus beguiled by Ulick's Irish wit, we did not for some time feel that we could not walk for ever. Lady Culling Smith complained of being stiff and tired, and we were compelled to the carriage again, and presently heavy dews of evening falling, we were advised to let down those fairy-board shutters I described to you, which was done with care and cost of nails. I did it at last, and oh! How I wished it up again when we were boxed up, and caged in without the power of seeing more than glimpses of our danger—glimpses heightening imagination, and if we were to be overturned all this glass to be broken into our eyes and ears.

Well! well! I will not wear your sympathy and patience eighteen times out, with the history of the eighteen sloughs we went, or were got, through at the imminent peril of our lives. Why the carriage was not broken to pieces I cannot tell, but an excellent strong carriage it was, thank Heaven and the builder whoever he was.

I should have observed to you that while we yet could look about us, we had continually seen, to increase our sense of vexation, Nimmo's new road looking like a gravel walk running often parallel to our path of danger, and yet for want of being finished there it was, useless, and most tantalizing.

Before it grew quite dark, Sir Culling tapped at our dungeon window, and bid us look out at a beautiful place, a paradise in the wilds; "Look out? How?" "Open the little window at your ear, and this just before you—push the bolt back." "But I can't."

With the help of an ivory-cutter lever, however, I did accomplish it, and saw indeed a beautiful place belonging, our giant guide told us, to Dean Mahon, well-wooded and most striking in this desert.

It grew dark, and Sir Culling, very brave, walking beside the carriage, when we came to the next bad step, sank above his knees; how they dragged him out I could not see, and there were we in the carriage stuck fast in a slough, which, we were told, was the last but one before Ballinahinch Castle, when my eyes were blessed with a twinkling light in the distance—a boy with a lantern. And when, breathless, he panted up to the side of the carriage and thrust up lantern and note (we still in the slough), how glad I was to see him and it! and to hear him say, "Then Mr. Martin's very unaasy about yees—so he is."

"I am very glad of it—very glad indeed," said I. The note in a nice lady's hand from Mrs. Martin greeted us with the assurance that Miss Edgeworth and her English friends should be welcome at Ballinahinch Castle.

Then from our mob another shout! another heave! another drag, and another lift by the spokes of the wheels. Oh! if they had broken!—but they did not, and we were absolutely out of this slough. I spare you the next and last, and then we wound round the *Lake-road* in the dark, on the edge of Ballinahinch Lake on Mr. Martin's new road, as our dear giant told us, and I thought we should never get to the house, but at last we saw a chimney on fire, at least myriads of sparks and spouts of flame, but before we reached it, it abated and we came to the door without seeing what manner of house or castle it might be, till the hall door opened and a butler—half an angel he appeared to us—appeared at the door. But then in the midst of our impatience I was to let down and buckle up these fairy boards—at last swinging and slipping it was accomplished, and out we got, but with my foot still on the step we all called out to tell the butler we were afraid some chimney was on fire. Without deigning even to look up at the chimney, he smiled and motioned us the way we should go. He was as we saw at first view, and found afterwards, the most imperturbable of men.

And now that we are safely housed, and housed in a castle too, I will leave you, my dear Pakenham, for the present. . . .

CONNEMARA TRAVELS CONTINUED.

March 12th

. . . What became of the chimney on fire, I cannot tell—the Imperturbable was probably right in never minding it; he was used to its ways of burning out, and being no more thought of.

He showed us into a drawing-room, where we saw by firelight a lady alone—Mrs. Martin, tall and thin, in deep mourning. Though by that light, but dimly visible, and by our eyes *dazed* as they were just coming out of the dark, but imperfectly seen, yet we could not doubt at first sight that she was a lady in the highest sense of the word, perfectly a gentlewoman. And her whole manner of receiving us, and the ease of her motions, and of her conversation, in a few moments convinced me that she must at some time of her life have been accustomed to live in the best society—the best society in Ireland; for it was evident from her accent that she was a *native*—high-life Dublin tone of about forty years ago. The curls on her forehead, mixed with grey, prematurely grey, like your mother's, much older than the rest of her person.

She put us at ease at once, by beginning to talk to us, as if she was well acquainted with my family—and so she was from William, who had prepossessed her in our favour, yet she did not then allude to him, though I could not but understand what she meant to convey— I liked her.

Then came in, still by firelight, from a door at the further end of the room, a young lady, elegantly dressed in deep mourning. "My daughter—Lady Culling Smith—Miss Edgeworth:" slight figure, head held up and thrown back. She had the resolution to come to the very middle of the room and make a deliberate and profound curtsey, which a dancing-master of Paris would have approved; seated herself upon the sofa, and seemed as if she never intended to speak. Mrs. Martin showed us up to our rooms, begging us not to dress unless we liked it before dinner; and we did not like it, for we were very much tired, and it was now between eight and nine o'clock. Bedchambers spacious. Dinner, we were told, was ready whenever we pleased, and, well pleased, down we went: found Mr. Martin in the drawing-room—a large Connemara gentleman, white, massive face; a stoop forward in his neck the consequence of a shot in the Peninsular war.

"Well! Will you come to dinner? Dinner's ready. Lady Culling Smith, take my arm; Sir Culling, Miss Edgeworth."

A fine large dining-room, and standing at the end of the table an odd-looking person, below the middle height, youngish, but the top and back of his head perfectly bald, like a bird's skull, and at each temple a thick bunch of carroty red curly hair, thick red whiskers and light blue eyes, very fair skin and carnation colour. He wore a long green coat, and some abominable coloured thing round his throat, and a look as if he could not look at you and would. I wondered what was to become of this man, and he looked as if he wondered too. But Mr. Martin, turning abruptly, said, "McHugh! where are you, man? McHugh, sit down man, here!"

And McHugh sat down. I afterwards found he was an essential person in the family: McHugh here, McHugh there; very active, acute, and ready, and bashful, a dare-devil kind of man, that would ride, and boat, and shoot in any weather, and would at any moment hazard his life to save a fellow-creature's. Miss Martin sat opposite to me, and with the light of branches of wax candles full upon her, I saw that she was very young, about seventeen, very fair, hair which might be called red by rivals and auburn by friends, her eyes blue grey, prominent, like pictures I have seen by Leonardo da Vinci.

But Miss Martin must not make me forget the dinner, and such a dinner! London *bon vivants* might have blessed themselves! Venison such as Sir Culling declared could not be found in England, except from one or two immense parks of noblemen favoured above their peers; salmon, lobsters, oysters, game, all well cooked and well served, and well placed upon the table: nothing loaded, all *in* good taste, as well as *to* the taste; wines, such as I was not worthy of, but Sir Culling knew how to praise them; champagne, and all manner of French wines.

In spite of a very windy night, I slept admirably well, and wakened with great curiosity to see what manner of place we were in. From the front windows of my room, which was over the drawing-room, I looked down a sudden slope to the only trees that could be seen, far or near, and only on the tops of them. From the side window a magnificent but desolate prospect of an immense lake and bare mountains.

When I went down, and to the hall door at which we had entered the night before, I was surprised to see neither mountains, lake, nor river—all flat as a pancake—a wild, boundless sort of common, with showers of stones; no avenue or regular approach, no human habitation within view: and when I walked up the road and turned to look at the castle, nothing could be less like a castle. From the drawing I send you (who it was done by I will tell you by-and-by), you would imagine it a real castle, bosomed high in trees. Such flatterers as those portrait-painters of places are! And yet it is all true enough, if you see it from the right point of view. Much I wished to see more of the inhabitants of this castle, but we were to pursue our way to Clifden this day; and with these thoughts balancing in my mind of *wish* to stay, and *ought* to go, I went to breakfast—coffee, tea, hot rolls, ham, all luxuries.

Isabella did not make her appearance, but this I accounted for by her having been much tired. She had complained of rheumatic pains, but I had thought no more about them. Little was I aware of all that was to be. *"L'homme propose: Dieu dispose."* Lady Culling Smith at last appeared, hobbling, looking in torture, leaning on her husband's arm, and trying to smile on our hospitable hosts, all standing up to receive her. Never did I see a human creature in the course of one night so changed. When she was to sit down, it was impossible: she could not bend her knees, and fell back in Sir Culling's arms. He was excessively frightened. His large, powerful host carried her up stairs, and she was put to bed by her thin, scared-looking, but excellent and helpful maid; and this was the beginning of an illness which lasted above three weeks. Little did we think, however, at the beginning how bad it would be. We thought it only rheumatism, and I wrote to Honora that we should be detained a few days longer—from day to day put off. Lady Culling Smith grew alarmingly ill. There was only one half-fledged doctor at Clifden: the Martins disliked him, but he was sent for, and a puppy he proved, thinking of nothing but his own shirt-buttons and fine curled hair. Isabella grew worse and worse—fainting-fits; and Mrs. and Miss Martin, both accustomed to prescribe for the country-people in want of all medical advice in these lone regions, went to their pharmacopœias and medicine chest, and prescribed various strong remedies, and ran up and down stairs, but could not settle what the patient's disease was, whether gout or rheumatism; and these required quite different treatment: hands and lips were swelled and inflamed, but not enough to say it was positively gout, then there was fear of drawing the gout to the stomach, and if it was not gout!—All was terror and confusion; and poor Sir Culling, excessively fond of Isabella, stood in tears beside her bed. He had sat up two nights with her, and was now seized with asthmatic spasms himself in his chest. It was one of the worst nights you can imagine, blowing a storm and raining cats and dogs. Mr. and Mrs. Martin and Sir Culling thought Lady Smith so dangerously ill, that it was necessary to send a man on horseback thirty miles to Outerard for a physician: and who could be sent such a night? one of the Galway postillions on one of the post-horses (you will understand that we were obliged to keep these horses and postillions at Ballinahinch, as no other horses could be procured). The postillion was to be *knocked up,* and Sir Culling and Mr. Martin went to some den to waken him.

Meanwhile I was standing alone, very sorrowful, on the hearth in the great drawing-room, waiting to hear how it could be managed, when in came Mr. McHugh, and coming quite close up to me, said, "Them Galway boys will not know the way across the bogs as I should: I'd be at Outerard in half the time. I'll go if they'll let me, and with all the pleasure in life."

"Such a night as this! Oh no, Mr. McHugh!"

"Oh yes; why not?" said he. And this good-hearted, wild creature would have gone that instant, if we would have let him!

However, we would not, and he gave instructions to the Galway boy how to keep clear of the sloughs and bog-holes; observing to me that "them stranger horses are good for little in Connemara—nothing like a Connemara pony for that!" As Ulick Burke said, "The ponies are such knowing little creatures, when they come to a slough they know they'd sink in, and their legs of no use to them, they lie down till the men that can stand drag them over with their legs kneeling under them."

The Galway boy got safe to Outerard, and next morning brought back Dr. Davis, a very clever, agreeable man, who had had a great deal of experience, having begun life as an army surgeon: at any rate, he was not thinking of himself, but of his patient. He thought Isabella dangerously ill—unsettled gout. I will not tire you with all the history of her illness, and all our terrors; but never would I have left home on this odd journey if I could have foreseen this illness. I cannot give you an idea of my loneliness of feeling, my utter helplessness, from the impossibility of having the advantage of the sympathy and sense of any of my own family. We had not, for one whole week, the comfort of even any one letter from any of our distant friends. We had expected to be by this time at Castlebar, and we had desired Honora to direct our letters there. Sir Culling with great spirit sent a Connemara messenger fifty miles to Castlebar for the letters, and when he came back he brought but one!

No mail-coach road comes near here: no man on horseback could undertake to carry the letters regularly. They are carried three times a week from Outerard to Clifden, thirty-six miles, by three gossoons, or more properly bogtrotters, and very hard work it is for them. One runs a day and a night, and then sleeps a day and a night, and then another takes his turn; and each of these boys has £15 a year. I remember seeing one of these postboys leaving Ballinahinch Castle, with his leather bag on his back, across the heath and across the bog, leaping every now and then, and running so fast! his bare, white legs thrown up among the brown heath. These postboys were persons of the greatest consequence to us: they brought us news from home, and to poor Lady Culling Smith accounts of her baby, and of her friends in England. We began to think we should never see any of them again.

I cannot with sufficient gratitude describe to you the hospitality and unvaried kindness of Mr. and Mrs. Martin during all these trials. Mr. Martin, rough man as he seemed outside, was all soft and tender within, and so very considerate for the English servants. Mrs. Martin told me that he said to her, "I am afraid that English man and maid must be very uncomfortable here—so many things to which they have been used, which we have not for them! Now we have no beer, you know, my dear, and English servants are always used to beer." So Mr. Martin gave them cider instead, and every day he took to each of them himself a glass of excellent port wine; and to Isabella, as gout-cordial, he gave Bronte, the finest, Sir Culling said, he ever tasted. And never all the time did Mr. and Mrs. Martin omit anything it was in their power to do to make us comfortable, and to relieve us from the dreadful feeling of being burthensome and horrible intruders! They did succeed in putting me completely at ease, as far as they were concerned. I do not think I could have got through all the anxiety I felt during Lady Culling Smith's illness, and away from all my own people, and waiting so shockingly long for letters, if it had not been for the kindness of Mrs. Martin, and the great fondness I soon felt for her. She is not literary; she is very religious—what would be called VERY GOOD, and yet she suited me, and I grew very fond of her, and she of me. Little things that I could feel better than describe inclined me to her, and our minds were open to one another from the first day. Once, towards the end, I believe, of the first week, when I began some sentence with an apology for some liberty I was taking, she put her hand upon my arm, and with a kind, reproachful look exclaimed, "Liberty! I thought we were past that long since: are not we?"

She told me that she had actually been brought up with a feeling of reverence for my father, and particularly for me, by a near relation of hers, old Mr. Kirwan, the President of the Royal Irish Academy, who was a great friend of my father's and puffer of me in early days. Then her acquaintance afterwards with Mr. Nimmo carried on the connection. She told me he showed her that copy of *Harry and Lucy* which you had in making the index, and showed her the bridge which he helped me over when Harry was building it. But what touched and won me first and most in Mrs. Martin was the manner in which she spoke of William—her true feeling for his character. "Whenever he could get me alone," she said, "he would talk to me of Honora or Mrs. Edgeworth and his aunt Mary and you."

Some of the expressions she repeated I could not but feel sure were his, and they were so affectionate towards me, I was much touched. *Too besides* Mrs. Martin made herself very agreeable by her quantity of anecdotes, and her knowledge of the people with whom she had lived in her youth, of whom she could, with great ability and admirable composed drollery, give the most characteristic traits.

Miss Martin—though few books beyond an *Edinburgh* or *Quarterly Review* or two appeared in the sitting-room—has books in quantities in a closet in her own room, which is within her mother's; and "every morning," said Mrs. Martin, "she comes into me while I am dressing, and pours out upon me an inundation of learning, fresh and fresh, all she has been reading for hours before I am up. Mary has read prodigiously."

I found Mary one of the most extraordinary persons I ever saw. Her acquirements are indeed prodigious: she has more knowledge of books, both scientific and learned, than any female creature I ever saw or heard of at her age—heraldry, metaphysics, painting and painters' lives, and tactics; she had a course of fortification from a French officer, and of engineering from Mr. Nimmo. She understands Latin, Greek, and Hebrew, and I don't know how many modern languages. French she speaks perfectly, learned from the French officer who taught her fortification, M. du Bois, who was one of Buonaparte's legion of honour, and when the Emperor was *ousted,* fled from France, and earned his bread at Ballinahinch by teaching French, which Miss

Martin talks as if she had been a native, but not as if she had been in good Parisian society; with an odd mixture of a *ton de garnison* which might be expected from a pupil of one of Buonaparte's officers. She imbibed from him such an admiration, such an enthusiasm for Buonaparte, that she cannot bear a word said to his disparagement; and when Sir Culling sometimes offended in that way, Miss Martin's face and neck grew carnation colour, and down to the tips of her fingers she blushed with indignation.

Her father the while smiled and winked at me. The father as well as the mother dote upon her; and he has a softened way of always calling her "my child" that interested me for both. "My child, never mind; what signifies about Buonaparte?"

One morning we went with Miss Martin to see the fine green Connemara marble-quarries. Several of the common people gathered round while we were looking at the huge blocks: these people Miss Martin called her TAIL. Sir Culling wished to obtain an answer to a question from some of these people, which he desired Miss Martin to ask for him, being conscious that, in his English tone, it would be unintelligible. When the question had been put and answered, Sir Culling objected: "But Miss Martin, you did not put the question exactly as I requested you to state it."

"No," said she, with colour raised and head thrown back, "No, because I knew how to put it so that people could understand it. *Je sais mon métier de reine.*"

This trait gives you an idea of her character and manner, and of the astonishment of Sir Culling at her want of sympathy with his really liberal and philanthropic views for Ireland, while she is full of her tail, her father's fifty-miles-long avenue, and Æschylus and Euripides, in which she is admirably well read. Do think of a girl of seventeen, in the wilds of Connemara, intimately acquainted with all the beauties of Æschylus and Euripides, and having them as part of her daily thoughts!

There are immense caves on this coast which were the *free-traders'* resort, and would have been worth any money to Sir Walter. "Quite a scene and a country for him," as Miss Martin one day observed to me; "don't you think your friend Sir Walter Scott would have liked our people and our country?"

It is not exactly a feudal state, but the *tail* of a feudal state. Dick Martin, father of the present man, was not only lord of all he surveyed, but lord of all the lives of the people: now the laws of the land have come in, and rival proprietors have sprung up in rival castles. Hundreds would still, I am sure, start out of their bogs for Mr. Martin, but he is called *Mister,* and the prestige is over. The people in Connemara were all very quiet and submissive till some *refugee Terry-alts** took asylum in these bog and mountain fastnesses. They spread their principles and soon the clan combined against their chief, and formed a plan of seizing Ballinahinch Castle, and driving him and all the Protestant gentry out of the country. Mr. Martin is a man of desperate courage, some skill as an officer, and *prodigious* bodily strength, which altogether stood him in stead in time of great danger. I cannot tell you the whole long story, but I will mention one anecdote which will show you how like the stories in Walter Scott are the scenes that have been lately passing in Connemara. Mr. Martin summoned one of his own followers, who had he knew joined the Terry-alts, to give up a gun lent to him in days of trust and favour: no answer to the summons. A

---

* Rebels of Clare, after the Union.

second, a third summons: no effect. Mr. Martin then warned the man that if he did not produce the gun at the next sessions, he would come and seize it. The man appeared at the house where Mr. Martin holds his sessions—about the size of Lovell's schoolroom, and always fuller than it can hold: Mr. Martin espied from his end of the room his friend with the gun, a powerfully strong man, who held his way on, and stood full before him.

"You sent for my gun, your honour, did you?"

"I did—three times; it is well you have brought it at last; give it to me."

The man kneeled down on one knee, and putting the gun across the other knee, broke it asunder, and throwing the pieces to Mr. Martin, cried, "There it is for you. I swore that was the only way you should ever have it, dead or alive. You have warned me, and now I warn you; take care of yourself."

He strode out of the crowd. But he was afterwards convicted of Terry-alt practices and transported. Now all is perfectly quiet, and Mr. Martin goes on doing justice in his own peculiar fashion every week. When the noise, heat, and crowd in his sessions court become beyond all bearing, he roars with his stentorian voice to clear the court; and if that be not done forthwith, he with his own two Herculean arms seizes the loudest two disputants, knocks their heads together, thrusts them bawling as they go out of the door and flings them asunder.

In his own house there never was a more gentle, hospitable, good-natured man, I must say again and again, or else I should be a very ungrateful woman.

Miss Martin has three ponies, which she has brought every day to the great Wyatt window of the library, where she feeds them with potatoes. One of them is very passionate; and once the potatoes being withheld a moment too long at the hall door he fell into a rage, pushed in at the door after her, and she ran for her life, got up stairs and was safe.

I asked what he would have done if he had come up to her?

"Set his two feet on my shoulders, thrown me down, and trampled upon me."

The other day the smith hurt his foot in shoeing him, and up he reared, and up jumped the smith on the raised part of his forge—the pony jumped after him, and if the smith had not scrambled behind his bellows, "would have killed him to be sure."

After hearing this I declined riding this pony, though Miss Martin pressed me much, and assured me he was as quiet as a lamb—provided I would never strike him or look cross. Once she got me up on his back, but I looked so miserable, she took me down again. She described to me her nursing of one of these ponies; "he used to stand with his head over my shoulder while I rubbed his nose for an hour together; but I suppose I must throw off these Bedouin habits before I go to London."

They are now spending the season in town. I had an opportunity of seeing her perfect freedom from coquetry in company with a Mr. Smith—no relation of Sir Culling's—a very handsome fine gentleman who came here unexpectedly. He was the person who gave me the sketch of Ballinahinch Castle, which Sophy has copied for you, and which I send.

All this time poor Isabella has been left by me in torture in her bed. At the end of three weeks she was pronounced out of danger, and in spite of the kind remonstrances of our hospitable hosts, not tired of the sick or the well, on a very wet odious day away we went. As there are no inns or place where an invalid could pass the night, I wrote to beg a night's lodging at Renvyle, Mr. Blake's. He and Mrs. Blake, who wrote *Letters from the Irish Highlands*, were not at home, in Galway on a visit, but they answered most politely that they begged me to consider their house as my own, and wrote to their agent who was at Renvyle to receive us.

Captain Bushby, of the Water Guard—married to a niece of Joanna Baillie's—was very kind in accompanying us on our first day's journey. "I must see you safe out," said he. "Safe out" is the common elision for safe out of Connemara. And really it was no easy matter to get us safe out; but I spare you a repetition of sloughs; we safely reached Renvyle, where the agent received us in a most comfortable well-furnished, well-carpeted, well-lighted library, filled with books—excellent dining-room beyond, and here Lady Smith had a day's rest, without which she could not have proceeded, and well for her she had such a comfortable resting place.

Next day we got into *Joyce's Country* and had hot potatoes and cold milk, and Renvyle cold fowl at The Lodge, as it is styled, of Big Jacky Joyce—one of the descendants of the ancient proprietors, and quite an original Irish character. He had heard my name often, he said, from Mr. Nimmo, and knew I was a writing lady, and a friend to Ireland, and he was civil to me, and I was civil to him, and after eyeing Sir Culling and Lady Smith, and thinking, I saw, that she was affecting to be languishing, and then perceiving that she was really weak and ill, he became cordial to the whole party, and entertained us for two hours, which we were obliged to wait for the going out of the tide before we could cross the sands. Here was an arm of the sea, across which Mr. Nimmo had been employed to build a bridge, and against Big Jack Joyce's advice, he would build it where Jack prophesied it would be swept away in the winter, and twice the bridge was built, and twice it was swept away, and still Nimmo said it was the fault of the masons; the embankment and his theory could not be wrong, and a third time he built the bridge, and there we saw the ruins of it on the sands— all the embankments swept away and all we had for it was to be dragged over the sand by men—the horses taken off. We were pushed down into a gully-hole five feet deep, and thence pulled up again; how it was I cannot tell you, for I shut my eyes and resigned myself, gave up my soul and was much surprised to find it in my body at the end of the operation: Big Jacky Joyce and his merry men having somehow managed it . . .

RETROSPECT.

. . . But now that it is all over, and I can balance pains and pleasures, I declare that, upon the whole, I had more pleasure than pain from this journey; the perils of the road were far overbalanced by the diversion of seeing the people, and the seeing so many to me perfectly new characters and modes of living. The anxiety of Isabella's illness, terrible as it was, and the fear of being ill myself and a burthen upon their hands, and even the horrid sense of remoteness and impossibility of communication with my own friends, were altogether overbalanced by the extraordinary kindness, and tenderness, and generous hospitality of the Martins. It will do my heart good all the days of my life to have experienced such kindness, and to have seen so much good in human nature as I saw with them—red McHugh included. I am sure I have a friend in Mrs. Martin: it is an extraordinary odd feeling to have made a friend at sixty-six years of age! You my dear young Pakenham, can't understand this; but you will live, I hope, to understand it, and perhaps to say, "Now I begin to comprehend what Maria, poor old soul! meant by that *odd* feeling at the end of her Connemara journey! . . ."

T. M. HEALY

On Bicycles: A Speech

July 7, 1898

I am aware of that, but we are now dealing with an important matter upon the Report stage. I do say that if this is to be considered the Bill ought to be recommitted, and notice given to us so that we could have an opportunity of discussing this penal clause in Committee. We should have some information in advance from the Government as to whether they intend, if they do intend to accept this proposal, as I am afraid, from the ominous silence of the Chief Secretary, and the fact that he brought in a Bill of the same mischievous character a year ago, that we have some grounds for a lurking suspicion that he is going to accept it. We should have notice of it, for this reason. The first thing I would suggest is that after the word "bicycle" to insert the words "or carriage." We could then discuss the entire question of vehicular traffic, which is practically what it amounts to. The cyclist has just as much right to be protected from being run down as a carriage. Why should I be run down in the dark by a carriage which carries no lamps, or by a car that refuses to carry anything? Carriages with indiarubber tyres are become very popular, and they are becoming noiseless like bicycles; therefore, I think it is essential, if this law is to be applied to one section of the community on wheels it is only right to apply it to all sections. We have had no notice of this because I do not think a penal clause has ever been proposed at the Report stage of a Bill without some notice to the House of the intention of the Government to accept it. That is one of my objections, but there is another. I object to the people of Ireland being fined £100,000 for the benefit of Birmingham manufacturers. There are something like a quarter of a million bicycles in Ireland, and lamps are made at Birmingham, and no lamps are made in Ireland, and no bells are made in Ireland. Now, I believe that no bicyclist, unless he is a fool, rides without a bell, but, generally speaking, lamps are not necessary in Ireland. I would not object to this proposal so much in the case of Dublin or Belfast, and I would not object to cyclists being compelled to carry lights if it is also made to apply to the grocer's cart and the milkman's cart, as well as to every cyclist. But so far as the general country is concerned, you might go ten miles without meeting a car, a cart, or anything whatever, either on wheels or on legs, in many of the remote parts of the country. Therefore, to legislate for Ireland, as a whole, as if it was all to be treated upon the same basis, is, in my opinion, an absurdity. There may be a case for it in Belfast and Dublin, but there certainly is no case whatever for it in a great many of the rural districts of the country. But in addition to these points I think this view should be considered. If a man is driving a car, or a cart, he is not often injured in case of accidents, although his horse may be injured; but the bicyclist is nearly always injured if anything runs into him. He is riding at his peril, and that is far more than can be said of the man on the car or cart. If you consider the way in which bicyclists are treated as a rule by those in

ON BICYCLES

charge of cars or carriages, I venture to say that the necessity for regulations is in the opposite direction, for the danger is rather the other way about. On the magisterial bench in Ireland there seem to be a number of old gouty gentlemen who themselves are unable to ride, and they seem to have the very strongest prejudice against any cyclist who happens to be brought before them, and this Amendment will give them a chance of coming down on cyclists in general with a very severe voice. As a matter of fact I do not think that there has been any invention of recent years, for men and women, which has given such excellent and healthy enjoyment to the population. Certainly, as I understand it, this clause might fairly take up five or six days, if it is to be considered in a proper spirit and from a thorough point of view. Why, every line of it is reeking with matter upon which Amendments ought to be moved. If the Government are determined to shut out every other type of vehicle from their consideration, and confine this law to bicycles, then, of course, we shall have a very enjoyable afternoon. But I would ask the Government to remember this: we brought before the House in the Committee stage the very important question of traction engines, and we pointed out that there was some necessity for some provision being made in regard to the cutting up of roads by traction engines, and we showed how, in the county of Cork, a road was thrown out of use from this cause, because the grand jury were unable to do anything more to the road. It appears that a pneumatic tyre is to be put under a penal law, while you allow a traction engine to cut up the roads with impunity. It does appear to me that this is a class of traffic which requires regulating, and you do not propose to give favourable consideration to an Amendment of that kind. This proposal has nothing whatever to do with the scope of the Bill, and it is a proposal to transfer from the grand jury for their existing powers entirely new legislation, not germane to the Measure of the Government, and which ought to be introduced in a special Bill dealing with the subject.

(From *Hansard*, Vol. 61.)

T. M. HEALY

On the Boer War: A Speech
February 7, 1900

These are the people you want to put over the Dutch in South Africa. You want a settlement. You want the two races to mingle hand in hand waving the Union Jack and singing "Rule Britannia," and you would put in ascendency over the Dutch such men as have made their ascendency in Ireland hateful, and who call your own Irish soldiers "rebels." What wonder, then, if there is disaffection! I understand the principles of Pirate Smith who hoisted his black flag at Bristol and made war with all and sundry for the sake of booty. He had not a Bible on board. He swore by the Jolly Roger and not by the Ten Commandments. You want to syndicate Christianity, and take the Twelve Apostles into your limited liability company. Then you hold up your hands like the pharisee and invite other nations to rejoice that the English possess such virtues. The Irish people are a feeble folk, and the only advantage which the Irish have is that we are able to contemplate your virtues at close quarters. But the Dutch, you see, are 7,000 miles away. Therefore misunderstandings may crop up between you and the Dutch. They have not the advantage which the Irish have in this House of seeing the British constantly, of reading your newspapers, and chanting Rudyard Kipling. But I am told that Rudyard Kipling is an author whom it is extremely difficult to translate into Dutch. Therefore, I am inclined to doubt the theory that in the furnace of this war the Afrikander and the Briton will be fused by the bloody flux of battle. No, we are here to-day to testify in the name and for the cause of race nationality. As I have already said, you may win. All your calculations are based upon that. If you win you will think that the results have justified your efforts. You will not think of the statesmanship of Gladstone, who held that there were bounds beyond which empire should not go, that there were limits even to British strength, and that by excessive effort, the extensor and contractor muscles of even the British right arm might tire. You disdain Gladstonian Councils, and you will go on and on and on in so far as time and circumstances permit you, and as long as you are successful you chant hosannas to the glories of your jingo statesmen. Is this wisdom? By what means do you hope to keep the Empire you have got? By what means do you hope to conciliate the races which you govern? Do you think the excuses on which you annex territory satisfy anyone but yourselves? I remember in 1879, when you were thinking of annexing Burma. The Tory Government was about to go out, but nobody knew that in India, where Reuter's telegrams are the great adjunct of civilisation, as anybody who turns up the history of that time will see. There came over suddenly one day a telegram from Rangoon, "King Thebaw is drinking." I do not think the hon. Baronet the Member for Carlisle was much disturbed at that. I had never heard of King Thebaw myself, and I was a little more surprised when

I read the next day, "The king is drinking still." A week elapsed, and then came a telegram, "King Thebaw has murdered his mother-in-law and three maiden aunts." Nothing more was heard for two days, and then there arrived another telegram, "Thebaw is drinking still." Shortly after this there were troops on the frontier. This was something like the Uitlanders' grievance. But before righteousness could invade Burma the Beaconsfield Ministry fell, and another five years elapsed in which Thebaw and his misfortunes, his want of temperance and the loss of his maiden aunts were entirely ignored by the British public. In June, 1885, a most appropriate circumstance occurred, for we put out the Gladstone Government over a dispute about the whisky tax, and within a week Baron Reuter telegraphed from Burma, "Thebaw is drinking still," and within a month or two after that you made war on Burma and King Thebaw was himself a Uitlander. Your pretext for taking Johannesburg is just the same. There, there is gold, and in Burma there were rubies, and commercial principles must triumph over backward native ways. Your policy is a policy of grab, and I do think it is pitiable that a nation whose qualities are great, whose courage is indomitable, whose resources are endless, should have, at this day, the canker of corruption eating at her heart. The principles which made you great are forgotten. The principles which make the British name a terror are represented by a statue of Cromwell outside Westminster Hall. You put up that statue to the memory of the author of the massacre of Drogheda after "quarter" had been promised to its garrison, at the very moment when your own forces are besieged in Ladysmith. Where was your historic conscience? We represent a small country and a small fraction of the Queen's dominions, but we have memories and we have hopes, and here lift up the voice of that country in protest against your policy, and we declare that the men of Ireland will never join you in any composition of wrong or of injustice.

(From *Hansard*, Vol. 78.)

JOHN EGLINTON

The Beginnings of Joyce

As I think of Joyce a haunting figure rises up in my memory. A pair of burning dark-blue eyes, serious and questioning, is fixed on me from under the peak of a nautical cap; the face is long, with a slight flush suggestive of dissipation, and an incipient beard is permitted to straggle over a very pronounced chin, under which the open shirt-collar leaves bare a full womanish throat. The figure is fairly tall and very erect, and gives a general impression of a kind of seedy hauteur; and every passer-by glances with a smile at the white tennis shoes (borrowed, as I gather from a mention of them in *Ulysses*). It was while walking homeward one night across Dublin that I was joined by this young man, whose appearance was already familiar to me; and although I cannot remember any of the strange sententious talk in which he instantly engaged, I have only to open the *Portrait of the Artist as a Young Man* to hear it again. "When we come to the phenomena of artistic conception, artistic gestation and artistic reproduction I require a new terminology and a new personal experience." I have never felt much interest in literary æsthetics, and he seemed to set a good deal of store by his system, referring, I recollect, to some remark made to him by "one of his disciples," but I liked listening to his careful intonation and full vowel sounds, and as he recited some of his verses, "My love is in a light attire," I remember noticing the apple in his throat, the throat of a singer; for Mr. Joyce has turned out to be an exception to a sweeping rule laid down by the late Sir J. P. Mahaffy, who used to say that he had never known a young man with a good tenor voice who did not go to the devil. Some ladies of the pavement shrieked at us as we crossed over O'Connell Bridge. I remember that we talked of serious matters, and at one point he impressed me by saying: "If I knew I were to drop dead before I reached that lamp-post, it would mean no more to me than it will mean to walk past it." Why did this young man seek out my acquaintance? Well, writing folk are interested in one another, and there were peculiarities in the occasion of the present writer's inglorious attempts at authorship about which it may be well to say something, as the relation may help indirectly to define the nature of Joyce's own portentous contribution to Irish literature.

James Joyce was one of a group of lively and eager-minded young men in the University College (a Jesuit house), amongst whom he had attained a sudden ascendancy by the publication in the *Fortnightly Review*, when he was only nineteen, of an article on Ibsen's play, *When We Dead Awaken*. The talk of these young men, their ribald wit and reckless manner of life, their interest in everything new in literature and philosophy (in this respect they far surpassed the students of Trinity College) are all reproduced in Joyce's writings; for his art seems to have found in this period the materials on which it was henceforth to work. Dublin was certainly at this moment a centre of vigorous potentialities.

THE BEGINNINGS OF JOYCE

The older culture was still represented with dignity by Dowden, Mahaffy and others; political agitation was holding back its energies for a favourable opportunity, while the organization of Sinn Fein was secretly ramifying throughout the country; the language movement was arrogant in its claims; the Irish Literary Theatre was already famous; and besides Yeats and Synge, A.E. and George Moore, there were numerous talkers, of incalculable individuality. There was hardly any one at that time who did not believe that Ireland was on the point of some decisive transformation. What, then, was wanting to this movement? for it has passed away, leaving Ireland more intensely what it has always been, a more or less disaffected member of the British Commonwealth of nations. That Ireland should achieve political greatness appeared then to most of us to be an idle dream; but in the things of the mind and of the spirit it seemed not a folly to think that Ireland might turn its necessity of political eclipse to glorious gains. A regenerate and thoughtful Ireland, an Ireland turned inwards upon itself in reverie, might recover inexhaustible sources of happiness and energy in its own beauty and aloofness, through a generous uprush of wisdom and melody in its poets and thinkers. It was not in the interest of the constituted spiritual authorities in Ireland that such a dream should ever be realized: a new movement of the human mind in Ireland was indeed precisely what was feared; the noisy language movement, the recrudescence of political agitation, outrage, assassination—any thing was preferable to that! There was a moment nevertheless when it seemed possible that this might be the turn events would take. Among other hopeful indications, a little magazine was started, under the editorship of the present writer, and A.E. boldly recommended "The Heretic" for a title, but the somewhat less compromising name, *Dana, a Magazine of Independent Thought,* was chosen. The fruitfulness of the moment was revealed in the number of eminent writers who contributed freely to its pages (Shaw and Chesterton promised contributions): Joyce, who chortled as he pocketed half a sovereign for a poem, was the only one to receive remuneration. Yeats held aloof, talking cuttingly of "Fleet Street atheism".

Joyce is, as all his writings show, Roman in mind and soul; for, generally speaking, to the Romanized mind the quest of truth, when it is not impious, is witless. What he seemed at this period I have attempted to describe, but what he really was is revealed in his *Portrait of the Artist as a Young Man,* a work completed in Trieste just ten years later. Religion had been with him a profound adolescent experience, torturing the sensitiveness which it awakened; all its floods had gone over him. He had now recovered, and had no objection to "Fleet Street atheism," but "independent thought" appeared to him an amusing disguise of the proselytizing spirit, and one night as we walked across town he endeavoured, with a certain earnestness, to bring home to me the extreme futility of ideals represented in *Dana,* by describing to me the solemn ceremonial of High Mass. (Dost thou remember these things, O Joyce, thou man of meticulous remembrance?) The little magazine laboured through a year, and the chief interest of the volume formed by its twelve numbers is now, no doubt, that it contains the series of sketches by George Moore, *Moods and Memories,* afterwards embodied in *Memoirs of My Dead Life.* It might have had a rare value now in the book market if I had been better advised one evening in the National Library, when Joyce came in with the manuscript of a serial story which he offered for publication. He observed me silently as I read, and when I handed it back to him with the timid observation that I did not care to publish what was to myself incomprehensible, he replaced it silently in his pocket.

I imagine that what he showed me was some early attempt in fiction, and that I was not really guilty of rejecting any work of his which has become famous. Joyce at this time was in the making, as is shown by the fact that the friends and incidents of this period have remained his principal subject matter. Chief among these friends was the incomparable "Buck Mulligan," Joyce's name for a now famous Dublin doctor—wit, poet, mocker, enthusiast, and, unlike most of his companions, blest with means to gratify his romantic caprices. He had a fancy for living in towers, and when I first heard of him had the notion of establishing himself at the top of the Round Tower at Clondalkin; afterwards he rented from the Admiralty the Martello Tower at Sandycove, which presently became the resort of poets and revolutionaries, something between one of the "Hell-Fire Clubs" of the eighteenth century and the Mermaid Tavern. Joyce was certainly very unhappy, proud and impecunious: no one took him at his own valuation, yet he held his own by his unfailing "recollectedness" and by his sententious and pedantic wit, shown especially in the limericks on the various figures in the literary movement, with which from time to time he regaled that company of roysterers and midnight bathers. Buck Mulligan's conversation, or rather his vehement and whimsical oratory, is reproduced with such exactness in *Ulysses* that one is driven to conclude that Joyce even then was "taking notes"; as to Joyce himself, he was exactly like his own hero Stephen Dedalus, who announced to his private circle of disciples that "Ireland was of importance because it belonged to him." He had made up his mind at this period, no doubt with vast undisclosed purposes of authorship, to make the personal acquaintance of everyone in Dublin of repute in literature. With Yeats he amused himself by delivering the sentence of the new generation, and "Never," said Yeats, "have I encountered so much pretension with so little to show for it." He was told that Lady Gregory, who was giving a literary party at her hotel, had refused to invite himself, and he vowed he would be there. We were all a little uneasy, and I can still see Joyce, with his air of half-timid effrontery, advancing toward his unwilling hostess and turning away from her to watch the company. Withal, there was something lovable in Joyce, as there is in every man of genius: I was sensible of the mute appeal of his liquid-burning gaze, though it was long afterwards that I was constrained to recognize his genius.

As already noted, Nature had endowed him with one remarkable advantage, an excellent tenor voice, and there is still, I have read, in existence a copy of the program of a Dublin concert, in which the names of the singers appear thus, perhaps only in alphabetical order:

1. *Mr. James A. Joyce*
2. *Mr. John M'Cormack*

He had persuaded himself to enter as a competitor in the Irish Musical Festival, the Feis Ceoil, but when a test-piece was handed to him, he looked at it, guffawed, and marched off the platform. Who but Joyce himself could have surmised at this moment the inhibition of his dæmon, or the struggle that may have been enacted in his dauntless and resourceful spirit? Perhaps it was then that he slipped past the Sirens Rock on the road to his destiny. Our dæmon, as Socrates pointed out, will only tell us what *not* to do, and if Joyce's dæmon had made the mistake of saying to him in so many words,

"Thou shalt be the Dante of Dublin, a Dante with a difference, it is true, as the Liffey is a more prosaic stream than the Arno: still, Dublin's Dante!" he might quite likely (for who is altogether satisfied with the destiny meted out to him?) have drawn back and "gone to the devil" with his fine tenor voice. He chose, what was for him no doubt the better part, his old vagabond impecunious life. One morning, just as the National Library opened, Joyce was announced; he seemed to wish for somebody to talk to, and related quite ingenuously how in the early hours of the morning he had been thrown out of the tower, and had walked into town from Sandycove. In reading the early chapters of *Ulysses* I was reminded of this incident, for this day, at least in its early portion, must have been for Joyce very like the day celebrated in that work, and I could not help wondering whether the idea of it may not have dawned upon him as he walked along the sands that morning.

Certain it is that he had now had his draught of experience: all the life which he describes in his writings now lay behind him. Suddenly we heard that he had married, was a father, and had gone off to Trieste to become a teacher in the Berlitz School there. It must have been two or three years later that he looked into the National Library for a few minutes, marvellously smartened up and with a short trim beard. The business which had brought him back had some connection, curiously enough, with the first introduction into Dublin of the cinema. The mission was a failure, and he was also much disgusted by the scruples of a Dublin publisher in reprinting a volume of short stories, of which all the copies had been destroyed in a fire. (It was not until 1914 that *Dubliners* was published in London.) "I am going back to civilization," were the last words

I heard from him. He has not, I believe, been in Dublin since.

From this point Joyce becomes for me, in retrospect, an heroic figure. He had "stooped under a dark tremendous sea of cloud," confident that he would "emerge some day": "using for my defence the only weapons I allow myself to use, silence, exile and cunning." Pause on that word "exile," a favourite one with Joyce. Why was it necessary for him to conjure up the grandiose image of his rejection by his countrymen? Ireland, though famous for flights of wild geese, banishes nobody, and Dublin had no quarrel with her Dante; and we have seen what he thought of the little group of those who were intent on blowing into flame the spark of a new spiritual initiative: the only people, be it said, of whom Catholic Ireland could be conceived of as anxious to rid herself. Still, a sensitive artist, reduced to impecunious despair as Joyce was at this period, might feel, in the very obscurity in which he was suffered to steal away out of Dublin, a sentence of banishment no less stern in its indifference than Florence's fiery sentence on her Dante:

> I go to encounter for the millionth time the reality of experience and to forge in the smithy of my soul the uncreated consciousness of my race.

He must have met with many curious adventures and suffered many a grief in the winning of his soul: but the strange thing is that in all his experience of the cities of men and of their minds and manners; while a new life claimed him and the desire of return departed from him; while his intellect consolidated itself through study and the acquisition of many languages: the city he had abandoned remained the home and subject matter of all his awakening invention. Dublin was of importance because it belonged to him. Demonstrably, he must have carried with him into his exile a mass of written material, but it was long before he learned how to deal with it, or to recognize, probably with some reluctance, in the merry imp of mockery which stirred within him, the spirit which was at length to take him by the hand and lead him out into the large spaces of literary creation.

His mind meanwhile retained some illusions: for example, that he was a poet. He has in fact published more than one volume of poems; but I will take A.E.'s word for it that most of them "might have been written by almost any young versifying sentimentalist." Another illusion was that he could write, in the ordinary sense, a novel; for *A Portrait of the Artist as a Young Man*, which took him ten years to write, is no more a novel than is Moore's *Confessions of a Young Man*. In style it is, for the most part, pompous and self-conscious, and in general we may say of it that it is one of those works which becomes important only when the author has done or written something else. That Joyce should have been able to make *Ulysses* out of much the same material gives the book now an extraordinary interest. It tells us a great deal about Joyce himself which we had hardly suspected, and both its squalor and its assumption wear quite a different complexion when we know that the author eventually triumphed over the one and vindicated the other. Genius is not always what it is supposed to be, self-realization: it is often a spirit to which the artist has to sacrifice himself; and until Joyce surrendered himself to his genius, until he died and came to life in his Mephistopheles of mockery, he remained what Goethe called *"ein trüber Gast auf der dunklen Erden"*.

I confess that when I read *Ulysses* I took Stephen Dedalus (Joyce himself) for the hero, and the impression seemed justified by the phrase at the end of the book when Stephen falls asleep: "at rest, he has travelled." The commentators, however, all appear to be agreed that Mr. Leopold Bloom is Ulysses, and they refer to the various episodes "Nausicaa," "The Oxen of the Sun," "The Nekuia," and so forth, with an understanding which I envy them. All the same, I am convinced that the only person concerned in the narrative who comes out as a real hero is the author himself. What kind of hero after all is brought to mind by the name Ulysses if not a hero long absent from his kingdom, returning, after being the sport of the gods for ten years, in triumph and vengeance? And it was after nearly as many years of absence as Ulysses from the country "which belonged to him," that Joyce turned up again for us in Dublin, with a vengeance! Certain it is that when he decided to scrap the scholastic habiliments of his mind, the poor disguise of a seedy snobbishness, and in lieu thereof endued himself with the elemental diabolism of *Ulysses*, he was transfigured. A thousand unexpected faculties and gay devices were liberated in his soul. The discovery of a new method in literary art, in which the pen is no longer the slave of logic and rhetoric made of this Berlitz School teacher a kind of public danger, threatening the corporate existence of "literature" as established in the minds and affections of the older generation.

He found this method, as the concluding pages of the *Portrait* suggest to us, in his diary: a swift notation, at their point of origination, of feelings and perceptions. In one way Joyce is no less concerned with style than was R. L. Stevenson: yet we mark in this pupil of the Irish Jesuits a spirit very different from the goodwill of the Scottish Protestant towards English literature. He is aware, like Stevenson, of every shade of style in English, and there is a chapter in *Ulysses* which presents a historic conspectus of English prose from its Anglo-Saxon beginnings down to the personal oddities of Carlyle, Henry James and others, and modern slang. But whereas, with Stevenson, English prose style, according to his own cheerful comparison, is a torch lit from one generation to another, our Romano-Celtic Joyce nurses an ironic detachment from the whole of the English tradition. Indeed, he is its enemy. Holding his ear to the subconscious, he catches his meanings unceremoniously as they rise, in hit-or-miss vocables. English is only one of the languages which he knows: they say he speaks Italian like a native, German, Spanish, Portuguese, and various other idioms; and he knows these languages not through books but as living organisms, their shop-talk and slang rather than their poets; they are companions to him, powerful agents, genii who bear him into the caverns whence they originated. And at the end of it all, it must have seemed to him that he held English, his country's spiritual enemy, in the hollow of his hand, for the English language too came at his call to do his bidding. George Moore used to talk with envy of those English writers who could use "the whole of the language," and I really think that Joyce must be added to Moore's examples of this power—Shakespeare, Whitman, Kipling. This language found itself constrained by its new master to perform tasks to which it was unaccustomed in the service of pure literature; against the grain it was forced to reproduce Joyce's fantasies in all kinds of juxtapositions, neologisms, amalgamations, truncations, words that are only found scrawled up in public lavatories, obsolete words, words in limbo or belike in the womb of time. It assumed every intonation and locution of Dublin, London, Glasgow, New York, Johannesburg. Like a devil taking pleasure in forcing a virgin to speak obscenely, so Joyce rejoiced darkly in causing the language of Milton and Wordsworth to utter all but unimaginable filth and treason.

Such is Joyce's Celtic revenge, and it must be owned that he has succeeded in making logic and rhetoric less sure of themselves among our younger writers. As an innovator in the art of fiction I conceive him to be less formidable. Mankind has never failed to recognize a good story-teller, and never will. They say that Joyce, when he is in good humour among his disciples, can be induced to allow them to examine a key to the elaborate symbolism of the different episodes, all pointing inward to a central mystery, undivulged, I fancy. *Ulysses*, in fact, is a mock-heroic, and at the heart of it is that which lies at the heart of all mockery, an awful inner void. None but Joyce and his dæmon know that void: the consciousness of it is perhaps the "tragic sense" which his disciples claim that he has introduced into English literature. But is there then no serious intention in *Ulysses*? As Joyce's most devout interpreters are at variance with respect to the leading motive, we may perhaps without much loss assume its seriousness to be nothing but the diabolic gravity with which the whole work is conducted throughout its mystifications. Yet the original motive may have been quite a simple one. Near the centre of the book, in that chapter known as the "Oxen of the Sun," which, in Mr. Stuart Gilbert's words, "ascends in orderly march the gamut of English styles," "culminating in a futurist cacophony of syncopated slang," there is a passage over which the reader may pause:

There are sins or (let us call them as the world calls them) evil memories which are hidden away by man in the darkest places of the heart but they abide there and wait. He may suffer their memory to grow dim, let them be as though they

THE BEGINNINGS OF JOYCE

had not been and all but persuade himself that they were not or at least were otherwise. Yet a chance word will call them forth suddenly and they will rise up to confront him in the most various circumstances, a vision or a dream, or while timbrel and harp soothe his senses or amid the cool silver tranquillity of the evening or at the feast at midnight when he is now filled with wine. Not to insult over him will the vision come as over one that lies under her wrath, not for vengeance to cut him off from the living but shrouded in the piteous vesture of the past, silent, remote, reproachful.

The "timbrel and harp" make me a little wary, but though some writer is doubtless parodied (Ruskin?), does there not seem here for once to be a relaxation of some significance, in the strain of mockery?

The conception of the Irish Jew, Leopold Bloom, within whose mind we move through a day of Dublin life, is somewhat of a puzzle. Buck Mulligan we know, and the various minor characters; and in the interview of the much enduring Stephen with the officials of the National Library, the present writer experiences a twinge of recollection of things actually said. But Bloom, if he be a real character, belongs to a province of Joyce's experience of which I have no knowledge. He is, I suppose, the jumble of ordinary human consciousness in the city, in any city, with which the author's experience of men and cities had deepened his familiarity: a slowly progressing host of instincts, appetites, adaptations, questions, curiosities, held at short tether by ignorance and vulgarity; and the rapid notation which I conceive Joyce to have discovered originally in his diary served admirably well to record these mental or psychic processes. Bloom's mind is the mind of the crowd, swayed by every vicissitude, but he is distinguished through race-endowment by a detachment from the special crowd-consciousness of the Irish, while his familiarity with the latter makes him the fitting instrument of the author's encyclopædic humour. Bloom, therefore, is an impersonation rather than a type: not a character, for a character manifests itself in action, and in *Ulysses* there is no action. There is only the rescue of Stephen from a row in a brothel, in which some have discovered a symbolism which might have appealed to G. F. Watts, the Delivery of Art by Science and Common Sense. But the humour is vast and genial. There are incomparable flights in *Ulysses:* the debate, for instance, in the Maternity Hospital on the mystery of birth; and above all, I think, the scene near the end of the book in the cabmen's shelter, kept by none other than Skin-the-Goat, the famous jarvey of the Phœnix Park murders. Here the author proves himself one of the world's great humorists. The humour as always is pitiless, but where we laugh we love, and after his portrait of the sailor in this chapter I reckon Joyce after all a lover of men.

When Joyce produced *Ulysses* he had shot his bolt. Let us put it without any invidiousness. He is a man of one book, as perhaps the ideal author always is. Besides, he is not specially interested in "literature," not at all events as a well-wisher. A man who adds something new to literature often hates the word, as the poet shrinks from the tomb even though it be in Westminster Abbey. Usually he is interested in something quite apart from literature, added unto it by him. As for Joyce, his interest is in language and the mystery of words. He appears at all events to have done with "literature," and we leave him with the plea for literature that it exists mainly to confer upon mankind a deeper and more general insight and corresponding powers of expression. Language is only ready to become the instrument of the modern mind when its development is complete, and it is when words are invested with all kinds of associations that they are the more or less adequate vehicles of thought and knowledge. And after "literature" perhaps comes something else.

ROBERT LYND

On Never Going to the British Museum

How enthusiastic the natural man is over museums and art galleries! Something in me responds as I read in a leading article in *The Times* that "there is no reason why almost any Londoner should not, if the museums and galleries were always open for nothing, be able to constitute himself a connoisseur of beauty." Not for me, I know, to constitute myself a connoisseur of beauty after this fashion, but even I, who seldom enter a museum or art gallery except during a visit to a foreign town, have dreamed of spending long days in public buildings, from the walls of which the world's genius looked down on me, a trembling initiate, or in which the world's knowledge was preserved in glass cases to be passed on to me as an almost private possession. Before I came to London I thought of it chiefly as a city of theatres, concert halls, and museums and galleries of the arts. I imagined that any sane Londoner, outside his working hours, would be either listening to music or looking at pictures on such occasions as he was not reading a book or seeing a play. It is odd what a hunger for the arts one had at that age, as though perpetually hoping to discover in a book or a picture the keys of Heaven. The very names of certain authors and artists made one vibrate with a sense of impending revelation, even if one had never read or seen a line of their work. I remember my excitement on first hearing the name of Walter Savage Landor, and how I went out with the first shillings I had and bought his verse in the Canterbury Poets and his prose in the Camelot Classics and all but persuaded myself for months, though with more and more difficulty, that here were the keys, or were going to be the keys, at last. Then there was Schubert. Then there was Wagner. One went to one's first Wagner opera in the sure and certain hope that a new door would be opened, and lo! doors vaster even than one had dreamed swung wide on their hinges. Those were days in which it was possible to go to the opera twice in a day and not feel weary—to sit through *Mignon* in the afternoon and to go to *Lohengrin* in the evening. If London seemed desirable then, it was chiefly as a city in which the opera lasted, not for a week only, but for a season. Had it been foretold me that a time would come when *The Ring* would be produced in London and when I, though a Londoner by settlement, would remain away from it, not merely with cheerfulness, but almost with a feeling of relief, I should have laughed at the falsehood. But *The Ring* has been produced in London more than once since then, and I have not heard it yet. I doubt if I shall ever hear it. I no longer expect to find the keys just there. I do not even buy Wagner rolls for the piano-player. Yet I would once have sworn that Wagner was greater than St. Paul or Robert Louis Stevenson.

As for the museums and picture galleries, how great was their lure three hundred miles away! The picture galleries, perhaps, were less exciting in prospect than the concert rooms, and the British Museum than the picture galleries. But, as at least half of my friends were painters, I had an ardent enough faith in Turner and Rembrandt and Velazquez to believe that they were the possessors of the keys if I could but find them. I had always felt a foreigner and an ignoramus in the presence of pictures, enjoying them rather as one enjoys a strange town in which a language is being spoken that one does not understand, but I had no doubt that I had only to become familiar with them in order to be as powerfully affected by them as I was by music. The British Museum, too, would disclose to me the secrets of Greece, where there was beauty not only in the faces of men and women but in their words—nay (which is most difficult of all), in their very actions. More than this, the reading-room was there to convert me into a scholar, if I wished, with shelves of learning that Faust might have envied. To go to London, indeed, was to go on a pilgrimage to a city which was a vast storehouse of beauty and wisdom that were to be had almost for the asking. It may seem all the more unaccountable that, on arriving in London, a lonely loafer in a lonely attic in Pimlico, I immediately went out and bought a map of the town and spent my first evening in a seat in the gallery of the old Gaiety Theatre. Had you been as deeply in love with Miss Marie Studholme as I was in my 'teens, I do not think you would have regarded this as too base a declension from the ideal. Love transforms even *The Toreador* into something more charming and desirable than the lost plays of Menander. The next day a man whom I had known as a medical student and who was acting as *locum tenens* somewhere in the East End called on me, and, after showing me the house where the Baroness Burdett-Coutts lived (which everybody, for some strange reason, used to show me) and the house where the Duke of Devonshire lived, and Buckingham Palace and St. James's Palace and Mooney's, took me off later in the day to Whitechapel, where, after a dish of tripe, we spent the evening getting into the way of actors and actresses behind the scenes at the Christmas pantomime. I confess I should have preferred to buy a seat, and I should have preferred still more not to see the pantomime at all, but I was in the hands of fate, which seemed to be bearing me further and further away from Schubert and G. F. Watts—how we worshipped him in those days!—and Phidias. Next to call on me was a painter whom I had known since we were small boys. He took me out and put me on to the top of a horse-bus, pointed out the house where the Baroness Burdett-Coutts lived and the house where the Duke of Devonshire lived, and ultimately led me into a public-house in Fleet Street, explaining as we went in: "Old Johnson used to come here." Well, an association with Dr. Johnson was at least ennobling, but this was not the reading-room of the British Museum. Then my friend took me out to Hampstead and into an inn, afterwards famous in song as the Old Bull and Bush, explaining after the fashion of a man of letters, "Old Hazlitt used to come here." That night I spent with him at Hampstead. On the next afternoon he proposed that we should go to Battersea on a visit to the studio of another artist whose name has become a household word since then. When we reached the Pier Hotel at Albert Bridge, he said, "Let's go in here," and, as we waited to be served, he speculated on the possibility that "old Whistler used to come here" when he was painting his *Battersea Bridge*. Never before had I lived in such a whirl of literary and artistic associations. I might not be seeing many pictures or reading many books, but I was following in the footsteps of the great painters and the great writers with an almost dog-like fidelity. My friend was a perfect master of the literary geography of London, though, indeed, when he led me into a most unpromising-looking tavern in St. Martin's Lane on the plea that "old Stevenson used to come here," I began to suspect that he was playing on my credulity. Still, there were pauses between the lessons, during which we did visit the Turner rooms in the National Gallery and gaze at *Rain, Steam and Speed* as at one of the wonders of the world in ruins. My friend's chief method of expressing his enthusiasm, as he stood before a picture he liked, was to say merely, "By God, old chap!" or "By God, Willie!" or "By God, Rupert!" and to nod his head, as if in despair of ever rivalling so great a miracle. And so he spoke before the blue cloak of the Mother of God in a Titian, or before the ox and the ass and the divine nursery under a hill of roads winding among cypresses in a Fra Filippo Lippi, or before a base king portrayed by Velazquez or before Rembrandt portrayed by himself. And, indeed, if we idled a good deal of our time in other places, he talked by preference even there of writers and artists—of Hazlitt and Lamb and Sir Thomas Browne, of Turner and Corot and Millet, and above all of Wordsworth, whom he revered as a poet but detested as a man. I cannot, by an odd chance, remember his ever once saying, "Old Wordsworth used to come here."

Thus my pilgrimage to London was, as it were, defeated at the very outset. And even today I have heard little of that music and seen few of those pictures and read few of those books that were once like the stars circling round the star of guidance in a dark world. I seldom hear any good music except such as I play with my own feet. I do not go to one opera in a year. I have been once in the Tate Gallery since the war, and not even once in the National Gallery. I have been in the British Museum, but only in order to see a civil servant. I am always on the point of breaking through this indolence and taking up the pilgrimage at the point at which I dropped out of it so many years ago, but, when it comes to the practical issue whether I shall go to a picture gallery or go home, I invariably find myself mounting a bus and going home. Theoretically, I still haunt museums and galleries and concert halls. If they were closed I should feel an infinitely poorer man, as though my income of possible pleasures had been cut down. I love the National Gallery and the British Museum, indeed, as noble reserves of pleasure on which I can draw at need. I can bear not visiting them, but I could not bear so easily not having them to visit.

Hence I join ardently in every protest against closing a museum or charging for admission to it. I do not like the potential I who visits such places to be hampered. It is not that I myself mind paying sixpence, but the potential I (who, as I have said, frequents museums much more than I do) might not have a sixpence. And, after all, the museums and art galleries exist for potential visitors as well as for actual visitors. They are a part of the rich surroundings of our lives. They make London almost worth living in, whereas without them it would be a wilderness. I like to feel that somewhere or other in the neighbourhood troops of people are shuffling round high rooms, peering at pictures and staring at statues and paying a puzzled reverence to antiquity. They are our representatives in the public appreciation of the arts just as the people who attend political meetings are our representatives in keeping alive the flame of democratic government. Do not think that one enjoys a picture or a statue the less for never having seen it. The *Mona Lisa* never seemed so wonderful as before one had been to Paris, and the *Winged Victory* would have been as lovely as winds and waters

ON NEVER GOING TO THE BRITISH MUSEUM 69

in the imagination even though one had never been to the Louvre or seen so much as a photograph of it. There is a pleasure in knowing that a thing exists in the same world with us. There is another pleasure in knowing that a thing exists in the same neighbourhood with us. London does not mean to me merely the people and the plane trees I see from the top of the bus on my way to the office, or the pavements and policemen, the lamps and the loiterers, I see out of the window of a taxi on my way to dinner. It means all the great composers constantly coming to life again in concert halls and theatres, all the great painters surviving in the quiet paradise of the National Gallery, all the great sculptors and all the great authors, a majestic congregation in the British Museum. Why, it is a pleasure, when walking along Adelphi Terrace, to feel "Bernard Shaw lives there," even though he is not to be seen at the window. It is a pleasure, too, to enjoy the art of the day by proximity and to know that somewhere or other the pictures of Mr. Augustus John and Mr. Henry Lamb and Mr. Nevinson are being exhibited, though the show is usually over before one has had time to go to it. And it is a pleasure to be contemporary with Mr. Arnold Bax and Mr. Arthur Bliss and to live in a constant anticipation of hearing their work otherwise than through one's admirable representative, the regular concert goer. The pleasures of proximity have never yet had justice done to them. It is chiefly they, however, that make London so much more desirable a city to live in than Birmingham or Manchester. It is because they mean so much to us that, if the British Museum or National Gallery were burnt down, we should regard it not only as a public calamity but as one of the great personal calamities of our lives.

PLAYS

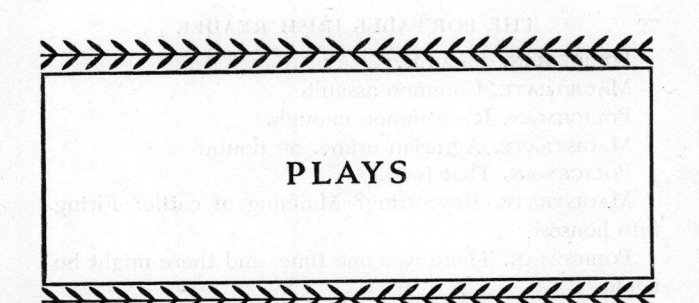

LADY GREGORY

Spreading the News

CHARACTERS

BARTLEY FALLON
MRS. FALLON
JACK SMITH
SHAWN EARLY
TIM CASEY
JAMES RYAN
MRS. TARPEY
MRS. TULLY
A POLICEMAN
(JO MULDOON)
A REMOVABLE
MAGISTRATE

SCENE: *The outskirts of a Fair. An Apple Stall.* MRS. TARPEY *sitting at it.* MAGISTRATE *and* POLICEMAN *enter.*

MAGISTRATE. So that is the Fair Green. Cattle and sheep and mud. No system. What a repulsive sight!

POLICEMAN. That is so, indeed.

MAGISTRATE. I suppose there is a good deal of disorder in this place?

POLICEMAN. There is.

MAGISTRATE. Common assault.

POLICEMAN. It's common enough.

MAGISTRATE. Agrarian crime, no doubt?

POLICEMAN. That is so.

MAGISTRATE. Boycotting? Maiming of cattle? Firing into houses?

POLICEMAN. There was one time, and there might be again.

MAGISTRATE. That is bad. Does it go any farther than that?

POLICEMAN. Far enough, indeed.

MAGISTRATE. Homicide, then! This district has been shamefully neglected! I will change all that. When I was in the Andaman Islands, my system never failed. Yes, yes, I will change all that. What has that woman on her stall?

POLICEMAN. Apples mostly—and sweets.

MAGISTRATE. Just see if there are any unlicensed goods underneath—spirits or the like. We had evasions of the salt tax in the Andaman Islands.

POLICEMAN (*sniffing cautiously and upsetting a heap of apples*). I see no spirits here—or salt.

MAGISTRATE (*to* MRS. TARPEY). Do you know this town well, my good woman?

MRS. TARPEY (*holding out some apples*). A penny the half-dozen, your honour.

POLICEMAN (*shouting*). The gentleman is asking do you know the town? He's the new magistrate!

MRS. TARPEY (*rising and ducking*). Do I know the town? I do, to be sure.

MAGISTRATE (*shouting*). What is its chief business?

MRS. TARPEY. Business, is it? What business would the people here have but to be minding one another's business?

SPREADING THE NEWS

MAGISTRATE. I mean what trade have they?

MRS. TARPEY. Not a trade. No trade at all but to be talking.

MAGISTRATE. I shall learn nothing here.

(JAMES RYAN *comes in, pipe in mouth. Seeing* MAGISTRATE *he retreats quickly, taking pipe from mouth.*)

MAGISTRATE. The smoke from that man's pipe had a greenish look; he may be growing unlicensed tobacco at home. I wish I had brought my telescope to this district. Come to the post-office, I will telegraph for it. I found it very useful in the Andaman Islands.

(MAGISTRATE *and* POLICEMAN *go out left.*)

MRS. TARPEY. Bad luck to Jo Muldoon, knocking my apples this way and that way. (*Begins arranging them.*) Showing off he was to the new magistrate.

(*Enter* BARTLEY FALLON *and* MRS. FALLON.)

BARTLEY. Indeed it's a poor country and a scarce country to be living in. But I'm thinking if I went to America it's long ago the day I'd be dead!

MRS. FALLON. So you might, indeed. (*She puts her basket on a barrel and begins putting parcels in it, taking them from under her cloak.*)

BARTLEY. And it's a great expense for a poor man to be buried in America.

MRS. FALLON. Never fear, Bartley Fallon, but I'll give you a good burying the day you'll die.

BARTLEY. Maybe it's yourself will be buried in the graveyard of Cloonmara before me, Mary Fallon, and I myself that will be dying unbeknownst some night, and no one a-near me. And the cat itself may be gone straying through the country, and the mice squealing over the quilt.

MRS. FALLON. Leave off talking of dying. It might be twenty years you'll be living yet.

BARTLEY (*with a deep sigh*). I'm thinking if I'll be

living at the end of twenty years, it's a very old man I'll be then!

Mrs. Tarpey (*turns and sees them*). Good morrow, Bartley Fallon; good morrow, Mrs. Fallon. Well, Bartley, you'll find no cause for complaining today; they are all saying it was a good fair.

Bartley (*raising his voice*). It was not a good fair, Mrs. Tarpey. It was a scattered sort of a fair. If we didn't expect more, we got less. That's the way with me always; whatever I have to sell goes down and whatever I have to buy goes up. If there's ever any misfortune coming to this world, it's on myself it pitches, like a flock of crows on seed potatoes.

Mrs. Fallon. Leave off talking of misfortunes, and listen to Jack Smith that is coming the way, and he singing.

(*Voice of* Jack Smith *heard singing*):

I thought, my first love,
    There'd be but one house between you and me,
And I thought I would find
    Yourself coaxing my child on your knee.
Over the tide
    I would leap with the leap of a swan,
Till I came to the side
    Of the wife of the red-haired man!

(Jack Smith *comes in; he is a red-haired man, and is carrying a hayfork.*)

Mrs. Tarpey. That should be a good song if I had my hearing.

Mrs. Fallon (*shouting*). It's "The Red-haired Man's Wife."

Mrs. Tarpey. I know it well. That's the song that has a skin on it! (*She turns her back to them and goes on arranging her apples.*)

Mrs. Fallon. Where's herself, Jack Smith?

JACK SMITH. She was delayed with her washing; bleaching the clothes on the hedge she is, and she daren't leave them, with all the tinkers that do be passing to the fair. It isn't to the fair I came myself, but up to the Five Acre Meadow I'm going, where I have a contract for the hay. We'll get a share of it into tramps today. (*He lays down hayfork and lights his pipe.*)

BARTLEY. You will not get it into tramps today. The rain will be down on it by evening, and on myself too. It's seldom I ever started on a journey but the rain would come down on me before I'd find any place of shelter.

JACK SMITH. If it didn't itself, Bartley, it is my belief you would carry a leaky pail on your head in place of a hat, the way you'd not be without some cause for complaining.

(*A voice heard, "Go on, now, go on out o' that. Go on I say."*)

JACK SMITH. Look at that young mare of Pat Ryan's that is backing into Shaughnessy's bullocks with the dint of the crowd! Don't be daunted, Pat, I'll give you a hand with her. (*He goes out, leaving his hayfork.*)

MRS. FALLON. It's time for ourselves to be going home. I have all I bought put in the basket. Look at there, Jack Smith's hayfork he left after him! He'll be wanting it. (*Calls*) Jack Smith! Jack Smith!—He's gone through the crowd—hurry after him, Bartley, he'll be wanting it.

BARTLEY. I'll do that. This is no safe place to be leaving it. (*He takes up fork awkwardly and upsets the basket.*) Look at that now! If there is any basket in the fair upset, it must be our own basket! (*He goes out to right.*)

MRS. FALLON. Get out of that! It is your own fault, it is. Talk of misfortunes and misfortunes will come. Glory be! Look at my new egg-cups rolling in every part—and my two pound of sugar with the paper broke—

MRS. TARPEY (*turning from stall*). God help us, Mrs. Fallon, what happened to your basket?

MRS. FALLON. It's himself that knocked it down, bad manners to him. (*Putting things up.*) My grand sugar that's destroyed, and he'll not drink his tea without it. I had best go back to the shop for more, much good may it do him!

(*Enter* TIM CASEY.)

TIM CASEY. Where is Bartley Fallon, Mrs. Fallon! I want a word with him before he'll leave the fair. I was afraid he might have gone home by this, for he's a temperate man.

MRS. FALLON. I wish he did go home! It'd be best for me if he went home straight from the fair green, or if he never came with me at all! Where is he, is it? He's gone up the road (*jerks elbow*) following Jack Smith with a hayfork. (*She goes out to left.*)

TIM CASEY. Following Jack Smith with a hayfork! Did ever any one hear the like of that. (*Shouts*) Did you hear that news, Mrs. Tarpey?

MRS. TARPEY. I heard no news at all.

TIM CASEY. Some dispute I suppose it was that rose between Jack Smith and Bartley Fallon, and it seems Jack made off, and Bartley is following him with a hayfork!

MRS. TARPEY. Is he now? Well, that was quick work! It's not ten minutes since the two of them were here, Bartley going home and Jack going to the Five Acre Meadow; and I had my apples to settle up, that Jo Muldoon of the police had scattered, and when I looked round again Jack Smith was gone, and Bartley Fallon was gone, and Mrs. Fallon's basket upset, and

SPREADING THE NEWS

all in it strewed upon the ground—the tea here—the two pound of sugar there—the egg-cups there— Look, now, what a great hardship the deafness puts upon me, that I didn't hear the commencement of the fight! Wait till I tell James Ryan that I see below; he is a neighbour of Bartley's, it would be a pity if he wouldn't hear the news!

(*She goes out. Enter* SHAWN EARLY *and* MRS. TULLY.)

TIM CASEY. Listen, Shawn Early! Listen, Mrs. Tully, to the news! Jack Smith and Bartley Fallon had a falling out, and Jack knocked Mrs. Fallon's basket into the road, and Bartley made an attack on him with a hayfork, and away with Jack, and Bartley after him. Look at the sugar here yet on the road!

SHAWN EARLY. Do you tell me so? Well, that's a queer thing, and Bartley Fallon so quiet a man!

MRS. TULLY. I wouldn't wonder at all. I would never think well of a man that would have that sort of a mouldering look. It's likely he has overtaken Jack by this.

(*Enter* JAMES RYAN *and* MRS. TARPEY.)

JAMES RYAN. That is great news Mrs. Tarpey was telling me! I suppose that's what brought the police and the magistrate up this way. I was wondering to see them in it a while ago.

SHAWN EARLY. The police after them? Bartley Fallon must have injured Jack so. They wouldn't meddle in a fight that was only for show!

MRS. TULLY. Why wouldn't he injure him? There was many a man killed with no more of a weapon than a hayfork.

JAMES RYAN. Wait till I run north as far as Kelly's bar to spread the news! (*He goes out.*)

TIM CASEY. I'll go tell Jack Smith's first cousin that is standing there south of the church after selling his lambs. (*Goes out.*)

MRS. TULLY. I'll go telling a few of the neighbours I see beyond to the west. (*Goes out.*)

SHAWN EARLY. I'll give word of it beyond at the east of the green. (*Is going out when* MRS. TARPEY *seizes hold of him.*)

MRS. TARPEY. Stop a minute, Shawn Early, and tell me did you see red Jack Smith's wife, Kitty Keary, in any place?

SHAWN EARLY. I did. At her own house she was, drying clothes on the hedge as I passed.

MRS. TARPEY. What did you say she was doing?

SHAWN EARLY (*breaking away*). Laying out a sheet on the hedge. (*He goes.*)

MRS. TARPEY. Laying out a sheet for the dead! The Lord have mercy on us! Jack Smith dead, and his wife laying out a sheet for his burying! (*Calls out*) Why didn't you tell me that before, Shawn Early? Isn't the deafness the great hardship? Half the world might be dead without me knowing of it or getting word of it at all! (*She sits down and rocks herself.*) O my poor Jack Smith! To be going to his work so nice and so hearty, and to be left stretched on the ground in the full light of the day!

(*Enter* TIM CASEY.)

TIM CASEY. What is it, Mrs. Tarpey? What happened since?

MRS. TARPEY. O my poor Jack Smith!

TIM CASEY. Did Bartley overtake him?

MRS. TARPEY. O the poor man!

TIM CASEY. Is it killed he is?

MRS. TARPEY. Stretched in the Five Acre Meadow!

TIM CASEY. The Lord have mercy on us! Is that a fact?

MRS. TARPEY. Without the rites of the Church or a ha'porth!

TIM CASEY. Who was telling you?

MRS. TARPEY. And the wife laying out a sheet for his corpse. (*Sits up and wipes her eyes.*) I suppose they'll wake him the same as another?

(*Enter* MRS. TULLY, SHAWN EARLY, *and* JAMES RYAN.)

MRS. TULLY. There is great talk about this work in every quarter of the fair.

MRS. TARPEY. Ochone! cold and dead. And myself maybe the last he was speaking to!

JAMES RYAN. The Lord save us! Is it dead he is?

TIM CASEY. Dead surely, and his wife getting provision for the wake.

SHAWN EARLY. Well, now, hadn't Bartley Fallon great venom in him?

MRS. TULLY. You may be sure he had some cause. Why would he have made an end of him if he had not? (*To* MRS. TARPEY, *raising her voice.*) What was it rose the dispute at all, Mrs. Tarpey?

MRS. TARPEY. Not a one of me knows. The last I saw of them, Jack Smith was standing there, and Bartley Fallon was standing there, quiet and easy, and he listening to "The Red-haired Man's Wife."

MRS. TULLY. Do you hear that, Tim Casey? Do you hear that, Shawn Early and James Ryan? Bartley Fallon was here this morning listening to red Jack Smith's wife, Kitty Keary that was! Listening to her and whispering with her! It was she started the fight so!

SHAWN EARLY. She must have followed him from her own house. It is likely some person roused him.

TIM CASEY. I never knew, before, Bartley Fallon was great with Jack Smith's wife.

MRS. TULLY. How would you know it? Sure it's not in the streets they would be calling it. If Mrs. Fallon didn't know of it, and if I that have the next house to them didn't know of it, and if Jack Smith himself didn't know of it, it is not likely you would know of it, Tim Casey.

SHAWN EARLY. Let Bartley Fallon take charge of her from this out so, and let him provide for her. It is little pity she will get from any person in this parish.

TIM CASEY. How can he take charge of her? Sure he has a wife of his own. Sure you don't think he'd turn souper and marry her in a Protestant church?

JAMES RYAN. It would be easy for him to marry her if he brought her to America.

SHAWN EARLY. With or without Kitty Keary, believe me it is for America he's making at this minute. I saw the new magistrate and Jo Muldoon of the police going into the post-office as I came up—there was hurry on them—you may be sure it was to telegraph they went, the way he'll be stopped in the docks at Queenstown!

MRS. TULLY. It's likely Kitty Keary is gone with him, and not minding a sheet or a wake at all. The poor man, to be deserted by his own wife, and the breath hardly gone out yet from his body that is lying bloody in the field!

(*Enter* MRS. FALLON.)

MRS. FALLON. What is it the whole of the town is talking about? And what is it you yourselves are talking about? Is it about my man Bartley Fallon you are talking? Is it lies about him you are telling, saying that he went killing Jack Smith? My grief that ever he came into this place at all!

SPREADING THE NEWS

JAMES FALLON. Be easy now, Mrs. Fallon. Sure there is no one at all in the whole fair but is sorry for you!

MRS. FALLON. Sorry for me, is it? Why would any one be sorry for me? Let you be sorry for yourselves, and that there may be shame on you for ever and at the day of judgment, for the words you are saying and the lies you are telling to take away the character of my poor man, and to take the good name off of him, and to drive him to destruction! That is what you are doing!

SHAWN EARLY. Take comfort now, Mrs. Fallon. The police are not so smart as they think. Sure he might give them the slip yet, the same as Lynchehaun.

MRS. TULLY. If they do get him, and if they do put a rope around his neck, there is no one can say he does not deserve it!

MRS. FALLON. Is that what you are saying, Bridget Tully, and is that what you think? I tell you it's too much talk you have, making yourself out to be such a great one, and to be running down every respectable person! A rope, is it? It isn't much of a rope was needed to tie up your own furniture the day you came into Martin Tully's house, and you never bringing as much as a blanket, or a penny, or a suit of clothes with you and I myself bringing seventy pounds and two feather beds. And now you are stiffer than a woman would have a hundred pounds! It is too much talk the whole of you have. A rope is it? I tell you the whole of this town is full of liars and schemers that would hang you up for half a glass of whisky. (*Turning to go.*) People they are you wouldn't believe as much as daylight from without you'd get up to have a look at it yourself. Killing Jack Smith indeed! Where are you at all, Bartley, till I bring you out of this? My nice quiet little man! My decent comrade! He that is as kind and as harmless as an innocent beast of the field! He'll be doing no harm at all if he'll shed the blood of some of you after this day's work! That much would be no harm at all. (*Calls out.*) Bartley! Bartley Fallon! Where are you? (*Going out.*) Did any one see Bartley Fallon?

(*All turn to look after her.*)

JAMES RYAN. It is hard for her to believe any such a thing, God help her!

(*Enter* BARTLEY FALLON *from right, carrying hayfork.*)

BARTLEY. It is what I often said to myself, if there is ever any misfortune coming to this world it is on myself it is sure to come!

(*All turn round and face him.*)

BARTLEY. To be going about with this fork and to find no one to take it, and no place to leave it down, and I wanting to be gone out of this— Is that you, Shawn Early? (*Holds out fork.*) It's well I met you. You have no call to be leaving the fair for a while the way I have, and how can I go till I'm rid of this fork? Will you take it and keep it until such time as Jack Smith—

SHAWN EARLY (*backing*). I will not take it, Bartley Fallon, I'm very thankful to you!

BARTLEY (*turning to apple stall*). Look at it now, Mrs. Tarpey, it was here I got it; let me thrust it in under the stall. It will lie there safe enough, and no one will take notice of it until such time as Jack Smith—

MRS. TARPEY. Take your fork out of that! Is it to put trouble on me and to destroy me you want? putting it there for the police to be rooting it out maybe. (*Thrusts him back.*)

BARTLEY. That is a very unneighbourly thing for you to do, Mrs. Tarpey. Hadn't I enough care on me with that fork before this, running up and down with it like the swinging of a clock, and afeard to lay it down in any

SPREADING THE NEWS 83

place! I wish I never touched it or meddled with it at all!

JAMES RYAN. It is a pity, indeed, you ever did.

BARTLEY. Will you yourself take it, James Ryan? You were always a neighbourly man.

JAMES RYAN (*backing*). There is many a thing I would do for you, Bartley Fallon, but I won't do that!

SHAWN EARLY. I tell you there is no man will give you any help or any encouragement for this day's work. If it was something agrarian now—

BARTLEY. If no one at all will take it, maybe it's best to give it up to the police.

TIM CASEY. There'd be a welcome for it with them surely! (*Laughter.*)

MRS. TULLY. And it is to the police Kitty Keary herself will be brought.

MRS. TARPEY (*rocking to and fro*). I wonder now who will take the expense of the wake for poor Jack Smith?

BARTLEY. The wake for Jack Smith!

TIM CASEY. Why wouldn't he get a wake as well as another? Would you begrudge him that much?

BARTLEY. Red Jack Smith dead! Who was telling you?

SHAWN EARLY. The whole town knows of it by this.

BARTLEY. Do they say what way did he die?

JAMES RYAN. You don't know that yourself, I suppose, Bartley Fallon? You don't know he was followed and that he was laid dead with the stab of a hayfork?

BARTLEY. The stab of a hayfork!

SHAWN EARLY. You don't know, I suppose, that the body was found in the Five Acre Meadow?

BARTLEY. The Five Acre Meadow!

TIM CASEY. It is likely you don't know that the police are after the man that did it?

BARTLEY. The man that did it?

MRS. TULLY. You don't know, maybe, that he was

made away with for the sake of Kitty Keary, his wife?

BARTLEY. Kitty Keary, his wife! (*Sits down bewildered.*)

MRS. TULLY. And what have you to say now, Bartley Fallon?

BARTLEY (*crossing himself*). I to bring that fork here, and to find that news before me! It is much if I can ever stir from this place at all, or reach as far as the road!

TIM CASEY. Look, boys, at the new magistrate, and Jo Muldoon along with him! It's best for us to quit this.

SHAWN EARLY. That is so. It is best not to be mixed in this business at all.

JAMES RYAN. Bad as he is, I wouldn't like to be an informer against any man.

(*All hurry away except* MRS. TARPEY, *who remains behind her stall. Enter* MAGISTRATE *and* POLICEMAN.)

MAGISTRATE. I knew the district was in a bad state, but I did not expect to be confronted with a murder at the first fair I came to.

POLICEMAN. I am sure you did not, indeed.

MAGISTRATE. It was well I had not gone home. I caught a few words here and there that roused my suspicions.

POLICEMAN. So they would, too.

MAGISTRATE. You heard the same story from everyone you asked?

POLICEMAN. The same story—or if it was not altogether the same, anyway it was no less than the first story.

MAGISTRATE. What is that man doing? He is sitting alone with a hayfork. He has a guilty look. The murder was done with a hayfork!

POLICEMAN (*in a whisper*). That's the very man they say did the act; Bartley Fallon himself!

MAGISTRATE. He must have found escape difficult—

he is trying to brazen it out. A convict in the Andaman Islands tried the same game, but he could not escape my system! Stand aside— Don't go far— Have the handcuffs ready. (*He walks up to* BARTLEY, *folds his arms, and stands before him.*) Here, my man, do you know anything of John Smith?

BARTLEY. Of John Smith! Who is he, now?

POLICEMAN. Jack Smith, sir—Red Jack Smith!

MAGISTRATE (*coming a step nearer and tapping him on the shoulder*). Where is Jack Smith?

BARTLEY (*with a deep sigh, and shaking his head slowly*). Where is he, indeed?

MAGISTRATE. What have you to tell?

BARTLEY. It is where he was this morning, standing in this spot, singing his share of songs—no, but lighting his pipe—scraping a match on the sole of his shoe—

MAGISTRATE. I ask you, for the third time, where is he?

BARTLEY. I wouldn't like to say that. It is a great mystery, and it is hard to say of any man, did he earn hatred or love.

MAGISTRATE. Tell me all you know.

BARTLEY. All that I know— Well, there are the three estates; there is Limbo, and there is Purgatory, and there is—

MAGISTRATE. Nonsense! This is trifling! Get to the point.

BARTLEY. Maybe you don't hold with the clergy so? That is the teaching of the clergy. Maybe you hold with the old people. It is what they do be saying, that the shadow goes wandering, and the soul is tired, and the body is taking a rest— The shadow! (*Starts up.*) I was nearly sure I saw Jack Smith not ten minutes ago at the corner of the forge, and I lost him again— Was it his ghost I saw, do you think?

MAGISTRATE (*to* POLICEMAN). Conscience-struck! He will confess all now!

BARTLEY. His ghost to come before me! It is likely it was on account of the fork! I do have it and he to have no way to defend himself the time he met with his death!

MAGISTRATE (*to* POLICEMAN). I must note down his words. (*Takes out notebook.*) (*To* BARTLEY): I warn you that your words are being noted.

BARTLEY. If I had ha' run faster in the beginning, this terror would not be on me at the latter end! Maybe he will cast it up against me at the day of judgment— I wouldn't wonder at all at that.

MAGISTRATE (*writing*). At the day of judgment—

BARTLEY. It was soon for his ghost to appear to me— is it coming after me always by day it will be, and stripping the clothes off in the night time?—I wouldn't wonder at all at that, being as I am an unfortunate man!

MAGISTRATE (*sternly*). Tell me this truly. What was the motive of this crime?

BARTLEY. The motive, is it?

MAGISTRATE. Yes; the motive; the cause.

BARTLEY. I'd sooner not say that.

MAGISTRATE. You had better tell me truly. Was it money?

BARTLEY. Not at all! What did poor Jack Smith ever have in his pockets unless it might be his hands that would be in them?

MAGISTRATE. Any dispute about land?

BARTLEY (*indignantly*). Not at all! He never was a grabber or grabbed from any one!

MAGISTRATE. You will find it better for you if you tell me at once.

BARTLEY. I tell you I wouldn't for the whole world

wish to say what it was—it is a thing I would not like to be talking about.

MAGISTRATE. There is no use in hiding it. It will be discovered in the end.

BARTLEY. Well, I suppose it will, seeing that mostly everybody knows it before. Whisper here now. I will tell no lie; where would be the use? (*Puts his hand to his mouth, and* MAGISTRATE *stoops.*) Don't be putting the blame on the parish, for such a thing was never done in the parish before—it was done for the sake of Kitty Keary, Jack Smith's wife.

MAGISTRATE (*to* POLICEMAN). Put on the handcuffs. We have been saved some trouble. I knew he would confess if taken in the right way.

(POLICEMAN *puts on handcuffs.*)

BARTLEY. Handcuffs now! Glory be! I always said, if there was ever any misfortune coming to this place it was on myself it would fall. I to be in handcuffs! There's no wonder at all in that.

(*Enter* MRS. FALLON, *followed by the rest. She is looking back at them as she speaks.*)

MRS. FALLON. Telling lies the whole of the people of this town are; telling lies, telling lies as fast as a dog will trot! Speaking against my poor respectable man! Saying he made an end of Jack Smith! My decent comrade! There is no better man and no kinder man in the whole of the five parishes! It's little annoyance he ever gave to any one! (*Turns and sees him.*) What in the earthly world do I see before me? Bartley Fallon in charge of the police! Handcuffs on him! O Bartley, what did you do at all at all?

BARTLEY. O Mary, there has a great misfortune come upon me! It is what I always said, that if there is ever any misfortune—

Mrs. Fallon. What did he do at all, or is it bewitched I am?

Magistrate. This man has been arrested on a charge of murder.

Mrs. Fallon. Whose charge is that? Don't believe them! They are all liars in this place! Give me back my man!

Magistrate. It is natural that you should take his part, but you have no cause of complaint against your neighbours. He has been arrested for the murder of John Smith, on his own confession.

Mrs. Fallon. The saints of heaven protect us! And what did he want killing Jack Smith?

Magistrate. It is best you should know all. He did it on account of a love affair with the murdered man's wife.

Mrs. Fallon (*sitting down*). With Jack Smith's wife! With Kitty Keary!—Ochone, the traitor!

The Crowd. A great shame, indeed. He is a traitor, indeed.

Mrs. Tully. To America he was bringing her, Mrs. Fallon.

Bartley. What are you saying, Mary? I tell you—

Mrs. Fallon. Don't say a word! I won't listen to any word you'll say! (*Stops her ears.*) O, isn't he the treacherous villain? Ochone go deo!

Bartley. Be quiet till I speak! Listen to what I say!

Mrs. Fallon. Sitting beside me on the ass car coming to the town, so quiet and so respectable, and treachery like that in his heart!

Bartley. Is it your wits you have lost or is it I myself that have lost my wits?

Mrs. Fallon. And it's hard I earned you, slaving, slaving—and you grumbling, and sighing, and cough-

SPREADING THE NEWS

ing, and discontented, and the priest wore out anointing you, with all the times you threatened to die!

BARTLEY. Let you be quiet till I tell you!

MRS. FALLON. You to bring such a disgrace into the parish. A thing that was never heard of before!

BARTLEY. Will you shut your mouth and hear me speaking?

MRS. FALLON. And if it was for any sort of a fine handsome woman, but for a little fistful of a woman like Kitty Keary, that's not four feet high hardly, and not three teeth in her head unless she got new ones! May God reward you, Bartley Fallon, for the black treachery in your heart and the wickedness in your mind, and the red blood of poor Jack Smith that is wet upon your hand!

(*Voice of* JACK SMITH *heard singing*):

    The sea shall be dry.
        The earth under mourning and ban!
    Then loud shall he cry
        For the wife of the red-haired man!

BARTLEY. It's Jack Smith's voice—I never knew a ghost to sing before— It is after myself and the fork he is coming! (*Goes back. Enter* JACK SMITH.) Let one of you give him the fork and I will be clear of him now and for eternity!

MRS. TARPEY. The Lord have mercy on us! Red Jack Smith! The man that was going to be waked!

JAMES RYAN. Is it back from the grave you are come?

SHAWN EARLY. Is it alive you are, or is it dead you are?

TIM CASEY. Is it yourself at all that's in it?

MRS. TULLY. Is it letting on you were to be dead?

MRS. FALLON. Dead or alive, let you stop Kitty Keary, your wife, from bringing my man away with her to America!

JACK SMITH. It is what I think, the wits are gone astray on the whole of you. What would my wife want bringing Bartley Fallon to America?

MRS. FALLON. To leave yourself, and to get quit of you she wants, Jack Smith, and to bring him away from myself. That's what the two of them had settled together.

JACK SMITH. I'll break the head of any man that says that! Who is it says it? (*To* TIM CASEY.) Was it you said it? (*To* SHAWN EARLY.) Was it you?

ALL TOGETHER (*backing and shaking their heads*). It wasn't I said it!

JACK SMITH. Tell me the name of any man that said it!

ALL TOGETHER (*pointing to* BARTLEY). It was *him* that said it!

JACK SMITH. Let me at him till I break his head!

(BARTLEY *backs in terror. Neighbours hold* JACK SMITH *back.*)

JACK SMITH (*trying to free himself*). Let me at him! Isn't he the pleasant sort of a scarecrow for any woman to be crossing the ocean with! It's back from the docks of New York he'd be turned (*trying to rush at him again*), with a lie in his mouth and treachery in his heart, and another man's wife by his side, and he passing her off as his own! Let me at him can't you. (*Makes another rush, but is held back.*)

MAGISTRATE (*pointing to* JACK SMITH). Policeman, put the handcuffs on this man. I see it all now. A case of false impersonation, a conspiracy to defeat the ends of justice. There was a case in the Andaman Islands, a murderer of the Mopsa tribe, a religious enthusiast—

POLICEMAN. So he might be, too.

MAGISTRATE. We must take both these men to the scene of the murder. We must confront them with the body of the real Jack Smith.

JACK SMITH. I'll break the head of any man that will find my dead body!

MAGISTRATE. I'll call more help from the barracks. (*Blows* POLICEMAN's *whistle.*)

BARTLEY. It is what I am thinking, if myself and Jack Smith are put together in the one cell for the night, the handcuffs will be taken off him, and his hands will be free, and murder will be done that time surely!

MAGISTRATE. Come on! (*They turn to the right.*)

LORD DUNSANY

A Night at an Inn

DRAMATIS PERSONAE

Merchant Sailors
 A. E. SCOTT-FORTESCUE (*the* TOFF), *a dilapidated gentleman*
 WILLIAM JONES (BILL)   ALBERT THOMAS
 JACOB SMITH (SNIGGERS)

1ST PRIEST OF KLESH   3RD PRIEST OF KLESH
2ND PRIEST OF KLESH   KLESH

The curtain rises on a room in an inn.

SNIGGERS *and* BILL *are talking, the* TOFF *is reading a paper.* ALBERT *sits a little apart.*

SNIGGERS. What's his idea, I wonder?
BILL. I don't know.
SNIGGERS. And how much longer will he keep us here?

BILL. We've been here three days.

SNIGGERS. And 'aven't seen a soul.

BILL. And a pretty penny it cost us when he rented the pub.

SNIGGERS. 'Ow long did 'e rent the pub for?

BILL. You never know with him.

SNIGGERS. It's lonely enough.

BILL. 'Ow long did you rent the pub for, Toffy?

(*The* TOFF *continues to read a sporting paper; he takes no notice of what is said.*)

SNIGGERS. 'E's *such* a toff.

BILL. Yet 'e's clever, no mistake.

SNIGGERS. Those clever ones are the beggars to make a muddle. Their plans are clever enough, but they don't work, and then they make a mess of things much worse than you or me.

BILL. Ah.

SNIGGERS. I don't like this place.

BILL. Why not?

SNIGGERS. I don't like the looks of it.

BILL. He's keeping us here because here those niggers can't find us. The three heathen priests what was looking for us so. But we want to go and sell our ruby soon.

ALBERT. There's no sense in it.

BILL. Why not, Albert?

ALBERT. Because I gave those black devils the slip in Hull.

BILL. You give 'em the slip, Albert?

ALBERT. The slip, all three of them. The fellows with the gold spots on their foreheads. I had the ruby then and I give them the slip in Hull.

BILL. How did you do it, Albert?

ALBERT. I had the ruby and they were following me. . . .

A NIGHT AT AN INN

BILL. Who told them you had the ruby? You didn't show it?

ALBERT. No. . . . But they kind of know.

SNIGGERS. They kind of know, Albert?

ALBERT. Yes, they know if you 've got it. Well, they sort of mouched after me, and I tells a policeman, and he says, oh they were only three poor niggers and they wouldn't hurt me. Ugh! When I thought of what they did in Malta to poor old Jim.

BILL. Yes and to George in Bombay before we started.

SNIGGERS. Ugh!

BILL. Why didn't you give 'em in charge?

ALBERT. What about the ruby, Bill?

BILL. Ah!

ALBERT. Well, I did better than that. I walks up and down through Hull. I walks slow enough. And then I turns a corner and I runs. I never seen a corner but I turns it. But sometimes I let a corner pass just to fool them. I twists about like a hare. Then I sits down and waits. No priests.

SNIGGERS. What?

ALBERT. No heathen black devils with gold spots on their face. I give 'em the slip.

BILL. Well done, Albert.

SNIGGERS (*after a sigh of content*). Why didn't you tell us?

ALBERT. 'Cause 'e won't let you speak. 'E 's got 'is plans and 'e thinks we 're silly folk. Things must be done 'is way. And all the time I 've give 'em the slip. Might 'ave 'ad one o' them crooked knives in him before now but for me who give 'em the slip in Hull.

BILL. Well done, Albert.

SNIGGERS. Do you hear that, Toffy? Albert has give 'em the slip.

THE TOFF. Yes, I hear.

SNIGGERS. Well, what do you say to that?

THE TOFF. Oh . . . Well done, Albert.

ALBERT. And what a' you going to do?

THE TOFF. Going to wait.

ALBERT. Don't seem to know what 'e 's waiting for.

SNIGGERS. It 's a nasty place.

ALBERT. It 's getting silly, Bill. Our money's gone and we want to sell the ruby. Let 's get on to a town.

BILL. But 'e won't come.

ALBERT. Then we 'll leave him.

SNIGGERS. We 'll be all right if we keep away from Hull.

ALBERT. We 'll go to London.

BILL. But 'e must 'ave 'is share.

SNIGGERS. All right. Only let 's go. (*To the* TOFF.) We 're going, do you hear? Give us the ruby.

THE TOFF. Certainly.

(*He gives them a ruby from his waistcoat pocket; it is the size of a small hen's egg. He goes on reading his paper.*)

ALBERT. Come on, Sniggers.

(*Exeunt* ALBERT *and* SNIGGERS.)

BILL. Good-bye, old man. We 'll give you your fair share, but there 's nothing to do here, no girls, no halls, and we must sell the ruby.

THE TOFF. I 'm not a fool, Bill.

BILL. No, no, of course not. Of course you ain't, and you 've helped us a lot. Good-bye. You 'll say good-bye

THE TOFF. Oh, yes. Good-bye.

(*Still reads paper. Exit* BILL. *The* TOFF *puts a revolver on the table beside him and goes on with his paper.*)

SNIGGERS (*out of breath*). We 've come back, Toffy.

THE TOFF. So you have.

ALBERT. Toffy—how did they get here?

A NIGHT AT AN INN

THE TOFF. They walked, of course.

ALBERT. But it 's eighty miles.

SNIGGERS. Did you know they were here, Toffy?

THE TOFF. Expected them about now.

ALBERT. Eighty miles.

BILL. Toffy, old man—what are we to do?

THE TOFF. Ask Albert.

BILL. If they can do things like this there 's no one can save us but you, Toffy—I always knew you were a clever one. We won't be fools any more. We 'll obey you, Toffy.

THE TOFF. You 're brave enough and strong enough. There isn't many that would steal a ruby eye out of an idol's head, and such an idol as that was to look at, and on such a night. You 're brave enough, Bill. But you 're all three of you fools. Jim would have none of my plans and where 's Jim? And George. What did they do to him?

SNIGGERS. Don't, Toffy!

THE TOFF. Well, then, your strength is no use to you. You want cleverness; or they 'll have you the way that they had George and Jim.

ALL. Ugh!

THE TOFF. These black priests would follow you round the world in circles. Year after year, till they got their idol's eye. And if we died with it they 'd follow our grandchildren. That fool thinks he can escape men like that by running round three streets in the town of Hull.

ALBERT. God's truth, *you* 'aven't escaped them, because they 're *'ere*.

THE TOFF. So I supposed.

ALBERT. You *supposed?*

THE TOFF. Yes, I believe there 's no announcement in the society papers. But I took this country seat especially to receive them. There 's plenty of room if you dig, it is pleasantly situated, and, what is most important, it is in a very quiet neighbourhood. So I am at home to them this afternoon.

BILL. Well, you're a deep one.

THE TOFF. And remember you've only my wits between you and death, and don't put your futile plans against those of an educated gentleman.

ALBERT. If you're a gentleman why don't you go about among gentlemen instead of the likes of us?

THE TOFF. Because I was too clever for them as I am too clever for you.

ALBERT. Too clever for them?

THE TOFF. I never lost a game of cards in my life.

BILL. You never lost a game!

THE TOFF. Not when there was money on it.

BILL. Well, well.

THE TOFF. Have a game of poker?

ALL. No, thanks.

THE TOFF. Then do as you're told.

BILL. All right, Toffy.

SNIGGERS. I saw something just then. Hadn't we better draw the curtains?

THE TOFF. No.

SNIGGERS. What?

THE TOFF. Don't draw the curtains.

SNIGGERS. Oh, all right.

BILL. But, Toffy, they can see us. One doesn't let the enemy do that. I don't see why. . . .

THE TOFF. No, of course you don't.

BILL. Oh, all right, Toffy. (*All begin to pull out revolvers.*)

THE TOFF (*putting his own away*). No revolvers, please.

ALBERT. Why not?

THE TOFF. Because I don't want any noise at my

A NIGHT AT AN INN

party. We might get guests that hadn't been invited. *Knives* are a different matter.

(*All draw knives. The* TOFF *signs to them not to draw them yet. The* TOFF *has already taken back his ruby.*)

BILL. I think they 're coming, Toffy.

THE TOFF. Not yet.

ALBERT. When will they come?

THE TOFF. When I am quite ready to receive them. Not before.

SNIGGERS. I should like to get this over.

THE TOFF. Should you? Then we 'll have them now.

SNIGGERS. Now?

THE TOFF. Yes. Listen to me. You shall do as you see me do. You will all pretend to go out. I 'll show you how. I 've got the ruby. When they see me alone they will come for their idol's eye.

BILL. How can they tell like this which of us has it?

THE TOFF. I confess I don't know, but they seem to.

SNIGGERS. What will you do when they come in?

THE TOFF. I shall do nothing.

SNIGGERS. What?

THE TOFF. They will creep up behind me. Then my friends, Sniggers and Bill and Albert, who gave them the slip, will do what they can.

BILL. All right, Toffy. Trust us.

THE TOFF. If you 're a little slow you will see enacted the cheerful spectacle that accompanied the demise of Jim.

SNIGGERS. Don't, Toffy. We 'll be there all right.

THE TOFF. Very well. Now watch me.

(*He goes past the windows to the inner door right; he opens it inwards, and then under cover of the open door he slips down on his knees and closes it, remaining on the inside, appearing to have gone out. He signs to the others, who understand. Then he appears to re-enter in the same manner.*)

THE TOFF. Now. I shall sit with my back to the door. You go out one by one so far as our friends can make out. Crouch very low, to be on the safe side. They mustn't see you through the window.

(BILL *makes his sham exit.*)

THE TOFF. Remember, no revolvers. The police are, I believe, proverbially inquisitive.

(*The other two follow* BILL. *All three are now crouching inside the door right. The* TOFF *puts the ruby beside him on the table. He lights a cigarette. The door in back opens so slowly that you can hardly say at what moment it began. The* TOFF *picks up his paper.*

A Native of India wriggles along the floor ever so slowly, seeking cover from chairs. He moves left where the TOFF *is. The three sailors are right.* SNIGGERS *and* ALBERT *lean forward.* BILL's *arm keeps them back. An armchair had better conceal them from the Indian. The black* PRIEST *nears the* TOFF.

BILL *watches to see if any more are coming. Then he leaps forward alone (he has taken his boots off) and knifes the* PRIEST.

The PRIEST *tries to shout, but* BILL's *left hand is over his mouth.*

The TOFF *continues to read his sporting paper. He never looks round.*)

BILL (*sotto voce*). There's only one, Toffy. What shall we do?

THE TOFF (*without turning his head*). Only one?

BILL. Yes.

THE TOFF. Wait a moment. Let me think. (*Still apparently absorbed in his paper.*) Ah, yes. You go back, Bill. We must attract another guest. Now are you ready?

BILL. Yes.

THE TOFF. All right. You shall now see my demise at my Yorkshire residence. You must receive guests for me. (*He leaps up in full view of the window, flings up both arms and falls on to the floor near the dead* PRIEST.) Now be ready. (*His eyes close.*)

(*There is a long pause. Again the door opens, very, very slowly. Another* PRIEST *creeps in. He has three golden spots upon his forehead. He looks round, then he creeps up to his companion and turns him over and looks inside each of his clenched hands. Then he looks at the recumbent* TOFF. *Then he creeps towards him.* BILL *slips after him and knifes him like the other, with his left hand over his mouth.*)

BILL (*sotto voce*). We've only got two, Toffy.

THE TOFF. Still another.

BILL. What'll we do?

THE TOFF (*sitting up*). Hum.

BILL. This is the best way, much.

THE TOFF. Out of the question. Never play the same game twice.

BILL. Why not, Toffy?

THE TOFF. Doesn't work if you do.

BILL. When?

THE TOFF. I have it, Albert. You will now walk into the room. I showed you how to do it.

ALBERT. Yes.

THE TOFF. Just run over here and have a fight at this window with these two men.

ALBERT. But they're——

THE TOFF. Yes, they're dead, my perspicuous Albert. But Bill and I are going to resuscitate them. Come on.

(BILL *picks up a body under the arms.*)

THE TOFF. That's right, Bill. (*Does the same.*) Come and help us, Sniggers. (SNIGGERS *comes.*) Keep low, keep low. Wave their arms about, Sniggers. Don't show yourself. Now, Albert, over you go. Our Albert is slain. Back you get, Bill. Back, Sniggers. Still, Albert. Mustn't move when he comes. Not a muscle.

(*A face appears at the window and stays for some time. Then the door opens and looking craftily round the third* PRIEST *enters. He looks at his companions' bodies and turns round. He suspects something. He takes up one of the knives and with a knife in each hand he puts his back to the wall. He looks to the left and right.*)

THE TOFF. Come on, Bill.

(*The* PRIEST *rushes to the door. The* TOFF *knifes the last* PRIEST *from behind.*)

THE TOFF. A good day's work, my friends.

BILL. Well done, Toffy. Oh, you are a deep one.

ALBERT. A deep one if ever there was one.

SNIGGERS. There ain't any more, Bill, are there?

THE TOFF. No more in the world, my friend.

BILL. Ay, that's all there are. There were only three in the temple. Three priests and their beastly idol.

ALBERT. What is it worth, Toffy? Is it worth a thousand pounds?

THE TOFF. It's worth all they've got in the shop. Worth just whatever we like to ask for it.

ALBERT. Then we're millionaires now.

THE TOFF. Yes, and what is more important, we no longer have any heirs.

BILL. We'll have to sell it now.

ALBERT. That won't be easy. It's a pity it isn't small and we had half a dozen. Hadn't the idol any other on him?

BILL. No, he was green jade all over and only had this one eye. He had it in the middle of his forehead, and was a long sight uglier than anything else in the world.

A NIGHT AT AN INN

Sniggers. I 'm sure we ought all to be very grateful to Toffy.

Bill. And indeed we ought.

Albert. If it hadn't 'ave been for him——

Bill. Yes, if it hadn't a' been for old Toffy.

Sniggers. He 's a deep one.

The Toff. Well, you see, I just have a knack of foreseeing things.

Sniggers. I should think you did.

Bill. Why I don't suppose anything happens that our Toff doesn't foresee. Does it, Toffy?

The Toff. Well, I don't think it does, Bill. I don't think it often does.

Bill. Life is no more than just a game of cards to our old Toff.

The Toff. Well, we 've taken these fellows' trick.

Sniggers (*going to the window*). It wouldn't do for any one to see them.

The Toff. Oh, nobody will come this way. We 're all alone on a moor.

Bill. Where will we put them?

The Toff. Bury them in the cellar, but there 's no hurry.

Bill. And what then, Toffy?

The Toff. Why then we 'll go to London and upset the ruby business. We have really come through this job very nicely.

Bill. I think the first thing that we ought to do is to give a little supper to old Toffy. We 'll bury these fellows tonight.

Albert. Yes, let 's.

Sniggers. The very thing.

Bill. And we 'll all drink his health.

Albert. Good old Toffy.

SNIGGERS. He ought to have been a general or a premier. (*They get bottles from cupboard, etc.*)

THE TOFF. Well, we 've earned our bit of a supper. (*They sit down.*)

BILL (*glass in hand*). Here 's to old Toffy who guessed everything.

ALBERT and SNIGGERS. Good old Toffy.

BILL. Toffy who saved our lives and made our fortunes.

ALBERT and SNIGGERS. Hear. Hear.

THE TOFF. And here 's to Bill who saved me twice tonight.

BILL. Couldn't have done it but for your cleverness, Toffy.

SNIGGERS. Hear, hear. Hear, hear.

ALBERT. He foresees everything.

BILL. A speech, Toffy. A speech from our general.

ALL. Yes, a speech.

SNIGGERS. A speech.

THE TOFF. Well, get me some water. This whisky 's too much for my head, and I must keep it clear till our friends are safe in the cellar.

BILL. Water. Yes, of course. Get him some water, Sniggers.

SNIGGERS. We don't use water here. Where shall I get it?

BILL. Outside in the garden.

(*Exit* SNIGGERS.)

ALBERT. Here 's to fortune. (*They all drink.*)

BILL. Here 's to Albert Thomas, Esquire. (*He drinks.*)

THE TOFF. Albert Thomas, Esquire. (*He drinks.*)

ALBERT. And William Jones, Esquire.

THE TOFF. William Jones, Esquire.

(*The* TOFF *and* ALBERT *drink.*)

(*Re-enter* SNIGGERS *terrified.*)

A NIGHT AT AN INN

The Toff. Hullo, here's Jacob Smith, Esquire, J.P., *alias* Sniggers, back again.

Sniggers. Toffy, I've been a-thinking about my share in that ruby. I don't want it, Toffy, I don't want it.

The Toff. Nonsense, Sniggers, nonsense.

Sniggers. You shall have it, Toffy, you shall have it yourself, only say Sniggers has no share in this 'ere ruby. Say it, Toffy, say it.

Bill. Want to turn informer, Sniggers?

Sniggers. No, no. Only I don't want the ruby, Toffy. . . .

The Toff. No more nonsense, Sniggers, we're all in together in this, if one hangs we all hang; but they won't outwit me. Besides, it's not a hanging affair, they had their knives.

Sniggers. Toffy, Toffy, I always treated you fair, Toffy. I was always one to say, give Toffy a chance. Take back my share, Toffy.

The Toff. What's the matter? What are you driving at?

Sniggers. Take it back, Toffy.

The Toff. Answer me, what are you up to?

Sniggers. I don't want my share any more.

Bill. Have you seen the police?

(Albert *pulls out his knife*.)

The Toff. No, no knives, Albert.

Albert. What then?

The Toff. The honest truth in open court, barring the ruby. We were attacked.

Sniggers. There's no police.

The Toff. Well, then, what's the matter?

Bill. Out with it.

Sniggers. I swear to God . . .

Albert. Well?

The Toff. Don't interrupt.

SNIGGERS. I swear I saw something *what I didn't like.*
THE TOFF. What you didn't like?
SNIGGERS (*in tears*). O Toffy, Toffy, take it back. Take my share. Say you take it.
THE TOFF. What has he seen?

(*Dead silence only broken by* SNIGGERS's *sobs. Then stony steps are heard. Enter a hideous Idol. It is blind and gropes its way. It gropes its way to the ruby and picks it up and screws it into a socket in the forehead.* SNIGGERS *still weeps softly, the rest stare in horror. The Idol steps out, not groping. Its steps move off, then stop.*)

THE TOFF. Oh, great heavens!
ALBERT (*in a childish, plaintive voice*). What is it, Toffy?
BILL. Albert, it is that obscene idol (*in a whisper*) come from India.
ALBERT. It is gone.
BILL. It has taken its eye.
SNIGGERS. We are saved.
A VOICE (*off*). (*With outlandish accent.*) Meestaire William Jones, Able Seaman.

(*The* TOFF *has never spoken, never moved. He only gazes stupidly in horror.*)

BILL. Albert, Albert, what is this?

(*He rises and walks out. One moan is heard.* SNIGGERS *goes to the window. He falls back sickly.*)

ALBERT (*in a whisper*). What has happened?
SNIGGERS. I have seen it. I have seen it, oh, I have seen it. (*He returns to table.*)
THE TOFF (*laying his hand very gently on* SNIGGERS's *arm, speaking softly and winningly*). What was it, Sniggers?
SNIGGERS. I have seen it.

ALBERT. What?
SNIGGERS. Oh!
VOICE. Meestaire Albert Thomas, Able Seaman.
ALBERT. Must I go, Toffy? Toffy, must I go?
SNIGGERS (*clutching him*). Don't move.
ALBERT (*going*). Toffy, Toffy.   (*Exit.*)
VOICE. Meestaire Jacob Smith, Able Seaman.
SNIGGERS. I can't go, Toffy. I can't go. I can't do it.
(*He goes.*)
VOICE. Meestaire Arnold Everett Scott-Fortescue, late Esquire, Able Seaman.
THE TOFF. I did not foresee it.   (*Exit.*)

CURTAIN

JOHN M. SYNGE

Riders to the Sea

CHARACTERS

MAURYA (*an old woman*)   BARTLEY (*her son*)
CATHLEEN (*her daughter*)   NORA (*a younger daughter*)
MEN and WOMEN

SCENE. *An Island off the West of Ireland.*
(*Cottage kitchen, with nets, oil-skins, spinning-wheel, some new boards standing by the wall, etc.* CATHLEEN, *a girl of about twenty, finishes kneading cake, and puts it down in the pot-oven by the fire; then wipes her hands, and begins to spin at the wheel.* NORA, *a young girl, puts her head in at the door.*)

NORA (*in a low voice*). Where is she?

CATHLEEN. She's lying down, God help her, and may be sleeping, if she's able.

(NORA *comes in softly, and takes a bundle from under her shawl.*)

CATHLEEN (*spinning the wheel rapidly*). What is it you have?

NORA. The young priest is after bringing them. It's a shirt and a plain stocking were got off a drowned man in Donegal.

(CATHLEEN *stops her wheel with a sudden movement, and leans out to listen.*)

NORA. We're to find out if it's Michael's they are, some time herself will be down looking by the sea.

CATHLEEN. How would they be Michael's, Nora. How would he go the length of that way to the far north?

NORA. The young priest says he's known the like of it. "If it's Michael's they are," says he, "you can tell herself he's got a clean burial by the grace of God, and if they're not his, let no one say a word about them, for she'll be getting her death," says he, "with crying and lamenting."

(*The door which* NORA *half closed is blown open by a gust of wind.*)

CATHLEEN (*looking out anxiously*). Did you ask him would he stop Bartley going this day with the horses to the Galway fair?

NORA. "I won't stop him," says he, "but let you not be afraid. Herself does be saying prayers half through the night, and the Almighty God won't leave her destitute," says he, "with no son living."

CATHLEEN. Is the sea bad by the white rocks, Nora?

NORA. Middling bad, God help us. There's a great roaring in the west, and it's worse it'll be getting when the tide's turned to the wind. (*She goes over to the table with the bundle.*) Shall I open it now?

CATHLEEN. Maybe she'd wake up on us, and come in before we'd done. (*Coming to the table.*) It's a long time we'll be, and the two of us crying.

NORA (*goes to the inner door and listens*). She's moving about on the bed. She'll be coming in a minute.

CATHLEEN. Give me the ladder, and I'll put them up in the turf-loft, the way she won't know of them at all, and maybe when the tide turns she'll be going down to see would he be floating from the east.

(*They put the ladder against the gable of the chimney; CATHLEEN goes up a few steps and hides the bundle in the turf-loft. MAURYA comes from the inner room.*)

MAURYA (*looking up at CATHLEEN and speaking querulously*). Isn't it turf enough you have for this day and evening?

CATHLEEN. There's a cake baking at the fire for a short space (*throwing down the turf*) and Bartley will want it when the tide turns if he goes to Connemara.

(NORA *picks up the turf and puts it round the pot-oven.*)

MAURYA (*sitting down on a stool at the fire*). He won't go this day with the wind rising from the south and west. He won't go this day, for the young priest will stop him surely.

NORA. He'll not stop him, mother, and I heard Eamon Simon and Stephen Pheety and Colum Shawn saying he would go.

MAURYA. Where is he itself?

NORA. He went down to see would there be another boat sailing in the week, and I'm thinking it won't be long till he's here now, for the tide's turning at the green head, and the hooker's tacking from the east.

CATHLEEN. I hear someone passing the big stones.

NORA (*looking out*). He's coming now, and he in a hurry.

BARTLEY (*comes in and looks round the room. Speaking sadly and quietly*). Where is the bit of new rope, Cathleen, was bought in Connemara?

CATHLEEN (*coming down*). Give it to him, Nora; it's on a nail by the white boards. I hung it up this morning, for the pig with the black feet was eating it.

NORA (*giving him a rope*). Is that it, Bartley?

MAURYA. You'd do right to leave that rope, Bartley, hanging by the boards. (BARTLEY *takes the rope.*) It will be wanting in this place, I'm telling you, if Michael is washed up tomorrow morning, or the next morning, or any morning in the week, for it's a deep grave we'll make him by the grace of God.

BARTLEY (*beginning to work with the rope*). I've no halter the way I can ride down on the mare, and I must go now quickly. This is the one boat going for two weeks or beyond it, and the fair will be a good fair for horses I heard them saying below.

MAURYA. It's a hard thing they'll be saying below if the body is washed up and there's no man in it to make the coffin, and I after giving a big price for the finest white boards you'd find in Connemara. (*She looks round at the boards.*)

BARTLEY. How would it be washed up, and we after looking each day for nine days, and a strong wind blowing a while back from the west and south?

MAURYA. If it wasn't found itself, that wind is raising the sea, and there was a star up against the moon, and it rising in the night. If it was a hundred horses, or a thousand horses you had itself, what is the price of a thousand horses against a son where there is one son only?

RIDERS TO THE SEA

BARTLEY (*working at the halter, to* CATHLEEN). Let you go down each day, and see the sheep aren't jumping in on the rye, and if the jobber comes you can sell the pig with the black feet if there is a good price going.

MAURYA. How would the like of her get a good price for a pig?

BARTLEY (*to* CATHLEEN). If the west wind holds with the last bit of the moon let you and Nora get up weed enough for another cock for the kelp. It's hard set we'll be from this day with no one in it but one man to work.

MAURYA. It's hard set we'll be surely the day you're drown'd with the rest. What way will I live and the girls with me, and I an old woman looking for the grave?

(BARTLEY *lays down the halter, takes off his old coat, and puts on a newer one of the same flannel.*)

BARTLEY (*to* NORA). Is she coming to the pier?

NORA (*looking out*). She's passing the green head and letting fall her sails.

BARTLEY (*getting his purse and tobacco*). I'll have half an hour to go down, and you'll see me coming again in two days, or in three days, or maybe in four days if the wind is bad.

MAURYA (*turning round to the fire, and putting her shawl over her head*). Isn't it a hard and cruel man won't hear a word from an old woman, and she holding him from the sea?

CATHLEEN. It's the life of a young man to be going on the sea, and who would listen to an old woman with one thing and she saying it over?

BARTLEY (*taking the halter*). I must go now quickly. I'll ride down on the red mare, and the grey pony'll run behind me. . . . The blessing of God on you. (*He goes out.*)

MAURYA (*crying out as he is in the door*). He's gone

now, God spare us, and we'll not see him again. He's gone now, and when the black night is falling I'll have no son left me in the world.

CATHLEEN. Why wouldn't you give him your blessing and he looking round in the door? Isn't it sorrow enough is on every one in this house without your sending him out with an unlucky word behind him, and a hard word in his ear?

(MAURYA *takes up the tongs and begins raking the fire aimlessly without looking round.*)

NORA (*turning towards her*). You're taking away the turf from the cake.

CATHLEEN (*crying out*). The Son of God forgive us, Nora, we're after forgetting his bit of bread. (*She comes over to the fire.*)

NORA. And it's destroyed he'll be going till dark night, and he after eating nothing since the sun went up.

CATHLEEN (*turning the cake out of the oven*). It's destroyed he'll be, surely. There's no sense left on any person in a house where an old woman will be talking for ever.

(MAURYA *sways herself on her stool.*)

CATHLEEN (*cutting off some of the bread and rolling it in a cloth; to* MAURYA). Let you go down now to the spring well and give him this and he passing. You'll see him then and the dark word will be broken, and you can say "God speed you," the way he'll be easy in his mind.

MAURYA (*taking the bread*). Will I be in it as soon as himself?

CATHLEEN. If you go now quickly.

MAURYA (*standing up unsteadily*). It's hard set I am to walk.

CATHLEEN (*looking at her anxiously*). Give her the stick, Nora, or maybe she'll slip on the big stones.

RIDERS TO THE SEA

NORA. What stick?

CATHLEEN. The stick Michael brought from Connemara.

MAURYA (*taking a stick* NORA *gives her*). In the big world the old people do be leaving things after them for their sons and children, but in this place it is the young men do be leaving things behind for them that do be old. (*She goes out slowly.* NORA *goes over to the ladder.*)

CATHLEEN. Wait, Nora, maybe she'd turn back quickly. She's that sorry, God help her, you wouldn't know the thing she'd do.

NORA. Is she gone round by the bush?

CATHLEEN (*looking out*). She's gone now. Throw it down quickly, for the Lord knows when she'll be out of it again.

NORA (*getting the bundle from the loft*). The young priest said he'd be passing tomorrow, and we might go down and speak to him below if it's Michael's they are surely.

CATHLEEN (*taking the bundle*). Did he say what way they were found?

NORA (*coming down*). "There were two men," says he, "and they rowing round with poteen before the cocks crowed, and the oar of one of them caught the body, and they passing the black cliffs of the north."

CATHLEEN (*trying to open the bundle*). Give me a knife, Nora, the string's perished with the salt water, and there's a black knot on it you wouldn't loosen in a week.

NORA (*giving her a knife*). I've heard tell it was a long way to Donegal.

CATHLEEN (*cutting the string*). It is surely. There was a man in here a while ago—the man sold us that knife—and he said if you set off walking from the rocks beyond, it would be seven days you'd be in Donegal.

NORA. And what time would a man take, and he floating?

(CATHLEEN *opens the bundle and takes out a bit of a stocking. They look at them eagerly.*)

CATHLEEN (*in a low voice*). The Lord spare us, Nora! isn't it a queer hard thing to say if it's his they are surely?

NORA. I'll get his shirt off the hook the way we can put the one flannel on the other. (*She looks through some clothes hanging in the corner*) It's not with them, Cathleen, and where will it be?

CATHLEEN. I'm thinking Bartley put it on him in the morning, for his own shirt was heavy with the salt in it (*pointing to the corner*). There's a bit of a sleeve was of the same stuff. Give me that and it will do.

(NORA *brings it to her and they compare the flannel.*)

CATHLEEN. It's the same stuff, Nora; but if it is itself aren't there great rolls of it in the shops of Galway, and isn't it many another man may have a shirt of it as well as Michael himself?

NORA (*who has taken up the stockings and counted the stitches, crying out*). It's Michael, Cathleen, it's Michael; God spare his soul, and what will herself say when she hears this story, and Bartley on the sea?

CATHLEEN (*taking the stocking*). It's a plain stocking.

NORA. It's the second one of the third pair I knitted, and I put up three score stitches, and I dropped four of them.

CATHLEEN (*counts the stitches*). It's that number is in it (*crying out*). Ah, Nora, isn't it a bitter thing to think of him floating that way to the far north, and no one to keen him but the black hags that do be flying on the sea?

NORA (*swinging herself round, and throwing out her arms on the clothes*). And isn't it a pitiful thing when there is nothing left of a man who was a great rower and fisher, but a bit of an old shirt and a plain stocking?

CATHLEEN (*after an instant*). Tell me is herself coming, Nora? I hear a little sound on the path.

NORA (*looking out*). She is, Cathleen. She's coming up to the door.

CATHLEEN. Put these things away before she'll come in. Maybe it's easier she'll be after giving her blessing to Bartley, and we won't let on we've heard anything the time he's on the sea.

NORA (*helping* CATHLEEN *to close the bundle*). We'll put them here in the corner.

(*They put them into a hole in the chimney corner.* CATHLEEN *goes back to the spinning-wheel.*)

NORA. Will she see it was crying I was?

CATHLEEN. Keep your back to the door the way the light'll not be on you.

(NORA *sits down at the chimney corner, with her back to the door.* MAURYA *comes in very slowly, without looking at the girls, and goes over to her stool at the other side of the fire. The cloth with the bread is still in her hand. The girls look at each other, and* NORA *points to the bundle of bread.*)

CATHLEEN (*after spinning for a moment*). You didn't give him his bit of bread?

(MAURYA *begins to keen softly, without turning round.*)

CATHLEEN. Did you see him riding down?

(MAURYA *goes on keening.*)

CATHLEEN (*a little impatiently*). God forgive you; isn't it a better thing to raise your voice and tell what you seen, than to be making lamentation for a thing that's done? Did you see Bartley, I'm saying to you.

MAURYA (*with a weak voice*). My heart's broken from this day.

CATHLEEN (*as before*). Did you see Bartley?

MAURYA. I seen the fearfulest thing.

CATHLEEN (*leaves her wheel and looks out*). God forgive you; he's riding the mare now over the green head, and the grey pony behind him.

MAURYA (*starts, so that her shawl falls back from her head and shows her white tossed hair. With a frightened voice*). The grey pony behind him.

CATHLEEN (*coming to the fire*). What is it ails you, at all?

MAURYA (*speaking very slowly*). I've seen the fearfulest thing any person has seen, since the day Bride Dara seen the dead man with the child in his arms.

CATHLEEN and NORA. Uah. (*They crouch down in front of the old woman at the fire.*)

NORA. Tell us what it is you seen.

MAURYA. I went down to the spring well, and I stood there saying a prayer to myself. Then Bartley came along, and he riding on the red mare with the grey pony behind him. (*She puts up her hands, as if to hide something from her eyes.*) The Son of God spare us, Nora!

CATHLEEN. What is it you seen?

MAURYA. I seen Michael himself.

CATHLEEN (*speaking softly*). You did not, mother; it wasn't Michael you seen, for his body is after being found in the far north, and he's got a clean burial by the grace of God.

MAURYA (*a little defiantly*). I'm after seeing him this day, and he riding and galloping. Bartley came first on the red mare; and I tried to say "God speed you," but something choked the words in my throat. He went by quickly; and "the blessing of God on you," says he, and I could say nothing. I looked up then, and I crying, at the grey pony, and there was Michael upon it—with fine clothes on him, and new shoes on his feet.

CATHLEEN (*begins to keen*). It's destroyed we are from this day. It's destroyed, surely.

NORA. Didn't the young priest say the Almighty God wouldn't leave her destitute with no son living?

MAURYA (*in a low voice, but clearly*). It's little the like of him knows of the sea. . . . Bartley will be lost now, and let you call in Eamon and make me a good coffin out of the white boards, for I won't live after them. I've had a husband, and a husband's father, and six sons in this house—six fine men, though it was a hard birth I had with every one of them and they coming to the world—and some of them were found and some of them were not found, but they're gone now the lot of them. . . . There were Stephen, and Shawn, were lost in the great wind, and found after in the Bay of Gregory of the Golden Mouth, and carried up the two of them on the one plank, and in by that door. (*She pauses for a moment, the girls start as if they heard something through the door that is half open behind them.*)

NORA (*in a whisper*). Did you hear that, Cathleen? Did you hear a noise in the north-east?

CATHLEEN (*in a whisper*). There's someone after crying out by the seashore.

MAURYA (*continues without hearing anything*). There was Sheamus and his father, and his own father again, were lost in a dark night, and not a stick or sign was seen of them when the sun went up. There was Patch after was drowned out of a curragh that turned over. I was sitting here with Bartley, and he a baby, lying on my two knees, and I seen two women, and three women, and four women coming in, and they crossing themselves, and not saying a word. I looked out then, and there were men coming after them, and they holding a thing in the half of a red sail, and water dripping out of it—it was a dry day, Nora—and leaving a track to the door. (*She pauses again with her hand stretched out towards the door. It opens softly and old women begin to come in, crossing themselves on the threshold, and kneeling down in front of the stage with red petticoats over their heads.*)

MAURYA (*half in a dream, to* CATHLEEN). Is it Patch, or Michael, or what is it at all?

CATHLEEN. Michael is after being found in the far north, and when he is found there how could he be here in this place?

MAURYA. There does be a power of young men floating round in the sea, and what way would they know if it was Michael they had, or another man like him, for when a man is nine days in the sea, and the wind blowing, it's hard set his own mother would be to say what man was it.

CATHLEEN. It's Michael, God spare him, for they're after sending us a bit of his clothes from the far north. (*She reaches out and hands* MAURYA *the clothes that belonged to* MICHAEL. MAURYA *stands up slowly and takes them in her hands.* NORA *looks out.*)

NORA. They're carrying a thing among them and there's water dripping out of it and leaving a track by the big stones.

CATHLEEN (*in a whisper to the women who have come in*). Is it Bartley it is?

ONE OF THE WOMEN. It is surely, God rest his soul.

(*Two younger women come in and pull out the table. Then men carry in the body of Bartley, laid on a plank, with a bit of a sail over it, and lay it on the table.*)

RIDERS TO THE SEA

CATHLEEN (*to the women, as they are doing so*). What way was he drowned?

ONE OF THE WOMEN. The grey pony knocked him into the sea, and he was washed out where there is a great surf on the white rocks.

(MAURYA *has gone over and knelt down at the head of the table. The women are keening softly and swaying themselves with a slow movement.* CATHLEEN *and* NORA *kneel at the other end of the table. The men kneel near the door.*)

MAURYA (*raising her head and speaking as if she did not see the people around her*). They're all gone now, and there isn't anything more the sea can do to me. . . . I'll have no call now to be up crying and praying when the wind breaks from the south, and you can hear the surf is in the east, and the surf is in the west, making a great stir with the two noises, and they hitting one on the other. I'll have no call now to be going down and getting Holy Water in the dark nights after Samhain, and I won't care what way the sea is when the other women will be keening. (*To* NORA.) Give me the Holy Water, Nora, there's a small sup still on the dresser.

(NORA *gives it to her.*)

MAURYA (*drops* MICHAEL'S *clothes across* BARTLEY'S *feet, and sprinkles the Holy Water over him*). It isn't that I haven't prayed for you, Bartley, to the Almighty God. It isn't that I haven't said prayers in the dark night till you wouldn't know what I'd be saying; but it's a great rest I'll have now, and it's time surely. It's a great rest I'll have now, and great sleeping in the long nights after Samhain, if it's only a bit of wet flour we do have to eat, and maybe a fish that would be stinking. (*She kneels down again, crossing herself, and saying prayers under her breath.*)

CATHLEEN (*to an old man*). Maybe yourself and Eamon would make a coffin when the sun rises. We have fine white boards herself bought, God help her, thinking Michael would be found, and I have a new cake you can eat while you'll be working.

THE OLD MAN (*looking at the boards*). Are there nails with them?

CATHLEEN. There are not, Colum; we didn't think of the nails.

ANOTHER MAN. It's a great wonder she wouldn't think of the nails, and all the coffins she's seen made already.

CATHLEEN. It's getting old she is, and broken.

(MAURYA *stands up again very slowly and spreads out the pieces of* MICHAEL's *clothes beside the body, sprinkling them with the last of the Holy Water.*)

NORA (*in a whisper to* CATHLEEN). She's quiet now and easy; but the day Michael was drowned you could hear her crying out from this to the spring well. It's fonder she was of Michael, and would any one have thought that?

CATHLEEN (*slowly and clearly*). An old woman will be soon tired with anything she will do, and isn't it nine days herself is after crying and keening, and making great sorrow in the house?

MAURYA (*puts the empty cup mouth downwards on the table, and lays her hands together on* BARTLEY's *feet*). They're all together this time, and the end is come. May the Almighty God have mercy on Bartley's soul, and on Michael's soul, and on the souls of Sheamus and Patch, and Stephen and Shawn (*bending her head*); and may He have mercy on my soul, Nora, and on the soul of every one is left living in the world. (*She pauses, and the keen rises a little more loudly from the women, then sinks away.*)

MAURYA (*continuing*). Michael has a clean burial in the far north, by the grace of the Almighty God. Bartley will have a fine coffin out of the white boards, and a deep grave surely. What more can we want than that? No man at all can be living for ever, and we must be satisfied. (*She kneels down again and the curtain falls slowly.*)

POLITICAL ECONOMY

GEORGE BERKELEY, BISHOP OF CLOYNE

Questions from *The Querist*

Q. 1. Whether there ever was, is, or will be an industrious nation poor, or an idle rich?

Q. 2. Whether a people can be called poor, where the common sort are well fed, clothed, and lodged?

Q. 7. Whether the real end and aim of men be not power? and whether he who could have every thing else at his wish or will, would value money?

Q. 15. Whether a general good taste in a people would not greatly conduce to their thriving? and whether an uneducated gentry be not the greatest of national evils?

Q. 20. Whether the creating of wants be not the likeliest way to produce industry in a people? and whether, if our peasants were accustomed to eat beef and wear shoes, they would not be more industrious?

Q. 42. Whether if human labour be the true source of wealth, it doth not follow that idleness of all things shall be discouraged in a wise state?

Q. 51. Whether by how much the less particular folk think for themselves, the public be not so much the more obliged to think for them?

Q. 58. Whether necessity is not to be hearkened to before convenience, and convenience before luxury?

Q. 59. Whether to provide plentifully for the poor, be not feeding the root, the substance whereof will shoot upwards into the branches, and cause the top to flourish?

Q. 63. Whether a people, who had provided themselves with the necessaries of life in good plenty, would not soon extend their industry to new arts, and new branches of commerce?

Q. 70. Whether human industry can produce, from such cheap materials, a manufacture of so great value, by any other art as by those of sculpture and painting?

Q. 71. Whether pictures and statues are not in fact so much treasure? and whether Rome and Florence would not be poor towns without them?

Q. 130. Whether the number and welfare of the subjects be not the true strength of the crown?

Q. 140. Whether we are not undone by fashions made for other people? and whether it be not madness in a poor nation to imitate a rich one?

Q. 158. When the root yieldeth insufficient nourishment, whether men do not top the tree to make the lower branches thrive?

Q. 167. Whether the vanity and luxury of a few ought to stand in competition with the interest of a nation?

Q. 176. Whether a nation might not be considered as a family?

Q. 193. Whether the collected wisdom of ages and nations be not found in books?

Q. 195. Whether a wise state hath any interest nearer heart than the education of youth?

Q. 214. Whether as seed equally scattered produceth a goodly harvest, even so an equal distribution of wealth doth not cause a nation to flourish?

Q. 367. Whether there can be a greater reproach on the leading men and the patriots of a country, than that the people should want employment?

Q. 443. Whether we may not obtain that as friends, which it is vain to hope for as rivals?

JAMES BRYCE

The House at Work

AN ENGLISHMAN expects to find his House of Commons reproduced in the House of Representatives. He has the more reason for this notion because he knows that the latter was modelled on the former, has borrowed many of its rules and technical expressions, and regards the procedure of the English chamber as a storehouse of precedents for its own guidance.[1] The notion is delusive. Resemblances of course there are. But an English parliamentarian who observes the American House at work is more impressed by the points of contrast than by those of similarity. The life and spirit of the two bodies are wholly different.

The room in which the House meets is in the south wing of the Capitol, the Senate and the Supreme Court

---

[1] *Both the Senate and the House of Representatives have recognized Jefferson's Manual of Parliamentary Practice as governing the House when none of its own rules (or of the joint rules of Congress) are applicable. This manual prepared by President Jefferson, is based on English precedents.*

being lodged in the north wing. It is more than thrice as large as the English House of Commons, with a floor about equal in area to that of Westminster Hall, 139 feet long by 93 feet wide and 36 feet high. Light is admitted through the ceiling. There are on all sides deep galleries running backwards over the lobbies, and capable of holding two thousand five hundred persons. The proportions are so good that it is not till you observe how small a man looks at the farther end, and how faint ordinary voices sound, that you realize its vast size. The seats are arranged in curved concentric rows looking towards the Speaker, whose handsome marble chair is placed on a raised marble platform projecting slightly forward into the room, the clerks and the mace below in front of him, in front of the clerks the official stenographers, to the right the seat of the sergeant-at-arms. Each member has a revolving arm-chair, with a roomy desk in front of it, where he writes and keeps his papers. Behind these chairs runs a railing, and behind the railing is an open space into which some classes of strangers may be brought, where sofas stand against the wall, and where smoking is practised, even by strangers, though the rules forbid it.

When you enter, your first impression is of noise and turmoil, a noise like that of short sharp waves in a Highland loch, fretting under a squall against a rocky shore. The raising and dropping of desk lids, the scratching of pens, the clapping of hands to call the pages, keen little boys who race along the gangways, the pattering of many feet, the hum of talking on the floor and in the galleries, make up a din over which the Speaker with the sharp taps of his hammer, or the orators straining shrill throats, find it hard to make themselves audible. Nor is it only the noise that gives the impression of disorder. Often three or four members are on their feet at once, each shouting to catch the Speaker's attention. Others, tired of sitting still, rise to stretch themselves, while the Western visitor, long, lank, and imperturbable, leans his arms on the railing, chewing his cigar, and surveys the scene with little reverence. Less favourable conditions for oratory cannot be imagined, and one is not surprised to be told that debate was more animated and practical in the much smaller room which the House formerly occupied.

Not only is the present room so big that only a powerful and well-trained voice can fill it, but the desks and chairs make a speaker feel as if he were addressing furniture rather than men, while of the members few seem to listen to the speeches. It is true that they sit in the House instead of running frequently out into the lobbies, but they are more occupied in talking or writing, or reading newspapers, than in attending to the debate. To attend is not easy, for only a shrill voice can overcome the murmurous roar; and one sometimes finds the newspapers, in describing an unusually effective speech, observe that "Mr. So-and-So's speech drew listeners about him from all parts of the House." They could not hear him where they sat, so they left their places to crowd in the gangways near him. "Speaking in the House," says an American writer, "is like trying to address the people in the Broadway omnibuses from the kerbstone in front of the Astor House. . . . Men of fine intellect and of good ordinary elocution have exclaimed in despair that in the House of Representatives the mere physical effort to be heard uses up all the powers, so that intellectual action becomes impossible. The natural refuge is in written speeches or in habitual silence, which one dreads more and more to break."

It is hard to talk calm good sense at the top of your voice, hard to unfold a complicated measure. A speaker's vocal organs react upon his manner, and his manner on the substance of his speech. It is also hard to thunder at an unscrupulous majority or a factious minority when they do not sit opposite to you, but beside you, and perhaps too much occupied with their papers to turn round and listen to you. The Americans think this an advantage, because it prevents scenes of disorder. They may be right; but what order gains oratory loses. It is admitted that the desks encourage inattention by enabling men to write their letters; but though nearly everybody agrees that they would be better away, nobody supposes that a proposition to remove them would succeed.[1] So too the huge galleries add to the area the voice has to fill; but the public like them, and might resent a removal to a smaller room. The smoking shocks an Englishman, but not more than the English practice of wearing hats in both Houses of Parliament shocks an American. Interruption, cries of "Divide," interjected remarks, are not more frequent—when I have been present they seemed to be much less frequent—than in the House of Commons. Approval is expressed more charily, as is usually the case in America. Instead of "Hear, hear," there is a clapping of hands and hitting of desks. Applause is sometimes given from the galleries; and occasionally at the end of a session both the members below and the strangers in the galleries above have been known to join in singing some popular ditty.

There is little good speaking. I do not mean merely that fine oratory, oratory which presents valuable thoughts in eloquent words, is rare, for it is rare in all assemblies. But in the House of Representatives a set speech upon any subject of importance tends to become

---

[1] *The House decided in 1859, at the end of one Congress, that the desks should be removed from the Hall (as the House is called), but in the next succeeding session the old arrangement was resumed.*

not an exposition or an argument but a piece of elaborate and high-flown declamation. Its author is often wise enough to send direct to the reporters what he has written out, having read aloud a small part of it in the House. When it has been printed *in extenso* in the *Congressional Record* (leave to get this done being readily obtained), he has copies struck off and distributes them among his constituents. Thus everybody is pleased and time is saved.[1]

That there is not much good business debating, by which I mean a succession of comparatively short speeches addressed to a practical question, and hammering it out by the collision of mind with mind, arises not from any want of ability among the members, but from the unfavourable conditions under which the House acts. Most of the practical work is done in the standing committees, while much of the House's time is consumed in pointless discussions, where member after member delivers himself upon large questions, not likely to be brought to a definite issue. Many of the speeches thus called forth have a value as repertories of facts, but the debate as a whole is unprofitable and languid. On the other hand the five-minute debates which take place, when the House imposes that limit of time, in Committee of the Whole on the consideration of a bill reported from a standing committee, are often lively, pointed, and effective. The topics which excite most interest and are best discussed are those of taxation and the appropriation of money, more particularly to public works, the improvement of rivers and harbours, erection of Federal buildings, and so forth. This kind of business is indeed to most of its members the

---

[1] I was told that formerly speeches might be printed in the Record as a matter of course, but that, a member having used this privilege to print and circulate a poem, the right was restrained.

chief interest of Congress, the business which evokes the finest skill of a tactician and offers the severest temptations to a frail conscience. As a theatre or school either of political eloquence or political wisdom, the House has been inferior not only to the Senate but to most European assemblies. Nor does it enjoy much consideration at home. Its debates are very shortly reported in the Washington papers as well as in those of Philadelphia and New York. They are not widely read except in very exciting times, and do little to instruct or influence public opinion.

This is of course only one part of a legislature's functions. An assembly may despatch its business successfully and yet shine with few lights of genius. But the legislation on public matters which the House turns out is scanty in quantity and generally mediocre in quality. What is more, the House tends to avoid all really grave and pressing questions, skirmishing round them, but seldom meeting them in the face or reaching a decision which marks an advance. If one makes this observation to an American, he replies that at this moment there are few such questions lying within the competence of Congress, and that in his country representatives must not attempt to move faster than their constituents. This latter remark is eminently true; it expresses a feeling which has gone so far that Congress conceives its duty to be to follow and not to seek to lead public opinion. The harm actually suffered so far is not grave. But the European observer cannot escape the impression that Congress might fail to grapple with a serious public danger, and is at present hardly equal to the duty of guiding and instructing the political intelligence of the nation.

In all assemblies one must expect abundance of unreality and pretence, many speeches obviously addressed to the gallery, many bills meant to be circulated but not to be seriously proceeded with. However, the House seems to indulge itself more freely in this direction than any other chamber of equal rank. Its galleries are large, holding 2500 persons. But it talks and votes, I will not say to the galleries, for the galleries cannot hear it, but as if every section of American opinion was present in the room. It adopts unanimously resolutions which perhaps no single member in his heart approves of, but which no one cares to object to, because it seems not worth while to do so. This habit sometimes exposes it to a snub, such as that administered by Bismarck in the matter of the resolution of condolence with the German Parliament on the death of Lasker, a resolution harmless indeed but so superfluous as to be almost obtrusive. A practice unknown to Europeans is of course misunderstood by them, and sometimes provokes resentment. Bills are frequently brought into the House proposing to effect impossible objects by absurd means, which astonish a visitor, and may even cause disquiet in other countries, while few people in America notice them, and no one thinks it worth while to expose their emptiness. American statesmen keep their pockets full of the loose cash of empty compliments and pompous phrases, and become so accustomed to scatter it among the crowd that they are surprised when a complimentary resolution or electioneering bill, intended to humour some section of opinion at home, is taken seriously abroad. The House is particularly apt to err in this way, because having no responsibility in foreign policy, and little sense of its own dignity, it applies to international affairs the habits of election meetings.

Watching the House at work, and talking to the members in the lobbies, an Englishman naturally asks himself how the intellectual quality of the body compares with that of the House of Commons. His American friends have prepared him to expect a marked inferiority. They are fond of running down congressmen. The cultivated New Englanders and New Yorkers do this out of intellectual fastidiousness, and in order to support the rôle which they unconsciously fall into when talking to Europeans. The rougher Western men do it because they would not have congressmen either seem or be better in any way than themselves, since that would be opposed to republican equality. A stranger who has taken literally all he hears is therefore surprised to find so much character, shrewdness, and keen though limited intelligence among the representatives. Their average business capacity is not below that of members of the House of Commons. True it is that great lights, such as usually adorn the British chamber, are absent: true also that there are fewer men who have received a high education which has developed their tastes and enlarged their horizons. The want of such men seriously depresses the average. It is raised, however, by the almost total absence of two classes hitherto well represented in the British Parliament, the rich, dull parvenu, who has bought himself into public life, and the perhaps equally unlettered young sporting or fashionable man who, neither knowing nor caring anything about politics, has come in for a county or (before 1885) a small borough, on the strength of his family estates. Few congressmen sink to so low an intellectual level as these two sets of persons, for congressmen have almost certainly made their way by energy and smartness, picking up a knowledge of men and things "all the time." In respect of width of view, of capacity for penetrating thought on political problems, representatives are scarcely above the class from which they came, that of second-rate lawyers or farmers,

THE HOUSE AT WORK   131

less often merchants or petty manufacturers. They do not pretend to be statesmen in the European sense of the word, for their careers, which have made them smart and active, have given them little opportunity for acquiring such capacities. As regards manners they are not polished, because they have not lived among polished people; yet neither are they rude, for to get on in American politics one must be civil and pleasant. The standard of parliamentary language, and of courtesy generally, has tended to rise during the last few decades; and scenes of violence and confusion such as occasionally convulse the French chamber, and were common in Washington before the War of Secession, are now rare.

On the whole, the most striking difference between the House of Representatives and European popular assemblies is its greater homogeneity. The type is marked; the individuals vary little from the type. In Europe all sorts of persons are sucked into the vortex of the legislature, nobles and landowners, lawyers, physicians, business men, artisans, journalists, men of learning, men of science. In America five representatives out of six are politicians pure and simple, members of a class as well defined as any one of the above-mentioned European classes. The American people, though it is composed of immigrants from every country, and occupies a whole continent, tends to become more uniform than most of the great European peoples; and this characteristic is palpable in its legislature.

Uneasy lies the head of an ambitious congressman,[1] for the chances are at least even that he will lose his

---

[1] *The term "Congressman" is commonly used to describe a member of the House of Representatives, though of course it ought to include senators also. So in England "Member of Parliament" means members of the House of Commons, though it covers all persons who have seats in the House of Lords.*

seat at the next election. It was observed in 1788 that half of the members of each successive State legislature were new members, and this average has been usually maintained in the Federal legislature, rather less than half keeping their seats from one Congress to the next. In England the proportion of members re-elected from Parliament to Parliament is much higher. Any one can see how much influence this constant change in the composition of the American House must have upon its legislative efficiency.

I have kept to the last the feature of the House which Europeans find the strangest.

It has parties, but they are headless. There is neither Government nor Opposition; neither leaders nor whips. No person holding any Federal office or receiving any Federal salary, can be a member of it. That the majority may be and often is opposed to the President and his cabinet, does not strike Americans as odd, because they proceed on the theory that the legislative ought to be distinct from the executive authority. Since no minister sits, there is no official representative of the party which for the time being holds the reins of the executive government. Neither is there any unofficial representative. And as there are no persons whose opinions expressed in debate are followed, so there are none whose duty it is to bring up members to vote, to secure a quorum, to see that people know which way the bulk of the party is going.

So far as the majority has a chief, that chief is the Speaker, who has been chosen by them as their ablest and most influential man; but as the Speaker seldom joins in debate (though he may do so by leaving the chair, having put some one else in it), the chairman of the most important committee, that of Ways and Means, enjoys a sort of eminence, and comes nearer than any one else to the position of leader of the House.[1] But his authority does not always enable him to secure coöperation for debate among the best speakers of his party, putting up now one now another, after the fashion of an English prime minister, and thereby guiding the general course of the discussion.

The minority do not formally choose a leader, nor is there usually any one among them whose career marks him out as practically the first man, but the person whom they have put forward as their party candidate for the Speakership, giving him what is called "the complimentary nomination," has a sort of vague claim to be so regarded. This honour amounts to very little. In the forty-eighth Congress the Speaker of the last preceding Congress received such a complimentary nomination from the Republicans against Mr. Carlisle, whom the Democratic majority elected. But the Republicans immediately afterwards refused to treat their nominee as leader, and left him, on some motion which he made, in a ridiculously small minority. Of course when an exciting question comes up, some man of marked capacity and special knowledge will often become virtually leader, in either party, for the purposes of the debates upon it. But he will not necessarily command the votes of his own side.

How then does the House work?

If it were a Chamber, like those of France or Germany, divided into four or five sections of opinion, none of which commands a steady majority, it would not work at all. But parties are few in the United States, and their cohesion tight. There are usually two only, so nearly equal in strength that the majority cannot afford to dissolve into groups like those of France. Hence upon

[1] *The Chairman of the Committee on Appropriations has perhaps as much real power.*

all large national issues, whereon the general sentiment of the party has been declared, both the majority and the minority know how to vote, and vote solid.

If the House were, like the English House of Commons, to some extent an executive as well as a legislative body—one by whose co-operation and support the daily business of government had to be carried on—it could not work without leaders and whips. This it is not. It neither creates, nor controls, nor destroys, the Administration, which depends on the President, himself the offspring of a direct popular mandate.

"Still," it may be replied, "the House has important functions to discharge. Legislation comes from it. Supply depends on it. It settles the tariff, and votes money for the civil and military services, besides passing measures to cure the defects which experience must disclose in the working of every government, every system of jurisprudence. How can it satisfy these calls upon it without leaders and organization?"

To a European eye, it does not seem to satisfy them. It votes the necessary supplies, but not wisely, giving sometimes too much, sometimes too little money, and taking no adequate securities for the due application of the sums voted. For many years past it has fumbled over both the tariff problem and the currency problem. It produces few useful laws, and leaves on one side many grave practical questions. An Englishman is disposed to ascribe these failures to the fact that as there are no leaders, there is no one responsible for the neglect of business, the miscarriage of bills, the unwise appropriation of public funds. "In England," he says, "the ministry of the day bears the blame of whatever goes wrong in the House of Commons. Having a majority, it ought to be able to do what it desires. If it pleads that its measures have been obstructed, and that it cannot under the faulty procedure of the House of Commons accomplish what it seeks, it is met, and crushed, by the retort that in such case it ought to have the procedure changed. What else is its majority good for but to secure the efficiency of Parliament? In America there is no person against whom similar charges can be brought. Although conspicuous folly or perversity on the part of the majority tends to discredit them collectively with the public, and may damage them at the next presidential or congressional election, still responsibility, to be effective, ought to be fixed on a few conspicuous leaders. Is not the want of such men, men to whom the country can look, and whom the ordinary members will follow, the cause of some of the faults which are charged on Congress, of its hesitations, its inconsistencies and changes, its ignoble surrenders to some petty clique, its deficient sense of dignity, its shrinking from troublesome questions, its proclivity to jobs?"

Two American statesmen to whom such a criticism was submitted, replied as follows: "It is not for want of leaders that Congress has forborne to settle the questions mentioned, but because the division of opinion in the country regarding them has been faithfully reflected in Congress. The majority has not been strong enough to get its way; and this has happened, not only because abundant opportunities for resistance arise from the methods of doing business, but still more because no distinct impulse or mandate towards any particular settlement of these questions has been received from the country. It is not for Congress to go faster than the people. When the country knows and speaks its mind, Congress will not fail to act." The significance of this reply lies in its pointing to a fundamental difference between the conception of the respective positions and duties of a representative body and of the nation at large entertained by Americans, and the conception which has hitherto prevailed in Europe. Europeans have thought of a legislature as belonging to the governing class. In America there is no such class. Europeans think that the legislature ought to consist of the best men in the country, Americans that it should be a fair average sample of the country. Europeans think that it ought to lead the nation, Americans that it ought to follow the nation.

Without some sort of organization, an assembly of three hundred and thirty men would be a mob, so necessity has provided in the system of committees a substitute for the European party organization. This system will be explained in the next chapter; for the present it is enough to observe that when a matter which has been (as all bills are) referred to a committee, comes up in the House to be dealt with there, the chairman of the particular committee is treated as a leader *pro hac vice,* and members who knew nothing of the matter are apt to be guided by his speech or his advice given privately. If his advice is not available, or is suspected because he belongs to the opposite party, they seek direction from the member in charge of the bill, if he belongs to their own party, or from some other member of the committee, or from some friend whom they trust. When a debate arises unexpectedly on a question of importance, members are often puzzled how to vote. The division being taken, they get some one to move a call of yeas and nays, and while this slow process goes on, they scurry about asking advice as to their action, and give their votes on the second calling over if not ready on the first. If the issue is one of serious consequence to the party, a recess is demanded by the majority, say for two hours. The House then adjourns, each party "goes into caucus" (the Speaker possibly announcing the fact), and debates the matter with closed doors. Then the House resumes, and each party votes solid according to the determination arrived at in caucus. In spite of these expedients, surprises and scratch votes are not uncommon.

I have spoken of the din of the House of Representatives, of its air of restlessness and confusion, contrasting with the staid gravity of the Senate, of the absence of dignity both in its proceedings and in the bearing and aspect of individual members. All these things notwithstanding, there is something impressive about it, something not unworthy of the continent for which it legislates.

This huge gray hall, filled with perpetual clamour, this multitude of keen and eager faces, this ceaseless coming and going of many feet, this irreverent public, watching from the galleries and forcing its way on to the floor, all speak to the beholder's mind of the mighty democracy, destined in another century to form one half of civilized mankind, whose affairs are here debated. If the men are not great, the interests and the issues are vast and fateful. Here, as so often in America, one thinks rather of the future than of the present. Of what tremendous struggles may not this hall become the theatre in ages yet far distant, when the parliaments of Europe have shrunk to insignificance?

(From *The American Commonwealth*.)

A.E.

Thoughts from *The National Being*

THE building up of a civilization is at once the noblest and the most practical of all enterprises, in which human faculties are exalted to their highest, and beauties and majesties are manifested in multitude as they are never by solitary man or by disunited peoples. In the highest civilizations the individual citizen is raised above himself and made part of a greater life, which we may call the National Being. He enters into it, and it becomes an oversoul to him, and gives to all his works a character and grandeur and a relation to the works of his fellow-citizens, so that all he does conspires with the labours of others for unity and magnificence of effect. So ancient Egypt, with its temples, sphinxes, pyramids, and symbolic decorations, seems to us as if it had been created by one grandiose imagination; for even the lesser craftsmen, working on the mummy case for the tomb, had much of the mystery and solemnity in their work which is manifest in temple and pyramid. So the city States in ancient Greece in their day were united by ideals to a harmony of art and architecture and literature. Among the Athenians at their highest the ideal of the State so wrought upon the individual that its service became the overmastering passion of life, and in that great oration of Pericles, where he told how the Athenian ideal inspired the citizens so that they gave their bodies for the commonwealth, it seems to have been conceived of as a kind of oversoul, a being made up of immortal deeds and heroic spirits, influencing the living, a life within their life, moulding their spirits to its likeness. It appears almost as if in some of these ancient famous communities the national ideal became a kind of tribal deity, that began first with some great hero who died and was immortalized by the poets, and whose character, continually glorified by them, grew at last so great in song that he could not be regarded as less than a demi-god. We can see in ancient Ireland that Cuchulain, the dark sad man of the earlier tales, was rapidly becoming a divinity, a being who summed up in himself all that the bards thought noblest in the spirit of their race; and if Ireland had a happier history no doubt one generation of bardic chroniclers after another would have moulded that half-mythical figure into the Irish ideal of all that was chivalrous, tender, heroic, and magnanimous, and it would have been a star to youth, and the thought of it a staff to the very noblest. Even as Cuchulain alone at the ford held it against a host, so the ideal would have upheld the national soul in its darkest hours, and stood in many a lonely place in the heart. The national soul in a theocratic State is a god; in an aristocratic age it assumes the character of a hero; and in a democracy it becomes a multitudinous being, definite in character if the democracy is a real social organism. But where the democracy is only loosely held together by the social order, the national being is vague in character, is a mood too feeble to inspire large masses of men to high policies in times of peace, and in times of war it communicates frenzy, panic, and delirium.

None of our modern States create in us such an impression of being spiritually oversouled by an ideal as the great States of the ancient world. The leaders of nations too have lost that divine air that many leaders of men wore in the past, and which made the populace rumour them as divine incarnations. It is difficult to know to what to attribute this degeneration. Perhaps the artists who create ideals are to blame. In ancient

Ireland, in Greece, and in India, the poets wrote about great kings and heroes, enlarging on their fortitude of spirit, their chivalry and generosity, creating in the popular mind an ideal of what a great man was like; and men were influenced by the ideal created, and strove to win the praise of the bards and to be recrowned by them a second time in great poetry. So we had Cuchulain and Oscar in Ireland; Hector of Troy, Theseus in Greece; Yudisthira, Rama, and Arjuna in India, all bard-created heroes moulding the minds of men to their image. It is the great defect of our modern literature that it creates few such types. How hardly could one of our modern public men be made the hero of an epic. It would be difficult to find one who could be the subject of a genuine lyric. Whitman, himself the most democratic poet of the modern world, felt this deficiency in the literature of the later democracies, and lamented the absence of great heroic figures. The poets have dropped out of the divine procession, and sing a solitary song. They inspire nobody to be great, and failing any finger-post in literature pointing to true greatness our democracies too often take the huckster from his stall, the drunkard from his pot, the lawyer from his court, and the company promoter from the director's chair, and elect them as representative men. We certainly do this in Ireland. It is—how many hundred years since greatness guided us? In Ireland our history begins with the most ancient of any in a mythical era when earth mingled with heaven. The gods departed, the half-gods also, hero and saint after that, and we have dwindled down to a petty peasant nationality, rural and urban life alike mean in their externals. Yet the cavalcade, for all its tattered habiliments, has not lost spiritual dignity. There is still some incorruptible spiritual atom in our people. We are still in some relation to the divine order; and while that incorrupted spiritual atom still remains all things are possible if by some inspiration there could be revealed to us a way back or forward to greatness, an Irish polity in accord with national character.

In formulating an Irish polity we have to take into account the change in world conditions. A theocratic State we shall have no more. Every nation, and our own along with them, is now made up of varied sects, and the practical dominance of one religious idea would let loose illimitable passions, the most intense the human spirit can feel. The way out of the theocratic State was by the drawn sword and was lit by the martyr's fires. The way back is unthinkable for all Protestant fears or Catholic aspirations. Aristocracies, too, become impossible as rulers. The aristocracy of character and intellect we may hope shall finally lead us, but no aristocracy so by birth will renew its authority over us. The character of great historic personages is gradually reflected in the mass. The divine right of kings is followed by the idea of the divine right of the people, and democracies finally become ungovernable save by themselves. They have seen and heard too much of pride and greatness not to have become, in some measure, proud and defiant of all authority except their own. It may be said the history of democracies is not one to fill us with confidence, but the truth is the world has yet to see the democratic State, and of the yet untried we may think with hope. Beneath the Athenian and other ancient democratic States lay a substratum of humanity in slavery, and the culture, beauty, and bravery of these extraordinary peoples were made possible by the workers in an underworld who had no part in the bright civic life.

We have no more a real democracy in the world today. Democracy in politics has in no country led to democracy in its economic life. We still have autocracy in industry as firmly seated on its throne as theocratic king ruling in the name of a god, or aristocracy ruling by military power; and the forces represented by these twain, superseded by the autocrats of industry, have become the allies of the power which took their place of pride. Religion and rank, whether content or not with the subsidiary place they now occupy, are most often courtiers of Mammon and support him on his throne. For all the talk about democracy our social order is truly little more democratic than Rome was under the Caesars, and our new rulers have not, with all their wealth, created a beauty which we could imagine after-generations brooding over with uplifted heart.

The people in theocratic States like Egypt or Chaldea, ruled in the name of gods, saw rising out of the plains in which they lived an architecture so mysterious and awe-inspiring that they might well believe the master-minds who designed the temples were inspired from the Oversoul. The aristocratic States reflected the love of beauty which is associated with aristocracies. The oligarchies of wealth in our time, who have no divine sanction to give dignity to their rule nor traditions of lordly life like the aristocracies, have not in our day created beauty in the world. But whatever of worth the ancient systems produced was not good enough to make permanent their social order. Their civilizations, like ours, were built on the unstable basis of a vast working-class with no real share in the wealth and grandeur it helped to create. The character of his kingdom was revealed in dream to Nebuchadnezzar by an image with a golden head and feet of clay, and that image might stand as symbol of the empires the world has known. There is in all a vast population living in an underworld of labour whose freedom to vote confers on them no real power, and who are most often scorned and neglected by those who profit by their labours. Indifference turns to fear and hatred if labour organizes and gathers power, or makes one motion of its myriad hands towards the sceptre held by the autocrats of industry. When this class is maddened and revolts, civilization shakes and totters like cities when the earthquake stirs beneath their foundations. Can we master these arcane human forces? Can we, by any device, draw this submerged humanity into the light and make them real partners in the social order, not partners merely in the political life of the nation, but, what is of more importance, in its economic life? If we build our civilization without integrating labour into its economic structure, it will wreck that civilization, and it will do that more swiftly today than two thousand years ago, because there is no longer the disparity of culture between high and low which existed in past centuries. The son of the artisan, if he cares to read, may become almost as fully master of the wisdom of Plato or Aristotle as if he had been at a university. Emerson will speak to him of his divinity; Whitman, drunken with the sun, will chant to him of his inheritance of the earth. He is elevated by the poets and instructed by the economists. But there are not thrones enough for all who are made wise in our social order, and failing even to serve in the social heaven these men will spread revolt and reign in the social hell. They are becoming too many for higher places to be found for them in the national economy. They are increasing to a multitude which must be considered, and the framers of a national polity must devise a life for them where their new-found dignity of spirit will not be abased.

Men no more will be content under rulers of industry they do not elect themselves than they were under political rulers claiming their obedience in the name of God. They will not for long labour in industries where they have no power to fix the conditions of their employment, as they were not content with a political system which allowed them no power to control legislation. Ireland must begin its imaginative reconstruction of a civilization by first considering that type which, in the earlier civilizations of the world, has been slave, serf, or servile, working either on land or at industry, and must construct with reference to it. These workers must be the central figures, and how their material, intellectual, and spiritual needs are met must be the test of value of the social order we evolve.

I have not in all this written anything about the relations of Ireland with other countries, or even with our neighbours, in whose political household we have lived for so many centuries in intimate hostility. I have considered this indeed, but did not wish, nor do I now wish, in anything I may write, to say one word which would add to that old hostility. Race hatred is the cheapest and basest of all national passions, and it is the nature of hatred, as it is the nature of love, to change us into the likeness of that which we contemplate. We grow nobly like what we adore, and ignobly like what we hate; and no people in Ireland became so anglicized in intellect and temperament, and even in the manner of expression, as those who hated our neighbours most. All hatreds long persisted in bring us to every baseness for which we hated others. The only laws which we cannot break with impunity are divine laws, and no law is more eternally sure in its workings than that which condemns us to be even as that we condemned. Hate is

THE NATIONAL BEING 145

the high commander of so many armies that an inquiry into the origin of this passion is at least as needful as histories of other contemporary notorieties. Not emperors or parliaments alone raise armies, but this passion also. It will sustain nations in defeat. When everything seems lost this wild captain will appear and the scattered forces are reunited. They will be as oblivious of danger as if they were divinely inspired, but if they win their battle it is to become like the conquered foe. All great wars in history, all conquests, all national antagonisms, result in an exchange of characteristics. It is because I wish Ireland to be itself, to act from its own will and its own centre, that I deprecate hatred as a force in national life. It is always possible to win a cause without the aid of this base helper, who betrays us ever in the hour of victory.

When a man finds the feeling of hate for another rising vehemently in himself, he should take it as a warning that conscience is battling in his own being with that very thing he loathes. Nations hate other nations for the evil which is in themselves; but they are as little given to self-analysis as individuals, and while they are right to overcome evil, they should first try to understand the genesis of the passion in their own nature. If we understand this, many of the ironies of history will be intelligible. We will understand why it was that our countrymen in Ulster and our countrymen in the rest of Ireland, who have denounced each other so vehemently, should at last appear to have exchanged characteristics: why in the North, having passionately protested against physical force movements, no-rent manifestos, and contempt for Imperial Parliament, they should have come themselves at last to organize a physical force movement, should threaten to pay no taxes, and should refuse obedience to an Act of Parliament. We will understand also why it was their opponents came themselves to address to Ulster all the arguments and denunciations Ulster had addressed to them. I do not point this out with intent to annoy, but to illustrate by late history a law in national as well as human psychology. If this unpopular psychology I have explained was adopted everywhere as true, we would never hear expressions of hate. People would realize they were first revealing and then stabbing their own characters before the world.

Nations act towards other nations as their own citizens act towards each other. When slavery existed in a State, if that nation attacked another it was with intent to enslave. Where there is a fierce economic competition between citizen and citizen then in war with another nation, the object of the war is to destroy the trade of the enemy. If the citizens in any country could develop harmonious life among themselves they would manifest the friendliest feelings towards the people of other countries. We find that it is just among groups of people who aim at harmonious life, co-operators and socialists, that the strongest national impulses to international brotherhood arise; and wars of domination are brought about by the will of those who within a State are dominant over the fortunes of the rest. Ireland, a small country, can only maintain its national identity by moral and economic forces. Physically it must be overmastered by most other European nations. Moral forces are really more powerful than physical forces. One Christ changed the spiritual life of Europe; one Buddha affected more myriads in Asia.

The co-operative ideal of brotherhood in industry has helped to make stronger the ideal of the brotherhood of humanity, and no body of men in any of the countries in the great War of our time regarded it with more genuine sorrow than those who were already beginning to promote schemes for international co-operation. It must be mainly in movements inspired with the ideal of the brotherhood of man, that the spirit will be generated which, in the future, shall make the idea of war so detestable that statesmen will find it is impossible to think of that solution of their disputes as they would think now of resorting to private assassination of political opponents. The great tragedy of Europe was brought about, not by the German Emperor, nor by Sir Edward Grey, nor by the Czar, nor by any of the other chiefs ostensibly controlling foreign policy, but by the nations themselves. These men may have been agents, but their action would have been impossible if they did not realize that there was a vast body of national feeling behind them not opposed to war. Their citizens were in conflict with each other already, generating the moods which lead on to war. Emperors, foreign secretaries, ambassadors, cabinet ministers are not really powerful to move nations against their will. On the whole, they act with the will of the nations, which they understand. Let any one ruler try, for example, to change by edict the religion of his subjects, and a week would see him bereft of place and power. They could not do this, because the will of the nation would be against it. They resort to war and prepare for it because the will of the nation is with them, and this throws us back on the private citizens, who finally are individually and collectively responsible for the actions of the State. In the everlasting battle between good and evil, private soldiers are called upon to fight as well as the captains, and it is only through the intensive cultivation by individuals and races of the higher moral and intellectual qualities, until in intensity they outweigh the mood and passion of the rest, that war will finally become obsolete as the court of appeal. When there is a panic of fire in a crowded building men are suddenly tested as to character. Some will become frenzied madmen, fighting and trampling their way out. Others will act nobly, forgetting themselves. They have no time to think. What they are in their total make up as human beings, overbalanced either for good or evil, appears in an instant. Even so, some time in the heroic future, some nation in a crisis will be weighed and will act nobly rather than passionately, and will be prepared to risk national extinction rather than continue existence at the price of killing myriads of other human beings, and it will oppose moral and spiritual forces to material forces, and it will overcome the world by making gentleness its might, as all great spiritual teachers have done. It comes to this, we cannot overcome hatred by hatred or war by war, but by the opposites of these. Evil is not overcome by evil but by good; and any race like the Irish, eager for national life, ought to learn this truth—that humanity will act towards their race as their race acts towards humanity. The noble and the base alike beget their kin. Empires, ere they disappear, see their own mirrored majesty arise in the looking-glass of time. Opposed to the pride and pomp of Egypt were the pride and pomp of Chaldea. Echoing the beauty of the Greek city state were many lovely cities made in their image. Carthage evoked Rome. The British Empire, by the natural balance and opposition of things, called into being another empire with a civilization of coal and steel, and with ambitions for colonies and for naval power, and with that image of itself it must wrestle for empire. The great armadas that throng the seas, the armed millions upon the earth betray the fear in the minds of races, nay, the inner spiritual certitude the soul has, that pride and lust of power must yet be humbled by their kind. They must at last meet their equals face to face, called to them as steel to magnet by some inner affinity. This is a law of life both for individuals and races, and, when this is realized, we know nothing will put an end to race conflicts except the equally determined and heroic development of the spiritual, moral, and intellectual forces which disdain to use the force and fury of material powers.

We may be assured that the divine law is not mocked, and it cannot be deceived. As men sow so do they reap. The anger we create will rend us; the love we give will return to us. Biologically, everything breeds true to its type: moods and thoughts just as much as birds and beasts and fishes. When I hear people raging against England or Germany or Russia I know that rage will beget rage, and go on begetting it, and so the whole devilish generation of passions will be continued. There are no nations to whom the entire and loyal allegiance of man's spirit could be given. It can only go out to the ideal empires and nationalities in the womb of time, for whose coming we pray. Those countries of the future we must carve out of the humanity of today, and we can begin building them up within our present empires and nationalities just as we are building up the co-operative movement in a social order antagonistic to it. The people who are trying to create these new ideals in the world are outposts, sentinels, and frontiersmen thrown out before the armies of the intellectual and spiritual races yet to come into being. We can all enlist in these armies and be comrades to the pioneers. I hope many will enlist in Ireland. I would cry to our idealists to come out of this present-day Irish Babylon, so filled with sectarian, political, and race hatreds, and to work for the future. I believe profoundly, with the most extreme of Nationalists, in the future of Ireland,

and in the vision of light seen by Bridget which she saw and confessed between hopes and tears to Patrick, and that this is the Isle of Destiny and the destiny will be glorious and not ignoble, and when our hour is come we will have something to give to the world, and we will be proud to give rather than to grasp. Throughout their history Irishmen have always wrought better for others than for themselves, and when they unite in Ireland to work for each other, they will direct into the right channel all that national capacity for devotion to causes for which they are famed. We ought not only to desire to be at peace with each other, but with the whole world, and this can only be brought about by the individual citizen at all times protesting against sectarian and national passions, and taking no part in them, coming out of such angry parties altogether, as the people of the Lord were called by the divine voice to come out of Babylon. It may seem a long way to set things right, but it is the swift way and the royal road, and there is no other; and nobody, no prophet crying before his time, will be listened to until the people are ready for him. The congregation must gather before the preacher can deliver what is in him to say. The economic brotherhood which I have put forward as an Irish ideal would, in its realization, make us at peace with ourselves, and if we are at peace with ourselves we will be at peace with our neighbours and all other nations, and will wish them the good-will we have among ourselves, and will receive from them the same good-will. I do not believe in legal and formal solutions of national antagonisms. While we generate animosities among ourselves we will always display them to other nations, and I prefer to search out how it is national hatreds are begotten, and to show how that cancer can be cut out of the body politic.

It seems inevitable that the domination of the individual by the State must become ever greater. It is in the evolutionary process. The amalgamation of individuals into nationalities and empires is as much in the cosmic plan as the development of highly organized beings out of unicellular organisms. I believe this process will continue until humanity itself is so psychically knit together that, as a being, it will manifest some form of cosmic consciousness in which the individual will share. Our spiritual intuitions and the great religions of the world alike indicate some such goal as that to which this turbulent cavalcade of humanity is wending. A knowledge of this must be in our subconscious being, or we would find the sacrifices men make for the State otherwise inexplicable. The State, though now ostensibly secular, makes more imperious claims on man than the ancient gods did. It lays hold of life. It asserts its right to take father, brother, and son, and to send them to meet death in its own defence. It denies them a choice or judgment as to whether its action is right or wrong. Right or wrong, the individual must be prepared to give his body for the commonwealth, and when one gives the body unresistingly, one gives the soul also. The marvellous thing about the authority of the State is that it is recognized by the vast majority of citizens. During eras of peace the citizen may be always in conflict with the policy of the State. He may call it a tyranny, but yet when it is in peril he will die to preserve for it an immortal life. The hold the State establishes over the spirit of man is the more wonderful when we look rearward on history, and see with what labour and sacrifice the State was established. But we see also how readily, once the union has been brought about, men will die to preserve it, even although it is a tyranny, a bad State. For what do they die unless the spirit in man has some inner certitude that the divine event to which humanity tends is a unity of its multitudinous life, and that a State—even a bad State—must be preserved by its citizens, because it is at least an attempt at organic unity? It is a simulacrum of the ideal; it contains the germ or possibility of that to which the spirit of man is travelling. It disciplines the individual in service to that greater being in which it will find its fulfilment, and a bad State is better than no State at all. To be without a State is to prowl backwards from the divinity before us to the beast behind us.

The power the State exerts is a spiritual power, acting on or through the will of man. The volunteer armies do not really march to die with more readiness than the conscript armies. The sacrifice is not readily explicable by material causes. There is no material reason why the proletarian—who has no property to defend, who is more or less sure as a skilled craftsman of employment under any ruler—should concern himself whether his ruler be King, Kaiser, or President. But not one in a hundred proletarians really thinks like that. It is not the hope of personal profit works upon men to risk life. Let some exploiter of industry desire to employ a thousand men at dangerous work, with the risks of death or disablement equal to those of war; let it be known that one in six will be killed and another be disabled, and what sum will purchase the service of workers? They will risk life for the State, though given a bare subsistence or a pay which they would describe as inhuman if offered by one of the autocrats of industry. Men working for the State will make the most extraordinary sacrifices; but they stand stubbornly and sullenly as disturbers and blockers of all industry which is run for private profit. Is it not clear of the two policies for the State to adopt, to promote personal interests among its citizens or to unite men for the general good, that the first path is full of danger to the State, while through the other men will march cheerfully, though it be to death, in defence of the State. Something, a real life above the individual, acts through the national being, and would almost suggest to us that Heaven cannot fully manifest its will to humanity through the individual, but must utter itself through multitudes. There must be an orchestration of humanity ere it can echo divine melodies. In real truth we are all seeking in the majesties we create for union with a greater Majesty.

I wrote in an earlier page that the ancient conception of Nature as a manifestation of spirit was incarnating anew in the minds of modern thinkers; that Nature was no longer conceived of as material or static in condition, but as force and continual motion; that they were trying to identify human will with this arcane energy, and let the forces of Nature manifest with more power in society. The real nature of these energies manifesting in humanity I do not know, but they have been hinted at in the Scriptures, the oracles of the Oversoul, which speak of the whole creation labouring upwards and the entry of humanity into the Divine Mind, and of the reintrocession of That Itself with all Its myriad unity into Deity, so that God might be all in all. I believe profoundly that men do not hold the ideas of liberty or solidarity, which have moved them so powerfully, merely as phantasies which are pleasant to the soul or make ease for the body; but because, whether they struggle passionately for liberty or to achieve a solidarity, in working for these two ideals, which seem in conflict, they are divinely supported, in unison with the divine nature, and energies as real as those the scientist studies—as electricity, as magnetism, heat or light—do descend into the soul and reinforce it with elemental energy. We are here for the purposes of soul, and there can be no purpose in individualizing the soul if essential freedom is denied to it and there is only a destiny. Wherever essential freedom, the right of the spirit to choose its own heroes and its own ideals, is denied, nations rise in rebellion. But the spirit in man is wrought in a likeness to Deity, which is that harmony and unity of Being which upholds the universe; and by the very nature of the spirit, while it asserts its freedom, its impulses lead it to a harmony with all life, to a solidarity or brotherhood with it.

All these ideals of freedom, of brotherhood, of power, of justice, of beauty, which have been at one time or another the fundamental idea in civilizations, are heaven-born, and descended from the divine world, incarnating first in the highest minds in each race, perceived by them and transmitted to their fellow-citizens; and it is the emergence or manifestation of one or other of these ideals in a group which is the beginning of a nation; and the more strongly the ideal is held the more powerful becomes the national being, because the synchronous vibration of many minds in harmony brings about almost unconsciously a psychic unity, a coalescing of the subconscious being of many. It is that inner unity which constitutes the national being.

The idea of the national being emerged at no recognizable point in our history in Ireland. It is older than any name we know. It is not earth-born, but the synthesis of many heroic and beautiful moments, and these, it must be remembered, are divine in their origin. Every heroic deed is an act of the spirit, and every perception of beauty is vision with the divine eye, and not with the mortal sense. The spirit was subtly intermingled with the shining of old romance, and it is no mere phantasy which shows Ireland at its dawn in a misty light thronged with divine figures, and beneath and nearer to us demi-gods and heroes fading into recognizable men. The bards took cognizance only of the most notable personalities who preceded them, and of these only the acts which had a symbolic or spiritual significance; and these grew thrice refined as generations of poets in enraptured musings along by the mountains or in the woods brooded upon their heritage of story, until, as it passed from age to age, the accumulated beauty grew greater than the beauty of the hour. The dream began to enter into the children of our race, and turn their thoughts from earth to that world in which it had its inception.

It was a common belief among the ancient peoples that each had a national genius or deity who presided over them, in whose all-embracing mind they were contained, and who was the shepherd of their destinies. We can conceive of the national spirit in Ireland as first manifesting itself through individual heroes or kings, and as the history of famous warriors laid hold of the people, extending its influence until it created therein the germs of a kindred nature.

An aristocracy of lordly and chivalrous heroes is bound in time to create a great democracy by the reflection of their character in the mass, and the idea of the divine right of kings is succeeded by the idea of the divine right of the people. If this sequence cannot be traced in any one respect with historical regularity, it is because of the complexity of national life, its varied needs, the vicissitudes of history, and its infinite changes of sentiment. But the threads are all taken up in the end; and ideals which were forgotten and absent from the voices of men will be found, when reourred to, to have grown to a rarer and more spiritual beauty in their quiet abode in the heart. The seeds which were sown at the beginning of a race bear their flowers and fruits towards its close, and already antique names begin to stir us again with their power, and the antique ideals to reincarnate in us and renew their dominion over us.

They may not be recognized at first as a re-emergence of ancient moods. The democratic economics of the ancient clans have vanished almost out of memory, but the mood in which they were established reappears in those who would create a communal or co-operative life in the nation into which those ancient clans long since have melted. The instinct in the clans to waive aside the weak and to seek for an aristocratic and powerful character in their leaders reappears in the rising generation, who turn from the utterer of platitudes to men of real intellect and strong will. The object of democratic organization is to bring out the aristocratic character in leadership, the vivid original personalities who act and think from their own will and their own centres, who bring down fire from the heaven of their spirits and quicken and vivify the mass, and make democracies also to be great and fearless and free. A nation is dead where men acknowledge only conventions. We must find out truth for ourselves, becoming first initiates and finally masters in the guild of life. The intellect of Ireland is in chains where it ought to be free, and we have individualism in our economics which ought to be co-ordinated and sternly disciplined out of the iniquity of free profiteering. To quicken the intellect and imagination of Ireland, to co-ordinate our economic life for the general good, should be the objects of national policy, and will subserve the evolutionary purpose. The free imagination and the aspiring mind alone climb into the higher spheres and deflect for us the ethereal currents.

It is the multitude of aristocratic thinkers who give glory to a people and make them of service to other nations, and it is by the character of the social order and the quality of brotherhood in it our civilization will endure. Without love we are nothing.

(From *The National Being*.)

FICTION

C. E. MONTAGUE

Another Temple Gone

THEY say that there may be a speck of quiet lodged at the central point of a cyclone. Round it everything goes whirling. It alone sits at its ease, as still as the end of an axle that lets the wheel, all about it, whirl any wild way it likes.

That was the way at Gartumna in those distant years when the "land war" was blowing great guns all over the rest of the County Clare. Gartumna lay just at the midst of that tempest. But not a leaf stirred in the place. You paid your rent if you could; for the coat that the old colonel had on his back—and he never out of the township—was that worn you'd be sorry. Suppose you hadn't the cash, still you were not "put out of it." All that you'd have to suffer was that good man buzzing about your holding, wanting to help; he would be all in a fidget trying to call to mind the way that some heathen Dane, that he had known when a boy, used to bedevil salt butter back into fresh—that, or how Montenegrins would fatten a pig on any wisp of old trash that would come blowing down the high road. A kind man, though he never got quit of the queer dream he had that he knew how to farm.

Another practising Christian we had was Father O'Reilly. None of the sort that would charge you half the girl's fortune before they'd let the young people set foot in the church. And, when it was done, he'd come to the party and sing the best song of any one there. However, at practical goodness Tom Farrell left the entire field at the post. Tom had good means: a farm in fee-simple—the land, he would often tell us, the finest in Ireland, "every pitaty the weight of the world if you'd take it up in your hand"; turf coming all but in at the door to be cut; besides, the full of a creel of fish in no more than the time you'd take dropping a fly on the stream: the keeper had married Tom's sister. People would say "Ach, the match Tom would be for a girl!" and gossips liked counting the "terrible sum" that he might leave when he'd die if only he knew how to set any sort of value on money. But this he did not. The widow Burke, who knew more about life than a body might think, said Tom would never be high in the world because no one could come and ask for a thing but he'd give it them. Then, as she warmed to the grateful labour of letting you know what was what, the widow might add: "I question will Tom ever make a threepenny piece, or a penny itself, out of that old construction he has away there in the bog."

At these words a hearer would give a slight start and glance cannily round, knowing that it would be no sort of manners to give a decent body like Sergeant Maguire the botheration and torment of hearing the like of that said out aloud. But the sergeant would never be there. For he too had his fine social instincts. He would be

ANOTHER TEMPLE GONE

half a mile off, intent on his duty, commanding the two decent lads that were smoking their pipes, one on each of his flanks, in the tin police hut away down the road. Gartumna did not doubt that this tactful officer knew more than he ever let on. A man of his parts must surely have seen, if not smelt, that no unclean or common whisky, out of a shop, had emitted the mellow sunshine transfiguring recent christenings and wakes. But who so coarse as to bring a functionary so right-minded up against the brute choice between falling openly short in professional zeal and wounding the gentle bosom of Gartumna's peace?

And yet the widow's sonorous soprano, or somebody else's, may have been raised once too often on this precarious theme. For, on one of the warmest June mornings that ever came out of the sky, Sergeant Maguire paraded his whole army of two, in line, on a front of one mile, with himself as centre file and file of direction, and marched out in this extremely open order into the fawn-coloured wilderness of the bog. "You'll understand, the two of yous," he had said to his right flank, Constable Boam, and to Constable Duffy, his left, "that this is a sweeping or dhragging movement that we're making."

The sun was high already—your feverish early starts were no craze of the sergeant's. The air over the bog had tuned up for the day to its loudest and most multitudinous hum and hot click of grasshoppers and bees; all the fawn surface swam in a water-coloured quiver of glare; the coarse, juiceless grass and old roots, leathery and slippery, tripped up the three beaters' feet. Hour by hour the long morning greased and begrimed the three clean-shaven, good-soldier faces that had set out on the quest; noon came blazingly on—its savage vertical pressure seemed to quell and mute with an excess of heat the tropical buzz of all the basking bog life that the morning's sunshine had inspirited; another hour and the bog was swooning, as old poets say, under the embraces of the sun her friend, when a thin column of more intensely quivering air, a hundred yards off to the sergeant's half-left, betrayed some source of an ardour still more fiery than the sun's. Just for the next five or ten minutes, no more, the sergeant had some good stalking. Then it was all over. The hunting was done: nothing left but to whistle in his flank men and go over the haul.

The tub and worm of the illicit still had not been really hidden; they were just formally screened with a few blocks of turf as though in silent appeal to the delicacy of mankind to accept as adequate this symbolic tribute to the convention of a seemly reticence. Farrell, a little, neatly-made, fine-featured man with a set, contained face, but with all the nervousness of him quivering out into the restless tips of his small, pointed fingers, gazed at the three stolid uniformed bulks, so much grosser than he, while they disrobed his beloved machinery of that decent light vesture of turf and rummaged with large, coarse hands among the mysteries of his craft. He wore the Quakerish black suit and the broad and low-crowned soft black hat in which a respectable farmer makes his soul on a Sunday morning. Silent, and seemingly not shamed, nor yet enraged, neither the misdemeanant caught in the act nor the parent incensed by a menace to its one child, he looked on, grave and almost compassionate. So might the high priestess of Vesta have looked when the Gaulish heathen came butting into the shrine and messed about with the poker and tongs of the goddess's eternal flame. How could the poor benighted wretches know the mischief that they might be doing the world?

Sergeant Maguire, too, may have had his own sense of our kind's tragic blindness quickened just then—that a man, a poor passionate man, should so rush upon his own undoing! "Ach, it's a pity of you, Farrell," he presently said. "A pity! You with the grand means that you have of your own! An' you distillin' pocheen!"

"Pocheen!" The little, precise, nervous voice of Farrell ran up into a treble of melancholy scorn. With an austere quality in his movements he drew a brown stoneware jar from among some heaped cubes of turf that the barbarians had not yet disarranged. From another recess he took a squat tumbler. Into this he poured from the jar enough to fill a liqueur-glass smaller than most. "Tell me," he bade almost sternly, holding the tumbler out to Maguire, "d'ye call that pocheen?"

"Ye can take a sup first," was the canny reply. Maguire had heard how Eastern kings always made cooks and premiers taste first.

Farrell absorbed the tot, drop by drop. He did not cross himself first, but there was something about his way of addressing himself to the draught that would make you think of a man crossing himself before some devout exercise, or taking the shoes from off his feet before stepping on holy ground. As the potion irrigated his soul he seemed to draw off from the touch of this clamorous world into some cloistral retreat. From these contemplative shades he emerged, controlling a sigh, a little time after the last drop had done its good office. He poured out for Maguire.

"Well, here's luck," said the sergeant, raising the glass, "and a light sentence beyond." The good fellow's tone conveyed what the etiquette of the service would not allow him to say—that in the day of judgment every mitigating circumstance would be freshly remembered.

Up to this his fortieth year Maguire, conversing with the baser liquors of this world and not with philtres of transfiguration, had counted it sin to drink his whisky as if it would burn him. So the whole of the tot was now about to descend his large-bore throat in close order, as charges of shot proceed through the barrel of a gun. But the needful peristaltic action of the gullet had scarcely commenced when certain tidings of great joy were taken in at the palate and forwarded express to an astonished brain. "Mother of God!" the sergeant exclaimed. "What sort of hivven's delight is this you've invented for all souls in glory?"

A sombre satisfaction gleamed out of Farrell's monkish face. Truth was coming into its own, if only too late. The heathen were seeing the light. "It's the stuff," he said, gravely, "that made the old gods of the Greeks and Romans feel sure they were gods."

"Be cripes, they were right," asseverated Maguire. He was imbibing drop by drop now, as the wise poets of all times have done, and not as the topers, the swillers of cocktails, punch and cup, and the like, things only fit to fill up the beasts that perish. Not hoggishness only, but infinite loss would it have seemed to let any one drop go about its good work as a mere jostled atom, lost in a mob of others. If ever the bounty of heaven should raise a bumper crop of Garricks on earth, you would not use them as so many supers, would you?

Farrell, after a short pause to collect his thoughts, was stating another instalment of the facts. "There's a soul and a body," he said, "to everything else, the same as ourselves. Any malt you'll have drunk, to this day, was the body of whisky only—the match of these old lumps of flesh that we're all of us draggin' about till we die. The soul of the stuff's what you've got in your hand."

ANOTHER TEMPLE GONE

"It is that," said the sergeant, and chewed the last drop like a lozenge. He now perceived that the use of large, bold, noble figures of speech, like this of Farrell's, was really the only way to express the wonderful thoughts filling up a man's mind when he is at his best. That was the characteristic virtue of Farrell's handiwork. Its merely material parts were, it is true, pleasant enough. They seemed, while you sipped, to be honey, warm sunshine embedded in amber and topaz, the animating essence of lustrous brown velvet, and some solution of all the mellowest varnish that ever ripened for eye or ear the glow of Dutch landscape or Cremona fiddle. No sooner, however, did this potable sum of all the higher physical embodiments of geniality and ardour enter your frame than a major miracle happened in the domain of the spirit: you suddenly saw that the most freely soaring poetry, all wild graces and quick turns and abrupt calls on your wits, was just the most exact, business-like way of treating the urgent practical concerns of mankind.

So the sergeant's receivers were well tuned to take in great truths when Farrell, first measuring out the due dram for Constable Duffy, resumed, "You'll remember the priest that died on us last year?"

"I do that, rest his soul," said each of the other two Catholics. Constable Boam was only a lad out of London, jumped by some favour into the force. But a good lad.

"Ye'll remember," Farrell continued, "the state he was in, at the end? Perished with thinness, and he filled with the spirit of God the way you'd see the soul of him shining out through the little worn webbin' of flesh he had on, the match for a flame that's in one of the Chinese lanterns you'd see made of paper. Using up the whole of his body, that's what the soul of him was—convertin' the flesh of it bit by bit into soul till hardly a tittle of body was left to put in the ground. You could lift the whole with a finger."

"Now, aren't ye the gifted man?" The words seemed to break, of themselves, out of Constable Duffy. Rapt with the view of entire new worlds of thought, and the feel of new powers for tackling them, Duffy gazed open-lipped and wide-eyed at Farrell the giver.

Farrell's face acknowledged, with no touch of wicked pride, this homage to truth. *"Non nobis, Domine."* Austere, sacerdotal, Farrell inspected the second enraptured proselyte. Then he went on, his eyes well fixed on some object or other far out on the great bog's murmurous waste—the wilfully self-mesmerizing stare of the mystic far gone. "The body's the real old curse. Not a thing in the world but it's kept out of being the grand thing it's got the means in it to be if it hadn't a hunk of a body always holding it back. You can't even have all the good there is in a song without some old blether of words would go wrong on your tongue as likely as not. And in Ireland the glory an' wonder that's sent by the will of God to gladden the heart of a man has never got shut till this day of sour old mashes of barley and malt and God alone knows what sort of dish-washin's fit to make a cow vomit, or poisons would blister half of the lining off the inside of an ass."

Constable Duffy was no man of words. But just at this moment he gained his first distinct view of philosophy's fundamental distinction between matter and form; the prospect so ravished his whole being that as he handed in the drained tumbler to Farrell he murmured in a kind of pensive ecstasy, "Hurroosh to your soul!" and for a long time afterwards was utterly lost in the joys of contemplation.

Constable Boam's reversionary interest in paradise

had now matured. While Farrell ministered to Boam, the grapes of the new wine of thought began abruptly to stammer through the lips of the sergeant. "Aye! Every man has a pack of old trash discommodin' his soul. Pitaties and meal and the like—worked up into flesh on the man. An' the whole of it made of the dirt in the fields, a month or two back! The way it's a full barrow-load of the land will be walking on every two legs that you'd see shankin' past! It's what he's come out of. And what he goes back into being. Aye, and what he can't do without having, as long as he lasts. An' yet it's not he. An' yet he must keep a fast hold on it always, or else he'll be dead. An' yet I'll engage he'll have to be fighting it always—it and the sloth it would put on the grand venomous life he has in him. God help us, it's difficult." Along the mazy path that has ever followed in the wake of Socrates the sergeant's mind slowly tottered, clinging at each turn to some reminiscence of Farrell's golden words, as a child makes its first adventurous journey on foot across the wide nursery floor, working from chair to chair for occasional support.

"Sorra a scrap of difficulty about it," Farrell assured him, "once you've got it firm set in your mind that it's all an everlastin' turnin' of body into soul that's required. All of a man's body that's nothing at all but body is nothing but divvil. The job is to cut a good share of it right out of you, clever and clean, an' then to inspirit the whole of the bit you have left with all the will and force of your soul till it's soul itself that the whole has become, or the next thing to the whole, the way the persons that lay you out after you die and the soul has quitted would wonder to see the weeny scrap that was left for anybody to wake. You could take anything that there is in the world and go on scourin' and scourin' away at the dross it has about it and so releasin' the workin's of good till you'd have the thing that was nine parts body and one part soul at the start changed to the other way round, aye and more. By the grace of God that's the work I've been at in this place. Half-way am I now, as you can see for yourselves, to transformin' the body of anny slushy old drink you'd get in a town into the soul of all kindness an' joy that our blessed Lord put into the water the good people had at the wedding. Nothin' at all to do but walk straight on, the way I was going, to work the stuff up to the pitch that you'd not feel it wettin' your throat, but only the love of God and of man an' the true wisdom of life, and comperhension of this and of that, flowin' softly into your mind. Divvil a thing stood in me way, save only"—here the mild-hearted fanatic stooped for a moment from the heights where his spirit abode to note with a wan smile of indulgence a little infirmity of mankind's—"a few of the boys do be lying around in the bog, the way they have me worn with the fear they'd lap the stuff hot out of the tub and be killed if I'd turn me back for one instant."

"They'll quit, from this out," the sergeant said, with immense decision. "I'll not have anny mischievous trash of the sort molestin' a man at his work."

"Ow, it's a wonderful country!" Constable Boam breathed to himself. The words had been rising to Boam's Cockney lips at almost every turn of affairs since his landfall at Kingstown. Now they came soft and low, soft and low. A peace passing all understanding had just invaded the wondering Englishman's mind.

Let not the English be tempted to think that by no other race can a law be dodged for a long time without scandal. Neither the sergeant nor either man of his

ANOTHER TEMPLE GONE

force was ever a shade the worse for liquor that summer. To Tom's priestly passion for purging more and yet more of the baser alloys out of the true cult there responded a lofty impulse, among the faithful, to keep undeflowered by any beastlike excess the magical garden of which he had given them the key.

For it was none of your common tavern practice to look in at Tom's when the loud afternoon hum of the bees was declining reposefully towards the cool velvety playtime of bats and fat moths. All that plays and the opera, lift of romance and the high, vibrant pitch of great verse are to you lucky persons of culture; travel, adventure, the throwing wide open of sudden new windows for pent minds to stare out, the brave stir of mystical gifts in the heart, gleams of enchanting light cast on places unthought of, annunciatory visits of that exalting sense of approach to some fiery core of all life, watch-tower and power-house both, whence he who attains might see all manner of things run radiantly clear in their courses and passionately right. The police did not offer this account of their spiritual sensations at Tom's, any more than the rest of Gartumna did. But all this, or a vision of this, was for mankind to enjoy as it took its ease on the crumbling heaps of dry turf by the still, what time the inquisitive owls were just beginning to float in soundless circles overhead. From some dull and chilly outer rim of existence each little group of Tom's friends would draw in together towards a glowing focus at which the nagging "No," "No," "No" of life's common hardness was sure to give place to the benedictive "Yes," "Yes," "O yes" of a benignly penetrative understanding of earth, heaven, and everything else. Who such a beast as to attempt to debauch the delicate fairy conducting these mysteries? Too good to imperil, they seemed, besides, too wonderful to end. Dust, all the same, hath dimmed Helen's eyes, which seemed to so many people as if their light could not go out.

All revolutions, some pundits say, are, at bottom, affairs of finance. And Mrs. Burke had diagnosed truly. Tom bore within him the germ of that mortal illness of giving away all before him. His reign in all hearts at Gartumna resembled that of the *Roi Soleil* over France, both in the measureless glory of its meridian and in the fundamental insolvency of its afternoon. He had always given the work of his hands, to the worthy, free and without price. The fitness to receive was all; something sacramental about the consumption of his latest masterpiece by small, close-drawn parties of beautiful souls made the passing of coin at such seasons abhorrent to Tom. "Would you have me keep a shebeen?" he had indignantly asked, when the sergeant made a stout, shamefaced effort to pay. So from day to day they kept up an urbane routine, month after month. Tom would always proffer the squat glass with a shy, tentative gesture; this made it clear that in the sight of God, so to speak, no such freedom had ever been taken, or thought, before. The sergeant would always accept in the jocose, casual tone of a martinet making one playful and really quite absurd exception to his rules, the case being one which, anyhow, cannot recur so that there need be no uneasiness about setting up a precedent now. But all summers end, and urbanity butters no parsnips.

The brownness of later August was deepening round Tom's place of research before he saw that the thing couldn't go on as it was. He suddenly saw it, about ten o'clock one morning. That evening, when the day's tide of civilian beneficiaries had tactfully receded from the still, and the police, their normal successors, had laid rifle and helmet aside, Tom held up his dreadful secret from minute to minute while the grey moth of twilight darkened on into brown moth-coloured night. He tried to begin telling, but found he couldn't trust both his voice and his face at the same time. As soon as his face could no longer be clearly seen he worked up a prodigious assumption of calm and said to the three monumental silhouettes planted black on their three plinths of turf, "I'm ruined! Apt you'll be to find me quit out of the place if you come back in two days or three."

The sergeant leapt off his plinth, levered up by the shock; "God help us!" he said. "What wild trash are you just after gabbing?"

"Me fortune's destroyed," Tom pursued. His face had crumpled up with distress as soon as he began; but the kind darkness hid that: his voice was in fairly good preservation. "I borrowed the full of the worth of me holding to get—" and no doubt he was going on, "get along with the work I'm at here," but felt, perhaps, that this would not be quite the thing, considering. So he broke off and said only, "The back of me hand to the Jew mortgagee that's foreclosin'."

"God help us!" again said the sergeant. "And we drinking the creature out of house and home a good while back! Men—!" He abruptly stiffened all the muscles of Duffy and Boam with the cogent parade voice that braces standing-easy into standing-at-ease. Then he thought for a moment. Oh, there was plenty to think of. Tom, the decent body, put out of his farm by the sheriff. Police aid, no doubt, requisitioned. The whole district, perhaps, in a hullabaloo, like all those around it. The Garden of Eden going straight back to prairie. He must be firm. "Men," he resumed, "are we standin' by to see a man ruined that's done the right thing by ourselves? I'll engage it's a mod'rate share only of cash he'll require to get on in peace with his work. An' the three of us unmarried men, with full pay and allowances!"

The heart of the ancient and good-natured people of England aligned itself instantly with the chivalrous spirit of the Gael. "Thet's right, sawgeant," said Constable Boam.

Constable Duffy's range of expression had not the width to cover fully the whole diversity of life. He ejaculated, "Hurroosh to your souls! Five shillin's a week."

"Sime 'ere," subjoined Boam.

"Mine's ten," said Maguire, "I've got me rank to remember."

So swiftly and smoothly may any man's business pass, with seeming success, into a small limited company. Farrell, the innocent Farrell, took heart afresh and toiled on at the disengagement of Bacchus, the actual godhead, from out his too, too solid coatings of flesh. The force stilled the first wild fears of its heart and felt it was getting good value for its money—a quiet beat for the body, and for the soul an ever open line of communication with the Infinite. Through all Gartumna a warning shudder had run at the first crisis. Now the world seemed safe again; the civilian lamb lay down once more besides the three large lions of the law, dreaming it to be enough that these were no man-eaters. Children all, chasing a butterfly farther and farther into the wilds, under a blackening sky. While they chased, the good old Resident Magistrate, Ponting, was dying of some sudden internal queerness he had, he that had never done harm to a soul if looking the other way could prevent it. And into Old Ponto's seat was climbing a raging dragon of what a blind world calls efficiency.

Major Coburn came, in fact, of that redoubtable

ANOTHER TEMPLE GONE

breed of superdragons, the virtuous, masterful, hundred-eyed cavalry sergeants who carve their way to commissions somewhat late in their careers. Precise as some old maids of exemplary life, as fully posted up in the tricks of the crowd that they have left as a schoolboy turned by magic into a master, they burn with a fierce clear flame of desire to make up the enjoyable arrears of discipline that they might, under luckier stars, have exercised in their youth. Being the thing that he was, how could the man Coburn fail to do harm, with all the harm that there was crying out to be done?

He sent for Sergeant Maguire. Quin, the district inspector—quite enough of an Argus himself without extra prompting—was there when the sergeant marched into the major's room. To outward view at this moment Maguire was fashioned out of first-rate wood. Within, he was but a tingling system of apprehensions. First, with gimlet eyes the two superiors perforated his outer timbers in numerous places, gravely demoralizing the nerve centres within. When these exploratory borings had gone pretty far the crimelessness of Gartumna was touched upon—in a spirit of coarse curiosity far, far from felicitation.

Maguire faintly propounded the notion that keeping the law was just a hobby rife among the wayward natives.

"They're queer bodies," he said in conclusion.

No fantasy like that could be expected to weigh with a new broom possessed with its first fine passion for sweeping. "Don't tell *me*," the major snapped. His voice vibrated abominably with menace. "You know as well as I do, sergeant, the sort of a squadron it is where a man's never crimed." He paused, to let this baleful thrust tell its tale in the agonized sergeant's vitals. Then he went on, "And you know what it means," and again he paused and the four gimlet eyes resumed their kindly task of puncturing him at assorted points.

To Maguire's previous distresses was now added the choice mortification which always attends the discovery that you have been firing off an abstract and friarly morality at heavily armour-plated men of the world. With no loss of penetrative power, the major continued, "Screening—that's what it means. Sergeants who need the stripes taking off them—that's what it means. Go back to your duty and see to it."

Sergeant Maguire withdrew.

"He'd not comperhend. He'd not comperhend," the sergeant despairfully told himself, over and over again, as he legged back the four miles to Gartumna under the early-falling September dew. If only the darkened mind of Major Coburn *could* gain understanding! Anybody on earth, you might think, if he had any wit at all to know good from bad, must see that this was a case in a thousand—that here, if ever in man's history, the spirit which giveth life was being borne down by the letter that killeth. But that body Coburn!—Maguire had been a soldier: he knew those middle-aged rankers. "Shut-headed cattle!" he groaned to himself. "No doin' anny-thing with them." The dew was quite heavy. Sundown, autumn, and all that was best in the world going the way of honeysuckle and rose. Before he reached the tin hut one of the longest in human use among melancholy's standard dyes had suffused pretty deeply the tissues of the sergeant's mind.

It seemed next morning as if that summer's glowing pomp of lustrous months were taking its leave with a grand gesture of self-revival on the eve of extinction, as famous actors will bend up every nerve in order to be most greatly their old selves on the night of farewell. Midsummer heat was burning again, and the quicksilvery haze shimmered over the bog when Maguire went out alone to see Farrell, just as the sergeant remembered it on the day when the scorched air from the furnace first showed him the still. Farrell, a little leaner now, a little less natty in his clothes, a little more absent-eyed with the intensity of a single absorption, raised from his work the patiently welcoming face of genius called away by affairs of this world from its heavenly traffic with miracles.

"All destroyed, Tom," the sergeant said quickly. The longer he waited to bash in the unsuspecting up-turned face of Farrell's childlike happiness the more impracticable would it have grown. "The glory," he added by way of detail, "is departed entirely."

Farrell stared. He did not yet take it in well enough to be broken.

"It's this devastatin' divvil," the sergeant went on, "that they've sent us in lieu of Old Ponto—God rest his kind soul!"

Farrell did not seem to have even heard of that sinister accession. They say there were Paris fiddlers who fiddled right through the French Revolution and did not hear about the Bastille or the Terror. Live with the gods and deal with the Absolute Good, and Amurath's succession to Amurath may not excite you.

"God help the man—can't he see he's destroyed?" Fretful and raw from a night of wakeful distress, the sergeant spoke almost crossly, although it was for Tom that he felt most sorely in all that overshadowed world.

The worker in the deep mine whence perfection is hewn peered, as it were, half-abstractedly up the shaft. Not otherwise might some world-leading thinker in Moscow have looked partly up from his desk to hear, with semi-interested ears, that a Bolshevik mob was burning the house.

The disorganized sergeant veered abruptly all the way round from pettishness to compunction. "Dear knows," he said, "that it's sorry I am for ye, Tom." He collected himself to give particulars of the catastrophe. "A hustlin' kind of a body," he ended, "et up with zeal till he'd turn the grand world that we have into a parcel of old rags and bones and scrap iron before you could hold him at all. An' what divvil's work would he have me be at, for a start, but clap somebody into the jug, good, bad, or indifferent? *Now* do ye see? There isn't a soul in the place but yourself that does the least taste of a thing that anny court in the wide world could convict for. What with you and the old priest and the new, and the old colonel below, you've made the whole of the people a very fair match for the innocent saints of God. An' this flea of a creature you couldn't even trust to be quiet an' not stravadin' out over the bog by himself like a spy, the way he'd soon have the whole set of us suppin' tribulation with a spoon of sorrow."

Farrell subsided on one of the seat-like piles of sunned peat. The fearful truth had begun to sink in. He sat for a while silent, tasting the bitter cup.

The heat that day was a wonder. Has anyone reading this ever been in the Crown Court at Assizes when three o'clock on a torrid dog-day comes in the dead vast and middle of some commonplace murder case, of poignant interest to no one except the accused? Like breeze and bird and flower in the song, judge and usher, counsel and witnesses, all the unimperilled parties alike "confess the hour." Questions are slowly thought of by the Bar and languidly put; the lifeless answers are listlessly heard; motes of dust lazily stirring in shafts of glare thrown from side windows help to drowse you as though they were poppy seeds to inhale: all eyes,

ANOTHER TEMPLE GONE

except one pair, are beginning to glaze; the whole majestic machine of justice seems to flag and slow down as if it might soon subside into utter siesta, just where it is, like a sun-drugged Neapolitan paviour asleep on his unfinished pavement. Only the shabby party penned in the dock is proof against all the pharmacopœia of opiates. Ceaselessly shifting his feet, resettling his neckcloth, hunting from each sleepy face to the next for some gleam of hope for himself, he would show, were any one there not too deeply lulled to observe, how far the proper quality and quantity of torment is capable of resisting the action of nature's own anodynes.

Out in the bog a rude likeness of that vigil of pain, set amidst the creeping peace of the lotus, was now being staged. Under the rising heat of that tropical day the whole murmurous pulse of the bog, its flies and old bees, all its audible infestation with life seemed to be sinking right down into torpor while Sergeant Maguire's woebegone narrative dribbled off into silence and Tom came to the last of his hopeless questions. Questions? No; mere ineffectual sniffings among the bars of the closed cage of their fate. They both lay back on the warm turf, some ten feet apart, Tom staring up blankly straight into the unpitying blue while the sergeant stuck it out numbly within the darkened dome of his helmet, held over his face, striving within the rosy gloom of that tabernacle to gather up all his strength for the terrible plunge.

The plunge had to come. The sergeant rose on one elbow. He marshalled his voice. "There's the one way of it, Tom," he got out at last. "Will you quit out of this and away to the States before I lose all me power to keep a hand off you?"

Farrell partly rose, too. His mind had not yet journeyed so far as the sergeant's along the hard road

"I'll make up the fare from me savings," the sergeant said humbly.

Farrell turned upon him a void, desolate face. The sergeant hurried on: "The three of us down below will clear up when you're gone. An' we'll sling the still for you into the bog-hole. Aye, be sections, will we. An' everything."

Farrell seemed to be eyeing at every part of its bald surface the dead wall of necessity. That scrutiny ended, he quietly said, "Me heart's broke," and lay back again flat on the peat. So did the sergeant. Nothing stirred for awhile except the agonized quiver and quake of the burnt air over the homely drain-pipe chimney of Tom's moribund furnace.

The sergeant wangled a day's leave of absence to go down to Queenstown the day Farrell sailed for New York. Farrell, absently waving a hand from some crowded lower deck of the departing ship, was a figure of high tragic value. Happy the mole astray above ground, or the owl routed out into the sun by bad boys, compared with the perfect specialist cast out upon a bewilderingly general world. The sergeant came away from the quay with his whole spirit laid waste—altruistic provinces and egoistic alike; his very soul sown with salt. He had been near the centre of life all the summer and felt the beat of its heart; now he was somewhere far out on its chill, charmless periphery—"As the earth when leaves are dead." He had not read Shelley. Still, just the same thing.

"I've done my duty," he said in an almost God-cursing tone as the three of them sat in the tin hut that night, among ashes, and heard the hard perpetual knock of the rain on the roof, "an' I've done down meself."

"Aye, and the whole of us," Constable Duffy lamented, not meaning reproach, but sympathy only; just his part in the common threnody, antiphone answering unto phone.

Constable Boam had a part in it, too: " 'Eaven an' 'Ell, 'Eaven an' 'Ell!"—he almost chanted his dreary conspectus of their vicissitudes. "Ow! a proper mix-up! Gord! it's a wonderful country!"

Nothing more was heard of Farrell. He may have died before he could bring back into use, beside the waters of Babylon, that one talent which 'twas death to hide. Or the talent itself may have died out in his bosom. Abrupt terminations have ere now been put to the infinite; did not Shakespeare dry up, for no visible cause, when he moved back to Stratford? All that we know is that Tom's genius can never have got into its full swing in the States. For, if it had, the States could never have gone to the desperate lengths that they afterwards did against the god of his worship.

E. Œ. SOMERVILLE AND MARTIN ROSS

Trinket's Colt

IT WAS Petty Sessions day in Skebawn, a cold, grey day of February. A case of trespass had dragged its burden of cross summonses and cross swearing far into the afternoon, and when I left the bench my head was singing from the bellowings of the attorneys, and the smell of their clients was heavy upon my palate.

The streets still testified to the fact that it was market day, and I evaded with difficulty the sinuous course of carts full of soddenly screwed people, and steered an equally devious one for myself among the groups anchored round the doors of the public-houses. Skebawn possesses, among its legion of public-houses, one establishment which timorously, and almost imperceptibly, proffers tea to the thirsty. I turned in there, as was my custom on court days, and found the little dingy den, known as the Ladies' Coffee-room, in the occupancy of my friend Mr. Florence McCarthy Knox, who was drinking strong tea and eating buns with serious simplicity. It was a first and quite unexpected glimpse of that domesticity that has now become a marked feature in his character.

"You're the very man I wanted to see," I said as I sat down beside him at the oilcloth-covered table; "a man I know in England who is not much of a judge of character has asked me to buy him a four-year-old down here, and as I should rather be stuck by a friend than a dealer, I wish you'd take over the job."

Flurry poured himself out another cup of tea, and dropped three lumps of sugar into it in silence.

Finally he said, "There isn't a four-year-old in this country that I'd be seen dead with at a pig fair."

This was discouraging, from the premier authority on horse-flesh in the district.

"But it isn't six weeks since you told me you had the finest filly in your stables that was ever foaled in the County Cork," I protested; "what's wrong with her?"

"Oh, is it that filly?" said Mr. Knox with a lenient smile; "she's gone these three weeks from me. I swapped her and six pounds for a three-year-old Ironmonger colt, and after that I swapped the colt and nineteen pounds for that Bandon horse I rode last week at your place, and after that again I sold the Bandon horse for seventy-five pounds to old Welply, and I had to give him back a couple of sovereigns luck-money. You see I did pretty well with the filly after all."

"Yes, yes—oh, rather," I assented, as one dizzily accepts the propositions of a bimetallist; "and you don't know of anything else——?"

The room in which we were seated was closely screened from the shop by a door with a muslin-curtained window in it; several of the panes were broken, and at this juncture two voices that had for some time carried on a discussion forced themselves upon our attention.

"Begging your pardon for contradicting you, ma'am," said the voice of Mrs. McDonald, proprietress of the tea-shop, and a leading light in Skebawn Dissenting circles, shrilly tremulous with indignation, "if the servants I recommend you won't stop with you, it's no fault of mine. If respectable young girls are set picking grass out of your gravel, in place of their proper work, certainly they will give warning!"

The voice that replied struck me as being a notable one, well-bred and imperious.

"When I take a barefooted slut out of a cabin, I don't expect her to dictate to me what her duties are!"

Flurry jerked up his chin in a noiseless laugh. "It's my grandmother!" he whispered. "I bet you Mrs. McDonald don't get much change out of her!"

"If I set her to clean the pigsty I expect her to obey me," continued the voice in accents that would have made me clean forty pigsties had she desired me to do so.

"Very well, ma'am," retorted Mrs. McDonald, "if that's the way you treat your servants, you needn't come here again looking for them. I consider your conduct is neither that of a lady nor a Christian!"

"Don't you, indeed?" replied Flurry's grandmother.

"Well, your opinion doesn't greatly distress me, for, to tell you the truth, I don't think you're much of a judge."

"Didn't I tell you she'd score?" murmured Flurry, who was by this time applying his eye to a hole in the muslin curtain. "She's off," he went on, returning to his tea. "She's a great character! She's eighty-three if she's a day, and she's as sound on her legs as a three-year-old! Did you see that old shandrydan of hers in the street a while ago, and a fellow on the box with a red beard on him like Robinson Crusoe? That old mare that was on the near side—Trinket her name is—is mighty near clean bred. I can tell you her foals are worth a bit of money."

I had heard of old Mrs. Knox of Aussolas; indeed, I had seldom dined out in the neighbourhood without hearing some new story of her and her remarkable *ménage*, but it had not yet been my privilege to meet her.

"Well, now," went on Flurry in his slow voice, "I'll tell you a thing that's just come into my head. My grandmother promised me a foal of Trinket's the day I was one-and-twenty, and that's five years ago, and deuce a one I've got from her yet. You never were at Aussolas? No, you were not. Well, I tell you the place there is like a circus with horses. She has a couple of score of them running wild in the woods, like deer."

"Oh, come," I said, "I'm a bit of a liar myself——"

"Well, she has a dozen of them anyhow, rattling good colts too, some of them, but they might as well be donkeys, for all the good they are to me or any one. It's not once in three years she sells one, and there she has them walking after her for bits of sugar, like a lot of dirty lapdogs," ended Flurry with disgust.

"Well, what's your plan? Do you want me to make her a bid for one of the lapdogs?"

"I was thinking," replied Flurry, with great deliberation, "that my birthday's this week, and maybe I could work a four-year-old colt of Trinket's she has out of her in honour of the occasion."

"And sell your grandmother's birthday present to me?"

"Just that, I suppose," answered Flurry with a slow wink.

A few days afterwards a letter from Mr. Knox informed me that he had "squared the old lady, and it would be all right about the colt." He further told me that Mrs. Knox had been good enough to offer me, with him, a day's snipe shooting on the celebrated Aussolas bogs, and he proposed to drive me there the following Monday, if convenient. Most people found it convenient to shoot the Aussolas snipe bog when they got the chance. Eight o'clock on the following Monday morning saw Flurry, myself, and a groom packed into a dogcart, with portmanteaus, gun-cases, and two rampant red setters.

It was a long drive, twelve miles at least, and a very cold one. We passed through long tracts of pasture country, fraught, for Flurry, with memories of runs, which were recorded for me, fence by fence, in every one of which the biggest dog-fox in the country had gone to ground, with not two feet—measured accurately on the handle of the whip—between him and the leading hound; through bogs that imperceptibly melted into lakes, and finally down and down into a valley, where the fir-trees of Aussolas clustered darkly round a glittering lake, and all but hid the grey roofs and pointed gables of Aussolas Castle.

"There's a nice stretch of a demesne for you," remarked Flurry, pointing downwards with the whip, "and one little old woman holding it all in the heel of her fist. Well able to hold it she is, too, and always was, and she'll live twenty years yet, if it's only to spite the whole lot of us, and when all's said and done goodness knows how she'll leave it!"

"It strikes me you were lucky to keep her up to her promise about the colt," I said.

Flurry administered a composing kick to the ceaseless strivings of the red setters under the seat.

"I used to be rather a pet with her," he said, after a pause; "but mind you, I haven't got him yet, and if she gets any notion I want to sell him I'll never get him, so say nothing about the business to her."

The tall gates of Aussolas shrieked on their hinges as they admitted us, and shut with a clang behind us, in the faces of an old mare and a couple of young horses, who, foiled in their break for the excitements of the outer world, turned and galloped defiantly on either side of us. Flurry's admirable cob hammered on, regardless of all things save his duty.

"He's the only one I have that I'd trust myself here with," said his master, flicking him approvingly with the whip; "there are plenty of people afraid to come here at all, and when my grandmother goes out driving she has a boy on the box with a basket full of stones to peg at them. Talk of the dickens, here she is herself!"

A short, upright old woman was approaching, preceded by a white woolly dog with sore eyes and a bark like a tin trumpet; we both got out of the trap and advanced to meet the lady of the manor.

I may summarize her attire by saying that she looked as if she had robbed a scarecrow; her face was small and incongruously refined, the skinny hand that she extended to me had the grubby tan that bespoke the professional gardener, and was decorated with a magnificent diamond ring. On her head was a massive purple velvet bonnet.

"I am very glad to meet you, Major Yeates," she said with an old-fashioned precision of utterance; "your grandfather was a dancing partner of mine in old days at the Castle, when he was a handsome young aide-de-camp there, and I was—— You may judge for yourself what I was."

She ended with a startling little hoot of laughter, and I was aware that she quite realized the world's opinion of her, and was indifferent to it.

Our way to the bogs took us across Mrs. Knox's home farm, and through a large field in which several young horses were grazing.

"There now, that's my fellow," said Flurry, pointing to a fine-looking colt, "the chestnut with the white diamond on his forehead. He'll run into three figures before he's done, but we'll not tell that to the old lady!"

The famous Aussolas bogs were as full of snipe as usual, and a good deal fuller of water than any bogs I had ever shot before. I was on my day, and Flurry was not, and as he is ordinarily an infinitely better snipe shot than I, I felt at peace with the world and all men as we walked back, wet through, at five o'clock.

The sunset had waned, and a big white moon was making the eastern tower of Aussolas look like a thing in a fairy tale or a play when we arrived at the hall door. An individual, whom I recognized as the Robinson Crusoe coachman, admitted us to a hall, the like of which one does not often see. The walls were panelled with dark oak up to the gallery that ran round three sides of it, the balusters of the wide staircase were heavily carved, and blackened portraits of Flurry's ancestors on the spindle side stared sourly down on their descendant as he tramped upstairs with the bog mould on his hobnailed boots.

We had just changed into dry clothes when Robinson Crusoe shoved his red beard round the corner of the door, with the information that the mistress said we were to stay for dinner. My heart sank. It was then barely half-past five. I said something about having no evening clothes and having to get home early.

"Sure the dinner'll be in another half hour," said Robinson Crusoe, joining hospitably in the conversation; "and as for evening clothes—God bless ye!"

The door closed behind him.

"Never mind," said Flurry, "I dare say you'll be glad enough to eat another dinner by the time you get home." He laughed. "Poor Slipper!" he added inconsequently, and only laughed again when I asked for an explanation.

Old Mrs. Knox received us in the library, where she was seated by a roaring turf fire, which lit the room a good deal more effectively than the pair of candles that stood beside her in tall silver candlesticks. Ceaseless and implacable growls from under her chair indicated the presence of the woolly dog. She talked with confounding culture of the books that rose all round her to the ceiling; her evening dress was accomplished by means of an additional white shawl, rather dirtier than its congeners; as I took her in to dinner she quoted Virgil to me, and in the same breath screeched an objurgation at a being whose matted head rose suddenly into view from behind an ancient Chinese screen, as I have seen the head of a Zulu woman peer over a bush.

Dinner was as incongruous as everything else. Detestable soup in a splendid old silver tureen that was nearly as dark in hue as Robinson Crusoe's thumb; a perfect salmon, perfectly cooked, on a chipped kitchen dish; such cut glass as is not easy to find nowadays;

sherry that, as Flurry subsequently remarked, would burn the shell off an egg; and a bottle of port, draped in immemorial cobwebs, wan with age, and probably priceless. Throughout the vicissitudes of the meal Mrs. Knox's conversation flowed on undismayed, directed sometimes at me—she had installed me in the position of friend of her youth—and talked to me as if I were my own grandfather—sometimes at Crusoe, with whom she had several heated arguments, and sometimes she would make a statement of remarkable frankness on the subject of her horse-farming affairs to Flurry, who, very much on his best behaviour, agreed with all she said, and risked no original remark. As I listened to them both, I remembered with infinite amusement how he had told me once that a pet name she had for him was "Tony Lumpkin," and no one but herself knew what she meant by it. It seemed strange that she made no allusion to Trinket's colt or to Flurry's birthday, but, mindful of my instructions, I held my peace.

As, at about half-past eight, we drove away in the moonlight, Flurry congratulated me solemnly on my success with his grandmother. He was good enough to tell me that she would marry me to-morrow if I asked her, and he wished I would, even if it was only to see what a nice grandson he'd be for me. A sympathetic giggle behind me told me that Michael, on the back seat, had heard and relished the jest.

We had left the gates of Aussolas about half a mile behind when, at the corner of a by-road, Flurry pulled up. A short squat figure arose from the black shadow of a furze bush and came out into the moonlight, swinging its arms like a cabman and cursing audibly.

"Oh murdher, oh murdher, Misther Flurry! What kept ye at all? 'Twould perish the crows to be waiting here the way I am these two hours———"

"Ah, shut your mouth, Slipper!" said Flurry, who, to my surprise, had turned back the rug and was taking off his driving coat, "I couldn't help it. Come on, Yeates, we've got to get out here."

"What for?" I asked, in not unnatural bewilderment.

"It's all right. I'll tell you as we go along," replied my companion, who was already turning to follow Slipper up the by-road. "Take the trap on, Michael, and wait at the River's Cross." He waited for me to come up with him, and then put his hand on my arm. "You see, Major, this is the way it is. My grandmother's given me that colt right enough, but if I waited for her to send him over to me I'd never see a hair of his tail. So I just thought that as we were over here we might as well take him back with us, and maybe you'll give us a help with him; he'll not be altogether too handy for a first go off."

I was staggered. An infant in arms could scarcely have failed to discern the fishiness of the transaction, and I begged Mr. Knox not to put himself to this trouble on my account, as I had no doubt I could find a horse for my friend elsewhere. Mr. Knox assured me that it was no trouble at all, quite the contrary, and that, since his grandmother had given him the colt, he saw no reason why he should not take him when he wanted him; also, that if I didn't want him he'd be glad enough to keep him himself; and finally, that I wasn't the chap to go back on a friend, but I was welcome to drive back to Shreelane with Michael this minute if I liked.

Of course I yielded in the end. I told Flurry I should lose my job over the business, and he said I could then marry his grandmother, and the discussion was abruptly closed by the necessity of following Slipper over a locked five-barred gate.

Our pioneer took us over about half a mile of country, knocking down stone gaps where practicable and scrambling over tall banks in the deceptive moonlight. We found ourselves at length in a field with a shed in one corner of it; in a dim group of farm buildings a little way off a light was shining.

"Wait here," said Flurry to me in a whisper; "the less noise the better. It's an open shed, and we'll just slip in and coax him out."

Slipper unwound from his waist a halter, and my colleagues glided like spectres into the shadow of the shed, leaving me to meditate on my duties as Resident Magistrate, and on the questions that would be asked in the House by our local member when Slipper had given away the adventure in his cups.

In less than a minute three shadows emerged from the shed, where two had gone in. They had got the colt.

"He came out as quiet as a calf when he winded the sugar," said Flurry; "it was well for me I filled my pockets from grandmamma's sugar basin."

He and Slipper had a rope from each side of the colt's head; they took him quickly across a field towards a gate. The colt stepped daintily between them over the moonlit grass; he snorted occasionally, but appeared on the whole amenable.

The trouble began later, and was due, as trouble often is, to the beguilements of a short cut. Against the maturer judgment of Slipper, Flurry insisted on following a route that he assured us he knew as well as his own pocket, and the consequence was that in about five minutes I found myself standing on top of a bank hanging on to a rope, on the other end of which the colt dangled and danced, while Flurry, with the other rope, lay prone in the ditch, and Slipper administered to the bewildered colt's hind quarters such chastisement as could be ventured on.

I have no space to narrate in detail the atrocious difficulties and disasters of the short cut. How the colt set to work to buck, and went away across a field, dragging the faithful Slipper, literally *ventre à terre,* after him, while I picked myself in ignominy out of a briar patch, and Flurry cursed himself black in the face. How we were attacked by ferocious cur dogs, and I lost my eye-glass; and how, as we neared the River's Cross, Flurry espied the police patrol on the road, and we all hid behind a rick of turf while I realized in fullness what an exceptional ass I was, to have been beguiled into an enterprise that involved hiding with Slipper from the Royal Irish Constabulary.

Let it suffice to say that Trinket's infernal offspring was finally handed over on the high road to Michael and Slipper, and Flurry drove me home in a state of mental and physical overthrow.

I saw nothing of my friend Mr. Knox for the next couple of days, by the end of which time I had worked up a high polish on my misgivings, and had determined to tell him that under no circumstances would I have anything to say to his grandmother's birthday present. It was like my usual luck that, instead of writing a note to this effect, I thought it would be good for my liver to walk across the hills to Tory Cottage and tell Flurry so in person.

It was a bright, blustery morning, after a muggy day. The feeling of spring was in the air, the daffodils were already in bud, and crocuses showed purple in the grass on either side of the avenue. It was only a couple of miles to Tory Cottage by the way across the hills; I walked fast, and it was barely twelve o'clock when I saw its pink walls and clumps of evergreens below me. As I looked down at it the chiming of Flurry's hounds in the kennels came to me on the wind; I stood still to listen, and could almost have sworn that I was hearing again the clash of Magdalen bells, hard at work on May morning.

The path that I was following led downwards through a larch plantation to Flurry's back gate. Hot wafts from some hideous cauldron at the other side of a wall apprised me of the vicinity of the kennels and their cuisine, and the fir-trees round were hung with gruesome and unknown joints. I thanked heaven that I was not a master of hounds, and passed on as quickly as might be to the hall door.

I rang two or three times without response; then the door opened a couple of inches and was instantly slammed in my face. I heard the hurried paddling of bare feet on oil-cloth, and a voice, "Hurry, Bridgie, hurry! There's quality at the door!"

Bridgie, holding a dirty cap on with one hand, presently arrived and informed me that she believed Mr. Knox was out about the place. She seemed perturbed, and she cast scared glances down the drive while speaking to me.

I knew enough of Flurry's habits to shape a tolerably direct course for his whereabouts. He was, as I had expected, in the training paddock, a field behind the stable yard, in which he had put up practice jumps for his horses. It was a good-sized field with clumps of furze in it, and Flurry was standing near one of these with his hands in his pockets, singularly unoccupied. I supposed that he was prospecting for a place to put up another jump. He did not see me coming, and turned with a start as I spoke to him. There was a queer expression of mingled guilt and what I can only describe as divilment in his grey eyes as he greeted me. In my dealings with Flurry Knox, I have since formed the habit of sitting tight, in a general way, when I see that expression.

"Well, who's coming next, I wonder!" he said, as he shook hands with me; "it's not ten minutes since I had two of your d——d peelers here searching the whole place for my grandmother's colt!"

"What!" I exclaimed, feeling cold all down my back; "do you mean the police have got hold of it?"

"They haven't got hold of the colt anyway," said Flurry, looking sideways at me from under the peak of his cap, with the glint of the sun in his eye. "I got word in time before they came."

"What do you mean?" I demanded; "where is he? For heaven's sake don't tell me you've sent the brute over to my place!"

"It's a good job for you I didn't," replied Flurry, "as the police are on their way to Shreelane this minute to consult you about it. *You!*" He gave utterance to one of his short diabolical fits of laughter. "He's where they'll not find him, anyhow. Ho ho! It's the funniest hand I ever played!"

"Oh yes, it's devilish funny, I've no doubt," I retorted, beginning to lose my temper, as is the manner of many people when they are frightened; "but I give you fair warning that if Mrs. Knox asks me any questions about it, I shall tell her the whole story."

"All right," responded Flurry; "and when you do, don't forget to tell her how you flogged the colt out on to the road over her own bounds ditch."

"Very well," I said hotly, "I may as well go home and send in my papers. They'll break me over this——"

"Ah, hold on, Major," said Flurry soothingly, "it'll be all right. No one knows anything. It's only on spec the old lady sent the bobbies here. If you'll keep quiet it'll all blow over."

"I don't care," I said, struggling hopelessly in the toils; "if I meet your grandmother, and she asks me about it, I shall tell her all I know."

"Please God you'll not meet her! After all, it's not once in a blue moon that she——" began Flurry. Even as he said the words his face changed. "Holy fly!" he ejaculated, "isn't that her dog coming into the field? Look at her bonnet over the wall! Hide, hide for your life!" He caught me by the shoulder and shoved me down among the furze bushes before I realized what had happened.

"Get in there! I'll talk to her."

I may as well confess that at the mere sight of Mrs. Knox's purple bonnet my heart had turned to water. In that moment I knew what it would be like to tell her how I, having eaten her salmon, and capped her quotations, and drunk her best port, had gone forth and helped to steal her horse. I abandoned my dignity, my sense of honour; I took the furze prickles to my breast and wallowed in them.

Mrs. Knox had advanced with vengeful speed; already she was in high altercation with Flurry at no great distance from where I lay; varying sounds of battle reached me, and I gathered that Flurry was not —to put it mildly—shrinking from that economy of truth that the situation required.

"Is it that curby, long-backed brute? You promised him to me long ago, but I wouldn't be bothered with him!"

The old lady uttered a laugh of shrill derision. "Is it likely I'd promise you my best colt? And still more, is it likely that you'd refuse him if I did?"

"Very well, ma'am." Flurry's voice was admirably indignant. "Then I suppose I'm a liar and a thief."

"I'd be more obliged to you for the information if I hadn't known it before," responded his grandmother with lightning speed; "if you swore to me on a stack of Bibles you knew nothing about my colt I wouldn't believe you! I shall go straight to Major Yeates and ask his advice. I believe *him* to be a gentleman, in spite of the company he keeps!"

I writhed deeper into the furze bushes, and thereby discovered a sandy rabbit run, along which I crawled, with my cap well over my eyes, and the furze needles stabbing me through my stockings. The ground shelved a little, promising profounder concealment, but the bushes were very thick, and I laid hold of the bare stem of one to help my progress. It lifted out of the ground in my hand, revealing a freshly cut stump. Something snorted, not a yard away; I glared through the opening, and was confronted by the long, horrified face of Mrs. Knox's colt, mysteriously on a level with my own.

Even without the white diamond on his forehead I should have divined the truth; but how in the name of wonder had Flurry persuaded him to couch like a woodcock in the heart of a furze brake? For a full minute I lay as still as death for fear of frightening him, while the voices of Flurry and his grandmother raged on alarmingly close to me. The colt snorted, and blew long breaths through his wide nostrils, but he did not move. I crawled an inch or two nearer, and after a few seconds of cautious peering I grasped the position. They had buried him.

A small sandpit among the furze had been utilized as a grave; they had filled him in up to his withers with sand, and a few furze bushes, artistically disposed around the pit, had done the rest. As the depth of

Flurry's guile was revealed, laughter came upon me like a flood; I gurgled and shook apoplectically, and the colt gazed at me with serious surprise, until a sudden outburst of barking close to my elbow administered a fresh shock to my tottering nerves.

Mrs. Knox's woolly dog had tracked me into the furze, and was now baying the colt and me with mingled terror and indignation. I addressed him in a whisper, with perfidious endearments, advancing a crafty hand towards him the while, made a snatch for the back of his neck, missed it badly, and got him by the ragged fleece of his hind quarters as he tried to flee. If I had flayed him alive he could hardly have uttered a more deafening series of yells, but, like a fool, instead of letting him go, I dragged him towards me, and tried to stifle the noise by holding his muzzle. The tussle lasted engrossingly for a few seconds, and then the climax of the nightmare arrived.

Mrs. Knox's voice, close behind me, said, "Let go my dog this instant, sir! Who are you——"

Her voice faded away, and I knew that she also had seen the colt's head.

I positively felt sorry for her. At her age there was no knowing what effect the shock might have on her. I scrambled to my feet and confronted her.

"Major Yeates!" she said. There was a deathly pause. "Will you kindly tell me," said Mrs. Knox slowly, "am I in Bedlam, or are you? And *what is that?*"

She pointed to the colt, and that unfortunate animal, recognizing the voice of his mistress, uttered a hoarse and lamentable whinny. Mrs. Knox felt around her for support, found only furze prickles, gazed speechlessly at me, and then, to her eternal honour, fell into wild cackles of laughter.

So, I may say, did Flurry and I. I embarked on my

explanation and broke down; Flurry followed suit and broke down too. Overwhelming laughter held us all three, disintegrating our very souls. Mrs. Knox pulled herself together first.

"I acquit you, Major Yeates, I acquit you, though appearances are against you. It's clear enough to me you've fallen among thieves." She stopped and glowered at Flurry. Her purple bonnet was over one eye. "I'll thank you, sir," she said, "to dig out that horse before I leave this place. And when you've dug him out you may keep him. I'll be no receiver of stolen goods!"

She broke off and shook her fist at him. "Upon my conscience, Tony, I'd give a guinea to have thought of it myself!"

(From *Some Experiences of an Irish R.M.*)

CHARLES LEVER

The Priest's Supper

AT THE conclusion of our last chapter we left our quondam antagonist, Mr. Beamish, stretched at full length upon a bed practising homœopathy by administering hot punch to his fever, while we followed our chaperon, Dr. Finucane, into the presence of the Reverend Father Brennan.

The company into which we now, without any ceremony on our parts, introduced ourselves, consisted of from five-and-twenty to thirty persons, seated around a large oak table, plentifully provided with materials for drinking, and cups, goblets, and glasses of every shape and form. The moment we entered, the doctor

THE PRIEST'S SUPPER

stepped forward, and, touching Father Malachi on the shoulder—for so I rightly guessed him to be—presented himself to his relative, by whom he was welcomed with every demonstration of joy. While their recognitions were exchanged, and while the doctor explained the reasons of our visit, I was enabled undisturbed and unnoticed, to take a brief survey of the party.

Father Malachi Brennan, P.P. of Carrigaholt, was what I had often pictured to myself as the *beau-ideal* of his caste; his figure was short, fleshy, and enormously muscular, and displayed proportions which wanted but height to constitute a perfect Hercules; his legs, so thick in the calf, so taper in the ankle, looked like nothing I know, except, perhaps, the metal balustrades of Carlisle bridge; his face was large and rosy, and the general expression a mixture of unbounded good-humour and inexhaustible drollery, to which the restless activity of his black and arched eyebrows greatly contributed: and his mouth, were it not for a trace of sensuality and voluptuousness about the nether lip, had been actually handsome; his head was bald, except a narrow circle close above the ears, which was marked by a ring of curly dark hair, sadly insufficient, however, to conceal a development behind, that, if there be truth in phrenology, bodes but little happiness to the disciples of Miss Martineau.

Add to these external signs a voice rich, fluent, and racy, with the mellow "Doric" of his country, and you have some faint resemblance of one "every inch a priest." The very antipodes to the *bonhomie* of this figure confronted him as croupier at the foot of the table. This, as I afterwards learned, was no less a person than Mr. Donovan, the coadjutor or "curate"—a tall, spare, ungainly looking man of about five-and-thirty, with a pale, ascetic countenance, the only readable expression of which vibrated between low suspicion and intense vulgarity; over his low, projecting forehead hung down a mass of straight red hair; indeed—for nature is not a politician—it almost approached an orange hue. This was cut close to the head all round, and displayed in their full proportions a pair of ears, which stood out "in relief," like turrets from a watch-tower, and with pretty much the same object; his skin was of that peculiar colour and texture, to which not all "the water in great Neptune's ocean" could impart a look of cleanliness, while his very voice, hard, harsh, and inflexible, was unprepossessing and unpleasant. And yet, strange as it may seem, he, too, was a type of his order; the only difference being, that Father Malachi was an older coinage, with the impress of Douay or St. Omer's, whereas Mr. Donovan was the shining metal, fresh stamped from the mint of Maynooth.

While thus occupied in my surveillance of the scene before me, I was roused by the priest saying—

"Ah, Fin, my darling, you needn't deny it; you're at the old game as sure as my name is Malachi, and ye'll never be easy nor quiet till ye're sent beyond the sea, or maybe have a record of your virtues on half a ton of marble in the churchyard yonder."

"Upon my honour, upon the sacred honour of a De Courcy——"

"Well, well, never mind it now; ye see ye're just keeping your friends cooling themselves there in the corner —introduce me at once."

"Mr. Lorrequer, I'm sure——"

"My name is Curzon," said the adjutant, bowing.

"A mighty pretty name, though a little profane; well, Mr. Curseon," for so he pronounced it, "ye're as welcome as the flowers in May; and it's mighty proud I am to see ye here."

"Mr. Lorrequer, allow me to shake your hand—I've heard of ye before."

There seemed nothing very strange in that; for go where I would through this country, I seemed as generally known as ever was Brummell in Bond Street.

"Fin tells me," continued Father Malachi, "that ye'd rather not be known down here, in regard of a reason," and here he winked. "Make yourself quite easy; the King's writ was never but once in these parts; and the 'original and true copy' went back to Limerick in the stomach of the server; they made him eat it, Mr. Lorrequer, but it's as well to be cautious, for there are a good number here. A little dinner, a little quarterly dinner we have among us, Mr. Curseon, to be social together, and raise a 'thrifle' for the Irish College at Rome, where we have a probationer or two ourselves."

"As good as a station, and more drink," whispered Fin into my ear. "And now," continued the priest, "ye must just permit me to re-christen ye both, and the contribution will not be the less for what I'm going to do; and I'm certain you'll not be worse for the change, Mr. Curseon—though 'tis only for a few hours, ye'll have a dacent name."

As I could see no possible objection to this proposal, nor did Curzon either, our only desire being to maintain the secrecy necessary for our antagonist's safety, we at once assented; when Father Malachi took me by the hand, but with such a total change in his whole air and deportment, that I was completely puzzled by it. He led me forward to the company with a good deal of that ceremonious reverence I have often admired in Sir Charles Vernon, when conducting some full-blown dowager through the mazes of a Castle minuet. The desire to laugh outright was almost irresistible as the Rev. Father stood at arms-length from me, still holding my hand, and bowing to the company, pretty much in the style of a manager introducing a blushing débutante to an audience. A moment more and I must have inevitably given way to a burst of laughter, when what was my horror to hear the priest present me to the company as their "excellent, worthy, generous, and patriotic young landlord, Lord Kilkee. Cheer, every mother's son of ye; cheer, I say!" And certainly precept was never more strenuously backed by example, for he huzza'd till I thought he would burst a blood-vessel; may I add, I almost wished it, such was the insufferable annoyance, the chagrin, this announcement gave me; and I waited with eager impatience for the din and clamour to subside, to disclaim every syllable of the priest's announcement, and take the consequences of my baptismal epithet, cost what it might. To this I was impelled by many and important reasons. Situated as I was with respect to the Callonby family, my assumption of their name at such a moment might get abroad, and the consequences to me be inevitable ruin; and independent of my natural repugnance to such sailing under false colours, I saw Curzon laughing almost to suffocation at my wretched predicament, and (so strong within me was the dread of ridicule) I thought, "What a pretty narrative he is concocting for the mess this minute." I rose to reply; and whether Father Malachi with his intuitive quickness guessed my purpose or not, I cannot say, but he certainly resolved to out-manœuvre me, and he succeeded; while with one hand he motioned to the party to keep silence, with the other he took hold of Curzon, but with no peculiar or very measured respect, and introduced him as Mr. M'Neesh, the new Scotch steward and improver—a character at that time whose popularity might compete with a tithe-proctor or an exciseman. So completely did this *tactique* turn the

THE PRIEST'S SUPPER

tables upon the poor adjutant, who the moment before was exulting over me, that I utterly forgot my own woes, and sat down convulsed with mirth at his situation—an emotion certainly not lessened as I saw Curzon passed from one to the other at table, "like a pauper to his parish," till he found an asylum at the very foot, in juxta with the engaging Mr. Donovan, a propinquity, if I might judge from their countenances, uncoveted by either party.

While this was performing, Dr. Finucane was making his recognitions with several of the company, to whom he had been long known during his visits to the neighbourhood. I now resumed my place on the right of the father, abandoning for the present all intention of disclaiming my rank, and the campaign was opened. The priest now exerted himself to the utmost to recall conversation into the original channels, and if possible to draw off attention from me, which he still feared might, perhaps, elicit some unlucky announcement on my part. Failing in his endeavours to bring matters to their former footing, he turned the whole brunt of his attentions to the worthy doctor on his left.

"How goes on the law, Fin?" said he; "any new proofs, as they call them, forthcoming?"

What Fin replied I could not hear, but the allusion to the "suit" was explained by Father Malachi informing us that the only impediment between his cousin and the title of Kinsale lay in the unfortunate fact that his grandmother, "rest her sowl," was not a man.

Dr. Finucane winced a little under the manner in which this was spoken; but returned the fire by asking if the bishop was down lately in that quarter. The evasive way in which "the father" replied stimulated my curiosity; but before it could be satisfied Father Malachi called out, "Mickey Oulahan! Mickey, I say, hand his lordship over 'the groceries' "—thus he designated a square decanter, containing about two quarts of whisky, and a bowl heaped high with sugar. "A dacent boy is Mickey, my lord, and I'm happy to be the means of making him known to you." I bowed with condescension, while Mr. Oulahan's eyes sparkled like diamonds at the recognition.

"He has only two years of his lease to run, and a 'long charge' " (*Anglicé*, a large family), continued the priest.

"I'll not forget him, you may depend upon it," said I.

"Do you hear that?" said Father Malachi, casting a glance of triumph round the table, while a general buzz of commendation on priest and patron went round, with many such phrases as, "Och thin," "It's his riv'rence *can* do it," "Na bocklish," "And why not," etc. As for me, I have already "confessed" to my crying sin, a fatal, irresistible inclination to follow the humour of the moment wherever it led me; and now I found myself as active a partisan in quizzing Mickey Oulahan, as though I was not myself a party included in the jest. I was thus fairly launched into my inveterate habit, and nothing could arrest my progress.

One by one the different individuals round the table were presented to me, and made known their various wants, with an implicit confidence in my power of relieving them, which I with equal readiness ministered to. I lowered the rent of every man at table. I made a general jail delivery, an act of grace (I blush to say) which seemed to be peculiarly interesting to the present company. I abolished all arrears—made a new line of road through an impassable bog, and over an inaccessible mountain—and conducted water to a mill, which (I learned in the morning) was always worked by wind. The decanter had scarcely completed its

THE PRIEST'S SUPPER

third circuit of the board, when I bid fair to be the most popular specimen of the peerage that ever visited the "far west." In the midst of my career of universal benevolence, I was interrupted by Father Malachi, whom I found on his legs, pronouncing a glowing eulogium on his cousin's late regiment, the famous North Cork.

"That was the corps!" said he. "Bid them do a thing, and they'd never leave off; and so, when they got orders to retire from Wexford, it's little they cared for the comforts of baggage, like many another regiment, for they threw away everything but their canteens, and never stopped till they ran to Ross, fifteen miles farther than the enemy followed them. And when they were all in bed the same night, fatigued and tired with their exertions, as ye may suppose, a drummer's boy called out in his sleep—'Here they are! they're coming!'—they all jumped up and set off in their shirts, and got two miles out of town before they discovered it was a false alarm."

Peal after peal of laughter followed the priest's encomium on the doctor's regiment; and, indeed, he himself joined most heartily in the mirth, as he might well afford to do, seeing that a braver or better corps than the North Cork Ireland did not possess.

"Well," said Fin, "it's easy to see ye never can forget what they did at Maynooth."

Father Malachi disclaimed all personal feeling on the subject; and I was at last gratified by the following narrative, which I regret deeply I am not enabled to give in the doctor's own words; but writing as I do from memory (in most instances), I can only convey the substance:—

It was towards the latter end of the year '98—the year of the troubles—that the North Cork was ordered, "for their sins," I believe, to march from their snug quarters in Fermoy, and take up a position in the town of Maynooth—a very considerable reverse of fortune to a set of gentlemen extremely addicted to dining out, and living at large upon a very pleasant neighbourhood. Fermoy abounded in gentry; Maynooth at that time had few, if any, excepting his Grace of Leinster, and he lived very privately, and saw no company. Maynooth was stupid and dull—there were neither belles nor balls; Fermoy (to use the doctor's well-remembered words) had "great feeling," and "very genteel young ladies, that carried their handkerchiefs in bags, and danced with the officers."

They had not been many weeks in their new quarters when they began to pine over their altered fortunes, and it was with a sense of delight, which a few months before would have been incomprehensible to them, they discovered that one of their officers had a brother, a young priest in the college. He introduced him to some of his *confrères,* and the natural result followed. A visiting acquaintance began between the regiment and such of the members of the college as had liberty to leave the precincts: who, as time ripened the acquaintance into intimacy, very naturally preferred the cuisine of the North Cork to the meagre fare of "the refectory." At last, seldom a day went by without one or two of their reverences finding themselves guests at the mess. The North Corkians were of a most hospitable turn, and the fathers were determined the virtue should not rust for want of being exercised; they would just drop in to say a word to "Captain O'Flaherty about leave to shoot in the demesne," as Carton was styled; or, they had a "frank from the Duke for the Colonel," or some other equally pressing reason; and they would contrive to be caught in the middle of a very droll story just as the "roast beef" was playing. Very little entreaty then suf-

THE PRIEST'S SUPPER

ficed—a short apology for the *dérèglements* of dress, and a few minutes more found them seated at the table without further ceremony on either side.

Among the favourite guests from the college two were peculiarly in estimation—"the Professor of the Humanities," Father Luke Mooney; and the Abbé D'Array, "the Lecturer on Moral Philosophy and Belles Lettres"; and certain it is, pleasanter fellows, or ones more gifted with the "convivial bump," never existed. He of the Humanities was a droll dog—a member of the Curran club, the "Monks of the Screw"—told an excellent story, and sang the "Cruiskeen Lawn" better than did any before or since him; the moral philosopher, though of a different *genre*, was also a most agreeable companion—an Irishman transplanted in his youth to St. Omer's, who had grafted upon his native humour a considerable share of French smartness and repartee. Such were the two who ruled supreme in all the festive arrangements of this jovial regiment, and were at last as regular at table as the adjutant and the paymaster; and so might they have continued, had not prosperity, that, in its blighting influence upon the heart, spares neither priests nor laymen, and is equally severe upon mice (see Æsop's fable) and moral philosophers, actually deprived them for the "nonce" of reason, and tempted them to their ruin. You naturally ask, What did they do? Did they venture upon allusions to the retreat upon Ross? Nothing of the kind. Did they, in that vanity which wine inspires, refer by word, act, or innuendo, to the well-known order of their Colonel, when reviewing his regiment in "the Phœnix," to "advance two steps backwards, and dress by the gutter"? Far be it from them: though indeed either of these had been esteemed light in the balance compared with their real crime. "Then, what was their failing?—come, tell it, and burn ye!"

They actually, *horresco referens*, quizzed the major *coram* the whole mess!—Now, Major John Jones had only lately exchanged the North Cork from the "Darry Ragement," as he called it. He was a red-hot Orangeman, a deputy-grand something, and vice-chairman of the "Prentice Boys" beside. He broke his leg when a schoolboy, by a fall incurred in tying an orange handkerchief around King William's august neck in College Green, on the 12th of July, and three several times had closed the gates of Derry with his own loyal hands, on the famed anniversary; in a word, he was one, that if his Church had enjoined penance as an expiation for sin, would have looked upon a trip to Jerusalem on his bare knees, as a very light punishment for the crime on his conscience, that he sat at table with two buck priests from Maynooth, and carved for them, like the rest of the company!

Poor Major Jones, however, had no such solace, and the canker-worm ate daily deeper and deeper into his pining heart. During the three or four weeks of their intimacy with his regiment, his martyrdom was awful. His figure wasted, and his colour became a deeper tinge of orange, and all around averred that there would soon be a "move up" in the corps, for the major had evidently "got his notice to quit" this world and its pomps and vanities. He felt "that he was dying," to use Haines Bayley's beautiful and apposite words, and meditated an exchange; but that, from circumstances, was out of the question. At last, subdued by grief, and probably his spirit having chafed itself smooth by such constant attrition, he became, to all seeming, calmer; but it was only the calm of a broken and weary heart. Such was Major Jones at the time, when, *suadente diabolo*, it seemed meet to Fathers Mooney and D'Array to make him the butt of their raillery. At first he could

THE PRIEST'S SUPPER

not believe it; the thing was incredible—impossible; but when he looked around the table, when he heard the roars of laughter, long, loud, and vociferous; when he heard his name bandied from one to the other across the table with some vile jest tacked to it "like a tin kettle to a dog's tail," he awoke to the full measure of his misery—the cup was full. Fate had done her worst, and he might have exclaimed with Lear, "spit, fire—spout, rain!" there was nothing in store for him of further misfortune.

A drum-head court-martial—a hint "to sell out"—ay, a sentence of "dismissed the service," had been mortal calamities, and, like a man, he would have borne them; but that he, Major John Jones, D.G.S., C.P.B., etc. etc., who had drunk the "pious, glorious, and immortal," sitting astride of "the great gun of Athlone," should come to this! Alas, and alas! He retired that night to his chamber a "sadder if not a wiser man"; he dreamed that the "statue" had given place to the unshapely figure of Leo X., and that "Lundy now stood where Walker stood before." He jumped from his bed in a moment of enthusiasm, he vowed his revenge, and he kept his vow.

That day the Major was "acting field-officer." The various patrols, sentries, picquets, and outposts were all under his especial control; and it was remarked that he took peculiar pains in selecting the men for night duty, which, in the prevailing quietness and peace of that time, seemed scarcely warrantable.

Evening drew near, and Major Jones, summoned by the "oft-heard beat," wended his way to the mess. The officers were dropping in, and true as "the needle to the pole," came Father Mooney and the Abbé. They were welcomed with the usual warmth, and, strange to say, by none more than the Major himself, whose hilarity knew no bounds.

How the evening passed I shall not stop to relate; suffice it to say, that a more brilliant feast of wit and jollification not even the North Cork ever enjoyed. Father Luke's drollest stories, his very quaintest humour, shone forth, and the Abbé sang a new *Chanson à Boire,* that Béranger might have envied.

"What are you about, my dear Father D'Array?" said the Colonel; "you are surely not rising yet; here's a fresh cooper of port just come in; sit down, I entreat."

"I say it with grief, my dear colonel, we must away; the half-hour has just chimed, and we must be within 'the gates' before twelve. The truth is, the superior has been making himself very troublesome about our 'carnal amusements,' as he calls our innocent mirth, and we must therefore be upon our guard."

"Well, if it must be so, we shall not risk losing your society altogether for an hour or so now; so, one bumper to our next meeting—to-morrow, mind; and now, M. l'Abbé, *au revoir.*"

The worthy fathers finished their glasses, and taking a most affectionate leave of their kind entertainers, sallied forth under the guidance of Major Jones, who insisted upon accompanying them part of the way, as "from information he had received, the sentries were doubled in some places, and the usual precautions against surprise all taken." Much as this polite attention surprised the objects of it, his brother officers wondered still more; and no sooner did they perceive the Major and his companions issue forth, than they set out in a body to watch where this most novel and unexpected complaisance would terminate.

When the priests reached the door of the barrack-yard, they again turned to utter their thanks to the Major, and entreat him once more "not to come a step farther. There now, Major, we know the path well, so

THE PRIEST'S SUPPER

just give us the pass, and don't stay out in the night air."

"*Ah oui, Monsieur Jones,*" said the Abbé, "*retournez, je vous prie.* We are, I may say, *chez nous. Ces braves gens, les* North Cork, know us by this time."

The Major smiled, while he still pressed his services to see them past the picquets; but they were resolved and would not be denied.

"With the word for the night, we want nothing more," said Father Luke.

"Well then," said the Major, in the gravest tone, and he was naturally grave, "you shall have your way, but remember to call out loud, for the first sentry is a little deaf, and a very passionate, ill-tempered fellow to boot."

"Never fear," said Father Mooney, laughing; "I'll go bail he'll hear me."

"Well—the word for the night is—'Bloody end to the Pope'; don't forget, now, 'Bloody end to the Pope';" and with these words he banged the door between him and the unfortunate priests; and as bolt was fastened after bolt, they heard him laughing to himself like a fiend.

"And big bad luck to ye, Major Jones, for the same, every day ye see a paving-stone," was the faint sub-audible ejaculation of Father Luke, when he was recovered enough to speak.

"*Sacristi! que nous sommes attrapés,*" said the Abbé, scarcely able to avoid laughing at the situation in which they were placed.

"Well, there's the quarter chiming now; we've no time to lose.—Major Jones! Major, darling! don't now, ah don't! sure ye know we'll be ruined entirely; there now, just change it, like a dacent fellow—the devil's luck to him, he's gone! Well, we can't stay here in the rain all night, and be expelled in the morning afterwards—so come along."

They jogged on for a few minutes in silence, till they came to that part of the "Duke's" demesne wall where the first sentry was stationed. By this time the officers, headed by the Major, had quietly slipped out of the gate, and were following their steps at a convenient distance.

The fathers had stopped to consult together what they should do in this trying emergency—when their whisper being overheard, the sentinel called out gruffly, in the genuine dialect of his country, "Who goes *that?*"

"Father Luke Mooney, and the Abbé D'Array," said the former, in his most bland and insinuating tone of voice, a quality he most eminently possessed.

"Stand and give the countersign."

"We are coming from the mess, and going home to the college," said Father Mooney, evading the question, and gradually advancing as he spoke.

"Stand, or I'll *shot* ye!" said the North Corkian.

Father Luke halted, while a muttered "Blessed Virgin" announced his state of fear and trepidation.

"D'Array, I say, what are we to do?"

"The countersign," said the sentry, whose figure they could perceive in the dim distance of about thirty yards.

"Sure ye'll let us pass, my good lad, and ye'll have a friend in Father Luke the longest day ye live, and ye might have a worse in time of need; ye understand?"

Whether he did understand or not, he certainly did not heed, for his only reply was the short click of his gun-lock, that bespeaks a preparation to fire.

"There's no help now," said Father Luke; "I see he's a haythen; and bad luck to the Major, I say again"; and this in the fulness of his heart he uttered aloud.

"That's not the countersign," said the inexorable sentry, striking the butt-end of the musket on the

THE PRIEST'S SUPPER

ground with a crash that smote terror into the hearts of the priests.

Mumble—mumble——"to the Pope," said Father Luke, pronouncing the last words distinctly, after the approved practice of a Dublin watchman, on being awoke from his dreams of rows and riot by the last toll of the Post-office, and not knowing whether it has struck "twelve" or "three," sings out the word "o'clock" in a long sonorous drawl, that wakes every sleeping citizen, and yet tells nothing how "time speeds on his flight."

"Louder," said the sentry, in a voice of impatience.

——"to the Pope."

"I don't hear the first part."

"Oh, then," said the priest, with a sigh that might have melted the heart of anything but a sentry, "Bloody end to the Pope; and may the saints in heaven forgive me for saying it."

"Again," called out the soldier; "and no muttering."

"Bloody end to the Pope," cried Father Luke, in bitter desperation.

"Bloody end to the Pope," echoed the Abbé.

"Pass, Bloody end to the Pope, and good-night," said the sentry, resuming his rounds, while a loud and uproarious peal of laughter behind told the unlucky priests they were overheard by others, and that the story would be over the whole town in the morning.

Whether it was that the penance for their heresy took long in accomplishing, or that they never could summon courage sufficient to face their persecutor, certain it is, the North Cork saw them no more, nor were they ever observed to pass the precincts of the college while that regiment occupied Maynooth.

Major Jones himself, and his confederates, could not have more heartily relished this story than did the party to whom the doctor related it. Much, if not all, the amusement it afforded, however, resulted from his inimitable mode of telling, and the power of mimicry with which he conveyed the dialogue with the sentry: and this, alas, must be lost to my readers, at least to that portion of them not fortunate enough to possess Dr. Finucane's acquaintance.

"Fin! Fin! your long story has nearly famished me," said the padre, as the laugh subsided; "and there you sit now with the jug at your elbow this half-hour; I never thought you would forget our old friend Martin Hanegan's Aunt."

"Here's to her health," said Fin; "and your reverence will give us the chant."

"Agreed," said Father Malachi, finishing a bumper; and after giving a few preparatory hems, he sang the following "singularly wild and beautiful poem," as someone calls Christabel:—

> "Here's a health to Martin Hanegan's aunt,
>   And I'll tell ye the reason why;
> She eats bekase she is hungry,
>   And drinks bekase she is dry.
>
> And if ever a man
>   Stopped the course of a can,
> Martin Hanegan's aunt would cry—
>   'Arrah, fill up your glass,
>   And let the jug pass;
> How d'ye know but your neighbour's dhry?'"

"Come, my lord and gentlemen, *da capo*, if ye please —fill up your glass"; and the *chanson* was chorused with a strength and vigour that would have astonished the Philharmonic.

The mirth and fun now grew fast and furious; and Father Malachi, rising with the occasion, flung his reckless drollery and fun on every side, sparing none, from his cousin to the coadjutor. It was now that peculiar period in the evening's enjoyment, when an expert and practical chairman gives up all interference or management, and leaves everything to take its course; this then was the happy moment selected by Father Malachi to propose the little "conthribution." He brought a plate from a side table, and placing it before him, addressed the company in a very brief but sensible speech, detailing the object of the institution he was advocating, and concluding with the following words:—"And now ye'll just give whatever ye like, according to your means in life, and what ye can spare"; the admonition like the "morale" of an income-tax, having the immediate effect of pitting each man against his neighbour, and suggesting to their already excited spirit all the ardour of gambling, without, however, a prospect of gain.

The plate was first handed to me, in honour of my "rank," and having deposited upon it a handful of small silver, the priest ran his finger through the coin, and called out—

"Five pounds! at least; not a farthing less, as I am a sinner. Look then—see, now; they tell ye, the gentlemen don't care for the like of ye! but see for yourselves. May I trouble y'r lordship to pass the plate to Mr. Mahony—he's impatient, I see."

Mr. Mahony, about whom I perceived very little of the impatience alluded to, was a grim-looking old Christian, in a rabbitskin waistcoat, with long flaps, who fumbled in the recesses of his breeches-pocket for five minutes, and then drew forth three shillings which he laid upon the plate, with what I fancied very much resembled a sigh.

"Six and sixpence, is it? or five shillings?—all the same, Mr. Mahony, and I'll not forget the thrifle you were speaking about this morning anyway"; and here he leaned over as if interceding with me for him, but in reality to whisper into my ear, "The greatest miser from this to Castlebar."

"Who's that put down the half-guinea in goold?" (and this time he spoke the truth). "Who's that, I say?"

"Tim Kennedy, your reverence," said Tim, stroking his hair down with one hand, and looking proud and modest at the same moment.

"Tim, ye're a credit to us any day, and I always said so.—It's a gauger he'd like to be, my lord," said he, turning to me, in a kind of stage whisper. I nodded and muttered something, when he thanked me most profoundly, as if his suit had prospered.

"Mickey Oulahan—the lord's looking at ye, Mickey." This was said *pianissimo* across the table, and had the effect of increasing Mr. Oulahan's donation from five shillings to seven—the last two being pitched in very much in the style of a gambler making his final coup, and crying *va banque*. "The Oulahans were always dacent people—dacent people, my lord."

"Be gorra, the Oulahans was niver dacenter nor the Molowneys, anyhow," said a tall, athletic young fellow, as he threw down three crown pieces, with an energy that made every coin leap from the plate.

"They'll do now," said Father Brennan; "I'll leave them to themselves"; and truly the eagerness to get the plate and put down the subscription fully equalled the rapacious anxiety I have witnessed in an old maid at loo to get possession of a thirty-shilling pool, be the same more or less, which lingered on its way to her, in the hands of many a fair competitor.

"Mr. M'Neesh"—Curzon had hitherto escaped all notice—"Mr. M'Neesh, to your good health," cried Father Brennan. "It's many a secret they'll be getting out o' ye down there about the Scotch husbandry."

THE PRIEST'S SUPPER

Whatever poor Curzon knew of "drills," certainly did not extend to them when occupied by turnips. This allusion of the priest's being caught up by the guests at the foot of the table, they commenced a series of inquiries into different Scotch plans of tillage—his brief and unsatisfactory answers to which, they felt sure, were given in order to evade imparting information. By degrees, as they continued to press him with questions, his replies grew more short, and a general feeling of dislike on both sides was not very long in following.

The father saw this, and determining with his usual tact to repress it, called on the adjutant for a song. Now, whether he had but one in the world, or whether he took this mode of retaliating for the annoyances he had suffered, I know not; but true it is, he finished his tumbler at a draught, and with a voice of no very peculiar sweetness, though abundantly loud, began "The Boyne Water."

He had just reached the word "battle" in the second line, upon which he was bestowing what he meant to be a shake, when, as if the word suggested it, it seemed the signal for a general engagement. Decanters, glasses, jugs, candlesticks—ay, and the money-dish, flew right and left—all originally intended, it is true, for the head of the luckless adjutant, but as they now and then missed their aim, and came in contact with the "wrong man," invariably provoked retaliation, and in a very few minutes the battle became general.

What may have been the doctor's political sentiments on this occasion I cannot even guess; but he seemed bent upon performing the part of a "convivial Lord Stanley," and maintaining a dignified neutrality. With this apparent object, he mounted upon the table, to raise himself, I suppose, above the din and commotion of party clamour, and, brandishing a jug of scalding water, bestowed it with perfect impartiality on the combatants on either side. This Whig plan of conciliation, however well intended, seemed not to prosper with either party; and many were the missiles directed at the ill-starred doctor. Meanwhile Father Malachi, whether following the pacific instinct of his order, in seeking an asylum in troublesome times, or equally moved by old habit to gather coin in low places (much of the money having fallen), was industriously endeavouring to insert himself beneath the table; in this, with one vigorous push, he at last succeeded, but in so doing lifted it from its legs; and thus destroying poor "Fin's" gravity, precipitated him, jug and all, into the thickest of the fray, where he met with that kind reception such a benefactor ever receives at the hands of a grateful public. I meanwhile hurried to rescue Curzon, who, having fallen to the ground, was getting a cast of his features taken in pewter, for such seemed the operation a stout farmer was performing on the adjutant's face with a quart. With considerable difficulty, notwithstanding my supposed "lordship," I succeeded in freeing him from his present position; and he, concluding, probably, that enough had been done for one "sitting," most willingly permitted me to lead him from the room. I was soon joined by the doctor, who assisted me in getting my poor friend to bed; which being done, he most eagerly entreated me to join the company. This, however, I firmly but mildly declined, very much to his surprise; for, as he remarked, "They'll all be like lambs now, for they don't believe there's a whole bone in his body."

Expressing my deep sense of the Christian-like forbearance of the party, I pleaded fatigue, and bidding Fin good-night, adjourned to my bedroom; and here,

THE PRIEST'S SUPPER

although the arrangements fell somewhat short of the luxurious ones appertaining to my late apartment at Callonby, they were most grateful at the moment; and having "addressed myself to slumber," I fell fast asleep, and only awoke late the following morning to wonder where I was: from any doubts as to which I was speedily relieved by the entrance of the priest's barefooted "colleen," to deposit on my table a bottle of soda-water, and announce breakfast, with his reverence's compliments.

Having made a hasty toilet I proceeded to the parlour, which, however late events might have impressed it upon my memory, I could scarcely recognize. Instead of the long oak table and the wassail-bowl, there stood near the fire a small round table, covered with a snow-white cloth, upon which shone in unrivalled brightness a very handsome tea equipage—the hissing kettle on one hob was *vis-à-vis*'d by a gridiron with three newly taken trout frying under the reverential care of Father Malachi himself—a heap of eggs, ranged like shot in an ordnance yard, stood in the middle of the table, while a formidable pile of buttered toast browned before the grate—the morning papers were airing upon the hearth—everything bespoke that attention to comfort and enjoyment one likes to discover in the house where chance may have domesticated him for a day or two.

"Good-morning, Mr. Lorrequer. I trust you have rested well," said Father Malachi as I entered.

"Never better; but where are our friends?"

"I have been visiting and comforting them in their affliction, and I may with truth assert it is not often my fortune to have three as sickly-looking guests. That was a most unlucky affair last night, and I must apologize."

"Don't say a word, I entreat: I saw how it all occurred, and am quite sure if it had not been for poor Curzon's ill-timed melody——"

"You are quite right," said the father, interrupting me. "Your friend's taste for music—bad luck to it!—was the *teterrima causa belli.*"

"And the subscription," said I; "how did it succeed?"

"Oh, the money went in the commotion; and although I have got some seven pounds odd shillings of it, the war was a most expensive one to me. I caught old Mahony very busy under the table during the fray; but let us say no more about it now—draw over your chair. Tea or coffee? there's the rum if you like it *chassé.*"

I immediately obeyed the injunction, and commenced a vigorous assault upon the trout, caught, as he informed me, "within twenty perches of the house."

"Your poor friend's nose is scarcely regimental," said he, "this morning; and as for Fin, he was never remarkable for beauty, so, though they might cut and hack, they could scarcely disfigure him; as Juvenal says—isn't it Juvenal?—

'Vacuus viator cantabit ante Latronem':

or in the vernacular—

'The empty traveller may whistle
Before the robber and his pistol.'

There's the Chili vinegar—another morsel of the trout?"

"I thank you; what excellent coffee, Father Malachi!"

"A secret I learned at St. Omer's some thirty years since. Any letters, Bridget?"—to a damsel that entered with a packet in her hand.

"A gossoon from Kilrush, y'r reverence, with a bit of a note for the gentleman there."

"For me!—ah, true enough. 'Harry Lorrequer, Esq.,

Kilrush—try Carrigaholt.'" So ran the superscription—the first part being in a lady's handwriting; the latter very like the "rustic paling" of the worthy Mrs. Healy's style. The seal was a large one, bearing a coronet at top, and the motto, in old Norman-French, told me it came from Callonby.

With what a trembling hand and beating heart I broke it open and yet feared to read it—so much of my destiny might be in that simple page. For once in my life my sanguine spirit failed me; my mind could take in but one casualty, that Lady Jane had divulged to her family the nature of my attentions, and that in the letter before me lay a cold mandate of dismissal from her presence for ever.

(From *Harry Lorrequer*.)

LIAM O'FLAHERTY

The Tramp

THERE were eight paupers in the convalescent yard of the workhouse hospital. The yard was an oblong patch of cement with the dining-room on one side and a high red-brick wall on the other. At one end was the urinal and at the other a little tarred wooden shed where there was a bathroom and a washhouse. It was very cold, for the sun had not yet risen over the buildings that crowded out the yard almost from the sky. It was a raw, bleak, February morning, about eight o'clock.

The paupers had just come out from breakfast and stood about uncertain what to do. What they had eaten only made them hungry and they stood shivering, making muffs of their coat-sleeves, their little black woolen caps perched on their heads, some still chewing a last mouthful of bread, others scowling savagely at the ground as they conjured up memories of hearty meals eaten some time in the past.

As usual Michael Deignan and John Finnerty slouched off into the washhouse and leaned against the sink, while they banged their boots on the floor to keep warm. Deignan was very tall and lean. He had a pale melancholy face and there was something the matter with the iris of his right eye. It was not blue like the other eye, but of an uncertain yellowish colour that made one think, somehow, that he was a sly, cunning, deceitful fellow, a totally wrong impression. His hair was very grey around the temples and fair elsewhere. The fingers of his hands were ever so long and thin and he was always chewing at the nails and looking at the ground, wrapped in thought.

"It's very cold," he said in a thin, weak, listless voice. It was almost inaudible.

"Yes," replied Finnerty gruffly, as he started up and heaved a loud sigh. "Ah—" he began and then he stopped, snorted twice to clear his nose, and let his head fall on his chest. He was a middle-sized, thickset fellow, still in good condition and fat in the face, which was round and rosy, with grey eyes and very white teeth. His black hair was grown long and curled about his ears. His hands were round, soft and white, like a schoolmaster's.

The two of them stood leaning their backs against the washstand and stamped their feet in a moody silence for several minutes and then the tramp, who had been admitted to the hospital the previous night, wandered into the washhouse. He appeared silently at the entrance of the shed and paused there for a moment while his tiny blue eyes darted around piercingly yet softly, just like a graceful wild animal might look through a clump of trees in a forest. His squat low body, standing between the tarred doorposts of the shed with the concrete wall behind and the grey sky overhead, was after a fashion menacing with the power and vitality it seemed to exude. So it seemed at least to the two dejected, listless paupers within the shed. They looked at the tramp with a mournful vexed expression and an envious gleam in their eyes and a furrowing of their foreheads and a shrinking of their flesh from this fresh dominant coarse lump of aggressive wandering life, so different to their own jaded, terror-stricken lives. Each thought, "Look at the red fat face of that vile tramp. Look at his fierce insulting eyes, that stare you in the face as boldly as a lion, or a child, and are impudent enough to have a gentle expression at the back of them, unconscious of malice. Look at that huge black beard that covers all his face and neck except the eyes and the nose and a narrow red slit for the mouth. My God, what throat muscles and what hair on his chest, on a day like this too, when I would die of cold to expose my chest that way!"

So each thought and neither spoke. As the tramp grinned foolishly—he just opened his beard, exposed red lips and red gums with stray blackened teeth scattered about them and then closed the beard again—the two paupers made no response. The two of them were educated men, and without meaning it they shrank from associating with the unseemly dirty tramp on terms of equality, just as they spent the day in the washhouse in the cold, so as to keep away from the other paupers.

The tramp took no further notice of them. He went

to the back of the shed and stood there looking out of the door and chewing tobacco. The other two men, conscious of his presence and irritated by it, fidgeted about and scowled. At last the tramp looked at Deignan, grinned, fumbled in his coat pocket, took out a crumpled cigarette and handed it to Deignan with another grin and a nodding of his head. But he did not speak.

Deignan had not smoked a cigarette for a week. As he looked at it for a moment in wonder, his bowels ached with desire for the little thin, crumpled, dirt-stained roll of tobacco held between the thumb and forefinger of the tramp's gnarled and mud-caked hand. Then with a contortion of his face as he tried to swallow his breath he muttered, "You're a brick," and stretched out a trembling hand. In three seconds the cigarette was lit and he was inhaling the first delicious puff of drug-laden smoke. His face lit up with a kind of delicious happiness. His eyes sparkled. He took three puffs and was handing the cigarette to his friend when the tramp spoke.

"No, keep it yerself, towny," he said in his even, effortless, soft voice. "I've got another for him."

And then when the two paupers were smoking, their listlessness vanished and they became cheerful and talkative. The two cigarettes broke down the barriers of distrust and contempt between themselves and the tramp. His unexpected act of generosity had counteracted his beard and the degraded condition of his clothes. He was not wearing a pauper's uniform, but a patched corduroy trousers and numbers of waistcoats and tattered coats of all colours, piled indiscriminately on his body and held together not by buttons but by a cord tied around his waist. They accepted him as a friend. They began to talk to him.

"You just came in for the night?" asked Deignan. There was still a condescending tone in the cultured accents.

The tramp nodded. Then after several seconds he rolled his tobacco to the other cheek, spat on the floor and hitched up his trousers.

"Yes," he said, "I walked from Drogheda yesterday and I landed in Dublin as tired as a dog. I said to myself that the only place to go was in here. I needed a wash, a good bed, and a rest, and I had only ninepence, a piece of steak, a few spuds, and an onion. If I bought a bed they'd be all gone and now I've had a good sleep, a warm bath, and I still have my ninepence and my grub. I'll start off as soon as I get out at eleven o'clock and maybe walk fifteen miles before I put up for the night somewhere."

"But how did you get into the hospital ward?" asked Finnerty, eyeing the tramp with a jealous look. The cigarette had accentuated Finnerty's feeling of hunger, and he was irritated at the confident way the tramp talked of walking fifteen miles that day and putting up somewhere afterwards.

"How did I get in?" said the tramp. "That's easy. I got a rash on my right leg this three years. It always gets me into the hospital when I strike a workhouse. It's easy."

Again there was a silence. The tramp shuffled to the door and looked out into the yard. The sky overhead was still grey and bleak. The water that had been poured over the concrete yard to wash it two hours before still glistened in drops and lay in little pools here and there. There was no heat in the air to dry it.

The other six paupers, three old men with sticks, two young men, and a youth whose pale face was covered with pimples, were all going about uncertainly, talking in a tired way and peering greedily in through the windows of the dining-room, where old Neddy, the pauper in charge of the dining-room, was preparing the bread and milk for the dinner ration. The tramp glanced around at all this and then shrugged his shoulders and shuffled back to the end of the washhouse.

"How long have you been in here?" he asked Deignan.

Deignan stubbed the remainder of his cigarette against his boot, put the quenched piece in the lining of his cap and then said, "I've been here six months."

"Educated man?" said the tramp. Deignan nodded. The tramp looked at him, went to the door and spat and then came back to his former position:

"I'll say you're a fool," he said quite coolly. "There doesn't look to be anything the matter with you. In spite of your hair, I bet you're no more than thirty-five. Eh?"

"That's just right about my age, but—"

"Hold on," said the tramp. "You are as fit as a fiddle, this is a spring morning, and yer loafing in here and eating yer heart out with hunger and misery instead of taking to the roads. What man! You're mad. That's all there's to it." He made a noise with his tongue as if driving a horse and began to clap his hands on his bare chest. Every time he hit his chest there was a dull heavy sound like distant thunder. The noise was so loud that Deignan could not speak until the tramp stopped beating his chest. He stood wriggling his lips and winking his right eye in irritation against what the tramp had said and jealousy of the man's strength and endurance, beating his bare hairy chest that way on such a perishing day. The blows would crush Deignan's ribs and the exposure would give him pneumonia.

"It's all very well for you to talk," he began querulously. Then he stopped and looked at the tramp. It occurred to him that it would be ridiculous to talk to a tramp about personal matters. But there was something aggressive and dominant and yet absolutely unemotional in the tramp's fierce stare that drove out that feeling of contempt. Instead Deignan felt spurred to defend himself. "How could you understand me?" he continued. "As far as you can see I am all right. I have no disease but a slight rash on my back and that comes from underfeeding, from hunger and . . . depression. My mind is sick. But of course you don't understand that."

"Quite right," said Finnerty, blowing cigarette smoke through his nostrils moodily. "I often envy those who don't think. I wish I were a farm labourer."

"Huh." The tramp uttered the exclamation in a heavy roar. Then he laughed loudly and deeply, stamped his feet and banged his chest. His black beard shook with laughter. "Mother of Mercy," he cried, "I'll be damned but you make me laugh, the two of you."

The two shuffled with their feet and coughed and said nothing. They became instantly ashamed of their contemptuous thoughts for the tramp, he who a few minutes before had given them cigarettes. They suddenly realized that they were paupers, degraded people, and contemptible people for feeling superior to a fellow-man because he was a tramp. They said nothing. The tramp stopped laughing and became serious.

"Now, look here," he said to Deignan, "what were you in civilian life, as they say to soldiers, what did you do before you came in here?"

"Oh, the last job I had was a solicitor's clerk," murmured Deignan, biting his nails. "But that was only a stopgap, I can't say that I ever had anything permanent. Somehow I always seemed to drift. When I left college

I tried for the Consular Service and failed. Then I stayed at home for a year at my mother's place in Tyrone. She has a little estate there. Then I came to Dublin here. I got disgusted hanging around at home. I fancied everybody was pitying me. I saw everybody getting married or doing something while I only loafed about, living on my mother. So I left. Landed here with two portmanteaux and eighty-one pounds. It's six years ago next fifteenth of May. A beautiful sunny day it was, too."

Deignan's plaintive voice drifted away into silence and he gnawed his nails and stared at the ground. Finnerty was trying to get a last puff from the end of his cigarette. He was trying to hold the end between his thumbs and puckered up his lips as if he were trying to drink boiling milk. The tramp silently handed him another cigarette and then he turned to Deignan.

"What did ye do with eighty-one quid?" he said. "Did ye drink it or give it to the women?"

Finnerty, cheered by the second cigarette which he had just lit, uttered a deep guffaw and said, "Ha, the women blast them, they're the curse of many a man's life," but Deignan started up and his face paled and his lips twitched.

"I can assure you," he said, "that I never touched a woman in my life." He paused as if to clear his mind of the horror that the tramp's suggestion had aroused in him. "No, I can't say I drank it. I can't say I did anything at all. I just drifted from one job to another. Somehow, it seemed to me that nothing big could come my way and that it didn't matter very much how I spent my life, because I would be a failure anyway. Maybe I did drink too much once in a while, or dropped a few pounds at a race meeting, but nothing of any account. No, I came down just because I seemed naturally to drift downwards and I couldn't muster up courage to stop myself. I . . . I've been here six months . . . I suppose I'll die here."

"Well I'll be damned," said the tramp. He folded his arms on his chest, and his chest heaved in and out with his excited breathing. He kept looking at Deignan and nodding his head. Finnerty who had heard Deignan's story hundreds of times with numberless details shrugged his shoulders, sniffed and said: "Begob, it's a funny world. Though I'm damn sure that I wouldn't be here only for women and drink."

"No?" said the tramp. "How do you make that out?"

"No, by Jiminy," said Finnerty, blowing out a cloud of blue smoke through his mouth as he talked. "I'd be a rich man today only for drink and women." He crossed his feet and leaned jauntily back against the washstand, with his hands held in front of him, the fingers of the right hand tapping the back of the left. His fat round face, with the heavy jaw, turned sideways towards the doorway, looked selfish, stupid and cruel. He laughed and said in an undertone, "Oh boys, oh boys, when I come to think of it." Then he coughed and shrugged his shoulders. "Would you believe it," he said turning to the tramp, "I've spent five thousand pounds within the last twelve months? It's a fact. Upon my soul I have. I curse the day I got hold of that money. Until two years ago I was a happy man, I had one of the best schools in the south of Ireland. Then an aunt of mine came home from America and stayed in the house with my mother and myself. She died within six months and left mother five thousand pounds. I got it out of the old woman's hands, God forgive me, and then. . . . Oh well," Finnerty shook his head solemnly, raised his eyebrows and sighed. "I'm not sorry," he continued, leering at a black spot on the concrete floor of the washhouse. "I could count the number of days I was sober on my fingers and thumbs. And now I'd give a month of my life for a cup of tea and a hunk of bread." He stamped about clapping his hands and laughing raucously. His bull neck shook when he laughed. Then he scowled again and said, "Wish I had a penny. That's nine o'clock striking. I'm starving with the hunger."

"Eh? Hungry?" The tramp had fallen into a kind of doze while Finnerty had been talking. He started up, scratched his bare neck and then rummaged within his upper garments mumbling to himself. At last he drew forth a little bag from which he took three pennies. He handed the pennies to Finnerty. "Get chuck for the three of us," he said.

Finnerty's eyes gleamed, he licked his lower lip with his tongue and then he darted out without saying a word.

In the workhouse hospital a custom had grown up, since goodness knows when, that the pauper in charge of the dining-room was allowed to filch a little from the hospital rations, of tea, bread, and soup, and then sell them to the paupers again as extras at nine o'clock in the morning for a penny a portion. This fraudulent practice was overlooked by the ward-master; for he himself filched all his rations from the paupers' hospital supply and he did it with the connivance of the workhouse master, who was himself culpable in other ways and was therefore prevented by fear from checking his subordinates. But Finnerty did not concern himself with these things. He dived into the dining-room, held up the three pennies before old Neddy's face and whispered "Three." Neddy, a lean wrinkled old pauper with a very thick red under-lip like a Negro, was standing in front of the fire with his hands folded under his dirty check apron. He counted the three pennies, mumbling, and then put them in his pocket. During twenty years he had collected ninety-three pounds in that manner. He had no relatives to whom he could bequeath the money, he never spent any and he never would leave the workhouse until his death, but he kept on collecting the money. It was his only pleasure in life. When he had collected a shilling in pennies he changed it into silver and the silver in due course into banknotes.

"They say he has a hundred pounds," thought Finnerty, his mouth dry with greed, as he watched Neddy put away the pennies. "Wish I knew where it was. I'd strangle him here and now and make a run for it. A hundred pounds. I'd eat and eat and eat and then I'd drink and drink."

The tramp and Deignan never spoke a word until Finnerty came back, carrying three bowls of tea and three hunks of bread on a white deal board. Deignan and Finnerty immediately began to gulp their tea and tear at the bread, but the tramp merely took a little sip at the tea and then took up his piece of bread, broke it in two, and gave a piece to each of the paupers.

"I'm not hungry," he said. "I've got my dinner with me, and as soon as I get out along the road in the open country I'm going to sit down and cook it. And it's going to be a real spring day, too. Look at that sun."

The sun had at last mounted the wall. It was streaming into the yard lighting up everything. It was not yet warm, but it was cheering and invigorating. And the sky had become a clear pure blue colour.

"Doesn't it make ye want to jump and shout?" cried the tramp, joyously stamping about. He had become very excited, seeing the sun.

"I'm afraid I'd rather see a good dinner in front of me," muttered Finnerty with his mouth full of bread.

"What about you, towny?" said the tramp, standing

in front of Deignan. "Wouldn't ye like to be walking along a mountain road now with a river flowing under yer feet in a valley and the sun tearing at yer spine?"

Deignan looked out wistfully, smiled for a moment dreamily and then sighed and shook his head. He sipped his tea and said nothing. The tramp went to the back of the shed. Nobody spoke until they had finished the bread and tea. Finnerty collected the bowls.

"I'll take these back," he said, "and maybe I might get sent over to the cookhouse for something."

He went away and didn't come back. The tramp and Deignan fell into a contemplative doze. Neither spoke until the clock struck ten. The tramp shrugged himself and coming over to Deignan, tapped him on the arm.

"I was thinking of what you said about . . . about how you spent your life, and I thought to myself, 'Well, that poor man is telling the truth and he's a decent fellow, and it's a pity to see him wasting his life in here.' That's just what I said to myself. As for that other fellow. He's no good. He's a liar. He'll go back again to his school or maybe somewhere else. But neither you nor I are fit to be respectable citizens. The two of us were born for the road, towny. Only you never had the courage of your convictions."

The tramp went to the door and spat. Deignan had been looking at him in wonder while he was talking and now he shifted his position restlessly and furrowed his forehead.

"I can't follow you," he said nervously and he opened his mouth to continue, when again he suddenly remembered that the man was a tramp and that it would not be good form to argue with him on matters of moral conduct.

"Of course ye can't," said the tramp, shuffling back to his position. Then he stuck his hands within his sleeves and shifted his tobacco to his other cheek. "I know why you can't follow me. You're a Catholic, you believe in Jesus Christ and the Blessed Virgin and the priests and a heaven hereafter. You like to be called respectable and to pay your debts. You were born a free man like myself, but you didn't have the courage . . ."

"Look here, man," cried Deignan in a shocked and angry voice, "stop talking that rubbish. You have been very kind about—er—cigarettes and food, but I can't allow you to blaspheme our holy religion in my presence. Horrid. Ugh."

The tramp laughed noiselessly. There was silence for several moments. Then the tramp went up to Deignan, shook him fiercely by the right arm and shouted in his ear, "You're the biggest fool I ever met." Then he laughed aloud and went back to his place. Deignan began to think that the tramp was mad and grew calm and said nothing.

"Listen here," said the tramp. "I was born disreputable. My mother was a fisherman's daughter and my lawful father was a farm labourer, but my real father was a nobleman and I knew it when I was ten years old. That's what gave me a disreputable outlook on life. My father gave mother money to educate me, and of course she wanted to make me a priest. I said to myself, I might as well be one thing as another. But at the age of twenty-three when I was within two years of ordination a servant girl had a child and I got expelled. She followed me, but I deserted her after six months. She lost her looks after the birth of the child. I never clapped eyes on her or the child since." He paused and giggled. Deignan bit his lip and his face contorted with disgust.

"I took to the road then," said the tramp. "I said to

myself that it was a foolish game trying to do anything in this world but eat and sleep and enjoy the sun and the earth and the sea and the rain. That was twenty-two years ago. And I'm proud to say that I never did a day's work since and never did a fellow-man an injury. That's my religion and it's a good one. Live like the birds, free. That's the only way for a free man to live. Look at yourself in a looking-glass. I'm ten years older than you and yet you look old enough to be my father. Come, man, take to the road with me today. I know you're a decent fellow, so I'll show you the ropes. In six months from now you'll forget you were ever a pauper or a clerk. What d'ye say?"

Deignan mused, looking at the ground.

"Anything would be better than this," he muttered. "But . . . Good Lord, becoming a tramp! I may have some chance of getting back to respectable life from here, but once I became a tramp I should be lost."

"Lost? What would you lose?"

Deignan shrugged his shoulders.

"I might get a job. Somebody might discover me here. Somebody might die. Anything might happen. But if I went on the road . . ." He shrugged his shoulders again.

"So you prefer to remain a pauper?" said the tramp with an impudent, half-contemptuous grin. Deignan winced and he felt a sudden mad longing grow within his head to do something mad and reckless.

"You're a fine fellow," continued the tramp, "you prefer to rot in idleness here with old men and useless wrecks to coming out into the free air. What man! Pull yerself together and come over now with me and apply for yer discharge. We'll foot it out together down south. What d'ye say?"

"By Jove, I think I will!" cried Deignan with a gleam

in his eyes. He began to trot excitedly around the shed, going to the door and looking up at the sky, and coming back again and looking at the ground, fidgeting with his hands and feet. "D'ye think, would it be all right?" he kept saying to the tramp.

"Sure it will be all right," the tramp kept answering. "Come on with me to the ward master and ask for your discharge."

But Deignan would not leave the shed. He had never in all his life been able to come to a decision on an important matter.

"Do you think, would it be all right?" he kept saying.

"Oh damn it and curse it for a story," said the tramp at last, "stay where you are and good day to you. I'm off."

He shuffled out of the shed and across the yard. Deignan put out his hand and took a few steps forward.

"I say—" he began and then stopped again. His brain was in a whirl thinking of green fields, mountain rivers, hills clad in blue mists, larks singing over clover fields, but something made him unable to loosen his legs, so that they could run after the tramp.

"I say—" he began again, and then he stopped and his face shivered and beads of sweat came out on his forehead.

He could not make up his mind.

MARY LAVIN

Lilacs

"THAT dunghill isn't doing anybody any harm and it's not going out of where it is as long as I'm in this house!" said Phelim Molloy.

"But if it could only be put somewhere else," said his wife Ros, "and not right under the window of the room where we eat our bit of food!"

"Didn't you tell me, yourself, a minute ago, you could smell it from the other end of the town? If that's the case I don't see what's going to be the good in moving it from one side of the yard to the other."

"What I don't see," said his daughter Kate, "is the need in us dealing in dung at all."

"There you are!" said Phelim. "There you are! I knew all along that was what you had in the back of your mind; both of you; and the one inside too!"—he beckoned backwards with his head towards the door behind him. "You wanted to be rid of it altogether, not just to shift it from one place to another. Why on earth can't women speak out what they mean? That's a thing always puzzled me."

"Leave Stacy out of it, Phelim," said Ros; "Stacy has one of her headaches."

"And what gave it to her I'd like to know?" said Phelim. "I'm supposed to think it was the smell of the dung gave it to her, but I know more than to be taken in by women's nonsensical notions."

"Don't talk so loud, Phelim," said Ros; "she might be asleep."

"It's a great wonder any of you can sleep a wink atall any night with the smell of that poor harmless heap of dung, out there, that's bringing in good money week after week."

He turned to his daughter.

"It paid for your education at a fine boarding-school."

He turned to Ros.

"And it paid for Stacy's notions about the violin and the piano, both of which is rotting within there in the room; and not a squeak of a tune ever I heard out of the one or other of them since the day they came into the house!"

"He won't give in," said Ros to her daughter. "We may as well keep our breath."

"You may as well," said Phelim. "That's a true thing anyway." He went over to the yard door. When he opened the door the faint odor of stale manure that hung already about the kitchen was thickened by a hot odor of new manure from the yard. Kate followed her father to the door and banged it shut after him.

As the steel taps on Phelim's shoes rang on the cobbles the two women stood at the window looking out at him. He took up a big yard brush made of twigs tied to a stick with leather thongs, and he started to brush up dry clots of manure that had fallen from the carts as they travelled from the gate to the dung trough. The dung trough itself was filled to the top and moisture from the manure was running in yellow streaks down the sides. The manure was brown and it was stuck all over with bright stripes of yellow straw.

"You'll have to keep at him, Mother," said Kate.

"There's not much use," said Ros.

"Something will have to be done. That's all about it!" said Kate. "Only last night at the concert in the Town Hall, just after the lights went down, I heard the new people, that took the bakehouse across the street, telling someone that they couldn't open a window since they came to the town with the terrible smell that was coming from somewhere; I could have died with shame, Mother. I didn't hear what answer they got but when the lights went up for the interval I saw they were sitting beside Mamie Murtagh, and you know what that one would be likely to say! My whole pleasure in the evening was spoiled, I can assure you."

"You take things too much to heart, Kate," said Ros. "There's Stacy inside there and if it wasn't for the smell of it I don't believe she'd mind us having it atall. She says to me sometimes, 'Wouldn't it be lovely, Mother, if there was a smell of lilacs every time we opened the door?' "

"Stacy makes me tired," said Kate, "with her talk about lilacs and lilacs! What does she ever do to try and improve things?"

"She's very timid," said Ros.

"That's all the more reason," said Kate, "my father would listen to her if she'd only speak to him."

"Stacy would never have the heart to cross anyone."

"Stacy's a fool."

"It's the smell that gives her the headaches all the same," said Ros. "Ever since she came home from boarding-school she's been getting her headaches every Wednesday regular the very minute the first cartload comes in across the yard."

"Isn't that what I'm saying!" said Kate impatiently, taking down a brown raincoat from a peg behind the door. "I'm going out for a walk and I won't be back till that smell has died down a bit. You can tell him that too, if he's looking for me."

When Kate went out Ros took down a copper tea caddy from the dresser and threw a few grains of tea into a brown earthen teapot. Then she poured a long stream of boiling water into the teapot from the great sooty kettle that hung over the flames. She poured out a cup of the tea and put sugar and milk in it, and a spoon. She didn't bother with a saucer and she took the cup over to the window and set it on the sill to cool while she watched Phelim sweeping in the yard.

In her heart there seemed to be a dark clot of malignance towards him because of the way he thwarted them over the dunghill. But as she looked out at him he put his hand to his back every once in a while, and Ros felt the black clot thinning away. Before the tea was cool enough to swallow, her blood was running bright and free in her veins again and she was thinking of the days when he used to call her by the old name.

She couldn't rightly remember when it was she first started calling herself Ros, or whether it was Phelim started it. Or it might have been someone outside the family altogether. But it was a good name no matter where it came from, a very suitable name for an old woman. It would be only foolishness to go on calling her Rose after she was faded and all dried up. She looked at her hands. They were thin as claws. She went over to the yard door.

"There's tea in the teapot, Phelim," she called out, and she left the door open. She went into the room where the two girls slept.

"Will I take you in a nice cup of nice hot tea, Stacy?" she said, leaning over the big bed.

"Is it settled?" said Stacy, sitting up.

"No," said Ros, pulling across the curtain, "it's to stay where it is."

"I hope he isn't upset?" said Stacy.

"No. He's sweeping the yard," said Ros, "and there's a hot cup of tea in the teapot for him if he likes to take it. You're a good girl, Stacy. How's your poor head?"

"I wouldn't want to upset him," said Stacy. "My head is a bit better. I think I'll get up."

It was, so, to Stacy that Ros turned on the night Phelim was taken bad with the bright pain low in the small of his back. When he died in the early hours of the morning, Ros kept regretting that she had crossed him over the dunghill.

"You have no call to regret anything, Mother," said Stacy. "You were ever and always calling him in out of the yard for cups of tea, morning, noon, and night. I often heard you, days I'd have one of my headaches. You've no call at all for regret."

"Why wouldn't I call him in to a cup of tea on a cold day?" said Ros. "There's no thanks for that. He was the best man that ever lived."

"You did all you could for him, Mother," said Kate, "and there's no need to be moaning and carrying on like that!"

"Let you not say anything," said Ros. "It was you was the one was always at me to talk to him about the dunghill. I wish I never crossed him."

"That was the only thing you ever crossed him over, Mother," said Stacy, "and the smell was really very hard to put up with."

Phelim was laid out in the parlor beyond the kitchen. He was coffined before the night but the lid was left off the coffin. Ros and the girls stayed up all night in the room. The neighbours stayed in the house but they sat in the kitchen where they threw sods of turf on the fire when they were needed and threw handfuls of tea leaves into the teapot now and again, and brought tea in to the Molloys.

Kate and Stacy sat one each side of their mother and mourned the man they were looking at, lying dead in a sheaf of undertaker linen crimp. They mourned him as

LILACS

they knew him for the last ten years, a heavy man with a red face who was seldom seen out of his big red rubber boots.

Ros mourned the Phelim of the red rubber boots but she mourned many another Phelim. She mourned him back beyond the time his face used to flush up when he went out in the air. She mourned him the time he never put a hat on when he was going out in the yard. She mourned him when his hair was thick although it was greying at the sides. She mourned him when he wore a big moustache sticking out stiff on each side. But most of all she mourned him for the first time when he had no hair on his face at all, and when his cheeks were always glossy from being out in the weather. That was the time he had to soap down his curls. That was the time he led her in a piece off the road when they were coming from Mass one Sunday.

"Rose," he said. "I've been thinking. There's a pile of money to be made out of manure. I've been thinking that if I got a cart and collected a bit here and a bit there for a few pence I might be able to sell in big loads for a lot more than I paid for it."

"Is that so?" she said. She remembered it well.

"And do you know what I've been thinking too?" he said. "I've been thinking that if I put by what I saved I might have enough by this time next year to take a lease of the little cottage on the Mill Road."

"The one with the church window in the gable end?" she said.

"And the two fine sheds," he said.

"The one with the ivy all down one side?" she said, but she knew well the one he meant.

"That's the very one," said Phelim. "How would you like to live there? With me, I mean."

"Manure has a terrible dirty smell," she said.

"You could plant flowers, maybe."

"I'd have to plant ones with a strong perfume," she said, "rockets and mignonette."

"Any ones you like. You'd have nothing else to do all day."

She remembered well how innocent he was then, for all that he was twenty, and thinking to make a man of himself by taking a wife. His face was white like a girl's, with patches of pink on his cheeks. He was handsome. There were prettier girls by far than her would have given their eyes to be led in a piece off the road, just for a bit of talk and gassing from Phelim Molloy— let alone a real proposal.

"Will you, Rose?" said Phelim. "There's a pile of money in manure, even if the people around these parts don't set any store by it."

The colour was blotching over his cheeks the way the wind blotched a river. He was nervous. He was putting his foot up on the bar of the gate where they were standing and the next minute he was taking it down again. She didn't like the smell of manure, then, any more than after, but she liked Phelim.

"It's dirty stuff," she said. And that was her last protest.

"I don't know so much about that," said Phelim. "There's a lot in the way you think about things. Do you know, Rose, sometimes when I'm driving along the road I look down at the dung that's dried into the road and I think to myself that you couldn't ask much prettier than it, the way it flashes by under the horses' feet in pale gold rings." Poor Phelim! There weren't many men would think of things like that.

"All right, so," she said. "I will."

"You will?" said Phelim. "You will!"

The sun spilled down just then and the dog-roses swayed back and forwards in the hedge.

"Kiss me so," he said.

"Not here!" she said. The people were passing on the road and looking down at them. She got as pink as the pink dog-roses.

"Why not?" said Phelim. "If you're going to marry me you must face up to everything. You must do as I say always. You must never be ashamed of anything."

She hung her head but he put his hand under her chin.

"If you don't kiss me right now, Rose Magarry, I'll have nothing more to do with you."

The way the candles wavered round the corpse was just the way the dog-roses wavered in the wind that day.

Ros shed tears for the little dog-roses. She shed tears for the blushes she had in her cheeks. She shed tears for the soft kissing lips of young Phelim. She shed tears for the sunny splashes of gold dung on the roads. And her tears were quiet and steady, like the crying of the small thin rains in windless weather.

When the cold white morning came at last the neighbours got up and stamped their feet on the flags outside the door. They went home to wash and get themselves ready for the funeral.

When the funeral was over Ros came back to the lonely house between her two daughters. Kate looked well in black. It made her thinner and her high colour looked to advantage. Stacy looked the same as ever. The chairs and tables were all pushed against the wall since they took the coffin out. One or two women stayed behind and there were hot tea and cold meat. There was a smell of guttered-out candles and a heavy smell of lilies.

Stacy drew in a deep breath.

"Oh, Kate!" she said. "Smell!"

Kate gave her a harsh look.

"Don't remind her," she said, "or she'll be moaning again."

But Ros was already looking out in the yard and the tears were streaming from her eyes again down the easy runnels of her dried and wrinkled face.

"Oh, Phelim," she said. "Why did I ever cross you? Wasn't I the bad old woman to cross you over a little heap of dirt and yellow straw?"

Kate bit her lip.

"Don't take any notice of her," she said to the women. She turned to Stacy. "Take in our hats and coats," she said, "and put a sheet over them." She turned back to the women. "Black is a divil to take the dust," she said, "and a divil to clean." But all the time she was speaking she was darting glances at Ros.

Ros was moaning louder.

"You're only tormenting yourself, Mother," she said. "He was a good man, one of the best, but he was an obstinate man over that dunghill, so you've no call to be upsetting yourself on the head of that!"

"It was out of the dung he made his first few shillings."

"How long ago was that!" said Kate. "And was that any reason for persecuting us all for the last five years with the smell of it coming up under the window, you might say?"

"I think we'll be going, Kate," said the women.

"We're much obliged to you for your kindness in our trouble," said Ros and Kate together.

The women went out quietly.

"Are they gone?" said Stacy, coming out of the inside room, looking out the window at the women going down the road.

"Is it the dunghill you were talking about?" she said. "Because tomorrow's Wednesday!"

"I know that," said Ros.

"The smell isn't so bad today, is it?" said Stacy. "Or was it the smell of the flowers drove it out?"

"I wish to goodness you'd look at it in a more serious light, Stacy," said Kate. "It's not alone the smell of it, but the way people look at us when they hear what we deal in."

"It's nothing to be ashamed of," said Ros. "It was honest dealing, and that's more than most in this town can say!"

"What do you know about the way people talk, Mother?" said Kate. "If you were away at boarding-school, like Stacy and me, you'd know, then, what it felt like to have to admit your father was making his money out of horse dung."

"I don't see what great call was on you to tell them!" said Ros.

"Listen to that!" said Kate. "It's easily seen you were never at boarding-school, Mother."

Stacy had nearly forgotten the boarding-school, but she remembered a bit about it then.

"We used to say our father dealt in fertilizer," she said. "But someone looked it up in a dictionary and found out it was only a fancy name for manure."

"Your father would have laughed at that," said Ros.

"It's not so funny at all," said Kate.

"Your father had a wonderful sense of humour," said Ros.

"He was as obstinate as a rock, that's one thing," said Kate.

"When we knew that was the case," said Ros, "why did we cross him? We might have known he wouldn't give in. I wish I never crossed him."

The old woman folded her knotted hands and sat down by the fire in the antique attitude of grieving womankind.

Kate could talk to Stacy when they were in the far corner of the kitchen getting down the cups and saucers from the dresser.

"I never thought she was so old-looking."

"She looked terribly old at the graveside," said Stacy. "Make her take her tea by the fire."

"Will you drink down a nice cup of tea, here by the fire, Mother?" said Stacy, going over to the old woman.

Ros took the cup out of the saucer and put the spoon into it. "Leave that back," she said, pushing away the saucer. She took the cup over to the window-sill.

"It only smells bad on hot days," she said, looking out.

"But summer is ahead of us!" said Kate, spinning round sharply and looking at the old woman.

"It is and it isn't," said Ros. "In the January of the year it's as true to say you have put the summer behind you as it is to say it is ahead of you."

"Mother?"

Kate came over and, pushing aside the geranium on the window-ledge, she leaned her arm there and stared back into her mother's face.

"Mother," she said. "You're not, by any chance, thinking of keeping on the dunghill?"

"I'm thinking of one thing only," said Ros. "I'm thinking of him and he young, with no hair on his lip, one day—and the next day, you might say, him lying within on the table and the women washing him for his burial."

LILACS

"I wish you'd give over tormenting yourself, Mother."

"I'm not tormenting myself atall," said Ros. "I like thinking about him."

"He lived to a good age," said Kate.

"I suppose you'll be saying that about me one of these days," said Ros, "and it no time ago I was sitting up straight behind the horse's tail, on my father's buggy, with my white blouse on me and my gold chain dangling and my hair halfway down my back. The road used to be flashing by under the clittering horse-hooves, and the gold dung dried into bright gold rings."

"Stacy," said Kate, that night when they were in bed, "I don't like to see her going back over the old days like she was all day. It's a bad sign. I hope we won't be laying her alongside Father one of these days."

"Oh, Kate," said Stacy, "don't remind me of poor Father. All the time she was talking about crossing him over the dung I was thinking of the hard things I was saying against him the last time my head was splitting and he was leading in the clattering carts over the cobblestones and the dirty smell of the dung rising up on every wind."

"You've no call to torment yourself, Stacy," said Kate.

"That's what you said to Mother."

"It's true what I say, no matter which of you I say it to. There was no need in having the dunghill atall. It was nothing but obstinacy. Start to say your beads now and you'll sleep before you've said the first decade. And don't be twitching the clothes off me. Move over."

It seemed to Stacy that she had only begun the second decade of her beads, when her closed eyes began to ache with a hard white light shining down on them without pity. She couldn't sleep with that hard light on her eyes. She couldn't open her eyes either, because the light pressed down so weightily on her lids. Perhaps, as Kate had said, it was morning and she had fallen asleep? Stacy forced her lids open. The window square was blinding white with hard venomous daylight. The soft night had gone. There was another day for them, and Father was out in the green churchyard where the long grass was always wet even in yellow sunlight.

Stacy lay cold. Her eyes were wide and scopeless and her feet were touching against the chilled iron rail at the foot of the bed. She looked around the whitewashed room and she looked out of the low window, that was shaped like the window of a church, at the cold crinkled edges of the corrugated sheds. Stacy longed for it to be summer, though summer was a long way off. She longed for the warm winds to be daffing through the trees and the dallops of grass to be dry enough for flopping down on, right where you were in the middle of a field. And she longed for it to be the time when the tight hard beads of the lilacs looped out into the soft pear shapes of blossom, in other people's gardens.

And then, as soft as the scent of lilac steals through early summer air, the thought came slowly into Stacy's mind that poor dear Father, sleeping in the long gravegrasses, might not mind them having lilacs now where the dunghill used to be. For it seemed already to Stacy that the dunghill was gone now that poor Father himself was gone. She curled up in the blankets and closed her eyes again, and so it was a long time before she knew for certain that there was a sound of knocking on the big yard gate and a sound of a horse shaking his brass trappings and pawing the cobbles with his forefoot. She raised her head a little off the pillow. There was the sound of a wooden gatewing flapping back against the wall. There was a rattle of horse-hooves and steel-bound cartwheels going over the cobbles. "Kate!

LILACS

Kate!" she shouted, and she shook Kate till she wakened with a flush of frightened red to her cheeks. "Kate," she said, "I thought I heard Father leading in a load of manure across the yard!"

Kate's flush deepened.

"Stacy, if you don't control yourself, your nerves will get the better of you completely. Where will you be then?" But as Kate spoke they heard the dray board of a cart being loosened in the yard and chains fell down on the cobbles with a ringing sound.

Kate sprang out of bed, throwing back the clothes right over the brass footrail, and left Stacy shivering where she lay, with the freezing air making snaps at her legs and her arms and her white neck. Kate stared out of the window.

"I knew this would happen," she said, "I could have told you!" Stacy got out of bed slowly and came over across the cold floor in her bare feet. She pressed her face against the icy glass. She began to cry in a thin wavering way like a child. Her nose was running, too—like a child's.

In the yard Ros was leading in a second cart of manure, and talking in a high voice to the driver of the empty cart that was waiting its turn to pass out. She was dressed in her everyday clothes that weren't black, but brown—the dark primitive colour of the earth and the earth's decaying refuse. The cart she led was piled high with rude brown manure, stuck all over with bright stripes of yellow straw, and giving off a hot steam. The steam rose up unevenly like thumby fingers of a clumsy hand and it reached for the faces of the staring women that were indistinct behind the fog their breaths put on the glass.

"Get dressed!" said Kate. "We'll go down together."

Ros was warming her hands by the fire when they

went into the kitchen. There was a strong odour of manure. Kate said nothing but she went over and banged the yard door shut. Stacy said nothing. Stacy stood. Ros looked up.

"Well?" said Ros.

"Well?" said Kate, after her, and she said it louder than Ros had said it.

The two women faced each other across the deal table. Stacy sat down on the chair that Ros had just left, and she began to cry in her thin wavy voice.

"Shut up, Stacy!" said Kate.

"Say what you have to say, Kate," said Ros, and in the minds of all three of them there was the black thought that bitter words could lash out endlessly, now that there was no longer a man in the house to come in across the yard with a heavy boot and stand in the doorway slapping his hands together and telling them to quit chewing the rag and lay the table for the meal.

"Say what you have to say," said Ros.

"You know what we have to say," said Kate.

"Well don't say it, so," said Ros, "if that's all it is." She went towards the door.

"Mother!" Stacy went after her and caught the corner of her mother's old skirt. "You were always saying it would be nice if it was once out of there."

"Isn't that my only regret, Stacy?" said Ros. "That was the only thing I crossed him over."

"But you were right, Mother."

"Was I?" said Ros, but not in the voice of one asking a question. "Sometimes an old woman talks about things she knows nothing about. Your father always said it wasn't right to be ashamed of anything that was honest. Another time he said money was money, no matter where it came from. That was a true thing to say. He was always saying true things. Did you hear the priest

LILACS

yesterday when we were coming away from the grave? 'God help all poor widows!' he said."

"What has that got to do with what we're talking about?" said Kate.

"A lot," said Ros. "Does it never occur to the two of you that it mightn't be so easy for three women, and no man, to keep a house going and fires lighting and food on the table; to say nothing at all about dresses and finery?"

"I suppose that last is meant for me!" said Kate.

"That's just like what Father himself would say," said Stacy, but no one heard her. Kate had suddenly moved over near her mother and was leaning with her back against the white rim of the table. When she spoke it was more kindly.

"Did you find out how his affairs were fixed, Mother?" she said.

"I did," said Ros and she looked at her daughter with cold eyes. "I did," she said again, and that was all she said as she went out the door.

The smell that came in the door made Stacy put her arm over her face and bury her nose in the crook of her elbow. But Kate drew herself up and her fine firm bosom swelled. She breathed in a strong breath.

"Pah!" she said. "How I hate it!"

"Think if it was a smell of lilacs!" said Stacy. "Lovely lilacs."

"I wish you'd stop crying," said Kate. "You can't blame her, after all, for not wanting to go against him and he dead. It's different for us."

Stacy's face came slowly out of the crook of her arm. She had a strange wondering look.

"Maybe when you and I are all alone, Kate?" she said, and then as she realized what she was saying she put her arm up quickly over her face in fright. "Not that I meant any harm," she said. "Poor Mother, poor Mother."

Kate looked at her with contempt.

"You should learn to control your tongue, Stacy. And in any case I wish you wouldn't be always talking as if we were never going to get married."

"I sometimes think we never will," said Stacy.

Kate shook out the tablecloth with a sharp flap in the warm air.

"Maybe *you* won't," she said. "I don't believe you will, as a matter of fact. But I will." She threw the tablecloth across the back of a chair and looked into the small shaving mirror belonging to their father that still hung on the wall.

In the small mirror Kate could see only her eyes and nose, unless she stood back far from it. And when she did that, as well as seeing herself, she could see the window and she could see through the window, the yard and any one in it. And so, after she had seen that she looked just as she thought she would look, she stepped back a little from the glass and began to follow the moving reflections of her mother that she saw in the glass. There seemed a greater significance in seeing her mother in this unreal way than there would have been in seeing her by looking directly out the window. The actions of Ros as she gathered up the fallen fragments of dung seemed to be symbolic of a great malevolent energy directed against her daughters.

"I didn't need to be so upset last night going to bed," she said to Stacy bitterly. "There's no fear of her going after my poor father. She's as hardy as a tree!"

But Ros Molloy wasn't cut out to be a widow. If Phelim had been taken from her before the dog-roses had faded on their first summer together she could

LILACS

hardly have moaned him more than she did, an old woman, cold and shivering, tossing in her big brass bed all alone.

The girls eased her work for her at every turn of the hand, but on Wednesday mornings they let her get up alone to open the gates at six o'clock and let in the carts of manure. But they didn't sleep.

As often as not Stacy got up, onto the cold floor in her bare feet, and stood at the window looking out. She crossed her arms over her breast to keep in what warmth she had taken from the blankets, and she told Kate what was going on outside.

"Did she look up at the window?" Kate asked every morning.

"No," Stacy said.

"Get back into bed so, and don't give her the satisfaction of knowing you're watching her."

"Kate."

"What?"

"You don't think I ought to slip down and see if the kettle is boiling for her when she comes in, do you, Kate?"

"You know what I think," said Kate. "Will you get back into bed and not be standing there freezing!"

"She has only her thin coat on," said Stacy.

Kate leaned up on one elbow, carefully humping up the clothes with her, pegged to her shoulder.

"By all the pulling and rattling that I hear, she's doing enough to keep up her circulation, without her having any clothes atall on her."

"She shouldn't be lifting things the way she is," said Stacy.

"And whose fault is it if she is?" said Kate, slumping back into the hollows of the bed. "Get back here into bed you, and stop watching out at her doing things there's no need in her doing atall. That's just what she wants; to have someone watching out at her."

"She's not looking this way at all, Kate."

"Oh, isn't she? Let me tell you what it is, that woman has eyes in the back of her head!"

"Oh, Kate," said Stacy and she ran over to the bed and threw herself in across Kate, sobbing. Kate lay still for a minute listening to her and then she leaned up on her other elbow and humped the clothes up over the other shoulder. Stacy slept between her and the wall. "What in the name of God ails you now?" she asked.

"Don't you remember, Kate? That's what she used to say to us when we were small. She used to stand up straight and stiff, with her gold chain on her, and say that we had better not do anything wrong behind her back because she had eyes in the back of her head."

Kate flopped back again.

"We all have to get old," she said.

"I know," said Stacy, "but all the same you'd hate to see the gold chain dangling down below her waist, like I did the other day, when she took it out of her black box and put it on her."

Kate sat up again.

"She's not wearing it, is she?"

"She put it back in the box."

Kate flopped back once more. Her face was flushed from the sudden jerks she gave in the cold morning air.

"I should hope she put it back," she said, "that chain is worth a lot of money since the price of gold went up."

Stacy lay still with her eyes closed. There was something wrong, but she didn't know just what it was. All she wanted was to get the dunghill taken away out of the yard and a few lilacs put there instead. But it seemed as if there were more than that bothering Kate.

LILACS

She wondered what it could be? She had always thought herself and Kate were the same, the same way of looking at things and that, but lately Kate seemed to be changed.

Kate was getting old. Stacy took no account of age but Kate was getting old. Kate took account of everything. Stacy might have been getting old too, if she was taking account of things, but she wasn't. It seemed no length ago to Stacy since they came home from the convent. She couldn't tell you what year it was. She was never definite about anything. Her head was filled with nonsense, Kate said.

"What do you think about when you're lying inside there with a headache?" Kate wanted to know oftentimes.

"Things," Stacy said.

She would only be thinking of things; this thing and that thing; things of no account; silly things. Like the times she lay in bed and thought of a big lilac tree sprouting up through the boards of the floor, bending the big bright nails, sending splinters of wood flying till they hit off the window-panes. The tree always had big pointed bunches of lilac blossom all over it; more blossoms than leaves. That just showed, Stacy thought, what nonsense it was. You never saw more blossoms than leaves. But the blossoms weighed down towards her where she lay shivering, and they touched her face.

It was nonsense like that that went dawdling through her mind one morning, when the knocking at the gate outside kept up for so long that she began to think her mother must have slept it out.

"Do you think she slept it out, Kate?"

"That might teach her," said Kate.

"Maybe I ought to slip down and let them in?"

"Stay where you are."

But Stacy had to get up.

"I'll just look in her door," she said.

Stacy went out and left the door open.

"Hurry back and shut the door," said Kate, calling after her.

But Stacy didn't hurry. Stacy didn't come back either.

"Stacy! Stacy!" Kate called out.

She lifted her head off her pillow to listen.

"Stacy? Is there anything wrong?"

Kate sat up in the cold.

"Stacy! Can't you answer a person?"

Kate got out on the floor.

She found Stacy lying in a heap at her mother's bedside and she hardly needed to look to know that Ros was dead. She as good as knew—she said afterwards—that Stacy would pass out the minute there was something unpleasant.

No wonder Stacy had no lines on her face. No wonder she looked a child, in spite of her years. Stacy got out of a lot of worry, very neatly, by just flopping off in a faint. Poor Ros was washed, and her eyes got shut and her habit put on her, before Stacy came round to her senses again.

"It looks as if you're making a habit of this," said Kate, when Stacy fainted again, in the cemetery this time, and didn't have to listen, as Kate did, to the sound of the sods clodding down on the coffin.

"But I did hear them, Kate," Stacy protested. "I did. I heard them distinctly. But I was a bit confused in my mind still at the time and I thought it was the sound of the horse-hooves clodding along the road."

"What horse-hooves? Are you going mad?"

"You remember, Kate. Surely you remember. The ones Mother was always telling us about. Her hair hung down her back and her gold chain dangled, and while she was watching the road flashing by under the clittering horse-hooves she used to think how pretty the gold dung was, dried into bright disks."

"That reminds me!" said Kate. "Tomorrow is Wednesday."

Although Stacy's face was wet with the moisture of her thin scalding tears, she smiled and clasped her hands together.

"Oh, Kate!" she said; and then, in broad daylight, standing in the middle of the floor in her new serge mourning dress that scraped the back of her neck all the time, she saw a heavy lilac tree nod at her with its lovely pale blooms bobbing.

"Which of us will get up?" Kate was saying, and watching Stacy while she was saying it.

"Get up?"

"To let them in."

"To let who in?"

"Who do you think? The men with the manure, of course." Kate spoke casually but when she looked at Stacy she stamped her foot on the floor.

"Don't look so stupid, Stacy. There isn't any time now to let them know. We can't leave them hammering at the gate after coming miles, maybe. Someone will have to go down and open the gate for them."

When Stacy heard the first rap on the gate she hated to think of Kate's having to get up.

"I'll get up, Kate," she said. "Stay where you are."

But she got no answer. Kate was walking out across the yard at the time, dressed and ready, and she had the gate thrown back against the wall before the men had time to raise their hands for a second rap.

Stacy dressed as quickly as she could, to have the kettle on as a surprise for Kate. It was the least she might do.

But when Stacy went down the fire was blazing up the chimney and there was a trace of tea in a cup on the table. Poor Kate, thought Stacy, she must have been awake half the night in case she'd let the time slip. Wasn't she great! Stacy felt very stupid. She was no good at all. Kate was great. Here was their great moment. Here was the time for getting rid of a nuisance, and if it was up to her to tell the men not to bring any more cartloads she honestly believed she'd be putting it off for weeks and be afraid to do it in the end, maybe. But Kate was great. Kate made no bones about it. Kate didn't say a word about how she was going to do it, or what she was going to say. She just slipped out of bed and made a cup of tea and went out in the yard and took command of everything. Kate was great.

"What did you say?" asked Stacy, when Kate came in.

"How do you mean?" said Kate and looked at her irritably. "What on earth gave you such a high colour at this hour of the morning? I never saw you with so much colour in your face before."

But the colour was fading out already.

"Didn't you tell them not to bring any more?" she asked.

Kate looked as if she were going to say something, and then she changed her mind. Then she changed her mind again, or else she thought of something different to say.

"I didn't like to give them the hard word," she said.

Stacy flushed again.

"I see what you mean," she said: "Ease off quietly?"

"Yes," said Kate. "Yes, we could do that. Or I was thinking of another plan."

Stacy knelt up on a hard deal chair and gripped the back of it. There was something very exciting in hearing Kate talk and plan. It gave Stacy a feeling that they had a great responsibility and authority and that they were standing on their own feet.

"You mightn't like the idea," said Kate, "at first."

"Oh, I'm sure I'll love it," said Stacy.

"It's this then," said Kate. "I was thinking last night that instead of doing away with the dunghill we should take in twice as much manure for a while till we made twice as much money, and then we could get out of this little one-story house altogether."

Stacy was looking out the window.

"Well?" said Kate.

Stacy laid her face against the glass.

"Oh for goodness' sake stop crying," said Kate; "I was only making a suggestion." She began to clatter the cups on the dresser. She looked back at Stacy. "I thought, you see, that after a bit we might move over to Rowe House. It's been idle a long time. I don't think they'd want very much for it, and it's two-story, what's more, with a front entrance and steps going up to the hall door."

Stacy dried her face in the crook of her arm and began to put back the cups that Kate had taken down from the dresser, because the table was already set. Her face had the strained and terrible look that people with weak natures have when they force their spirits beyond their bounds.

"I'll never leave the house," she said; "never as long as I live."

"Stay in it, so!" said Kate. "And rot in it for all I care. But I'm getting out of it first chance I get! And that dunghill isn't stirring from where it is until I have a fine fat dowry out of it."

She went into the bedroom and banged the door, and Stacy sat down looking at the closed door. Then she looked out the window. Then she got up and ran her hand down over the buttons of her bodice. They were all closed properly. She took the tea caddy and began to put two careful spoonfuls of tea into the teapot. When the tea was some minutes made, she went over to the closed door. Once again she ran her hand down the buttons of her bodice; and then she called Kate.

"Your tea is getting cold," she said, and while she waited for an answer her heart beat out its fear upon her hollow chest.

But Kate was in a fine good humour when she came out, with her arms piled up with dresses and hats and cardboard boxes covered with rose-scattered wallpaper. She left the things down on the window-sill and pulled her chair in to the table.

"Is this loaf bread or turnover?" she said. "It tastes very good. Sit down yourself, Stacy," and after a mouthful of the hot tea she nodded her head at the things on the window-sill.

"There's no point in having a room idle, is there?" she said. "I may as well move into Mother's room."

There was no more mention of the dunghill. Kate attended to it. Stacy didn't have her headaches as bad as she used to have them. Not giving in to them was the best cure yet. Kate was right. There was only a throbbing. It wasn't bad.

Stacy and Kate got on great. At least there was no fighting. But the house was as uneasy as a house where two women live alone. At night you felt it most. So Stacy was glad at the back of everything when Con O'Toole began dropping in, although she didn't like him and she thought the smell of stale tobacco that was all over the house next day was worse than the smell of the dung.

"Do you like the smell of his pipe, Kate?" said Stacy one day.

"I never noticed," said Kate.

"I think it's worse than the smell of the dung!" said Stacy with a gust of bravery.

"I thought we agreed on saying 'fertilizer' instead of that word you just used," said Kate, stopping up in the dusting.

"That was when we were at boarding-school!" said Stacy, going on with the dusting.

"I beg your pardon," said Kate, "it was when we were mixing with the right kind of people. I wish you wouldn't be so forgetful."

But next morning Kate came into the parlor when Stacy was nearly finished with the dusting. She threw out her firm chest and drew in a deep breath.

"Pah!" she said. "It *is* disgusting. I'll make him give up using it as soon as we take up residence at Rowe House. But don't say anything about it to him. He mightn't take it well. Of course I can say anything I like to him. He'll take anything from me. But it's better to wait till after we're married and not come on him with everything all at once."

That was the first Stacy heard about Kate's getting married, but of course if she had only thought about it she'd have seen the way the wind was blowing. But she took no account of anything.

After the first mention of the matter, however, Kate could hardly find time to talk about anything else, right up to the fine blowsy morning that she was hoisted up on the car by Con, in her new peacock blue outfit, and her mother's gold chain dangling. Stacy was almost squeezed out of the doorway by the crowd of well-wishers waving them off. They all came back into the house. Such a mess! Chairs pulled about! Crumbs on the cushions! Confetti! Wine spilled all over the carpet! And the lovely iced cake all cut into! Such a time as there would be cleaning it all up! And Stacy thought that when she'd be putting things back in their places would be a good time to make a few changes. That chair with the red plush would be better on the other side of the piano. And she'd leave the sofa out a bit from the wall.

"Will you be lonely, Miss Stacy?" said someone.

"You should get someone in, to keep you company, Miss Stacy," said someone else.

"At night anyway," they all said.

They were very kind. Stacy loved hearing them all making plans for her. It was so good-natured. But this was the first time she'd ever got a chance to make a few plans for herself, and she wished they'd hurry up and go.

They didn't stay so very long. They were soon all gone, except Jasper Kane. Jasper liked Stacy, apart from his being the family solicitor and knowing her father so well.

"Might I inquire, Miss Stacy, what is the first thing you're planning to do, now that you are your own mistress?"

Stacy went over to the window.

"I'm going to plant a few lilac trees, Mr. Kane," she said, because she felt she could trust him. Her father always did.

"Oh!" said Jasper, and he looked out the window too. "Where?" he said.

"There!" said Stacy, pointing out of the back window. "There where the dunghill is now." She drew a brave breath. "I'm getting rid of the dunghill, you see," she said.

Jasper stayed looking out of the window at the dunghill. Then he looked at Stacy. He was an old man.

"But what will you live on, Miss Stacy?" he said.

SEÁN O'FAOLÁIN

A Born Genius

I

PROUT LANE (better known as Little Hell) was wrapped in a softly waving veil of mist and Pat Lenihan, leaning against his doorpost, was staring into it; even as earlier in the afternoon when he had been caught by old Phillips, at the office window of the vinegar factory, staring down into the darkening marshes.

"Lenihan," he had raged, "if I came into this office twenty times a day I'd find you eating your pen with your gob to that window. What the blazes do you be looking at, anyway?"

And shoving up his glasses, he had peered out at the brown evening fog rising through the pollarded willows, mingling as it rose with the barely descending rain. Then he had looked back at Lenihan, and as if slightly in doubt of his clerk's sanity, he had left the room with a low, minatory "Get on with it."

Lenihan smiled to himself as he recalled the question. What had he been looking at, indeed, but at his boat—when it would be finished—chugging out between the forts at the harbour mouth, cutting through the waves and the mists over the open sea?

He was clerk to the old vinegar factory—an easy, even a pleasant job. There was not a great deal of work to be done; the factory was on the outskirts of the city, one might almost say in the country, and Phillips, the manager and owner, was easy to get on with. Besides, Lenihan knew he was not a very satisfactory clerk and not every employer would have put up with him. That afternoon incident at the window was typical. There were other times when Phillips had been known to roar up from the yard to the office window:

"Lenihan, will you stop that blasted singing?"

And the sweet, tenor voice, that like a thrush in full music had been trilling up and down the scales with swollen throat for the last half-hour, would fall silent in the middle of a run. Then old Phillips would sniff through his great red beak of a nose and with a sigh the workmen would take up their shovels or their hods again, and up in his office Lenihan would raise his shoulders as if to bear a sudden weight before he returned with a sigh to his ledgers.

Even the workmen knew he was not a satisfactory clerk. When they came to the office window on Saturday for the week's pay they might find him sweating with excitement and nervousness over a pile of notes and silver, counting the amounts over and over again, forgetting to which envelope each little pile belonged, making wrong calculations, and finally getting so utterly confused that the men themselves would have to come to his aid before he got it all correct.

In return he occasionally sang for them. If he passed by as they lay resting after the midday meal they would grasp his hands and sleeves and legs and beseech him for a song. They did not care what song he sang—anything so long as they heard him. Not that he always agreed: he would explain that a singer must be very careful of his voice, *so* careful. If he did sing, he would draw himself up, take the key from a tuning-fork, puff out his voice in a little cough, face the marsh, the sluggish stream, and the leaning poplars, as if they were an audience, and with as much care as if he were in the greatest theatre in the world, sing for the four or five old workers lying about him, all stained white with magnesia. He would give them "Flow On, Thou Silent

A BORN GENIUS

River," or "The Gypsy's Warning," which is, he explained, really a song for a contralto, or their favourite, the tenor's part from "The Moon Hath Raised Her Lamp Above" out of Benedict's *Lily of Killarney*. Gently he would sing:

> "Do not trust him, gentle maiden,
> Gentle maiden, trust him not . . ."

while the men swung their heads in time and winked at one another in delight and admiration.

> "Over in the green grave yonder,
> Lies the gypsy's only child . . .
> Soon she perished, now she's sleeping,
> In that cold and silent grave. . . ."

When he finished he would go away at once with a little bow and a military salute, blushing faintly if he overheard their praise as he went.

"Ah! God!" one would say. "He have a massive voice."

"A marvel!" they would reply in unison.

"But, of course," the first would lean forward to whisper confidentially, "he's a born genius!"

Only Flyer, his brother, would lean back very stiffly, silent as a waxwork image. Presently, he knew, they would turn to him for the latest news of Pat's doings, and then he would tell them—what matter if they had heard it all fifty times before. Meanwhile he sat silent, his two hands holding his paunch, his two swivel eyes gazing sadly into one another.

"Well, Flyer!" they ask at last. "What is he up to now?"

Before he began Flyer would shake his head mightily by way of emphasis, as if he were trying to shake his eyes straight or fix his head down properly into his shoulders.

"Pat," he whispers very solemnly and oracularly, "is

a marvel!" Then with a sudden roar he leans forward to them. "He's after painting two swans," he bellows dramatically, "on deh kitchen windas. Wan is facing wan way and d'oder is facing d'oder way. And I swear to God," Flyer continues with the gestures of an orator speaking to thousands, "I swear to God dis day"—here he looks both ways to the sky—"ye'd tink dey'd fly away while ye'd be looking at 'em. And what's more, he's after making a sunny-house outside o' deh winda, and he have geraniums, and lilies, and posies, and nasturtiums and I dunno what else put growin' dere. So dat so help me God dis day"—again Flyer implores the sky—"you'd tink deh swans was floatin' in a garden! And deh garden was floating in through deh winda! And dere was no winda! But you all flowers"—here he swims through the air with his outflung hands—"and all swans and all garden . . ."

He never finished his account of anything, his head taken by a kind of gigantic Vitus's dance and his eyes starting from his head. He was subnormal, the factory liar. Pat scarcely ever spoke to him, he was ashamed of him.

The men firmly believed Flyer's tales; wasn't there, at the back of the drying-shed where the white chunks of magnesia were stacked on shelves to cake, and had been, for years now, the monument he carved for his sister's grave? It was a huge block of grey vermicular stone which the rains of winter had begun to peel and crumble as if it were plaster. For almost a year he had toiled at it, day and night, in every spare moment, lying on his stomach on the cold stone, kneeling beside it on the clay, getting into all sorts of postures as he hacked away. For that year he never went to a concert or exercised his voice. He worked so hard that old Phillips, seeing him tapping away at the stone during the spare moments of the lunch-hour, used to sniff and say: "If you worked as hard as that for me, Lenihan, by George, you'd nearly be worth your hire!"

But when it was all ready except the inscription he had spoiled it. He went at his sister's name in a fury of impatience to be finished, working into the night by candlelight, with the bull-frogs croaking below him in the moon-blanched marsh. Then he stared in horror at the result: all the S's and N's were upside down—it read like Russian script. A month later he began at the name again, carving out a horizontal piece to obliterate what he had done. This time, he got all the S's and N's right, but by some accursed fate he forgot everything else, and the name now read:

SUSANNANAN LENINAN.

He never completed his task and the monument now lay—as he said bitterly, like a huge letter-box to Heaven for "Susannanan Leninan"—covered with a sack, forgotten, unfinished behind the drying-sheds. And now, wasn't he making a motor-boat!

The veils of mist continued to float in from the sea, as solid as a fog. With a sigh he closed the door and returned to the fire. Summer was ending. He took up a piece of wood-carving that he had begun last winter and with a small gouge he scraped at the vein in a leaf. He had the house to himself—Flyer was boozing in the pub at the end of the lane and his mother was gone to the chapel to her Confraternity. He laid the piece of wood aside and lit a cigarette and hummed a bar or two from a song—Schubert's "Serenade." Then he turned to the grand piano, and when he had searched for and found the key and shook out the music, he dusted the worn keys with his silk handkerchief.

II

Directly opposite the narrow mouth of Little Hell, or so it appears to the eye, are the slopes of Montenotte —tonight no more than a crowd of winking lights hanging, like the stars, but in a lower darkness. From where she had stepped on a mound of ruins somewhere behind Prout Lane, Mrs. John Delaney looked across at those hundred faint lights of which at least a couple might be the windows of her home and the lamps at her lodge-gates. She could even distinguish the lay of her own road where the lamps curved in a steady series. Far down to the right, too, she could see through the mists another faint line of lights where the river swung out to meet the harbour, and she halted for an extra second to stare into the impenetrable darkness beyond all, from where the wind blew chill about her legs and blew the mist into her eyes and penetrated her furs. It would be hard for her to say which view of the harbour was more familiar to her—from this side of the city, a narrow ribbon of river threading between factory chimneys and the roofs of houses; from her garden, there across the valley, widening and narrowing to river-lochs, the great country-houses scattered deep in trees into which she could almost fling a pebble. For it was not really so long ago since, from a lane-way door not a mile from this lane, she had stood as a young girl looking at this self-same night-view, taking a breath of air after hours of practice at the piano, and at the "Jewel Song" from *Faust*, and "Absent," and "Flow On, Thou Silent River," and "The Gypsy's Warning," and all the rest of them, to be allowed to sing one of which was her reward for an hour's oh'ing and ah'ing at the scales. Leaning against a crumbling wall she hummed to herself:

> "Do not trust him, gentle maiden,
> Gentle maiden, trust him not . . .
> Soon she perished . . ."

She pulled herself up suddenly—at this rate she would not get her calls finished by midnight. She saw a solitary lamp ahead of her at the end of a passage and made for it; perhaps Ninety-Two B was at that end of the lane, and for the sixth time she smacked her lips in annoyance at not having had the sense to ask for precise directions, or, at least, to bring some kind of torch.

And yet they were always telling her at the Society that she was their best woman for dispensing charity. Occasionally she wondered why. There were occasions on which she forgot she had been a lane-child herself, or tried to persuade herself that the Society and the lane-people did not know that it was her voice, and the help of the nuns in her school, that had lifted her out of the rut, that it was her voice alone that had opened the way for her into amateur theatricals where she met her husband. It was her one vanity, her one hopeless self-deception. For even if they had not remembered her, the lanes would have seen the mark of their kind in her deep chest, and her strong arms, and her frosty complexion, and her hard lips—her only inheritance from her mother, a woman who had carried a basket of fish on her back around Cork, day after day, for thirty years. That was the real reason why the Society always sent her to the worst lanes; they knew well that the lane-people knew, and would not try to impose on her with a sorrowful tale and a whining voice; that the only weapon left to the poor people was flattery, and that would not succeed with such as her. It was because of that lane-cunning, as strong in her as in them, that she would not knock now at a door to ask the way. It was old wisdom to her—"What they didn't know didn't trouble them."

But when she reached the lamp and its lights fell on the number to her left, she knew she was utterly lost in this forest of slummery. She was about to walk back the way she had come when suddenly from behind the lighted cabin window by her shoulder a piano flung out in great strong drops of sound the prelude to an old familiar arrangement of Schubert's "Serenade" and immediately a fine tenor voice opened the duet, though where the contralto or baritone should reply there was silence except for the gently throbbing beat of the accompaniment. Her heart beat faster than the time of the music as in one of these half-silences she knocked at that door. The music halted and the door opened. Because the light was strong behind him she could not see Lenihan's face.

"Can you tell me," she said, "where I can find number Ninety-Two B?"

At the first word she recognized the voice.

"Yes, of course. But I'm afraid you won't find it yourself. Wait one minute," he said, diving back into the kitchen, "and I'll get my hat and show you."

She lowered her head to step down into the earthen-floored cabin. She saw the grand piano, almost as long as the whole room; it was grey with a layer of dust and coal-ash. A smoke-darkened plaster-cast of an angel hung over the wide, low grate. Pieces of wood shaped like monstrous bones leaned in a corner—the ribs of his boat. When he turned she gave him one quick look, and he, caught by the full shock of surprise, cried out:

"Trixie Flynn!"

"Pat Lenihan!" she reproached. "Why did you never come to see me and welcome me home?"

A BORN GENIUS

Her voice was deep, rich, pouting.

"I couldn't, Trixie. I couldn't somehow. What brings you here at this hour of the night?"

"The Saint Vincent de Pauls sent me. Mrs. Cahill in Ninety-Two B is sick."

She had recovered completely from her surprise and she arranged her hair as she looked at him from under her eyebrows.

"Sit down!" he said.

His voice was shaking and he shut the door and leaned against it.

"The old favourite," she said, looking at the score on the piano.

"I haven't sung for nearly a year and a half," he said.

"Why?"

"I'm making a boat," he murmured, almost as if he were a child caught wrong-doing.

"A boat!"

She was shocked.

"Pat Lenihan! A boat! And you with your voice!"

"Ah!" he cried miserably. "It's all very well for you, Trixie. You caught the tide. You've been to Paris and Milan. I read about your concert last March, below in the Opera House."

She grimaced with lips and eyebrows and shrugged her shoulders in disdain.

"*Un rien.* A bagatelle."

"And you got married, too," he whispered.

"Aha!" she trilled. "I often thought we'd get together, Pat. But, *chi le sa?*"

His lips twitched and his eyes strayed to a photograph on the piano. She went over to it, and he followed. There she, as a buxom Marguerite, knelt and looked up at Lenihan in the tights and doublet of Faust.

"And you've been singing in Manchester and Liverpool," he said, looking at her as she looked at the photograph.

"It's my wonderful year," she laughed. "Back from Milan! Married! Several recitals! But"—she pouted again in a deep, sad voice—"you never came to see *ta petite* Marguerite!"

"See what?" asked Lenihan.

"Me!" she pouted, swaying before him.

"Oh! You don't want me now," cried Lenihan.

He slammed down the lid of the piano. The wires vibrated.

"I'll never sing another song!" he declared.

She was about to argue with him, but he interrupted her savagely.

"What's the use?" he cried. "Who hears me? And if they did, what difference would it make? Who could tell in this hole of a city whether I was good or bad? I suppose if the truth were known I wouldn't be taken in the chorus of a travelling Moody-Manners."

"I heard you outside the window," she said. "You were in good voice."

"I'm not. I couldn't be. I haven't practised for eighteen months. It's all a lot of damned tomfoolery. Look at all the hours I've wasted—the nights. And what good did it do me? I know I have a voice. But it isn't a great voice. I never even got as much as a penny out of it. Not that I want it. Of course the Opera House is a bagatelle to you, as you call it. What are we here but a lot of country boys playing at amateur operatics?"

"Why don't you sing in a choir, Pat?" she asked. "You'd make some money that way."

"A choir!"

His voice was like the sour beer that stank in the vinegar factory.

"And what would I sing in a choir?"

Through his nose he began to intone horribly:

> "Tantum ergo Sacramentum
> Novo cedat Ritui . . ."

"Stop, Pat!"

They were silent for a minute or two.

"I want to sing my old part in that serenade, Pat," she said gently.

"No."

"Please, Pat!"

"No! No! No!"

She went to the piano and, leaving a wave of scent in the air as she swished by him, began to turn the music with the ample gestures of a prima donna. As she sat, and with her white fingers plucked out the modulated sounds, the music seemed to mingle sweetly with the scent. She saw, looking over her shoulder at him, that he was wavering.

"Have you never been to any of my concerts, Pat?"

He shook his head. She flung out a few notes like a blackbird full of pride in its song.

"Come on, Pat!" She smiled at him again.

He flung his mood aside and stood by her, his hands clasped tremblingly across his chest, his eyes lost in the dark corner of the room. They began:

> "Leise flehen meine Lieder
> Durch die Nacht zu dir,
> In den stillen Hain hernieder,
> Liebchen, komm zu mir . . ."

Her rich, finely trained voice poured into the room and out of it through the lanes. Responding to it his body swayed to and fro as he drew up from his chest the most powerful volume of song he could command. Once where she had a bar or two to sing alone he glanced down at her. Her great bosom, too, rose to the notes, and it was white and suède-smooth in the lamplight. Looking at her, he almost missed a note. He sang with an almost uncontrolled passion the remainder of the song.

When it was finished he fell into a chair by the piano and covered his eyes with his hands.

"My God!" he said. "What a voice! What a marvellous voice!"

He thought he caught the vibration of triumph and pity in her throat as she said:

"Pat! You really have a very nice voice."

Outside the window, in spite of the rain, they suddenly heard a chattering group of men, women, and children, trying to peep through the window-slits and the key-hole. He was glad of the interruption and, jerking his head, he led her to the back-door and across the yard to another lane.

"Come and see me, Pat!" she said. He did not reply. From time to time she said: "Isn't it wet?" Or: "Mind this hole!" But still he did not reply. At the door of Ninety-Two B, she said again:

"Won't you come to see me? Ah! *S'il vous plaît? Mon cher* Pat? *Mon petit* Pat?"

"Yes, yes, yes," he said shortly. "I'll come. Maybe. Good night, Trixie."

"*Au revoir, mon petit* Pat."

The light of the cabin windows fell on him at intervals, as he went. Then the mist and the dark covered him from her sight.

III

To her surprise, when she heard from him, three months later just before the Christmas holidays, he was in New York. It was a picture postcard of the New

York Philharmonic Orchestra with his address and two sentences:

Having a grand time. Richard Trübner has taken me in hand and has great hopes of me. Pat.

With the cunning of the born guttersnipe she went at once to Little Hell on two or three entirely superfluous calls and at each house she said when leaving:

"I hear you've lost Mr. Lenihan from the lane."

Before she left the slum she had heard more about him than he would ever have written to her in a hundred letters, and as she was driven back to Montenotte she smiled to think how neatly everything she had heard fitted in with all her previous knowledge of Pat Lenihan—his silence about himself, his poverty, the strain of bitterness and irreligion in him. He had never told her, for example, that he lived in Prout Lane or that he had for years supported his mother and sister. And she recalled, suddenly, how when five years before they were meeting frequently for some amateur operetta he had told her of the monument he was going to carve for his sister's grave. She had said, probing inquisitively:

"And you'll put your father's name on it, too, of course?"

"No! I will not," he had snapped back, and, flushing, walked away.

Well! Here was the secret out at last.

"Ah, sure, Mrs. Delaney," they had said to her in Prout Lane. "That boy could do any mortal thing he liked. D'ye see his house? 'Twould take the sight of your eyes, Mrs. Delaney. It's massive. Oh, sure, his father will make a C'ruso out of him. The two of ye will charm Cork."

She had to halt their flattery several times. She wanted to hear about Pat Lenihan.

"His father? 'Nt ye know? Fifteen years ago— No! I'm tellin' a lie—twelve years ago his father ran away from his mother to America. He left her with five children, the blackguard. Three of 'em died since. Susie was the last to go. An' all this time the father is sending for the boy. His mother says, an' Flyer says— but you wouldn't mind Flyer—his mother says the father is rotten with money. But the blackguard never sent a penny since the day he left. Oh, Pat's future is cut out for him. Sure he's a genius. He'd charm the married women. And"—with a burst of hypocritical and delighted laughter—"sure you'd charm the married men, Mrs. Delaney!"

She envied him. She was to have her first child in the spring and her singing days, she felt, were nearly done. For all her promise of triumphant nights and audiences applauding in the gloom across the footlights, she was falling into the routine of a little tawdry provincial city. From this on the most she could hope for would be an occasional recital in Cork, with more frequent gratis appearances at charity concerts to help her husband to get contracts for churches or convent buildings or for hospitals or schools managed by religious. She did not reply to the postcard. She felt too envious.

IV

New York was wine to Pat Lenihan, and because it was under snow the silence of it filled into his heart. All he could hear above the perpetual whistling of the chains on the automobiles, and the muffled honk of their horns, was the long sad squawk of a train-siren cleaving the frozen air, and the low tolling of a bell where an engine drew its load through Manhattan, somewhere to the north. The air was cold, exhilarating and pure. A few last gentle flakes were added to those clotting the trees in the Park, and the low sun, a burning moon, blazed on every twig. The tall, tapering buildings, dim and pale, glittered with their own thousand lights as they rose through the sky.

He was driving in a taxi, back from his singing-lesson, to his room in a little down-town Theological Seminary on Ninth Avenue and Twenty-First Street. He had laughed to think what they would say in Cork if they heard he was living in such a place. But two weeks after his arrival in New York his father had got him a letter to the Dean, and because it was cheaper and less frigid than a hotel he had stayed there ever since. Not that he saw his father; the introduction was sent to him, and though that was nearly four months ago he was about to meet his father tonight for the first time.

Ever since the tender disappeared into the early-morning mist at Queenstown four months or so ago, leaving him on the liner, he had been filled by that miracle of elation that comes only once in life to every man, that fills him when chance at last opens for him some long-desired road. He had never in all his life been so excited as when he stepped off the boat and looked expectantly around the wharf; for half his dreams had been of the day when his father would return with him, successful and wealthy, to live, reconciled to his mother, in Ireland. But he saw nobody and nobody came to meet him. He was planning to go to his father's business address, the only one he knew, when at the customs desk they handed him a letter in which his father explained that he had been called away suddenly to Cleveland on business and they would see one another in a few weeks' time.

"There is, to be sure," his father wrote, "a good deal of money in singing and my Pat must have the best teachers money can buy. Meanwhile you must have a good time."

The letter mentioned several theatres; one called Earl Carroll's Vanities was a "real bully show." Lenihan smiled at the Americanese, and because he could not meet his father, went that evening to see something that his father had liked. He came out, unhappy and troubled, his eyes and mind soiled by gaudy images of red and purple curtains and sham marble pillars and naked women. Had he not come by chance on a symphony concert and snatched an hour filled with the thunder and whisper of a Beethoven concerto (it was the "Emperor") he would have had nothing but an unpleasant memory for his first night in New York, a memory that might have shattered his miracle for ever.

After that he lived his own life and the miraculous elation of hope blossomed once more. After another three weeks his father wrote again. He was now in Chicago and in a few weeks they would meet. Meanwhile Pat must begin to study, "for my Pat must make a name for himself and I'll help my boy to it while I have a dollar left." Things went on like that for another three months, some of the letters containing large cheques, and still Lenihan had not met his father. By now, too, his mother was writing long letters from Cork, charging him in an agony of fear with hiding something from her, and Lenihan spent a good part of his leisure time writing long letters to both of them. But his master was by now much more hopeful, and even enthusiastic, and Lenihan could already see, a year away, perhaps, the night of his debut—the little concert-hall, for it would be a very modest beginning, the accompanist looking to him for the signal, the

A BORN GENIUS

scattered audience of connoisseurs and critics, and then the notices the following morning in the Press giving him his first taste of fame.

It was characteristic of his elation that he found even Ninth Avenue beautiful. And yet, at any rate around Twenty-First Street, it is merely a dirty, paper-strewn cobbled street, darkened and made raucous by an overhead railway. There is the usual Greek fruit-store, the usual wide-windowed restaurant and lunch-counter, white-tiled like a public lavatory at home in Ireland, and with such names as Charlie's Lunch or The Coffee Pot; an old-clothes shop, a cheap Sicilian haberdasher strayed up from Macdougal Street; there was a Palmist and Phrenologist, with big-breasted Polish gypsies always offering themselves in the doorway. The tram-cars raced along the avenue under the thunder of the overhead railway. Only when the snow covers the dirt and the smells and dulls the noise is the place really tolerable. Yet, to Lenihan, it had the charm of a foreign city, the one place that remained indelible in all its details on his memory when he returned to Ireland, that filthy avenue banked in snow, made doubly white by the black girders of the overhead; and side by side for all its length all those vital struggling immigrant homes. That long noisy street remained with him as a poignantly lovely memory, a thing more vital and brutal than he could ever explain.

And it was all the more poignant and bitter when he discovered that for all the four months he was in New York his father had watched him coming out of the archway of the Seminary in the morning and going in, often very late at night, getting no more in return for his patient vigil than the briefest glance at his son's face raised questioningly to the sky, or, after dark, the outline of his son's back under the lamplight.

In the hall, now, by the telephone booth he stood waiting, and though it was twelve years since they had met, and the old man had grown scant-haired and yellow-skinned and hard-mouthed, they recognized each other at once. But they could say nothing but: "How are you, my son?" and: "How are you, Father?"—looking shyly at each other, smiling and saying nothing, because they had nothing in common they dared talk about.

"Let's go and have a cup of cawfee," said the father at last, and he took his son by the arm and led him across to the white counter of Charlie's Lunch.

In the bright light of the restaurant Lenihan noticed that his father's hands were trembling, and that they were rough with work, and that his suit was odorous of the steam-press.

"You've come from Detroit, Father?"

"What?" said the father, taken by surprise.

"You wrote me from Detroit last time, Father," said Lenihan.

"Yeah!"

As the white-hatted curate brought them the coffee the father spoke about Detroit to his son, inventing the names of the streets and the squares and the parks.

"'Nt you like New Yawrk?" he asked then, and in spite of the succession of nasals his intonation was pure Cork.

"I do, indeed," said Lenihan.

The old man began at once in a very fast voice to make his confession to his son, but he went round and round it and he could not approach the actual point. He talked instead in a confused way about America and its customs, about democracy and the liberties of America, about freedom of thought and tolerance and cosmopolitanism, and though Lenihan tried very hard to follow him he could not, and finally he gave it up and, barely listening, merely said: "Yes," or "No," or "Indeed?" or "Do you say so?" He was trying to think how he could get to the point of suggesting to his father that he ought to return to his home and wife in Cork. Suddenly he observed how excited and nervous the old man was, and how his eyes were shifting here and there as his talk grew slower and more deliberate. He felt his father was coming to the point, and he waited for his opportunity, almost trembling himself with hope and expectation.

"Of course," his father was saying, "you are a young maan still, Pat. A very young maan. And in Ireland a maan has little chance of meeting with experience. But you are a clever young maan and I hope you have understanding."

"I hope so, sir," said Lenihan.

The old man looked at him from eye to eye, and said solemnly and deliberately:

"A maan's married life is sacred to him."

"Father!" said Lenihan, grasping his father's hand. How rough it was and how it shook as he held it!

"Yes, Pat?"

"Father, come home to my mother."

With a shock he realized that he had often and often said those words before to his father when he used to meet him as a child, wandering drunk in the streets. His father looked at him. There was silence for a moment and then an overhead train thundered by.

"Pat!" said his father.

"Yes."

"Pat, I want you to stay here."

"But you can go home without me," he was beginning to argue when the old man interrupted him.

"Pat, boy, I'll make a success of you. I'm very fond

of you, and I always was. Aren't you my first son, and why shouldn't I? I have a father's love for you, Pat. My boy! I've done a lot of rotten things, Pat, but you don't hold them against me? You wouldn't hold things out against your old dad?"

A group of men came in and sat at the counter near them.

"Come upstairs, Pat," said the father, taking his hand.

"Upstairs?" said Lenihan.

"Yes," said the father, leading him through the shop. "I know the man here," he explained.

He was like a hare doubling before the dog. He lied at every hand's turn. Upstairs in the room over the shop the first thing Lenihan saw was a panorama of Queenstown and in surprise he turned to his father.

"Yes, Pat?" faltered the old man.

"Queenstown!" said Lenihan in delight.

"Aye," smiled his father, still unable to confess.

"How did it get here?"

"Yes, Pat."

And he laughed with foolish delight, in spite of his nervousness, because at last someone else besides himself was enjoying the old familiar scene.

"Look at the old Deepwater Quay!" said Lenihan. "And look at Spike! and Haulbowline! Isn't it grand!"

Then he stopped, his eyes wandering to the fireplace over which hung an Irish flag, the old green with the yellow harp, and crossing it an Italian flag, the quartered shield in the white centre. Beneath it on the mantelpiece was a photograph. He went towards it. It was himself and Trixie Flynn as Faust and Marguerite. When he wheeled on his father the old man was looking up at him like a dog about to be kicked or a schoolboy waiting for punishment. But before the confession could come the door was flung open and in raced two lovely little black-haired boys, and after them strode a dark-eyed, big-chested Italian woman.

"Whoo! Pop!" cried the children, leaping up joyously at old Lenihan. "We been shoppin'!"

And they began to show him their New Year toys until, seeing the stranger, they fell suddenly quiet.

"Anita!" said old Lenihan. "This is Pat."

It was plain that he had told her at least some of the truth—how much Lenihan never knew; probably that he was a widower and this was his son. Afterwards it tore Lenihan's heart to think the old man had not been able to keep it secret that he had a son whom he loved. Now, however, as the woman looked at him, searching his face for the face of his mother, Lenihan began to think of Prout Lane, wrapped in its veils of mist, and of his mother, hurrying to the chapel to her Confraternity at night, and he let his eyes fall, and taking his hat he went slowly out of the room. His father raced down the stairs to stop him, persuading and entreating him, step by step, as he insisted on descending to the street.

That night when he had at last got rid of his father, Lenihan packed his bag and took the Shore Line midnight to Boston, his taxi racing with whistling chains through the snow-covered avenues, past the great floodlit towers of the city's buildings, closed for the night, past the theatres he had begun to know so well, dark now and silent, and empty, the shops at rest, the sidewalks deserted, into the great station where the foyer was full of light and life, and the waiting line of Pullmans beyond stood silent and dark, ready for its journey, under the sad whistle of the siren and the low tolling of its bell.

He stayed in Boston for the better part of a year.

abandoning all his ambitions and hopes. There was no looking out of the office window here, no singing at the lunch-hour for the workmen, no intervals in which he might at his ease exercise his voice. Having saved his fare, and a little more, he returned to Ireland for Christmas.

Not until he was seated in the train from Queenstown to Cork did it occur to him that in those four months in New York his father must have spent on him the best part of his life's savings, that his father was a poor man—that his father probably was quite fond of him. A light snow, rare event in Southern Ireland, was blowing past the carriage-windows, and in it he saw Ninth Avenue and the black girders of the overhead and, for the first time, his father's face at the window of Charlie's Lunch peering out anxiously to see him leave the Seminary in the morning, peering out at night in the hope of seeing him return, and doing that day after day, week after week, afraid to meet his son, and yet aching to talk with him and maybe persuade him to stay with him for the rest of his life. The old fellow, thought Lenihan, must have gone to a great deal of trouble and humiliation persuading the Dean to allow me to stay at the Seminary; and then he thought of all the devices, all the lies, all the subterfuges his father had employed, and all to no greater result than five minutes' painful argument as they stepped down the stairs of the restaurant-cum-haberdasher's shop in Ninth Avenue; and, afterwards, still more painful because bitter and insulting, the pleading and the quarrelling in the little room of the Theological Seminary over the way. Through the whirling snow-flakes, curling about the bare beech-boughs, and melting on the dark drooping laurels and the tattered hedges, he saw only, and now with a sudden but tardy pity, that his father's sin had borne bitter fruit.

The train rolled into the city, over the red bridge into the railway-station, and as he stepped from it and saw his mother coming forward in search of him through the crowd, full of joy at the thought that she was about to see her son again—the sorrow of her husband's early desertion long since forgotten—Lenihan realized that he was divided in pity between these two, and that, for being divided, he could never as long as he lived be at ease again with either.

In the old covered car, as they drove into the city, and up the hills again to Prout Lane, Lenihan told his mother the truth about her husband. But when she began to weep for herself and curse her husband with sudden blasphemy, Lenihan found that he had no longer any hate or resentment left in him. After that, when the news spread through the lane, he refused to talk of it with anybody, and if they insisted on upbraiding his father he would merely say: "Little good it did him," or: "The poor old sod, I pity him sometimes."

v

All that day a stream of lane-people kept trickling in to welcome the genius home. They had expected a night of jollification, but they were just as pleased with the drama of the weeping mother, Flyer drunken and fractious on the porter intended for the feast, and Pat sitting glum and silent by the fire. His piano he had sold before he went to America, never thinking to need it again; his window-flowers were withered stumps; the fire had taken his wood-carvings one by one, as well as the unfinished portions of his boat that used to lean in the corners of the kitchen.

"Didn't I have a clean kitchen for you, Pat?" his mother wailed. "And what news you brought me! Look at that lovely red marbled wall-paper we got for you, fourpence a dozen, and Flyer to put it up for you with his own two hands. Oh! What a home-coming!" she wailed at each new comforting gossip, until at last he drove out of the house and down to the river's edge to look at the skeleton of his boat, and to look, in the dusk, at the marshes of the vinegar factory. Then the only shelter from the night and his loneliness was the dark lights of Montenotte and Trixie Flynn.

It was no pleasure to him to visit her. Earlier in the afternoon he had observed from an old poster that they were now calling her "Madame Flynn-Delaney, Cork's Own Nightingale," and as he read it he had groaned aloud, like a man in pain. This rat-eaten place still had, he thought bitterly, as he walked through its tawdry front streets whose finery was only the thickness of a brick, and into its ware-house back streets that looked as if they had been rusting and crumbling for centuries, all the mannerisms and unconscious humour ascribed to it by the sniggering Levers and Prouts and Thackerays of a hundred years ago. With a kind of sour joy he began to roam about the city, trying to keep from visiting Montenotte—O romantic mount of Night!—associating his own misery with the shades of the Spensers and the Warbecks and the Walters—for he refused to ally even his thoughts with the people themselves—the dukes and earls and lords-lieutenant and secretaries whose petty glories were the only ones the place had ever seen. Everywhere he went he sought with deliberate malice for the signs of decayed grandeur—streets of Georgian houses full of cheap shops, a puny bridge called after Wellington, a wide street dubbed a Square and given to Nelson, a horse-trough presented to a Berwick, a wretched slum street to the whole House of Hanover, and every sooty, mud-deep quay partitioned off here to a Grenville, or a Wandesford, or a Camden, or a Lancaster, a George, a Charlotte, an Albert. All the exiled down-at-heels sighing for St. James's and Pall Mall, with their flea-bitten servants and tarnished finery, had been offered the immortality of their names on the walls of a jakes in this city of exile. But all the time, as if in spite of himself, he approached nearer and nearer to Montenotte. The bored souls of provincial towns are all like that—feeding on one another without pleasure like leeches.

He had been afraid that she would ask him too many questions about his father and his own plans. She seemed far more interested in showing him her baby and in telling him about the contract for the new cathedral that all the architects in Cork were trying to wheedle out of the Bishop. Then her husband came in for dinner and with him her sister-in-law and her brother, and they prevailed on Lenihan to stay. It was a good dinner but noisy with cross-talk, and Delaney bored them with talk about the cathedral: the people who were manœuvring for the contract, distant relations of the Bishop that were being approached by this person and that, the best sites for the cathedral, the soil, the stone, the style, explaining the advantages of Romanesque with his knife and his napkin and a loaf of bread, deriding Pugin because he had filled Ireland with plaster Gothic.

"My God! I'd rather concrete," he would declare. "Though concrete wasn't as popular once as it is now. That's what your Americans"—to Lenihan—"did for us. I remember a competition twelve years ago and I was the first student to suggest a concrete church. 'How in the name of God,' said the adjudicator—it was Sir

Edwin Lutyens—'how in the name of almighty God,' says he, 'could that roof stand?' 'Oh, it's concrete, Sir Edwin,' says I. 'Indeed,' says Sir Edwin, 'an' I suppose the spire is made of cast-iron?' But, you know," Delaney went on in spite of the laughter, "you could have a concrete roof in a Romanesque church. And it wouldn't be a smaller church. You'd make in the height what you'd lose in the width; you could have galleries . . ."

And so on and on while Lenihan kept thinking: "I'm back; back in garrulous, windbag Cork." And his mind filled with images of New York and Boston and he ceased to hear Delaney's talk except as the babble of a stream.

After dinner, whisky and port and coffee were handed around and there was much sniggering in a corner over a *risqué* French pictorial. But Lenihan put such a good face on things that he managed to lift out of his mood into a good humour, and while the rain blown up from the harbour lashed the streaming panes and the fire crackled with drops falling in the chimney he and Trixie sang a comical duet from the *Yeomen of the Guard* while Delaney pranced around the room holding his glass to the ceiling, coming in on the refrain very flat and out of tune. Then he went off to drive his guests home and Lenihan and Trixie were left alone, talking over the fire in a darkened room, of the great singers they had heard, she of Melba, and Patti, and Tonnalerre, and Clara Butt, he of Kennerley Rumford and Caruso and his master Trübner. She began to complain sadly of her life in Cork and he said he could well believe her.

"I have my child, of course," she said, "and I'd die for her. I'd lay down the last drop of my blood for that child," she declared with flashing eyes, and her bosom panted and her voice rose.

The wine was going to both their heads, and Lenihan found himself telling her that her sentiments did her great honour. But then, there was her husband, she said, and her voice fell. There was John gone off to the club now and he wouldn't be back until morning; and she allowed Lenihan to pat her on the hand. He felt he had never liked her so much as tonight, and as she leaned forward and encouraged him to speak he told her readily all about his father. As he left they halted in the door to hum a bar from the "Serenade," and he kissed her hand in good-bye.

Then, as he tramped in a midnight downpour back up to the little sleeping cabins of Prout Lane he felt that he had no right to betray the old man's shame, and late as it was he wrote and posted a letter to Trixie warning her that she had his confidence and imploring her to tell nobody what she had heard. She wrote a long and warm letter in reply saying that she was honoured by his confidence and would respect it. She wrote:

"Don't I understand, Pat, only too well that such things are best kept quiet in a city like this? There are always people trying to dig out your past in Cork. As for your father, have nothing to do with the old devil. You never know what he'd try to make out of this. Leave him severely alone, neither writing to him nor communicating with him in any way. . . ."

Again Lenihan saw his father peering out of Charlie's Lunch for that morning and evening glimpse of himself leaving the Seminary, and thinking of it he decided he would never again visit this coarse woman, wandering instead at night, in and out of the back streets, searching always for old names and old memories, sometimes for snatches of accidental beauty where the shadows of a lamp in an archway made a design of glooms, or lights that were more like shadows, or where an empty blank gable-end towered dark over a lane, or a whitewashed cottage shone like snow under its purple roof. What was he, after all, but another like those Sydneys and Coburgs and Adelaides and the rest of them, whoever they were, another exile tortured by the empty days and the companionless nights?

In the end he went back to her. After all, they were the only two people in Cork who really knew what singing meant. And when he did go, late one evening, she was so childishly glad to see him, and so unhappy about her husband, that he felt he had been harsh and unkind and readily agreed to sing with her at a forthcoming concert. But it happened that just that night a priest called to bless the house. "Father Shanahan," she whispered to Lenihan as he came in, "the Bishop's secretary"; and, as he went upstairs to pray over the house: "God forgive me, I have my house blessed by half the priests in Cork." He was a pale-haired saturnine man, with a voice as high-pitched as a girl's, and his eyes were soft with innocence or humility, and immediately he entered the room Trixie began to be charming to him and flirt with him in a loud voice and with much winking. His answers, however, were so awkward that to Lenihan Trixie's talk seemed improper and gross. He pretended to be playing with the baby, leaning over the pram and glaring down at it as if he were about to choke it. Presently he found himself being intrigued into giving a half-promise to sing the "Adeste" with Trixie at the parish choir next Sunday, though it enraged him to see his half-promise passed on at once as if it were a personal gift of Trixie's to the parish. But she was so charming about it that the little priest grew more and more awkward and finally took his leave, and Lenihan, who had disliked priests at all times, preferred to go with him. Yet the following night he was back at her house again, and again she was delighted to see him, and after that he took to visiting her regularly. There was no other house open to him.

VI

In April he was taken back in the vinegar factory, and little by little the marshes under the office window began to sprout in green patches, and at the lunch-hour he could walk abroad in the fields more and more often under dry skies and broken clouds and work longer and longer in the evenings at his boat. He began to feel less resentful of Cork. The loveliness of the country encroaching on and compensating for the empty town, the promise of long Sundays in summer among the inlets within and without the harbour, where the bright green hills dipped down to the blue sea, and the white line of waves seemed never to move—all this weaned him gradually back to his old self, and the memory of the heavy winter passed from him.

He was in that happy mood one Sunday as he went to sing at a charity matinee with Trixie. She was waiting for him in the corridor and at once she called him aside to her dressing-room. In the artificial light her hair shone—so much bronze wire piled on her head—and her rich bosom displayed generously in her low-cut evening-gown of pink and silver looked as if a touch would reveal that it had a nap on it like a peach or snow-white suède. He took her by her bare, braceleted arm.

"Is it the contract?" he asked eagerly.

"No."

She was awkward. He felt there was something wrong.

"Pat! They are beginning to talk about us. You mustn't come so often."

The music of the orchestra rolled up to them as the stage-door was opened and shut.

"Who is talking about us?" he asked, flushing with shame.

"Well! Father Shanahan is dropping hints."

"Oh!"

"My husband says it's unwise."

"It's the contract you're thinking of, Trixie."

"I'm not, Pat. But you know Cork?"

With a sudden impulse of defiance of the mean, tattling city he put his arms around her and kissed her, and she did not resist him, returning his kiss even more warmly than he gave it. It seemed natural to her to kiss him, to hold him in her great maternal arms. A knock on the door called them to their duet and they went down the corridor to the stage whispering to each other to be calm, to be calm. But as on that first night when she came to his house in Prout Lane, they sang the duet in a rivalry of almost wild passion, accelerating the tempo of the melancholy serenade until the accompanist found himself never nearer than a quarter of a bar behind. The audience sensed their emotion in Lenihan's flushed cheeks and in the woman by her high-flung chin and flashing eyes, and sharing in that emotion, several seconds before the song ended, they sent their clamorous, thundering applause up from the gloom beyond the bright encircling footlights. In the wings, Delaney, trembling for his contract, waited for his wife; he implored her to be careful—the Bishop was in the house and Shanahan was somewhere on the stage. But beyond the billowing curtain the applause rose and fell in wave on wave until they came forward to sing again, choosing with an almost incredible lack of discretion the love-duet from *The Lily of Killarney*. By the prompter's box Father Shanahan looked on with tightened lips and disapproving eyes as Lenihan rose breathlessly to:

> "I come, I come, my heart's delight!
> My heart's delight!
> My heart's delight . . ."

sung so feelingly that when it was over and he reached the side of the stage he collapsed in a chair. They brought him a glass of water, and as he sipped it mechanically he saw Delaney come in from the auditorium, in a fury, and lead his wife to her room, and little Father Shanahan looking at them with a cold look in his innocent eyes.

After that painful scene he dared not visit her again, and indeed she wrote to warn him not to come to her. Fortunately it was summer and he could now work for long hours in the evenings at his boat. As he saw it, as it were, come to life under his hands he became as happy as a woman with child. July came and the trestles under his boat were deep in buttercups, and as he worked the salmon leaped up the falls, splashing, bow-bent silver. During those days he seemed to be tireless, and when the darkness drove him home to his cabin-kitchen he worked late into the night making cabinets to exchange with a local firm of furnishers for the timber and the brass and iron and glass fittings he needed. It was August and a woodbine trailed its tendrils from the hedges over the flank of his boat. As with his sister's tombstone he worked in a fever of impatience to be finished. It was so hot that he had to put a tarpaulin over the keel and it burned his hand to lean on it. September came and under his boat were fox-gloves, and the wild-arum in its tight wrapping. October followed and the denuded trees showed the red berry of the dog-rose, burning like the holly-berry on its branch. It seemed as if he would not have his boat launched that autumn, but before the month died he had painted the name on her prow—*The Trickster;* and dared write to Delaney asking if he and his wife would come to launch his boat.

That Sunday, after singing in the choir, she came, and the boat was lowered down the slip and it breasted the water and floated there in broken ripples of colour. Lenihan rushed forward to thank her, but her husband was impatient to be gone and she would not delay.

All he could say was:

"Thanks. Is he still angry?"

"Yes. He says you lost him that contract."

"Didn't you get it after all?" he cried.

"No," she said. "We heard last night that Cassidy got it."

But Delaney sounded his horn impatiently and she turned to go.

For a week Lenihan was delighted with his boat. He almost slept in it. He visited it before his work every morning. He raced down at the lunch-hour to see and fondle it. Then the engineers from whom he had ordered the engine told him it would never be of any use to him. He argued with them for hours, but they only shrugged their shoulders at him. The timbers were too far apart and flimsy to bed the engine on them; the stern-post would not bear piercing for the propeller-shaft; the sheer of the quarter made it impossible to lead the shaft through at the proper angle.

As in the case of his sister's tombstone he never went near it again. It lay moored under the alders until marauding boys knocked a hole in it, and sinking halfway in the shallow mud, it grew slimy and green and hulk-like. You can see it there today—for it has outlived poor Lenihan—but only if you peer closely enough into the fibrous shadows of the bank, where it is almost indistinguishable from the air-searching roots of the trees.

The evening Lenihan discovered that it would never take him out to the misty sea, never nuzzle the swaying flowers that glisten in the carmined inlets of the harbour, it was grey with the first cold rains of November. He stood by his door in Prout Lane, biting his nails, and staring across the dark valley of the Lee at the hanging lights of Montenotte, while the slowly waving mist veiled the moon, a warm haze floated up from the sea, persistent as a fog. Winter had begun again, and again the boredom of the empty days and nights. He could hear the people talking beyond the dividing wall. His mother was gone to the chapel to her Confraternity. Flyer was boozing in the pub at the end of the lane.

Searching for the key of his piano—a second-hand, cheap affair—he wiped the dust from the yellow keys and sat to play the Schubert "Serenade." As the worn keys plucked out the drops of sound his voice rose gently to the words. Suddenly he stopped and listened. He rushed to the door and flung it wide. He saw the mist curling about the gas-lamp overhead and the lighted cabin windows as they vanished down the winding lane. Slowly he closed the door and returned to his song. The voices in the next house had fallen silent: his fingers drew the notes in slow procession.

> "Lass auch dir die Brust bewegen,
> Liebchen, höre mich,
> Bebend harr' ich dir entgegen,
> Komm, beglücke mich . . ."

He could not finish. He began it, several times, and each time he paused, and sat listening for a noise at the door.

SEUMAS O'KELLY

The Weaver's Grave

A STORY OF OLD MEN

I

MORTIMER HEHIR, the weaver, had died, and they had come in search of his grave to Cloon na Morav, the Meadow of the Dead. Meehaul Lynskey, the nail-maker, was first across the stile. There was excitement in his face. His long warped body moved in a shuffle over the ground. Following him came Cahir Bowes, the stonebreaker, who was so beaten down from the hips forward, that his back was horizontal as the back of an animal. His right hand held a stick which propped him up in front, his left hand clutched his coat behind, just above the small of the back. By these devices he kept himself from toppling head over heels as he walked. Mother earth was the brow of Cahir Bowes by magnetic force, and Cahir Bowes was resisting her fatal kiss to the last. And just now there was animation in the face he raised from its customary contemplation of the ground. Both old men had the air of those who had been unexpectedly let loose. For a long time they had lurked somewhere in the shadows of life, the world having no business for them, and now, suddenly, they had been remembered and called forth to perform an office which nobody else on earth could perform. The excitement in their faces as they crossed over the stile into Cloon na Morav expressed a vehemence in their belated usefulness. Hot on their heels came two dark, handsome, stoutly built men, alike even to the cord that tied their corduroy trousers under their knees, and, being grave-diggers, they carried flashing spades. Last of all, and after a little delay, a firm white hand was laid on the stile, a dark figure followed, the figure of a woman whose palely sad face was picturesquely, almost dramatically, framed in a black shawl which hung from the crown of the head. She was the widow of Mortimer Hehir, the weaver, and she followed the others into Cloon na Morav, the Meadow of the Dead.

To glance at Cloon na Morav as you went by on the hilly road, was to get an impression of a very old burial-ground; to pause on the road and look at Cloon na Morav was to become conscious of its quiet situation, of winds singing down from the hills in a chant for the dead; to walk over to the wall and look at the mounds inside was to provoke quotations from Gray's "Elegy"; to make the sign of the cross, lean over the wall, observe the gloomy lichened background of the wall opposite, and mark the things that seemed to stray about, like yellow snakes in the grass, was to think of Hamlet moralizing at the graveside of Ophelia, and hear him establish the identity of Yorrick. To get over the stile and stumble about inside, was to forget all these things and to know Cloon na Morav for itself. Who could tell the age of Cloon na Morav? The mind could only swoon away into mythology, paddle about in the dotage of paganism, the toothless infancy of Christianity. How many generations, how many septs, how many clans, how many families, how many people, had gone into

Cloon na Morav? The mind could only take wing on the romances of mathematics. The ground was billowy, grotesque. Several partially suppressed insurrections—a great thirsting, worming, pushing and shouldering under the sod—had given it character. A long tough growth of grass wired it from end to end, Nature, by this effort, endeavouring to control the strivings of the more daring of the insurgents of Cloon na Morav. No path here; no plan or map or register existed; if there ever had been one or the other it had been lost. Invasions and wars and famines and feuds had swept the ground and left it. All claims to interment had been based on powerful traditional rights. These rights had years ago come to an end—all save in a few outstanding cases, the rounding up of a spent generation. The overflow from Cloon na Morav had already set a new cemetery on its legs a mile away, a cemetery in which limestone headstones and Celtic crosses were springing up like mushrooms, advertising the triviality of a civilization of men and women, who, according to their own epitaphs, had done exactly the two things they could not very well avoid doing: they had all, their obituary notices said, been born and they had all died. Obscure quotations from Scripture were sometimes added by way of apology. There was an almost unanimous expression of forgiveness to the Lord for what had happened to the deceased. None of this lack of humour in Cloon na Morav. Its monuments were comparatively few, and such of them as it had not swallowed were well within the general atmosphere. No obituary notice in the place was complete; all were either wholly or partially eaten up by the teeth of time. The monuments that had made a stout battle for existence were pathetic in their futility. The vanity of the fashionable of dim ages made one weep. Who on earth could have brought in the white marble slab to Cloon na Morav? It had grown green with shame. Perhaps the lettering, once readable upon it, had been conscientiously picked out in gold. The shrieking winds and the fierce rains of the hills alone could tell. Plain heavy stones, their shoulders rounded with a chisel, presumably to give them some off-handed resemblance to humanity, now swooned at fantastic angles from their settings, as if the people to whose memory they had been dedicated had shouldered them away as an impertinence. Other slabs lay in fragments on the ground, filling the mind with thoughts of Moses descending from Mount Sinai and, waxing angry at sight of his followers dancing about false gods, casting the stone tables containing the Commandments to the ground, breaking them in pieces—the most tragic destruction of a first edition that the world has known. Still other heavy square dark slabs, surely creatures of a pagan imagination, were laid flat down on numerous short legs, looking sometimes like representations of monstrous black cockroaches, and again like tables at which the guests of Cloon na Morav might sit down, goblin-like, in the moon-light, when nobody was looking. Most of the legs had given way and the tables lay overturned, as if there had been a quarrel at cards the night before. Those that had kept their legs exhibited great cracks or fissures across their backs, like slabs of dark ice breaking up. Over by the wall, draped in its pattern of dark green lichen, certain families of dim ages had made an effort to keep up the traditions of the Eastern sepulchres. They had showed an aristocratic reluctance to take to the common clay in Cloon na Morav. They had built low casket-shaped houses against the gloomy wall, putting an enormously heavy iron door with ponderous iron rings—like the rings on a pier by the sea at one end, a tremendous lock—one wondered what Goliath kept the key—finally cementing the whole thing up and surrounding it with spiked iron railings. In these contraptions very aristocratic families locked up their dead as if they were dangerous wild animals. But these ancient vanities only heightened the general democracy of the ground. To prove a traditional right to a place in its community was to have the bond of your pedigree sealed. The act of burial in Cloon na Morav was in itself an epitaph. And it was amazing to think that there were two people still over the sod who had such a right—one Mortimer Hehir, the weaver, just passed away, the other Malachi Roohan, a cooper, still breathing. When these two survivors of a great generation got tucked under the sward of Cloon na Morav its terrific history would, for all practical purposes, have ended.

II

Meehaul Lynskey, the nailer, hitched forward his bony shoulders and cast his eyes over the ground—eyes that were small and sharp, but unaccustomed to range over wide spaces. The width and the wealth of Cloon na Morav were baffling to him. He had spent his long life on the look-out for one small object so that he might hit it. The colour that he loved was the golden glowing end of a stick of burning iron; wherever he saw that he seized it in a small sconce at the end of a long handle, wrenched it off by a twitch of the wrist, hit it with a flat hammer several deft taps, dropped it into a vessel of water, out of which it came a cool and perfect nail. To do this thing several hundred times six days in the week, and pull the chain of a bellows at short intervals, Meehaul Lynskey had developed an extraordinary dexterity of sight and touch, a swiftness of business that no mortal man could exceed, and so long as he had been

THE WEAVER'S GRAVE

pitted against nail-makers of flesh and blood he had more than held his own; he had, indeed, even put up a tremendous but an unequal struggle against the competition of nail-making machinery. Accustomed as he was to concentrate on a single, glowing, definite object, the complexity and disorder of Cloon na Morav unnerved him. But he was not going to betray any of these professional defects to Cahir Bowes, the stonebreaker. He had been sent there as an ambassador by the caretaker of Cloon na Morav, picked out for his great age, his local knowledge, and his good character, and it was his business to point out to the twin grave-diggers, sons of the caretaker, the weaver's grave, so that it might be opened to receive him. Meehaul Lynskey had a knowledge of the place, and was quite certain as to a great number of grave sites, while the caretaker, being an official without records, had a profound ignorance of the whole place.

Cahir Bowes followed the drifting figure of the nail-maker over the ground, his face hitched up between his shoulders, his eyes keen and grey, glint-like as the mountains of stones he had in his day broken up as road material. Cahir, no less than Meehaul, had his knowledge of Cloon na Morav and some of his own people were buried here. His sharp, clear eyes took in the various mounds with the eye of a prospector. He, too, had been sent there as an ambassador, and as between himself and Meehaul Lynskey he did not think there could be any two opinions; his knowledge was superior to the knowledge of the nailer. Whenever Cahir Bowes met a loose stone on the grass quite instinctively he turned it over with his stick, his sharp old eyes judging its grain with a professional swiftness, then cracking at it with his stick. If the stick were a hammer the stone, attacked on its most vulnerable spot, would fall to pieces like glass. In stones Cahir Bowes saw not sermons but seams. Even the headstones he tapped significantly with the ferrule of his stick, for Cahir Bowes had an artist's passion for his art, though his art was far from creative. He was one of the great destroyers, the reducers, the makers of chaos, a powerful and remorseless critic of the Stone Age.

The two old men wandered about Cloon na Morav, in no hurry whatever to get through with their business. After all they had been a long time pensioned off, forgotten, neglected, by the world. The renewed sensation of usefulness was precious to them. They knew that when this business was over they were not likely to be in request for anything in this world again. They were ready to oblige the world, but the world would have to allow them their own time. The world, made up of the two grave-diggers and the widow of the weaver, gathered all this without any vocal proclamation. Slowly, mechanically as it were, they followed the two ancients about Cloon na Morav. And the two ancients wandered about with the labour of age and the hearts of children. They separated, wandered about silently as if they were picking up old acquaintances, stumbling upon forgotten things, gathering up the threads of days that were over, reviving their memories, and then drew together, beginning to talk slowly, almost casually, and all their talk was of the dead, of the people who lay in the ground about them. They warmed to it, airing their knowledge, calling up names and complications of family relationships, telling stories, reviving all virtues, whispering at past vices, past vices that did not sound like vices at all, for the long years are great mitigators and run in splendid harness with the coyest of all the virtues, Charity. The whispered scandals of Cloon na Morav were seen by the twin grave-diggers and the widow of the weaver through such a haze of antiquity that they were no longer scandals but romances. The rake and the drab, seen a good way down the avenue, merely look picturesque. The grave-diggers rested their spades in the ground, leaning on the handles in exactly the same graveyard pose, and the pale widow stood in the background, silent, apart, patient, and, like all dark, tragic looking women, a little mysterious.

The stonebreaker pointed with his quivering stick at the graves of the people whom he spoke about. Every time he raised that forward support one instinctively looked, anxious and fearful, to see if the clutch were secure on the small of the back. Cahir Bowes had the sort of shape that made one eternally fearful for his equilibrium. The nailer, who, like his friend the stonebreaker, wheezed a good deal, made short, sharp gestures, and always with the right hand; the fingers were hooked in such a way, and he shot out the arm in such a manner, that they gave the illusion that he held a hammer and that it was struck out over a very hot fire. Every time Meehaul Lynskey made this gesture one expected to see sparks flying.

"Where are we to bury the weaver?" one of the grave-diggers asked at last.

Both old men laboured around to see where the interruption, the impertinence, had come from. They looked from one twin to the other, with gravity, indeed anxiety, for they were not sure which was which, or if there was not some illusion in the resemblance, some trick of youth to baffle age.

"Where are we to bury the weaver?" the other twin repeated, and the strained look on the old men's faces deepened. They were trying to fix in their minds which of the twins had interrupted first and which last. The eyes of Meehaul Lynskey fixed on one twin with the instinct of his trade, while Cahir Bowes ranged both and eventually wandered to the figure of the widow in the background, silently accusing her of impatience in a matter which it would be indelicate for her to show haste.

"We can't stay here for ever," said the first twin.

It was the twin upon whom Meehaul Lynskey had fastened his small eyes, and, sure of his man this time, Meehaul Lynskey hit him.

"There's many a better man than you," said Meehaul Lynskey, "that will stay here for ever." He swept Cloon na Morav with the hooked fingers.

"Them that stays in Cloon na Morav for ever," said Cahir Bowes with a wheezing energy, "have nothing to be ashamed of—nothing to be ashamed of. Remember that, young fellow."

Meehaul Lynskey did not seem to like the intervention, the help, of Cahir Bowes. It was a sort of implication that he had not—*he*, mind you,—had not hit the nail properly on the head.

"Well, where are we to bury him, anyway?" said the twin, hoping to profit by the chagrin of the nailer—the nailer who, by implication, had failed to nail.

"You'll bury him," said Meehaul Lynskey, "where all belonging to him is buried."

"We come," said the other twin, "with some sort of intention of that kind." He drawled out the words, in imitation of the old men. The skin relaxed on his handsome dark face and then bunched in puckers of humour about the eyes; Meehaul Lynskey's gaze, wandering for once, went to the handsome dark face of the other twin and the skin relaxed and then bunched in puckers of humour about *his* eyes, so that Meehaul Lynskey had an unnerving sensation that these young grave-diggers were purposely confusing him.

THE WEAVER'S GRAVE

"You'll bury him," he began with some vehemence, and was amazed to again find Cahir Bowes taking the words out of his mouth, snatching the hammer out of his hand, so to speak.

"——where you're told to bury him," Cahir Bowes finished for him.

Meehaul Lynskey was so hurt that his long slanting figure moved away down the graveyard, then stopped suddenly. He had determined to do a dreadful thing. He had determined to do a thing that was worse than kicking a crutch from under a cripple's shoulder; that was like stealing the holy water out of a room where a man lay dying. He had determined to ruin the last day's amusement on this earth for Cahir Bowes and himself by prematurely and basely disclosing the weaver's grave!

"Here," called back Meehaul Lynskey, "is the weaver's grave, and here you will bury him."

All moved down to the spot, Cahir Bowes going with extraordinary spirit, the ferrule of his terrible stick cracking on the stones he met on the way.

"Between these two mounds," said Meehaul Lynskey, and already the twins raised their twin spades in a sinister movement, like swords of lancers flashing at a drill.

"Between these two mounds," said Meehaul Lynskey, "is the grave of Mortimer Hehir."

"Hold on!" cried Cahir Bowes. He was so eager, so excited, that he struck one of the grave-diggers a whack of his stick on the back. Both grave-diggers swung about to him as if both had been hurt by the one blow.

"Easy there," said the first twin.

"Easy there," said the second twin.

"Easy yourselves," cried Cahir Bowes. He wheeled about his now quivering face on Meehaul Lynskey.

"What is it you're saying about the spot between the mounds?" he demanded.

"I'm saying," said Meehaul Lynskey vehemently, "that it's the weaver's grave."

"What weaver?" asked Cahir Bowes.

"Mortimer Hehir," replied Meehaul Lynskey. "There's no other weaver in it."

"Was Julia Rafferty a weaver?"

"What Julia Rafferty?"

"The midwife, God rest her."

"How could she be a weaver if she was a midwife?"

"Not a one of me knows. But I'll tell you what I do know and know rightly: that it's Julia Rafferty is in that place and no weaver at all."

"Amn't I telling you it's the weaver's grave?"

"And amn't I telling you it's not?"

"That I may be as dead as my father but the weaver was buried there."

"A bone of a weaver was never sunk in it as long as weavers was weavers. Full of Raffertys it is."

"Alive with weavers it is."

"Heavenlyful Father, was the like ever heard: to say that a grave was alive with dead weavers."

"It's full of them—full as a tick."

"And the clean grave that Mortimer Hehir was never done boasting about—dry and sweet and deep and no way bulging at all. Did you see the burial of his father ever?"

"I did, in troth, see the burial of his father—forty year ago if it's a day."

"Forty year ago—it's fifty-one year come the sixteenth of May. It's well I remember it and it's well I have occasion to remember it, for it was the day after that again that myself ran away to join the soldiers, my

THE WEAVER'S GRAVE

aunt hot foot after me, she to be buying me out the week after, I a high-spirited fellow morebetoken."

"Leave the soldiers out of it and leave your aunt out of it and stick to the weaver's grave. Here in this place was the last weaver buried, and I'll tell you what's more. In a straight line with it is the grave of——"

"A straight line, indeed! Who but yourself, Meehaul Lynskey, ever heard of a straight line in Cloon na Morav? No such thing was ever wanted or ever allowed in it."

"In a straight direct line, measured with a rule——"

"Measured with crooked, stumbling feet, maybe feet half reeling in drink."

"Can't you listen to me now?"

"I was always a bad warrant to listen to anything except sense. Yourself ought to be the last man in the world to talk about straight lines, you with the sight scattered in your head, with the divil of sparks flying under your eyes."

"Don't mind me sparks now, nor me sight neither, for in a straight measured line with the weaver's grave was the grave of the Cassidys."

"What Cassidys?"

"The Cassidys that herded for the O'Sheas."

"Which O'Sheas?"

"O'Shea Ruadh of Cappakelly. Don't you know any one at all, or is it gone entirely your memory is?"

"Cappakelly *inagh!* And who cares a whistle about O'Shea Ruadh, he or his seed, breed and generations? It's a rotten lot of landgrabbers they were."

"Me hand to you on that. Striving ever they were to put their red paws on this bit of grass and that perch of meadow."

"Hungry in themselves even for the cutaway bog."

"And Mortimer Hehir a decent weaver, respecting every man's wool."

"His forehead pallid with honesty over the yarn and the loom."

"If a bit broad-spoken when he came to the door for a smoke of the pipe."

"Well, there won't be a mouthful of clay between himself and O'Shea Ruadh now."

"In the end what did O'Shea Ruadh get after all his striving?"

"I'll tell you that. He got what land suits a blind fiddler."

"Enough to pad the crown of the head and tap the sole of the foot! Now you're talking."

"And the devil a word out of him now no more than any one else in Cloon na Morav."

"It's easy talking to us all about land when we're packed up in our timber boxes."

"As the weaver was when he got sprinkled with the holy water in that place."

"As Julia Rafferty was when they read the prayers over her in that place, she a fine, buxom, cheerful woman in her day, with great skill in her business."

"Skill or no skill, I'm telling you she's not there, wherever she is."

"I suppose you want me to take her up in my arms and show her to you?"

"Well then, indeed, Cahir, I do not. 'Tisn't a very handsome pair you would make at all, you not able to stand much more hardship than Julia herself."

From this there developed a slow, laboured, aged dispute between the two authorities. They moved from grave to grave, pitting memory against memory, story against story, knocking down reminiscence with reminiscence, arguing in a powerful intimate obscurity that no outsider could hope to follow, blasting knowledge with knowledge, until the whole place seemed strewn with the corpses of their arguments. The two grave-diggers followed them about in a grim silence; impatience in their movements, their glances; the widow keeping track of the grand tour with a miserable feeling, a feeling, as site after site was rejected, that the tremendous exclusiveness of Cloon na Morav would altogether push her dead man, the weaver, out of his privilege. The dispute ended, like all epics, where it began. Nothing was established, nothing settled. But the two old men were quite exhausted, Meehaul Lynskey sitting down on the back of one of the monstrous cockroaches, Cahir Bowes leaning against a tombstone that was half-submerged, its end up like the stern of a derelict at sea. Here they sat glaring at each other like a pair of grim vultures.

The two grave-diggers grew restive. Their business had to be done. The weaver would have to be buried. Time pressed. They held a consultation apart. It broke up after a brief exchange of views, a little laughter.

"Meehaul Lynskey is right," said one of the twins.

Meehaul Lynskey's face lit up. Cahir Bowes looked as if he had been slapped on the cheeks. He moved out from his tombstone.

"Meehaul Lynskey is right," repeated the other twin. They had decided to break up the dispute by taking sides. They raised their spades and moved to the site which Meehaul Lynskey had urged upon them.

"Don't touch that place," Cahir Bowes cried, raising his stick. He was measuring the back of the grave-digger again when the man spun round upon him, menace in his handsome dark face.

"Touch me with that stick," he cried, "and I'll——'

Some movement in the background, some agitation

in the widow's shawl, caused the grave-digger's menace to dissolve, the words to die in his mouth, a swift flush mounting the man's face. A faint smile of gratitude swept the widow's face like a flash. If was as if she had cried out, "Ah, don't touch the poor old, cranky fellow! you might hurt him." And it was as if the grave-digger had cried back: "He has annoyed me greatly, but I don't intend to hurt him. And since you say so with your eyes I won't even threaten him."

Under pressure of the half threat, Cahir Bowes shuffled back a little way, striking an attitude of feeble dignity, leaning out on his stick while the grave-diggers got to work.

"It's the weaver's grave, surely," said Meehaul Lynskey.

"If it is," said Cahir Bowes, "remember his father was buried down seven feet. You gave into that this morning."

"There was no giving in about it," said Meehaul Lynskey. "We all know that one of the wonders of Cloon na Morav was the burial of the last weaver seven feet, he having left it as an injunction on his family. The world knows he went down the seven feet."

"And remember this," said Cahir Bowes, "that Julia Rafferty was buried no seven feet. If she is down three feet it's as much as she went."

Sure enough, the grave-diggers had not dug down more than three feet of ground when one of the spades struck hollowly on unhealthy timber. The sound was unmistakable and ominous. There was silence for a moment. Then Cahir Bowes made a sudden short spurt up a mound beside him, as if he were some sort of mechanical animal wound up, his horizontal back quivering. On the mound he made a superhuman effort to straighten himself. He got his ears and his blunt nose

THE WEAVER'S GRAVE

into a considerable elevation. He had not been so upright for twenty years. And raising his weird countenance, he broke into a cackle that was certainly meant to be a crow. He glared at Meehaul Lynskey, his emotion so great that his eyes swam in a watery triumph.

Meehaul Lynskey had his eyes, as was his custom, upon one thing, and that thing was the grave, and especially the spot on the grave where the spade had struck the coffin. He looked stunned and fearful. His eyes slowly withdrew their gimlet-like scrutiny from the spot, and sought the triumphant crowing figure of Cahir Bowes on the mound.

Meehaul Lynskey looked as if he would like to say something, but no words came. Instead he ambled away, retired from the battle, and standing apart, rubbed one leg against the other, above the back of the ankles, like some great insect. His hooked fingers at the same time stroked the bridge of his nose. He was beaten.

"I suppose it's not the weaver's grave," said one of the grave-diggers. Both of them looked at Cahir Bowes.

"Well, you know it's not," said the stonebreaker. "It's Julia Rafferty you struck. She helped many a one into the world in her day, and it's poor recompense to her to say she can't be at rest when she left it." He turned to the remote figure of Meehaul Lynskey and cried: "Ah-ha, well you may rub your ignorant legs. And I'm hoping Julia will forgive you this day's ugly work."

In silence, quickly, with reverence, the twins scooped back the clay over the spot. The widow looked on with the same quiet, patient, mysterious silence. One of the grave-diggers turned on Cahir Bowes.

"I suppose you know where the weaver's grave is?" he asked.

Cahir Bowes looked at him with an ancient tartness, then said:

"You suppose!"

"Of course, you know where it is."

Cahir Bowes looked as if he knew where the gates of heaven were, and that he might—or might not—enlighten an ignorant world. It all depended! His eyes wandered knowingly out over the meadows beyond the graveyard. He said:

"I do know where the weaver's grave is."

"We'll be very much obliged to you if you show it to us."

"Very much obliged," endorsed the other twin.

The stonebreaker, thus flattered, led the way to a new site, one nearer to the wall, where were the plagiarisms of the Eastern sepulchres. Cahir Bowes made little journeys about, measuring so many steps from one place to another, mumbling strange and unintelligible information to himself, going through an extraordinary geometrical emotion, striking the ground hard taps with his stick.

"Glory be to the Lord," cried Meehaul Lynskey, "he's like the man they had driving the water for the well in the quarry field, he whacking the ground with his magic hazel wand."

Cahir Bowes made no reply. He was too absorbed in his own emotion. A little steam was beginning to ascend from his brow. He was moving about the ground like some grotesque spider weaving an invisible web.

"I suppose now," said Meehaul Lynskey, addressing the marble monument, "that as soon as Cahir hits the right spot one of the weavers will turn about below. Or maybe he expects one of them to whistle up at him out of the ground. That's it; devil a other! When we hear the whistle we'll all know for certain where to bury the weaver."

Cahir Bowes was contracting his movements, so that he was now circling about the one spot, like a dog going to lie down.

Meehaul Lynskey drew a little closer, watching eagerly, his grim yellow face, seared with yellow marks from the fires of his workshop, tightened up in a sceptical pucker. His half-muttered words were bitter with an aged sarcasm. He cried:

"Say nothing; he'll get it yet, will the man of knowledge, the know-all, Cahir Bowes! Give him time. Give him until this day twelve month. Look at that for a right-about-turn on the left heel. Isn't the nimbleness of that young fellow a treat to see? Are they whistling to you from below, Cahir? Is it dancing to the weaver's music you are? That's it, devil a other."

Cahir Bowes was mapping out a space on the grass with his stick. Gradually it took, more or less, the outline of a grave site. He took off his hat and mopped his steaming brow with a red handkerchief, saying:

"There is the weaver's grave."

"God in Heaven," cried Meehaul Lynskey, "will you look at what he calls the weaver's grave? I'll say nothing at all. I'll hold my tongue. I'll shut up. Not one word will I say about Alick Finlay, the mildest man that ever lived, a man full of religion, never at the end of his prayers! But, sure, it's the saints of God that get the worst of it in this world, and if Alick escaped during life, faith he's in for it now, with the pirates and the body-snatchers of Cloon na Morav on top of him."

A corncrake began to sing in the near-by meadow, and his rasping notes sounded like a queer accompaniment to the words of Meehaul Lynskey. The grave-diggers, who had gone to work on the Cahir Bowes site, laughed a little, one of them looking for a moment at Meehaul Lynskey, saying:

"Listen to that damned old corncrake in the meadow! I'd like to put a sod in his mouth."

The man's eye went to the widow. She showed no emotion one way or the other, and the grave-digger got back to his work. Meehaul Lynskey, however, wore the cap. He said:

"To be sure! I'm to sing dumb. I'm not to have a word out of me at all. Others can rattle away as they like in this place, as if they owned it. The ancient good old stock is to be nowhere and the scruff of the hills let rampage as they will. That's it, devil a other. Castles falling and dunghills rising! Well, God be with the good old times and the good old mannerly people that used to be in it, and God be with Alick Finlay, the holiest——"

A sod of earth came through the air from the direction of the grave, and, skimming Meehaul Lynskey's head, dropped somewhere behind. The corncrake stopped his notes in the meadow, and Meehaul Lynskey stood statuesque in a mute protest, and silence reigned in the place while the clay sang up in a swinging rhythm from the grave.

Cahir Bowes, watching the operations with intensity, said:

"It was nearly going astray on me."

Meehaul Lynskey gave a little snort. He asked:

"What was?"

"The weaver's grave."

"Remember this: the last weaver is down seven feet. And remember this: Alick Finlay is down less than Julia Rafferty."

He had no sooner spoken when a fearful thing happened. Suddenly out of the soft cutting of the earth a spade sounded harsh on tinware, there was a crash, less harsh, but painfully distinct, as if rotten boards were falling together, then a distinct subsidence of the earth. The work stopped at once. A moment's fearful silence followed. It was broken by a short, dry laugh from Meehaul Lynskey. He said:

"God be merciful to us all! That's the latter end of Alick Finlay."

The two grave-diggers looked at each other. The shawl of the widow in the background was agitated. One twin said to the other:

"This can't be the weaver's grave."

The other agreed. They all turned their eyes upon Cahir Bowes. He was hanging forward in a pained strain, his head quaking, his fingers twitching on his stick. Meehaul Lynskey turned to the marble monument and said with venom:

"If I was guilty I'd go down on my knees and beg God's pardon. If I didn't I'd know the ghost of Alick Finlay, saint as he was, would leap upon me and guzzle me—for what right would I have to set anybody at him with driving spades when he was long years in his grave?"

Cahir Bowes took no notice. He was looking at the ground, searching about, and slowly, painfully, began his web-spinning again. The grave-diggers covered in the ground without a word. Cahir Bowes appeared to get lost in some fearful maze of his own making. A little whimper broke from him now and again. The steam from his brow thickened in the air, and eventually he settled down on the end of a headstone, having got the worst of it. Meehaul Lynskey sat on another stone facing him, and they glared, sinister and grotesque, at each other.

"Cahir Bowes," said Meehaul Lynskey, "I'll tell you what you are, and then you can tell me what I am."

"Have it whatever way you like," said Cahir Bowes. "What is it that I am?"

"You're a gentleman, a grand oul' stonebreaking gentleman. That's what you are, devil a other!"

The wrinkles on the withered face of Cahir Bowes contracted, his eyes stared across at Meehaul Lynskey, and two yellow teeth showed between his lips. He wheezed:

"And do you know what you are?"

"I don't."

"You're a nailer, that's what you are, a damned nailer."

They glared at each other in a quaking, grim silence.

And it was at this moment of collapse, of deadlock, that the widow spoke for the first time. At the first sound of her voice one of the twins perked his head, his eyes going to her face. She said in a tone as quiet as her whole behaviour:

"Maybe I ought to go up to the Tunnel Road and ask Malachi Roohan where the grave is."

They had all forgotten the oldest man of them all, Malachi Roohan. He would be the last mortal man to enter Cloon na Morav. He had been the great friend of Mortimer Hehir, the weaver, in the days that were over, and the whole world knew that Mortimer Hehir's knowledge of Cloon na Morav was perfect. Maybe Malachi Roohan would have learned a great deal from him. And Malachi Roohan, the cooper, was so long bed-ridden that those who remembered him at all thought of him as a man who had died a long time ago.

"There's nothing else for it," said one of the twins, leaving down his spade, and immediately the other twin laid his spade beside it.

The two ancients on the headstones said nothing. Not even *they* could raise a voice against the possibilities of Malachi Roohan, the cooper. By their terrible aged silence they gave consent, and the widow turned to walk out of Cloon na Morav. One of the grave-diggers took out his pipe. The eyes of the other followed the widow, he hesitated, then walked after her. She became conscious of the man's step behind her as she got upon the stile, and turned her palely sad face upon him. He stood awkwardly, his eyes wandering, then said:

"Ask Malachi Roohan where the grave is, the exact place."

It was to do this the widow was leaving Cloon na Morav; she had just announced that she was going to ask Malachi Roohan where the grave was. Yet the man's tone was that of one who was giving her extraordinarily acute advice. There was a little half-embarrassed note of confidence in his tone. In a dim way the widow thought that, maybe, he had accompanied her to the stile in a little awkward impulse of sympathy. Men were very curious in their ways sometimes. The widow was a very well-mannered woman, and she tried to look as if she had received a very valuable direction. She said:

"I will. I'll put that question to Malachi Roohan."

And then she passed out over the stile.

III

The widow went up the road, and beyond it struck the first of the houses of the near-by town. She passed through faded streets in her quiet gait, moderately grief-stricken at the death of her weaver. She had been his fourth wife, and the widowhoods of fourth wives have not the rich abandon, the great emotional cataclysm, of first, or even second, widowhoods. It is a little chastened in its poignancy. The widow had a nice feeling that it would be out of place to give way to any of the characteristic manifestations of normal widowhood. She shrank from drawing attention to the fact that she had been a fourth wife. People's memories become so extraordinarily acute to family history in times of death! The widow did not care to come in as a sort of dramatic surprise in the gossip of the people about the weaver's life. She had heard snatches of such gossip at the wake the night before. She was beginning to understand why people love wakes and the intimate personalities of wakehouses. People listen to, remember, and believe what they hear at wakes. It is more precious to them than anything they ever hear in school, church, or playhouse. It is hardly because they get certain entertainment at the wake. It is more because the wake is a grand review of family ghosts. There one hears all the stories, the little flattering touches, the little unflattering bitternesses, the traditions, the astonishing records, of the clans. The woman with a memory speaking to the company from a chair beside a laid-out corpse carries more authority than the bishop allocuting from his chair. The wake is realism. The widow had heard a great deal at the wake about the clan of the weavers, and noted, without expressing any emotion, that she had come into the story not like other women, for anything personal to her own womanhood—for beauty, or high spirit, or temper, or faithfulness, or unfaithfulness—but simply because she was a fourth wife, a kind of curiosity, the back-wash of Mortimer Hehir's romances. The widow felt a remote sense of injustice in all this. She had said to herself that widows who had been fourth wives deserved more sympathy than widows who had been first wives, for the simple reason that fourth widows had never been, and could never be, first wives! The thought

THE WEAVER'S GRAVE

confused her a little, and she did not pursue it, instinctively feeling that if she did accept the conventional view of her condition she would only crystallize her widowhood into a grievance that nobody would try to understand, and which would, accordingly, be merely useless. And what was the good of it, anyhow? The widow smoothed her dark hair on each side of her head under her shawl.

She had no bitter and no sweet memories of the weaver. There was nothing that was even vivid in their marriage. She had no complaints to make of Mortimer Hehir. He had not come to her in any fiery love impulse. It was the marriage of an old man with a woman years younger. She had recognized him as an old man from first to last, a man who had already been thrice through a wedded experience, and her temperament, naturally calm, had met his half-stormy, half-petulant character, without suffering any sort of shock. The weaver had tried to keep up to the illusion of a perennial youth by dyeing his hair, and marrying one wife as soon as possible after another. The fourth wife had come to him late in life. She had a placid understanding that she was a mere flattery to the weaver's truculent egoism.

These thoughts, in some shape or other, occupied, without agitating, the mind of the widow as she passed a dark shadowy figure through streets that were clamorous in their quietudes, painful in their lack of all the purposes for which streets have ever been created. Her only emotion was one which she knew to be quite creditable to her situation: a sincere desire to see the weaver buried in the grave to which the respectability of his family and the claims of his ancient house fully and fairly entitled him to. The proceedings in Cloon na Morav had been painful, even tragical, to the widow. The weavers had always been great authorities and zealous guardians of the ancient burial place. This function had been traditional and voluntary with them. This was especially true of the last of them, Mortimer Hehir. He had been the greatest of all authorities on the burial places of the local clans. His knowledge was scientific. He had been the grand savant of Cloon na Morav. He had policed the place. Nay, he had been its tyrant. He had over and over again prevented terrible mistakes, complications that would have appalled those concerned if they were not beyond all such concerns. The widow of the weaver had often thought that in his day Mortimer Hehir had made his solicitation for the place a passion, unreasonable, almost violent. They said that all this had sprung from a fear that had come to him in his early youth that through some blunder an alien, an inferior, even an enemy, might come to find his way into the family burial place of the weavers. This fear had made him what he was. And in his later years his pride in the family burial place became a worship. His trade had gone down, and his pride had gone up. The burial ground in Cloon na Morav was the grand proof of his aristocracy. That was the coat-of-arms, the estate, the mark of high breeding, in the weavers. And now the man who had minded everybody's grave had not been able to mind his own. The widow thought that it was one of those injustices which blacken the reputation of the whole earth. She had felt, indeed, that she had been herself slack not to have learned long ago the lie of this precious grave from the weaver himself; and that he himself had been slack in not properly instructing her. But that was the way in this miserable world! In his passion for classifying the rights of others, the weaver had obscured his own. In his long and entirely successful battle in keeping alien corpses out of his own aristocratic pit he had made his own corpse alien to every pit in the place. The living high priest was the dead pariah of Cloon na Morav. Nobody could now tell except, perhaps, Malachi Roohan, the precise spot which he had defended against the blunders and confusions of the entire community, a dead-forgetting, indifferent, slack lot!

The widow tried to recall all she had ever heard the weaver say about his grave, in the hope of getting some clue, something that might be better than the scandalous scatter-brained efforts of Meehaul Lynskey and Cahir Bowes. She remembered various detached things that the weaver, a talkative man, had said about his grave. Fifty years ago since that grave had been last opened, and it had then been opened to receive the remains of his father. It had been thirty years previous to that since it had taken in his father, that is, the newly dead weaver's father's father. The weavers were a long-lived lot, and there were not many males of them; one son was as much as any one of them begot to pass to the succession of the loom; if there were daughters they scattered, and their graves were continents apart. The three wives of the late weaver were buried in the new cemetery. The widow remembered that the weaver seldom spoke of them, and took no interest in their resting place. His heart was in Cloon na Morav and the sweet, dry, deep, aristocratic bed he had there in reserve for himself. But all his talk had been generalization. He had never, that the widow could recall, said anything about the site, about the signs and measurements by which it could be identified. No doubt, it had been well known to many people, but they had all died. The weaver had never realized what their slipping away might mean to himself. The position of the grave was so intimate to his own mind that it never occurred to him that it could be obscure to the minds of others. Mortimer Hehir had passed away like some learned and solitary astronomer who had discovered a new star, hugging its beauty, its exclusiveness, its possession to his heart, secretly rejoicing how its name would travel with his own through heavenly space for all time—and forgetting to mark its place among the known stars grouped upon his charts. Meehaul Lynskey and Cahir Bowes might now be two seasoned astronomers of venal knowledge looking for the star which the weaver, in his love for it, had let slip upon the mighty complexity of the skies.

The thing that is clearest to the mind of a man is often the thing that is most opaque to the intelligence of his bosom companion. A saint may walk the earth in the simple belief that all the world beholds his glowing halo; but all the world does not; if it did the saint would be stoned. And Mortimer Hehir had been as innocently proud of his grave as a saint might be ecstatic of his halo. He believed that when the time came he would get a royal funeral—a funeral fitting to the last of the line of great Cloon na Morav weavers. Instead of that they had no more idea of where to bury him than if he had been a wild tinker of the roads.

The widow, thinking of these things in her own mind, was about to sigh when, behind a window pane, she heard the sudden bubble of a roller canary's song. She had reached, half absent-mindedly, the home of Malachi Roohan, the cooper.

IV

The widow of the weaver approached the door of Malachi Roohan's house with an apologetic step, pawing the threshold a little in the manner of peasant women—a mannerism picked up from shy animals—before she stooped her head and made her entrance.

THE WEAVER'S GRAVE

Malachi Roohan's daughter withdrew from the fire a face which reflected the passionate soul of a cook. The face cooled as the widow disclosed her business.

"I wouldn't put it a-past my father to have knowledge of the grave," said the daughter of the house, adding, "The Lord a mercy on the weaver."

She led the widow into the presence of the cooper.

The room was small and low and stuffy, indifferently served with light by an unopenable window. There was the smell of old age, of decay, in the room. It brought almost a sense of faintness to the widow. She had the feeling that God had made her to move in the ways of old men—passionate, cantankerous, egoistic old men, old men for whom she was always doing something, always remembering things, from missing buttons to lost graves.

Her eyes sought the bed of Malachi Roohan with an unemotional, quietly sceptical gaze. But she did not see anything of the cooper. The daughter leaned over the bed, listened attentively, and then very deftly turned down the clothes, revealing the bust of Malachi Roohan The widow saw a weird face, not in the least pale or lined, but ruddy, with a mahogany bald head, a head upon which the leathery skin—for there did not seem any flesh—hardly concealed the stark outlines of the skull. From the chin there strayed a grey beard, the most shaken and whipped-looking beard that the widow had ever seen; it was, in truth, a very miracle of a beard, for one wondered how it had come there, and having come there, how it continued to hang on, for there did not seem anything to which it could claim natural allegiance. The widow was as much astonished at this beard as if she saw a plant growing in a pot without soil. Through its gaps she could see the leather of the skin, the bones of a neck, which was indeed a neck.

Over this head and shoulders the cooper's daughter bent and shouted into a crumpled ear. A little spasm of life stirred in the mummy. A low, mumbling sound came from the bed. The widow was already beginning to feel that, perhaps, she had done wrong in remembering that the cooper was still extant. But what else could she have done? If the weaver was buried in a wrong grave she did not believe that his soul would ever rest in peace. And what could be more dreadful than a soul wandering on the howling winds of the earth? The weaver would grieve, even in heaven, for his grave, grieve, maybe, as bitterly as a saint might grieve who had lost his halo. He was a passionate old man, such an old man as would have a turbulent spirit. He would surely——. The widow stifled the thoughts that flashed into her mind. She was no more superstitious than the rest of us, but——. These vague and terrible fears, and her moderately decent sorrow, were alike banished from her mind by what followed. The mummy on the bed came to life. And, what was more, he did it himself. His daughter looked on with the air of one whose sensibilities had become blunted by a long familiarity with the various stages of his resurrections. The widow gathered that the daughter had been well drilled; she had been taught how to keep her place. She did not tender the slightest help to her father as he drew himself together on the bed. He turned over on his side, then on his back, and stealthily began to insinuate his shoulder blades on the pillow, pushing up his weird head to the streak of light from the little window. The widow had been so long accustomed to assist the aged that she made some involuntary movement of succour. Some half-seen gesture by the daughter, a sudden lifting of the eyelids on the face of the patient, disclosing a pair of blue eyes, gave the widow instinctive pause. She remained where she was, aloof like the daughter of the house. And as she caught the blue of Malachi Roohan's eyes it broke upon the widow that here in the essence of the cooper there lived a spirit of extraordinary independence. Here, surely, was a man who had been accustomed to look out for himself, who resented the attentions, even in these days of his flickering consciousness. Up he wormed his shoulder blades, his mahogany skull, his leathery skin, his sensational eyes, his miraculous beard, to the light and to the full view of the visitor. At a certain stage of the resurrection—when the cooper had drawn two long, stringy arms from under the clothes—his daughter made a drilled movement forward, seeking something in the bed. The widow saw her discover the end of a rope, and this she placed in the hands of her indomitable father. The other end of the rope was fastened to the iron rail of the foot of the bed. The sinews of the patient's hands clutched the rope, and slowly, wonderfully, magically, as it seemed to the widow, the cooper raised himself to a sitting posture in the bed. There was dead silence in the room except for the laboured breathing of the performer. The eyes of the widow blinked. Yes, there was that ghost of a man hoisting himself up from the dead on a length of rope reversing the usual procedure. By that length of rope did the cooper hang on to life, and the effort of life. It represented his connection with the world, the world which had forgotten him, which marched past his window outside without knowing the stupendous thing that went on in his room. There he was, sitting up in the bed, restored to view by his own unaided efforts, holding his grip on life to the last. It cost him something to do it, but he did it. It would take him longer and longer every day to grip along that length of rope; he would fail ell by ell, sinking back to the last helplessness on his rope, descending into eternity as a vessel is lowered on a rope into a dark, deep well. But there he was now, still able for his work, unbeholding to all, self-dependent and alive, looking a little vaguely with his blue eyes at the widow of the weaver. His daughter swiftly and quietly propped pillows at his back, and she did it with the air of one who was allowed a special privilege.

"Nan!" called the old man to his daughter.

The widow, cool-tempered as she was, almost jumped on her feet. The voice was amazingly powerful. It was like a shout, filling the little room with vibrations. For four things did the widow ever after remember Malachi Roohan—for his rope, his blue eyes, his powerful voice, and his magic beard. They were thrown on the background of his skeleton in powerful relief.

"Yes, Father," his daughter replied, shouting into his ear. He was apparently very deaf. This infirmity came upon the widow with a shock. The cooper was full of physical surprises.

"Who's this one?" the cooper shouted, looking at the widow. He had the belief that he was delivering an aside.

"Mrs. Hehir."

"Mrs. Hehir—what Hehir would she be?"

"The weaver's wife."

"The weaver? Is it Mortimer Hehir?"

"Yes, Father."

"In troth I know her. She's Delia Morrissey, that married the weaver; Delia Morrissey that he followed to Munster, a raving lunatic with the dint of love."

A hot wave of embarrassment swept the widow. For a moment she thought the mind of the cooper was wandering. Then she remembered that the maiden

THE WEAVER'S GRAVE

name of the weaver's first wife was, indeed, Delia Morrissey. She had heard it, by chance, once or twice.

"Isn't it Delia Morrissey herself we have in it?" the old man asked.

The widow whispered to the daughter:

"Leave it so."

She shrank from a difficult discussion with the spectre on the bed on the family history of the weaver. A sense of shame came to her that she could be the wife to a contemporary of this astonishing old man holding on to the life rope.

"I'm out!" shouted Malachi Roohan, his blue eyes lighting suddenly. "Delia Morrissey died. She was one day eating her dinner and a bone stuck in her throat. The weaver clapped her on the back, but it was all to no good. She choked to death before his eyes on the floor. I remember that. And the weaver himself near died of grief after. But he married secondly. Who's this he married secondly, Nan?"

Nan did not know. She turned to the widow for enlightenment. The widow moistened her lips. She had to concentrate her thoughts on a subject which, for her own peace of mind, she had habitually avoided. She hated genealogy. She said a little nervously:

"Sara MacCabe."

The cooper's daughter shouted the name into his ear.

"So you're Sally MacCabe, from Looscaun, the one Mortimer took off the blacksmith? Well, well, that was a great business surely, the pair of them hot-tempered men, and your own beauty going to their heads like strong drink."

He looked at the widow, a half-sceptical, half-admiring expression flickering across the leathery face. It was such a look as he might have given to Dergorvilla of Leinster, Deirdre of Uladh, or Helen of Troy.

The widow was not the notorious Sara MacCabe from Looscaun; that lady had been the second wife of the weaver. It was said they had led a stormy life, made up of passionate quarrels and partings, and still more passionate reconciliations, Sara MacCabe from Looscaun not having quite forgotten or wholly neglected the blacksmith after her marriage to the weaver. But the widow again only whispered to the cooper's daughter:

"Leave it so."

"What way is Mortimer keeping?" asked the old man.

"He's dead," replied the daughter.

The fingers of the old man quivered on the rope.

"Dead? Mortimer Hehir dead?" he cried. "What in the name of God happened him?"

Nan did not know what happened him. She knew that the widow would not mind, so, without waiting for a prompt, she replied:

"A weakness came over him, a sudden weakness."

"To think of a man being whipped off all of a sudden like that!" cried the cooper. "When that's the way it was with Mortimer Hehir what one of us can be sure at all? Nan, none of us is sure! To think of the weaver, with his heart as strong as a bull, going off in a little weakness! It's the treacherous world we live in, the treacherous world, surely. Never another yard of tweed will he put up on his old loom! Morty, Morty, you were a good companion, a great warrant to walk the hills, whistling the tunes, pleasant in your conversation and as broad-spoken as the Bible."

"Did you know the weaver well, Father?" the daughter asked.

"Who better?" he replied. "Who drank more pints with him than what myself did? And indeed it's to his wake I'd be setting out, and it's under his coffin my shoulder would be going, if I wasn't confined to my rope."

He bowed his head for a few moments. The two women exchanged a quick, sympathetic glance.

The breathing of the old man was the breathing of one who slept. The head sank lower.

The widow said:

"You ought to make him lie down. He's tired."

The daughter made some movement of dissent; she was afraid to interfere. Maybe the cooper could be very violent if roused. After a time he raised his head again. He looked in a new mood. He was fresher, more wide-awake. His beard hung in wisps to the bedclothes.

"Ask him about the grave," the widow said.

The daughter hesitated a moment, and in that moment the cooper looked up as if he had heard, or partially heard. He said:

"If you wait a minute now I'll tell you what the weaver was." He stared for some seconds at the little window.

"Oh, we'll wait," said the daughter, and turning to the widow, added, "won't we, Mrs. Hehir?"

"Indeed we will wait," said the widow.

"The weaver," said the old man suddenly, "was a dream."

He turned his head to the women to see how they had taken it.

"Maybe," said the daughter, with a little touch of laughter, "maybe Mrs. Hehir would not give in to that."

The widow moved her hands uneasily under her shawl. She stared a little fearfully at the cooper. His blue eyes were clear as lake water over white sand.

"Whether she gives in to it, or whether she doesn't give in to it," said Malachi Roohan, "it's a dream Mortimer Hehir was. And his loom, and his shuttles, and his warping bars, and his bobbin, and the threads that he put upon the shifting racks, were all a dream. And the only thing he ever wove upon his loom was a dream."

The old man smacked his lips, his hard gums whacking. His daughter looked at him with her head a little to one side.

"And what's more," said the cooper, "every woman that ever came into his head, and every wife he married, was a dream. I'm telling you that, Nan, and I'm telling it to you of the weaver. His life was a dream, and his death is a dream. And his widow there is a dream. And all the world is a dream. Do you hear me, Nan, this world is all a dream?"

"I hear you very well, Father," the daughter sang in a piercing voice.

The cooper raised his head with a jerk, and his beard swept forward, giving him an appearance of vivid energy. He spoke in a voice like a trumpet blast:

"And I'm a dream!"

He turned his blue eyes on the widow. An unnerving sensation came to her. The cooper was the most dreadful old man she had ever seen, and what he was saying sounded the most terrible thing she had ever listened to. He cried:

"The idiot laughing in the street, the king looking at his crown, the woman turning her head to the sound of a man's step, the bells ringing in the belfry, the man walking his land, the weaver at his loom, the cooper handling his barrel, the Pope stooping for his red slippers—they're all a dream. And I'll tell you why they're a dream: because this world was meant to be a dream."

"Father," said the daughter, "you're talking too much. You'll over-reach yourself."

The old man gave himself a little pull on the rope. It

THE WEAVER'S GRAVE

was his gesture of energy, a demonstration of the fine fettle he was in. He said:

"You're saying that because you don't understand me."

"I understand you very well."

"You only think you do. Listen to me now, Nan. I want you to do something for me. You won't refuse me?"

"I will not refuse you, Father; you know very well I won't."

"You're a good daughter to me, surely, Nan. And do what I tell you now. Shut close your eyes. Shut them fast and tight. No fluttering of the lids now."

"Very well, Father."

The daughter closed her eyes, throwing up her face in the attitude of one blind. The widow was conscious of the woman's strong, rough features, something good-natured in the line of the large mouth. The old man watched the face of his daughter with excitement. He asked:

"What is it that you see now, Nan?"

"Nothing at all, Father."

"In troth you do. Keep them closed tight and you'll see it."

"I see nothing only——"

"Only what? Why don't you say it?"

"Only darkness, Father."

"And isn't that something to see? Isn't it easier to see darkness than to see light? Now, Nan, look into the darkness."

"I'm looking, Father."

"And think of something—anything at all—the stool before the kitchen fire outside."

"I'm thinking of it."

"And do you remember it?"

"I do well."

"And when you remember it what do you want to do—sit on it, maybe?"

"No, Father."

"And why wouldn't you want to sit on it?"

"Because—because I'd like to see it first, to make sure."

The old man gave a little crow of delight. He cried: "There it is! You want to make sure that it is there, although you remember it well. And that is the way with everything in this world. People close their eyes and they are not sure of anything. They want to see it again before they believe. There is Nan, now, and she does not believe in the stool before the fire, the little stool she's looking at all her life, that her mother used to seat her on before the fire when she was a small child. She closes her eyes, and it is gone! And listen to me now, Nan—if you had a man of your own and you closed your eyes you wouldn't be too sure he was the man you remembered, and you'd want to open your eyes and look at him to make sure he was the man you knew before the lids dropped on your eyes. And if you had children about you and you turned your back and closed your eyes and tried to remember them you'd want to look at them to make sure. You'd be no more sure of them than you are now of the stool in the kitchen. One flash of the eyelids and everything in this world is gone."

"I'm telling you, Father, you're talking too much."

"I'm not talking half enough. Aren't we all uneasy about the world, the things in the world that we can only believe in while we're looking at them? From one season of our life to another haven't we a kind of belief that some time we'll waken up and find everything different? Didn't you ever feel that, Nan? Didn't you think things would change, that the world would be a new place altogether, and that all that was going on around us was only a business that was doing us out of something else? We put up with it while the little hankering is nibbling at the butt of our hearts for the something else! All the men there be who believe that some day The Thing will happen, that they'll turn round the corner and waken up in the new great Street!"

"And sure," said the daughter, "maybe they are right, and maybe they will waken up."

The old man's body was shaken with a queer spasm of laughter. It began under the clothes on the bed, worked up his trunk, ran along his stringy arms, out into the rope, and the iron foot of the bed rattled. A look of extraordinarily malicious humour lit up the vivid face of the cooper. The widow beheld him with fascination, a growing sense of alarm. He might say anything. He might do anything. He might begin to sing some fearful song. He might leap out of bed.

"Nan," he said, "do you believe you'll swing round the corner and waken up?"

"Well," said Nan, hesitating a little, "I do."

The cooper gave a sort of peacock crow again. He cried:

"Och! Nan Roohan believes she'll waken up! Waken up from what? From a sleep and from a dream, from this world! Well, if you believe that, Nan Roohan, it shows you know what's what. You know what the thing around you, called the world, is. And it's only dreamers who can hope to waken up—do you hear me, Nan; it's only dreamers who can hope to waken up."

"I hear you," said Nan.

"The world is only a dream, and a dream is nothing at all! We all want to waken up out of the great nothingness of this world."

"And, please God, we will," said Nan.

"You can tell all the world from me," said the cooper, "that it won't."

"And why won't we, Father?"

"Because," said the old man, "we ourselves are the dream. When we're over the dream is over with us. That's why."

"Father," said the daughter, her head again a little to one side, "you know a great deal."

"I know enough," said the cooper shortly.

"And maybe you could tell us something about the weaver's grave. Mrs. Hehir wants to know."

"And amn't I after telling you all about the weaver's grave? Amn't I telling you it is all a dream?"

"You never said that, Father. Indeed you never did."

"I said everything in this world is a dream, and the weaver's grave is in this world, below in Cloon na Morav."

"Where in Cloon na Morav? What part of it, Father? That is what Mrs. Hehir wants to know. Can you tell her?"

"I can tell her," said Malachi Roohan. "I was at his father's burial. I remember it above all burials, because that was the day the handsome girl, Honor Costello, fell over a grave and fainted. The sweat broke out on young Donohoe when he saw Honor Costello tumbling over the grave. Not a marry would he marry her after that, and he sworn to it by the kiss of her lips. 'I'll marry no woman that fell on a grave,' says Donohoe. 'She'd maybe have a child by me with turned-in eyes or a twisted limb.' So he married a farmer's daughter, and the same morning Honor Costello married a cattle drover. Very well, then. Donohoe's wife had no child at all. She was a barren woman. Do you hear me, Nan? A barren woman she was. And such childer as Honor Costello had by the drover! Yellow hair they had, heavy

THE WEAVER'S GRAVE

as seaweed, the skin of them clear as the wind, and limbs as clean as a whistle! It was said the drover was of the blood of the Danes, and it broke out in Honor Costello's family!"

"Maybe," said the daughter, "they were Vikings."

"What are you saying?" cried the old man testily. "Ain't I telling you it's Danes they were. Did any one ever hear a greater miracle?"

"No one ever did," said the daughter, and both women clicked their tongues to express sympathetic wonder at the tale.

"And I'll tell you what saved Honor Costello," said the cooper. "When she fell in Cloon na Morav she turned her cloak inside out."

"What about the weaver's grave, Father? Mrs. Hehir wants to know."

The old man looked at the widow; his blue eyes searched her face and her figure; the expression of satirical admiration flashed over his features. The nostrils of the nose twitched. He said:

"So that's the end of the story! Sally MacCabe, the blacksmith's favourite, wants to know where she'll sink the weaver out of sight! Great battles were fought in Looscaun over Sally MacCabe! The weaver thought his heart would burst, and the blacksmith damned his soul for the sake of Sally MacCabe's idle hours."

"Father," said the daughter of the house, "let the dead rest."

"Ay," said Malachi Roohan, "let the foolish dead rest. The dream of Looscaun is over. And now the pale woman is looking for the black weaver's grave. Well, good luck to her!"

The cooper was taken with another spasm of grotesque laughter. The only difference was that this time it began by the rattling of the rail of the bed, travelled along the rope, down his stringy arms dying out somewhere in his legs in the bed. He smacked his lips, a peculiar harsh sound, as if there was not much meat to it.

"Do I know where Mortimer Hehir's grave is?" he said ruminatingly. "Do I know where me rope is?"

"Where is it, then?" his daughter asked. Her patience was great.

"I'll tell you that," said the cooper. "It's under the elm tree of Cloon na Morav. That's where it is surely. There was never a weaver yet that did not find rest under the elm tree of Cloon na Morav. There they all went as surely as the buds came on the branches. Let Sally MacCabe put poor Morty there; let her give him a tear or two in memory of the days that his heart was ready to burst for her, and believe you me no ghost will ever haunt her. No dead man ever yet came back to look upon a woman!"

A furtive sigh escaped the widow. With her handkerchief she wiped a little perspiration from both sides of her nose. The old man wagged his head sympathetically. He thought she was the long dead Sally MacCabe lamenting the weaver! The widow's emotion arose from relief that the mystery of the grave had at last been cleared up. Yet her dealings with old men had taught her caution. Quite suddenly the memory of the handsome dark face of the grave-digger who had followed her to the stile came back to her. She remembered that he said something about "the exact position of the grave." The widow prompted yet another question:

"What position under the elm tree?"

The old man listened to the question; a strained look came into his face.

"Position of what?" he asked.

"Of the grave."

"Of what grave?"

"The weaver's grave."

Another spasm seized the old frame, but this time it came from no aged merriment. It gripped his skeleton and shook it. It was as if some invisible powerful hand had suddenly taken him by the back of the neck and shaken him. His knuckles rattled on the rope. They had an appalling sound. A horrible feeling came to the widow that the cooper would fall to pieces like a bag of bones. He turned his face to his daughter. Great tears had welled into the blue eyes, giving them an appearance of childish petulance, then of acute suffering.

"What are you talking to me of graves for?" he asked, and the powerful voice broke. "Why will you be tormenting me like this? It's not going to die I am, is it? Is it going to die I am, Nan?"

The daughter bent over him as she might bend over a child. She said:

"Indeed, there's great fear of you. Lie down and rest yourself. Fatigued out and out you are."

The grip slowly slackened on the rope. He sank back, quite helpless, a little whimper breaking from him. The daughter stooped lower, reaching for a pillow that had fallen in by the wall. A sudden sharp snarl sounded from the bed, and it dropped from her hand.

"Don't touch me!" the cooper cried. The voice was again restored, powerful in its command. And to the amazement of the widow she saw him again grip along the rope and rise in the bed.

"Amn't I tired telling you not to touch me?" he cried. "Have I any business talking to you at all? Is it gone my authority is in this house?"

He glared at his daughter, his eyes red with anger, like a dog crouching in his kennel, and the daughter stepped back, a wry smile on her large mouth. The widow stepped back with her, and for a moment he held the women with their backs to the wall by his angry red eyes. Another growl and the cooper sank back inch by inch on the rope. In all her experience of old men the widow had never seen anything like this old man; his resurrections and his collapse. When he was quite down the daughter gingerly put the clothes over his shoulders and then beckoned the widow out of the room.

The widow left the house of Malachi Roohan, the cooper, with the feeling that she had discovered the grave of an old man by almost killing another.

V

The widow walked along the streets, outwardly calm, inwardly confused. Her first thought was "the day is going on me!" There were many things still to be done at home; she remembered the weaver lying there, quiet at last, the candles lighting about him, the brown habit over him, a crucifix in his hands—everything as it should be. It seemed ages to the widow since he had really fallen ill. He was very exacting and peevish all that time. His death agony had been protracted, almost melodramatically violent. A few times the widow had nearly run out of the house, leaving the weaver to fight the death battle alone. But her common sense, her good nerves, and her religious convictions had stood to her, and when she put the pennies on the weaver's eyes she was glad she had done her duty to the last. She was glad now that she had taken the search for the grave out of the hands of Meehaul Lynskey and Cahir Bowes; Malachi Roohan had been a sight, and she would never forget him, but he had known what nobody else knew. The widow, as she ascended a little upward sweep of the road to Cloon na Morav, noted that the sky beyond it was more vivid, a red band of light having struck across the grey-blue, just on the horizon. Up against this red background was the dark outline of landscape, and especially Cloon na Morav. She kept her eyes upon it as she drew nearer. Objects that were vague on the landscape began to bulk up with more distinction.

She noted the back wall of Cloon na Morav, its green lichen more vivid under the red patch of the skyline. And presently, above the green wall, black against the vivid sky, she saw elevated the bulk of one of the black cockroaches. On it were perched two drab figures, so grotesque, so still, that they seemed part of the thing itself. One figure was sloping out from the end of the tombstone so curiously that for a moment the widow thought it was a man who had reached down from the table to see what was under it. At the other end of the table was a slender warped figure, and as the widow gazed upon it she saw a sign of animation. The head and face, bleak in their outlines, were raised up in a gesture of despair. The face was turned flush against the sky, so much so that the widow's eyes instinctively sought the sky too. Above the slash of red, in the west, was a single star, flashing so briskly and so freshly that it might have never shone before. For all the widow knew, it might have been a young star frolicking in the heavens with all the joy of youth. Was that, she wondered, at what the old man, Meehaul Lynskey, was gazing. He was very, very old, and the star was very, very young! Was there some protest in the gesture of the head he raised to that thing in the sky; was there some mockery in the sparkle of the thing of the sky for the face of the man? Why should a star be always young, a man aged so soon? Should not a man be greater than a star? Was it this Meehaul Lynskey was thinking? The widow could not say, but something in the thing awed her. She had the sensation of one who surprises a man in some act that lifts him above the commonplaces of existence. It was as if Meehaul Lynskey were discovered prostrate before some altar, in the throes of a religious agony. Old men were, the widow felt, very, very strange, and she did not know that she would ever understand them. As she looked at the bleak head of Meehaul Lynskey up, against the vivid patch of the sky, she wondered if there could really be something in that head which would make him as great as a star, immortal as a star? Suddenly Meehaul Lynskey made a movement. The widow saw it quite distinctly. She saw the arm raised, the hand go out, with its crooked fingers, in one, two, three quick, short taps in the direction of the star. The widow stood to watch, and the gesture was so familiar, so homely, so personal, that it was quite understandable to her. She knew then that Meehaul Lynskey was not thinking of any great things at all. He was only a nailer! And seeing the Evening Star sparkle in the sky he had only thought of his workshop, of the bellows, the irons, the fire, the sparks, and the glowing iron which might be made into a nail while it was hot! He had in imagination seized a hammer and made a blow across interstellar space at Venus! All the beauty and youth of the star frolicking on the pale sky above the slash of vivid redness had only suggested to him the making of yet another nail! If Meehaul Lynskey could push up his scarred yellow face among the stars of the sky he would only see in them the sparks of his little smithy.

Cahir Bowes was, the widow thought, looking down at the earth, from the other end of the tombstone, to see if there were any hard things there which he could smash up. The old men had their backs turned upon

THE WEAVER'S GRAVE 339

each other. Very likely they had had another discussion since, which ended in this attitude of mutual contempt. The widow was conscious again of the unreasonableness of old men, but not much resentful of it. She was too long accustomed to them to have any great sense of revolt. Her emotion, if it could be called an emotion, was a settled, dull toleration of all their little bigotries.

She put her hand on the stile for the second time that day, and again raised her palely sad face over the graveyard of Cloon na Morav. As she did so she had the most extraordinary experience of the whole day's sensations. It was such a sensation as gave her at once a wonderful sense of the reality and the unreality of life. She paused on the stile, and had a clear insight into something that had up to this moment been obscure. And no sooner had the thing become definite and clear than a sense of the wonder of life came to her. It was all very like the dream Malachi Roohan had talked about.

In the pale grass, under the vivid colours of the sky, the two grave-diggers were lying on their backs, staring silently up at the heavens. The widow looked at them as she paused on the stile. Her thoughts of these men had been indifferent, subconscious, up to this instant. They were handsome young men. Perhaps if there had been only one of them the widow would have been more attentive. The dark handsomeness did not seem the same thing when repeated. Their beauty, if one could call it beauty, had been collective, the beauty of flowers, of dark, velvety pansies, the distinctive marks of one faithfully duplicated on the other. The good looks of one had, to the mind of the widow, somehow nullified the good looks of the other. There was too much borrowing of Peter to pay Paul in their well-favoured features. The first grave-digger spoiled the illusion of individuality in the second grave-digger. The widow had not thought so, but she would have agreed if anybody whispered to her that a good-looking man who wanted to win favour with a woman should never have so complete a twin brother. It would be possible for a woman to part tenderly with a man, and, if she met his image and likeness around the corner, knock him down. There is nothing more powerful, but nothing more delicate in life than the valves of individuality. To create the impression that humanity was a thing which could be turned out like a coinage would be to ruin the whole illusion of life. The twin grave-diggers had created some sort of such impression, vague, and not very insistent, in the mind of the widow, and it had made her lose any special interest in them. Now, however, as she hesitated on the stile, all this was swept from her mind at a stroke. That most subtle and powerful of all things, personality, sprang silently from the twins and made them, to the mind of the widow, things as far apart as the poles. The two men lay at length, and exactly the same length and bulk, in the long, grey grass. But, as the widow looked upon them, one twin seemed conscious of her presence, while the other continued his absorption in the heavens above. The supreme twin turned his head, and his soft, velvety brown eyes met the eyes of the widow. There was welcome in the man's eyes. The widow read that welcome as plainly as if he had spoken his thoughts. The next moment he had sprung to his feet, smiling. He took a few steps forward, then, self-conscious, pulled up. If he had only jumped up and smiled the widow would have understood. But those few eager steps forward and then that stock stillness! The other twin rose reluctantly, and as he did so the widow was conscious of even physical differences in the brothers. The eyes were not the same.

THE WEAVER'S GRAVE

No such velvety soft lights were in the eyes of the second one. He was more sheepish. He was more phlegmatic. He was only a plagiarism of the original man! The widow wondered how she had not seen all this before. The resemblance between the twins was only skin deep. The two old men, at the moment the second twin rose, detached themselves slowly, almost painfully, from their tombstone, and all moved forward to meet the widow. The widow, collecting her thoughts, piloted her skirts modestly about her legs as she got down from the narrow stonework of the stile and stumbled into the contrariness of Cloon na Morav. A wild sense of satisfaction swept her that she had come back the bearer of useful information.

"Well," said Meehaul Lynskey, "did you see Malachi Roohan?" The widow looked at his scorched, sceptical, yellow face, and said:

"I did."

"Had he any word for us?"

"He had. He remembers the place of the weaver's grave." The widow looked a little vaguely about Cloon na Morav.

"What does he say?"

"He says it's under the elm tree."

There was silence. The stonebreaker swung about on his legs, his head making a semi-circular movement over the ground, and his sharp eyes were turned upward, as if he were searching the heavens for an elm tree. The nailer dropped his underjaw and stared tensely across the ground, blankly, patiently, like a fisherman on the edge of the shore gazing over an empty sea. The grave-digger turned his head away shyly, like a boy, as if he did not want to see the confusion of the widow; the man was full of the most delicate mannerisms. The other grave-digger settled into a stolid attitude, then the skin bunched up about his brown eyes in puckers of humour. A miserable feeling swept the widow. She had the feeling that she stood on the verge of some collapse.

"Under the elm tree," mumbled the stonebreaker.

"That's what he said," added the widow. "Under the elm tree of Cloon na Morav."

"Well," said Cahir Bowes, "when you find the elm tree you'll find the grave."

The widow did not know what an elm tree was. Nothing had ever happened in life as she knew it to render any special knowledge of trees profitable, and therefore desirable. Trees were good; they made nice firing when chopped up; timber, and all that was fashioned out of timber, came from trees. This knowledge the widow had accepted as she had accepted all the other remote phenomena of the world into which she had been born. But that trees should have distinctive names, that they should have family relationships, seemed to the mind of the widow only an unnecessary complication of the affairs of the universe. What good was it? She could understand calling fruit trees fruit trees and all other kinds simply trees. But that one should be an elm and another an ash, that there should be name after name, species after species, giving them peculiarities and personalities, was one of the things that the widow did not like. And at this moment, when the elm tree of Malachi Roohan had raised a fresh problem in Cloon na Morav, the likeness of old men to old trees—their crankiness, their complexity, their angles, their very barks, bulges, gnarled twistiness, and kinks —was very close, and brought a sense of oppression to the sorely-tried brain of the widow.

"Under the elm tree," repeated Meehaul Lynskey. "The elm tree of Cloon na Morav." He broke into an aged cackle of a laugh. "If I was any good at all at making a rhyme I'd make one about that elm tree, devil a other but I would."

The widow looked around Cloon na Morav, and her eyes, for the first time in her life, were consciously searching for trees. If there were numerous trees there she could understand how easy it might be for Malachi Roohan to make a mistake. He might have mistaken some other sort of tree for an elm—the widow felt that there must be plenty of other trees very like an elm. In fact, she reasoned that other trees, do their best, could not help looking like an elm. There must be thousands and millions of people like herself in the world who pass through life in the belief that a certain kind of tree was an elm when, in reality, it may be an ash or an oak or a chestnut or a beech, or even a poplar, a birch, or a yew. Malachi Roohan was never likely to allow anybody to amend his knowledge of an elm tree. He would let go his rope in the belief that there was an elm tree in Cloon na Morav, and that under it was the weaver's grave—that is, if Malachi Roohan had not, in some ghastly aged kink, invented the thing. The widow, not sharply, but still with an appreciation of the thing, grasped that a dispute about trees would be the very sort of dispute in which Meehaul Lynskey and Cahir Bowes would, like the very old men that they were, have revelled. Under the impulse of the message she had brought from the cooper they would have launched out into another powerful struggle from tree to tree in Cloon na Morav; they would again have strewn the place with the corpses of slain arguments, and in the net result they would not have been able to establish anything either about elm trees or about the weaver's grave. The slow, sad gaze of the widow for trees in Cloon na Morav brought to her, in these circumstances, both pain and relief. It was a relief that Meehaul Lynskey and Cahir Bowes could not challenge each other to a battle of trees; it was a pain that the tree of Malachi Roohan was nowhere in sight. The widow could see for herself that there was not any sort of a tree in Cloon na Morav. The ground was enclosed upon three sides by walls, on the fourth by a hedge of quicks. Not even old men could transform a hedge into an elm tree. Neither could they make the few struggling briars clinging about the railings of the sepulchres into anything except briars. The elm tree of Malachi Roohan was now non-existent. Nobody would ever know whether it had or had not ever existed. The widow would as soon give the soul of the weaver to the howling winds of the world as go back and interview the cooper again on the subject.

"Old Malachi Roohan," said Cahir Bowes with tolerant decision, "is doting."

"The nearest elm tree I know," said Meehaul Lynskey, "is half a mile away."

"The one above at Carragh?" questioned Cahir Bowes.

"Ay, beside the mill."

No more was to be said. The riddle of the weaver's grave was still the riddle of the weaver's grave. Cloon na Marov kept its secret. But, nevertheless, the weaver would have to be buried. He could not be housed indefinitely. Taking courage from all the harrowing aspects of the deadlock, Meehaul Lynsky went back, plump and courageously to his original allegiance.

"The grave of the weaver is there," he said, and he struck out his hooked fingers in the direction of the disturbance of the sod which the grave-diggers had made under pressure of his earlier enthusiasm.

Cahir Bowes turned on him with a withering, quavering glance.

"Aren't you afraid that God would strike you where you stand?" he demanded.

"I'm not—not a bit afraid," said Meehaul Lynskey. "It's the weaver's grave."

"You say that," cried Cahir Bowes, "after what we all saw and what we all heard?"

"I do," said Meehaul Lynskey, stoutly. He wiped his lips with the palm of his hand, and launched out into one of his arguments, arguments, as usual, packed with particulars.

"I saw the weaver's father lowered in that place. And I'll tell you, what's more, it was Father Owen MacCarthy that read over him, he a young red-haired curate in this place at the time, long before ever he became parish priest of Benelog. There was I, standing in this exact spot, a young man, too, with a light moustache, holding me hat in me hand, and there one side of me—maybe five yards from the marble stone of the Keernahans—was Patsy Curtin that drank himself to death after, and on the other side of me was Honor Costello, that fell on the grave and married the cattle drover, a big, loose-shouldered Dane."

Patiently, half absent-mindedly, listening to the renewal of the dispute, the widow remembered the words of Malachi Roohan, and his story of Honor Costello, who fell on the grave over fifty years ago. What memories these old men had! How unreliable they were, and yet flashing out astounding corroborations of each other. Maybe there was something in what Meehaul Lynskey was saying. Maybe—but the widow checked her thoughts. What was the use of it all? This grave could not be the weaver's grave; it had been grimly demonstrated to them all that it was full of stout coffins. The widow, with a gesture of agitation, smoothed her hair down the gentle slope of her head under the shawl. As she did so her eyes caught the eyes of the grave-digger; he was looking at her! He withdrew his eyes at once, and began to twitch the ends of his dark moustache with his fingers.

"If," said Cahir Bowes, "this be the grave of the weaver, what's Julia Rafferty doing in it? Answer me that, Meehaul Lynskey."

"I don't know what's she doing in it, and what's more, I don't care. And believe you my word, many a queer thing happened in Cloon na Morav that had no right to happen in it. Julia Rafferty, maybe, isn't the only one that is where she had no right to be."

"Maybe she isn't," said Cahir Bowes, "but it's there she is, anyhow, and I'm thinking it's there she's likely to stay."

"If she's in the weaver's grave," cried Meehaul Lynskey, "what I say is, out with her!"

"Very well, then, Meehaul Lynskey. Let you yourself be the powerful man to deal with Julia Rafferty. But remember this, and remember it's my word, that touch one bone in this place and you touch all."

"No fear at all have I to right a wrong. I'm no back-slider when it comes to justice, and justice I'll see done among the living and the dead."

"Go ahead, then, me hearty fellow. If Julia herself is in the wrong place somebody else must be in her own place, and you'll be following one rightment with another wrongment until in the end you'll go mad with the tangle of dead men's wrongs. That's the end that's in store for you, Meehaul Lynskey."

Meehaul Lynskey spat on his fist and struck out with the hooked fingers. His blood was up.

"That I may be as dead as my father!" he began in a traditional oath, and at that Cahir Bowes gave a little cry and raised his stick with a battle flourish. They went up and down the dips of the ground, rising and falling on the waves of their anger, and the widow stood where she was, miserable and downhearted, her feet growing stone cold from the chilly dampness of the ground. The twin, who did not now count, took out his pipe and lit it, looking at the old men with a stolid gaze. The twin who now counted walked uneasily away, bit an end off a chunk of tobacco, and came to stand in the ground in a line with the widow, looking on with her several feet away; but again the widow was conscious of the man's growing sympathy.

"They're a nice pair of boyos, them two old lads," he remarked to the widow. He turned his head to her. He was very handsome.

"Do you think they will find it?" she asked. Her voice was a little nervous, and the man shifted on his feet, nervously responsive.

"It's hard to say," he said. "You'd never know what to think. Two old lads, the like of them, do be very tricky."

"God grant they'll get it," said the widow.

"God grant," said the grave-digger.

But they didn't. They only got exhausted as before, wheezing and coughing, and glaring at each other as they sat down on two mounds.

The grave-digger turned to the widow.

She was aware of the nice warmth of his brown eyes.

"Are you waking the weaver again tonight?" he asked.

"I am," said the widow.

"Well, maybe some person—some old man or woman from the country—may turn up and be able to tell where the grave is. You could make inquiries."

"Yes," said the widow, but without any enthusiasm, "I could make inquiries."

The grave-digger hesitated for a moment, and said more sympathetically, "We could all, maybe, make inquiries." There was a softer personal note, a note of adventure, in the voice.

The widow turned her head to the man and smiled at him quite frankly.

"I'm beholding to you," she said and then added with a little wounded sigh, "Everyone is very good to me."

The grave-digger twirled the ends of his moustache.

Cahir Bowes, who had heard, rose from his mound and said briskly, "I'll agree to leave it at that." His air was that of one who had made an extraordinary personal sacrifice. What he was really thinking was that he would have another great day of it with Meehaul Lynskey in Cloon na Morav tomorrow. He'd show that oul' fellow, Lynskey, what stuff Boweses were made of.

"And I'm not against it," said Meehaul Lynskey. He took the tone of one who was never to be outdone in magnanimity. He was also thinking of another day of effort tomorrow, a day that would, please God, show the Boweses what the Lynskeys were like.

With that the party came straggling out of Cloon na Morav, the two old men first, the widow next, the grave-diggers waiting to put on their coats and light their pipes.

There was a little upward slope on the road to the town, and as the two old men took it the widow thought they looked very spent after their day. She wondered if Cahir Bowes would ever be able for that hill. She would give him a glass of whisky at home, if there was any left in the bottle. Of the two, and as limp and slack as his body looked, Meehaul Lynskey appeared the better able for the hill. They walked together, that is to say, abreast, but they kept almost the width of the road between each other, as if this gulf expressed the breach of friendship between them on the head of the dispute about the weaver's grave. They had been making liars of each other all day, and they would, please God, make liars of each other all day tomorrow. The widow, understanding the meaning of this hostility, had a faint sense of amusement at the contrariness of old men. How could she tell what was passing in the head which Cahir Bowes hung, like a fuchsia drop, over the road? How could she know of the strange rise and fall of the thoughts, the little frets, the tempers, the faint humours, which chased each other there? Nobody —not even Cahir Bowes himself—could account for them. All the widow knew was that Cahir Bowes stood suddenly on the road. Something had happened in his brain, some old memory cell long dormant had become nascent, had a stir, a pulse, a flicker of warmth, of activity, and swiftly as a flash of lightning in the sky, a glow of lucidity lit up his memory. It was as if a searchlight had suddenly flooded the dark corners of his brain. The immediate physical effect on Cahir Bowes was to cause him to stand stark still on the road, Meehaul Lynskey going ahead without him. The widow saw Cahir Bowes pivot on his heels, his head, at the end of the horizontal body, swinging round like the movement of a hand on a runaway clock. Instead of pointing up the hill homeward the head pointed down the hill and back to Cloon na Morav. There followed the most extraordinary movements—shufflings, gyrations—that the widow had ever seen. Cahir Bowes wanted to run like mad away down the road. That was plain. And Cahir Bowes believed that he was running like mad away down the road. That was also evident. But what he actually did was to make little jumps on his feet, his stick rattling the ground in front, and each jump did not bring him an inch of ground. He would have gone more rapidly in his normal shuffle. His efforts were like a terrible parody on the springs of a kangaroo. And Cahir Bowes, in a voice that was now more a scream than a cackle, was calling out unintelligible things. The widow, looking at him, paused in wonder, then over her face there came a relaxation, a colour, her eyes warmed, her expression lost its settled pensiveness, and all her body was shaken with uncontrollable laughter. Cahir Bowes passed her on the road in his fantastic leaps, his abortive buck-jumps, screaming and cracking his stick on the ground, his left hand still gripped tightly on the small of his back behind, a powerful brake on the small of his back.

Meehaul Lynskey turned back and his face was shaken with an aged emotion as he looked after the stonebreaker. Then he removed his hat and blessed himself.

"The cross of Christ between us and harm," he exclaimed. "Old Cahir Bowes has gone off his head at last. I thought there was something up with him all day. It was easily known there was something ugly working in his mind."

The widow controlled her laughter and checked herself, making the sign of the cross on her forehead, too. She said:

"God forgive me for laughing and the weaver with the habit but fresh upon him."

The grave-digger who counted was coming out somewhat eagerly over the stile, but Cahir Bowes, flourishing his stick, beat him back again and then himself reentered Cloon na Morav. He stumbled over the grass, now rising on a mound, now disappearing altogether in a dip of the ground, travelling in a giddy course like a

THE WEAVER'S GRAVE

hooker in a storm; again, for a long time, he remained submerged, showing, however, the eternal stick, his periscope, his indication to the world that he was about his business. In a level piece of ground, marked by stones with large mottled white marks upon them, he settled and cried out to all, and calling God to witness, that this surely was the weaver's grave. There was scepticism, hesitation, on the part of the grave-diggers, but after some parley, and because Cahir Bowes was so passionate, vehement, crying and shouting, dribbling water from the mouth, showing his yellow teeth, pouring sweat on his forehead, quivering on his legs, they began to dig carefully in the spot. The widow, at this, re-arranged the shawl on her head and entered Cloon na Morav, conscious, as she shuffled over the stile, that a pair of warm brown eyes were, for a moment, upon her movements and then withdrawn. She stood a little way back from the digging and waited the result with a slightly more accelerated beating of the heart. The twins looked as if they were ready to strike something unexpected at any moment, digging carefully, and Cahir Bowes hung over the place, cackling and crowing, urging the men to swifter work. The earth sang up out of the ground, dark and rich in colour, gleaming like gold, in the deepening twilight in the place. Two feet, three feet, four feet of earth came up, the spades pushing through the earth in regular and powerful pushes, and still the coast was clear. Cahir Bowes trembled with excitement on his stick. Five feet of a pit yawned in the ancient ground. The spade work ceased. One of the grave-diggers looked up at Cahir Bowes and said:

"You hit the weaver's grave this time right enough. Not another grave in the place could be as free as this."

The widow sighed a quick little sigh and looked at

the face of the other grave-digger, hesitated, then allowed a remote smile of thankfulness to flit across her palely sad face. The eyes of the man wandered away over the darkening spaces of Cloon na Morav.

"I got the weaver's grave surely," cried Cahir Bowes, his old face full of a weird animation. If he had found the Philosopher's Stone he would only have broken it. But to find the weaver's grave was an accomplishment that would help him into a wisdom before which all his world would bow. He looked around triumphantly and said:

"Where is Meehaul Lynskey now; what will the people be saying at all about his attack on Julia Rafferty's grave? Julia will haunt him, and I'd sooner have any one at all haunting me than the ghost of Julia Rafferty. Where is Meehaul Lynskey now? Is it ashamed to show his liary face he is? And what talk had Malachi Roohan about an elm tree? Elm tree, indeed! If it's trees that is troubling him now let him climb up on one of them and hang himself from it with his rope! Where is that old fellow, Meehaul Lynskey, and his rotten head? Where is he, I say? Let him come in here now to Cloon na Morav until I be showing him the weaver's grave, five feet down and not a rib or a knuckle in it, as clean and beautiful as the weaver ever wished it. Come in here, Meehaul Lynskey, until I hear the lies panting again in your yellow throat."

He went in his extraordinary movement over the ground, making for the stile all the while talking.

Meehaul Lynskey had crouched behind the wall outside when Cahir Bowes led the diggers to the new site, his old face twisted in an attentive, almost agonizing emotion. He stood peeping over the wall, saying to himself:

"Whisht, will you! Don't mind that old madman. He

THE WEAVER'S GRAVE

hasn't it at all. I'm telling you he hasn't it. Whisht, will you! Let him dig away. They'll hit something in a minute. They'll level him when they find out. His brain has turned. Whisht, now, will you, and I'll have that rambling old lunatic, Cahir Bowes, in a minute. I'll leap in on him. I'll charge him before the world. I'll show him up. I'll take the gab out of him. I'll lacerate him. I'll lambaste him. Whisht, will you!"

But as the digging went on and the terrible cries of triumph arose inside Meehaul Lynskey's knees knocked together. His head bent level to the wall, yellow and grimacing, nerves twitching across it, a little yellow froth gathering at the corners of the mouth. When Cahir Bowes came beating for the stile Meehaul Lynskey rubbed one leg with the other, a little below the calf, and cried brokenly to himself:

"God in Heaven, he has it! He has the weaver's grave."

He turned about and slunk along in the shadow of the wall up the hill, panting and broken. By the time Cahir Bowes had reached the stile Meehaul Lynskey's figure was shadowily dipping down over the crest of the road. A sharp cry from Cahir Bowes caused him to shrink out of sight like a dog at whom a weapon had been thrown.

The eyes of the grave-digger who did not now count followed the figure of Cahir Bowes as he moved to the stile. He laughed a little in amusement, then wiped his brow. He came up out of the grave. He turned to the widow and said:

"We're down five feet. Isn't that enough in which to sink the weaver in? Are you satisfied?"

The man spoke to her without any pretence at fine feeling. He addressed her as a fourth wife should be addressed. The widow was conscious but unresentful of the man's manner. She regarded him calmly and without any resentment. On her part there was no resentment either, no hypocrisy, no make-believe. Her unemotional eyes followed his action as he stuck his spade into the loose mould on the ground. A cry from Cahir Bowes distracted the man, he laughed again, and before the widow could make a reply he said:

"Old Cahir is great value. Come down until we hear him handling the nailer."

He walked away down over the ground.

The widow was left alone with the other gravedigger. He drew himself up out of the pit with a sinuous movement of the body which the widow noted. He stood without a word beside the pile of heaving clay and looked across at the widow. She looked back at him and suddenly the silence became full of unspoken words, of flying, ringing emotions. The widow could see the dark green wall, above it the band of still deepening red, above that the still more pallid grey sky, and directly over the man's head the gay frolicking of the fresh star in the sky. Cloon na Morav was flooded with a deep, vague light. The widow scented the fresh wind about her, the cool fragrance of the earth, and yet a warmth that was strangely beautiful. The light of the man's dark eyes were visible in the shadow which hid his face. The pile of earth beside him was like a vague shape of miniature bronze mountains. He stood with a stillness which was tense and dramatic. The widow thought that the world was strange, the sky extraordinary, the man's head against the red sky a wonder, a poem, above it the sparkle of the great young star. The widow knew that they would be left together like this for one minute, a minute which would be as a flash and as eternity. And she knew now that sooner or later this man would come to her and that she would welcome him. Below at the stile the voice of Cahir Bowes was cackling in its aged notes. Beyond this the stillness was the stillness of heaven and earth. Suddenly a sense of faintness came to the widow. The whole place swooned before her eyes. Never was this world so strange, so like the dream that Malachi Roohan had talked about. A movement in the figure of the man beside the heap of bronze had come to her as a warning, a fear, and a delight. She moved herself a little in response, made a step backward. The next instant she saw the figure of the man spring across the open black mouth of the weaver's grave to her.

A faint sound escaped her and then his breath was hot on her face, his mouth on her lips.

Half a minute later Cahir Bowes came shuffling back, followed by the twin.

"I'll bone him yet," said Cahir Bowes. "Never you fear I'll make that old nailer face me. I'll show him up at the weaver's wake tonight!"

The twin laughed behind him. He shook his head at his brother, who was standing a pace away from the widow. He said:

"Five feet."

He looked into the grave and then looked at the widow, saying:

"Are you satisfied?"

There was silence for a second or two, and when she spoke the widow's voice was low but fresh, like the voice of a young girl. She said:

"I'm satisfied."

FRANK O'CONNOR
Song Without Words

EVEN if there were only two men left in the world and both of them to be saints, they wouldn't be happy even then. One of them would be bound to try and improve the other. That is the nature of things.

There were two men one time in the big monastery near our place called Brother Arnold and Brother Michael. In private life Brother Arnold was a postman, but as he had a great name as a cattle doctor they put him in charge of the monastery cows. He had the sort of face you'd expect to see advertising somebody's tobacco; a big, innocent, good-humoured face with a pair of blue eyes that always had a twinkle in them. Of course, by the rule he was supposed to look sedate and go round in a composed and measured way, but wherever Brother Arnold went his eyes went along with him, to see what devilment would he see on the way, and the eyes would give a twinkle and the hands would slip out of the long white sleeves and he'd be beckoning and doing sign talk on his fingers till further orders.

Now, one day it happened that he was looking for a bottle of castor oil and he suddenly remembered that he'd lent it to Brother Michael in the stables. Brother Michael was a fellow he didn't get on too well with at all; a dour, silent sort of man that kept himself to himself. He was a man of no great appearance, with a mournful, wizened little face and a pair of weak, red-rimmed eyes—for all the world the sort of man that, if you shaved off his beard, clapped a bowler hat on his head and a fag in his mouth, wouldn't need any other reference to get a job in a stables.

There wasn't any sign of him around the stable yard,

SONG WITHOUT WORDS

but that was only natural because he wouldn't be wanted till the other monks came back from the fields, so Brother Arnold banged in the stable door and went to look for the bottle himself. He didn't see the bottle but he saw something else he'd rather not have seen, and that was Brother Michael, hiding in one of the horse-boxes. He was standing against the partition, hoping he wouldn't be noticed, with something hidden behind his back and the look of a little boy that's just been caught at the jam. Something told Brother Arnold he was the most unwelcome man in the world at that minute. He got red and waved his hand by way of showing that he hadn't seen anything and that if he had it was none of his business, and away with him out and back to his own quarters.

It came as a bit of a shock to him. You could see plain enough that the other man was up to something nasty and you could hardly help wondering what it was. It was funny; he always noticed the same thing when he was in the world; it was the quiet, sneaky fellows that were always up to mischief. In chapel he looked at Brother Michael and he got the impression that Brother Michael was also looking at him; a sneaky sort of look to make sure he wouldn't be spotted. Next day again when they met in the yard he caught Brother Michael looking at him, and he gave him back a cold look and nod as much as to say he had him taped.

The day after Brother Michael beckoned him to come over to the stable for a minute, as if there was one of the horses sick. Brother Arnold knew well it wasn't one of the horses, but he went all the same. He was curious to know what explanation he would be offered. Brother Michael closed the door carefully after him and then leaned back against the jamb of the door with his legs crossed and his hands behind his back, a real foxy look. Then he nodded in the direction of the horse-box as much as to say "Remember the day you saw me in there?" Brother Arnold nodded. He wasn't likely to forget it. So then Brother Michael put his hand up his sleeve and held out a folded newspaper. Brother Arnold grinned as much as to say "Are you letting on now that that was all you were up to, reading a paper?" but the other man pressed it into his hands. He opened it without any great curiosity, thinking it might be some local paper the man got for the news from home. He glanced at the name of it, and then a light broke on him. His whole face lit up as if you'd switched an electric torch on behind, and at last he burst out laughing. He couldn't help himself. Brother Michael didn't laugh, but he gave a dry little cackle which was as near as he ever got to a laugh. The name of the paper was *The Irish Racing News*. Brother Michael pointed to a heading about the Curragh and then pointed at himself. Brother Arnold shook his head and gave him another look as if he was waiting for another good laugh out of him. Brother Michael scratched his head for something to show what he meant. He was never much good at the sign language. Then he picked up the sweeping brush and straddled it. He pulled up his skirts; he stretched his left hand out, holding the handle of the brush and began flogging the air behind him, with a grim look on his leathery little puss. And then Brother Arnold nodded and nodded and put up his thumbs to show he understood. He saw now that the reason Brother Michael behaved so queerly was because he read racing papers on the sly, and he read racing papers on the sly because in private life he was a jockey on the Curragh.

He was still laughing away like mad with his blue eyes dancing, and then he remembered all the things

SONG WITHOUT WORDS 359

he thought about Brother Michael and bowed his head and beat his breast by way of asking pardon. After that he took another look at the paper. A mischievous twinkle came into his eyes and he pointed the paper at himself. Brother Michael pointed back at him, a bit puzzled. Brother Arnold chuckled and nodded and stuffed the paper up his own sleeve. Then Brother Michael winked and gave the thumbs-up sign, and in that slow cautious way of his he went down the stable and reached up to the top of the wall where the stable roof sloped down. That was his hiding hole. He took down several more and gave them to Brother Arnold.

For the rest of the day Brother Arnold was in the best of humour. He winked and smiled at everyone round the farm till they were all wondering what the joke was. All that evening and long after he went to his cubicle, he rubbed his hands and giggled with delight every time he thought of it; it gave him a warm, mellow feeling as if his heart had expanded to embrace all humanity.

It wasn't till next morning that he had a chance of looking at the papers himself. He took them out and spread them on a rough desk under a feeble electric-light bulb high up in the roof. It was four years since last he'd seen a paper of any sort, and then it was only a bit of a local newspaper that one of the carters had brought wrapped about a bit of bread and butter. Brother Arnold had palmed it as neatly as any conjurer; hidden it away in his desk and studied it as if it was a bit of a lost Greek play. There was nothing on it but a bit of a County Council wrangle about the appointment of seven warble-fly inspectors, but by the time he was finished with it he knew it by heart. So he didn't just glance at the papers the way a man would in the train to pass the time. He nearly ate them. Blessed bits of words like fragments of tunes coming to him out of a past life; paddocks and point-to-points and two-year-olds; and there he was in the middle of a racecourse crowd on a spring day, with silver streamers of light floating down the sky like heavenly bunting. He was a handsome fellow in those days. He had only to close his eyes and he could see the refreshment tent again, with the golden light leaking like spilt honey through the rents in the canvas, and there was the little girl he used to be sparking, sitting on an upturned lemonade box. "Ah, Paddy," she said, "sure there's bound to be racing in Heaven." She was fast; too fast for Brother Arnold, who was a quiet-going sort of fellow, and he never got over the shock when he found out that she was running another fellow all the time. But now, all he could remember of her was her smile, and afterwards, whenever his eyes met Brother Michael's he longed to give him a hearty slap on the back and say "Michael, there's bound to be racing in Heaven," and then a grin spread over his big sunny face, and Brother Michael, without once losing that casual, melancholy air, replied with a wall-faced flicker of the horny eyelid; a tick-tack man's signal; a real expressionless, horsy look of complete understanding.

One day Brother Michael came in and took out a couple of papers. On one of them he pointed to the horses he'd marked; on the other to the horses that came up. He didn't show any sign of jubilation. He just winked, a leathery sort of a wink, and Brother Arnold gaped as he saw the list of winners. It filled him with wonder to think that where so many clever people lost, a simple little monk, living hundreds of miles away, could foresee it all. The more he thought of it, the more excited he got. He went to the door, reached up his long arm and took down a loose stone from the wall above it. Brother Michael nodded slowly three or four times as much as to say "Well, you're a caution!" Brother Arnold grinned broadly. He might have been saying "That's nothing." Then he took down a bottle and handed it to Brother Michael. The jockey gave him one look; his face didn't change, but he took out the cork and sniffed. Still his face never changed. Then all at once he went to the door, gave a quick glance up and a quick glance down and raised the bottle to his mouth. The beer was strong; it made him redden and cough. He cleaned the neck of the bottle with his sleeve before he gave it back. A shudder went through him and his little eyes watered as he watched Brother Arnold's throttle moving on well-oiled hinges. The big man put the bottle back in its hiding-place and beckoned to Brother Michael that he could go there himself whenever he liked. Brother Michael shook his head but Brother Arnold nodded earnestly. His fingers moved like lightning while he explained how a farmer whose cow he had cured left a bottle in the yard for him every week.

Now, Brother Michael's success made Brother Arnold want to try his hand, and whenever Brother Michael gave him a copy of a racing paper with his own selections marked, Brother Arnold gave it back with his, and then they contented themselves as well as they could till the results turned up, three or four days late. It was a new lease of life to the little jockey, for what comfort is it to a man even if he has all the winners when there isn't a soul in the whole world he can tell? He felt now if only he could have a bob each way on a horse, he'd never ask any more of life. Unfortunately, he hadn't a bob. That put Brother Arnold thinking. He was a resourceful chap, and it was he who invented the dockets, valued for so many Hail Marys. The man who lost had to pay up in prayers for the other man's intention. It was an ingenious scheme and it worked admirably.

At first Brother Arnold had a run of luck. But it wasn't for nothing that the other man had been a jockey. He was too hardy to make a fool of himself, even over a few Hail Marys, and everything he did was carefully planned. Brother Arnold began carefully enough, but the moment he struck it lucky, he began to gamble wildly. Brother Michael had often seen it happen on the Curragh, and he remembered the fate of the men it happened to. Fellows he'd known with big houses and cars were now cadging drinks on the streets of Dublin. "Aha, my lad," he said to himself, thinking of his companion, "God was very good to you the day he called you in here where you couldn't do harm to yourself or those belonged to you."

Which, by the way, was quite uncalled for, because in the world Brother Arnold's only weakness was for a drop of stout, and it never did him any harm, but Brother Michael was rather given to a distrust of human nature; the sort of man who goes looking for a moral in everything, even when there's no moral in it. He tried to make Brother Arnold take a proper interest in the scientific side of betting, but the man seemed to take it all as a great joke, a flighty sort of fellow. He bet more and more wildly, with that foolish good-natured grin on his face, and after a while Brother Michael found himself being owed the deuce of a lot of prayers. He didn't like that either. It gave him scruples of conscience and finally turned him against betting in any shape or form. He tried to get Brother Arnold to drop it, but Brother Arnold only looked hurt and a little indignant, like a child you've told to stop his game. Brother Michael had that weakness on his conscience too. It suggested that he was getting too attached to Brother Arnold, as in fact he was. He had to admit it. There was something warm and friendly about the man that you couldn't help liking.

Then one day he went in to Brother Arnold and found him with a pack of cards in his hand. They were a very old pack that had more than served their time in some farmer's house. They gave Brother Michael a turn, just to look at them. Brother Arnold made the gesture of dealing them out and Brother Michael shook his head. Brother Arnold blushed and bit his lip, but he persisted. All the doubts Brother Michael had been having for weeks turned to conviction. This was the primrose path with a vengeance; one thing leading to another. Brother Arnold grinned and shuffled the deck; Brother Michael, biding his time, cut for deal and Brother Arnold won. He dealt two hands of five and showed the five of hearts as trump. Just because he was still waiting for a sign, Brother Michael examined his own hand. His face got grimmer. It wasn't the sort of sign he had been expecting, but it was a sign all the same: four hearts all in a bunch; the ace, the jack, two other trumps and the three of spades. All he had to do was surrender the spade and pick up the five of trumps, and there he was with an unbeatable hand. Was that luck? Was that coincidence, or was it the Old Boy himself, taking a hand and trying to draw him deeper down into the mud? He liked to find the moral in things, and the moral in this was as plain as a pikestaff though it went to his heart to admit it. He was a lonesome, melancholy little man and the horses had meant a lot to him in his bad spells. At times it seemed as if they were the only thing that kept him from going clean dotty. How was he going to face maybe twenty or thirty years more of life, never knowing what horses were running or what jocks were up—Derby Day, Punchestown, Leopardstown and the Curragh, all going by and he knowing no more of them than if he was dead?

"O Lord," he thought bitterly, "a fellow gives up the whole world for You, his chance of a wife and kids, his home and his family, his friends and his job, and goes off to a bare mountain where he can't even tell his troubles to the man alongside him; and still he keeps something back. One little thing to remind him of what he gave up. With me 'twas the horses and with this man 'twas the sup of beer, and I daresay there's fellows inside that have a bit of a girl's hair hidden somewhere they can go and look at it now and again. I suppose we all have our little hiding hole, if the truth was known, but as small as it is, the whole world is in it, and bit by bit it grows on us again till the day You find us out."

Brother Arnold was waiting for him to play. He gave a great sigh and put his hand on the desk. Brother Arnold looked at it and then looked at him. Brother Michael idly took away the spade and added the heart, and still Brother Arnold couldn't see. Then Brother Michael shook his head and pointed down through the floor. Brother Arnold bit his lip again as though he were on the point of crying, threw down his own hand and walked away to the other end of the cow-house. Brother Michael left him so for a few moments. He could see the struggle that was going on in the man; he could almost hear the Old Boy whispering in his ear that he, Brother Michael, was only an old woman (Brother Michael had heard that before); that life was long and that a man might as well be dead and buried as not have some little thing to give him an innocent bit of amusement—the sort of plausible whisper that put many a man on the gridiron. He knew that however hard it was now, Brother Arnold would be thankful to him in the next world. "Brother Michael," he'd say, "I don't know what I'd ever have done without the example you gave me."

Then Brother Michael went up and touched him gently on the shoulder. He pointed to the bottle, the racing paper and the cards in turn. Brother Arnold heaved a terrible sigh but he nodded. They gathered them up between them, the cards and the bottle and the papers, hid them under their habits to avoid all occasion of scandal and went off to confess their crimes to the Prior.

JAMES JOYCE

Mr. Bloom Takes a Walk

BY LORRIES along Sir John Rogerson's quay Mr Bloom walked soberly, past Windmill lane, Leask's the linseed crusher's, the postal telegraph office. Could have given that address too. And past the sailors' home. He turned from the morning noises of the quayside and walked through Lime street. By Brady's cottages a boy for the skins lolled, his bucket of offal linked, smoking a chewed fagbutt. A smaller girl with scars of eczema on her forehead eyed him, listlessly holding her battered caskhoop. Tell him if he smokes he won't grow. O let him! His life isn't such a bed of roses! Waiting outside pubs to bring da home. Come home to ma, da, Slack hour: won't be many there. He crossed Townsend street, passed the frowning face of Bethel. El, yes: house of: Aleph, Beth. And past Nichols' the undertaker's. At eleven it is. Time enough. Daresay Corny Kelleher bagged that job for O'Neill's. Singing with his eyes shut. Corny. Met her once in the park. In the dark. What a lark. Police tout. Her name and address she then told with my tooraloom tooraloom tay. O, surely he begged it. Bury him cheap in a whatyoumaycall. With my tooraloom, tooraloom, tooraloom, tooraloom.

In Westland row he halted before the window of the Belfast and Oriental Tea Company and read the legends of leadpapered packets: choice blend, finest quality, family tea. Rather warm. Tea. Must get some from Tom Kernan. Couldn't ask him at a funeral, though. While his eyes still read blandly he took off his hat quietly inhaling his hairoil and sent his right hand with slow grace over his brow and hair. Very warm morning. Under their dropped lids his eyes found the tiny bow of the leather headband inside his high grade hat. Just there. His right hand came down into the bowl of his hat. His fingers found quickly a card behind the headband and transferred it to his waistcoat pocket.

So warm. His right hand once more more slowly went over again: choice blend, made of the finest Ceylon brands. The far east. Lovely spot it must be: the garden of the world, big lazy leaves to float about on, cactuses, flowery meads, snaky lianas they call them. Wonder is it like that. Those Cinghalese lobbing around in the sun, in *dolce far niente*. Not doing a hand's turn all day. Sleep six months out of twelve. Too hot to quarrel. Influence of the climate. Lethargy. Flowers of idleness. The air feeds most. Azotes. Hothouse in Botanic gardens. Sensitive plants. Waterlilies. Petals too tired to. Sleeping sickness in the air. Walk on roseleaves. Imagine trying to eat tripe and cowheel. Where was the chap I saw in that picture somewhere? Ah, in the dead sea, floating on his back, reading a book with a parasol open.

MR. BLOOM TAKES A WALK

Couldn't sink if you tried: so thick with salt. Because the weight of the water, no, the weight of the body in the water is equal to the weight of the. Or is it the volume is equal of the weight? It's a law something like that. Vance in high school cracking his fingerjoints, teaching. The college curriculum. Cracking curriculum. What is weight really when you say the weight? Thirty-two feet per second, per second. Law of falling bodies: per second, per second. They all fall to the ground. The earth. It's the force of gravity of the earth is the weight.

He turned away and sauntered across the road. How did she walk with her sausages? Like that something. As he walked he took the folded *Freeman* from his sidepocket, unfolded it rolled it lengthwise in a baton and tapped it at each sauntering step against his trouserleg. Careless air: just drop in to see. Per second, per second. Per second for every second it means. From the curbstone he darted a keen glance through the door of the postoffice. Too late box. Post here. No-one. In.

He handed the card through the brass grill.

—Are there any letters for me? he asked.

While the postmistress searched a pigeonhole he gazed at the recruiting poster with soldiers of all arms on parade: and held the top of his baton against his nostrils, smelling freshprinted rag paper. No answer probably. Went too far last time.

The postmistress handed him back through the grill his card with a letter. He thanked and glanced rapidly at the typed envelope.

Henry Flower, Esq,
c/o P. O. Westland Row,
City.

Answered anyhow. He slipped card and letter into his sidepocket, reviewing again the soldiers on parade. Where's old Tweedy's regiment? Castoff soldier. There:

bearskin cap and hackle plume. No, he's a grenadier. Pointed cuffs. There he is: royal Dublin fusiliers. Redcoats. Too showy. That must be why the women go after them. Uniform. Easier to enlist and drill. Maud Gonne's letter about taking them off O'Connell street at night: disgrace to our Irish capital. Griffith's paper is on the same tack now: an army rotten with venereal disease: overseas or halfseasover empire. Half baked they look: hypnotised like. Eyes front. Mark time. Table: able. Bed: ed. The King's own. Never see him dressed up as a fireman or a bobby. A mason, yes.

He strolled out of the postoffice and turned to the right. Talk: as if that would mend matters. His hand went into his pocket and a forefinger felt its way under the flap of the envelope, ripping it open in jerks. Women will pay a lot of heed, I don't think. His fingers drew forth the letter and crumpled the envelope in his pocket. Something pinned on: photo perhaps. Hair? No.

M'Coy. Get rid of him quickly. Take me out of my way. Hate company when you.

—Hello, Bloom. Where are you off to?

—Hello, M'Coy. Nowhere in particular.

—How's the body?

—Fine. How are you?

—Just keeping alive, M'Coy said.

His eyes on the black tie and clothes he asked with low respect:

—Is there any . . . no trouble I hope? I see you're. . .

—O no, Mr Bloom said. Poor Dignam, you know. The funeral is today.

—To be sure, poor fellow. So it is. What time?

A photo it isn't. A badge maybe.

—E . . . eleven, Mr Bloom answered.

MR. BLOOM TAKES A WALK 369

—I must try to get out there, M'Coy said. Eleven, is it? I only heard it last night. Who was telling me? Holohan. You know Hoppy?

—I know.

Mr Bloom gazed across the road at the outsider drawn up before the door of the Grosvenor. The porter hoisted the valise up on the well. She stood still, waiting, while the man, husband, brother, like her, searched his pockets for change. Stylish kind of coat with that roll collar, warm for a day like this, looks like blanketcloth. Careless stand of her with her hands in those patch pockets. Like that haughty creature at the polo match. Women all for caste till you touch the spot. Handsome is and handsome does. Reserved about to yield. The honourable Mrs and Brutus is an honourable man. Possess her once take the starch out of her.

—I was with Bob Doran, he's on one of his periodical bends, and what do you call him Bantam Lyons. Just down there in Conway's we were.

Doran, Lyons in Conway's. She raised a gloved hand to her hair. In came Hoppy. Having a wet. Drawing back his head and gazing far from beneath his veiled eyelids he saw the bright fawn skin shine in the glare, the braided drums. Clearly I can see today. Moisture about gives long sight perhaps. Talking of one thing or another. Lady's hand. Which side will she get up?

—And he said: *Sad thing about our poor friend Paddy! What Paddy?* I said. *Poor little Paddy Dignam,* he said.

Off to the country: Broadstone probably. High brown boots with laces dangling. Wellturned foot. What is he fostering over that change for? Sees me looking. Eye out for other fellow always. Good fallback. Two strings to her bow.

—*Why?* I said. *What's wrong with him?* I said.

Proud: rich: silk stockings.

—Yes, Mr Bloom said.

He moved a little to the side of M'Coy's talking head. Getting up in a minute.

—*What's wrong with him?* he said. *He's dead,* he said. And, faith, he filled up. *Is it Paddy Dignam?* I said. I couldn't believe it when I heard it. I was with him no later than Friday last or Thursday was it in the Arch. *Yes,* he said. *He's gone. He died on Monday, poor fellow.*

Watch! Watch! Silk flash rich stockings white. Watch!

A heavy tramcar honking its gong slewed between.

Lost it. Curse your noisy pugnose. Feels locked out of it. Paradise and the peri. Always happening like that. The very moment. Girl in Eustace street hallway Monday was it settling her garter. Her friend covering the display of. *Esprit de corps*. Well, what are you gaping at?

—Yes, yes, Mr Bloom said after a dull sigh. Another gone.

—One of the best, M'Coy said.

The tram passed. They drove off towards the Loop Line bridge, her rich gloved hand on the steel grip. Flicker, flicker: the laceflare of her hat in the sun: flicker, flick.

—Wife well, I suppose? M'Coy's changed voice said.

—O yes, Mr Bloom said. Tiptop, thanks.

He unrolled the newspaper baton idly and read idly:

> *What is home without*
> *Plumtree's Potted Meat?*
> *Incomplete.*
> *With it an abode of bliss.*

MR. BLOOM TAKES A WALK

—My missus has just got an engagement. At least it's not settled yet.

Valise tack again. By the way no harm. I'm off that, thanks.

Mr Bloom turned his largelidded eyes with unhasty friendliness.

—My wife too, he said. She's going to sing at a swagger affair in the Ulster hall, Belfast, on the twenty-fifth.

—That so? M'Coy said. Glad to hear that, old man. Who's getting it up?

Mrs Marion Bloom. Not up yet. Queen was in her bedroom eating bread and. No book. Blackened court cards laid along her thigh by sevens. Dark lady and fair man. Cat furry black ball. Torn strip of envelope.

Love's
Old
Sweet
Song
Comes lo-ve's old. . .

—It's a kind of tour, don't you see? Mr Bloom said thoughtfully. *Sweet song.* There's a committee formed. Part shares and part profits.

M'Coy nodded, picking at his moustache stubble.

—O well, he said. That's good news.

He moved to go.

—Well, glad to see you looking fit, he said. Meet you knocking around.

—Yes, Mr Bloom said.

—Tell you what, M'Coy said. You might put down my name at the funeral, will you? I'd like to go but I mightn't be able, you see. There's a drowning case at Sandycove may turn up and then the coroner and myself would have to go down if the body is found. You just shove in my name if I'm not there, will you?

—I'll do that, Mr Bloom said, moving to get off. That'll be all right.

—Right, M'Coy said brightly. Thanks, old man. I'd go if I possibly could. Well, tolloll. Just C. P. M'Coy will do.

—That will be done, Mr Bloom answered firmly.

Didn't catch me napping that wheeze. The quick touch. Soft mark. I'd like my job. Valise I have a particular fancy for. Leather. Capped corners, riveted edges, double action lever lock. Bob Cowley lent him his for the Wicklow regatta concert last year and never heard tidings of it from that good day to this.

Mr Bloom, strolling towards Brunswick street, smiled. My missus has just got an. Reedy freckled soprano. Cheeseparing nose. Nice enough in its way: for a little ballad. No guts in it. You and me, don't you know? In the same boat. Softsoaping. Give you the needle that would. Can't he hear the difference? Think he's that way inclined a bit. Against my grain somehow. Thought that Belfast would fetch him. I hope that smallpox up there doesn't get worse. Suppose she wouldn't let herself be vaccinated again. Your wife and my wife.

Wonder is he pimping after me?

Mr Bloom stood at the corner, his eyes wandering over the multicoloured hoardings. Cantrell and Cochrane's Ginger Ale (Aromatic). Clery's summer sale. No, he's going on straight. Hello. *Leah* tonight: Mrs Bandman Palmer. Like to see her in that again. *Hamlet* she played last night. Male impersonator. Perhaps he was a woman. Why Ophelia committed suicide? Poor papa! How he used to talk about Kate Bateman in that! Outside the Adelphi in London waited all the afternoon to get in. Year before I was born that was: sixty-five. And Ristori in Vienna. What is this the right name is?

MR. BLOOM TAKES A WALK 373

By Mosenthal it is. Rachel, is it? No. The scene he was always talking about where the old blind Abraham recognizes the voice and puts his fingers on his face.

—Nathan's voice! His son's voice! I hear the voice of Nathan who left his father to die of grief and misery in my arms, who left the house of his father and left the God of his father.

Every word is so deep, Leopold.

Poor papa! Poor man! I'm glad. I didn't go into the room to look at his face. That day! O dear! O dear! Ffoo! Well, perhaps it was the best for him.

Mr Bloom went round the corner and passed the drooping nags of the hazard. No use thinking of it any more. Nosebag time. Wish I hadn't met that M'Coy fellow.

He came nearer and heard a crunching of gilded oats, the gently champing teeth. Their full buck eyes regarded him as he went by, amid the sweet oaten reek of horsepiss. Their Eldorado. Poor jugginses! Damn all they know or care about anything with their long noses stuck in nosebags. Too full for words. Still they get their feed all right and their doss. Gelded too: a stump of black guttapercha wagging limp between their haunches. Might be happy all the same that way. Good poor brutes they look. Still their neigh can be very irritating.

He drew the letter from his pocket and folded it into the newspaper he carried. Might just walk into her here. The lane is safer.

He passed the cabman's shelter. Curious the life of drifting cabbies, all weathers, all places, time or setdown, no will of their own. *Voglio e non*. Like to give them an odd cigarette. Sociable. Shout a few flying syllables as they pass. He hummed:

*Là ci darem la mano
La la lala la la.*

He turned into Cumberland street and, going on some paces, halted in the lee of the station wall. No-one. Meade's timberyard. Piled balks. Ruins and tenements. With careful tread he passed over a hopscotch court with its forgotten pickeystone. Not a sinner. Near the timberyard a squatted child at marbles, alone, shooting the taw with a cunnythumb. A wise tabby, a blinking sphinx, watched from her warm sill. Pity to disturb them. Mohammed cut a piece out of his mantle not to wake her. Open it. And once I played marbles when I went to that old dame's school. She liked mignonette. Mrs Ellis's. and Mr? He opened the letter within the newspaper.

A flower. I think it's a. A yellow flower with flattened petals. Not annoyed then? What does she say?

Dear Henry,

I got your last letter to me and thank you very much for it. I am sorry you did not like my last letter. Why did you enclose the stamps? I am awfully angry with you. I do wish I could punish you for that. I called you naughty boy because I do not like that other word. Please tell me what is the real meaning of that word. Are you not happy in your home you poor little naughty boy? I do wish I could do something for you. Please tell me what you think of poor me. I often think of the beautiful name you have. Dear Henry, when will we meet? I think of you so often you have no idea. I have never felt myself so much drawn to a man as you. I feel so bad about. Please write me a long letter and tell me more. Remember if you do not I will punish you. So now you know what I will do to you, you naughty

MR. BLOOM TAKES A WALK

boy, if you do not write. O how I long to meet you. Henry dear, do not deny my request before my patience are exhausted. Then I will tell you all. Goodbye now, naughty darling. I have such a bad headache today and write *by return* to your longing

MARTHA.

P. S. Do tell me what kind of perfume does your wife use. I want to know.

He tore the flower gravely from its pinhold smelt its almost no smell and placed it in his heart pocket. Language of flowers. They like it because no-one can hear. Or a poison bouquet to strike him down. Then, walking slowly forward, he read the letter again, murmuring here and there a word. Angry tulips with you darling manflower punish your cactus if you don't please poor forgetmenot how I long violets to dear roses when we soon anemone meet all naughty nightstalk wife Martha's perfume. Having read it all he took it from the newspaper and put it back in his sidepocket.

Weak joy opened his lips. Changed since the first letter. Wonder did she write it herself. Doing the indignant: a girl of good family like me, respectable character. Could meet one Sunday after the rosary. Thank you: not having any. Usual love scrimmage. Then running round corners. Bad as a row with Molly. Cigar has a cooling effect. Narcotic. Go further next time. Naughty boy: punish: afraid of words, of course. Brutal, why not? Try it anyhow. A bit at a time.

Fingering still the letter in his pocket he drew the pin out of it. Common pin, eh? He threw it on the road. Out of her clothes somewhere: pinned together. Queer the number of pins they always have. No roses without thorns.

Flat Dublin voices bawled in his head. Those two

sluts that night in the Coombe, linked together in the rain.

> *O, Mairy lost the pin of her drawers.*
> *She didn't know what to do*
> *To keep it up*
> *To keep it up.*

It? Them. Such a bad headache. Has her roses probably. Or sitting all day typing. Eyefocus bad for stomach nerves. What perfume does your wife use? Now could you make out a thing like that?

To keep it up.

Martha, Mary. I saw that picture somewhere I forget now old master or faked for money. He is sitting in their house, talking. Mysterious. Also the two sluts in the Coombe would listen.

To keep it up.

Nice kind of evening feeling. No more wandering about. Just loll there: quiet dusk: let everything rip. Forget. Tell about places you have been, strange customs. The other one, jar on her head, was getting the supper: fruit, olives, lovely cool water out of the well stonecold like the hole in the wall at Ashtown. Must carry a paper goblet next time I go to the trottingmatches. She listens with big dark soft eyes. Tell her: more and more: all. Then a sigh: silence. Long long long rest.

Going under the railway arch he took out the envelope, tore it swiftly in shreds and scattered them towards the road. The shreds fluttered away, sank in the dank air: a white flutter then all sank.

Henry Flower. You could tear up a cheque for a hundred pounds in the same way. Simple bit of paper. Lord Iveagh once cashed a sevenfigure cheque for a million in the bank of Ireland. Shows you the money to be made out of porter. Still the other brother lord

MR. BLOOM TAKES A WALK 377

Ardilaun has to change his shirt four times a day, they say. Skin breeds lice or vermin. A million pounds, wait a moment. Twopence a pint, fourpence a quart, eightpence a gallon of porter, no, one and fourpence a gallon of porter. One and four into twenty: fifteen about. Yes, exactly. Fifteen millions of barrels of porter.

What was I saying barrels? Gallons. About a million barrels all the same.

An incoming train clanked heavily above his head, coach after coach. Barrels bumped in his head: dull porter slopped and churned inside. The bungholes sprang open and a huge dull flood leaked, flowing together, winding through mudflats all over the level land, a lazy pooling swirl of liquor bearing along wideleaved flowers of its froth.

He had reached the open backdoor of All Hallows. Stepping into the porch he doffed his hat, took the card from his pocket and tucked it again behind the leather headband. Damn it. I might have tried to work M'Coy for a pass to Mullingar.

Same notice on the door. Sermon by the very reverend John Conmee S. J. on saint Peter Claver and the African mission. Save China's millions. Wonder how they explain it to the heathen Chinee. Prefer an ounce of opium. Celestials. Rank heresy for them. Prayers for the conversion of Gladstone they had too when he was almost unconscious. The protestants the same. Convert Dr. William J. Walsh, D.D. to the true religion. Buddha their god lying on his side in the museum. Taking it easy with hand under his cheek. Josssticks burning. Not like Ecce Homo. Crown of thorns and cross. Clever idea Saint Patrick the shamrock. Chopsticks? Conmee: Martin Cunningham knows him: distinguished looking. Sorry I didn't work him about getting Molly into the choir instead of that Father Farley who looked a fool but wasn't. They're taught that. He's not going out in bluey specs with the sweat rolling off him to baptise blacks, is he? The glasses would take their fancy, flashing. Like to see them sitting round in a ring with blub lips, entranced, listening. Still life. Lap it up like milk, I suppose.

The cold smell of sacred stone called him. He trod the worn steps, pushed the swingdoor and entered softly by the rere.

Something going on: some sodality. Pity so empty. Nice discreet place to be next some girl. Who is my neighbor? Jammed by the hour to slow music. That woman at midnight mass. Seventh heaven. Women knelt in the benches with crimson halters round their necks, heads bowed. A batch knelt at the altar rails. The priest went along by them, murmuring, holding the thing in his hands. He stopped at each, took out a communion, shook a drop or two (are they in water?) off it and put it neatly into her mouth. Her hat and head sank. Then the next one: a small old woman. The priest bent down to put it into her mouth, murmuring all the time. Latin. The next one. Shut your eyes and open your mouth. What? *Corpus*. Body. Corpse. Good idea the Latin. Stupefies them first. Hospice for the dying. They don't seem to chew it; only swallow it down. Rum idea; eating bits of a corpse why the cannibals cotton to it.

He stood aside watching their blind masks pass down the aisle, one by one, and seek their places. He approached a bench and seated himself in its corner, nursing his hat and newspaper. These pots we have to wear. We ought to have hats modelled on our heads. They were about him here and there, with heads still bowed in their crimson halters, waiting for it to melt in their

MR. BLOOM TAKES A WALK 379

stomachs. Something like those mazzoth: it's that sort of bread: unleavened shewbread. Look at them. Now I bet it makes them feel happy. Lollipop. It does. Yes, bread of angels it's called. There's a big idea behind it, kind of kingdom of God is within you feel. First communicants. Hokypoky penny a lump. Then feel all like one smart family party, same in the theatre, all in the same swim. They do. I'm sure of that. Not so lonely. In our confraternity. Then come out a bit spreeish. Let off steam. Thing is if you really believe in it. Lourdes cure, waters of oblivion, and the Knock apparition, statues bleeding. Old fellow asleep near that confession box. Hence those snores. Blind faith. Safe in the arms of kingdom come. Lulls all pain. Wake this time next year.

He saw the priest stow the communion cup away, well in, and kneel an instant before it, showing a large grey bootsole from under the lace affair he had on. Suppose he lost the pin of his. He wouldn't know what to do to. Bald spot behind. Letters on his back I. N. R. I.? No: I. H. S. Molly told me one time I asked her. I have sinned: or no: I have suffered, it is. And the other one? Iron nails ran in.

Meet one Sunday after the rosary. Do not deny my request. Turn up with a veil and black bag. Dusk and the light behind her. She might be here with a ribbon round her neck and do the other thing all the same on the sly. Their character. That fellow that turned queen's evidence on the invincibles he used to receive the, Carey was his name, the communion every morning. This very church. Peter Carey. No, Peter Claver I am thinking of. Denis Carey. And just imagine that. Wife and six children at home. And plotting that murder all the time. Those crawthumpers, now that's a good name for them, there's always something shiftylooking about them.

They're not straight men of business either. O no she's not here: the flower: no, no. By the way did I tear up that envelope? Yes: under the bridge.

The priest was rinsing out the chalice: then he tossed off the dregs smartly. Wine. Makes it more aristocratic than for example if he drank what they are used to Guinness's porter or some temperance beverage Wheatley's Dublin hop bitters or Cantrell and Cochrane's ginger ale (aromatic). Doesn't give them any of it: shew wine: only the other. Cold comfort. Pious fraud but quite right: otherwise they'd have one old booser worse than another coming along, cadging for a drink. Queer the whole atmosphere of the. Quite right. Perfectly right that is.

Mr Bloom looked back towards the choir. Not going to be any music. Pity. Who has the organ here I wonder? Old Glynn he knew how to make that instrument talk, the *vibrato:* fifty pounds a year they say he had in Gardiner street. Molly was in fine voice that day, the *Stabat Mater* of Rossini. Father Bernard Vaughan's sermon first. Christ or Pilate? Christ, but don't keep us all night over it. Music they wanted. Footdrill stopped. Could hear a pin drop. I told her to pitch her voice against that corner. I could feel the thrill in the air, the full, the people looking up:

Quis est homo?

Some of that old sacred music is splendid. Mercadante: seven last words. Mozart's twelfth mass: the *Gloria* in that. Those old popes were keen on music, on art and statues and pictures of all kinds. Palestrina for example too. They had a gay old time while it lasted. Healthy too chanting, regular hours, then brew liqueurs. Benedictine. Green Chartreuse. Still, having eunuchs in their choir that was coming it a bit thick. What kind

MR. BLOOM TAKES A WALK

of voice is it? Must be curious to hear after their own strong basses. Connoisseurs. Suppose they wouldn't feel anything after. Kind of a placid. No worry. Fall into flesh don't they? Gluttons, tall, long legs. Who knows? Eunuch. One way out of it.

He saw the priest bend down and kiss the altar and then face about and bless all the people. All crossed themselves and stood up. Mr Bloom glanced about him and then stood up, looking over the risen hats. Stand up at the gospel of course. Then all settled down on their knees again and he sat back quietly in his bench. The priest came down from the altar, holding the thing out from him, and he and the massboy answered each other in Latin. Then the priest knelt down and began to read off a card:

—O God, our refuge and our strength. . .

Mr Bloom put his face forward to catch the words. English. Throw them the bone. I remember slightly. How long since your last mass? Gloria and immaculate virgin. Joseph her spouse. Peter and Paul. More interesting if you understood what it was all about. Wonderful organisation certainly, goes like clockwork. Confession. Everyone wants to. Then I will tell you all. Penance. Punish me, please. Great weapon in their hands. More than doctor or solicitor. Woman dying to. And I schschschschschsch. And did you chachachachacha? And why did you? Look down at her ring to find an excuse. Whispering gallery walls have ears. Husband learn to his surprise. God's little joke. Then out she comes. Repentance skindeep. Lovely shame. Pray at an altar. Hail Mary and Holy Mary. Flowers, incense, candles melting. Hide her blushes. Salvation army blatant imitation. Reformed prostitute will address the meeting. How I found the Lord. Squareheaded chaps those must be in

Rome: they work the whole show. And don't they rake in the money too? Bequests also: to the P. P. for the time being in his absolute discretion. Masses for the repose of my soul to be said publicly with open doors. Monasteries and convents. The priest in the Fermanagh will case in the witness box. No browbeating him. He had his answer pat for everything. Liberty and exaltation of our holy mother the church. The doctors of the church: they mapped out the whole theology of it.

The priest prayed:

—Blessed Michael, archangel, defend us in the hour of conflict. Be our safeguard against the wickedness and snares of the devil (may God restrain him, we humbly pray): and do thou, O prince of the heavenly host, by the power of God thrust Satan down to hell and with him those other wicked spirits who wander through the world for the ruin of souls.

The priest and the massboy stood up and walked off. All over. The women remained behind: thanksgiving.

Better be shoving along. Brother Buzz. Come around with the plate perhaps. Pay your Easter duty.

He stood up. Hello. Were those two buttons of my waistcoat open all the time. Women enjoy it. Annoyed if you don't. Why didn't you tell me before. Never tell you. But we. Excuse, miss, there's a (whh!) just a (whh!) fluff. Or their skirt behind, placket unhooked. Glimpses of the moon. Still like you better untidy. Good job it wasn't farther south. He passed, discreetly buttoning, down the aisle and out through the main door into the light. He stood a moment unseeing by the cold black marble bowl while before him and behind two worshippers dipped furtive hands in the low tide of holy water. Trams: a car of Prescott's dyeworks: a widow in her weeds. Notice because I'm in mourning myself. He

MR. BLOOM TAKES A WALK

covered himself. How goes the time? Quarter past. Time enough yet. Better get that lotion made up. Where is this? Ah yes, the last time. Sweny's in Lincoln place. Chemists rarely move. Their green and gold beaconjars too heavy to stir. Hamilton Long's, founded in the year of the flood. Huguenot churchyard near there. Visit some day.

He walked southward along Westland row. But the recipe is in the other trousers. O, and I forgot that latchkey too. Bore this funeral affair. O well, poor fellow, it's not his fault. When was it I got it made up last? Wait, I changed a sovereign I remember. First of the month it must have been or the second. O he can look it up in the prescriptions book.

The chemist turned back page after page. Sandy shrivelled smell he seems to have. Shrunken skull. And old. Quest for the philosopher's stone. The alchemists. Drugs age you after mental excitement. Lethargy then. Why? Reaction. A lifetime in a night. Gradually changes your character. Living all the day among herbs, ointments, disinfectants. All his alabaster lilypots. Mortar and pestle. Aq. Dist. Fol. Laur. Te Virid. Smell almost cure you like the dentist's doorbell. Doctor whack. He ought to physic himself a bit. Electuary or emulsion. The first fellow that picked an herb to cure himself had a bit of pluck. Simples. Want to be careful. Enough stuff here to chloroform you. Test: turns blue litmus paper red. Chloroform. Overdose of laudanum. Sleeping draughts. Lovephiltres. Paragoric poppysyrup bad for cough. Clogs the pores or the phlegm. Poisons the only cures. Remedy where you least expect it. Clever of nature.

—About a fortnight ago, sir?

—Yes, Mr Bloom said.

He waited by the counter, inhaling the keen reek of drugs, the dusty dry smell of sponges and loofahs. Lot of time taken up telling your aches and pains.

—Sweet almond oil and tincture of benzoin, Mr Bloom said, and then orangeflower water. . .

It certainly did make her skin so delicate white like wax.

—And white wax also, he said.

Brings out the darkness of her eyes. Looking at me, the sheet up to her eyes, Spanish, smelling herself, when I was fixing the links in my cuffs. Those homely recipes are often the best: strawberries for the teeth: nettles and rainwater: oatmeal they say steeped in buttermilk. Skinfood. One of the old queen's sons, duke of Albany was it? had only one skin. Leopold yes. Three we have. Warts, bunions and pimples to make it worse. But you want a perfume too. What perfume does your? *Peau d'Espagne.* That orangeflower. Pure curd soap. Water is so fresh. Nice smell these soaps have. Time to get a bath round the corner. Hammam. Turkish. Massage. Dirt gets rolled up in your navel. Nicer if a nice girl did it. Also I think I. Yes I. Do it in the bath. Curious longing I. Water to water. Combine business with pleasure. Pity no time for massage. Feel fresh then all day. Funeral be rather glum.

—Yes, sir, the chemist said. That was two and nine. Have you brought a bottle?

—No, Mr Bloom said. Make it up, please. I'll call later in the day and I'll take one of those soaps. How much are they?

—Fourpence, sir.

Mr Bloom raised a cake to his nostrils. Sweet lemony wax.

—I'll take this one, he said. That makes three and a penny.

MR. BLOOM TAKES A WALK

—Yes, sir, the chemist said. You can pay all together, sir, when you come back.

—Good, Mr Bloom said.

He strolled out of his shop, the newspaper baton under his armpit, the coolwrapped soap in his left hand.

At his armpit Bantam Lyons' voice and hand said:

—Hello, Bloom, what's the best news? Is that today's? Show us a minute.

Shaved off his moustache again, by Jove! Long cold upper lip. To look younger. He does look balmy. Younger than I am.

Bantam Lyons' yellow blacknailed fingers unrolled the baton. Wants a wash too. Take off the rough dirt. Good morning, have you used Pears' soap? Dandruff on his shoulders. Scalp wants oiling.

—I want to see about that French horse that's running today, Bantam Lyons said. Where the bugger is it?

He rustled the pleated pages, jerking his chin on his high collar. Barber's itch. Tight collar he'll lose his hair. Better leave him the paper and get shut of him.

—You can keep it, Mr Bloom said.

—Ascot. Gold cup. Wait, Bantam Lyons muttered. Half a mo. Maximum the second.

—I was just going to throw it away, Mr Bloom said.

Bantam Lyons raised his eyes suddenly and leered weakly.

—What's that? his sharp voice said.

—I say you can keep it, Mr Bloom answered. I was going to throw it away that moment.

Bantam Lyons doubted an instant, leering: then thrust the outspread sheets back on Mr Bloom's arms.

—I'll risk it, he said. Here, thanks.

He sped off towards Conway's corner. God speed scut.

Mr Bloom folded the sheets again to a neat square and lodged the soap in it, smiling. Silly lips of that chap. Betting. Regular hotbed of it lately. Messenger boys stealing to put on sixpence. Raffle for large tender turkey. Your Christmas dinner for threepence. Jack Fleming embezzling to gamble then smuggled off to America. Keeps a hotel now. They never come back. Fleshpots of Egypt.

He walked cheerfully towards the mosque of the baths. Remind you of a mosque redbaked bricks, the minarets. College sports today I see. He eyed the horseshoe poster over the gate of college park: cyclist doubled up like a cod in a pot. Damn bad ad. Now if they had made it round like a wheel. Then the spokes: sports, sports, sports: and the hub big: college. Something to catch the eye.

There's Hornblower standing at the porter's lodge. Keep him on hands: might take a turn in there on the nod. How do you do, Mr Hornblower? How do you do, sir?

Heavenly weather really. If life was always like that. Cricket weather. Sit around under sunshades. Over after over. Out. They can't play it here. Duck for six wickets. Still Captain Buller broke a window in the Kildare street club with a slog to square leg. Donnybrook fair more in their line. And the skulls we were acracking when M'Carthy took the floor. Heatwave. Won't last. Always passing, the stream of life, which in the stream of life we trace is dearer than them all.

Enjoy a bath now: clean trough of water, cool enamel, the gentle tepid stream. This is my body.

He foresaw his pale body reclined in it at full, naked, in a womb of warmth, oiled by scented melting soap, softly laved. He saw his trunk and limbs ririppled over and sustained, buoyed lightly upward, lemonyellow: his navel, bud of flesh: and saw the dark tangled curls of his bush floating, floating hair of the stream around the limp father of thousands, a languid floating flower.

(From *Ulysses*.)

NORAH HOULT

Mrs. Johnson

MRS. EMILY JOHNSON opened her eyes suddenly. The clock belonging to St. Matthew's Church had begun to strike. She moistened her dry lips and started to count:

"Two, three, four, five, six . . . not surely seven? Yes: seven."

Seven o'clock! Just fancy! She must have dozed off. It was only just after five when she had come in with a loaf of bread and quarter of margarine, and thought she would take a little rest before going out. And she had meant to be off early. A bad beginning! She must stir her pins now, and no mistake.

She threw off the blankets, and sat on the edge of the bed for a moment while her mind took stock of her body, searching to know how it felt. Her limbs were heavy and weak, and there was the same dull pain at the bottom of her back as there had been when she lay down.

"I don't feel a bit rested," she murmured. "Not a bit, I don't."

She sighed heavily, and went across to examine herself in the little wooden looking-glass that was propped on her chest of drawers. She took it off, and held it close to her eyes.

She was wearing a pink jumper of artificial silk over a magenta coloured petticoat. Her skirt she had slipped off when she lay down. Her hair, which was a peculiar grey-brown, the result of many sousings in guaranteed colour restorers and improvers, was greasy looking and part of it had come down, for Mrs. Johnson still fought shy of shingling. Her skin was a sickly yellow.

Mrs. Johnson gazed at herself with solicitude. "I do look bad," she thought. And then, not without pride, "No one could say as how I don't look bad."

But now another instinct put out its feeler and she searched the mirror for some more encouraging indication. She did not find it, and propped the mirror up again. "I look my age," she reflected with resignation as she took out hair-pins. "Leastways I look forty, though neither fair nor fat. Except," she added as an afterthought, "where I shouldn't be."

She set the kettle on the gas ring to boil. Feel better after a cup of tea, she reflected as she had reflected many times before.

She took it hot and strong, together with a piece of bread and margarine. Towards the end of her repast she fell to considering whether she should have a good wash or no. Custom and inclination insisted, "It's not as if I hadn't washed today," and "After just having the 'flu, you can't be too careful." On the other hand, perhaps it freshened you up. She decided she would bathe her face and neck and leave the rest.

She did so. She even cleaned her nails, and found a pad with which subsequently she polished them.

Afterwards she surveyed herself more hopefully: the tea and hot water had brought a little colour to her cheeks. She'd keep on her jumper after all. If you could only stand it there was nothing like a little bit of colour for making you look young.

She dabbed on some lip salve, both on her lips and cheeks. Not too much! The first thing was to look respectable, as of course in your way you were. And then white powder over her little chin and short broad nose. On her neck as well, to hide the creases. She had a genuine double chin tonight; that was lying in bed so long. Ah, well, it didn't show if you remembered to hold your head well up. Now her hat pulled well down; now the grey coat.

At the door in spite of her hurry she was filled with misgivings, and turned back to have another look at herself. She certainly looked very far from her real self; it had to be admitted. No one could look really well, even if they happened to be raging, tearing beauties, if they felt as ill as she did. Perhaps after all it would be better to wear a veil—not mind them being out of fashion.

With the veil attached she stared at herself keenly. Did it make her look older or younger? She wished she knew absolutely for sure.

Still, she had had it on when she got off with that fellow in Hyde Park last week, the Tuesday wasn't it? On the whole, perhaps, she'd stick to it. She really did feel so poorly.

She drew it up to bestow a parting lick of powder, and then, after listening a moment at the door, went softly downstairs. Yet not too softly, for though she wished to slip out unseen, she didn't want to be caught looking as if she wished to slip out unseen.

She was unfortunate, for the door of the front room opened as she reached the bottom stair, and Mrs. Lytton, the landlady, came out.

"I thought that was you, Mrs. Johnson, quiet though you was. Going out, are you?"

Mrs. Johnson licked her lips unconsciously, and then gave a propitiatory smile.

"Yes, I thought I would, Mrs. Lytton. It's a nice evening, isn't it?"

"I thought," said Mrs. Lytton staring her lodger full in the face, "you was maybe coming to pay me what you owe me."

For a brief second Mrs. Johnson thought of essaying injured dignity. But she was hopelessly outmatched, for, besides being large of bust and determined of feature and countenance, Mrs. Lytton was all dressed up. She was wearing a frock of black taffeta silk cut very low to display an expanse of pink chest, and round her neck hung three rows of pearls. It was evident, too, that her bright yellow hair had been newly waved.

Must be expecting someone, thought Mrs. Johnson. I wonder. . . . Aloud she said: "Now Mrs. Lytton, dear, you know yourself I 'aven't been able to get out for more than a week. You can't do much when you're sick in bed with the influenza, can you now?"

"Oh, I know you've been ill all right," retorted Mrs. Lytton. "Who should know it better than me that 'as 'ad to carry your meals up. You still owe me for that Bovril I got you."

"I know well how kind you've been," said Mrs. Johnson rapidly. "And when my lad sends me the usual, you shall 'ave it all. If I don't get a bit of something from somewhere first—and I'm sure I shall—you shall 'ave that."

"Thank you for nothing, Mrs. Johnson. I know well

enough when your son sends you the money, that is *if* he sends you it. He's missed, you know. And anyway it's not till Friday week. And you owe me three weeks' rent besides the ten bob I lent you because you was ill, or said you was, and the one and three I spent myself on the Bovril."

"*Said* I was ill," interjected Mrs. Johnson more in sorrow than in anger.

"And let me tell you straight and fair, from the horse's mouth, that I have no intention of waiting a fortnight to be paid. With one thing and another, Emily Johnson, I have put up with you till I am sick and tired. For friendship's sake. I'd not 'ave stood it from no one else. But there's reason in everything, and I've my living to make, I suppose, same as everyone else. I could get more than I'm asking you for your room as you know well. Giving it away I am out of kindness."

Mrs. Johnson recognized her cue.

"Now, Rose, I've always said to everyone that there's no kinder nor more generous woman than yourself," she stated with dramatic emphasis.

"Don't Rose me! And listen. Things can't go on no longer like this. They gotta stop. D'you understand me?"

There came a knock at the hall door.

Mrs. Lytton's attention left Mrs. Johnson, and went eagerly to the other side of the door. Then she turned back to Mrs. Johnson again, but only to dispose of her.

"I'll see you again, Emily, when you come back, and if there's no rent or nothing coming from you you'll have to make new arrangements. I have to see a friend now about a business matter."

She stood back, and Mrs. Johnson opened the door and slipped out past the man who was standing there without a word or a look back. It would never do to appear inquisitive with Rose. And in any case she had always been one to mind her own business and not interfere with other people. "Live and let live, that's my motto," she thought with satisfaction which terminated in a touch of bitterness. "If it had only been other people's I wouldn't be where I am today."

She had now turned into the Camberwell Road, and the shouts of children at play, people passing hurriedly, the lights, the trams, and the coloured enticing patches made by picture palaces and public-houses began to invigorate her. She forgot the pain in her back and stepped out fairly briskly, shooting little sideways glances about her. The familiar life of the streets, the easy security it gave, warmed her blood. There were so many things and people about: surely she could hardly miss going into something lucky. She had, she thought proudly, always been one for a bit of life and excitement; and even if she wasn't as young as some of the girls, she wasn't as old as others: no, not by a long chalk she wasn't.

Inevitably her mind began to turn over other considerations. Mrs. Johnson was not one of those who never knew quite how much they carried in their pocket or bag. Circumstances made such a fine carelessness impossible. And so without any need to refresh her memory by a look her thoughts went inside her imitation leather hand-bag, and added together the silver sixpence, the penny, the halfpenny, and the farthing which lay there together. It was all she had left of the ten shillings Rose had lent her. It would be better, she decided, to walk to the Elephant and get a penny 'bus from there over Westminster Bridge. Or would it save her more if she walked as far as Westminster, and then got a penny 'bus to the Circus? Once at the Circus she could slip into Long's, and see if there was any one there she knew. A Guinness would do her no end of good if she only got the chance of one.

The picture of the foaming brown glass which might be awaiting her quickened her footsteps. She walked at a steady pace down the Walworth Road, taking little heed of passersby. Experience had taught her that the busy streets of South-East London were no lucky hunting ground for her at that time in the evening. As she put it to herself, she was too refined for this side of the Bridge. And though she rarely took the recollection out of its pushed-back corner in her mind, it was in the Walworth Road, returning home with empty pockets late one night, that a man, a very low-down sort of man, had stopped suddenly in front of her and said, "Give you a bob?"

Mrs. Johnson had not come to that, as she told herself with regard to other unpleasant incidents from time to time. Yet its effect was sufficient to make her tread the Walworth Road with special circumspection. She was above it, at least when it took its pleasures.

So she walked primly along, her fairly red lips and whitely powdered skin thrown into shadow by her veil; and if she scorned the Walworth Road, it cannot be said that the Walworth Road, in busy mood just before the shops closed down, took any more notice of her.

At the Elephant she stood on the edge of the pavement for a moment undecided. She had been walking twenty-five minutes, and the pain at her back refused to be lulled any longer. She also felt a little dizzy in her head, and she thought petulantly how very noisy, how much more noisy than usual, everything was. For now the glamour had left the lights and bustle, and what had been gay and seductive appeared only harsh and clamorous. How hard the pavements were! Her toes felt hot and constricted and a corn began to throb. "Them patent shoes!" thought Mrs. Johnson with resignation. And then sorrowfully, "My poor feet!"

Meditating there upon the question of whether or no to take the 'bus, her wandering eye perceived a young woman approaching from the right towards her.

A young woman it was, who, unlike Mrs. Johnson, attracted a fair share of attention as she walked with airy indifference in front of 'buses, whose drivers' heads turned to watch her progress. For Miss Florrie Small possessed both an appearance and a figure, and showed the latter to advantage in a tightly-fitting costume of green velour cloth. Curves were to a degree out of fashion, but they still continued to possess a certain attraction, and Miss Small allowed herself a certain freedom of plumpness above her waist. For the rest she was careful about both her corsets and her diet. And on this occasion her little black felt toque with ear flaps combined smartness and becomingness in an exceptional degree.

But what drew the eyes of many women to Miss Small was the genuine skunk fur, large and magnificent, which hung regally over her shoulders. Tired, shabby women, of hen-like outline, as they pushed perambulators or plodded slowly on weary feet, let indifferent glances drop from Miss Small's pink, red and white countenance (for everyone made up in these days) to her fur. Then the glances, returning to her face, were no longer indifferent, but disapproving and even malevolent. One woman coming out with another from a public-house observed Miss Small for a fraction, and then nudged her companion, saying violently, "These 'ere tarts, they make me sick, they do!"

But Miss Small was inured to stares, and even to the occasional comments of her neighbourhood. She accepted them quite properly as a tribute to her exceptional smartness, and had they not been forthcoming in their customary degree, she would have hastened to the nearest public lavatory, there to expend, if need be, even a penny at the mirror in order to inquire after the cause. It was not that she appeared, as was the case with Mrs. Johnson, to take any heed, for the neighbourhood of the Elephant did not interest her professionally; but if she aroused little attention in the Walworth Road, there was little hope of her doing so in more competitive areas.

Like others, Mrs. Johnson observed Florrie's fur with interest, but when she raised her eyes to the wearer's comely if somewhat artificial countenance they contained only admiration and delighted interest, modified to a close observer by a rather uncertain appeal. As Miss Small arrived on the pavement, she raised her veil and advanced a little towards her.

"Why, it's Florrie!" cried Mrs. Johnson in a burst of joyful surprise. "Well! Fancy running into you!"

For a second Miss Small returned Mrs. Johnson's regard impassively. She knew the lady was apt to prove a hanger-on, and wisdom counselled her to walk on with a nod. On the other hand, in face of Mrs. Johnson's effusion, this would have been tantamount to a snub, and Florrie was temperamentally averse to snubbing people. After all, she reflected, she could easily shake her off later. There were points of etiquette that even Mrs. Johnson could not disregard.

"Hullo! Haven't seen you about lately," she said affably enough.

"No, you 'aven't," said Mrs. Johnson in the tone of one who confirms a great truth. "I've 'ad the 'flu. 'Ad it shockin' bad! I ain't been out of bed for a week."

"You don't look too bright."

"I don't. Nor I don't feel it."

There was a short silence, while Mrs. Johnson watched Florrie, and Florrie watched for a 'bus. It turned the corner.

"I was just waiting for a 'bus up West myself," said Mrs. Johnson. "If you don't mind my company, dear?"

"Not at all," said Florrie politely, if rather absently.

They got into the 'bus, Mrs. Johnson making a great show of drawing back politely to let Florrie mount first. They sat down on the left-hand side, and Florrie began to fumble in her bag.

"Going all the way to the Circus?" said Mrs. Johnson, trying to make her voice appear indifferent.

Florrie nodded.

"I'll have a tuppenny, too," said Mrs. Johnson brightly, surrendering her sixpence to the conductor. But as she took the four coppers handed back, she experienced a pang. Cut into her sixpence she had, and she only meant to have a penny fare. Suppose it was an unlucky evening? Well, it couldn't be helped. And a bit of company was worth it. You never knew.

She looked sideways at Florrie. Better not say anything about her fur. She didn't seem very talkative, and it was no use giving offence. It was certainly a new one. She would have liked to know who had paid for it.

But Florrie suddenly became affable. She had realized that the conductor had half anticipated that she would pay for Mrs. Johnson, and it had made her feel a little mean. After all she was in funds. She might stand the old girl a drink later.

So she asked for details of Mrs. Johnson's symptoms, and soon became really interested in the topic.

"It makes you feel so down in the dumps," said Mrs. Johnson.

"A friend of mine," replied Florrie, "once killed himself after having the 'flu."

"You don't say!"

"He did. Nice fellow he was, too, in his way. Very cheerful. Great sense of humour, you know. Always had a joke whenever you met him. He used to be in the Regent a lot with a lot of other chaps night after night. And always free with his money, you don't know! Why, he'd think nothing of taking on three girls at a time. And he wouldn't expect you to keep to beer! 'Order what you like, and how you like,' was what he'd always say. Well, after a while I missed him. He was never there. Of course I just thought that he was away or something." Florrie paused.

"Of course you would," agreed Mrs. Johnson, anxious to show her appreciation.

"So I was talking to a friend of his one evening. Jack Hulton, his name is—very like the fellow with the band, isn't it, the name I mean?—and I just happened to say, 'What's got Billy Richards these days'—that was his name, you know, Billy Richards. 'Where's Billy Richards?' I said, and he said, 'Haven't you heard?' and by the way he said it I knew there was something in the wind. 'No,' I said. 'What's up?' I said.

"Then he got telling me about it. Threw himself out of the window of an hotel or boarding-house or something in Torrington Square. At the top of the house it was. And when he was picked up he was as dead as frozen meat, poor fellow!"

"Dear, dear," said Mrs. Johnson.

"And believe me or believe me not it was just that he'd had 'flu. Everyone said so. Had it real bad, you know. And never got over it. Moped and wouldn't go about with his friends. Though he had no money troubles at all! Very good position, I believe, in something or other. Isn't it queer what people will do when they get as low as all that?"

Mrs. Johnson agreed. The story depressed her slightly. "Well," she started, "I always fight against it myself. What I say is . . ."

"And there was someone else I knew," interrupted Florrie.

With an expression of rapt attention Mrs. Johnson gave her ear to Florrie, while her eyes occasionally wandered past her through the window. They had left Trafalgar Square, and there was plenty to see.

Mrs. Johnson noticed many men unaccompanied, some walking fast, making for a dinner appointment, others strolling slowly with a watchful eye. Solitary women there were, too, walking slower or a trifle faster than usual because of their recognition that it was pleasure time. Mrs. Johnson marvelled, as she never ceased to marvel, at the number of taxis there were about, returning many of them from the theatre, others still busy taking late arrivals. And over all the uneasy throng, passing their various ways a little more watchfully than earlier in the day, the impassive sky stared down indifferently. It had watched men and women repeat themselves too often; or perhaps it was too far away to understand.

Mrs. Johnson felt lonely and chilled. She would have liked the evening before her to have been blotted out. Or if only it could have been all over, and she was going back to snuggle down in bed, and lose herself and her aches and pains in rest. "I do need a pick-me-up," she thought, self-pityingly.

"Here we are," said Florrie, breaking off from her narrative, as the 'bus drew up.

They crossed Piccadilly Circus together, going up

the south side of Shaftesbury Avenue. Florrie had resumed her social air of nonchalance, but the gulf between her and Mrs. Johnson had lessened. True, the glances that came their way rested on Florrie, but the glances were casual, and both of them felt less like duchess and poor dependent and more on the equality of two members of the same overcrowded and hard-working profession.

But when Florrie had mounted the stairs leading to the lounge of the public-house that was their destination, the dividing line between them became again tightly drawn. Men, men and women together and women alone, looking each of them up and down as they entered, classified them by professional standards. Florrie, it was evident, was a force to be reckoned with: she had smartness, she had an air, and she thus received the compliment of thoughtful appraisal. But the room passed over Mrs. Johnson in uninterested silence. She was easy to place, and her place was a low one.

Glancing round, Florrie received and returned a nod of recognition from two men sitting in the right-hand corner. But they were with two girls, and she did not choose to go over to them. She sat down at a table by the wall, facing the bar, at which one girl was already sitting. This girl was small and thin. She had applied a high colour to her sallow skin; her red mouth drooped; her brown eyes were sharp, and she appeared both sulky and on the defensive.

At Florrie she directed a suspicious glance, gathering her personality together against a rival better-dressed and better-looking than herself. Her pose endeavoured to suggest that she remained unimpressed. Mrs. Johnson she ignored after one glance.

Florrie, refreshed by the feeling of power the room

had given her, expanded. "What are you going to have?" she asked Mrs. Johnson. "A Guinness?"

"Thank you very much, I will," said Mrs. Johnson. And then added, for she could not afford to leave any vestige of doubt about the matter of paying, "It's very kind of you, dear."

"Well, that's that," said Florrie, and beckoned to the waiter. He came with celerity. Florrie was a good customer.

"A couple of Guinnesses, George, as quick as you like."

The waiter nodded and smiled. Before going away, he stared at the almost empty glass in front of the table's first occupant, whose name was Lily. It was a hard stare, and Lily, pretending not to notice, cursed inwardly. She had been sitting with the glass of bitter in front of her for nearly half an hour, and she knew she couldn't make it last out much longer. She gazed with an increased intensity at a man at the next table talking to two others. He had looked at her once; if he gave her the least bit more of encouragement she decided she would go over and sit at their table. It had a vacant seat, and there was no use missing the slightest opportunity. She was sick to death of walking about the streets with a headache, and being looked at as if she didn't exist.

Mrs. Johnson had also observed the waiter's look. She was sorry it was his night on, for he was a difficult person with whom to deal. She liked the other man with the long, drooping, dark moustache much better. He was good natured, and had sometimes exchanged an affable word with her. But this man allowed her no grace in the way of time; and his manner always made it perfectly clear that he regarded her as an intruder. "Get off or get out" was his motto.

He returned with the glasses of stout, and Florrie deposited a shilling and a sixpence on the red wine-marked tray as she asked him some question which Mrs. Johnson was unable to overhear. He replied reassuringly.

Mrs. Johnson started to drink, darting little birdlike glances at the people around her. When the waiter returned, Lily stared at him boldly. "A Bass, please," she said in a low, hoarse voice. It would be the last drink she could afford to treat herself to tonight, but perhaps it was worth waiting a little longer.

There was little conversation between the other two women. Florrie sipped her stout slowly and watched the door. Mrs. Johnson, who comprehended much of the art of living, concentrated on savouring her drink. Every time she raised her glass she experienced a thrill of satisfaction, and she followed the progress of the liquid down her throat with a tender observation. It didn't exactly warm you, but oh, how satisfying it was! Every time she placed her glass down she felt she had done much to add to her well-being. Two or three bottles a day, and, she thought, she would feel herself in no time. Self-confidence came gradually as her glass diminished, and she crossed her legs, and looked round boldly. She wished now she hadn't put the veil on when she had gone out. Men would have seen her in it when she came in, and it would certainly have given her age away.

Meanwhile Florrie became a little restless. She hated wasting time, and she knew she was not in the *milieu* to which her gifts entitled her. Sitting in a pub, a common pub, with an old hag of a finished and done-with prostitute was not suitable. But she had fixed up with Hemp to be free for him if he came along before nine. She finished off her drink in three large gulps and considered the question of ordering either another of the same or a Bass. The waiter was moving near, and as she caught his eye she remembered Mrs. Johnson, and hesitated.

She glanced at her companion, who in her engrossed enjoyment of her beverage had nearly come to the end of the glass without remembering that it was her bounden duty to make it stretch out to the utmost fraction of possible time. Now, however, she remembered, and raising the glass to her lips for appearance' sake, set it down untouched.

Florrie noticed the action, and was moved by it. After all, she thought, the poor thing had been ill. Who could tell? She herself might one day be in Mrs. Johnson's shoes, and then she'd be thankful for any small mercy. Besides, the little bitch opposite who looked at her in such an ugly way would be impressed. It would teach her that she, Florrie Small, was not one of those who never had a few shillings in her purse. And didn't mind spending them on others.

"Have a Bass with me?" she said to Mrs. Johnson with well simulated carelessness.

Joy and surprise caught at Mrs. Johnson. What amazing luck! It was a long time since she had been treated to two drinks running. She could hardly believe it.

"Ta!" she said, her amazement making her briefer than usual. But gratitude in rich profusion flowed from her to Florrie. She looked at her with shining eyes. What a fine, smart girl she was! There wasn't another one in the room to hold a candle to her. She deserved her luck with the men, her lovely fur; she did indeed. And she, Emily Johnson, didn't grudge it to her, if any one else did.

As the waiter left them with Florrie's order, a new-comer entered, and Florrie, seeing him, jerked into animation. Her face radiated welcome, and as he came up to her she held out her hand to be shaken, and inclined her head coyly to one side in an appealing attitude. Florrie knew how to behave, as well as what was due to her. Mrs. Johnson, glancing at her unobtrusively, noted the gleam of a gold side tooth with covetousness.

She also unobtrusively noticed Florrie's friend, and summed him up as sufficiently well off to be of importance, even though undistinguished, and not altogether at ease. He hadn't a hearty way with him, and Mrs. Johnson was inclined to be suspicious of the quiet ones. You never knew where you were with them.

After a few remarks, Florrie withdrew with him and her Bass to a table a little distance away which had just been vacated. Mrs. Johnson expected to be ignored, and she was. She was left alone with Lily.

They glanced at each other for a moment: Lily's gaze was hard and contemptuous. It was an unmistakable answer to Mrs. Johnson's vague expression of would-be friendliness. They both sat very still and aloof, slowly swallowing their ale, and watchful, at least so far as Lily was concerned, for every stray glance and every new-comer.

It was not long before Mrs. Johnson felt very much like talking to someone. She glanced at the small table next to her. Two small girls, tightly costumed, tightly hatted, and made up in precisely the same way and to the same degree, were sitting there talking earnestly. One, however, was dark and more vixenish than the other, and when her friend had finished what she was saying she leaned across to her, and said as one voicing a grave problem:

"But I thought he was very fond of you."

The other girl made no answer. She turned and

looked over her shoulder; then, catching Mrs. Johnson's sympathetic eye, looked through her.

"I thought he was fond of you," said the other girl again, but more urgently. Still met by silence, she sat back and raised her glass.

Mrs. Johnson's attention went to the other side of the room, where she saw a girl called Kate, very vivacious, bright of eye and flushed of cheek, sitting close to a table at which were two men, both rather grave and watchful and cautious. Kate was swinging a pretty leg, and at last she caught the eye of her neighbour. "Swing me just a little bit higher," she said gaily to him, adding, "I bet you don't mind how high."

Mrs. Johnson sighed. There was no denying some girls had the gift. She watched Kate, now engaged in conversation, with admiration, till her attention was called away by the appearance of two young men at her table.

They were both quite young: one had a smooth-skinned, round face, and a small, dark moustache. His hair was oiled, and his eyes sharp and closely set together. He appeared to be the leading spirit of the two, but the other one, Mrs. Johnson decided, was better-looking, with nice, wavy fair hair, well marked nose and jaw, and a frank, boyish look. "A bit like Cecil would have been, had he lived," reflected Mrs. Johnson, gazing at him with undisguised approval.

While they ordered whiskies she pondered on whether there was the remotest chance that she would be able to get off. Not much. She wouldn't be good enough for them. Too old! As a matter of fact she hadn't much of a chance sitting in this pub at all. Too much light; too much competition. Still, she'd wait a bit. It was a rest.

Their conversation concerned racing matters, and

Mrs. Johnson had to watch Lily's success with the dark man. "Would you like a cert. for the 3.30 to-morrow?" he had asked her.

"I know those certs.," replied Lily, showing her teeth, which were white and even. She giggled and glanced coquettishly at the other young man. She also favoured him. But she took care to look quickly back at the man who had first spoken to her, and giggled again.

"Well, take it or leave it," he said. He pulled out a bit of paper and pencil and wrote something upon it. "I'm not a tipster. Am I, Frank?"

His friend shook his head.

"But I've put more money in the way of my pals than any blinking cheat of a tipster. Now then, do you want this?"

"I'm sure I'm much obliged," said Lily, accepting the slip of paper. She read it, and put it away in her hand-bag.

Mrs. Johnson felt neglected, and she also felt sociable. She decided that this was the time to force herself into action. "I'd like to get hold of a winner myself," she said, smiling at the dark young man.

He looked at her ungraciously. "A bob's my charge," he said.

Mrs. Johnson was not quarrelsome, but neither was she devoid of spirit, and the dark young man became oppressive to her.

"Didn't see *her* pay you," she said, jerking her head towards Lily. Then, alarmed at her boldness, she gave a deprecating smile, intended to turn her remark into a joke. But the smile was a little late, and it was ignored.

"She's a friend of mine, aren't you, darling?" he said, staring coolly at Mrs. Johnson while he patted Lily's arm.

Lily giggled again.

"Course you are," she said, not troubling to glance at Mrs. Johnson.

"I've known you for donkey's years, haven't I?"

"But you didn't find me a donkey, did you?" he answered meaningly.

Lily went into a shriek of laughter. Pleased at his success, the young man beckoned her, and then bent and whispered in her ear. Again Lily shrieked with laughter.

Mrs. Johnson tried to catch the other young man's eye, hoping for a spark of sympathy, but failed. It was evident that, feeling somewhat uncomfortable, he was engaged in absenting his real self from the table. He was staring blankly at the wall; he hadn't bargained for women, and he was determined not to get involved.

Mrs. Johnson felt her mood change. The whole place became distasteful to her. She looked hard at the ashtray just in front of her, fighting against a dangerous impulse to turn on Lily and shout at her.

"Some people do think they're someone," she muttered. But no one took any notice. Indeed no one heard her except the good-looking young man, and he was still determinedly engaged in not being drawn into anything.

Mrs. Johnson took a resolve. She swallowed the last drops of her Bass, carefully took out a handkerchief from her bag, and wiped her lips with exaggerated precision. The action gave her the sense of being very much a lady, and for a few seconds the reflection that she was in reality superior to everybody else in the room comforted her.

She pulled down her veil and rose, darting as she did so a look intended to convey scorn and contempt at Lily, who did not observe the gesture. Then she looked from her round the room, including the rest of its occupants in her dismissal. Which of those girls had had a devoted husband, the same as her? she asked herself. And a little public of their own with garden and field at the back. None of them. Nor ever would. Prostitutes, that's what they were, and always would be.

As she passed across the room she noticed that Florrie and her gentleman friend were very much engaged in themselves. She half paused as she passed near them, hoping for a glance of recognition, which would have warmed her. But Florrie did not look up.

Mrs. Johnson felt a little queer as she walked down the steps. She had, she reflected, had only a couple of drinks, but then her stomach had been almost empty. "Wonder if I could run to two pennyworth of chips or something?" she muttered to herself, and paused at the door to consider the question. But the cold stare of the commissionaire standing there sent her on into the street.

The lights of Wardour Street blinked heartlessly at her. Instinctively she turned into the comparative quietness of Gerard Street, her mind going back in hostility to the place she had just left.

To herself she expressed the hope that that dirty little whore wouldn't get the young fellow. She knew their sort; they had only come in to get a few drinks, and exchange compliments with the girls to make them feel big. As for Lily herself . . . her thoughts lingered round the girl in bitterness. Then suddenly she felt herself to be old and tired, and the hatred left her. She tried to remember the special grudge she had had against the occupants of the table, and it seemed no longer important. After all she had got two drinks out of Florrie. How much had that fur she was wearing cost?

"Let me see," she asked herself. "How much did Jim

give for that fur he bought me out of his winnings at the Lewes races? A real, good skunk it was."

She stood for a few minutes by the gallery entrance to the Hippodrome, her mind reconstructing the event. She had been in the field, tying the goats to a fresh bit of grass, and he had called to her. There was a parcel for her, he had said. Yes, he had had it sent by post for a surprise. And how rare and pleased he had been at seeing her in it. Everybody, or nearly everybody, who came into the bar that evening he had called behind to have a look at it. It was fourteen pounds he had given for it, and that was cost price, because he had got it through a man he knew in the trade. Poor Jim! He was generous with his money when he had it. Too generous! Better for her today if he'd have been the saving kind. Ah, well! What was had to be!

She looked up and down the street. She would have liked to tell someone about her husband. How good he had been to her, never denying her anything if he could help it! What would he say if he could see where she had got to today!

There was nobody about: the two totties who had passed her had turned into Charing Cross Road. Wait! Wasn't that a man standing on the opposite side turned in her direction? She looked back, and then turned and walked slowly towards him.

As she drew near, he crossed, making a line that led past her, but looking hard at her as he came abreast. She coughed and stood still.

No! He had sheered off. Not to his liking evidently. Not much use following; he was walking quite fast now. Mrs. Johnson sighed and walked slowly on. She ought to have gone to the Park first of all. Perhaps she would go now. But she couldn't walk all that way without a bite. She weighed the claims of 'bus fares and a snack. The latter won, for she might feel equal to walking when she had got something inside her.

She hurried across to the other side of the road, and walked rapidly along. It was cold, and she shivered. A whisky now! A whisky would be the thing to give her help in getting hold of someone. It was no good trying to be gay and enticing without food or anything. Leastways not at her age.

Withdrawing into a corner, she took twopence from her purse ready to pass over the counter. It was against her practice to let anyone see into her purse; some people were nosy; liked to see how much cash you had; some of those girls, them that hadn't been brought up at all proper, were a bit too ready with their remarks.

Now she had only threepence halfpenny left. She felt a sharp pang of regretful kindness towards those meagre brown coins. They'd be gone before the night was out, she'd be bound. And then where'd she be? Not a sou in the world! Not a bloody sou!

At the door of the café she paused, almost relinquishing her intention. Fivepence halfpenny was, after all, a lot more than threepence halfpenny. There was the farthing, which came in for loaves of bread. But the smell of hot food caught at her nostrils too alluringly to be resisted, and she went inside.

There was nobody there she knew, for the place happened to be fairly empty at the time. Two girls were at the table eating heartily, and drinking out of big cups of coffee. A man and a girl were in a corner, and there was a girl sitting by herself smoking.

Mrs. Johnson ordered her sandwich from the white-jacketed young Jew behind the counter, and thought regretfully of the chips she might have had in its stead if she had only happened to be the other side of the river. These sandwiches were the best you could get up West for their price, and held a proud position among those who were initiated; but, after all, thought Mrs. Johnson, what she really needed was something spicy and hot. And a cup of coffee. Should she blow it all in, and order a cup? It was a difficult decision.

If she ordered a cup of coffee she would also feel entitled to a seat. Of course there was nothing actually to prevent her from sitting down with her sandwich, upon which she had liberally spread mustard; but Mrs. Johnson knew that she was in the bad books of the young Jew, and she hoped to placate him by standing. Once he had told her that you couldn't be expected to get a whole evening's rest for tuppence. "Was it," he had asked her with mock politeness, "reasonable?" and the resort was too convenient for Mrs. Johnson to wish to burn her boats entirely.

Eating as slowly as she dared, Mrs. Johnson had nearly come to the end of her sandwich when a young woman entered, quietly dressed in a grey flannel suit with a white jumper. She was pale, and though her dark eyes were lively and good natured, Mrs. Johnson did not know how to place her, since she sported very little make-up.

She ordered two ham sandwiches, and much to Mrs. Johnson's pleasure remained at the counter to eat them. For it was evident that she was disposed towards conversation, and not particular with whom she held it. So when Mrs. Johnson assiduously passed her the mustard, she was thanked with warmth.

"Very cold tonight," said Mrs. Johnson, encouraged.

"My God, isn't it! Cold as hell! Or I suppose hell isn't? What do you say, Tommy?"

She was addressing the Jew, who took, however, no notice. He knew Miss Agnes True, and did not care for her style.

As a retort to his silence, Agnes raised her eyebrows, and then turned down the corners of her mouth ludicrously, jerking her head back from Rosenbaum to Mrs. Johnson, who tittered, feeling that she was getting her own back to some extent. She decided she liked Agnes: not one of your stuck-up ones, she wasn't. A real, nice girl. And it was plain that she had had a few drinks. That might make her generous. You never knew your luck.

For a little while Agnes was silent, concentrating upon her food. Then she turned to Mrs. Johnson again.

"I have been in the old Hole. You know where I mean? Right! Got in with a chap what was as tight as an owl, and went on putting it away, too. 'Now my dear,' he says to me. 'I'm not going to ask you to take me home. I wouldn't insult you,' he says. 'But you can have as many drinks as you want.' And he meant it too. He ordered a double Scotch straight away. Some girls might have been too—you know what I mean—to take it. But what's the odds? That's what I say. A short life, and get through it as best you can, that's what I say."

"I wish I'd been there," said Mrs. Johnson. "I was just saying to myself that a drop of Scotch is what you want, my dear. I miss it, because you see my husband— he had a public-house of his own. And I've just had the 'flu something awful. I couldn't tell you what I feel like. It's as much as I can do just to stand up."

She raised her voice slightly in the hope that Rosenbaum would get the benefit of the last remark. Not though, she thought to herself, that his sort have any decency in them.

"You do look off it," said Agnes sympathetically. "You've come out too soon. That's what it is. You ought to have given yourself another day or two in bed."

"So I ought," said Mrs. Johnson. "I know that. But there you are. I've my living to make."

"That's right," said Agnes. "That's what it is. No time to stay at home and say your prayers. Go forth into the highways and byways and compel them to come in. That's our game. For better or for worse. For richer or for poorer. And mostly for poorer."

She laughed loudly, and not being sufficiently applauded proceeded to make her point clearer.

"That's a quotation from the Bible, though you may not know it. But I know it. Oh, yes! I know my Bible. When I went to Sunday School I got the prize. Believe me or believe me not, I got a bew-ti-ful prize."

"You *are* a lively one, you are," said Mrs. Johnson.

At the sound of her voice, the Jew suddenly turned.

"Can I get you anything else, madam?" he inquired with mock politeness. Mrs. Johnson shook her head.

"Are you going to stay here all night then?" he said, changing his voice disagreeably.

"All right, all right," said Mrs. Johnson. "You're in a hurry, aren't you?"

Agnes's presence had emboldened her, and she recognized her own courage with approbation. Funny how you never feel up to yourself when you're alone, she thought.

"Wait a mo," said Agnes, cramming the last of her sandwich into her mouth, "and I'll come with you, though the perfect gentleman here is so polite and pressing me to stay with him."

She laughed again, and Mrs. Johnson joined in her merriment. For a moment Rosenbaum took no notice, giving an attentive ear to a male customer who had just come in.

Then he turned full on Agnes, who had vexed him with her tongue before.

"Well, I must say you're one as I'd rather see your back than your face," he said, turning full on her. "You may be a nice, sweet little thing, but somehow I don't seem to see it."

"Don't you insult me, you dirty Jew," said Agnes in a raised voice. "I needn't put up with anything from you, and I'm not going to. You get your living mostly from us girls, don't you; and you'd better treat us proper. I've paid you, haven't I?"

Mrs. Johnson realized that they were rousing attention from the other occupants of the café. She became a little frightened. If Rosenbaum got really offended, he might refuse to serve her again. Complain to the police or something. It would be like him.

"Get out of here, both of you," said Rosenbaum. "Get out of here, or it will be the worse for you."

"How do you mean, it will be the worse for me, you bloody Jew," shouted Agnes. "What do you mean?"

"Come on, dear," said Mrs. Johnson. "Come on. Don't take any notice."

Agnes hesitated. The temptation to have a really good row, to turn and address the whole café, to relieve herself once and for all in glorious fashion was strong. But she sensed that Rosenbaum was waiting for her next move. And he had the authorities behind him.

"All right. But you shall hear from me further," she said with dignity. She looked round the café with a thoughtful air. But it did not appear as if any one was coming to her aid. Mrs. Johnson was already out in the street. So she shot a last arrow. "There's nothing I hate and despise more than the Jews who betrayed Our Lord, and who are responsible for every mean and dirty action under the sun," she said clearly, and went out to rejoin Mrs. Johnson.

They walked away from the door in silence, and then Agnes said as a final comment: "The b . . . ! The bloody b . . . of a Jew!"

Mrs. Johnson did not reply: she only shook her head once to imply that things had come to such a pass that they were beyond her. Pulling down her veil had turned her mind to another topic. She decided to consult Agnes.

"Do you think," she said after a short interval, "that wearing this veil makes me look old?"

Agnes glanced at her without bothering to give any careful survey, and then reassured her heartily: "Old, not a bit. You look as young as ever you were."

This was not exactly what Mrs. Johnson wanted.

"But would you say," she said, pushing her veil up, "that I look better without it."

But Agnes was in too expansive a mood to give herself to any survey of details.

"Christ!" she said. "What does it matter? If your name's up to click tonight, you'll click, veil or no veil. If it isn't, well then you won't, and that's all there is to it. Let's go and get a drink and hope for the best."

"I'd like to," said Mrs. Johnson, "but honest, dear, I'm cleaned right out."

Agnes looked at her searchingly. "I have heard that said before."

"It's the blessed truth," said Mrs. Johnson, stung into vehemence. "God strike me dead, if it isn't! 'Ere! Look!"

Agnes looked indifferently at the opened bag thrust under her eyes. A stick of rouge, a key, a box without a lid of compressed powder, and a very dirty, small powder-puff were its visible contents.

"Well, I suppose I shall have to treat you," she said. "If I wasn't on the streets already, I soon would be, what with all the things people get out of me for nothing."

Mrs. Johnson thought it wiser to be silent. Agnes was evidently in a mood when she might choose to quarrel with her at any moment. She followed her into the public-house lounge selected a little wearily. The snack she had eaten had not had the effect she hoped, for her back was hurting, and her head beginning to ache. Urgently, too, it came to her that it was time to get to business. She ought really to leave Agnes and walk about a little. She would never do any good as long as she was with someone young. But then perhaps a glass of something would pick her up.

The room they entered wore a subdued, almost dejected air. There were plenty of men, but they were men who had come to drink and talk, and only casual glances rested on Mrs. Johnson and Agnes as they sat down.

Agnes looked round searchingly. "That fellow I told you about isn't here," she said. "He said he'd come back here, and pick me up later. Much hopes of that, I don't think! Well, we'll have a bottle of the usual to keep us going."

She gave the order, and it was not till they had drunk a little that Agnes regained her former cheerfulness. "If I don't work myself off on someone tonight," she said loudly, "I shall run all the way home smiling at every man I see. And then I shall dance round my room. Why not? You get what's coming to you, and if it doesn't come, why worry?"

"That's what I say," said Mrs. Johnson. "It's no use meeting troubles half way. No use at all. And that's a fact."

She emptied her glass, and then putting it down, fortified to have a good stare round, found that it was impossible to remember the faces of any one after she had looked away. They were far off, and didn't seem at all important. Nevertheless she had to make them important. She kept her eyes fixed for some time on a fair, boyish-looking young man in a corner, who grew more and more uneasy under her half unconscious leer; and told herself that she must remember to keep a clear head. This was only her third drink: showed the way illness and starvation had affected her. Thinking of her hardships, she removed her gaze from the young man, to his great relief, and shook her head sadly as she studied the red tiled pattern of the table which glowed up at her with rich warmth.

Then, "Never mind," she told herself after a few moments. "You're as good as any of them here anyway."

She looked round again defiantly, and the young man, catching her eye, removed his regard hastily. She would have liked to find an occasion for asserting herself, for all at once it came to her that she had been far too meek with people. The way Rose had grown to ride roughshod over her lately! After all she had done for that woman in the past! When you had money and a home and a husband, people loved you. But if you were down, they'd all of them like to give you another push. If she only had Rose here now, she'd tell her what she thought of her. Such a mean fuss over a few weeks' rent. She turned to Agnes with an idea of telling her the story of her wrongs, but the girl began to speak first.

"I tell you what!" said Agnes, with the effect of uttering a new truth. "The matter with us is that we are too refined. It's the painted bird that gets the worm every time. Much more important than being early."

MRS. JOHNSON

Mrs. Johnson felt her mind grasp with astonishing clarity the immense significance of this utterance.

"That's right," she said, nodding her head several times. "We're too refined. Too quiet-like and decent for most of them."

"Decent's the word," interrupted Agnes. "Do you know what I was asked to do the other night? And for two pounds. Two pounds! I was supposed to make a beast of myself, if you please. Wait now, and I'll tell you the way it happened." Turning towards Mrs. Johnson, her eyes met those of a young man just coming into the room. He came towards her, and Mrs. Johnson, looking to see the cause of the delay in the narrative, saw with mixed feelings a young man standing by their table.

"Good evening, Mr. James," said Agnes, looking up with excitement flavoured by something resembling contempt in her eyes. "Or isn't it James tonight? You never know, you know. It might be one of the other holy apostles." She laughed loudly.

Mrs. Johnson reflected that Agnes was certainly a bit on. Seemed as if she cared for nobody. So flushed, too! And ordinarily she was such a pale girl.

"What's your poison?" said Mr. James, ignoring the sally, and pulling out a chair for himself.

"Just a wee drappie of the malt," said Agnes, adding absently, "as Harry Lauder says."

Mrs. Johnson looked hard at her empty glass, and then turned a fixed smile towards her companions, directed neither at Agnes nor at Mr. James, but hovering between them in the hope of winning some sort of recognition from one or the other.

Mr. James, pink and round faced, with thin hair already receding from his forehead, began to realize for the first time the presence of Mrs. Johnson, and glanced uneasily from her to Agnes, waiting for a cue. He didn't want to treat that elderly person, and because of her lack of attraction became suspicious. Perhaps she was the girl's mother. Perhaps he had been unwise in sitting down straight off. What he ought to have done was to sit down at another table, and wait till Agnes joined him, or the old hag sheered off. He withdrew himself a little and became thoughtful.

Agnes realized the cause of his uneasiness, and hastened to reassure him. "This lady here has just 'ad influenza. Do you know the joke, 'How did you get it?' 'I opened the window, and in flew Enza!' She has just done me the favour of having a drink with me till you turned up—for somehow I thought it might be little Jimmy's night out tonight. But she's saying that she can't keep away from her by-bye much longer, she feels so bad."

Mr. James looked at Mrs. Johnson for confirmation.

Mrs. Johnson was a little disappointed, but she admitted to herself that it was to have been expected.

"Yes, I am just off," she said, preserving her smile, though the glow of expectancy went from her eyes, leaving them rather like that of a hurt child determined not to cry.

Mr. James understood that there was nothing to be feared from this quarter, and in his relief expanded benevolently. After all, giving the old girl a drink would only mean another eightpence, and it would look well with Agnes, who was almost the only one of her profession with whom he felt at ease. In talking of her to his chosen intimates, he would close by saying solemnly, "And to look at her you would never know she was that sort. Just a quiet-looking, wholesome sort of girl, you'd think if you didn't know her."

To which someone or other could generally be relied upon to say, "But you know different," and then there would be a burst of laughter very flattering to Mr. James. Oh, Agnes was certainly an acquisition, if she did rag you rather when there was any one else about. So he turned to Mrs. Johnson, and said graciously, "Have a whisky before you go. It'll do you good."

"It's most kind of you. Thank you very much, I'm sure," said Mrs. Johnson, affecting a ladylike precise voice which somehow seemed natural to her at the moment. She finished up with a little bow, thinking to herself with a gleam of pleasure, "Refined, that's what I am."

The whiskies having arrived, Mr. James decided he might dismiss Mrs. Johnson from his mind. Agnes was leaning towards him now, talking rapidly, her face close against his. He did not follow all she was saying, and laughed rather as his instinct prompted him than by the light of his own appreciation. For he considered he was well away now from the safe shore; and sometimes he felt a little thrilled by his own bravery and would glance round to see what attention he was attracting; and sometimes he felt uneasy and afraid, and his eyes grew absent as he thought of what lay in front of him. But whenever Agnes paused he nodded, looked thoughtful for a moment, smiled, and then renewed his grip on what she was saying.

Meanwhile Mrs. Johnson, sipping her whisky, watched them passively. Her mind remained tranquil, for she was not jealous of Agnes, and inasmuch as she thought at all, she felt glad that Agnes was evidently fixed up all right. At the back of her mind, as yet unformulated, was the realization that her evening was running out, and that very shortly indeed she would have to try and do something about it. But she did not spoil the few precious moments in which she had a right to a comfortable seat, and was regarded with tolerance if not with approval by taking thought. People came and went; occasionally a burst of laughter or a raised voice struck her attention; her head became heavy, and she felt further and further away from the world of struggle and discomfort.

Abruptly her pleasant coma was dispelled. "Time, gentlemen, time!" came the harsh voice of the waiter, intruding on conversation, shattering reverie, disturbing observation. To Mrs. Johnson it was the strident voice of reality shouting at her to get a move on, and remember that she had her rent to pay.

"Eleven o'clock, and I haven't spoken to a man yet," Mrs. Johnson warned herself in something of a panic. She swallowed the last of the liquor remaining in her glass, and pushing back her chair rose to her feet, frowning and determined. One predominating thought mastered her: she must get out into the street and accost someone, any one, quick. But she remembered her manners. "Good night, dear," she said to Agnes, who nodded and laughed, and "Good night to you," she said to Mr. James, who gave a half-nod, and shuffled uneasily in his chair. She went out of the room and, a little unsteadily, down the stairs, followed by a long, high laugh, over whose significance she pondered vacantly.

Coming into Leicester Square, the bright lights, as they seemed, and throngs of hurrying people confused her. For a moment she wondered irritably if there was an accident or something, to account for so many people. And there was such a noise. Faces shot by her, gleaming with astonishing clarity, as if lit up by a powerful white light, and then in a moment vanished as if they had never been. There were two men arguing angrily outside the old Empire; just past them three girls coming along arm-in-arm, their red mouths opened by laughter. Again a placard bore down upon her suddenly and impressively, "The Wicked Shall Be Turned into Hell" it shouted at Mrs. Johnson, and passed by; while in its turn the unshaven face of a matchseller standing at the curb rose at her, and fixed her attention a few seconds owing to its aloofness. The matchseller was apart from the pushing, staring, talking people; he was too apart even to be a spectator. But he stayed his place like a scene-shifter who stands in the wings without a thought for the play, waiting till the end.

Crossing the road, Mrs. Johnson made her way down the short cut which leads into the Charing Cross Road. The fresh air steadied her a little, but she felt very tired and suddenly very lonely. It was because, she thought, there were so many millions of people about all talking to someone else except her alone. Outside the picture palace she paused, and laid a hand on her back.

"Christ! My back doesn't half ache," she said aloud, looking for sympathy from the commissionaire, who was impatiently awaiting the expected exit of the audience so that he could get home. Meanwhile he stared up and down, anxious not to lose any spectacle which he might add to his day's store before retiring into private life.

He was a big fellow with a fine moustache, and though he made no comment with regard to Mrs. Johnson's plaint, she continued to pause expectantly, for of a sudden she had become convinced that there existed a strong likeness between him and her dead husband. He gave her a glance at last, having failed to find anything or anybody worthy of his attention.

"Cheer up, mother," he said consolingly, "you'll soon be dead."

"It's very strange," said Mrs. Johnson, disregarding this piece of comfort. "It's very strange indeed, but you're just the image of my husband. The absolute spit of him!"

A page-boy coming out from the cinema heard, and a grin twisted the corners of his mouth. That was a good one to tell against Big Jim. The commissionaire, aware of him, said loudly, "Well, I'm not your husband. No. Nor likely to be if I can help it. So don't get ideas."

The boy laughed loudly, and two or three people passing paused and stared with expectant grins. Mrs. Johnson felt she was being made game of, and the mixed assortment of liquor inside her lighted a spurt of indignation.

"Don't you suggest anything against my husband," she said with tones that gathered loudness. "He owned a big hotel, he did, and took more money in an hour than you do in a month: for all you stand there as if you thought you was in a beauty competition." The crowd was increased by the first arrivals from the audience, and this time the laughter was against the commissionaire, who became annoyed.

"Here, none of your lip! Move along or I'll tell the police." And then added, instinctively finding the softest place in Mrs. Johnson's armour, "You're drunk, and at your age, too!"

Mrs. Johnson did not care to have the police brought into the conversation, even at her most irresponsible, and slowly she started to move on, saying, but not too loudly, "Don't be so free with your drunks, my fine fellow, or else if there's a law in the land, you'll be made sorry for it. Libel it is! The law of libel!"

She left him behind, and walked fairly fast. But she still continued to mutter to herself, and a few of the crowd, hoping to be provided with further entertainment, followed. Mrs. Johnson, turning suddenly, saw the white face of one of them, a young man, looming close by, and mistook his eager expression for sympathy.

"My husband was a fine man," she confided to him. "A fine, big man; could have knocked down that whipper-snapper as easy as easy." She shook her head in sad reminiscence. "But he died. He died of cancer."

The thought had suddenly flashed upon her with the vividness of a great discovery, and it seemed to her as if she was recounting for the first time a fact of the utmost moment. "Yes, dear! Cancer was eating his stomach out, month after month, so as he couldn't keep a bit of food inside him; and there he was looking as yellow as a Chinaman, him that 'ad never 'ad a day's illness in his life, so that it would break your heart to see him. . . ." She stopped, for the face had vanished, the young man's prudence having conquered his curiosity.

Mrs. Johnson crossed to St. Martin's Church, and then to Charing Cross Station, for the young man's presence had aroused her to a sense of her calling. With an effort she dismissed the pictures of her past which had occupied her mind. "Better have a look at myself," she thought, and in Charing Cross Ladies' Room, she remembered, there was a full length mirror at which you could powder and have a good long view of yourself without being charged. In some of these places you would get your head eaten off if you so much as took a peep in the looking-glass without paying the attendant. It was an unfair world!

Mrs. Johnson made her way into the station through the waiting-room, and downstairs. She stood in front of the mirror, and powdered her face generously while she debated within herself the question of paying out yet another penny in order to satisfy a demand of nature. She had forgotten that there was no free convenience provided here: always a catch, she told herself, somewhere. If she spent a penny, she'd only have . . . how much was it? Twopence halfpenny, or twopence three farthings, to be precise. On the other hand, if she waited till she got outside and then took a risk, she might get a policeman on to her. The commissionaire's threat had brought a sense of police persecution home to her. The way they walked so silently round corners just when you thought you were safe from observation! Besides, she had always kept herself respectable in those sorts of ways: not like some she could name. But, then, they'd never known any better; never been legally married and had a place of their own. She had.

Before leaving she had another long look at herself. There was no denying that she did look yellow. She turned to a smartly dressed young woman who was standing beside her, and, moved by the craving to receive some sympathy, coughed loudly, and put her hand to her throat.

The young woman, with a broad, pink face and a lot of fair hair bunched outside her ears, happened to be feeling pleased with herself, and therefore benevolently inclined. She was just about to set off in a taxi with a gentleman who was going to pay for a really smart hotel, and then some more: so meeting Mrs. Johnson's appealing eyes in the glass, she responded.

"Got a bad cough, haven't you?" she said.

"Oh, terrible," replied Mrs. Johnson eagerly. "I've just had the 'flu. I've never felt like I feel now in all my life before. It's cruel, that's what it is. Have you ever felt like it, I wonder? There's a pain that's just eating into my back, here. I feel sickish; my head aches that bad; and the soles of my poor feet make it so that I can hardly put one foot before another."

"Oh, yes, I've felt like that in my time," replied the girl, replacing a stick of rouge in her hand-bag; beautiful, expensive hand-bag it was, Mrs. Johnson noticed admiringly. "Scores of times, if it comes to that."

"Fancy that!" said Mrs. Johnson, gazing at her in a blend of admiration, wonder and appeal. Her mind worked rapidly. This girl seemed a friendly sort. No harm in trying it on.

"And the worst of it is," said Mrs. Johnson, "I haven't even got the price of my 'bus fare home. I was dying for a ——, and it's took my last penny. Now, what I'm going to do I don't really know. I'm not young and good-looking and smart like you, dearie, and it's hard to live. I suppose I shall have to walk all the way back to Camberwell, that's where I live, though I know I shall drop down in the street long before I get there."

"Nothing doing," said the girl briefly. She started to ascend the steps, and then with the thought of her own immediate lucrative future before her she repented, and pausing for a moment opened her bag. Perhaps God would see that *she* never knew want, if He saw her being generous to other people who hadn't her luck.

"Here you are," she said, going back and handing three coppers to Mrs. Johnson, who had come round to meet her, after a glance round to make sure that there was no attendant watching. "That'll pay your fare home anyway. As a matter of fact I'm pretty well cleaned out myself."

"Thank you very much, dear," said Mrs. Johnson, effusive and polite to the last, though a little disappointed. "Wouldn't have hurt her to make it a tanner," she commented to herself.

All dressed up as she was—pearl necklace and a beautiful cloth to her costume. Well, have to be thankful for small mercies, I suppose.

She stared at herself with mournful interest a little longer: her mind occupied with the old problem, to veil or not to veil. It looked so old-fashioned. But it did hide her wrinkles. Leave it perhaps.

At last she dragged herself away and slowly and heavily ascended the stairs, not even pausing for a last glance at herself in the mirror in the wall at the top, for a deep weariness not to be evaded or forgotten any longer had captured her whole being. It was true what she had told her late acquaintance: she ached all down her back; her stomach was a little uneasy; her legs felt so heavy that it was a weary business dragging them up the stairs. It wasn't fair, she told herself, to expect her to try and do anything. If Rose had a heart at all, she couldn't deny her a few more nights' rest. She had fivepence halfpenny now: whatever remained from her 'bus fare she would take to Rose. "See," she would say, "this is all I have, but if it's any good to you have it. Have it!" she would say. Perhaps Rose would lend her another ten bob if she got her in the right mood.

As she left the station, keeping close to the pavement, somebody pushed into her, nearly causing her to lose her balance. She waited a moment to steady herself, and then proceeded on her way, without enough heart in her even to place in his proper category the man who had shoved her. At the end of the Strand stood crowds of people waiting for their 'buses, almost, it seemed, blocking her way on purpose, as she moved pace by pace towards Trafalgar Square. She felt blinded by voices, the jostling rush, and whimpered a little out of tiredness as she moved through.

At the doorway of a chemist's shop at the corner she paused, and stood there thinking that she might give the world a last chance to do something for her. She waited passively, now and then recollecting herself enough to turn her head and single out the approaching figure of a man walking by himself. At these moments her lips would expand in an effort of invitation which remained fixed some time after the object which had inspired it had vanished from sight.

Before very long she felt someone pause beside her. Mrs. Johnson turned hopefully. But it was a policeman who confronted her. "Now then," he said, "hadn't you better be getting along?"

Mrs. Johnson looked for a moment—which seemed to her a long while—into the red face which loomed above her. Vast and meaningless it seemed to her until gradually its significance reached her brain. Then she turned without a word, making her way mechanically across Northumberland Avenue. Arrived at the other side, she looked behind to see if he were following her. No, he had turned the other way.

It's no use, she reflected, not without satisfaction. Everybody and everything was against her. It was Friday, too, an unlucky day Friday had always been for her. Better go home while there was still a 'bus to get. It was nearly twelve, and there wouldn't be one if she waited much longer. Hadn't had any luck. But she couldn't be expected to when she was feeling as she was. No one could.

Her 'bus came, and she watched it drawing up with satisfaction. Nice, friendly 'bus, that would take her home to bed. She was lucky in getting a corner seat, but, as she drew out tuppence for her ticket, a sense of the tragedy its giving up signified to her overcame her once more. "That's almost my last copper gone," she said aloud, looking round at the other passengers in the 'bus, and making her last bid that evening for a look or smile of sympathy with her child's eyes, half terrified, half proud. To be in such a hole!

But no one answered her. Any gaze that met hers withdrew with uneasy speed. The woman who sat next Mrs. Johnson nudged her neighbour, and exchanged with her a smile full of meaning. The man opposite gazed at his boots with great solemnity. Next to him a portly grocer thought with disgust, "Is the woman going to start begging? Here! In a 'bus! Scandalous!" And he frowned at her heavily in order that she should be discouraged from creating any such scene. And then one by one the eyes of the people who had overheard Mrs. Johnson returned to her, filled with carefully prepared impersonality. If she went on talking, or addressed someone, it might be amusing, the boldest thought. But be careful not to give her a chance to pick on them.

But the flicker of life had died in Mrs. Johnson. She offered no more entertainment, but sat awaiting the time she would get out and creep home to bed. It would not be safe to risk going past her proper fare stage, she decided. She wasn't going to pay another penny, no, not if she knew it. So that meant dragging herself along the dark, close-smelling Camberwell Road, which seemed to stretch itself out for ever. Sometimes she had to stop and lean against a wall, to get a moment's respite. "Christ!" she would mutter at such times, and once, when she felt very exhausted, "Lord Christ!" Perhaps she had knocked herself up proper. It was disgraceful that she should have been forced to go out that evening. And nothing had come of it. Nothing had come of it.

At last she turned the corner of her street. As she approached she thought of Rose, who might even be waiting up for her, and her steps faltered. The thing was to be very quiet going in: not let the old cat hear her. Very quietly she slipped the key into the lock, and stole in, closing the door noiselessly behind her. Holding her breath, she tiptoed upstairs, pausing ever and again to listen. But there was no sound. Rose must be asleep. Thank God for that!

Inside her little bedroom, she closed the door, and cautiously turned the key in the lock. She was in now, and she'd not be turned out again that night at least for any one. Not if Rose came and shouted ever so. Now she was safe. There was a whole night between her and the recurrence of unpleasantness. Florrie; Lily; the face of the dark man who had been so rude; Agnes, a gay sort that girl; the good-looking fair boy; Mr. James; the big commissionaire, old beast he was; the girl who had given her threepence—dressed up tart: flickered in her confused head as she undressed. Then she dismissed them. It was all over now. The evening was over. She'd get a little rest and peace now. Feel better tomorrow perhaps.

"At least," was her last coherent thought, "I got a few drinks for nothing. Some of those girls, prostitutes though they may be, have good hearts. I will say that for them."

JAMES STEPHENS

Schoolfellows

I

WE HAD been at school together and I remembered him perfectly well, for he had been a clever and prominent boy. He won prizes for being at the top of his class; and prizes for good behaviour; and prizes for games. Whatever prizes were going we knew that he should get them; and, although he was pleasant about it, he knew it himself.

He saw me first, and he shouted and waved his hat, but I had jumped on a tram already in motion. He ran after me for quite a distance; but the trams only stop at regular places, and he could not keep up: he fell behind, and was soon left far behind.

I had intended jumping off to shake his hand; but I thought, so fast did he run, that he would catch up; and then the tram went quicker and quicker; and quite a stream of cars and taxis were in the way; so that when the tram did stop he was out of sight. Also I was in a hurry to get home.

Going home I marvelled for a few moments that he should have run so hard after me. He ran almost—desperately.

"It would strain every ounce of a man's strength to run like that!" I said.

And his eyes had glared as he ran!

"Poor old chap!" I thought. "He must have wanted to speak to me very badly."

Three or four days afterwards I met him again; and we talked together for a while on the footpath. Then, at whose suggestion I do not remember, we moved into the bar of an hotel near by.

We drank several glasses of something; for which, noticing that his hat was crumpled and his coat sleeves shiny, I paid. We spoke of the old days at school and he told me of men whom he had met, but whom I had not heard of for a long time. Such old schoolfellows as I did know of I mentioned, and in every instance he took their addresses down on a piece of paper.

He asked what I was doing and how I was succeeding

and where I lived; and this latter information he pencilled also on his piece of paper.

"My memory is getting bad," he said with a smile.

Every few minutes he murmured into our schoolday conversation—

"Whew! Isn't it hot!"

And at other times, laughing a little, apologizing a little, he said:

"I am terribly thirsty today; it's the heat, I suppose."

I had not noticed that it was particularly hot; but we are as different in our skins as we are in our souls, and one man's heat may be tepid enough to his neighbour.

II

Then I met him frequently. One goes home usually at the same hour and by the same road; and it was on these home-goings and on this beaten track that we met.

Somehow, but by what subtle machinery I cannot recall, we always elbowed one another into a bar; and, as his hat was not getting less crumpled nor his coat less shiny, I paid for whatever liquor was consumed.

One can do anything for a long time without noticing it, and the paying for a few drinks is not likely to weigh on the memory. Still, we end by noticing everything; and perhaps I noticed it the earlier because liquor does not agree with me. I never mentioned that fact to any one, being slightly ashamed of it, but I knew it very woefully myself by the indigestion which for two or three days followed on even a modest consumption of alcohol.

So it was that setting homewards one evening on the habitual track I turned very deliberately from it; and, with the slightest feeling of irritation, I went homewards by another route; and each night that followed I took this new path.

I did not see him for some weeks, and then one evening he hailed me on the new road. When I turned at the call and saw him running—he was running—I was annoyed, and, as we shook hands, I became aware that it was not so much the liquor I was trying to sidetrack as my old schoolfellow.

He walked with me for quite a distance; and he talked more volubly than was his wont. He talked excitedly; and his eyes searched the streets ahead as they widened out before our steps, or as they were instantly and largely visible when we turned a corner. A certain malicious feeling was in my mind as we paced together; I thought:

"There is no public-house on this road."

Before we parted he borrowed a half-sovereign from me, saying that he would pay it back in a day or two, but I cheerfully bade adieu to the coin as I handed it over, and thought also that I was bidding a lengthy adieu to him.

"I won't meet him for quite a while," I said to myself; and that proved to be true.

III

Nevertheless when a fair month had elapsed I did meet him again, and we marched together in a silence which was but sparsely interrupted by speech.

He had apparently prospected my new route, for he informed me that a certain midway side-street was a short cut; and midway in this side-street we found a public-house.

I went into this public-house with the equable pulse of a man who has no true grievance; for I should have

SCHOOLFELLOWS

been able to provide against a contingency which even the worst equipped prophet might have predicted.

As often as his glass was emptied I saw that it was refilled; but, and perhaps with a certain ostentation, I refrained myself from the cup.

Of course, one drink leads to another and the path between each is conversational. My duty it appeared was to supply the drinks, but I thought it just that he should supply the conversation.

I had myself a fund of silence which might have been uncomfortable to a different companion, and against which he was forced to deploy many verbal battalions.

We had now met quite a number of times. He had exhausted our schooldays as a topic; he knew nothing about politics or literature or city scandal, and talk about weather dies of inanition in less than a minute; and yet —he may have groaned at the necessity—there had to be fashioned a conversational bridge which should unite drink to drink, or drinks must cease.

In such a case a man will talk about himself. It is one's last subject; but it is a subject upon which, given the preliminary push, one may wax eternally eloquent.

He rehearsed to me a serial tale of unmerited calamity, and of hardship by field and flood; of woes against which he had been unable to provide, and against which no man could battle; and of accidents so attuned to the chords of fiction that one knew they had to be true. He had been to rustic-sounding places in England and to Spanish-sounding places in America; and from each of these places an undefined but complete misfortune had uprooted him and chased him as with a stick. So by devious, circuitous, unbelievable routes he had come home again.

One cannot be utterly silent unless one is dead, and

then possibly one makes a crackle with one's bones; so I spoke:

"You are glad to be home again?" I queried.

He was glad; but he was glad dubiously and with reservations. Misfortune had his address, and here or elsewhere could thump a hand upon his shoulder.

His people were not treating him decently, it appeared. They had been content to see him return from outlandish latitudes, but since then they had not given him a fair show.

Domestic goblins hinted at, not spoken, but which one sensed to be grisly, half detached themselves from between the drinks. He was not staying with his people. They made him an allowance. You could not call it an allowance either: they paid him a weekly sum. Weekly sum was a large way of putting it, for you cannot do much on fifteen shillings a week; that sum per week would hardly pay for, for—

"The drinks," I put in brightly; for one cannot be persistently morose in jovial company.

"I must be off," I said, and I filled the chink of silence which followed on my remark with a waving hand and the bustle of my hasty departure.

IV

Two evenings afterwards he met me again.

We did not shake hands; and my salutation was so brief as not really to merit that name.

He fell in beside me and made a number of remarks about the weather; which, if they were as difficult to make as they were to listen to, must have been exceedingly troublesome to him. One saw him searching as in bottomless pits for something to say; and he hauled a verbal wisp from these profundities with the labour of one who drags miseries up a mountain.

The man was pitiable, and I pitied him. I went alternately hot and cold. I blushed for him and for myself; for the stones under our feet and for the light clouds that went scudding above our heads; and in another instant I was pale with rage at his shameful, shameless persistence. I thrust my hands into my pockets, because they were no longer hands but fists; and because they tingled and were inclined to jerk without authority from me.

We came to the midway, cross-street which as well as being a short cut was the avenue to a public-house; and he dragged slightly at the crossing as I held to my course.

"This is the longest way," he murmured.

"I prefer it," I replied.

After a moment he said:

"You always go home this way."

"I shall go a different way tomorrow," I replied.

"What way?" he enquired timidly.

"I must think that out," said I.

With that I stood and resolutely bade him good-bye. We both moved a pace from each other, and then he turned again, flurriedly, and asked me for the loan of half a crown. He wanted it to get a—a—a—

I gave it to him hurriedly and walked away, prickling with a sensation of weariness and excitement as of one who has been worried by a dog but has managed to get away from it.

Then I did not see him for two days, but of course I knew that I should meet him, and the knowledge was as exasperating as any kind of knowledge could be.

V

It was quite early in the morning; and he was waiting outside my house. He accompanied me to the tram, and on the way asked me for half a crown. I did not give it, and I did not reply to him.

As I was getting on the tram he lowered his demand and asked me urgently for sixpence. I did not answer nor look at him, but got on my tram and rode away in such a condition of nervous fury that I could have assaulted the conductor who asked me to pay my fare.

When I reached home that evening he was still waiting for me; at least, he was there, and he may have hung about all day; or he may have arrived just in time to catch me.

At the sight of him all the irritation which had almost insensibly been adding to and multiplying and storing itself in my mind, fused together into one sole consciousness of rage which not even a language of curses could make explicit enough to suit my need of expression. I swore when I saw him; and I cursed him openly when he came to me with the sly, timid, outfacing bearing, which had become for me his bearing.

He began at once; for all pretence was gone, and all the barriers of reserve and decency were down. He did not care what I thought of him; nor did he heed in the least what I said to him. He did not care about anything except only by any means; by every means; by cajolery, or savagery, or sentimentality, to get or screw or torment some money out of me.

I knew as we stood glaring and panting that to get the few pence he wanted he would have killed me with as little compunction as one would kill a moth which had fluttered into the room; and I knew that with as little pity I could have slaughtered him as he stood there.

He wanted sixpence, and I swore that I would see him dead before I gave it to him. He wanted twopence and I swore I would see him damned before I gave him a penny.

I moved away, but he followed me clawing my sleeve and whining:

"Twopence: you can spare twopence: what is twopence to you? If I had twopence and a fellow asked me for it I'd give it to him: twopence . . ."

I turned and smashed my fist into his face. His head jerked upwards, and he went staggering backwards and fell backwards into the road; as he staggered the blood jetted out of his nose.

He picked himself up and came over to me bloody, and dusty, and cautious, and deprecating, with a smile that was a leer . . .

"Now will you give me twopence?" he said.

I turned then and I ran from him as if I were running for my life. As I went I could hear him padding behind me, but he was in no condition, and I left him easily behind. And every time I saw him after that I ran.

ELIZABETH BOWEN

Look at All Those Roses

LOU exclaimed at that glimpse of a house in a sheath of startling flowers. She twisted round, to look back, in the open car, till the next corner had cut it out of sight. To reach the corner, it struck her, Edward accelerated, as though he were jealous of the rosy house—a house with gables, flat-fronted, whose dark windows stared with no expression through the flowers. The garden, with its silent, burning gaiety, stayed in both their minds like an apparition.

One of those conflicts between two silent moods had set up, with Lou and Edward, during that endless drive. Also, there is a point when an afternoon oppresses one with fatigue and a feeling of unreality. Relentless, pointless, unwinding summer country made nerves ache at the back of both their eyes. This was a late June Monday; they were doubling back to London through Suffolk by-roads, on the return from a week-end. Edward, who detested the main roads, had traced out their curious route before starting, and Lou now sat beside him with the map on her knees. They had to be back by eight, for Edward, who was a writer, to finish and post an article: apart from this, time was no object with them. They looked forward with no particular pleasure to London and unlocking the stuffy flat, taking in the milk, finding bills in the letterbox. In fact, they looked forward to nothing with particular pleasure. They were going home for the purely negative reason that there was nowhere else they could as cheaply go. The week-end had not been amusing, but at least it had been "away." Now they could foresee life for weeks ahead—until someone else invited them—the typewriter, the cocktail-shaker, the telephone, runs in the car out of London to nowhere special. Love when Edward got a cheque in the post, quarrels about people on the way home from parties—and Lou's anxiety always eating them. This future weighed on them like a dull burden. . . . So they had been glad to extend today.

But under a vacant sky, not sunny but full of diffused

glare, the drive had begun to last too long: they felt bound up in the tired impotence of a dream. The stretches of horizon were stupefying. The road bent round wedges of cornfield, blocky elms dark with summer: for these last ten miles the countryside looked abandoned; they passed dropping gates, rusty cattle-troughs and the thistly, tussocky, stale grass of neglected farms. There was nobody on the roads; perhaps there was nobody anywhere. . . . In the heart of all this, the roses looked all the odder.

"They were extraordinary," she said (when the first corner was turned) in her tired little dogmatic voice.

"All the more," he agreed, "when all the rest of the country looks something lived in by poor whites."

"I wish we lived *there*," she said. "It really looked like somewhere."

"It wouldn't if we did."

Edward spoke with some tartness. He had found he had reason to dread week-ends away: they unsettled Lou and started up these fantasies. Himself, he had no illusions about life in the country: life without people was absolutely impossible. What would he and she do with nobody to talk to but each other? Already, they had not spoken for two hours. Lou saw life in terms of ideal moments. She found few ideal moments in their flat.

He went on: "You know you can't stand earwigs. And we should spend our lives on the telephone."

"About the earwigs?"

"No. About ourselves."

Lou's smart little monkey face became dolorous. She never risked displeasing Edward too far, but she was just opening her mouth to risk one further remark when Edward jumped and frowned. A ghastly knocking had started. It seemed to come from everywhere, and at the same time to be a special attack on them. Then it had to be traced to the car's vitals: it jarred up Lou through the soles of her feet. Edward slowed to a crawl and stopped. He and she confronted each other with that completely dramatic lack of expression they kept for occasions when the car went wrong. They tried crawling on again, a few tentative yards; the knocking took up again with still greater fury.

"Sounds to me like a big end gone."

"Oh my goodness," she said.

All the same, she was truly glad to get out of the car. She stretched and stood waiting on the grass roadside while Edward made faces into the bonnet. Soon he flung round to ask what she would suggest doing: to his surprise (and annoyance) she had a plan ready. She would walk back to that house and ask if they had a telephone. If they had not, she would ask for a bicycle and bicycle to the place where the nearest garage was.

Edward snatched the map, but could not find where they were. Where they were seemed to be highly improbable. "I expect you," Lou said, "would rather stay with the car." "No, I wouldn't," said Edward, "anybody can have it. . . . You like to be sure where I am, don't you?" he added. He locked their few odd things up in the boot of the car with the suitcases, and they set off in silence. It was about a mile.

There stood the house, waiting. Why should a house wait? Most pretty scenes have something passive about them, but this looked like a trap baited with beauty, set ready to spring. It stood back from the road. Lou put her hand on the gate and, with a touch of bravado, the two filed up the paved path to the door. Each side of the path, hundreds of standard roses bloomed, overcharged with colour, as though this were their one hour. Crimson, coral, blue-pink, lemon and cold white, they

LOOK AT ALL THOSE ROSES 441

disturbed with fragrance the dead air. In this spellbound afternoon, with no shadows, the roses glared at the strangers, frighteningly bright. The face of the house was plastered with tea-roses: waxy cream when they opened but with vermilion buds.

The blistered door was propped open with a bizarre object, a lump of quartz. Indoors was the dark coldlooking hall. When they had come to the door they found no bell or knocker: they could not think what to do. "We had better cough," Lou said. So they stood there coughing, till a door at the end of the hall opened and a lady or woman looked out—they were not sure which. "Oh?" she said, with no expression at all.

"We couldn't find your bell."

"There they are," she said, pointing to two Swiss cowbells that hung on loops of string by the door she had just come out of. Having put this right, she continued to look at them, and out through the door past them, wiping her powerful-looking hands vaguely against the sides of her blue overall. They could hardly see themselves as intruders when their intrusion made so little effect. The occupying inner life of this person was not for an instant suspended by their presence. She was a shabby Amazon of a woman, with a sculptural clearness about the face. She must have lost contact with the outer world completely: there was now nothing to "place" her by. It is outside attachments—hopes, claims, curiosities, desires, little touches of greed—that put a label on one to help strangers. As it was, they could not tell if she were rich or poor, stupid or clever, a spinster or a wife. She seemed prepared, not anxious, for them to speak. Lou, standing close beside Edward, gave him a dig in a rib. So Edward explained to the lady how they found themselves, and asked if she had a telephone or a bicycle.

She said she was sorry to say she had neither. Her maid had a bicycle, but had ridden home on it. "Would you like some tea?" she said. "I am just boiling the kettle. Then perhaps you can think of something to do." This lack of grip of the crisis made Edward decide the woman must be a moron: annoyance contused his face. But Lou, who wanted tea and was attracted by calmness, was entirely won. She looked at Edward placatingly.

"Thank you," he said. "But I must do something at once. We haven't got all night; I've got to be back in London. Can you tell me where I can telephone from? I must get through to a garage—a good garage."

Unmoved, the lady said: "You'll have to walk to the village. It's about three miles away." She gave unexpectedly clear directions, then looked at Lou again. "Leave your wife here," she said. "Then she can have tea."

Edward shrugged; Lou gave a brief undecided sigh. How much she wanted to stop. But she never liked to be left. This partly arose from the fact that she was not Edward's wife: he was married to someone else and his wife would not divorce him. He might some day go back to her, if this ever became the way of least resistance. Or he might, if it were the way of even less resistance, move on to someone else. Lou was determined neither should ever happen. She did love Edward, but she also stuck to him largely out of contentiousness. She quite often asked herself why she did. It seemed important—she could not say why. She was determined to be a necessity. Therefore she seldom let him out of her sight—her idea of love was adhesiveness. . . . Knowing this well, Edward gave her a slightly malign smile, said she had far better stay, turned, and walked down the path without her. Lou, like a lost cat, went half-way to the door. "Your roses are wonderful . . ." she said, staring out with unhappy eyes.

"Yes, they grow well for us, Josephine likes to see them." Her hostess added: "My kettle will be boiling. Won't you wait in there?"

Lou went deeper into the house. She found herself in a long, low and narrow parlour, with a window at each end. Before she could turn round, she felt herself being looked at. A girl of about thirteen lay, flat as a board, in a wicker invalid carriage. The carriage was pulled out across the room, so that the girl could command the view from either window, the flat horizons that bounded either sky. Lying there with no pillow she had a stretched look. Lou stood some distance from the foot of the carriage: the dark eyes looked at her down thin cheekbones, intently. The girl had an unresigned, living face; one hand crept on the rug over her breast. Lou felt, here was the nerve and core of the house. . . . The only movement was made by a canary, springing to and fro in its cage.

"Hullo," Lou said, with that deferential smile with which one approaches an invalid. When the child did not answer, she went on: "You must wonder who I am?"

"I don't now; I did when you drove past."

"Then our car broke down."

"I know, I wondered whether it might."

Lou laughed and said: "Then you put the evil eye on it."

The child ignored this. She said: "This is not the way to London."

"All the same, that's where we're going."

"You mean, where you were going. . . . Is that your husband who has just gone away?"

"That's Edward: yes. To telephone. He'll be back."

Lou, who was wearing a summer suit, smart, now rather crumpled, of honey-yellow linen, felt Josephine look her up and down. "Have you been to a party?" she said, "or are you going to one?"

"We've just been staying away," Lou walked nervously down the room to the front window. From here she saw the same roses Josephine saw: she thought they looked like forced roses, magnetized into being. Magnetized, buds uncurled and petals dropped. Lou began to wake from the dream of the afternoon: her will stirred; she wanted to go; she felt apprehensive, threatened. "I expect you like to lie out of doors, with all those roses?" she said.

"No, not often: I don't care for the sky."

"You just watch through the window?"

"Yes," said the child, impatiently. She added: "What are the parts of London with most traffic?"

"Piccadilly Circus. Trafalgar Square."

"Oh, I would like to see those."

The child's mother's step sounded on the hall flags: she came in with the tea-tray. "Can I help you?" said Lou, glad of the interim.

"Oh, thank you. Perhaps you'd unfold that table. Put it over here beside Josephine. She's lying down because she hurt her back."

"My back was hurt six years ago," said Josephine. "It was my father's doing."

Her mother was busy lodging the edge of the tray on the edge of the tea-table.

"Awful for him," Lou murmured, helping unstack the cups.

"No, it's not," said Josephine. "He has gone away."

Lou saw why. A man in the wrong cannot live where there is no humanity. There are enormities you can only keep piling up. He had bolted off down that path, as

Edward had just done. Men cannot live with sorrow, with women who embrace it. Men will suffer a certain look in animals' eyes, but not in women's eyes. And men dread obstinacy, of love, of grief. You could stay with burning Josephine, not with her mother's patient, exalted face. . . . When her mother had gone again, to fetch the teapot and kettle, Josephine once more fastened her eyes on Lou. "Perhaps your husband will be some time," she said. "You're the first new person I have seen for a year. Perhaps he will lose his way."

"Oh, but then I should have to look for him!"

Josephine gave a fanatical smile. "But when people go away they sometimes quite go," she said. "If they always come back, then what is the good of moving?"

"I don't see the good of moving."

"Then stay here."

"People don't just go where they want; they go where they must."

"Must you go back to London?"

"Oh, I have to, you know."

"Why?"

Lou frowned and smiled in a portentous, grown-up way that meant nothing at all to either herself or Josephine. She felt for her cigarette case and, glumly, found it empty—Edward had walked away with the packet of cigarettes that he and she had been sharing that afternoon. He also carried any money she had.

"You don't know where he's gone to," Josephine pointed out. "If you had to stay, you would soon get used to it. We don't wonder where my father is."

"What's your mother's name?"

"Mrs. Mather. She'd like you to stay. Nobody comes to see us; they used to, they don't now. So we only see each other. They may be frightened of something—"

Mrs. Mather came back, and Josephine looked out of

the other window. This immediate silence marked a conspiracy, in which Lou had no willing part. While Mrs. Mather was putting down the teapot, Lou looked round the room, to make sure it was ordinary. This window-ended parlour was lined with objects that looked honest and worn without having antique grace. A faded room should look homely. But extinct paper and phantom cretonnes gave this a gutted air. Rooms can be whitened and gutted by too-intensive living, as they are by a fire. It was the garden, out there, that focused the senses. Lou indulged for a minute the astounding fancy that Mr. Mather lay at the roses' roots. . . . Josephine said sharply: "I don't want any tea," which made Lou realize that she would have to be fed and did not want to be fed in front of the stranger Lou still was. Mrs. Mather made no comment: she drew two chairs to the table and invited Lou to sit down. "It's rather sultry," she said. "I'm afraid your husband may not enjoy his walk."

"How far did you say it was?"

"Three miles."

Lou, keeping her wrist under the table, glanced down covertly at her watch.

"We are very much out of the way," said Mrs. Mather.

"But perhaps you like that?"

"We are accustomed to quiet," said Mrs. Mather, pouring out tea. "This was a farm, you know. But it was an unlucky farm, so since my husband left I have let the land. Servants seem to find that the place is lonely —country girls are so different now. My present servant is not very clear in her mind, but she works well and does not seem to feel lonely. When she is not working she rides home."

"Far?" said Lou, tensely.

LOOK AT ALL THOSE ROSES

"A good way," said Mrs. Mather, looking out of the window at the horizon.

"Then aren't you rather . . . alone?—I mean, if anything happened."

"Nothing more can happen," said Mrs. Mather. "And there are two of us. When I am working upstairs or am out with the chickens, I wear one of those bells you see in the hall, so Josephine can always hear where I am. And I leave the other bell on Josephine's carriage. When I work in the garden she can see me, of course." She slit the waxpaper top off a jar of jam. "This is my last pot of last year's damson," she said. "Please try some; I shall be making more soon. We have two fine trees."

"You should see mother climb them," said Josephine.

"Aren't you afraid of falling?"

"Why," said Mrs. Mather, advancing a plate of rather rich bread and butter. "I never eat tea, thank you," Lou said, sitting rigid, sipping round her cup of tea like a bird.

"She tninks if she eats she may have to stay here for ever," Josephine said. Her mother, taking no notice, spread jam on her bread and butter and started to eat in a calmly voracious way. Lou kept clinking her spoon against the teacup: every time she did this the canary started and fluttered. Though she knew Edward could not possibly come yet, Lou kept glancing down the garden at the gate. Mrs. Mather, reaching out for more bread and butter, saw, and thought Lou was looking at the roses. "Would you like to take some back to London?" she said.

Josephine's carriage had been wheeled out on the lawn between the rosebeds. She lay with eyes shut and forehead contracted, for overhead hung the dreaded space of the sky. But she had to be near Lou while Lou cut the roses. In a day or two, Lou thought, I should be wearing a bell. What shall I do with these if I ever do go? she thought, as she cut through the strong stems between the thorns and piled the roses on the foot of the carriage. I shall certainly never want to look at roses again. By her wrist watch it was six o'clock—two hours since Edward had started. All round, the country under the white stretched sky was completely silent. She went once to the gate.

"Is there any way from that village?" she said at last. "Any bus to anywhere else? Any taxi one could hire?"

"I don't know," said Josephine.

"When does your servant come back?"

"Tomorrow morning. Sometimes our servants never come back at all."

Lou shut the knife and said: "Well, those are enough roses." She supposed she could hear if whoever Edward sent for the car came to tow it away. The car, surely, Edward would not abandon? She went to the gate again. From behind her Josephine said: "Then please wheel me indoors."

"If you like. But I shall stay here."

"Then I will. But please put something over my eyes."

Lou got out her red silk handkerchief and laid this across Josephine's eyes. This made the mouth more revealing: she looked down at the small resolute smile. "If you want to keep on listening," the child said, "you needn't talk to me. Lie down and let's pretend we're both asleep."

Lou lay down on the dry cropped grass alongside the wheels of the carriage: she crossed her hands under her head, shut her eyes and lay stretched, as rigid as Josephine. At first she was so nervous, she thought the lawn vibrated under her spine. Then slowly she relaxed. There is a moment when silence, no longer resisted, rushes into the mind. She let go, inch by inch, of life, that since she was a child she had been clutching so desperately—her obsessions about this and that, her obsession about keeping Edward. How anxiously she had run from place to place, wanting to keep everything inside her own power. I should have stayed still: I shall stay still now, she thought. What I want must come to me: I shall not go after it. People who stay still generate power. Josephine stores herself up, and so what she wants happens, because she knows what she wants. I only think I want things; I only think I want Edward. (He's not coming and I don't care, I don't care.) I feel life myself now. No wonder I've been tired, only half getting what I don't really want. Now I want nothing; I just want a white circle.

The white circle distended inside her eyelids and she looked into it in an ecstasy of indifference. She knew she was looking at nothing—then knew nothing . . .

Josephine's voice, from up in the carriage, woke her. "You were quite asleep."

"Was I?"

"Take the handkerchief off: a motor's coming."

Lou heard the vibration. She got up and uncovered Josephine's eyes. Then she went to the foot of the carriage and got her roses together. She was busy with this, standing with her back to the gate, when she heard the taxi pull up, then Edward's step on the path. The taxi driver sat staring at the roses. "It's all right," Edward shouted, "they're sending out from the garage. They should be here any moment. But what people— God!—Look here, have you been all right?"

"Perfectly, I've been with Josephine."

"Oh, hullo, Josephine," Edward said, with a hasty exercise of his charm. "Well, I've come for this woman. Thank you for keeping her."

"It's quite all right, thank you. . . . Shall you be going now?"

"We must get our stuff out of the car: it will have to be towed to the garage. Then when I've had another talk to the garage people we'll take this taxi on and pick up a train. . . . Come on, Lou, come on! We don't want to miss those people! And we've got to get that stuff out of the car!"

"Is there such a hurry?" she said, putting down the roses.

"Of course, there's a hurry. . . ." He added, to Josephine: "We'll look in on our way to the station, when I've fixed up all this, to say good-bye to your mother." He put his hand on Lou's shoulder and punted her ahead of him down the path. "I'm glad you're all right," he said, as they got into the taxi. "You're well out of that, my girl. From what I heard in the village—"

"What, have you been anxious?" said Lou, curiously.

"It's a nervy day," said Edward, with an uneasy laugh, "and I had to put in an hour in the village emporium, first waiting for my call, then waiting for this taxi. (And this is going to cost us a pretty penny.) I got talking, naturally, one way and another. You've no idea what they said when they heard where I had parked you. Not a soul round there will go near the place. I must say—discounting gossip—there's a story there," said Edward. "They can't fix anything, but . . . Well, you see, it appears that this Mather woman . . ." Lowering his voice, so as not to be heard by the driver, Edward began to tell Lou what he had heard in the village about the abrupt disappearance of Mr. Mather.

OSCAR WILDE

Lord Arthur Savile's Crime

I

IT WAS Lady Windermere's last reception before Easter, and Bentinck House was even more crowded than usual. Six Cabinet Ministers had come on from the Speaker's Levée in their stars and ribands, all the pretty women wore their smartest dresses, and at the end of the picture-gallery stood the Princess Sophia of Carlsrühe, a heavy Tartar-looking lady, with tiny black eyes and wonderful emeralds, talking bad French at the top of her voice, and laughing immoderately at everything that was said to her. It was certainly a wonderful medley of people. Gorgeous peeresses chatted affably to violent radicals, popular preachers brushed coat-tails with eminent sceptics, a perfect bevy of bishops kept following a stout prima-donna from room to room, on the staircase stood several Royal Academicians, disguised as artists, and it was said that at one time the supper-room was absolutely crammed with geniuses. In fact, it was one of Lady Windermere's best nights, and the Princess stayed till nearly half-past eleven.

As soon as she had gone, Lady Windermere returned to the picture-gallery, where a celebrated political economist was solemnly explaining the scientific theory of music to an indignant virtuoso from Hungary, and began to talk to the Duchess of Paisley. She looked wonderfully beautiful with her grand ivory throat, her large blue forget-me-not eyes, and her heavy coils of golden hair. *Or pur* they were—not that pale straw colour that nowadays usurps the gracious name of gold, but such gold as is woven into sunbeams or hidden in strange amber; and they gave to her face something of the frame of a saint, with not a little of the fascination of a sinner. She was a curious psychological study. Early in life she had discovered the important truth that nothing looks so like innocence as an indiscretion; and by a series of reckless escapades, half of them quite harmless, she had acquired all the privileges of a personality. She had more than once changed her husband; indeed, Debrett credits her with three marriages; but as she had never changed her lover, the world had long ago ceased to talk scandal about her. She was now forty years of age, childless, and with that inordinate passion for pleasure which is the secret of remaining young.

Suddenly she looked eagerly round the room, and said, in her clear contralto voice, "Where is my cheiromantist?"

"Your what, Gladys?" exclaimed the Duchess, giving an involuntary start.

"My cheiromantist, Duchess; I can't live without him at present."

"Dear Gladys! you are always so original," murmured the Duchess, trying to remember what a cheiromantist really was, and hoping it was not the same as a cheiropodist.

"He comes to see my hand twice a week regularly," continued Lady Windermere, "and is most interesting about it."

"Good heavens!" said the Duchess to herself, "he is a sort of cheiropodist after all. How very dreadful. I hope he is a foreigner at any rate. It wouldn't be quite so bad then."

"I must certainly introduce him to you."

"Introduce him!" cried the Duchess; "you don't mean

to say he is here?" and she began looking about for a small tortoise-shell fan and a very tattered lace shawl, so as to be ready to go at a moment's notice.

"Of course he is here; I would not dream of giving a party without him. He tells me I have a pure psychic hand, and that if my thumb had been the least little bit shorter, I should have been a confirmed pessimist, and gone into a convent."

"Oh, I see!" said the Duchess, feeling very much relieved; "he tells fortunes, I suppose?"

"And misfortunes, too," answered Lady Windermere, "any amount of them. Next year, for instance, I am in great danger, both by land and sea, so I am going to live in a balloon, and draw up my dinner in a basket every evening. It is all written down on my little finger, or on the palm of my hand, I forget which."

"But surely that is tempting Providence, Gladys."

"My dear Duchess, surely Providence can resist temptation by this time. I think every one should have their hands told once a month, so as to know what not to do. Of course, one does it all the same, but it is so pleasant to be warned. Now if someone doesn't go and fetch Mr. Podgers at once, I shall have to go myself."

"Let me go, Lady Windermere," said a tall handsome young man, who was standing by, listening to the conversation with an amused smile.

"Thanks so much, Lord Arthur; but I am afraid you wouldn't recognize him."

"If he is as wonderful as you say, Lady Windermere, I couldn't well miss him. Tell me what he is like, and I'll bring him to you at once."

"Well, he is not a bit like a cheiromantist. I mean he is not mysterious, or esoteric, or romantic-looking. He is a little, stout man, with a funny, bald head, and great gold-rimmed spectacles; something between a family doctor and a country attorney. I'm really very sorry, but it is not my fault. People are so annoying. All my pianists look exactly like poets, and all my poets look exactly like pianists; and I remember last season asking a most dreadful conspirator to dinner, a man who had blown up ever so many people, and always wore a coat of mail, and carried a dagger up his shirt-sleeve; and do you know that when he came he looked just like a nice old clergyman, and cracked jokes all the evening? Of course, he was very amusing, and all that, but I was awfully disappointed; and when I asked him about the coat of mail, he only laughed, and said it was far too cold to wear in England. Ah, here is Mr. Podgers! Now, Mr. Podgers, I want you to tell the Duchess of Paisley's hand. Duchess, you must take your glove off. No, not the left hand, the other."

"Dear Gladys, I really don't think it is quite right," said the Duchess, feebly unbuttoning a rather soiled kid glove.

"Nothing interesting ever is," said Lady Windermere: *"on a fait le monde ainsi.* But I must introduce you. Duchess, this is Mr. Podgers, my pet cheiromantist. Mr. Podgers, this is the Duchess of Paisley, and if you say that she has a larger mountain of the moon than I have, I will never believe in you again."

"I am sure, Gladys, there is nothing of the kind in my hand," said the Duchess gravely.

"Your Grace is quite right," said Mr. Podgers, glancing at the little fat hand with its short square fingers, "the mountain of the moon is not developed. The line of life, however, is excellent. Kindly bend the wrist. Thank you. Three distinct lines on the *rascette!* You will live to a great age, Duchess, and be extremely happy. Ambition—very moderate, line of intellect not exaggerated, line of heart——"

"Now, do be indiscreet, Mr. Podgers," cried Lady Windermere.

"Nothing would give me greater pleasure," said Mr. Podgers, bowing, "if the Duchess ever had been, but I am sorry to say that I see great permanence of affection, combined with a strong sense of duty."

"Pray go on, Mr. Podgers," said the Duchess, looking quite pleased.

"Economy is not the least of your Grace's virtues," continued Mr. Podgers, and Lady Windermere went off into fits of laughter.

"Economy is a very good thing," remarked the Duchess complacently; "when I married Paisley he had eleven castles, and not a single house fit to live in."

"And now he has twelve houses, and not a single castle," cried Lady Windermere.

"Well, my dear," said the Duchess, "I like——"

"Comfort," said Mr. Podgers, "and modern improvements, and hot water laid on in every bedroom. Your Grace is quite right. Comfort is the only thing our civilization can give us."

"You have told the Duchess's character admirably, Mr. Podgers, and now you must tell Lady Flora's"; and in answer to a nod from the smiling hostess, a tall girl, with sandy Scotch hair, and high shoulder-blades, stepped awkwardly from behind the sofa, and held out a long, bony hand with spatulate fingers.

"Ah, a pianist! I see," said Mr. Podgers, "an excellent pianist, but perhaps hardly a musician. Very reserved, very honest, and with a great love of animals."

"Quite true!" exclaimed the Duchess, turning to Lady Windermere, "absolutely true! Flora keeps two dozen collie dogs at Macloskie, and would turn our town house into a menagerie if her father would let her."

"Well, that is just what I do with my house every Thursday evening," cried Lady Windermere, laughing, "only I like lions better than collie dogs."

"Your one mistake, Lady Windermere," said Mr. Podgers, with a pompous bow.

"If a woman can't make her mistakes charming, she is only a female," was the answer. "But you must read some more hands for us. Come, Sir Thomas, show Mr. Podgers yours"; and a genial-looking old gentleman, in a white waistcoat, came forward, and held out a thick rugged hand, with a very long third finger.

"An adventurous nature; four long voyages in the past, and one to come. Been shipwrecked three times. No, only twice, but in danger of a shipwreck your next journey. A strong Conservative, very punctual, and with a passion for collecting curiosities. Had a severe illness between the ages of sixteen and eighteen. Was left a fortune when about thirty. Great aversion to cats and radicals."

"Extraordinary!" exclaimed Sir Thomas; "you must really tell my wife's hand, too."

"Your second wife's," said Mr. Podgers quietly, still keeping Sir Thomas's hand in his. "Your second wife's. I shall be charmed"; but Lady Marvel, a melancholy-looking woman, with brown hair and sentimental eyelashes, entirely declined to have her past or her future exposed; and nothing that Lady Windermere could do would induce Monsieur de Koloff, the Russian Ambassador, even to take his gloves off. In fact, many people seemed afraid to face the odd little man with his stereotyped smile, his gold spectacles, and his bright, beady eyes; and when he told poor Lady Fermor, right out before every one, that she did not care a bit for music, but was extremely fond of musicians, it was generally felt that cheiromancy was a most dangerous science, and one that ought not to be encouraged, except in a *tête-à-tête*.

Lord Arthur Savile, however, who did not know anything about Lady Fermor's unfortunate story, and who had been watching Mr. Podgers with a great deal of interest, was filled with an immense curiosity to have his own hand read, and feeling somewhat shy about putting himself forward, crossed over the room to where Lady Windermere was sitting, and, with a charming blush, asked her if she thought Mr. Podgers would mind.

"Of course, he won't mind," said Lady Windermere, "that is what he is here for. All my lions, Lord Arthur, are performing lions, and jump through hoops whenever I ask them. But I must warn you beforehand that I shall tell Sybil everything. She is coming to lunch with me tomorrow, to talk about bonnets, and if Mr. Podgers finds out that you have a bad temper, or a tendency to gout, or a wife living in Bayswater, I shall certainly let her know all about it."

Lord Arthur smiled, and shook his head. "I am not afraid," he answered. "Sybil knows me as well as I know her."

"Ah! I am a little sorry to hear you say that. The proper basis for marriage is a mutual misunderstanding. No, I am not at all cynical, I have merely got experience, which, however, is very much the same thing. Mr. Podgers, Lord Arthur Savile is dying to have his hand read. Don't tell him that he is engaged to one of the most beautiful girls in London, because that appeared in the *Morning Post* a month ago."

"Dear Lady Windermere," cried the Marchioness of Jedburgh, "do let Mr. Podgers stay here a little longer.

He has just told me I should go on the stage, and I am so interested."

"If he has told you that, Lady Jedburgh, I shall certainly take him away. Come over at once, Mr. Podgers, and read Lord Arthur's hand."

"Well," said Lady Jedburgh, making a little *moue* as she rose from the sofa, "if I am not to be allowed to go on the stage, I must be allowed to be part of the audience at any rate."

"Of course; we are all going to be part of the audience," said Lady Windermere; "and now, Mr. Podgers, be sure and tell us something nice. Lord Arthur is one of my special favourites."

But when Mr. Podgers saw Lord Arthur's hand he grew curiously pale, and said nothing. A shudder seemed to pass through him, and his great bushy eyebrows twitched convulsively, in an odd, irritating way they had when he was puzzled. Then some huge beads of perspiration broke out on his yellow forehead, like a poisonous dew, and his fat fingers grew cold and clammy.

Lord Arthur did not fail to notice these strange signs of agitation, and, for the first time in his life, he himself felt fear. His impulse was to rush from the room, but he restrained himself. It was better to know the worst, whatever it was, than to be left in this hideous uncertainty.

"I am waiting, Mr. Podgers," he said.

"We are all waiting," cried Lady Windermere, in her quick, impatient manner, but the cheiromantist made no reply.

"I believe Arthur is going on the stage," said Lady Jedburgh, "and that, after your scolding, Mr. Podgers is afraid to tell him so."

Suddenly Mr. Podgers dropped Lord Arthur's right

hand, and seized hold of his left, bending down so low to examine it that the gold rims of his spectacles seemed almost to touch the palm. For a moment his face became a white mask of horror, but he soon recovered his *sang-froid*, and looking up at Lady Windermere, said with a forced smile, "It is the hand of a charming young man."

"Of course it is!" answered Lady Windermere, "but will he be a charming husband? That is what I want to know."

"All charming young men are," said Mr. Podgers.

"I don't think a husband should be too fascinating," murmured Lady Jedburgh pensively, "it is so dangerous."

"My dear child, they never are too fascinating," cried Lady Windermere. "But what I want are details. Details are the only things that interest. What is going to happen to Lord Arthur?"

"Well, within the next few months Lord Arthur will go on a voyage——"

"Oh yes, his honeymoon, of course!"

"And lose a relative."

"Not his sister, I hope?" said Lady Jedburgh, in a piteous tone of voice.

"Certainly not his sister," answered Mr. Podgers, with a deprecating wave of the hand, "a distant relative merely."

"Well, I am dreadfully disappointed," said Lady Windermere. "I have absolutely nothing to tell Sybil tomorrow. No one cares about distant relatives nowadays. They went out of fashion years ago. However, I suppose she had better have a black silk by her; it always does for church, you know. And now let us go to supper. They are sure to have eaten everything up, but we may find some hot soup. François used to make excellent soup once, but he is so agitated about politics at present, that I never feel quite certain about him. I do wish General Boulanger would keep quiet. Duchess, I am sure you are tired?"

"Not at all, dear Gladys," answered the Duchess, waddling towards the door. "I have enjoyed myself immensely, and the cheiropodist, I mean the cheiromantist, is most interesting. Flora, where can my tortoiseshell fan be? Oh, thank you, Sir Thomas, so much. And my lace shawl, Flora? Oh, thank you, Sir Thomas, very kind, I'm sure"; and the worthy creature finally managed to get downstairs without dropping her scent-bottle more than twice.

All this time Lord Arthur Savile had remained standing by the fireplace, with the same feeling of dread over him, the same sickening sense of coming evil. He smiled sadly at his sister, as she swept past him on Lord Plymdale's arm, looking lovely in her pink brocade and pearls, and he hardly heard Lady Windermere when she called to him to follow her. He thought of Sybil Merton, and the idea that anything could come between them made his eyes dim with tears.

Looking at him, one would have said that Nemesis had stolen the shield of Pallas, and shown him the Gorgon's head. He seemed turned to stone, and his face was like marble in its melancholy. He had lived the delicate and luxurious life of a young man of birth and fortune, a life exquisite in its freedom from sordid care, its beautiful boyish insouciance; and now for the first time he became conscious of the terrible mystery of Destiny, of the awful meaning of Doom.

How mad and monstrous it all seemed! Could it be that written on his hand, in characters that he could not read himself, but that another could decipher, was some fearful secret of sin, some blood-red sign of crime?

LORD ARTHUR SAVILE'S CRIME

Was there no escape possible? Were we no better than chessmen, moved by an unseen power, vessels the potter fashions at his fancy, for honour or for shame? His reason revolted against it, and yet he felt that some tragedy was hanging over him, and that he had been suddenly called upon to bear an intolerable burden. Actors are so fortunate. They can choose whether they will appear in tragedy or in comedy, whether they will suffer or make merry, laugh or shed tears. But in real life it is different. Most men and women are forced to perform parts for which they have no qualifications. Our Guildensterns play Hamlet for us, and our Hamlets have to jest like Prince Hal. The world is a stage, but the play is badly cast.

Suddenly Mr. Podgers entered the room. When he saw Lord Arthur he started, and his coarse, fat face became a sort of greenish-yellow colour. The two men's eyes met, and for a moment there was silence.

"The Duchess has left one of her gloves here, Lord Arthur, and has asked me to bring it to her," said Mr. Podgers finally. "Ah, I see it on the sofa! Good evening."

"Mr. Podgers, I must insist on your giving me a straightforward answer to a question I am going to put to you."

"Another time, Lord Arthur, but the Duchess is anxious. I am afraid I must go."

"You shall not go. The Duchess is in no hurry."

"Ladies should not be kept waiting, Lord Arthur," said Mr. Podgers, with his sickly smile. "The fair sex is apt to be impatient."

Lord Arthur's finely chiselled lips curled in petulant disdain. The poor Duchess seemed to him of very little importance at that moment. He walked across the room to where Mr. Podgers was standing, and held his hand out.

"Tell me what you saw there," he said. "Tell me the truth. I must know it. I am not a child."

Mr. Podgers's eyes blinked behind his gold-rimmed spectacles, and he moved uneasily from one foot to the other, while his fingers played nervously with a flash watch-chain.

"What makes you think that I saw anything in your hand, Lord Arthur, more than I told you?"

"I know you did, and I insist on your telling me what it was. I will pay you. I will give you a cheque for a hundred pounds."

The green eyes flashed for a moment, and then became dull again.

"Guineas?" said Mr. Podgers at last, in a low voice.

"Certainly. I will send you a cheque tomorrow. What is your club?"

"I have no club. That is to say, not just at present. My address is——, but allow me to give you my card"; and producing a bit of gilt-edge pasteboard from his waistcoat pocket, Mr. Podgers handed it, with a low bow, to Lord Arthur, who read on it,

Mr. SEPTIMUS R. PODGERS
Professional Cheiromantist
103a West Moon Street

"My hours are from ten to four," murmured Mr. Podgers mechanically, "and I make a reduction for families."

"Be quick," cried Lord Arthur, looking very pale, and holding his hand out.

Mr. Podgers glanced nervously round, and drew the heavy *portière* across the door.

"It will take a little time, Lord Arthur, you had better sit down."

"Be quick, sir," cried Lord Arthur again, stamping his foot angrily on the polished floor.

Mr. Podgers smiled, drew from his breast-pocket a small magnifying glass, and wiped it carefully with his handkerchief.

"I am quite ready," he said.

II

Ten minutes later, with face blanched by terror, and eyes wild with grief, Lord Arthur Savile rushed from Bentinck House, crushing his way through the crowd of fur-coated footmen that stood round the large striped awning, and seeming not to see or hear anything. The night was bitter cold, and the gas-lamps round the square flared and flickered in the keen wind; but his hands were hot with fever, and his forehead burned like fire. On and on he went, almost with the gait of a drunken man. A policeman looked curiously at him as he passed, and a beggar, who slouched from an archway to ask for alms, grew frightened, seeing misery greater than his own. Once he stopped under a lamp, and looked at his hands. He thought he could detect the stain of blood already upon them, and a faint cry broke from his trembling lips.

Murder! that is what the cheiromantist had seen there. Murder! The very night seemed to know it, and the desolate wind to howl it in his ear. The dark corners of the streets were full of it. It grinned at him from the roofs of the houses.

First he came to the Park, whose sombre woodland seemed to fascinate him. He leaned wearily up against the railings, cooling his brow against the wet metal, and listening to the tremulous silence of the trees. "Murder! murder!" he kept repeating, as though iteration could dim the horror of the word. The sound of his own voice made him shudder, yet he almost hoped that Echo might hear him, and wake the slumbering city from its dreams. He felt a mad desire to stop the casual passerby, and tell him everything.

Then he wandered across Oxford Street into narrow, shameful alleys. Two women with painted faces mocked at him as he went by. From a dark courtyard came a sound of oaths and blows, followed by shrill screams, and, huddled upon a damp door-step, he saw the crook-backed forms of poverty and eld. A strange pity came over him. Were these children of sin and misery predestined to their end, as he to his? Were they, like him, merely the puppets of a monstrous show?

And yet it was not the mystery, but the comedy of suffering that struck him; its absolute uselessness, its grotesque want of meaning. How incoherent everything seemed! How lacking in all harmony! He was amazed at the discord between the shallow optimism of the day, and the real facts of existence. He was still very young.

After a time he found himself in front of Marylebone Church. The silent roadway looked like a long riband of polished silver, flecked here and there by the dark arabesques of waving shadows. Far into the distance curved the line of flickering gas-lamps, and outside a little walled-in house stood a solitary hansom, the driver asleep inside. He walked hastily in the direction of Portland Place, now and then looking round, as though he feared that he was being followed. At the corner of Rich Street stood two men, reading a small bill upon a hoarding. An odd feeling of curiosity stirred him, and he crossed over. As he came near, the word "Murder," printed in black letters, met his eye. He started, and a deep flush came into his cheek. It was an advertisement

LORD ARTHUR SAVILE'S CRIME 465

offering a reward for any information leading to the arrest of a man of medium height, between thirty and forty years of age, wearing a billycock hat, a black coat, and check trousers, and with a scar upon his right cheek. He read it over and over again, and wondered if the wretched man would be caught, and how he had been scarred. Perhaps, some day, his own name might be placarded on the walls of London. Some day, perhaps, a price would be set on his head also.

The thought made him sick with horror. He turned on his heel, and hurried on into the night.

Where he went he hardly knew. He had a dim memory of wandering through a labyrinth of sordid houses, of being lost in a giant web of sombre streets, and it was bright dawn when he found himself at last in Piccadilly Circus. As he strolled home towards Belgrave Square, he met the great waggons on their way to Covent Garden. The white-smocked carters, with their pleasant sunburnt faces and coarse curly hair, strode sturdily on, cracking their whips, and calling out now and then to each other; on the back of a huge grey horse, the leader of a jangling team, sat a chubby boy, with a bunch of primroses in his battered hat, keeping tight hold of the mane with his little hands, and laughing; and the great piles of vegetables looked like masses of jade against the morning sky, like masses of green jade against the pink petals of some marvellous rose. Lord Arthur felt curiously affected, he could not tell why. There was something in the dawn's delicate loveliness that seemed to him inexpressibly pathetic, and he thought of all the days that break in beauty, and that set in storm. These rustics, too, with their rough, good-humoured voices, and their nonchalant ways, what a strange London they saw! A London free from the sin of night and the smoke of day, a pallid, ghost-like city, a desolate town of tombs! He wondered what they thought of it, and whether they knew anything of its splendour and its shame, of its fierce, fiery-coloured joys, and its horrible hunger, of all it makes and mars from morn to eve. Probably it was to them merely a mart where they brought their fruits to sell, and where they tarried for a few hours at most, leaving the streets still silent, the houses still asleep. It gave him pleasure to watch them as they went by. Rude as they were, with their heavy, hob-nailed shoes, and their awkward gait, they brought a little of Arcady with them. He felt that they had lived with Nature, and that she had taught them peace. He envied them all that they did not know.

By the time he had reached Belgrave Square the sky was a faint blue, and the birds were beginning to twitter in the gardens.

III

When Lord Arthur woke it was twelve o'clock, and the midday sun was streaming through the ivory-silk curtains of his room. He got up and looked out of the window. A dim haze of heat was hanging over the great city, and the roofs of the houses were like dull silver. In the flickering green of the square below some children were flitting about like white butterflies, and the pavement was crowded with people on their way to the Park. Never had life seemed lovelier to him, never had the things of evil seemed more remote.

Then his valet brought him a cup of chocolate on a tray. After he had drunk it, he drew aside a heavy *portière* of peach-coloured plush, and passed into the bathroom. The light stole softly from above, through thin slabs of transparent onyx, and the water in the marble tank glimmered like a moonstone. He plunged hastily in, till the cool ripples touched throat and hair, and then dipped his head right under, as though he would have wiped away the stain of some shameful memory. When he stepped out he felt almost at peace. The exquisite physical conditions of the moment had dominated him, as indeed often happens in the case of very finely wrought natures, for the senses, like fire, can purify as well as destroy.

After breakfast, he flung himself down on a divan, and lit a cigarette. On the mantel-shelf, framed in dainty old brocade, stood a large photograph of Sybil Merton, as he had seen her first at Lady Noel's ball. The small, exquisitely shaped head drooped slightly to one side, as though the thin, reed-like throat could hardly bear the burden of so much beauty; the lips were slightly parted, and seemed made for sweet music; and all the tender purity of girlhood looked out in wonder from the dreaming eyes. With her soft, clinging dress of *crêpe-de-chine,* and her large leaf-shaped fan, she looked like one of those delicate little figures men find in the olive-woods near Tanagra; and there was a touch of Greek grace in her pose and attitude. Yet she was not *petite*. She was simply perfectly proportioned— a rare thing in an age when so many women are either over life-size or insignificant.

Now as Lord Arthur looked at her, he was filled with the terrible pity that is born of love. He felt that to marry her, with the doom of murder hanging over his head, would be a betrayal like that of Judas, a sin worse than any the Borgia had ever dreamed of. What happiness could there be for them, when at any moment he might be called upon to carry out the awful prophecy written in his hand? What manner of life would be theirs while Fate still held this fearful fortune in the scales? The marriage must be postponed, at all costs.

Of this he was quite resolved. Ardently though he loved the girl, and the mere touch of her fingers, when they sat together, made each nerve of his body thrill with exquisite joy, he recognized none the less clearly where his duty lay, and was fully conscious of the fact that he had no right to marry until he had committed the murder. This done, he could stand before the altar with Sybil Merton, and give his life into her hands without terror of wrongdoing. This done, he could take her to his arms, knowing that she would never have to blush for him, never have to hang her head in shame. But done it must be first; and the sooner the better for both.

Many men in his position would have preferred the primrose path of dalliance to the steep heights of duty; but Lord Arthur was too conscientious to set pleasure above principle. There was more than mere passion in his love; and Sybil was to him a symbol of all that is good and noble. For a moment he had a natural repugnance against what he was asked to do, but it soon passed away. His heart told him that it was not a sin, but a sacrifice; his reason reminded him that there was no other course open. He had to choose between living for himself and living for others, and terrible though the task laid upon him undoubtedly was, yet he knew that he must not suffer selfishness to triumph over love. Sooner or later we are all called upon to decide on the same issue—of us all, the same question is asked. To Lord Arthur it came early in life—before his nature had been spoiled by the calculating cynicism of middle-age, or his heart corroded by the shallow, fashionable egotism of our day, and he felt no hesitation about doing his duty. Fortunately also, for him, he was no mere dreamer, or idle dilettante. Had he been so, he would have hesitated, like Hamlet, and let irresolution mar his purpose. But he was essentially practical. Life to

LORD ARTHUR SAVILE'S CRIME

him meant action, rather than thought. He had that rarest of all things, common sense.

The wild, turbid feelings of the previous night had by this time completely passed away, and it was almost with a sense of shame that he looked back upon his mad wanderings from street to street, his fierce emotional agony. The very sincerity of his sufferings made them seem unreal to him now. He wondered how he could have been so foolish as to rant and rave about the inevitable. The only question that seemed to trouble him was, whom to make away with; for he was not blind to the fact that murder, like the religions of the pagan world, requires a victim as well as a priest. Not being a genius, he had no enemies, and indeed he felt that this was not the time for the gratification of any personal pique or dislike, the mission in which he was engaged being one of great and grave solemnity. He accordingly made out a list of his friends and relatives on a sheet of notepaper, and after careful consideration, decided in favour of Lady Clementina Beauchamp, a dear old lady who lived in Curzon Street, and was his own second cousin by his mother's side. He had always been very fond of Lady Clem, as every one called her, and as he was very wealthy himself, having come into all Lord Rugby's property when he came of age, there was no possibility of his deriving any vulgar monetary advantage by her death. In fact, the more he thought over the matter, the more she seemed to him to be just the right person, and, feeling that any delay would be unfair to Sybil, he determined to make his arrangements at once.

The first thing to be done was, of course, to settle with the cheiromantist; so he sat down at a small Sheraton writing-table that stood near the window, drew a cheque for £105, payable to the order of Mr. Septimus

Podgers, and, enclosing it in an envelope, told his valet to take it to West Moon Street. He then telephoned to the stables for his hansom, and dressed to go out. As he was leaving the room he looked back at Sybil Merton's photograph, and swore that, come what may, he would never let her know what he was doing for her sake, but would keep the secret of his self-sacrifice hidden always in his heart.

On his way to the Buckingham, he stopped at a florist's, and sent Sybil a beautiful basket of narcissus, with lovely white petals and staring pheasants' eyes, and on arriving at the club went straight to the library, rang the bell, and ordered the waiter to bring him a lemon-and-soda, and a book on toxicology. He had fully decided that poison was the best means to adopt in this troublesome business. Anything like personal violence was extremely distasteful to him, and besides, he was very anxious not to murder Lady Clementina in any way that might attract public attention, as he hated the idea of being lionized at Lady Windermere's, or seeing his name figuring in the paragraphs of vulgar society-newspapers. He had also to think of Sybil's father and mother, who were rather old-fashioned people, and might possibly object to the marriage if there was anything like a scandal, though he felt certain that if he told them the whole facts of the case they would be the very first to appreciate the motives that had actuated him. He had every reason, then, to decide in favour of poison. It was safe, sure, and quiet, and did away with any necessity for painful scenes, to which, like most Englishmen, he had a rooted objection.

Of the science of poisons, however, he knew absolutely nothing, and as the waiter seemed quite unable to find anything in the library but *Ruff's Guide* and *Bailey's Magazine,* he examined the book-shelves himself, and finally came across a handsomely bound edition of the *Pharmacopœia,* and a copy of Erskine's *Toxicology,* edited by Sir Mathew Reid, the President of the Royal College of Physicians, and one of the oldest members of the Buckingham, having been elected in mistake for somebody else; a *contretemps* that so enraged the Committee, that when the real man came up they blackballed him unanimously. Lord Arthur was a good deal puzzled at the technical terms used in both books, and had begun to regret that he had not paid more attention to his classics at Oxford, when in the second volume of Erskine, he found a very interesting and complete account of the properties of aconitine, written in fairly clear English. It seemed to him to be exactly the poison he wanted. It was swift—indeed, almost immediate, in its effect—perfectly painless, and when taken in the form of a gelatine capsule, the mode recommended by Sir Mathew, not by any means unpalatable. He accordingly made a note, upon his shirt-cuff, of the amount necessary for a fatal dose, put the books back in their places, and strolled up St. James's Street, to Pestle and Humbey's, the great chemists. Mr. Pestle, who always attended personally on the aristocracy, was a good deal surprised at the order, and in a very deferential manner murmured something about a medical certificate being necessary. However, as soon as Lord Arthur explained to him that it was for a large Norwegian mastiff that he was obliged to get rid of, as it showed signs of incipient rabies, and had already bitten the coachman twice in the calf of the leg, he expressed himself as being perfectly satisfied, complimented Lord Arthur on his wonderful knowledge of toxicology, and had the prescription made up immediately.

Lord Arthur put the capsule into a pretty little silver *bonbonnière* that he saw in a shop window in Bond

Street, threw away Pestle and Humbey's ugly pill-box, and drove off at once to Lady Clementina's.

"Well, *monsieur le mauvais sujet,*" cried the old lady, as he entered the room, "why haven't you been to see me all this time?"

"My dear Lady Clem, I never have a moment to myself," said Lord Arthur, smiling.

"I suppose you mean that you go about all day long with Miss Sybil Merton, buying *chiffons* and talking nonsense? I cannot understand why people make such a fuss about being married. In my day we never dreamed of billing and cooing in public, or in private for that matter."

"I assure you I have not seen Sybil for twenty-four hours, Lady Clem. As far as I can make out, she belongs entirely to her milliners."

"Of course; that is the only reason you come to see an ugly old woman like myself. I wonder you men don't take warning. *On a fait des folies pour moi,* and here I am, a poor rheumatic creature, with a false front and a bad temper. Why, if it were not for dear Lady Jansen, who sends me all the worst French novels she can find, I don't think I could get through the day. Doctors are no use at all, except to get fees out of one. They can't even cure my heartburn."

"I have brought you a cure for that, Lady Clem," said Lord Arthur gravely. "It is a wonderful thing, invented by an American."

"I don't think I like American inventions, Arthur. I am quite sure I don't. I read some American novels lately, and they were quite nonsensical."

"Oh, but there is no nonsense at all about this, Lady Clem! I assure you it is a perfect cure. You must promise to try it"; and Lord Arthur brought the little box out of his pocket, and handed it to her.

"Well, the box is charming, Arthur. Is it really a present? That is very sweet of you. And is this the wonderful medicine? It looks like a *bonbon*. I'll take it at once."

"Good heavens! Lady Clem," cried Lord Arthur, catching hold of her hand, "you mustn't do anything of the kind. It is a homœopathic medicine, and if you take it without having heartburn, it might do you no end of harm. Wait till you have an attack, and take it then. You will be astonished at the result."

"I should like to take it now," said Lady Clementina, holding up to the light the little transparent capsule, with its floating bubble of liquid aconitine. I am sure it is delicious. The fact is that, though I hate doctors, I love medicines. However, I'll keep it till my next attack."

"And when will that be?" asked Lord Arthur eagerly. "Will it be soon?"

"I hope not for a week. I had a very bad time yesterday morning with it. But one never knows."

"You are sure to have one before the end of the month then, Lady Clem?"

"I am afraid so. But how sympathetic you are today, Arthur! Really, Sybil has done you a great deal of good. And now you must run away, for I am dining with some very dull people, who won't talk scandal, and I know that if I don't get my sleep now I shall never be able to keep awake during dinner. Good-bye, Arthur, give my love to Sybil, and thank you so much for the American medicine."

"You won't forget to take it, Lady Clem, will you?" said Lord Arthur, rising from his seat.

"Of course I won't, you silly boy. I think it is most kind of you to think of me, and I shall write and tell you if I want any more."

Lord Arthur left the house in high spirits, and with a feeling of immense relief.

That night he had an interview with Sybil Merton. He told her how he had been suddenly placed in a position of terrible difficulty, from which neither honour nor duty would allow him to recede. He told her that the marriage must be put off for the present, as until he had got rid of his fearful entanglements, he was not a free man. He implored her to trust him, and not to have any doubts about the future. Everything would come right, but patience was necessary.

The scene took place in the conservatory of Mr. Merton's house, in Park Lane, where Lord Arthur had dined as usual. Sybil had never seemed more happy, and for a moment Lord Arthur had been tempted to play the coward's part, to write to Lady Clementina for the pill, and to let the marriage go on as if there was no such person as Mr. Podgers in the world. His better nature, however, soon asserted itself, and even when Sybil flung herself weeping into his arms, he did not falter. The beauty that stirred his senses had touched his conscience also. He felt that to wreck so fair a life for the sake of a few months' pleasure would be a wrong thing to do.

He stayed with Sybil till nearly midnight, comforting her and being comforted in turn, and early the next morning he left for Venice, after writing a manly, firm letter to Mr. Merton about the necessary postponement of the marriage.

IV

In Venice he met his brother, Lord Surbiton, who happened to have come over from Corfu in his yacht. The two young men spent a delightful fortnight together. In the morning they rode on the Lido, or glided up and down the green canals in their long black gondola; in the afternoon they usually entertained visitors on the yacht; and in the evening they dined at Florian's, and smoked innumerable cigarettes on the Piazza. Yet somehow Lord Arthur was not happy. Every day he studied the obituary column in the *Times,* expecting to see a notice of Lady Clementina's death, but every day he was disappointed. He began to be afraid that some accident had happened to her, and often regretted that he had prevented her taking the aconitine when she had been so anxious to try its effect. Sybil's letters, too, though full of love, and trust, and tenderness, were often very sad in their tone, and sometimes he used to think that he was parted from her for ever.

After a fortnight Lord Surbiton got bored with Venice, and determined to run down the coast to Ravenna, as he heard that there was some capital cock-shooting in the Pinetum. Lord Arthur at first refused absolutely to come, but Surbiton, of whom he was extremely fond, finally persuaded him that if he stayed at Danielli's by himself he would be moped to death, and on the morning of the fifteenth they started, with a strong nor'-east wind blowing, and a rather choppy sea. The sport was excellent, and the free, open-air life brought the colour back to Lord Arthur's cheek, but about the twenty-second he became anxious about Lady Clementina, and, in spite of Surbiton's remonstrances, came back to Venice by train.

As he stepped out of his gondola on to the hotel steps, the proprietor came forward to meet him with a sheaf of telegrams. Lord Arthur snatched them out of his hand, and tore them open. Everything had been successful. Lady Clementina had died quite suddenly on the night of the seventeenth!

His first thought was for Sybil, and he sent her off a telegram announcing his immediate return to London. He then ordered his valet to pack his things for the night mail, sent his gondoliers about five times their proper fare, and ran up to his sitting-room with a light step and a buoyant heart. There he found three letters waiting for him. One was from Sybil herself, full of sympathy and condolence. The others were from his mother, and from Lady Clementina's solicitor. It seemed that the old lady had dined with the Duchess that very night, had delighted every one by her wit and *esprit*, but had gone home somewhat early, complaining of heartburn. In the morning she was found dead in her bed, having apparently suffered no pain. Sir Mathew Reid had been sent for at once, but, of course, there was nothing to be done, and she was to be buried on the twenty-second at Beauchamp Chalcote. A few days before she died she had made her will, and left Lord Arthur her little house in Curzon Street, and all her furniture, personal effects, and pictures, with the exception of her collection of miniatures, which was to go to her sister, Lady Margaret Rufford, and her amethyst necklace, which Sybil Merton was to have. The property was not of much value; but Mr. Mansfield, the solicitor, was extremely anxious for Lord Arthur to return at once, if possible, as there were a great many bills to be paid, and Lady Clementina had never kept any regular accounts.

Lord Arthur was very much touched by Lady Clementina's kind remembrance of him, and felt that Mr. Podgers had a great deal to answer for. His love of Sybil, however, dominated every other emotion, and the consciousness that he had done his duty gave him peace and comfort. When he arrived at Charing Cross, he felt perfectly happy.

The Mertons received him very kindly. Sybil made him promise that he would never again allow anything to come between them, and the marriage was fixed for the seventh of June. Life seemed to him once more bright and beautiful, and all his old gladness came back to him again.

One day, however, as he was going over the house in Curzon Street, in company with Lady Clementina's solicitor and Sybil herself, burning packages of faded letters, and turning out drawers of odd rubbish, the young girl suddenly gave a little cry of delight.

"What have you found, Sybil?" said Lord Arthur, looking up from his work, and smiling.

"This lovely little silver *bonbonnière*, Arthur. Isn't it quaint and Dutch? Do give it to me! I know amethysts won't become me till I am over eighty."

It was the box that had held the aconitine.

Lord Arthur started, and a faint blush came into his cheek. He had almost entirely forgotten what he had done, and it seemed to him a curious coincidence that Sybil, for whose sake he had gone through all that terrible anxiety, should have been the first to remind him of it.

"Of course you can have it, Sybil. I gave it to poor Lady Clem myself."

"Oh! thank you, Arthur; and may I have the *bonbon* too? I had no notion that Lady Clementina liked sweets. I thought she was far too intellectual."

Lord Arthur grew deadly pale, and a horrible idea crossed his mind.

"*Bonbon*, Sybil? What do you mean?" he said in a slow, hoarse voice.

"There is one in it, that is all. It looks quite old and dusty, and I have not the slightest intention of eating it. What is the matter, Arthur? How white you look!"

Lord Arthur rushed across the room, and seized the box. Inside it was the amber-coloured capsule, with its poison-bubble. Lady Clementina had died a natural death after all!

The shock of the discovery was almost too much for him. He flung the capsule into the fire, and sank on the sofa with a cry of despair.

v

Mr. Merton was a good deal distressed at the second postponement of the marriage, and Lady Julia, who had already ordered her dress for the wedding, did all in her power to make Sybil break off the match. Dearly, however, as Sybil loved her mother, she had given her whole life into Lord Arthur's hands, and nothing that Lady Julia could say could make her waver in her faith. As for Lord Arthur himself, it took him days to get over his terrible disappointment, and for a time his nerves were completely unstrung. His excellent common sense, however, soon asserted itself, and his sound, practical mind did not leave him long in doubt about what to do. Poison having proved a complete failure, dynamite, or some other form of explosive, was obviously the proper thing to try.

He accordingly looked again over the list of his friends and relatives, and, after careful consideration, determined to blow up his uncle, the Dean of Chichester. The Dean, who was a man of great culture and learning, was extremely fond of clocks, and had a wonderful collection of timepieces, ranging from the fifteenth century to the present day, and it seemed to Lord Arthur that this hobby of the good Dean's offered him an excellent opportunity for carrying out his scheme. Where to procure an explosive machine was, of course, quite another matter. The London Directory gave him no information on the point, and he felt that there was very little use in going to Scotland Yard about it, as they never seemed to know anything about the movements of the dynamite faction till after an explosion had taken place, and not much even then.

Suddenly he thought of his friend Rouvaloff, a young Russian of very revolutionary tendencies, whom he had met at Lady Windermere's in the winter. Count Rouvaloff was supposed to be writing a life of Peter the Great, and to have come over to England for the purpose of studying the documents relating to that Tsar's residence in this country as a ship carpenter; but it was generally suspected that he was a Nihilist agent, and there was no doubt that the Russian Embassy did not look with any favour upon his presence in London. Lord Arthur felt that he was just the man for his purpose, and drove down one morning to his lodgings in Bloomsbury, to ask his advice and assistance.

"So you are taking up politics seriously?" said Count Rouvaloff, when Lord Arthur had told him the object of his mission; but Lord Arthur, who hated swagger of any kind, felt bound to admit to him that he had not the slightest interest in social questions, and simply wanted the explosive machine for a purely family matter, in which no one was concerned but himself.

Count Rouvaloff looked at him for some moments in amazement, and then seeing that he was quite serious, wrote an address on a piece of paper, initialed it, and handed it to him across the table.

"Scotland Yard would give a good deal to know this address, my dear fellow."

"They shan't have it," cried Lord Arthur, laughing; and after shaking the young Russian warmly by the hand he ran downstairs, examined the paper, and told the coachman to drive to Soho Square.

There he dismissed him, and strolled down Greek Street, till he came to a place called Bayle's Court. He passed under the archway, and found himself in a curious *cul-de-sac*, that was apparently occupied by a French laundry, as a perfect network of clothes-lines was stretched across from house to house, and there was a flutter of white linen in the morning air. He walked right to the end, and knocked at a little green house. After some delay, during which every window in the court became a blurred mass of peering faces, the door was opened by a rather rough-looking foreigner, who asked him in very bad English what his business was. Lord Arthur handed him the paper Count Rouvaloff had given him. When the man saw it he bowed, and invited Lord Arthur into a very shabby front parlour on the ground floor, and in a few moments Herr Winckelkopf, as he was called in England, bustled into the room, with a very wine-stained napkin round his neck, and a fork in his left hand.

"Count Rouvaloff has given me an introduction to you," said Lord Arthur, bowing, "and I am anxious to have a short interview with you on a matter of business. My name is Smith, Mr. Robert Smith, and I want you to supply me with an explosive clock."

"Charmed to meet you, Lord Arthur," said the genial little German, laughing. "Don't look so alarmed, it is my duty to know everybody, and I remember seeing you one evening at Lady Windermere's. I hope her ladyship is quite well. Do you mind sitting with me while I finish my breakfast? There is an excellent *pâté*, and my friends are kind enough to say that my Rhine wine is better than any they get at the German Embassy," and before Lord Arthur had got over his surprise at being recognized, he found himself seated in the back-room, sipping the most delicious Marcobrünner out of a pale yellow hock-glass marked with the Imperial monogram, and chatting in the friendliest manner possible to the famous conspirator.

"Explosive clocks," said Herr Winckelkopf, "are not very good things for foreign exportation, as, even if they succeed in passing the Custom House, the train service is so irregular, that they usually go off before they have reached their proper destination. If, however, you want one for home use, I can supply you with an excellent article, and guarantee that you will be satisfied with the result. May I ask for whom it is intended? If it is for the police, or for any one connected with Scotland Yard, I am afraid I cannot do anything for you. The English detectives are really our best friends, and I have always found that by relying on their stupidity, we can do exactly what we like. I could not spare one of them."

"I assure you," said Lord Arthur, "that it has nothing to do with the police at all. In fact, the clock is intended for the Dean of Chichester."

"Dear me! I had no idea that you felt so strongly about religion, Lord Arthur. Few young men do nowadays."

"I am afraid you overrate me, Herr Winckelkopf," said Lord Arthur, blushing. "The fact is, I really know nothing about theology."

"It is a purely private matter then?"

"Purely private."

Herr Winckelkopf shrugged his shoulders, and left the room, returning in a few minutes with a round cake of dynamite about the size of a penny, and a pretty little French clock, surmounted by an ormolu figure of Liberty trampling on the hydra of Despotism.

Lord Arthur's face brightened up when he saw it. "That is just what I want," he cried, "and now tell me how it goes off."

"Ah! there is my secret," answered Herr Winckelkopf, contemplating his invention with a justifiable look of pride; "let me know when you wish it to explode, and I will set the machine to the moment."

"Well, today is Tuesday, and if you could send it off at once——"

"That is impossible; I have a great deal of important work on hand for some friends of mine in Moscow. Still, I might send it off tomorrow."

"Oh, it will be quite time enough!" said Lord Arthur politely, "if it is delivered tomorrow night or Thursday morning. For the moment of the explosion, say Friday at noon exactly. The Dean is always at home at that hour."

"Friday, at noon," repeated Herr Winckelkopf, and he made a note to that effect in a large ledger that was lying on a bureau near the fireplace.

"And now," said Lord Arthur, rising from his seat, "pray let me know how much I am in your debt."

"It is such a small matter, Lord Arthur, that I do not care to make any charge. The dynamite comes to seven and sixpence, the clock will be three pounds ten, and the carriage about five shillings. I am only too pleased to oblige any friend of Count Rouvaloff's."

"But your trouble, Herr Winckelkopf?"

"Oh, that is nothing! It is a pleasure to me. I do not work for money; I live entirely for my art."

Lord Arthur laid down £4, 2s. 6d. on the table, thanked the little German for his kindness, and, having succeeded in declining an invitation to meet some Anarchists at a meat-tea on the following Saturday, left the house and went off to the Park.

For the next two days he was in a state of the greatest excitement, and on Friday at twelve o'clock he drove down to the Buckingham to wait for news. All the afternoon the stolid hall-porter kept posting up telegrams from various parts of the country giving the results of horse-races, the verdicts in divorce suits, the state of the weather, and the like, while the tape ticked out wearisome details about an all-night sitting in the House of Commons, and a small panic on the Stock Exchange. At four o'clock the evening papers came in, and Lord Arthur disappeared into the library with the *Pall Mall*, the *St. James's*, the *Globe*, and the *Echo*, to the immense indignation of Colonel Goodchild, who wanted to read the reports of a speech he had delivered that morning at the Mansion House, on the subject of South African Missions, and the advisability of having black Bishops in every province, and for some reason or other had a strong prejudice against the *Evening News*. None of the papers, however, contained even the slightest allusion to Chichester, and Lord Arthur felt that the attempt must have failed. It was a terrible blow to him, and for a time he was quite unnerved. Herr Winckelkopf, whom he went to see the next day, was full of elaborate apologies, and offered to supply him with another clock free of charge, or with a case of nitro-glycerine bombs at cost price. But he had lost all faith in explosives, and Herr Winckelkopf himself acknowledged that everything is so adulterated nowadays, that even dynamite can hardly be got in a pure condition. The little German, however, while admitting that something must have gone wrong with the machinery, was not without hope that the clock might still go off, and instanced the case of a barometer that he had once sent to the military Governor at Odessa, which, though timed to explode in ten days, had not done so for something like three months. It was quite true that when it did go off, it merely succeeded in blowing a housemaid to atoms, the Governor having gone out of town six weeks before, but at least it showed that dynamite, as a destructive force, was, when under the control of machinery, a powerful, though a somewhat unpunctual agent. Lord Arthur was a little consoled by this reflection, but even here he was destined to disappointment, for two days afterwards, as he was going upstairs, the Duchess called him into her boudoir, and showed him a letter she had just received from the Deanery.

"Jane writes charming letters," said the Duchess; "you must really read her last. It is quite as good as the novels Mudie sends us."

Lord Arthur seized the letter from her hand. It ran as follows:—

THE DEANERY, CHICHESTER,
27th May.

My Dearest Aunt,

Thank you so much for the flannel for the Dorcas Society, and also for the gingham. I quite agree with you that it is nonsense their wanting to wear pretty things, but everybody is so Radical and irreligious nowadays, that it is difficult to make them see that they should not try and dress like the upper classes. I am sure I don't know what we are coming to. As papa has often said in his sermons, we live in an age of unbelief.

We have had great fun over a clock that an unknown admirer sent papa last Thursday. It arrived in a wooden box from London, carriage paid; and papa feels it must have been sent by someone who had read his remarkable sermon, "Is Licence Liberty?" for on top of the clock was a figure of a woman, with what papa said was the cap of Liberty on her head. I didn't think it very becoming myself, but papa said it was historical, so I suppose it is all right. Parker unpacked it, and papa put it on the mantelpiece in the library, and we were all sitting there on Friday morning, when just as the clock struck twelve, we heard a whirring noise, a little puff of smoke came from the pedestal of the figure, and the goddess of

Liberty fell off, and broke her nose on the fender! Maria was quite alarmed, but it looked so ridiculous, that James and I went off into fits of laughter, and even papa was amused. When we examined it, we found it was a sort of alarum clock, and that, if you set it to a particular hour, and put some gunpowder and a cap under a little hammer, it went off whenever you wanted. Papa said it must not remain in the library, as it made a noise, so Reggie carried it away to the schoolroom, and does nothing but have small explosions all day long. Do you think Arthur would like one for a wedding present? I suppose they are quite fashionable in London. Papa says they should do a great deal of good, as they show that Liberty can't last, but must fall down. Papa says Liberty was invented at the time of the French Revolution. How awful it seems!

I have now to go to the Dorcas, where I will read them your most instructive letter. How true, dear aunt, your idea is, that in their rank of life they should wear what is unbecoming. I must say it is absurd, their anxiety about dress, when there are so many more important things in this world, and in the next. I am so glad your flowered poplin turned out so well, and that your lace was not torn. I am wearing my yellow satin, that you so kindly gave me, at the Bishop's on Wednesday, and think it will look all right. Would you have bows or not? Jennings says that every one wears bows now, and that the underskirt should be frilled. Reggie has just had another explosion, and papa has ordered the clock to be sent to the stables. I don't think papa likes it so much as he did at first, though he is very flattered at being sent such a pretty and ingenious toy. It shows that people read his sermons, and profit by them.

Papa sends his love, in which James, and Reggie, and Maria all unite, and, hoping that Uncle Cecil's gout is better, believe me, dear aunt, ever your affectionate niece,

JANE PERCY.

PS.—Do tell me about the bows. Jennings insists they are the fashion.

Lord Arthur looked so serious and unhappy over the letter, that the Duchess went into fits of laughter.

"My dear Arthur," she cried, "I shall never show you a young lady's letter again! But what shall I say about the clock? I think it is a capital invention, and I should like to have one myself."

"I don't think much of them," said Lord Arthur, with a sad smile, and, after kissing his mother, he left the room.

When he got upstairs, he flung himself on a sofa, and his eyes filled with tears. He had done his best to commit this murder, but on both occasions he had failed, and through no fault of his own. He had tried to do his duty, but it seemed as if Destiny herself had turned traitor. He was oppressed with the sense of the barrenness of good intentions, of the futility of trying to be fine. Perhaps, it would be better to break off the marriage altogether. Sybil would suffer, it is true, but suffering could not really mar a nature so noble as hers. As for himself, what did it matter? There is always some war in which a man can die, some cause to which a man can give his life, and as life had no pleasure for him, so death had no terror. Let Destiny work out his doom. He would not stir to help her.

At half-past seven he dressed, and went down to the club. Surbiton was there with a party of young men, and he was obliged to dine with them. Their trivial conversation and idle jests did not interest him, and as soon as coffee was brought he left them, inventing some engagement in order to get away. As he was going out of the club, the hall-porter handed him a letter. It was from Herr Winckelkopf, asking him to call down the next evening, and look at an explosive umbrella, that went off as soon as it was opened. It was the very latest invention, and had just arrived from Geneva. He tore the letter up into fragments. He had made up his mind not to try any more experiments. Then he wandered down to the Thames Embankment, and sat for hours by the river. The moon peered through a mane of tawny clouds, as if it were a lion's eye, and innumerable stars spangled the hollow vault, like gold dust powdered on a purple dome. Now and then a barge swung out into the turbid stream, and floated away with the tide, and the railway signals changed from green to scarlet as the trains ran shrieking across the bridge. After some time, twelve o'clock boomed from the tall tower at Westminster, and at each stroke of the sonorous bell the night seemed to tremble. Then the railway lights went out, one solitary lamp left gleaming like a large ruby on a giant mast, and the roar of the city became fainter.

At two o'clock he got up, and strolled towards Blackfriars. How unreal everything looked! How like a strange dream! The houses on the other side of the river seemed built out of darkness. One would have said that silver and shadow had fashioned the world anew. The huge dome of St. Paul's loomed like a bubble through the dusky air.

As he approached Cleopatra's Needle he saw a man leaning over the parapet, and as he came nearer the man looked up, the gas-light falling full upon his face.

It was Mr. Podgers, the cheiromantist! No one could mistake the fat, flabby face, the gold-rimmed spectacles, the sickly feeble smile, the sensual mouth.

Lord Arthur stopped. A brilliant idea flashed across

him, and he stole softly up behind. In a moment he had seized Mr. Podgers by the legs, and flung him into the Thames. There was a coarse oath, a heavy splash, and all was still. Lord Arthur looked anxiously over, but could see nothing of the cheiromantist but a tall hat, pirouetting in an eddy of moonlit water. After a time it also sank, and no trace of Mr. Podgers was visible. Once he thought that he caught sight of the bulky misshapen figure striking out for the staircase by the bridge, and a horrible feeling of failure came over him, but it turned out to be merely a reflection, and when the moon shone out from behind a cloud it passed away. At last he seemed to have realized the decree of destiny. He heaved a deep sigh of relief, and Sybil's name came to his lips.

"Have you dropped anything, sir?" said a voice behind him suddenly.

He turned round, and saw a policeman with a bull's-eye lantern.

"Nothing of importance, sergeant," he answered, smiling, and hailing a passing hansom, he jumped in, and told the man to drive to Belgrave Square.

For the next few days he alternated between hope and fear. There were moments when he almost expected Mr. Podgers to walk into the room, and yet at other times he felt that Fate could not be so unjust to him. Twice he went to the cheiromantist's address in West Moon Street, but he could not bring himself to ring the bell. He longed for certainty, and was afraid of it.

Finally it came. He was sitting in the smoking-room of the club having tea, and listening rather wearily to Surbiton's account of the last comic song at the Gaiety, when the waiter came in with the evening papers. He took up the *St. James's*, and was listlessly turning over its pages, when this strange heading caught his eye:

SUICIDE OF A CHEIROMANTIST.

He turned pale with excitement, and began to read. The paragraph ran as follows:

> Yesterday morning, at seven o'clock, the body of Mr. Septimus R. Podgers, the eminent cheiromantist, was washed on shore at Greenwich, just in front of the Ship Hotel. The unfortunate gentleman had been missing for some days, and considerable anxiety for his safety had been felt in cheiromantic circles. It is supposed that he committed suicide under the influence of a temporary mental derangement, caused by overwork, and a verdict to that effect was returned this afternoon by the coroner's jury. Mr. Podgers had just completed an elaborate treatise on the subject of the Human Hand, that will shortly be published, when it will no doubt attract much attention. The deceased was sixty-five years of age, and does not seem to have left any relations.

Lord Arthur rushed out of the club with the paper still in his hand, to the immense amazement of the hall-porter, who tried in vain to stop him, and drove at once to Park Lane. Sybil saw him from the window, and something told her that he was the bearer of good news. She ran down to meet him, and, when she saw his face, she knew that all was well.

"My dear Sybil," cried Lord Arthur, "let us be married tomorrow!"

"You foolish boy! Why, the cake is not even ordered!" said Sybil, laughing through her tears.

VI

When the wedding took place, some three weeks later, St. Peter's was crowded with a perfect mob of smart people. The service was read in the most impressive manner by the Dean of Chichester, and everybody agreed that they had never seen a handsomer couple than the bride and bridegroom. They were more than handsome, however—they were happy. Never for a single moment did Lord Arthur regret all that he had suffered for Sybil's sake, while she, on her side, gave him the best things a woman can give to any man—worship, tenderness, and love. For them romance was not killed by reality. They always felt young.

Some years afterwards, when two beautiful children had been born to them, Lady Windermere came down on a visit to Alton Priory, a lovely old place, that had been the Duke's wedding present to his son; and one afternoon as she was sitting with Lady Arthur under a lime tree in the garden, watching the little boy and girl as they played up and down the rose-walk, like fitful sunbeams, she suddenly took her hostess's hand in hers, and said, "Are you happy, Sybil?"

"Dear Lady Windermere, of course I am happy. Aren't you?"

"I have no time to be happy, Sybil. I always like the last person who is introduced to me; but, as a rule, as soon as I know people I get tired of them."

"Don't your lions satisfy you, Lady Windermere?"

"Oh dear, no! lions are only good for one season. As soon as their manes are cut, they are the dullest creatures going. Besides, they behave very badly, if you are really nice to them. Do you remember that horrid Mr. Podgers? He was a dreadful impostor. Of course, I didn't mind that at all, and even when he wanted to borrow money I forgave him, but I could not stand his making love to me. He has really made me hate cheiromancy. I go in for telepathy now. It is much more amusing."

"You mustn't say anything against cheiromancy here,

Lady Windermere; it is the only subject that Arthur does not like people to chaff about. I assure you he is quite serious over it."

"You don't mean to say that he believes in it, Sybil?"

"Ask him, Lady Windermere, here he is"; and Lord Arthur came up the garden with a large bunch of yellow roses in his hand, and his two children dancing round him.

"Lord Arthur?"

"Yes, Lady Windermere."

"You don't mean to say that you believe in cheiromancy?"

"Of course I do," said the young man, smiling.

"But why?"

"Because I owe to it all the happiness of my life," he murmured, throwing himself into a wicker chair.

"My dear Lord Arthur, what do you owe to it?"

"Sybil," he answered, handing his wife the roses, and looking into her violet eyes.

"What nonsense!" cried Lady Windermere. "I never heard such nonsense in all my life."

AUTOBIOGRAPHY AND HISTORY

GEORGE MOORE

Mount Venus

THE past never changes; it is like a long picture-gallery. Many of the pictures are covered with grey cloths, as is usual in picture-galleries; but we can uncover any picture we wish to see, and not infrequently a cloth will fall as if by magic, revealing a forgotten one, and it is often as clear in outline and as fresh in paint as a Van der Meer.

That night in the Temple I met a memory as tender in colour and outline as the Van der Meer in the National Gallery. It was at the end of a long summer's day, five-and-twenty years ago, that I first saw her among some ruins in the Dublin mountains, and in her reappearance she seemed so startlingly like Ireland that I felt she formed part of the book I was dreaming, and that nothing of the circumstances in which I found her could be changed or altered. My thoughts fastened on to her, carrying me out of the Temple, back to Ireland, to the time when the ravages of the Land League had recalled me from the *Nouvelle Athènes*—a magnificent, young Montmartrian, with a blond beard *à la Capoul,* trousers hanging wide over the foot, and a hat so small that my sister had once mistaken it for her riding-hat.

And still in my Montmartrian clothes I had come back from the West with a story in my head, which could only be written in some poetical spot, probably in one of the old houses among the Dublin mountains, built there in the eighteenth century. And I had set out to look for one on a hot day in July, when the trees in Merrion Square seemed like painted trees, so still were they in the grey silence; the sparrows had ceased to twitter; the carmen spat without speaking, too weary to solicit my fare; and the horses continued to doze on the bridles. Even the red brick, I said, seems to weary in the heat. Too hot a day for walking, but I must walk if I'm to sleep tonight.

My way led through Stephen's Green, and the long decay of Dublin that began with the Union engaged my thoughts, and I fared sighing for the old-time mansions that had been turned into colleges and presbyteries. There were lodging-houses in Harcourt Street, and beyond Harcourt Street the town dwindled, first into small shops, then into shabby-genteel villas; at Terenure, I was among cottages, and within sight of purple hills, and when the Dodder was crossed, at the end of the village street, a great wall began, high as a prison wall; it might well have been mistaken for one, but the trees told it was a park wall, and the great ornamental gateway was a pleasant object. It came into sight suddenly —a great pointed edifice finely designed, and after ad-

MOUNT VENUS

miring it I wandered on, crossing an old grey bridge. The Dodder again, I said. The beautiful green country unfolded, a little melancholy for lack of light and shade, for lack, I added, of a ray to gild the fields. A beautiful country falling into ruin. The beauty of neglect—yet there is none in thrift. My eyes followed the long herds wandering knee-deep in succulent herbage, and I remembered that every other country I had seen was spoilt more or less by human beings, but this country was nearly empty, only an occasional herdsman to remind me of myself in this drift of ruined suburb, with a wistful line of mountains enclosing it, and one road curving among the hills, and everywhere high walls—parks, in the centre of which stand stately eighteenth-century mansions. How the eighteenth century sought privacy! I said, and walked on dreaming of the lives there were lived in these sequestered domains.

No road ever wound so beautifully, I cried, and there are no cottages, only an occasional ruin to make the road attractive. How much more attractive it is now, redeemed from its humanities—large families flowing over doorways, probably in and out of cesspools! I had seen such cottages in the West, and had wished them in ruins, for ruins are wistful, especially when a foxglove finds roothold in the crannies, and tall grasses flourish round the doorway, and withdrawing my eyes from the pretty cottage, I admired the spotted shade, and the road itself, now twisting abruptly, now winding leisurely up the hill, among woods ascending on my left and descending on my right. But what seemed most wonderful of all was the view that accompanied the road—glimpses of a great plain showing between comely trees shooting out of the hillside—a dim green plain, divided by hedges, traversed by long herds, and enclosed, if I remember rightly, by a line of low grey hills, far, ever so far, away.

All the same, the road ascends very steeply, I growled, beginning to doubt the veracity of the agent who had informed me that a house existed in the neighbourhood. In the neighbourhood, I repeated, for the word appeared singularly inappropriate. In the solitude, he should have said.

A little higher up in the hills a chance herdsman offered me some goat's milk; but it was like drinking Camembert cheese, and the least epicurean amongst us would prefer his milk and cheese separate. He had no other, and, in answer to my questions regarding a house to let, said there was one a mile up the road: Mount Venus.

Mount Venus! Who may have given it that name?

The question brought all his stupidity into his face, and after a short talk with him about his goats, I said I must be getting on to Mount Venus . . . if it be no more than a mile.

Nothing in Ireland lasts long except the miles, and the last mile to Mount Venus is the longest mile in Ireland; and the road is the steepest. It wound past another ruined cottage, and then a gateway appeared—heavy wrought-iron gates hanging between great stone pillars, the drive ascending through lonely grass-lands with no house in view, for the house lay on the further side of the hill, a grove of beech-trees reserving it as a surprise for the visitor. A more beautiful grove I have never seen, some two hundred years old, and the house as old as it—a long house built with picturesque chimney-stacks, well placed at each end, a resolute house, emphatic as an oath, with great steps before the door, and each made out of a single stone, a house at which one knocks timidly, lest mastiffs should rush out, eager for the strangling.

But no fierce voices answered my knocking, only a vague echo.

Maybe I'll find somebody in the back premises, and wandering through a gateway, I found myself among many ruins of barns and byres, and the ruin of what had once been a haggard; and I asked myself what were those strange ruins, and not finding any explanation, passed on, thinking the great stones had probably been used for the crushing of apples. Cider-presses? and I sought a living thing. No cow in the byre, nor pony in the stable, nor dog in the kennel, nor pig in the sty, nor gaunt Irish fowl stalking about the kitchen-door—the door which seemed to be the kitchen-door. An empty dovecot hung on the wall above it. Mount Venus without doves, I said, and sought for a pair on the sagging roofs. To my knocking no answer came, and, disappointed, I wandered back to the front of the house. At all events the view is open to me, and I descended the hillside towards the loveliest prospect that ever greeted mortal eyes.

At the end of the great yew hedge, hundreds of years old, the comely outline of Howth floated between sea and sky, spiritual, it seemed, on that grey day, as a poem by Shelley. One thought, too, of certain early pictures of Corot. The line of the shore was certainly drawn as beautifully as if he had drawn it, and the plain about the sea, filled with Dublin City, appeared in the distance a mere murky mass, with here and there a building, indicated, faintly, with Corot's beauty of touch. Nearer still the suburbs came trickling into the fields, the very fields through which I had passed, those in which I had seen herds of cattle feeding.

Then came a glimpse of a walled garden at the end of the yew hedge, a little lower down the shelving hillside, and, pulling a thorn-bush out of the gateway, I passed into a little wilderness of vagrant grasses and goats. A scheme for the restoration of Mount Venus started up in my mind; about two thousand pounds would have to be spent, but for that money I should live in the most beautiful place in the world. The Temple Church cannot compare with Chartres, nor Mount Venus with Windsor; a trifle, no doubt, in the world of art; but what a delicious trifle! . . . My dream died suddenly in the reflection that one country-house is generally enough for an Irish landlord, and I walked thinking if there were one among my friends who would restore Mount Venus sufficiently for the summer months, long enough for me to write my book, and to acquire a permanent memory of a beautiful thing which the earth was claiming rapidly, and which, in a few years, would have passed away.

By standing on some loose stones it was possible to look into the first-floor rooms, and I could see marble chimney-pieces set in a long room, up and down which I could walk while arranging my ideas; and when ideas failed me I could wander to the window and suckle my imagination on the view. This is the house I'm in search of, and there seems to be sufficient furniture for my wants. I'll return tomorrow. . . . But my pleasure will be lost if I've to wait till tomorrow. Somebody must be here. I'll try again. The silence that answered my knocking strengthened my determination to see Mount Venus that night, and I returned to the empty yard, and peeped and pried through all the out-houses, discovering at last a pail of newly peeled potatoes. There must be somebody about, and I waited, peeling the potatoes that remained unpeeled to pass the time.

I'm afraid I'm wasting your potatoes, I said to the woman who appeared in the doorway—a peasant woman wearing a rough, dark grey petticoat and heavy boots, men's boots (they were almost the first thing I noticed)—just the woman who I expected would come, the caretaker. She looked surprised when I told her of my knocking, and said she could not understand how it was she had not heard me, for she had been there all the time. She spoke with her head turned aside, showing a thin well-cut face with a shapely forehead, iron-grey hair, a nose, long and thin, with fine nostrils, and a mouth a pretty line, I think . . . but that is all I can say about her, for when I try to remember more I seem to lose sight of her. . . .

"You've come to see the house?"

She stopped and looked at me.

"Is there any reason why I shouldn't see it?"

"No, there's no reason why you shouldn't; only I thought nobody would ever come to see it again. If you'll wait a minute I'll fetch the key."

She doesn't speak like a caretaker, I thought, now more than ever anxious to go over the house with her.

"Is it a lease of the house you'd like, or do you wish only to hire it for the season, sir?"

"Only for the season, I said. It is to be let furnished?"

"There's not much furniture, but sufficient—"

"So long as there are beds, and a table to write upon, and a few chairs."

"Yes, there's that, and more than that," she answered, smiling. "This is the kitchen," and she showed me into a vast stone room; and the passages leading from the kitchen were wide and high, and built in stone. The walls seemed of great thickness, and when we came to the staircase, she said: "Mind you don't slip. The chairs are very slippery, but can easily be put right. The stonemason will only have to run his chisel over them."

"I'm more interested in the rooms in which I'm to live myself . . . if I take the house."

"These are the drawing-rooms," she said, and drew my attention to the chimney-piece.

"It's very beautiful," I answered, turning from the parti-coloured marbles to the pictures. All the ordinary subjects of pictorial art lined the walls, but I passed on without noticing any, so poor and provincial was the painting, until I came suddenly upon the portrait of a young girl. The painting was not less anonymous, but her natural gracefulness transpired in classical folds as she stood leaning on her bow, a Diana of the 'forties, looking across the greensward waiting to hear if the arrow had reached its mark.

Into what kind of old age has she drifted? I asked myself, and the recollection of the thin clear-cut eager face brought me back again to the portrait, and forgetful of the woman I had found in the out-house peeling potatoes for her dinner, I studied the face, certain that I had seen it before. But where?

"Several generations seem to be on the walls. Do you know anything about the people who lived in this house?"

"It was built about two hundred years ago, I should say."

"Who built it? Do you know its history?"

The woman did not answer, and we wandered into another room, and, noticing her face was turned from me, I said:

"I should like to hear something about the girl whose portrait I've been looking at. There's nothing to conceal? No story—"

"There's nothing in her story that any one need be ashamed of. But why do you ask?" And the manner in which she put the question still further excited my curiosity.

"Because it seems to me that I've seen the face before."

"Yes," she answered, "you have. The portrait in the next room is my portrait . . . as I was forty years ago. But I didn't think that any one would see the likeness."

"Your portrait!" I answered abruptly. "Yes, I can see the likeness." And I heard her say under her breath that she had been through a great deal of trouble, and her face was again turned from me as we walked into another room.

"But do you wish to take the house, sir? If not—"

"In some ways it would suit me well enough, but it's a long way to bring food up here. I'll write and let you know. And your portrait I shall always remember," I added, thinking to please her. But seeing that my remark failed to do so, I spoke of the dry well, and she told me there was another well: an excellent spring, only the cattle went there to drink; but it would be easy to put an iron fence round it.

I let her go and wandered whither she had advised me—to the cromlech, one of the grandest in Ireland. It could not fail to interest me, she had said, and I could not fail to find it if I followed the path round the hill. I would come to some ilex trees, and at the end of them, in the beech dell, I should find the altar.

And there I found a great rock laid upon three upright stones; one had fallen lately. In the words of a passing shepherd, the altar was out of repair.

"Even Druid altars do not survive the nineteenth century in Ireland," I answered, and still lingering under the ilex trees, for they were her trees, I thought of her in that time long ago, in the 'forties, when an artist came to Mount Venus to paint her portrait. A man of some talent, too, I said to myself, for he painted her in a beautiful attitude. Or was it she who gave him the attitude, leaning on her bow? Was it she who settled the folds about her limbs, and decided the turn of her head, the eyes looking across the greensward towards the target. Had she fled with somebody whom she had loved dearly and been deserted and cast away on that hillside? Does the house belong to her? Or is she the caretaker? Does she live there with a servant? Or alone, cooking her own dinner? None of my questions had she answered, and I invented story after story for her, all the way back to Dublin, through the grey evening in which no star appeared, only a red moon rising up through the woods like a fire in the branches.

(From *Hail and Farewell*.)

Bricriu's Feast

BRICRIU Poison-tongue held a great feast for Conchobar mac Nessa and for all the Ulstermen. The preparation of the feast took a whole year. For the entertainment of the guests a spacious house was built by him. He erected it at Dun Rudraige after the likeness of the Red Branch in Emain Macha. Yet it surpassed the buildings of that period entirely for material, for artistic design, and for beauty of architecture—its pillars and frontings splendid and costly, its carving and lintel-work famed for magnificence. The house was made in this fashion: on the plan of Tara's Mead-Hall, having nine compartments from fire to wall, each fronting of bronze thirty feet high, overlaid with gold. In the fore part of the palace a royal couch was erected for Conchobar high above those of the whole house. It was set with carbuncles and other precious stones which shone with a lustre of gold and silver, radiant with every hue, making night like day. Around it were placed the twelve couches of the twelve tribes of Ulster. The nature of the workmanship was on a par with the material of the edifice. It took a wagon team to carry each beam, and the strength of seven Ulstermen to fix each pole, while thirty of the chief artificers of Erin were employed on its erection and arrangement.

Then a balcony was made by Bricriu on a level with the couch of Conchobar and as high as those of the heroes of valour. The decorations of its fittings were magnificent. Windows of glass were placed on each side of it, and one of these was above Bricriu's couch, so that he could view the hall from his seat, as he knew the Ulstermen would not allow him within.

When Bricriu had finished building the hall and the balcony, supplying it with both quilts and blankets, beds and pillows, providing meat and drink, so that nothing was lacking, neither furnishings nor food, he straightway went to Emain Macha to meet Conchobar and the nobles of Ulster.

If fell upon a day when there was a gathering of the Ulstermen in Emain. He was at once made welcome, and was seated by the shoulder of Conchobar. Bricriu addressed himself to him as well as to the body of Ulstermen. "Come with me," said Bricriu, "to partake of a banquet with me."

"Gladly," rejoined Conchobar, "if that please the men of Ulster."

Fergus mac Roig and the nobles of Ulster made answer, "No; for if we go our dead will outnumber our living, when Bricriu has incensed us against each other."

"If ye come not, worse shall ye fare," said Bricriu.

"What then," asked Conchobar, "if the Ulstermen go not with thee?"

"I will stir up strife," said Bricrui, "between the kings, the leaders, the heroes of valour, and the yeomen, till they slay one another, man for man, if they come not to me to share my feast."

"That shall we not do to please thee," said Conchobar.

"I will stir up enmity between father and son so that it will come to mutual slaughter. If I do not succeed in doing so, I will make a quarrel between mother and daughter. If that does not succeed, I will set each of the Ulster women at variance, so that they come to deadly blows till their breasts become loathsome and putrid."

"Sure it is better to come," said Fergus.

"Do ye straightway take counsel with the chief Ulstermen," said Sencha son of Ailill.

"Unless we take counsel against this Bricriu, mischief will be the consequence," said Conchobar.

Thereupon all the Ulster nobles assembled in council. In discussing the matter Sencha counselled them thus: "Take hostages from Bricriu, since ye have to go with him, and set eight swordsmen about him so as to compel him to retire from the house as soon as he has laid out the feast."

Furbaide Ferbenn son of Conchobar brought Bricriu their reply and explained the whole matter.

"It is happily arranged," said Bricriu.

The men of Ulster straightway set out from Emain Macha, host, battalion, and company, under king, chieftain, and leader. Excellent and admirable the march of the brave and valiant heroes to the palace.

The hostages of the nobles had gone security on his behalf, and Bricriu accordingly considered how he should manage to set the Ulstermen at variance. His deliberation and self-scrutiny being ended, he betook himself to the presence of Loegaire the Triumphant son of Connad mac Iliach. "Hail now, Loegaire the Triumphant, thou mighty mallet of Breg, thou hot hammer of Meath, flame-red thunderbolt, thou victorious warrior of Ulster, what hinders the championship of Ulster being thine always?"

"If so I choose, it shall be mine," said Loegaire.

"Be thine the sovereignty of the nobles of Erin," said Bricriu, "if only thou act as I advise."

"I will indeed," said Loegaire.

"Sooth, if the Champion's Portion of my house be thine, the championship of Emain is thine forever. The Champion's Portion of my house is worth contesting, for it is not the portion of a fool's house," said Bricriu. "Belonging to it is a cauldron full of generous wine, with room enough for three of the valiant heroes of Ulster; furthermore a seven-year-old boar; nought has entered its mouth since it was little save fresh milk and fine meal in springtime, curds and sweet milk in summer, the kernel of nuts and wheat in autumn, beef and broth in winter; a cow-lord full seven-year-old; since it was a little calf neither heather nor twig-tops have passed its lips, nought but sweet milk and herbs, meadow-hay and corn. Add to this five-score cakes of wheat cooked in honey. Five-and-twenty bushels, that is what was supplied for these five-score cakes—four cakes from each bushel. Such is the champion's portion of my house. And since thou art the best hero among the men of Ulster, it is but just to give it to thee, and so I wish it. By the end of the day, when the feast is spread out, let thy charioteer get up, and it is to him the Champion's Portion will be given."

"Among them shall be dead men if it is not done so," said Loegaire. Bricriu laughed at that, for it pleased him well.

When he had done inciting Loegaire the Triumphant to enmity, Bricriu went to Conall the Victorious. "Hail to thee, Conall the Victorious! Thou art the hero of victories and of combats; great are the victories thou hast already scored over the heroes of Ulster. By the time the Ulstermen go into foreign bounds thou art three days and three nights in advance over many a ford; thou protectest their rear when returning so that an assailant may not spring past thee nor through thee nor over thee; what then should hinder the Champion's Portion of Emain being thine always?" Though great his treachery with regard to Loegaire, he showed twice as much with Conall the Victorious.

When he had satisfied himself with inciting Conall the Victorious to quarrel, he went to Cu Chulainn. "Hail to thee, Cu Chulainn! Thou victor of Breg, thou bright banner of the Liffey, darling of Emain, beloved of wives and of maidens, for thee today Cu Chulainn is no nickname, for thou art the champion of the Ulstermen. Thou wardest off their great feuds and forays; thou seekest justice for each man of them; thou attainest alone to what all the Ulstermen fail in; all the men of Ulster acknowledge thy bravery, thy valour, and thy achievements surpassing theirs. What meaneth therefore thy leaving of the Champion's Portion for someone else of the men of Ulster, since no one of the men of Erin is capable of contesting it against thee?"

"By the gods of my tribe," said Cu Chulainn, "his head shall he lose who comes to contest it with me." Thereafter Bricriu severed himself from them and followed the host as if no contention had been made among the heroes.

BRICRIU'S FEAST

Whereupon they entered Bricriu's stronghold, and each one occupied his couch therein, king, prince, noble, yeoman, and young hero. The half of the hall was set apart for Conchobar and his retinue of valiant Ulster heroes; the other half was reserved for the ladies of Ulster attending on Mugan daughter of Eochaid Fedlech, wife of Conchobar. Those who attended on Conchobar were the chief Ulster warriors with the body of youths and entertainers.

While the feast was being prepared for them, the musicians and players performed. The moment Bricriu spread the feast with its savouries he was ordered by the hostages to leave the hall. They straightway got up with their drawn swords in their hands to expel him. Whereupon Bricriu and his wife went out to the balcony. As he arrived at the threshold of the stronghold he called out, "That Champion's Portion, such as it is, is not the portion of a fool's house; do ye give it to the Ulster hero ye prefer for valour." And then he left them.

Then the waiters got up to serve the food. The charioteer of Loegaire the Triumphant, that is, Sedlang mac Riangabra, rose up and said to the distributors: "Give to Loegaire the Triumphant the Champion's Portion which is by you, for he alone is entitled to it before the other young heroes of Ulster."

Then Id mac Riangabra, charioteer to Conall the Victorious, got up and spoke to like effect. And Loeg mac Riangabra spoke as follows: "Bring it to Cu Chulainn; it is no disgrace for all the Ulstermen to give it to him; it is he that is most valiant among you."

"That's not true," said Conall the Victorious and Loegaire the Triumphant.

They got up upon the floor and donned their shields and seized their swords. They hewed at one another until half the hall was an atmosphere of fire with the clash of sword- and spear-edge, the other half one white sheet from the enamel of the shields. Great alarm got hold upon the stronghold; the valiant heroes shook; Conchobar himself and Fergus mac Roig were furious on seeing the injury and injustice of two men attacking one, namely Conall the Victorious and Loegaire the Triumphant attacking Cu Chulainn. There was no one among the Ulstermen who dared separate them until Sencha spoke to Conchobar: "Part the men," said he.

Thereupon Conchobar and Fergus intervened; the combatants immediately let drop their hands to their sides. "Execute my wish," said Sencha.

"Your will shall be obeyed," they responded.

"My wish, then," said Sencha, "is tonight to divide the Champion's Portion there among all the host, and after that to decide with reference to it according to the will of Ailill mac Matach, for it is accounted unlucky among the Ulstermen to close this assembly unless the matter be adjudged in Cruachan."

The feasting was then resumed; they made a circle about the fire and got drunken and merry.

Bricriu, however, and his queen were in their balcony. From his couch the condition of the palace was visible to him, and how things were going on. He exercised his mind as to how he should contrive to get the women to quarrel as he had the men. When Bricriu had done searching his mind, it just chanced as he could have wished that Fedelm Fresh-Heart came from the stronghold with fifty women in her train, in jovial mood. Bricriu observed her coming past him. "Hail to thee tonight, wife of Loegaire the Triumphant! Fedelm Fresh-Heart is no nickname for thee with respect to thy excellence of form and wisdom and of lineage. Conchobar, king of a province of Erin, is thy father, Loegaire the Triumphant thy husband; I should deem it but small honour to thee that any of the Ulster women should take precedence of thee in entering the banqueting-hall; only at thy heel should all the Ulster women tread. If thou comest first into the hall tonight, the sovereignty of the queenship shalt thou enjoy over all the ladies of Ulster for ever." Fedelm at that takes a leap over three ridges from the hall.

Thereafter came Lendabair daughter of Eogan mac Durthacht, wife of Conall the Victorious. Bricriu addressed her, saying, "Hail to thee, Lendabair! For thee that is no nickname; thou art the darling and pet of all mankind on account of thy splendour and of thy lustre. As far as thy husband hath surpassed all the heroes of mankind in valour and in comeliness, so far hast thou distinguished thyself above the women of Ulster." Though great the deceit he applied in the case of Fedelm, he applied twice as much in the case of Lendabair.

Then Emer came out with half a hundred women in her train. "Greeting and hail to thee, Emer daughter of Forgall Monach, wife of the best man in Erin! Emer of the Fair Hair is no nickname for thee; Erin's kings and princes contend for thee in jealous rivalry. As the sun surpasseth the stars of heaven, so far dost thou outshine the women of the whole world in form and shape and lineage, in youth and beauty and elegance, in good name and wisdom and address." Though great his deceit in the case of the other ladies, in that of Emer he used thrice as much.

The three companies thereupon went out until they met at a spot three ridges from the hall. None of them knew that Bricriu had incited them one against the other. To the hall they straightway return. Even and easy and graceful their carriage on the first ridge; scarcely did one of them raise one foot before the other.

But on the ridge following, their steps were shorter and quicker. On the ridge next to the house it was with difficulty each kept up with the other; so they raised their robes to the rounds of their hips to complete the attempt to go first into the hall. For what Bricriu had said to each of them with regard to the other was that whosoever entered first should be queen of the whole province. The amount of confusion then occasioned by the competition was as it were the noise of fifty chariots approaching. The whole stronghold shook and the warriors sprang to their arms and tried to kill one another within.

"Stay," cried Sencha; "they are not enemies who have come; it is Bricriu who has set to quarrelling the women who have gone out. By the gods of my tribe, unless the door be closed against them, our dead will outnumber our living." Thereupon the door-keepers closed the doors. Emer, the daughter of Forgall Monach, wife of Cu Chulainn, by reason of her speed, outran the others and put her back against the door, and straightway called upon the door-keepers before the other ladies came, so that the men within got up, each of them to open the door for his own wife that she might be the first to come in. "Bad outlook tonight," said Conchobar. He struck the silver sceptre that was in his hand against the bronze pillar of the couch, and the company sat down.

"Stay," said Sencha; "it is not a warfare of arms that shall be held here; it will be a warfare of words." Each woman went out under the protection of her husband, and then followed the "Ulster Women's War of Words."[1]

Thus did the men in the hall behave on hearing the

---

[1] *The series of rhetorical speeches in which the women enumerate the virtues of their respective husbands is omitted.*

laudatory addresses of the women—Loegaire and Conall each sprang into his hero's light, and broke a stave of the palace at a like level with themselves, so that in this way their wives came in. Cu Chulainn upheaved the palace just over against his bed, till the stars of heaven were to be seen from underneath the wattle. By that opening came his own wife with half a hundred of her attendants in her train, as also a hundred in waiting upon the other twain. Other ladies could not be compared with Emer, while no one at all was to be likened to Emer's husband. Thereupon Cu Chulainn let the palace down until seven feet of the wattle entered the ground; the whole stronghold shook, and Bricriu's balcony was laid flat to the earth in such a way that Bricriu and his queen toppled down until they fell into the ditch in the middle of the courtyard among the dogs. "Woe is me," cried Bricriu, as he hastily got up, "enemies have come into the palace." He took a turn round and saw how it was lop-sided and inclined entirely to one side. He wrung his hands, then betook himself within, so bespattered that none of the Ulstermen could recognize him.

Then from the floor of the house Bricriu made speech: "Alas! that I have prepared you a feast, O Ulstermen. My house is more to me than all my other possessions. Upon you, therefore, it is taboo to drink, to eat, or to sleep until you leave my house as you found it upon your arrival."

Thereupon the valiant Ulstermen went out of the house and tried to tug it, but they did not raise it so much that even the wind could pass between it and the earth. That matter was a difficulty for the Ulstermen. "I have no suggestion for you," said Sencha, "except that you entreat of him who left it lop-sided to set it upright."

Whereupon the men of Ulster told Cu Chulainn to

restore the house to its upright position, and Bricriu made a speech: "O King of the heroes of Erin, if thou set it not straight and erect, none in the world can do so." All the Ulstermen then entreated Cu Chulainn to solve the difficulty. That the banqueters might not be lacking for food or for ale, Cu Chulainn got up and tried to lift the house at a tug and failed. A distortion thereupon got hold of him, whilst a drop of blood was at the root of each single hair, and he drew his hair into his head, so that, looked on from above, his dark-yellow curls seemed as if they had been shorn with scissors, and taking upon himself the motion of a millstone he strained himself until a warrior's foot could find room between each pair of ribs.

His natural resources and fiery vigour returned to him, and he then heaved the house aloft and set it so that it reached its former level. Thereafter the consumption of the feast was pleasant to them, with the kings and the chieftains on the one side round about Conchobar the illustrious, the noble high-king of Ulster.

Again it was their hap to quarrel about the Champion's Portion. Conchobar with the nobles of Ulster interposed with the view of judging between the heroes. "Go to Cu Roi mac Dairi, the man who will undertake to intervene," said Conchobar.

"I accept that," said Cu Chulainn.

"I agree," said Loegaire.

"Let us go, then," said Conall the Victorious.

"Let horses be brought and thy chariot yoked, O Conall," said Cu Chulainn.

"Woe is me!" cried Conall.

"Every one," said Cu Chulainn, "knows the clumsiness of thy horses and the unsteadiness of thy going and thy turnout; thy chariot's movement is most heavy;

BRICRIU'S FEAST

each of the two wheels raises turf every way thy big chariot careers, so that for the space of a year there is a well-marked track easily recognized by the warriors of Ulster."

"Dost thou hear that, Loegaire?" said Conall.

"Woe is me!" said Loegaire. "But I am not to blame or reproach. I am nimble at crossing fords, and more, to breast the storm of spears, out-stripping the warriors of Ulster. Put not on me the pretence of kings and champions against single chariots in strait and difficult places, in woods and on confines, until the champion of a single chariot tries not to career before me."

Thereupon Loegaire had his chariot yoked and he leaped into it. He drove over the Plain-of-the-Two-Forks, of the Gap-of-the-Watch, over the Ford of Carpat Fergus, over the Ford of the Morrigu, to the Rowan Meadow of the Two Oxen in the Fews of Armagh, by the Meeting of the Four Ways past Dundalk, across Mag Slicech, westwards to the slope of Breg. A dim, dark, heavy mist overtook him, confusing him in such a way that it was impossible for him to fare farther. "Let us stay here," said Loegaire to his charioteer, "until the mist clears up." Loegaire alighted from his chariot, and his gillie put the horses into the meadow that was near at hand.

While there, the gillie saw a huge giant approaching him. Not beautiful his appearance: broad of shoulder and fat of mouth, with sack eyes and a bristly face; ugly, wrinkled, with bushy eyebrows; hideous and horrible and strong; stubborn and violent and haughty; fat and puffing; with big sinews and strong forearms; bold, audacious, and uncouth. A shorn black patch of hair on him, a dun covering about him, a tunic over it to the ball of his rump; on his feet old tattered brogues, on his back a ponderous club like the wheel-shaft of a mill.

"Whose horses are these, gillie?" he asked, as he gazed furiously at him.

"The horses of Loegaire the Triumphant."

"Yes! a fine fellow is he!" And as he thus spoke he brought down his club on the gillie and gave him a blow from top to toe.

The gillie gave a cry, whereupon Loegaire came up. "What is this you are doing to the lad?" asked Loegaire.

"It is by way of penalty for damage to the meadow," said the giant.

"I will come myself, then," said Loegaire; and they struggled together until Loegaire fled to Emain leaving his horses and gillie and arms.

Not long thereafter Conall the Victorious took the same way and arrived at the plain where the druidical mist overtook Loegaire. The like hideous black, dark cloud overtook Conall the Victorious, so that he was unable to see either heaven or earth. Conall thereupon leapt out and the gillie unharnessed the horses in the same meadow. Not long thereafter he saw the same giant coming towards him. He asked him whose servant he was.

"I am the servant of Conall the Victorious," he said.

"A good man he!" said the giant, and he raised his hands and gave the gillie a blow from top to toe. The fellow yelled. Then came Conall. He and the giant came to close quarters. Stronger were the wrestling turns of the giant, and Conall fled, as Loegaire had done, having left behind his charioteer and his horses, and came to Emain.

Cu Chulainn then went by the same way till he came to the same place. The like dark mist overtook him as fell upon the two preceding. Cu Chulainn sprang down, and Loeg brought the horses into the meadow. He had not long to wait until he saw the same man coming towards him. The giant asked him whose servant he was.

"Servant to Cu Chulainn."

"A good man he!" said the giant, plying him with the club.

Loeg yelled. Then Cu Chulainn arrived. He and the giant came to close quarters and either rained blows upon the other. The giant was worsted. He forfeited horses and charioteer, and Cu Chulainn brought along with him his fellows' horses, charioteers, and accoutrements, till he reached Emain in triumph.

"Thine is the Champion's Portion," said Bricriu to Cu Chulainn, and to the others, "well I know from your deeds that you are in no way on a par with Cu Chulainn."

"Not true, Bricriu," said they, "for we know it is one of his friends from the fairy world that came to him to play us mischief and coerce us with regard to the championship. We shall not forego our claim on that account."

The men of Ulster, with Conchobar and Fergus, failed to effect a settlement. And the conclusion the nobles in Conchobar's following arrived at was, to accompany the heroes and have the difficulty adjudged at the abode of Ailill mac Matach and of Medb of Cruachan Ai with reference to the Champion's Portion and the mutual rivalry of the women. Fine and lovely and majestic the march of the Ulstermen to Cruachan. Cu Chulainn, however, remained behind the host entertaining the Ulster ladies, performing nine feats with apples and nine with knives, in such wise that one did not interfere with the other.

Loeg mac Riangabra then went to speak to him in the

feat-stead and said: "You sorry simpleton, your valour and bravery have passed away, the Champion's Portion has gone from you; the Ulstermen have reached Cruachan long since."

"Indeed we had not at all perceived it, my Loeg. Yoke us the chariot, then," said Cu Chulainn. Loeg accordingly yoked it and off they started. By that time the Ulstermen had reached Mag Breg, Cu Chulainn, having been incited by his charioteer, travelled with such speed from Dun Rudraige, the Grey of Macha and the Black Sainglenn racing with his chariot across the whole province of Conchobar, across Sliab Fuait and across Mag Breg, that the third chariot arrived first in Cruachan.

In virtue then of the swiftness and impetuous speed with which all the valiant Ulstermen reached Cruachan under the lead of Conchobar and the body of chiefs, a great shaking seized Cruachan, till the war-arms fell from the walls to the ground, seizing likewise the entire host of the stronghold, till the men in the royal keep were like rushes in a stream. Medb thereupon spoke: "Since the day I took up home in Cruachan I have never heard thunder, there being no clouds." Thereupon Finnabair, daughter of Ailill and Medb, went to the balcony over the high porch of the stronghold. "Mother dear," said she, "I see a chariot coming along the plain."

"Describe it," said Medb, "its form, appearance, and style; the colour of the horses; how the hero looks, and how the chariot courses."[1]

---

[1] Here follows a conventional description in highly embroidered rhetoric of the chariots and personal appearance of Loegaire and Conall. This, as well as the description of Cu Chulainn's chariot, is omitted. The narrative is resumed with the description of Cu Chulainn himself, long famous with Gaelic literary men and professional story-tellers.

"In the chariot a dark, melancholy man, comeliest of the men of Erin. Around him a soft crimson pleasing tunic fastened across the breast, where it stands open, with a salmon-brooch of inlaid gold, against which his bosom heaves, beating in full strokes. A long-sleeved linen kirtle with a white hood, embroidered red with flaming gold. Set in each of his eyes eight red dragon gem-stones. His two cheeks blue-white and blood-red. He emits sparks of fire and burning breath, with a ray of love in his look. A shower of pearls, it seems, has fallen into his mouth. Each of his two eyebrows as black as the side of a black spit. On his two thighs rests a golden-hilted sword and fastened to the copper frame of the chariot is a blood-red spear with a sharp mettlesome blade on a shaft of wood well fitted to his hand. Over both his shoulders a crimson shield with a rim of silver, chased with figures of animals in gold. He leaps the hero's salmon-leap into the air and does many like swift feats besides. Such is the chief of a chariot-royal. Before him in that chariot is a charioteer, a very slender, tall, much-freckled man. On his head very curled bright-red hair, with a fillet of bronze upon his brow which prevents the hair from falling over his face. On both sides of his head patins of gold confine the hair. A shoulder-mantle about him with sleeves opening at the two elbows, and in his hand a goad of red gold with which he guides the horses.

"Truly, it is a drop before a shower; we recognize the man from his description," said Medb.

An ocean fury, a whale that rages, a fragment of flame and fire;
A bear majestic, a grandly moving billow,
  A beast in maddening anger:
In the crash of glorious battle
  Through the hostile foe he leaps,
  His shout the fury of doom;

A terrible bear, he is death to the herd of cattle:
Feat upon feat, head upon head he piles:
Praise ye the hearty one, he who is completely victor.
As fresh malt is ground in the mill shall we be ground by
　　Cu Chulainn.

"By the god of my people," said Medb, "I swear if it be in fury Cu Chulainn comes to us, like as a mill of ten spokes grinds very hard malt, so he alone will grind us into mould and gravel, should the whole province attend on us in Cruachan, unless his fury and violence are subdued."

"How do they come this time?" said Medb.

> Wrist to wrist and palm to palm,
> 　　Tunic to tunic they advance,
> Shield to shield and frame to frame,
> 　　A shoulder-to-shoulder band,
> Wood to wood and car to car,
> 　　This they all are, fond mother.
>
> As thunder when crashing on the roof,
> 　　With speed the chargers dash,
> As heavy seas which storms are shaking,
> 　　The earth in turn they pound;
> Anon it vibrates as they strike,
> Their strength and weight are like and like.
> 　　　Their name is noble,
> 　　　　No ill fame!

Then Medb made speech:

"Women to meet them, and many, half-naked,
Full-breasted and bare and beautiful, numerous;
Bring vats of cold water where wanting, beds ready for rest,
Fine food bring forth, and not scanty, but excellent,
Strong ale and sound and well malted, warriors' keep;
Let the gates of the stronghold be set open, open the enclosure.
The battalion that is rushing on won't kill us, I hope."

Thereupon Medb went out by the high door of the palace into the court, thrice fifty maidens in her train, with three vats of cold water for the three valiant heroes in front of the hosts, in order to alleviate their heat. Choice was straightway given them so as to ascertain whether a house apiece should be allotted them or one house among the three. "To each a house apart," said Cu Chulainn. Thereafter such as they preferred of the thrice fifty girls were brought into the house, fitted up with beds of surprising magnificence. Finnabair in preference to any other was brought by Cu Chulainn into the apartment where he himself was. On the arrival of the Ulstermen, Ailill and Medb with their whole household went and bade them welcome. "We are pleased," said Sencha son of Ailill, responding.

Thereupon the Ulstermen came into the stronghold, and the palace is left to them as recounted, viz., seven circles and seven compartments from fire to partition, with bronze frontings and carvings of red yew. Three stripes of bronze in the arching of the house, which was of oak, with a covering of shingles. It had twelve windows with glass in the openings. The couch of Ailill and Medb in the centre of the house, with silver frontings and stripes of bronze round it, with a silver wand by the partition facing Ailill, that would reach the mid hips of the house so as to check the inmates unceasingly. The Ulster heroes went round from one door of the palace to the other, and the musicians played while the guests were being prepared for. Such was the spaciousness of the house that it had room for the hosts of valiant heroes of the whole province in the retinue of Conchobar. Moreover, Conchobar and Fergus mac Roig were in Ailill's apartment with nine valiant Ulster heroes besides. Great feasts were then prepared for them and they were there until the end of three days and three nights.

Thereafter Ailill inquired of Conchobar with his Ulster retinue what was the purpose of his visit. Sencha related the matter on account of which they had come, viz., the three heroes' rivalry as to the Champion's Portion, and the ladies' rivalry as to precedence at feasts—"They could not stand being judged anywhere else than here by thee." At that Ailill was silent and was not in a happy mood. "Indeed," said he, "it is not to me this decision should be given as to the Champion's Portion, unless it be done from hatred."

"There is really no better judge," said Sencha.

"Well," said Ailill, "I require time to consider. For that then three days and three nights suffice for me," said Ailill.

"That would not forfeit friendship," answered Sencha.

The Ulstermen straightway bade farewell; being satisfied, they left their blessing with Ailill and Medb and their curse with Bricriu, for it was he who had incited them to strife. They then departed from the territory of Medb, having left Loegaire and Conall and Cu Chulainn to be judged by Ailill. The like supper as before was given to each of the heroes every night.

One night as their portion was assigned to them, three cats from the cave of Cruachan were let loose to attack them, that is, three beasts of magic. Conall and Loegaire made for the rafters, leaving their food with the beasts. In that wise they slept until the morrow. Cu Chulainn fled not from the beast which was attacking him. When it stretched its neck out for eating, Cu Chulainn gave a blow with his sword on the beast's head, but the blade glided off as it were from stone. Then the cat set itself down. Under the circumstances Cu Chulainn neither ate nor slept, but he kept his place. As soon as it was early morning the cats were gone. In such condition were the three heroes seen on the morrow.

"Does not that trial suffice for adjudging you?" asked Ailill.

"By no means," said Conall and Loegaire, "it is not against beasts we are striving but against men."

Ailill, having gone to his chamber, set his back against the wall. He was disquieted in mind, for he took the difficulty that faced him to be fraught with danger. He neither ate nor slept till the end of three days and three nights. "Coward!" Medb then called him; "if you do not decide, I will."

"Difficult for me to judge them," Ailill said; "it is a misfortune for one to have to do it."

"There is no difficulty," said Medb, "for Loegaire and Conall Cernach are as different as bronze and white bronze; and Conall Cernach and Cu Chulainn are as different as white bronze and red gold."

It was then, after she had pondered her advice, that Loegaire the Triumphant was summoned to Medb. "Welcome, O Loegaire the Triumphant," said she; "it is meet to give thee the Champion's Portion. We assign to thee the sovereignty of the heroes of Erin from this time forth, and the Champion's Portion, and a cup of bronze with a bird chased in silver on its bottom. In preference to every one else, take it with thee as a token of award. No one else is to see it until, at the day's end, thou hast come to the Red Branch of Conchobar. On the Champion's Portion being exhibited among you, then shalt thou bring forth thy cup in the presence of all the Ulster nobles. Moreover, the Champion's Portion is therein. None of the valiant Ulster heroes will dispute it further with thee. For the thing thou art to take away with thee shall be a token of genuineness in the estimation of all the Ulstermen." Thereupon the cup with its full of luscious wine was given to Loegaire the Triumphant. On the floor of the palace he swallowed the contents at a draught. "Now you have the feast of a champion," said Medb; "I wish you may enjoy it a hundred years at the head of all Ulster."

Loegaire thereupon bade farewell. Then Conall Cernach was likewise summoned to the royal presence. "Welcome," said Medb, "O Conall Cernach; proper it is to give thee the Champion's Portion, with a cup of white bronze besides, having a bird on the bottom of it chased in gold." Thereafter the cup was given to Conall with its full of luscious wine.

Conall bade farewell. A herald was then sent to fetch Cu Chulainn. "Come to speak with the king and queen," said the messenger. Cu Chulainn at the time was busy playing chess with Loeg mac Riangabra, his own charioteer. "No mocking!" he said; "you might try your lies on some other fool." He hurled one of the chessmen, and it pierced the centre of the herald's brain. He got his death blow therefrom, and fell between Ailill and Medb.

"Woe is me," said Medb; "sorely doth Cu Chulainn work on us his fury when his fit of rage is upon him." Whereupon Medb got up and came to Cu Chulainn and put her two arms round his neck.

"Try a lie upon another," said Cu Chulainn.

"Glorious son of the Ulstermen and flame of the heroes of Erin, it is no lie that is to our liking where thou art concerned. Were all Erin's heroes to come, to thee by preference would we grant the quest, for, in regard to fame, bravery, and valour, distinction, youth, and glory, the men of Erin acknowledge thy superiority."

Cu Chulainn got up. He accompanied Medb into the palace, and Ailill bade him a warm welcome. A cup of

BRICRIU'S FEAST

gold was given him full of luscious wine, and having on the bottom of it birds chased in precious stone. With it, in preference to every one else there was given him a lump, as big as his two eyes, of dragon-stone. "Now you have the feast of a champion," said Medb. "I wish you may enjoy it a hundred years at the head of all the Ulster heroes." "Moreover, it is our verdict," said Ailill and Medb, "inasmuch as thou art not to be compared with the Ulster warriors, neither is thy wife to be compared with their women. Nor is it too much, we think, that she should always precede all the Ulster ladies when entering the Mead-Hall." At that Cu Chulainn drank at one draught the full of the cup, and then bade farewell to the king, queen, and whole household.

Thereafter he followed his charioteer. "My plan," said Medb to Ailill, "is to keep those three heroes with us again tonight, and to test them further."

"Do as thou deemest right," said Ailill. The men were then detained and brought to Cruachan and their horses unyoked.

Their choice of food was given them for their horses. Conall and Loegaire told them to give oats two years old to theirs. But Cu Chulainn chose barley grains for his. They slept there that night. The women were apportioned among them. Finnabair, with a train of fifty damsels, was brought to the place of Cu Chulainn. Sadb the Eloquent, another daughter of Ailill and Medb, with fifty maids in attendance was ushered into the presence of Conall Cernach. Concend, daughter of Cet mac Matach, with fifty damsels along with her, was brought into the presence of Loegaire the Triumphant. Moreover, Medb herself was accustomed to visit the couch of Cu Chulainn. They slept there that night.

On the morrow they arose early in the morning and went to the house where the youths were performing the wheel-feat. Then Loegaire seized the wheel until it reached half up the sidewall. Upon that the youths laughed and cheered him. It was in reality a jeer, but it seemed to Loegaire a shout of applause. Conall then took the wheel. It was on the ground. He tossed it as high as the ridge-pole of the hall. The youths raised a shout at that. It seemed to Conall that it was a shout of applause and victory. To the youths it was a shout of scorn. Then Cu Chulainn took the wheel—it was in mid-air he caught it. He hurled it aloft till it cast the ridge-pole from off the hall; the wheel went a man's cubit into the ground in the outside enclosure. The youths raised a shout of applause and triumph in Cu Chulainn's case. It seemed to Cu Chulainn, however, it was a laugh of scorn and ridicule they then gave vent to.

Cu Chulainn then sought out the womenfolk and took thrice fifty needles from them. These he tossed up one after the other. Each needle went into the eye of another, till in that wise they were joined together. He returned to the women, and gave each her own needle into her own hand. The young warriors praised Cu Chulainn. Whereupon they bade farewell to the king, the queen, and household as well.

On the arrival of Loegaire, Conall, and Cu Chulainn at Emain Macha, the heroes of Ulster ceased their discussions and their babblings and fell to eating and enjoying themselves. It was Sualtam mac Roig, father of Cu Chulainn himself, who that night attended upon the Ulstermen. Moreover, Conchobar's ladder-vat was filled for them. Their portion having been brought into their presence, the waiters began to serve, but at the outset they withheld the Champion's Portion from distribution. "Why not give the Champion's Portion," said Dubtach Chafertongue, "to some one of the heroes; those three have not returned from the King of Cruachan, bringing no sure token with them, whereby the Champion's Portion may be assigned to one of them."

Thereupon Loegaire the Triumphant got up and lifted on high the bronze cup having the silver bird chased on the bottom. "The Champion's Portion is mine," said he, "and none may contest it with me."

"It is not," said Conall Cernach. "Not alike are the tokens we brought off with us. Yours is a cup of bronze, whereas mine is a cup of white bronze. From the difference between them the Champion's Portion clearly belongs to me."

"It belongs to neither of you," said Cu Chulainn as he got up and spoke. "You have brought no token that procures you the Champion's Portion. Yet the king and queen whom you visited were loath in the thick of distress to intensify the strife. But no less than your deserts have you received at their hands. The Champion's Portion remains with me, seeing I have brought a token distinguished above the rest."

He then lifted on high a cup of red gold having a bird chased on the bottom of it in precious dragonstone, the size of his two eyes. All the Ulster nobles in the train of Conchobar mac Nessa saw it. "Therefore it is I," he said, "who deserve the Champion's Portion, provided I have fair play."

"To thee we all award it," said Conchobar and Fergus and the Ulster nobles as well. "By the verdict of Ailill and Medb the Champion's Portion is yours." [1]

"I swear by my people's god," said Loegaire the Triumphant and Conall the Victorious, "that the cup you

---

[1] *At this point there is introduced a short episode in which the three competitors go to be tested by a strange personage called Ercol. The scene then shifts to the banqueting hall of Conchobar.*

have brought is purchased. Of the jewels and the treasures in your possession you have given to Ailill and Medb for it in order that a defeat might not be on record against you, and that the Champion's Portion might be given to no one else by preference. By my people's god, that judgment shall not stand; the Champion's Portion shall not be yours."

They then sprang up one after the other, their swords drawn. Straightway Conchobar and Fergus intervened, whereupon they let down their hands and sheathed their swords.

"Hold!" said Sencha, "do as I bid."

"We will," they said.[1]

The Ulstermen advised them to go to Cu Roi for judgment. To that too they agreed.

On the morning of the morrow the three heroes—Cu Chulainn, Conall, and Loegaire—set off to Cu Roi's stronghold (Cathair Con Roi). They unyoked their chariots at the gate of the hold, then entered the court. Whereupon Blathnat, Minn's daughter, wife of Cu Roi mac Dairi, bade them a warm welcome. That night on their arrival Cu Roi was not at home, but knowing they would come, he counselled his wife regarding the heroes until he should return from his Eastern expedition into Scythia. From the age of seven years, when he took up arms, until his death, Cu Roi had not reddened his sword in Erin, nor ever had the food of Erin passed his lips. Nor could Erin retain him for his haughtiness, renown, and rank, overbearing fury, strength, and gal-

---

[1] *The heroes are then sent to Budi mac m-Bain [Yellow son of Fair], and by him to Uath mac Imomain [Terror son of Great Fear]. The episode of Uath consists of a short version of the beheading incident which is recited in more detail later in the part called The Champion's Covenant [see below].*

lantry. His wife acted according to his wish in the matter of bathing and washing, providing them with refreshing drinks and beds most excellent. And they liked it well.

When bedtime was come, she told them that each was to take his night watching the fort until Cu Roi should return. "And, moreover, thus said Cu Roi, that you take your turn watching according to seniority." In whatsoever quarter of the globe Cu Roi should happen to be, every night he chanted a spell over his stronghold, so that the fort revolved as swiftly as a millstone. The entrance was never to be found after sunset.

The first night, Loegaire the Triumphant took the watch, inasmuch as he was the eldest of the three. As he kept watch into the later part of the night, he saw a giant approaching him as far as his eyes could see from the sea westwards. Exceedingly huge and ugly and horrible Loegaire thought him, for, in height, it seemed to him, he reached into the sky, and the reflection of the sea was visible between his legs. Thus did he come, his hands full of stripped oaks, each of which would form a burden for a wagon-team of six, at whose root not a stroke had been repeated after a single sword-stroke. One of the stakes he cast at Loegaire, who let it pass him. Twice or thrice he repeated it, but the stroke reached neither the skin nor the shield of Loegaire. Then Loegaire hurled a spear at him but it did not hit him.

The giant stretched his hand towards Loegaire. Such was its length that it reached across the three ridges that were between them as they were throwing at each other, and thus in his grasp the giant seized him. Though Loegaire was big and imposing, he fitted like a year-old child into the clutch of his opponent, who then ground him between his two palms as a chessman is turned in a groove. In that state, half-dead, the giant tossed him out over the fort, so that he fell into the mire of the ditch at the gate. The fort had no opening there, and the other men and inmates of the hold thought Loegaire had leapt outside over the fort, as a challenge for the other men to do likewise.

There they were until the day's end. When the night-watch began, Conall went out as sentry, for he was older than Cu Chulainn. Everything occurred as it did to Loegaire the first night.

The third night Cu Chulainn went on watch. That night the three Greys of Sescind Uarbeil, the three Ox-feeders of Breg, and the three sons of Big-fist the Siren met by appointment to plunder the stronghold. This too was the night of which it was foretold that the Spirit of the Lake by the fort would devour the whole population of the hold, man and beast.

Cu Chulainn, while watching through the night, had many uneasy forebodings. When midnight came he heard a terrific noise drawing near to him. "Holloa, holloa," Cu Chulainn shouted, "who is there? If friends they be, let them not stir; if foes, let them flee." Then they raised a terrific shout at him. Whereupon Cu Chulainn sprang upon them, so that the nine of them fell dead to the earth. He heaped their heads in disorder into the seat of watching and resumed his post. Another nine shouted at him. In like manner he killed three nines, making one cairn of them, heads and accoutrements.

While he was there far on into the night, tired and sad and weary, he heard the rising of the lake on high as if it were the booming of a very heavy sea. However deep his dejection, he could not resist going to see what caused the great noise he heard. He then perceived the upheaving monster, and it seemed to him to be thirty cubits in curvature above the loch. It raised itself on high into the air and sprang towards the fort, opening its mouth so that one of the halls could go into its gullet.

Then Cu Chulainn called to mind his swooping feat, sprang on high, and was as swift as a winnowing riddle right round the monster. He entwined his two arms about its neck, stretched his hand into its gullet, tore out the monster's heart, and cast it from him on the ground. Then the beast fell from the air and rested on the earth, after having sustained a blow on the shoulder. Cu Chulainn then plied it with his sword, hacked it to bits, and took the head with him into the sentry-seat along with the other heap of skulls.

While there, depressed and miserable in the morning dawn, he saw the giant approaching him westwards from the sea. "Bad night," says he.

"It will be worse for thee, thou oaf," said Cu Chulainn. Then the giant cast one of the branches at Cu Chulainn, who let it pass him. He repeated it twice or thrice, but it reached neither the skin nor the shield of Cu Chulainn. Cu Chulainn then hurled his spear at the giant, but it did not reach him. Whereupon the giant stretched out his hand towards Cu Chulainn to grip him as he had the others. Cu Chulainn leapt the hero's salmon-leap and called to mind his swooping feat with his sword drawn over the giant's head. As swift as a hare he was, and in mid-air circling round the giant, until he made a water-wheel of him.

"Life for life, O Cu Chulainn," he said.

"Give me my three wishes," said Cu Chulainn.

"Thou shalt have them as they come at a breath," he said.

The sovereignty of Erin's heroes be henceforth mine,
The Champion's Portion without dispute,
The precedence to my wife over the Ulster ladies for ever.

"It shall be thine," he said at once. Then he who had been talking with Cu Chulainn vanished, he knew not whither.

Then Cu Chulainn mused to himself as to the leap his fellows had leapt over the fort, for their leap was big and broad and high. Moreover, it seemed to him that it was by leaping that the valiant heroes had gone over it. He tried it twice and failed. "Alas!" said Cu Chulainn, "my exertions for the Champion's Portion have exhausted me, and now I lose it through not being able to take the leap the others took." As thus he mused, he assayed the following feats: he would spring backwards in mid-air a shot's distance from the fort, and then he would rebound from there until his forehead struck the fort. Then he would spring on high until all that was within the fort was visible to him, and again he would sink up to his knees in the earth owing to the pressure of his vehemence and violence. At another time he would not take the dew from off the tip of the grass by reason of his buoyancy of mood, vehemence of nature, and heroic valour. What with the fit and fury that raged upon him he stepped over the fort outside and alighted at the door of the hall. His two footprints are in the flag on the floor of the hold at the spot where the royal entrance was. Thereafter he entered the house and heaved a sigh.

Then Minn's daughter, Blathnat, wife of Cu Roi, spoke: "Truly not the sigh of one dishonoured, but a victor's sigh of triumph." The daughter of the king of the Isle of the Men of Falga (*i.e.*, Blathnat) knew full well of Cu Chulainn's evil plight that night. They were not long there when they beheld Cu Roi coming towards them, carrying into the house the standard of the three nines slain by Cu Chulainn, along with their heads and that of the monster. He put the heads from off his breast

BRICRIU'S FEAST

on to the floor of the stead, and spoke: "The gillie whose one night's trophies are these is a fit lad to watch the king's stronghold forever. The Champion's Portion, over which you have fallen out with the gallant youths of Erin, truly belongs to Cu Chulainn. The bravest of them, were he here, could not match him in number of trophies." Cu Roi's verdict upon them was:

The Champion's Portion to be Cu Chulainn's,
With the sovereignty of valour over all the Gael,
And to his wife the precedence on entering the Mead-Hall before all the ladies of Ulster.

And the value of seven bondmaidens in gold and silver Cu Roi gave to Cu Chulainn in reward for his one night's performance.

The three heroes of Ulster straightway bade Cu Roi farewell and kept on until they were seated in Emain Macha before the day closed. When the waiters came to deal and divide, they took the Champion's Portion with its share of ale out of the distribution that they might have it apart. "Indeed, sure are we," said Dubtach Chafertongue, "you think not tonight of contending for the Champion's Portion. Perhaps the man you sought out has undertaken to pass judgment."

Whereupon said the other folk to Cu Chulainn, "The Champion's Portion was not assigned to one of you in preference to the other. As to Cu Roi's judgment upon these three, not a whit did he concede to Cu Chulainn upon their arriving at Emain." Cu Chulainn then declared that he by no means coveted the winning of it; for the loss thence resulting to the winner would be on a par with the profit got from it. The championship was therefore not fully assigned until the advent of the Champion's Covenant in Emain, which follows.

One day as the Ulstermen were in Emain Macha, fatigued after the gathering and the games, Conchobar and Fergus mac Roig, with the Ulster nobles as well, proceeded from the playing field outside and seated themselves in the Red Branch of Conchobar. Neither Cu Chulainn nor Conall the Victorious nor Loegaire the Triumphant were there that night. But the hosts of Ulster's heroes were there. As they were seated, it being eventide, and the day drawing toward the close, they saw a big uncouth fellow of exceeding ugliness drawing nigh them into the hall. To them it seemed as if none of the Ulstermen would reach half his height. Horrible and ugly was the carle's disguise. Next his skin he wore an old hide with a dark dun mantle around him, and over him a great spreading club-tree branch the size of a winter-shed under which thirty bullocks could find shelter. Ravenous yellow eyes he had, protruding from his head, each of the twain the size of an ox-vat. Each finger was as thick as a person's wrist. In his left hand he carried a stock, a burden for twenty yoke of oxen. In his right hand was an axe weighing thrice fifty glowing molten masses of metal. Its handle would require a yoke of six to move it. Its sharpness such that it would lop off hairs, the wind blowing them against its edge.

In that guise he went and stood by the fork-beam beside the fire. "Is the hall lacking in room for you," said Dubtach Chafertongue to the uncouth clodhopper (*bachlach*), "that ye find no other place than by the fork-beam, unless ye wish to be an illumination to the house?—only sooner will a blaze be to the house than brightness to the household."

"Whatever property may be mine, you will agree that no matter how big I am the household will be lighted, while the hall will not be burned. That, however, is not my sole function; I have others as well. But neither in Erin nor in Alba nor in Europe nor in Africa nor in Asia, including Greece, Scythia, the Isles of Gades, the Pillars of Hercules, and Bregnon's Tower have I accomplished the quest on which I have come, nor a man to do me fair play regarding it. Since ye Ulstermen have excelled all the peoples of those lands in strength, prowess, and valour; in rank, magnanimity, and dignity; in truth, generosity, and worth, get one among you to grant the boon I ask."

"In truth it is not just that the honour of a province be carried off," said Fergus mac Roig, "because of one man who fails in keeping his word of honour. Death certainly is not a whit nearer to him than to you."

"It is not I that shun it."

"Make thy quest known to us, then," said Fergus.

"Only if fair play is offered me will I tell it."

"It is right to give fair play," said Sencha son of Ailill, "for it is not seemly for a great people to break a mutual covenant over any unknown individual. It seems to us, furthermore, that if you at last find a person such as you seek, you will find him here."

"Conchobar I put aside," said he, "for the sake of his sovereignty, and Fergus mac Roig also on account of his like privilege. These two excepted, come whosoever of you that may dare, that I may cut off his head tonight, he mine tomorrow night."

"Sure then there is no warrior here," said Dubtach, "after these two."

"By my troth there will be at this moment," cried Munremur mac Gerrcind as he sprung on to the floor of the hall. The strength of Munremur was as the strength of a hundred warriors, each arm having the might of a hundred "centaurs." "Bend down, bachlach," said Munremur, "that I may cut off thy head tonight, thou to cut off mine tomorrow."

"Were that the object of my quest I could get it anywhere," said the bachlach; "let us act according to our covenant—I to cut off your head tonight, you to avenge it tomorrow night."

"By my people's gods," said Dubtach Chafertongue, "death is thus for thee no pleasant prospect, should the man killed tonight attack thee on the morrow. It is given to thee alone if thou hast the power, being killed night after night, and to avenge it the next day."

"Truly I will carry out what you all as a body agree upon by way of counsel, strange as it may seem to you," said the bachlach. He then pledged the other to keep his troth in this contention as to fulfilling his tryst on the morrow.

With that Munremur took the axe from the bachlach's hand. Seven feet apart were its two angles. Then the bachlach put his neck across the block. Munremur dealt a blow across it with the axe until it stood in the block beneath, cutting off the head so that it lay by the base of the fork-beam, the house being filled with the blood.

Straightway the bachlach rose, recovered himself, clasped his head, block, and axe to his breast, and made his exit from the hall with the blood streaming from his neck. It filled the Red Branch on every side. Great was the people's horror, wondering at the marvel that had appeared to them. "By my people's gods," said Dubtach Chafertongue, "if the bachlach, having been killed tonight, come back tomorrow, he will not leave a man alive in Ulster."

The following night he returned, and Munremur shirked him. Then the bachlach began to urge his pact with Munremur. "Truly it is not right for Munremur not to fulfill his covenant with me."

That night, however, Loegaire the Triumphant was present. "Who of the warriors that contest Ulster's Champion's Portion will carry out a covenant with me tonight? Where is Loegaire the Triumphant?" said he.

"Here," said Loegaire. He pledged him, too, yet Loegaire did not keep his agreement. The bachlach returned on the morrow and similarly pledged Conall Cernach, who came not as he had sworn.

The fourth night the bachlach returned, and fierce and furious was he. All the ladies of Ulster came that night to see the strange marvel that had come to the Red Branch. That night Cu Chulainn was there also. Then the bachlach began to upbraid them. "Ye men of Ulster, your valour and your prowess are gone. Your warriors greatly covet the Champion's Portion, yet are unable to contest it. Where is the mad fellow called Cu Chulainn? I would like to know whether his word is better than the others."

"No covenant do I desire with you," said Cu Chulainn.

"Likely is that, thou wretched fly; greatly dost thou fear to die." Whereupon Cu Chulainn sprang towards him and dealt him a blow with the axe, hurling his head to the top rafter of the Red Branch until the whole hall shook. Cu Chulainn then again caught up the head and gave it a blow with the axe and smashed it. Thereafter the bachlach rose up.

On the morrow the Ulstermen were watching Cu Chulainn to see whether he would shirk the bachlach as the other heroes had done. As Cu Chulainn was awaiting the bachlach, they saw that great dejection seized him. It would have been fitting had they sung his dirge. They felt sure that his life would last only until the bachlach came. Then said Cu Chulainn with shame to Conchobar, "Thou shalt not go until my pledge to the bachlach is fulfilled; for death awaits me, and I would rather have death with honour."

They were there as the day was closing and they saw the bachlach approaching. "Where is Cu Chulainn?" said he.

"Here I am," he replied.

"Thou art dull of speech tonight, unhappy one; greatly you fear to die. Yet, though great your fear, death you have not shirked."

Thereafter Cu Chulainn stretched his neck across the block, which was of such size that his neck reached but half way. "Stretch out thy neck, thou wretch," cried the bachlach.

"Thou art keeping me in torment," said Cu Chulainn; "dispatch me quickly. Last night, by my troth, I tormented thee not. Verily I swear that if thou torment me I will make myself as long as a crane above you."

"I cannot slay thee," said the bachlach, "what with the shortness of your neck and your side and the size of the block."

Then Cu Chulainn stretched out his neck so that a warrior's foot would have fitted between any two of his ribs; his neck he stretched until his head reached the other side of the block. The bachlach raised his axe until it reached the roof-tree of the house. The creaking of the old hide that was about him and the crashing of the axe—both his arms being raised aloft with all his might—were as the loud noise of a wood tempest-tossed in a night of storm. Down it came then on his neck—its blunt side below, all the nobles of Ulster gazing upon them.

"O Cu Chulainn, arise! Of the warriors of Ulster and Erin, no matter their mettle, none is found to compare with thee in valour, bravery, and truthfulness. The sovereignty of the heroes of Erin to thee from this hour forth and the Champion's Portion undisputed, and to thy wife the precedence always of the ladies of Ulster in the Mead-Hall. And whosoever shall lay wager against thee from now, as my tribe swears I swear, all his life he will be in danger." Then the bachlach vanished. It was Cu Roi mac Dairi who in that guise had come to fulfill the promise he had given to Cu Chulainn.

(Translated from the Irish by George Henderson.)

The Cattle-Raid of Cooley

(Táin bó Cúalnge)

THE PILLOW-TALK

ONCE on a time, when Ailill and Medb had spread their royal bed in Cruachan, the stronghold of Connacht, such was the pillow-talk betwixt them:

Said Ailill, "True is the saying, O woman, 'She is a well-off woman that is a rich man's wife.'"

"Aye, that she is," answered the wife; "but wherefore say'st thou so?"

"For this," Ailill replied, "that thou art this day better off than the day that first I took thee."

Then answered Medb, "As well-off was I before I ever saw thee."

"It was a wealth, indeed, we never heard nor knew of," said Ailill; "but a woman's wealth was all thou hadst, and foes from lands next thine were wont to carry off the spoil and booty that they took from thee."

"Not so was I," said Medb; "the High King of Erin himself was my father, Eochaid Feidlich son of Finn son of Finnen son of Finnguin son of Rogen Ruad son of Rigen son of Blathacht son of Beothacht son of Enna Agnech son of Angus Turbech. Of daughters had he six: Derbriu, Ethne and Ele, Clothru, Mugain and Medb, myself, that was the noblest and seemliest of them all. It was I was the goodliest of them in bounty and gift-giving, in riches and treasures. It was I was best of them in battle and strife and combat. It was I that had fifteen hundred royal mercenaries of the sons of aliens exiled from their own land, and as many more of the sons of freemen of the land. These were as a standing household-guard," continued Medb; "hence hath my father bestowed one of the five provinces of Erin upon me, that is, the province of Cruachan; wherefore 'Medb of Cruachan' am I called. Men came from Finn son of Ross Ruad, king of Leinster, to seek me for a wife, and I refused him; and from Cairbre Niafer son of Ross Ruad, king of Tara, to woo me, and I refused him; and they came from Conchobar son of Fachtna Fathach, king of Ulster, and I refused him likewise. They came from Eochaid Bec, and I went not; for it is I that exacted a peculiar bride-gift, such as no woman ever required of a man of the men of Erin, namely, a husband without avarice, without jealousy, without fear. For should he be mean, the man with whom I should live, we were ill-matched together, inasmuch as I am great in largess and gift-giving, and it would be a disgrace for my husband if I should be better at spending than he, and for it to be said that I was superior in wealth and treasures to him, while no disgrace would it be were one as great as the other. Were my husband a coward, it were as unfit for us to be mated, for I by myself and alone break battles and fights and combats, and it would be a reproach for my husband should his wife be more full of life than himself,

THE CATTLE-RAID OF COOLEY

and no reproach our being equally bold. Should he be jealous, the husband with whom I should live, that too would not suit me, for there never was a time that I had not one man in the shadow of another. Howbeit, such a husband have I found, namely thyself, Ailill son of Ross Ruad of Leinster. Thou wast not churlish; thou wast not jealous; thou wast not a sluggard. It was I plighted thee, and gave purchase price to thee, which of right belongs to the bride—of clothing, namely, the raiment of twelve men, a chariot worth thrice seven bondmaids, the breadth of thy face of red gold, the weight of thy left forearm of white bronze. Whoso brings shame and sorrow and madness upon thee, no claim for compensation or satisfaction hast thou therefor that I myself have not, but it is to me the compensation belongs," said Medb, "for a man dependent upon a woman's maintenance is what thou art."

"Nay, not such was my state," said Ailill; "but two brothers had I; one of them over Tara, the other over Leinster; namely Finn over Leinster and Cairbre over Tara. I left the kingship to them because they were older but not superior to me in largess and bounty. Nor heard I of a province in Erin under woman's keeping but this province alone. And for this I came and assumed the kingship here as my mother's successor; for Mata of Muresc, daughter of Matach of Connacht, was my mother. And who could there be for me to have as my queen better than thyself, being, as thou wert, daughter of the High King of Erin?"

"Yet so it is," pursued Medb, "my fortune is greater than thine."

"I marvel at that," Ailill made answer, "for there is none that hath greater treasures and riches and wealth than I: indeed, to my knowledge there is not."

The Occasion of the Cattle-Raid

Then were brought to them the least precious of their possessions, that they might know which of them had the more treasures, riches, and wealth. Their pails and their cauldrons and their iron-wrought vessels, their jugs and their pots and their eared pitchers were fetched to them.

Likewise their rings and their bracelets and their thumb-rings and their golden treasures were fetched to them, and their apparel, both purple and blue and black and green.

Their numerous flocks of sheep were led in from fields and meadows and plains. These were counted and compared, and found to be equal, of like size, of like number; however, there was one uncommonly fine ram over Medb's sheep, and he was worth a bondmaid, but a corresponding ram was over the ewes of Ailill.

Their horses and steeds and studs were brought from pastures and paddocks. There was a noteworthy horse in Medb's herd and he was of the value of a bondmaid; a horse to match was found among Ailill's.

Then were their numerous droves of swine driven from woods and shelving glens and wolds. These were numbered and counted and claimed. There was a noteworthy boar with Medb, and yet another with Ailill.

Next they brought before them their droves of cattle and their herds and their roaming flocks from the brakes and the wastes of the province.

These were counted and numbered and claimed, and were the same for both, equal in size, equal in number, except only there was an especial bull of the bawn of Ailill, and he was the calf of one of Medb's cows, and

THE CATTLE-RAID OF COOLEY

Finnbennach (the White-Horned) was his name. But he, deeming it no honour to be in a woman's possession, had left and gone over to the herd of the king. And it was the same to Medb as if she owned not a pennyworth, forasmuch as she had not a bull of his size amongst her cattle.

Then it was that Mac Roth the messenger was summoned to Medb, and Medb strictly bade Mac Roth learn where might be found a bull of that likeness in any of the provinces of Erin. "In truth," said Mac Roth, "I know where the bull is that is best and better again, in the province of Ulster, in the district of Cooley, in the house of Daire mac Fiachna; the Donn of Cooley he is called."

"Go thou to him, Mac Roth, and ask for me of Daire the loan for a year of the Donn of Cooley, and at the year's end he shall have a reward for the loan, to wit, fifty heifers and the Donn of Cooley himself. And bear a further boon with thee, Mac Roth: should the borderfolk and those of the country grudge the loan of that rare jewel that is the Donn of Cooley, let Daire himself come with his bull, and he shall get a measure equalling his own land of the smooth Mag Ai and a chariot of the worth of thrice seven bondmaids and he shall enjoy my own closest intimacy."

Thereupon the foot-messengers went to the house of Daire mac Fiachna. This was the number wherewith Mac Roth went, namely, nine members of Medb's court. Welcome was lavished on Mac Roth in Daire's house—fitting welcome it was—chief messenger of all was Mac Roth. Daire asked of Mac Roth what had brought him upon the journey and why he had come. The messenger announced the cause for which he had come, and related the contention between Medb and Ailill.

"And it is to beg the loan of the Donn of Cooley to match the White-Horned of Connacht that I have come," said he; "and thou shalt receive the hire of his loan, that is, fifty heifers and the Donn of Cooley himself. And yet more I may add: come thyself with thy bull and thou shalt have of the land of the smooth soil of Mag Ai as much as thou ownest here, and a chariot of the worth of thrice seven bondmaids, and enjoy Medb's favors besides."

At these words Daire was well pleased, and he leaped for joy so that the seams of his flock-bed rent in twain beneath him.

"By the truth of our conscience," said he, "however the Ulstermen take it, whether well or ill, this time this jewel shall be delivered to Ailill and to Medb, the Donn of Cooley shall go into the land of Connacht." Well pleased was Mac Roth at the words of Daire son of Fiachna.

Thereupon the messengers were served, and straw and fresh rushes were spread under them. The choicest of food was brought to them and a feast was served to them and soon they were noisy and intoxicated. And a discourse took place between two of the messengers.

" 'Tis true what I say," spoke the one; "good is the man in whose house we are."

"Of a truth, he is good."

"Nay, is there one among all the men of Ulster better than he?" persisted the first.

"In truth, there is," answered the second messenger. "Better is Conchobar whose man he is, Conchobar who holds the kingship of the province. And though all the Ulstermen gathered around him, it were no shame for them. Yet is it passing good of Daire that what had been a task for the four mighty provinces of Erin to bear away from the land of Ulster, that is the Donn of Cooley, is surrendered so freely to us nine footmen."

Hereupon a third messenger had his say: "What is this ye dispute about?" he asked.

"That messenger says, 'A good man is the man in whose house we are.'"

"Yea, he is good," said the other.

"Is there among all the Ulstermen any that is better than he?" demanded the first messenger further.

"Aye, there is," answered the second messenger; "better is Conchobar whose man he is; and though all the Ulstermen gathered around him, it were no shame for them. Yet truly good it is of Daire, that what had been a task for four of the great provinces of Erin to bear away out of the borders of Ulster is handed over even to us nine footmen."

"I would not grudge to see a retch of blood and gore in the mouth whereout that was said; for were not the bull given willingly, yet should he be taken by force."

At that moment it was that Daire mac Fiachna's chief steward came into the house and with him a man with drink and another with food, and he heard the foolish words of the messenger; and anger came upon him and he set down their food and drink for them and he neither said to them, "Eat," nor did he say, "Eat not."

Straightway he went into the house where was Daire mac Fiachna and said, "Is it thou that hast given that notable jewel to the messengers, the Donn of Cooley?"

"Yea, it was I," Daire made answer.

"Indeed it was not the part of a king to give him. For it is true what they say: Unless thou hadst bestowed him of thy own free will, so wouldst thou yield him against thy will by the host of Ailill and Medb and the great cunning of Fergus mac Roig."

"I swear by the gods I worship," said Daire, "they shall in no wise take by foul means what they cannot take by fair!"

There they abode until morning. Early in the morning the messengers arose and proceeded to the house where Daire was. "Tell us, lord, how we may reach the place where the Donn of Cooley is kept."

"Nay then," said Daire; "if it were my custom to deal foully with messengers or with travelling folk or with them that go by the road, not one of you would depart alive!"

"How sayest thou?" said Mac Roth.

"Great cause there is," replied Daire: "ye said, unless I yielded willingly, I should yield to the might of Ailill's host and Medb's and the great cunning of Fergus."

"Even so," said Mac Roth, "whatever the runners drunken with thine ale or thy viands have said, it is not for thee to heed or mind, nor yet to be charged on Ailill and on Medb."

"For all that," answered Daire, "this time I will not give my bull, if I can help it!"

Back then the messengers went until they arrived at Cruachan, the stronghold of Connacht. Medb asked their tidings, and Mac Roth told them: that they had not brought the bull from Daire.

"And the reason?" demanded Medb.

Mac Roth recounted to her how the dispute arose. "There is no need to polish knots over such affairs as that, Mac Roth; for it was known," said Medb, "if the Donn of Cooley would not be given with their will, he would be taken in their despite, and taken he shall be!"

So far is recounted the Occasion of the Cattle-Raid.

THE CATTLE-RAID OF COOLEY 545

THE COMBAT OF CU CHULAINN AND FERDIAD

The four great provinces of Erin were side by side and against Cu Chulainn from Monday before Samain (Hallowe'en) to Wednesday after Spring-beginning, and without leave to work harm or vent their rage on the province of Ulster, while yet all the Ulstermen were sunk in their nine days' pains, and Conall Cernach sought out battle in strange foreign lands paying the tribute and tax of Ulster. Sad was the plight and strait of Cu Chulainn during that time, for he was not a day or a night without fierce, fiery combat waged on him by the men of Erin, until he killed Calatin with his seven and twenty sons and Fraech son of Fidach and performed many deeds and successes which are not enumerated here. Now this was sore and grievous to Medb and to Ailill.

Then the men of Erin took counsel who should be fit to send to the ford to fight and do battle with Cu Chulainn to drive him off from them.

With one accord they declared that it should be Ferdiad son of Daman son of Daire, the great and valiant warrior of the Fir Domnann, the horn-skin from Irrus Domnann, the irresistible force, and the battle-rock of destruction, the own dear foster-brother of Cu Chulainn. And fitting it was for him to go thither, for well-matched and alike was their manner of fight and of combat. Under the same instructress had they done skillful deeds of valour and arms, when learning the art with Scathach and with Uathach and with Aife. Yet was it the felling of an oak with one's fists, and the stretching of the hand into a serpent's den, and a going into the lair of a lion, for hero or champion in the world, aside from Cu Chulainn, to fight or combat with Ferdiad on whatever ford or river or mere he set his shield. And neither of them overmatched the other, save in the feat of the *gae bulga* (bag-spear) which Cu Chulainn possessed. Howbeit against this, Ferdiad was horn-skinned when fighting and in combat with a warrior on the ford; and they thought he could avoid the *gae bulga* and defend himself against it, because of the horn about him of such kind that neither arms nor multitude of edges could pierce it.

Then were messengers and envoys sent from Medb and Ailill to Ferdiad. Ferdiad denied them their request, and dismissed and sent back the messengers, and he went not with them, for he knew wherefore they would have him, to fight and combat with his friend, with his comrade and his foster-brother, Cu Chulainn.

Then did Medb despatch to Ferdiad the druids and the poets of the camp, and lampooners and hard-attackers to the end that they might make the three satires to stay him and the three scoffing speeches against him, to mock at him and revile and disgrace him, that they might raise three blisters on his face,—Blame, Blemish, and Disgrace, that he might not find a place in the world to lay his head, if he came not with them to the tent of Medb and Ailill.

Ferdiad came with them for the sake of his own honour and for fear of their bringing shame on him, since he deemed it better to fall by the shafts of valour and bravery and skill than to fall by the shafts of satire, abuse, and reproach. And when Ferdiad was come into the camp, Medb and Ailill beheld him, and great and most wonderful joy possessed them, and they sent him to where their trusty people were, and he was honoured and waited on, and choice, well-flavoured strong liquor was poured out for him until he became drunken and

THE CATTLE-RAID OF COOLEY

merry. Finnabair, daughter of Ailill and Medb, was seated at his side. It was Finnabair that placed her hand on every goblet and cup Ferdiad quaffed. She it was that gave him three kisses with every cup that he took. She it was that passed him sweet-smelling apples over the bosom of her tunic. This is what she ceased not to say, that her darling and her chosen sweetheart of the world's men was Ferdiad. And when Medb got Ferdiad drunken and merry, great rewards were promised him if he would make the fight and combat.

When now Ferdiad was satisfied, happy and joyful, Medb spoke, "Hail now, Ferdiad. Dost thou know the occasion wherefor thou art summoned to this tent?"

"I know not, in truth," Ferdiad replied; "unless it be that the nobles of the men of Erin are here. Why is it a less fitting time for me to be here than any other good warrior?"

"It is not that, indeed," answered Medb, "but to give thee a chariot worth four times seven bondmaids, and the apparel of two men and ten men, of cloth of every colour, and the equivalent of Mag Muirthemne of the rich soil of Mag Ai, and that thou shouldst be at all times in Cruachan, and wine be poured out for thee there; the freedom of thy descendants and thy race for ever, free of tribute, free of rent, without constraint to encamp or take part in our expeditions, without duress for thy son, or for thy grandson, or for thy great-grandson, till the end of time and existence; this leaf-shaped golden brooch of mine shall be thine, wherein are ten-score ounces, and ten-score half-ounces, and ten-score scruples, and ten-score quarters; Finnabair, my daughter and Ailill's, to be thy own wife, and my own most intimate friendship, if thou exactest that withal."

"He needs it not," they cried, one and all; "great are the rewards and gifts!"

Such were the words of Medb, and she spoke them here and Ferdiad responded:

Medb.   Great rewards in arm-rings,
           Share of plain and forest,
           Freedom of thy children
              From this day till Doom!
           Ferdiad son of Daman,
           More than thou couldst hope for,
           Why shouldst thou refuse it,
              That which all would take?

Ferdiad.   Naught I'll take without bond—
           No ill spearman am I—
           Hard on me tomorrow:
              Great will be the strife!
           He called Hound of Culann,
           How his thrust is grievous!
           No soft thing to stand him;
              Rude will be the wound!

Medb.   Champions will be surety,
           Thou needst not keep hostings.
           Reins and splendid horses
              Shall be given as pledge!
           Ferdiad, good, of battle,
           For that thou art dauntless,
           Thou shalt be my lover,
              Past all, free of pain!

Ferdiad.   Without bond I'll not go
           To engage in ford-feats;
           It will live till doomsday
              In full strength and force.
           Ne'er will I yield—who hears me,
           Whoe'er counts upon me—
           Without sun- and moon-oath,
              Without sea and land!

Medb.   Why then dost thou delay it?
           Bind it as it please thee,
           By kings' hands and princes',
              Who will stand for thee!

THE CATTLE-RAID OF COOLEY

          Lo, I will repay thee,
          Thou shalt have thine asking,
          For I know thou wilt slaughter
             Man that meets thee!

Ferdiad.   Nay, without six sureties—
          It shall not be fewer—
          Ere I do my exploits
             There where hosts will be!
          Should my will be granted,
          I expect, though unequal,
          That I'll meet in combat
             Cu Chulainn the brave!

Medb.   Domnall, then, or Cairbre,
          Niaman famed for slaughter,
          Or even poets,
             Natheless, thou shalt have.
          Bind thyself on Morann,
          Wouldst thou its fulfillment,
          Bind on smooth Man's Cairbre,
             And our two sons, bind!

Ferdiad.   Medb, with wealth of cunning,
          Whom no spouse can bridle,
          Thou it is that guardest
             Cruachan of the mounds!
          High thy fame and wild power!
          Mine the fine pied satin;
          Give thy gold and silver,
             Which were proffered me!

Medb.   To thee, foremost champion,
          I will give my ringed brooch.
          From this day till Sunday,
             Shall thy respite be!
          Warrior, mighty, famous,
          All the earth's fair treasures
          Shall to thee be given;
             Everything be thine!

          Finnabair of the champions,
          Queen of western Erin,
          When thou hast slain the Smith's **Hound**,
          Ferdiad, she is thine!

Ferdiad.   Should I have Finnabair to wife,
All of Ai and Cruachan too,
And to dwell for alway there,
I would not seek the deedful Cu Chulainn!

Equal skill to me and him—
Thus spoke Ferdiad—
The same nurses reared us both,
And with them we learned our art.

Not for fear of battle hard,
Noble Eochaid Fedlech's daughter,
Would I shun the Blacksmith's Hound,
But my heart bleeds for his love!

Medb.   Thou shalt have, dear bright-scaled man,
One swift, proud, high-mettled steed.
Thou shalt have domains and land
And shalt stay not from the fight!

Ferdiad.   But that Medb entreated so
And that poets' tongues did urge,
I'd not go for hard rewards
To contend with my own friend!

Medb.   Son of Daman of white cheeks,
Shouldst thou check this heroes' Hound,
For ever thy fame will live,
When thou comest from Ferdiad's Ford!

Then said they, one and all, those gifts were great.

" 'Tis true, they are great. But though they are," said Ferdiad, "with Medb herself I will leave them, and I will not accept them if it be to do battle or combat with my foster-brother, the man of my alliance and affection, and my equal in skill of arms, namely, with Cu Chulainn"; and he said:

Greatest toil, this, greatest toil,
Battle with the Hound of gore!
Liefer would I battle twice
With two hundred men of Fal (Ireland)!

> Sad the fight, and sad the fight,
> I and Hound of feats shall wage!
> We shall hack both flesh and blood;
> Skin and body we shall hew!
>
> Sad, O god, yea, sad, O god,
> That a woman us should part!
> My heart's half, the blameless Hound;
> Half the brave Hound's heart am I!
>
> Liefer would I, liefer far,
> Arms should slay me in fierce fight,
> Than the death of the heroes' Hound
> Should be food for ravenous birds!
>
> Tell him this, O tell him this,
> To the Hound of beauteous hue,
> Fearless Scathach hath foretold
> My fall on a ford through him!
>
> Woe to Medb, yea, woe to Medb,
> Who hath used her guile on us;
> She hath set me face to face
> 'Gainst Cu Chulainn—hard the toil!

"Ye men," said Medb, in the wonted fashion of stirring up disunion and dissension, as if she had not heard Ferdiad at all, "true is the word Cu Chulainn speaks."

"What word is that?" asked Ferdiad.

"He said, then," replied Medb, "he would not think it too much if thou shouldst fall by his hands in the choicest feat of his skill in arms, in the land whereto he should come."

"It was not just for him to speak so," said Ferdiad; "for it is not cowardice or lack of boldness that he hath ever seen in me by day or night. And I speak not so of him, for I have it not to say of him. And I swear by my arms of valour, if it be true that he spoke so, I will be the first man of the men of Erin to contend with him on the morrow, how loath soever I am to do so!"

And he gave his word in the presence of them all that he would go and meet Cu Chulainn. For it pleased Medb, if Ferdiad should fail to go, to have them as witnesses against him, in order that she might say that it was fear or dread that caused him to break his word.

"Blessing and victory upon thee for that!" said Medb; "it pleaseth me more than for thee to show fear and lack of boldness. For every man loves his own land, and how is it better for him to seek the welfare of Ulster, because his mother was descended from the Ulstermen, than for thee to seek the welfare of Connacht, as thou art the son of a king of Connacht?"

Then it was that Medb obtained from Ferdiad the easy surety of a covenant to fight and contend on the morrow with six warriors of the champions of Erin, or to fight and contend with Cu Chulainn alone, if to him this last seemed lighter. Ferdiad obtained of Medb the easy surety, as he thought, to send the aforesaid six men for the fulfillment of the terms which had been promised him, should Cu Chulainn fall at his hands.

There was a wonderful warrior of the Ulstermen present at that covenant, and that was Fergus mac Roig. Fergus betook him to his tent. "Woe is me, for the deed that will be done on the morning of the morrow!"

"What deed is that?" his tent-folk asked.

"My good fosterling Cu Chulainn will be slain!"

"Alas! who makes that boast?"

"Not hard to say: None other but his dear, devoted foster-brother, Ferdiad son of Daman. Why bear ye not my blessing," Fergus continued, "and let one of you go with a warning and mercy to Cu Chulainn, if perchance he will leave the ford on the morn of the morrow?"

"As we live," said they, "though it were thyself was on the ford of battle, we would not go near him to seek thee."

THE CATTLE-RAID OF COOLEY

"Come, my lad," cried Fergus, "get our horses for us, and yoke the chariot."

Then were Fergus's horses fetched for him and his chariot was yoked, and he came forward to the place of combat where Cu Chulainn was, to inform him of the challenge, that Ferdiad was to fight with him.

"A chariot comes hither towards us, O Cu Chulainn!" cried Loeg. For in this wise was the gillie, with his back towards his lord as the two played chess. He used to win every other game of draughts and chess from his master. Watch and guard of the four points of the compass was he besides.

"What manner of chariot is it?" asked Cu Chulainn.

"A chariot like to a royal fort, huge, with its yoke, strong, golden; with its great board of copper; with its shafts of bronze; with its two horses, black, swift, stout, strong-forked, thick-set, under beautiful shafts. One kingly, broad-eyed warrior is the combatant in the chariot. A curly, forked beard he wears that reaches below outside over the smooth lower part of his soft tunic, which would shelter fifty warriors on a day of storm and rain under the heavy shield of the warrior's beard. A bent buckler, white, beautiful, of many colours, he bears, with three stout-wrought chains, so that there is room from edge to edge for four troops of ten behind the leather of the shield which hangs upon the broad back of the warrior. A long, hard-edged, broad, red sword in a sheath woven and twisted of white silver. A strong, three-ridged spear, wound and banded with all-gleaming white silver he has lying across the chariot."

"Not difficult to recognize him," said Cu Chulainn; "it is my master Fergus that comes hither with a warning and with compassion for me, before all the four provinces of Erin."

Fergus drew nigh and sprang from his chariot. Cu

Chulainn bade him welcome. "Welcome is thy coming, O master Fergus!" cried Cu Chulainn. "If a flock of birds comes into the plain, thou shalt have a duck with the half of another. If a fish comes into the river-mouth, thou shalt have a salmon with the half of another. A handful of water-cress and a bunch of laver and a sprig of sea-grass and a drink of cold water from the sand thou shalt have thereafter."

"It is an outlaw's portion, that," said Fergus.

"'Tis true; 'tis an outlaw's portion is mine," answered Cu Chulainn.

"Truly intended, methinks, the welcome, O fosterling," said Fergus. "But were it for this I came, I should think it better to leave it. It is for this I am here, to inform thee who comes to fight and contend with thee at the morning hour early on the morrow."

"Even so we will hear it from thee," said Cu Chulainn.

"Thine own friend and comrade and foster-brother, the man thine own equal in feats and in skill of arms and in deeds, Ferdiad son of Daman son of Daire, the great and mighty warrior of the Fir Domnann."

"As my soul liveth," replied Cu Chulainn, "it is not to an encounter we wish our friend to come, and not for fear, but for love and affection of him; and almost I would prefer to fall by the hand of that warrior than for him to fall by mine."

"It is just for that," answered Fergus, "that thou shouldst be on thy guard and prepared. Say not that thou hast no fear of Ferdiad, for it is fitting that thou shouldst have fear and dread before fighting with Ferdiad. For unlike to all whom it fell to fight and contend with thee on the Cattle-Raid of Cooley on this occasion is Ferdiad son of Daman son of Daire, for he has a horny skin about him in battle against a man, a belt,

THE CATTLE-RAID OF COOLEY 555

equally strong, victorious in battle, and neither points nor edges are reddened upon it in the hour of strife and anger. For he is the fury of the lion, and the bursting of wrath, and the blow of doom, and the wave that drowns foes."

"Speak not thus!" cried Cu Chulainn, "for I swear by my arms of valour, the oath that my people swear, that every limb and every joint will be as a pliant rush in the bed of a river under the point of the sword, if he show himself to me on the ford! Truly I am here," said Cu Chulainn, "checking and staying four of the five grand provinces of Erin from Monday at Samain till the beginning of spring, and I have not left my post for a night's disport, through stoutly opposing the men of Erin on the Cattle-Raid of Cooley. And in all this time, I have not put foot in retreat before any one man nor before a multitude, and methinks just as little will I turn in flight before him."

And thus spoke he, that it was not fear of Ferdiad that caused his anxiety regarding the fight, but his love for him. And, on his part, so spoke Fergus, putting him on his guard because of Ferdiad's strength, and he said these words and Cu Chulainn responded:

Fergus.   O Cu Chulainn—splendid deed—
               Lo, it is time for thee to rise.
               Here in rage against thee comes
               Ferdiad, red-faced Daman's son!

Cu Chulainn. Here am I—no easy task—
               Holding Erin's men at bay;
               A foot I have never turned in flight
               In my fight with single foe!

Fergus.   Fierce the man with scores of deeds;
               No light thing him to subdue.
               Strong as hundreds—brave his mien—
               Point pricks not, edge cuts him not!

Cu Chulainn.	If we clash upon the ford, I and Ferdiad of known skill, We'll not part until we know; Fierce will be our weapon fight!
Fergus.	Greatest deed awaits thy hand: Fight with Ferdiad, Daman's son. Hard stern arms with stubborn edge, Shalt thou have, thou Culann's Hound!

After that, Fergus returned to the camp and halting-place of the men of Erin, lest the men of Erin should say he was betraying them or forsaking them, if he should remain longer than he did conversing with Cu Chulainn. And they took farewell of each other.

Now as regards the charioteer of Cu Chulainn after Fergus went from them: "What wilt thou do tonight?" asked Loeg.

"What, indeed?" said Cu Chulainn.

"It will be thus," said the charioteer: "Ferdiad will come to attack thee, with new beauty of plaiting and dressing of hair, and washing and bathing, and the four provinces of Erin with him to look at the combat. I would that thou shouldst go where thou wilt get a like adorning for thyself, to the place where is Emer Folt-chain (Emer of the Beautiful Hair), thy wife, daughter of Forgall Monach, at Cairthenn in Cluan da Dam (Two Oxen's Meadow) in Sliab Fuait, where thou wilt get even such an adorning for thyself."

"It is fitting to do so," said Cu Chulainn. Then Cu Chulainn went thither that night to Dun Delgan, his own stronghold, and passed the night with his wife. His doings from that time are not related here now.

As for Ferdiad, he betook himself to his tent and to his people, and imparted to them the easy surety which Medb had obtained from him to do combat and battle with six warriors on the morrow, or to do combat and battle with Cu Chulainn alone, if he thought it a lighter task. He made known to them also the fair terms he had obtained from Medb of sending the same six warriors for the fulfillment of the covenant she had made with him, should Cu Chulainn fall by his hands.

The folk of Ferdiad were not joyful, blithe, cheerful, or merry that night, but they were sad, sorrowful, and downcast, for they knew that here were the two champions and the two bulwarks in a gap for a hundred, the two pillars of battle and strife of the men of Erin of that time met in combat; one or the other of them would fall there or both would fall, and if it should be one of them, they believed it would be their king and their own lord that would fall there, for it was not easy to contend and do battle with Cu Chulainn on the Cattle-Raid of Cooley.

Ferdiad slept right heavily the first part of the night, but when the end of the night was come, his sleep and his heaviness left him. And the anxiousness of the combat and the battle came upon him. But most troubled in spirit was he that he should allow all the treasures to pass from him, and the maiden, by reason of the combat with one man. Unless he fought with that one man, he must needs fight with six champions on the morrow. What tormented him more than that was, should he once show himself on the ford to Cu Chulainn, he was certain he would never have power of head or of life ever after. And Ferdiad arose early on the morrow. And he charged his charioteer to take his horses and to yoke his chariot. The charioteer sought to dissuade him from that journey. "By our word," said the gillie, "it would be better for thee to remain than to go thither," said he; "for, not more do I commend it for thee than I condemn it."

"Hold thy peace about us, boy!" said Ferdiad, "for we

will brook no interference from any one concerning this journey. For the promise we gave to Medb and Ailill in the presence of the men of Erin, it would shame us to break it; for they would say it was fear or dread that caused us to break it. And, by my conscience, I would almost liefer fall myself by Cu Chulainn's hand than that he should fall by mine on this occasion. And should Cu Chulainn fall by my hand on the ford of combat, then shall Medb and many of the men of Erin fall by my hand because of the pledge they extorted from me, and I drunken and merry."

And in this manner he spoke, conversing with the charioteer, and he uttered these words, the little lay that follows, urging on the charioteer, and the servant responded:

Ferdiad.

> Let us haste to the encounter,
> To battle with this man;
> The ford we will come to,
>   Over which Badb will shriek!
> To meet with Cu Chulainn,
> To wound his slight body,
> To thrust the spear through him
>   So that he may die!

The Henchman.

> To stay it were better;
> Thy threats are not gentle;
> Death's sickness will one of you have,
>   And sad will ye part!
> To meet Ulster's noblest,
> To meet whence ill cometh;
> Long will men speak of it.
>   Alas, for thy course!

Ferdiad.

> Not fair what thou speakest;
> No fear has the warrior;
> We owe no one meekness;
>   We stay not for thee!
> Hush, gillie, about us!
> The time will bring strong hearts;
> More meet strength than weakness;
>   Let us on to the tryst!

THE CATTLE-RAID OF COOLEY

Ferdiad's horses were now brought forth and his chariot was hitched, and he set out from the camp for the ford of battle when yet day with its full light had not come there for him. "My lad," said Ferdiad, "it is not fitting that we make our journey without bidding farewell to the men of Erin. Turn the horses and the chariot for us towards the men of Erin." Thrice the servant turned the heads of the horses and the chariot towards the men of Erin.

Then he came upon Medb, letting her water from her on the floor of the tent. "Ailill, sleepest thou still?" asked Medb.

"Not so!" replied Ailill.

"Dost hear thy new son-in-law taking farewell of thee?"

"Is that what he does?" asked Ailill.

"It is that, truly," Medb answered; "but I swear by what my tribe swears, not on the same feet will the man who makes that greeting come back to you."

"Howbeit, we have profited by a happy alliance of marriage with him," said Ailill; "if only Cu Chulainn falls by his hand. I should be pleased if they both fell, yet I would prefer that Ferdiad should escape."

Ferdiad came to the ford of combat. "Look, my lad!" said Ferdiad, "is Cu Chulainn on the ford?"

"That he is not," replied the gillie.

"Look well for us," said Ferdiad.

"Cu Chulainn is not a little speck where he would be in hiding," answered the gillie.

"It is true, then, my lad; till this day Cu Chulainn has not heard of a goodly warrior coming to meet him on the Cattle-Raid of Cooley, and now when he has heard of one, he has left the ford."

"Shame for thee to slander Cu Chulainn in his absence. Rememberest thou not when ye gave battle to

German Garbglas above the borders of the Tyrrhene Sea, thou leftest thy sword with the hosts and it was Cu Chulainn who slew a hundred warriors till he reached it and brought it to thee? And mindest thou well where we were that night?" the gillie asked further.

"I know not," Ferdiad answered.

"At the house of Scathach's steward," said the other; "and thou wentest proudly in advance of us all into the house. The churl gave thee a blow with his three-pointed fork in the small of the back, so that thou flewest like a bolt out over the door. Cu Chulainn came in and gave the churl a blow with his sword, so that he made two pieces of him. I was their house-steward while you were in that place. If it were that day, thou wouldst not say thou wast a better warrior than Cu Chulainn."

"Wrong is what thou hast done, O gillie," said Ferdiad; "for I would not have come to the combat, hadst thou spoken thus to me at first. Why dost thou not lay the chariot-poles at my side and the skin-coverings under my head, so that I may sleep now?"

"Alas," said the gillie, "it is a sorry sleep before deer and a pack of wolves here!"

"How so, gillie? Art thou not able to keep watch and guard for me?"

"I am," the gillie answered; "unless they come in clouds or in the air to attack thee, they shall not come from east or from west to attack thee without warning, without notice."

"Come, gillie," said Ferdiad, "unharness the horses and spread for me the cushions and skins of my chariot under me here, so that I sleep off my heavy fit of sleep and slumber here, for I slept not the last part of the night with the anxiousness of the battle and combat."

The gillie unharnessed the horses; he unfastened the chariot under him, and spread beneath Ferdiad the

THE CATTLE-RAID OF COOLEY 561

chariot-cloths. He slept off the heavy fit of sleep that was on him. The gillie remained on watch and guard for him.

Now how Cu Chulainn fared is related here: He arose not till the day with its bright light had come to him, lest the men of Erin might say it was fear or fright of the champion he had, if he should arise early. And when the day with its full light had come, he passed his hand over his face and bade his charioteer take his horses and yoke them to his chariot. "Come, gillie," said Cu Chulainn, "take out our horses for us and harness our chariot, for an early riser is the warrior appointed to meet us, Ferdiad son of Daman son of Daire. If Ferdiad awaits us, he must needs think it long."

"The horses are taken out," said the gillie; "the chariot is harnessed. Mount, and be it no shame to thy valour to go thither!"

Cu Chulainn stepped into the chariot and they pressed forward to the ford. Then it was that the cutting, feat-performing, battle-winning, red-sworded hero, Cu Chulainn son of Sualtam, mounted his chariot, so that there shrieked around him the goblins and fiends and the sprites of the glens and the demons of the air; for the Tuatha De Danann were wont to set up their cries around him, to the end that the dread and the fear and the fright and the terror of him might be so much the greater in every battle and on every field, in every fight and in every combat wherein he went.

Not long had Ferdiad's charioteer waited when he heard something: a rush and a crash and a hurtling sound, and a din and a thunder, a clatter and a clash, namely, the shield-cry of feat-shields, and the jangle of javelins, and the deed-striking of swords, and the thud of the helmet, and the ring of spears, and the clang of the cuirass, and the striking of arms, the fury of feats, the straining of ropes, and the whir of wheels, and the creaking of the chariot, the tramping of horses' hoofs, and the deep voice of the hero and battle-warrior in grave speech with his servant on his way to the ford to attack his opponent.

The servant came and touched his master with his hand and awakened him. "Ferdiad, master," said the youth, "rise up! They are here to meet thee at the ford." Then Ferdiad arose and girt his body in his war-dress of battle and combat. And the gillie spoke these words:

> The roll of a chariot
> Its fair yoke of silver;
> A great man and stalwart
>   Overtops the strong car!
> Over Bri Ross, over Brane
> Their swift path they hasten;
> Past Old-tree Town's tree-stump,
>   Victorious they speed!
>
> A sly Hound that driveth,
> A fair chief that urgeth,
> A free hawk that speedeth
>   His steeds towards the south!
> Gore-coloured, the Cua,
> It is sure he will take us;
> We know—vain to hide it—
>   He brings us defeat!
>
> Woe to him on the hillock,
> The brave Hound before him;
> Last year I foretold it,
>   That some time he'd come!

"Come, gillie," said Ferdiad; "for what reason praisest thou this man ever since I am come from my house? And it is almost a cause for strife with thee that thou hast praised him thus highly. But Ailill and Medb have prophesied to me that this man will fall by my hand; and since it is for a reward, he shall quickly be torn

THE CATTLE-RAID OF COOLEY 563

asunder by me. Make ready the arms on the ford against his coming."

"Should I turn my face backward," said the gillie, "methinks the poles of that chariot yonder will pass through the back of my neck."

"Too much, my lad," said Ferdiad, "dost thou praise Cu Chulainn, for not a reward has he given thee for praising, but it is time to fetch help."

It was not long that Ferdiad's charioteer remained there when he saw something: "How beholdest thou Cu Chulainn?" asked Ferdiad of his charioteer.

"I behold," said he, "a beautiful five-pointed chariot, broad above, of white crystal, with a thick yoke of gold, with stout plates of copper, with shafts of bronze, with wheel-bands of bronze covered with silver, approaching with swiftness, with speed, with perfect skill; with a green shade, with a thin-framed, dry-bodied box surmounted with feats of cunning, straight-poled, as long as a warrior's sword. On this is room for a hero's seven arms, the fair seat for its lord; two wheels, dark, black; a pole of tin, with red enamel, of a beautiful colour; two inlaid, golden bridles. This chariot is placed behind two fleet steeds, nimble, furious, small-headed, bounding, large-eared, small-nosed, sharp-beaked, red-chested, gaily prancing, with inflated nostrils, broad-chested, quick-hearted, high-flanked, broad-hoofed, slender-limbed, over-powering and resolute. A grey, broad-hipped, small-stepping, long-maned horse, whose name is Liath (the Grey) of Macha, is under one of the yokes of the chariot; a black, crisp-maned, swift-moving, broad-backed horse, whose name is Dub (the Black) of Sainglenn, under the other. Like unto a hawk after its prey on a sharp tempestuous day, or to a tearing blast of wind of spring on a March day over the back of a plain, or unto a startled stag when first roused by the hounds in the first of the chase, are Cu Chulainn's two horses before the chariot, as if they were on glowing, fiery flags, so that they shake the earth and make it tremble with the fleetness of their course.

"In the front of this chariot is a man with fair, curly, long hair. There is around him a cloak, blue, Parthian purple. A spear with red and keen-cutting blades, flaming-red in his hand. The semblance of three heads of hair he has, namely, brown hair next to the skin of his head, blood-red hair in the middle, a crown of gold is the third head of hair.

"Beautiful is the arrangement of that hair so that it makes three coils down behind over his shoulders. Even as a thread of gold it seems, when its hue has been wrought over the edge of an anvil; or like to the yellow of bees whereon shines the sun on a summer's day is the shining of each single hair of his head. Seven toes he has on each of his feet and seven fingers on each of his hands and the brilliance of a very great fire is around his eye.

"Befitting him is the charioteer beside him, with curly, jet-black hair, shorn broad over his head. A cowled garment around him, open at the elbows. A horsewhip, very fine and golden in his hand, and a light-grey cloak wrapped around him, and a goad of white silver in his hand. He plies the goad whatever way would go the deed-renowned warrior that is in the chariot."

And Cu Chulainn reached the ford. Ferdiad waited on the south side of the ford; Cu Chulainn stood on the north side. Ferdiad bade welcome to Cu Chulainn. "Welcome is thy coming, O Cu Chulainn!" said Ferdiad.

"Truly spoken has seemed thy welcome always till

THE CATTLE-RAID OF COOLEY

now," answered Cu Chulainn; "but to-day I put no more trust in it. And, O Ferdiad," said Cu Chulainn, "it were fitter for me to bid thee welcome than that thou shouldst welcome me; for it is thou that are come to the land and the province wherein I dwell; and it is not fitting for thee to come to contend and do battle with me, but it were fitter for me to go to contend and do battle with thee. For before thee in flight are my women and my boys and my youths, my steeds and my troops of horses, my droves, my flocks and my herds of cattle."

"Good, O Cu Chulainn," said Ferdiad; "what has ever brought thee out to contend and do battle with me? For when we were together with Scathach and with Uathach and with Aife, thou wast not a man worthy of me, for thou wast my serving-man, even for arming my spear and dressing my bed."

"That was indeed true," answered Cu Chulainn; "because of my youth and my littleness did I so much for thee, but this is by no means my mood this day. For there is not a warrior in the world I would not drive off this day in the field of battle and combat."

It was not long before they met in the middle of the ford. And then it was that each of them cast sharp-cutting reproaches at the other, renouncing his friendship; and Ferdiad spoke these words there, and Cu Chulainn responded:

Ferdiad.   What led thee, O Cu,
        To fight a strong champion?
        Thy flesh will be gore-red
          Over smoke of thy steeds!
        Alas for thy journey,
        A kindling of firebrands;
        In sore need of healing,
        If home thou shouldst reach!

Cu Chulainn.	I have come before warriors
	  Around the herd's wild Boar,
	Before troops and hundreds,
	  To drown thee in deep.
	In anger, to prove thee
	In hundred-fold battle,
	Till on thee come havoc,
	  Defending thy head!

Ferdiad.	Here stands one to crush thee, 'Tis I will destroy thee, From me there shall come The flight of their warriors In the presence of Ulster, That long they'll remember The loss that was theirs!

Cu Chulainn.	How then shall we combat?
	For wrongs shall we heave sighs?
	Despite all, we'll go there,
	  To fight on the ford!
	Or is it with hard swords,
	Or even with red spear-points,
	Before hosts to slay thee,
	  If thy hour hath come?

Ferdiad.	Before sunset, before nightfall—
	If need be, then guard thee—
	I'll fight thee at Bairche,
	  Not bloodlessly fight!
	The Ulstermen call thee,
	"He has him!" Oh, hearken!
	The sight will distress them
	  That through them will **pass**!

Cu Chulainn.	In danger's gap fallen,
	At hand is thy life's term;
	On thee plied be weapons,
	  Not gentle the skill!
	One champion will slay thee;
	We both will encounter;
	No more shall lead forays,
	  From this day till doom!

THE CATTLE-RAID OF COOLEY

Ferdiad.   Away with thy warnings,
        Thou world's greatest braggart;
        Nor guerdon nor pardon,
          Low warrior, for thee!
        It is I that well know thee,
        Thou heart of a cageling—
        This lad merely tickles—
          Without skill or force!

Cu Chulainn.   When we were with Scathach,
        For wonted arms' training,
        Together we'd fare forth,
          To seek every fight.
        Thou wast my heart's comrade,
        My clan and my kinsman;
        Never found I one dearer;
          Thy loss would be sad!

Ferdiad.   Thou wager'st thine honour
        Unless we do battle;
        Before the cock crows,
          Thy head on a spit!
        Cu Chulainn of Cooley,
        Mad frenzy hath seized thee;
        All ill we'll wreak on thee,
          For thine is the sin!

"Come now, O Ferdiad," cried Cu Chulainn, "not meet was it for thee to come to contend and do battle with me, because of the instigation and intermeddling of Ailill and Medb, and because of the false promises that they made thee. Because of their deceitful terms and of the maiden Finnabair have many good men been slain. And all that came because of those promises of deceit, neither profit nor success did it bring them, and they have fallen by me. And none the more, O Ferdiad, shall it win victory or increase of fame for thee; and, as they all fell, shalt thou too fall by my hand!" Thus he spake, and he further uttered these words, and Ferdiad hearkened to him:

Come not nigh me, noble chief,
Ferdiad, comrade, Daman's son.
Worse for thee than it is for me;
Thou wilt bring sorrow to a host!

Come not nigh me against all right;
Thy last bed is made by me.
Why shouldst thou alone escape
From the prowess of my arms?

Shall not great feats thee undo,
Though thou art purple, horny-skinned?
And the maid thou boastest of,
Shall not, Daman's son, be thine!

Finnabair, Medb's fair daughter,
Great her charms though they may be,
Fair as is the damsel's form,
She is not for thee to enjoy!

Finnabair, the king's own chiild,
Is the lure, if truth be told;
Many they whom she has deceived
And undone as she has thee!

Break not, foolish one, oath with me;
Break not friendship, break not bond;
Break not promise, break not word;
Come not nigh me, noble chief!

Fifty chiefs obtained in plight
This same maid, a proffer vain.
Through me went they to their graves;
Spear-right all they had from me!

Were she my affianced wife,
Smiled on me this fair land's head,
I would not thy body hurt,
Right nor left, in front nor behind!

"Good, O Ferdiad," cried Cu Chulainn, "a pity it is for thee to abandon my alliance and my friendship for the sake of a woman that has been trafficked to fifty other warriors before thee, and it would be long before I

THE CATTLE-RAID OF COOLEY

would forsake thee for that woman. Therefore it is not right for thee to come to fight and combat with me; for when we were with Scathach and Uathach and Aife, we were together in practice of valour and arms of the world, and it was together we were used to seek out every battle and every battle-field, every combat and every contest, every wood and every desert, every covert and every recess." And thus he spoke and he uttered these words:

Cu Chulainn. We were heart-companions once;
We were comrades in the woods;
We were men that shared one bed,
When we slept the heavy sleep,
After hard and weary fights.
Into many lands, so strange,
Side by side we sallied forth,
And we ranged the woodlands through,
When with Scathach we learned arms!

Ferdiad. O Cu Chulainn, rich in feats,
Hard the trade we both have learned;
Treason hath overcome our love;
Thy first wounding hath been brought;
Think not of our friendship more,
Cu, it avails thee not!

"Too long are we now in this way," said Ferdiad; "and what arms shall we resort to to-day, O Cu Chulainn?"

"With thee is thy choice of weapons this day until night-time," answered Cu Chulainn, "for thou art he that first didst reach the ford."

"Rememberest thou at all," asked Ferdiad, "the choice of arms we were wont to practice with Scathach and with Uathach and with Aife?"

"Indeed, and I do remember," answered Cu Chulainn.

"If thou rememberest, let us begin with them."

They betook them to their choicest deeds of arms.

They took upon them two equally matched shields for feats, and their eight-edged targets for feats, and their eight small darts, and their eight straight swords, with ornaments of walrus-tooth, and their eight lesser ivoried spears which flew from them and to them like bees on a day of fine weather.

They cast no weapons that struck not. Each of them was busy casting at the other with those missiles from morning's early twilight until noon at midday, the while they overcame their various feats with the bosses and hollows of their feat-shields. However great the excellence of the throwing on either side, equally great was the excellence of the defence, so that during all that time neither bled nor reddened the other.

"Let us cease now from this bout of arms, O Cu Chulainn," said Ferdiad; "for it is not by such our decision will come."

"Yea, surely, let us cease, if the time hath come," answered Cu Chulainn.

Then they ceased. They threw their feat-tackle from them into the hands of their charioteers.

"To what weapons shall we resort next, O Cu Chulainn?" asked Ferdiad.

"Thine is the choice of weapons until nightfall," answered Cu Chulainn, "for thou art he who didst first reach the ford."

"Let us begin, then," said Ferdiad, "with our straight-cut, smooth-hardened throwing-spears, with cords of full-hard flax on them."

"Aye, let us begin then," assented Cu Chulainn.

Then they took on them two hard shields, equally strong. They fell to their straight-cut, smooth-hardened spears with cords of full-hard flax on them. Each of them was engaged in casting at the other with the spears from the middle of noon till yellowness came over the sun at the hour of evening's sundown. However great the excellence of the defence, equally great was the excellence of the throwing on either side, so that each of them bled and reddened and wounded the other during that time.

"Wouldst thou fain make a truce, O Cu Chulainn?" asked Ferdiad.

"It would please me," replied Cu Chulainn; "for whoso begins with arms has the right to desist."

"Let us leave off from this now, O Cu Chulainn," said Ferdiad.

"Aye, let us leave off, if the time has come," answered Cu Chulainn.

So they ceased; and they threw their arms from them into the hands of their charioteers.

Thereupon each of them went toward the other in the middle of the ford, and each of them put his hand on the other's neck and gave him three kisses in remembrance of his fellowship and friendship. Their horses were in one and the same paddock that night, and their charioteers at one and the same fire; and their charioteers made ready a litter-bed of fresh rushes for them with pillows for wounded men on them. Then came healing and curing folk to heal and cure them, and they laid healing herbs and grasses and a curing charm on their cuts and stabs, their gashes and many wounds. Of every healing herb and grass and curing charm that was brought from the fairy-mounds of Erin to Cu Chulainn and was applied to the cuts and stabs, to the gashes and many wounds of Cu Chulainn, a like portion thereof he sent across the ford westward to Ferdiad, to put on his wounds and his pools of gore, so that the men of Erin should not have it to say, should Ferdiad fall at his hands, it was more than his share of care had been given to him.

Of every food and of every savoury, soothing and strong drink that was brought by the men of Erin to Ferdiad, a like portion thereof he sent over the ford northwards to Cu Chulainn; for the purveyors of Ferdiad were more numerous than the purveyors of Cu Chulainn. All the men of Erin were purveyors to Ferdiad, to the end that he might keep Cu Chulainn off from them. But only the inhabitants of Mag Breg were purveyors to Cu Chulainn. They were wont to come daily, that is, every night, to converse with him.

They bided there that night. Early on the morrow they arose and went to the ford of combat.

"To what weapons shall we resort on this day, O Ferdiad?" asked Cu Chulainn.

"Thine is the choosing of weapons till night-time," Ferdiad made answer, "because it was I had my choice of weapons yesterday."

"Let us take, then," said Cu Chulainn, "to our great, well-tempered lances to-day, for we think that the thrusting will bring nearer the decisive battle to-day than did the casting of yesterday. Let our horses be brought to us and our chariots yoked, to the end that we engage in combat over our horses and chariots on this day."

"Good, let us do so," Ferdiad assented.

Thereupon they took full-firm broad-shields on them for that day. They took to their great, well-tempered lances on that day. Either of them began to pierce and to drive, to throw and to press down the other, from early morning's twilight till the hour of evening's close. If it were the wont of birds in flight to fly through the bodies of men, they could have passed through their bodies on that day and carried away pieces of blood and flesh through their wounds and their sores into the clouds and the air all around. And when the hour of evening's close was come, their horses were spent and the drivers were wearied, and they themselves, the hero warriors of valour, were exhausted.

"Let us give over now, O Ferdiad," said Cu Chulainn, "for our horses are spent and our drivers tired, and when they are exhausted, why should we too not be exhausted?" And in this manner he spoke, and uttered these words at that place:

> We need not our chariots break—
> This, a struggle fit for giants.
> Place the hobbles on the steeds,
> Now that the din of arms is over!

"Yea, we will cease, if the time has come," replied Ferdiad. They ceased then. They threw their arms away from them into the hands of their charioteers. Each of them came towards his fellow. Each laid his hand on the other's neck and gave him three kisses. Their horses were in the one pen that night, and their charioteers at one fire. . . . etc.

They abode there that night. Early on the morrow they arose and repaired to the ford of combat. Cu Chulainn marked an evil mien and a dark mood that day beyond every other on Ferdiad.

"It is evil thou appearest to-day, O Ferdiad," said Cu Chulainn; "thy hair has become dark to-day, and thine eye has grown drowsy and thine upright form and thy features and thy gait have gone from thee!"

"Truly not for fear nor for dread of thee has that happened to me to-day," answered Ferdiad; "for there is not in Erin this day a warrior I could not repel!"

"Alas! O Ferdiad," said Cu Chulainn, "a pity it is for thee to oppose thy foster-brother and comrade and friend on the counsel of any woman in the world!"

"A pity it is, O Cu Chulainn," Ferdiad responded. "But, should I part without a struggle with thee, I should be in ill repute forever with Medb and with the nobles of the four great provinces of Erin."

"A pity it is, O Ferdiad," said Cu Chulainn; "not on the counsel of all the men and women of the world would I desert thee or would do thee harm. And almost would it make a clot of gore of my heart to be combating with thee!"

And Cu Chulainn lamented and moaned, and he spoke these words and Ferdiad responded:

Cu Chulainn. Ferdiad, ah, if it be thou,
Well I know thou art doomed to die!
To have gone at a woman's hest,
Forced to fight thy sworn comrade!

Ferdiad. O Cu Chulainn—wise decree—
Loyal champion, hero true,
Each man is constrained to go
Beneath the sod that hides his grave!

Cu Chulainn. Finnabair, Medb's fair daughter,
Stately maiden though she be,
Not for love they'll give to thee,
But to prove thy kingly might!

Ferdiad. Proved was my might long since,
Thou Cu of gentle spirit.
Of one braver I've not heard,
Till to-day I have not found!

Cu Chulainn. Thou art he provoked this fight,
Son of Daman, Daire's son,
To have gone at woman's word,
Swords to cross with thine old friend!

Ferdiad. Should we then unfought depart,
Brothers though we are, bold Hound,
Ill would be my word and fame
With Ailill and Cruachan's Medb!

Cu Chulainn. Food has not yet passed his lips,
Nay, nor has he yet been born,
Son of king or blameless queen,
For whom I would work thee harm!

Ferdiad.	Culann's Hound, with floods of deeds, Medb, not thou, hath us betrayed; Fame and victory thou shalt have; Not on thee we lay our fault!
Cu Chulainn.	Clotted gore is my stout heart, Near I am parted from my soul; Wrongful it is—with hosts of deeds— Ferdiad, dear, to fight with thee!

After this colloquy Ferdiad spoke. "How much soever thou findest fault with me to-day," said Ferdiad, "for my ill-boding mien and evil doing, it will be as an offset to my prowess." And then he said, "To what weapons shall we resort to-day?"

"With thyself is the choice of weapons to-day until night-time come," replied Cu Chulainn, "for it was I that chose on the day gone by."

"Let us resort, then," said Ferdiad, "to our heavy, hard-smiting swords this day, for we trust that the smiting each other will bring us nearer to the decision of battle to-day than did our piercing each other yesterday."

"Let us go, then, by all means," responded Cu Chulainn.

Then they took two full-great long-shields upon them for that day. They turned to their heavy, hard-smiting swords. Each of them fell to strike and to hew, to lay low and cut down, to slay and undo his fellow, till as large as the head of a month-old child was each lump and each cut, each clutter and each clot of gore that each of them took from the shoulders and thighs and shoulder-blades of the other.

Each of them was engaged in smiting the other in this way from the twilight of the early morning till the hour of evening's close. "Let us leave off from this now, O Cu Chulainn!" said Ferdiad.

"Aye, let us leave off if the hour is come," said Cu Chulainn.

They parted then, and threw their arms away from them into the hands of their charioteers. Though in comparison it had been the meeting of two happy, blithe, cheerful, joyful men, their parting that night was of two that were sad, sorrowful, and full of suffering. They parted without a kiss, a blessing, or any other sign of friendship, and their servants disarmed the steeds and the heroes; no healing nor curing herbs were sent from Cu Chulainn to Ferdiad that night, and no food nor drink was brought from Ferdiad to him. Their horses were not in the same paddock that night. Their charioteers were not at the same fire.

They passed that night there. It was then that Ferdiad arose early on the morrow and went alone to the ford of combat, and dauntless and vengeful and mighty was the man that went thither that day, Ferdiad the son of Daman. For he knew that that day would be the decisive day of the battle and combat; and he knew that one or the other of them would fall there that day, or that they both would fall. It was then he donned his battle-garb of battle and fight and combat. He put his silken, glossy trews with its border of speckled gold next to his white skin. Over this, outside, he put his brown-leathern, well-sewed kilt. Outside of this he put a huge, goodly flagstone, the size of a millstone, the shallow stone of adamant which he had brought from Africa, and which neither points nor edges could pierce. He put his solid, very deep, iron kilt of twice molten iron over the huge goodly flag as large as a millstone, through fear and dread of the *gae bulga* on that day. About his head he put his crested war-cap of battle and fight and combat, whereon were forty carbuncle-gems beautifully adorning it and studded with red-enamel and crystal and rubies and with shining stones of the Eastern world. His angry, fierce-striking spear he seized in his right hand. On his left side he hung his curved battle-sword, which would cut a hair against the stream with its keenness and sharpness, with its gold pommel and its rounded hilt of red gold. On the arch-slope of his back he slung his massive, fine, buffalo shield of a warrior whereon were fifty bosses, wherein a boar could be shown in each of its bosses, apart from the great central boss of red gold. Ferdiad performed divers brilliant, manifold, marvellous feats on high that day, unlearned of any one before, neither from foster-mother nor from foster-father, neither from Scathach nor from Uathach nor from Aife, but he found them of himself that day in the face of Cu Chulainn.

Cu Chulainn likewise came to the ford, and he beheld the various, brilliant, manifold, wonderful feats that Ferdiad performed on high. "Thou seest yonder, O Loeg, my master, the divers bright, numerous, marvellous feats that Ferdiad performs one after the other, and therefore, O Loeg," cried Cu Chulainn, "if defeat be my lot this day, do thou prick me on and taunt me and speak evil to me, so that the more my spirit and anger shall rise in me. If, however, before me his defeat takes place, say thou so to me and praise me and speak me fair, to the end that greater may be my courage."

"It certainly shall be done so, if need be, O Cucuc," Loeg answered.

Then Cu Chulainn, too, girded on his war-harness of battle and fight and combat about him, and performed all kinds of splendid, manifold, marvellous feats on high that day which he had not learned from any one before, neither with Scathach nor with Uathach nor with Aife.

Ferdiad observed those feats, and he knew they would be plied against him in turn.

"What weapons shall we resort to to-day?" asked Cu Chulainn.

"With thee is the choice of weapons till night-time," Ferdiad responded.

"Let us go to the Feat of the Ford, then," said Cu Chulainn.

"Aye, let us do so," answered Ferdiad. Albeit Ferdiad spoke that, he deemed it the most grievous thing whereto he could go, for he knew that Cu Chulainn used to destroy every hero and every battle-soldier who fought with him in the Feat of the Ford.

Great indeed was the deed that was done on the ford that day. The two horses, the two champions, the two chariot-fighters of the west of Europe, the two bright torches of valour of the Gael, the two hands of dispensing favour and of giving rewards and jewels and treasures in the west of the northern world, the two veterans of skill and the two keys of bravery of the Gael, the man for quelling the variance and discord of Connacht, the man for guarding the cattle and herds of Ulster, to be brought together in an encounter as from afar, set to slay or to kill each other, through the sowing of dissension and the incitement of Ailill and Medb.

Each of them was busy hurling at the other in those deeds of arms from early morning's gloaming till the middle of noon. When midday came, the rage of the men became wild, and each drew nearer to the other.

Thereupon Cu Chulainn gave one spring once from the bank of the ford till he stood upon the boss of Ferdiad son of Daman's shield, seeking to reach his head and to strike it from above over the rim of the shield. Straightway Ferdiad gave the shield a blow with his left elbow, so that Cu Chulainn went from him like a bird onto the brink of the ford. Again Cu Chulainn

THE CATTLE-RAID OF COOLEY

sprang from the brink of the ford, so that he lighted upon the boss of Ferdiad's shield, that he might reach his head and strike it over the rim of the shield from above. Ferdiad gave the shield a thrust with his left knee, so that Cu Chulainn went from him like an infant onto the bank of the ford.

Loeg espied that. "Woe, then, O Cu Chulainn," cried Loeg, "it seems to me the battle-warrior that is against thee hath shaken thee as a woman shakes her child. He has washed thee as a cup is washed in the tub. He hath ground thee as a mill grinds soft malt. He hath pierced thee as a tool bores through an oak. He hath bound thee as the bindweed binds the trees. He hath pounced on thee as a hawk pounces on little birds, so that no more hast thou right or title or claim to valour or skill in arms till the very day of doom and of life, thou little imp of an elf-man!"

Thereat for the third time Cu Chulainn arose with the speed of the wind, and the swiftness of a swallow, and the dash of a dragon, and the strength of a lion into the clouds of the air, till he alighted on the boss of the shield of Ferdiad son of Daman, so as to reach his head that he might strike it from above over the rim of his shield. Then it was that the warrior gave the shield a violent powerful shake, so that Cu Chulainn flew from it into the middle of the ford, the same as if he had not sprung at all.

It was then the first distortion of Cu Chulainn took place, so that a swelling and inflation filled him like breath in a bladder, until he made a dreadful, many-coloured, wonderful bow of himself, so that as big as a giant or a sea-man was the hugely brave warrior towering directly over Ferdiad.

Such was the closeness of the combat they made, that

their heads encountered above and their feet below and their hands in the middle over the rims and bosses of their shields.

Such was the closeness of the combat they made, that their shields burst and split from their rims to their centres.

Such was the closeness of the combat they made, that their spears bent and turned and shivered from their tips to their rivets.

Such was the closeness of the combat they made, that the boccanach and the bannanach (the puck-faced sprites and the white-faced sprites) and the spirits of the glens and the uncanny beings of the air screamed from the rims of their shields and from the guards of their swords and from the tips of their spears.

Such was the closeness of the combat they made, that the steeds of the Gael broke loose affrighted and plunging with madness and fury, so that their chains and their shackles, their traces and their tethers snapped, and the women and children and the undersized, the weak and the madmen among the men of Erin broke out through the camp southwestward.

At that time they were at the edge-feat of the swords. It was then Ferdiad caught Cu Chulainn in an unguarded moment, and he gave him a thrust with his tusk-hilted blade, so that he buried it in his breast, and his blood fell into his belt, till the ford became crimsoned with the clotted blood from the battle-warrior's body. Cu Chulainn endured it not under Ferdiad's attack, with his death-bringing, heavy blows, and his long strokes and his mighty middle slashes at him.

Then Cu Chulainn bethought him of his friends from the fairy-mound and of his mighty folk who would come and defend him and of his scholars to protect him, whenever he would be hard-pressed in the combat. It

THE CATTLE-RAID OF COOLEY

was then that Dolb and Indolb arrived to help and to succour their friend, namely Cu Chulainn, and one of them went on either side of him and they smote Ferdiad, the three of them, and Ferdiad did not perceive the men from the fairy-mound. Then it was that Ferdiad felt the onset of the three together smiting his shield against him, and thence he called to mind that, when they were with Scathach and Uathach, learning together, Dolb and Indolb used to come to help Cu Chulainn out of every stress wherein he was.

Ferdiad spoke; "Not alike are our foster-brothership and our comradeship, O Cu Chulainn."

"How so, then?" asked Cu Chulainn.

"Thy friends of the fairy-folk have succoured thee, and thou didst not disclose them to me before," said Ferdiad.

"Not easy for me were that," answered Cu Chulainn, "for if the magic veil be once revealed to one of the sons of Mil, none of the Tuatha De Danann will have power to practise concealment or magic. And why complainest thou here, O Ferdiad?" said Cu Chulainn; "thou hast a horn skin whereby to multiply feats and deeds of arms on me, and thou hast not shown me how it is closed or how it is opened."

Then it was they displayed all their skill and secret cunning to one another, so that there was not a secret of either of them kept from the other except the *gae bulga*, which was Cu Chulainn's alone. Howbeit, when the fairy friends found Cu Chulainn had been wounded, each of them inflicted three great, heavy wounds on Ferdiad. It was then that Ferdiad made a cast to the right, so that he slew Dolb with that goodly cast. Then followed the two woundings and the two throws that overcame him, till Ferdiad made a second throw toward Cu Chulainn's left, and with that throw he stretched low and killed Indolb dead on the floor of the ford. Hence it is that the story-teller sang the verse:

> Why is this called Ferdiad's Ford,
> Even though three men on it fell?
> None the less it washed their spoils—
> It is Dolb's and Indolb's Ford!

What need to relate further! When the devoted, equally great sires and warriors, and the hard, battle-victorious wild champions that fought for Cu Chulainn had fallen, it greatly strengthened the courage of Ferdiad, so that he gave two blows for every blow of Cu Chulainn's. When Loeg mac Riangabra saw his lord being overcome by the crushing blows of the champion who oppressed him, Loeg began to stir up and rebuke Cu Chulainn, in such a way that a swelling and inflation filled Cu Chulainn from the top to the ground, so that he made a dreadful, wonderful bow of himself like a rainbow in a shower of rain, and he made for Ferdiad with the violence of a dragon or with the strength of a blood-hound.

And Cu Chulainn called for the *gae bulga* from Loeg mac Riangabra. This was its nature: in the stream it was made ready, and from between the fork of the foot it was cast; the wound of a single spear it gave when it entered the body, and thirty barbs it had when it opened, and it could not be drawn out of a man's flesh till the flesh had been cut about it.

Thereupon Loeg came forward to the brink of the river and to the place where the fresh water was dammed, and the *gae bulga* was sharpened and set in position. He filled the pool and stopped the stream and checked the tide of the ford. Ferdiad's charioteer watched the work, for Ferdiad had said to him early in the morning, "Now, gillie, do thou hold back Loeg from

THE CATTLE-RAID OF COOLEY 583

me to-day, and I will hold back Cu Chulainn from thee and thy men forever."

"This is a pity," said Ferdiad's charioteer; "no match for him am I; for a man to combat a hundred is he amongst the men of Erin, and that am I not. Still, however slight his help, it shall not come to his lord past me."

Thus were the charioteers: two brothers were they, namely, Id mac Riangabra and Loeg mac Riangabra. As for Id mac Riangabra, he was then watching his brother thus making the dam till he filled the pools and went to set the *gae bulga* downwards. It was then that Id went up and released the stream and opened the dam and undid the fixing of the *gae bulga*. Cu Chulainn became deep purple and red all over when he saw the setting undone of the *gae bulga*. He sprang from the top of the ground so that he alighted light and quick on the rim of Ferdiad's shield. Ferdiad gave a strong shake of the shield, so that he hurled Cu Chulainn the measure of nine paces out to the westward over the ford. Then Cu Chulainn called and shouted to Loeg to set about preparing the *gae bulga* for him. Loeg hastened to the pool and began the work. Id ran and opened the dam and released it before the stream. Loeg sprang at his brother and they grappled on the spot. Loeg threw Id and handled him sorely, for he was loath to use weapons on him. Ferdiad pursued Cu Chulainn westwards over the ford. Cu Chulainn sprang on the rim of the shield. Ferdiad shook the shield, so that he sent Cu Chulainn the space of nine paces eastwards over the ford. Cu Chulainn called and shouted to Loeg and bade him stop the stream and make ready the spear. Loeg attempted to come nigh it, but Ferdiad's charioteer opposed him, so that Loeg turned upon him and left him on the sedgy bottom of the ford. He gave him many a heavy blow with clenched fist on the face and countenance, so that he broke his mouth and his nose and put out his eyes and his sight, and left him lying wounded and full of terror. And forthwith Loeg left him and filled the pool and checked the stream and stilled the noise of the river's voice, and set in position the *gae bulga*. After some time Ferdiad's charioteer arose from his death-cloud, and set his hands on his face and countenance, and he looked away towards the ford of combat and saw Loeg fixing the *gae bulga*. He ran again to the pool and made a breach in the dike quickly and speedily, so that the river burst out in its booming, bounding, bellying, bank-breaking billows making its own wild course. Cu Chulainn became purple and red all over when he saw the setting of the *gae bulga* had been disturbed, and for the third time he sprang from the top of the ground and alighted on the edge of Ferdiad's shield, so as to strike him over the shield from above. Ferdiad gave a blow with his left knee against the leather of the bare shield, so that Cu Chulainn was thrown into the waves of the ford.

Thereupon Ferdiad gave three severe woundings to Cu Chulainn. Cu Chulainn cried and shouted loudly to Loeg to make ready the *gae bulga* for him. Loeg attempted to get near it, but Ferdiad's charioteer prevented him. Then Loeg grew very wroth at his brother, and he made a spring at him, and he closed his long, full-valiant hands over him, so that he quickly threw him to the ground and straightway bound him. And then he went from him quickly and courageously, so that he filled the pool and stayed the stream and set the *gae bulga*. And he cried out to Cu Chulainn that it was ready, for it was not to be discharged without a quick

THE CATTLE-RAID OF COOLEY 585

word of warning before it. Hence it is that Loeg cried out:

> Ware! beware the *gae bulga*,
> Battle-winning Culann's Hound! and the rest.

And he sent it to Cu Chulainn along the stream.

Thus it was that Cu Chulainn let fly the white *gae bulga* from the fork of his irresistible right foot. Ferdiad began to defend the ford against Cu Chulainn, so that the noble Cu Chulainn arose with the swiftness of a swallow and the wail of the storm-play in the rafters of the firmament, so that he laid hold of the breadth of his two feet of the bed of the ford, in spite of the champion. Ferdiad prepared for the feat according to the report thereof. He lowered his shield, so that the spear went over its edge into the watery, water-cold river. And he looked at Cu Chulainn, and he saw all his various venomous feats made ready, and he knew not to which of them he should first give answer, whether to the "Fist's breast-spear," or to the "Wild shield's broad-spear," or to the "Short spear from the middle of the palm," or to the white *gae bulga* over the fair, watery river.

When Ferdiad saw that his gillie had been thrown and heard the *gae bulga* called for, he thrust his shield down to protect the lower part of his body. Cu Chulainn gripped the short spear that was in his hand, cast it off the palm of his hand over the rim of the shield and over the edge of the corselet and hornskin, so that its farther half was visible after piercing Ferdiad's heart in his bosom. Ferdiad gave a thrust of his shield upwards to protect the upper part of his body, though it was help that came too late. Loeg sent the *gae bulga* down the stream, and Cu Chulainn caught it in the fork of his foot, and when Ferdiad raised his shield Cu Chulainn threw the *gae bulga* as far as he could cast underneath at Ferdiad, so that it passed through the strong, thick, iron apron of wrought iron, and broke in three parts the huge, goodly stone the size of a millstone, so that it cut its way through the body's protection into him, till every joint and every limb was filled with its barbs.

"Ah, that blow suffices," sighed Ferdiad. "I am fallen of that! But, yet one thing more: mightily didst thou drive with thy right *foot*. And it was not fair of thee for me not to fall by thy *hand*." And he yet spoke and uttered these words:

> O Cu of grand feats,
> Unfairly I am slain!
> Thy guilt clings to me;
> My blood falls on thee!
>
> No meed for the wretch
> Who treads treason's gap,
> Now weak is my voice;
> Ah, gone is my bloom!
>
> My ribs' armour bursts,
> My heart is all gore;
> I battled not well;
> I am smitten, O Cu!
>
> Unfair, side by side,
> To come to the ford.
> 'Gainst my noble ward
> Hath Medb turned my hand!
>
> There will come rooks and crows
> To gaze on my arms,
> To eat flesh and blood.
> A tale, Cu, for thee!

Thereupon Cu Chulainn hastened towards Ferdiad and clasped his two arms about him, and bore him with all his arms and his armour and his dress northwards over the ford, so that it would be with his face to the

THE CATTLE-RAID OF COOLEY

north of the ford, in Ulster, the triumph took place and not to the west of the ford with the men of Erin. Cu Chulainn laid Ferdiad there on the ground, and a cloud and a faint and a swoon came over Cu Chulainn there by the head of Ferdiad. Loeg espied it and the men of Erin all arose for the attack upon him.

"Come, O Cucuc," cried Loeg; "arise now from thy trance, for the men of Erin will now come to attack us, and it is not single combat they will allow us, now that Ferdiad son of Daman son of Daire is fallen by thee."

"What availeth it me to arise, O gillie," said Cu Chulainn, "now that this one is fallen by my hand?" In this wise the gillie spoke, and he uttered these words and Cu Chulainn responded:

Loeg.	Now arise, O Emain's Hound; Now most fits thee courage high. Ferdiad hast thou thrown—of hosts— God's fate! How thy fight was hard!
Cu Chulainn.	What avails me courage now? I'm oppressed with rage and grief, For the deed that I have done On his body sworded sore.
Loeg.	It becomes thee not to weep; Fitter for thee to exult! That red-speared one thee hath left Plaintful, wounded, steeped in gore!
Cu Chulainn.	Even had he cleaved my leg, And one hand had severed, too; Woe, that Ferdiad—who rode steeds— Shall not ever be in life!
Loeg.	Liefer far what has come to pass, To the maidens of the Red Branch; He to die, thou to remain; They grudge not that ye should part!

Cu Chulainn.	From the day I left Cooley, Seeking high and splendid Medb, Carnage has she had—with fame— Of her warriors whom I've slain!
Loeg.	Thou hast had no sleep in peace, In pursuit of thy great Cattle-Raid; Though thy troop was few and small, Oft thou wouldst rise at early morn!

Cu Chulainn began to lament and bemoan Ferdiad, and he spoke these words:

"Alas, O Ferdiad," said he, "it was thine ill fortune thou didst not take counsel with any of those that knew my real deeds of valour and arms, before we met in clash of battle!

"Unhappy for thee that Loeg mac Riangabra did not make thee blush in regard to our comradeship!

"Unhappy for thee that the truly faithful warning of Fergus thou did not take.

"Unhappy for thee that dear, trophied, triumphant, battle-victorious Conall counselled thee not in regard to our comradeship!

"For those men would not have spoken in obedience to the messages or desires or orders or false words of promise of the fair-haired woman of Connacht.

"For well do those men know that there will not be born a being that will perform deeds so tremendous and so great among the Connachtmen as I, till the very day of doom and of everlasting life, whether at handling of shield and buckler, at plying of spear and sword, at playing at draughts and chess, at driving of steeds and chariots."

And he spoke these warm words, sadly, sorrowfully in praise of Ferdiad:

"There shall not be found the hand of a hero that will wound warrior's flesh, like the cloud coloured Ferdiad!

THE CATTLE-RAID OF COOLEY 589

"There shall not be heard from the gap of danger the cry of the red-mouthed Badb to the winged shade-speckled flocks of phantoms!

"There shall not be one that will contend for Cruachan that will obtain covenants equal to thine, till the very day of doom and of life henceforward, O red-cheeked son of Daman!" said Cu Chulainn.

Then it was that Cu Chulainn arose and stood over Ferdiad. "Ah, Ferdiad," said Cu Chulainn, "greatly have the men of Erin deceived and abandoned thee, to bring thee to contend and do battle with me. For no easy thing is it to contend and do battle with me on the Cattle-Raid of Cooley! And yet never before have I found combat that was so sore or distressed me so as thy combat, save the combat with Oenfer Aife, mine own son." Thus he spoke and he uttered these words:

> Ah, Ferdiad, betrayed to death,
> Our last meeting, oh, how sad!
> Thou to die, I to remain.
> Ever sad our long farewell!
>
> When we over yonder dwelt
> With our Scathach, steadfast, true,
> This we thought, that till the end of time,
> Our friendship never would end!
>
> Dear to me thy noble blush;
> Dear thy comely, perfect form;
> Dear thine eye, blue-grey and clear;
> Dear thy wisdom and thy speech!
>
> Never strode to rending fight,
> Never wrath and manhood held,
> Nor slung shield across broad back,
> One like thee, Daman's red son!
>
> Never have I met till now,
> Since I slew Aife's only son,
> One thy peer in deeds of arms,
> Never have I found, Ferdiad!

> Finnabair, Medb's daughter fair,
> Beauteous, lovely though she be,
> As a gad round sand or stones,
> She was shown to thee, Ferdiad!

Then Cu Chulainn turned to gaze on Ferdiad. "Ah, my master Loeg," cried Cu Chulainn, "now strip Ferdiad and take his armour and garments off him, that I may see the brooch for the sake of which he entered on the combat and fight with me."

Loeg came up and stripped Ferdiad. He took his armour off him and he saw the brooch and he placed the brooch in Cu Chulainn's hand, and Cu Chulainn began to lament and mourn over Ferdiad, and he spoke these words:

> Alas, golden brooch;
> Ferdiad of the hosts,
> O good smiter, strong,
> Victorious thy hand!
>
> Thy hair blond and curled,
> A wealth fair and grand.
> Thy soft, leaf-shaped belt
> Around thee till death!
>
> Our comradeship dear;
> Thy noble eye's gleam;
> Thy golden-rimmed shield;
> Thy sword, worth treasures!
>
> Thy white-silver torque
> Thy noble arm binds.
> Thy chess-board worth wealth;
> Thy fair, ruddy cheek!
>
> To fall by my hand,
> I own was not just!
> It was no noble fight!
> Alas, golden brooch!
>
> Thy death at Cu's hand
> Was dire, O dear calf!
> Unequal the shield
> Thou hadst for the strife!

THE CATTLE-RAID OF COOLEY

> Unfair was our fight,
> Our woe and defeat!
> Fair the great chief;
> Each host overcome
> And put under foot!
> Alas, golden brooch!

"Come, O Loeg, my master," cried Cu Chulainn; "now cut open Ferdiad and take the *gae bulga* out, because I may not be without my weapons."

Loeg came and cut open Ferdiad and he took the *gae bulga* out of him. And Cu Chulainn saw his weapons bloody and red-stained by the side of Ferdiad, and he uttered these words:

> O Ferdiad, in gloom we meet.
> Thee I see both red and pale.
> I myself with unwashed arms;
> Thou liest in thy bed of gore!
>
> Were we yonder in the East,
> With Scathach and our Uathach,
> There would not be pallid lips
> Twixt us two, and arms of strife!
>
> Thus spoke Scathach trenchantly,
> Words of warning, strong and stern:
> "Go ye all to furious fight;
> German, blue-eyed, fierce will come!"
>
> Unto Ferdiad then I spoke,
> And to Lugaid generous,
> To the son of fair Baetan,
> German we would go to meet!
>
> We came to the battle-rock,
> Over Loch Linn Formait's shore,
> And four hundred men we brought
> From the Isles of the Athissech!
>
> As I and Ferdiad brave stood
> At the gate of German's fort,
> I slew Rinn the son of Nel;
> He slew Ruad son of Fornel!

Ferdiad slew upon the slope
Blath, son of Colba Red-sword.
Lugaid, fierce and swift, then slew
Mugairne of the Tyrrhene Sea!

I slew, after going in,
Four times fifty grim, wild men.
Ferdiad killed—a furious horde—
Dam Dremenn and Dam Dilenn!

We laid waste shrewd German's fort
O'er the broad bespangled sea.
German we brought home alive
To our Scathach of broad shield!

Then our famous nurse made fast
Our blood-pact of amity,
That our angers should not rise
Amongst the tribe of noble Elg!

Sad the morn, a day in March,
Which struck down weak Daman's son.
Woe is me, the friend is fallen
Whom I pledged in red blood's draught!

Were it there I saw thy death,
Midst the great Greeks' warrior-bands,
I'd not live on after thee,
But together we would die!

Woe, what us befell therefrom,
Us, dear Scathach's fosterlings,
Sorely wounded me, stiff with gore,
Thee to die the death for ever!

Woe, what us befell therefrom,
Us, dear Scathach's fosterlings,
Thee in death, me, strong, alive.
Valour is an angry strife!

"Good, O Cucuc," said Loeg, "let us leave this ford now; too long are we here!"

"Aye, let us leave it, O my master Loeg," replied Cu Chulainn. "But every combat and battle I have fought seems a game and a sport to me compared with the

THE CATTLE-RAID OF COOLEY

combat and battle of Ferdiad." Thus he spoke, and he uttered these words:

> All was play, all was sport,
> Till Ferdiad came to the ford!
> One task for both of us,
> Equal our reward.
> Our kind gentle nurse
> Chose him over all!
>
> All was play, all was sport,
> Till Ferdiad came to the ford!
> One our life, one our feat,
> One our skill in arms.
> Two shields gave Scathach
> To Ferdiad and me!
>
> All was play, all was sport,
> Till Ferdiad came to the ford!
> Dear the shaft of gold
> I smote on the ford.
> Bull-chief of tribes,
> Braver he than all!
>
> Only games and only sport,
> Till Ferdiad came to the ford!
> Loved Ferdiad seemed to me,
> After me would live for ever!
> Yesterday, a mountain's size—
> He is but a shade to-day!
>
> Only games and only sport,
> Till Ferdiad came to the ford!
> Lion, furious, flaming, fierce;
> Swollen wave that wrecks like doom!
>
> Three things countless on the Cattle-Raid
> Which have fallen by my hand:
> Hosts of cattle, men and steeds,
> I have slaughtered on all sides!
>
> Though the hosts were great,
> That came out of Cruachan wild,
> More than a third and less than half,
> Slew I in my direful sport!

> Never trod in battle's ring;
> Banba nursed not on her breast;
> Never sprang from sea or land,
> King's son that had larger fame!

Thus far the Combat of Ferdiad with Cu Chulainn and the Tragic Death of Ferdiad.

(Translated from the Irish by Dr. Joseph Dunn.)

STANDISH O'GRADY

The Outlawed Chieftain

INTRODUCTION

ONE of the most romantic incidents in the history of Elizabethan Ireland is the well-known story of the capture and captivity in Dublin and the escape thence of the famous warrior Hugh Roe O'Donnell. The flight was effected on Christmas Eve, 1591. After adventures and sufferings which I have elsewhere described, he was borne half dead with cold and hunger across the Wicklow hills, then covered with deep snow, into the wild gorge of Glenmalure to the protection of a warlike chieftain, Feagh MacHugh O'Byrne, whose principal stronghold was in that romantic glen. The boy's feet were frost-bitten and lamed. He was straightway put to bed, to use the phraseology of the times, "laid upon a bed of healing," and carefully nursed and tended by the old chieftain's best leeches. So Christmas time passed for the much-wronged Hugh Roe. Through the windows of his little hut he saw the snow-clad mountains, caught the gleam of a passing morion or polished

THE OUTLAWED CHIEFTAIN 595

battle-axe head as the chieftain's trusty sentinels paced to and fro. He heard the curious sounds incident to the daily life of Feagh's semi-barbarous mediæval stronghold, and the murmurings of Avonbeg swollen with melting snow rushing forward and downward to join the Avonmore. As he grew stronger faces famous in Irish history came and went about his couch, faces very kind and friendly to him, though terrible enough to the then rulers of Ireland. There came old Feagh the warrior and spoiler, and his wife the Lady Rose O'Byrne, the last reference to whom that I have discovered is an Order in Council that she should be burnt in the Castle Yard, presumably for high treason. There came Feagh's sons, Turlough and Felim and Raymond, all characters of historical dignity and interest; his son-in-law, the Brown Geraldine; and, not to extend the list of Hugh Roe's kind Glenmalure friends, Feagh's foster-son, Anthony O'More, chieftain designate, as I may say, of the Queen's County, which from time immemorial had been O'More territory, though now mainly occupied by grantees and Crown tenants. His name Anthony was shortened and softened into Owny; as Owny he figures in all contemporary documents, English and Irish. He was eldest son of a celebrated warrior and chieftain of the Queen's County named Rory Ogue O'More, and was at this time about the same age as Hugh Roe, that is to say, about nineteen. As every one was then known by a patronymic title, the boy's full style was Owny mac Rory Ogue O'More. A short time before this the Viceroy Fitzwilliam, whose eyes were fixed upon the lad wrote concerning him to Burleigh—"Owny mac Rory Ogue O'More hath lately taken weapon" (*i.e.* been solemnly invested with arms and knighted). "He is a lad of a bold and stirring spirit. The O'Mores look to him to be their captain." This boy became very famous afterwards in the Tyrone wars. There is a likeness of him in the first plate of the *Pacata Hibernia,* which has been reproduced in Miss Lawless's *History of Ireland,* in "The Story of the Nations" series. This fine boy, as yet without a stain of blood on his hands, was one of Hugh Roe's kind friends and frequent visitors when he lay on his couch of healing at Glenmalure. His father, Rory Ogue, is the chief character in the story which I am about to relate.

A few miles from Glenmalure, at Newcastle, there was settled these years an English gentleman of high birth and considerable influence in the State. He was Sir Harry Harrington, nephew of Sir Henry Sidney, and therefore first cousin of Sir Philip. Sir Harry Harrington of Newcastle, and old Feagh of Glenmalure were good friends and neighbours. They were quite intimate and neighbourly—a curious and significant fact, for Sir Harry was a member of the Council, and Feagh was in fact anything but a pillar of the State. Whoever observed Sir Harry closely would have seen that he lacked the little finger of the right hand, and whoever saw him stripped saw a body cut and scarred like a carbonado. Who did all this cutting and carving upon the body of Sir Harry Harrington of Newcastle? It was Rory Ogue O'More, father of Owny, Hugh Roe's new friend, and it is the story of that cutting and carving which I am about to relate. Rory Ogue and Sir Harry are the chief *dramatis personæ* of the story, the incidents of which I have collected from the Sidney State Papers, the Calendar of State Papers (Ireland), the notes of Sir John Harrington's translation of Ariosto, the Four Masters, Derrick's *Image of Ireland,* and Philip O'Sullivan's *Historia Hiberniæ.* In telling the story I assume the classical privilege of occasionally putting speeches into the mouths of the chief characters—speeches such as under the circumstances they were likely to have delivered.

CHAPTER I

RORY OGUE O'MORE

IN the year 1575 Sir Henry Sidney, "Big Henry of the Beer," as the Four Masters affectionately style him, came for the last time into Ireland as Chief Governor of the realm. Along with him came his nephew, Harry Harrington, the history of whose severe woundings and bodily harms I desire to tell.

Young Harrington was by Sir Henry appointed to the most dangerous and stirring service at the time to be found in Ireland—viz., that of the Queen's County, the ancient kingdom or principality of Leix. There the nation of the O'Mores were in fierce rebellion under their captain, Rory Ogue O'More, and young Harrington was bound to see there a great deal of warlike work of a peculiar and Irish variety. The land question in Leix was in course of solution according to sixteenth-century methods. It was, indeed, a most burning question, literally so; it had reduced to cinders not only Leix but a considerable proportion of the adjoining counties of Carlow, Meath, Dublin, the King's County, Kildare, and Kilkenny. Rory Ogue, in assertion of alleged ancestral rights there, which were denied by the Government, had wasted and burnt far and wide, burnt the open country and a great many walled towns, till the name of Rory was a terror in the land, and women silenced crying children with Rory's dreadful name. Rory turns up throughout the State Papers in as many forms as that old sea-god with whom Ulysses grappled in the midst of his seals. Now he was an army with banners and bag-pipes, cavalry and infantry, now a swift troop of plunderers destroying and fleeing, fleeing and destroying; his course, traceable in the night by lines of burning houses, in the day by pillars of smoke and the wailing of women. We find him a buttress of the State leaning on and leant on by the Government. We find him the turbulent lord besieging the castles of his neighbours, annexing the lands of his neighbours, while the weak Government, affecting slumber, looked out as it were with one eye half unclosed, on the *laisser-faire* principle. For our chieftainry, like the English baronage, asserted the right of private war, and the Government acquiesced. Thus we find in the annals for this reign the following curious entry—"Ulick, son of Richard Sassenagh, Earl of Clanricarde, and his brother Shane of the Clover, were at war with each other this year, but they were both at peace with the Government." Anon, Rory, sheathing his sword, rides to Dublin, to Court, as a great lord with his lifeguard and feudal retinue, creating a flutter in viceregal circles as well by his lofty bearing and his size, for he was a giant in stature, as by the fame of his exploits. Anon, he is on the war-path again, and this time against the State. Sometimes Rory was not heard of for weeks or months. Men hoped that he was dead or fled. The wasted lands revived, burnt towns and villages were timidly rebuilt, flocks and herds began to graze again in Leix. Here and there a timorous husbandman drove a scant furrow, praying God and His saints to keep Rory Ogue away. Men spoke of Rory as a thing of the past, and recounted dreadful tales as of ancient days. Suddenly, without premonitory symptoms, the chieftain again, in all his terrors and horrors, burst upon the half-settled country.

THE OUTLAWED CHIEFTAIN

He had been under leeches on "a bed of healing," had been in the south secretly with the Graces and Butlers, or on the other side of the Shannon with Shane of the Clover, a congenial spirit, refitting his shattered fortunes, collecting means for the renewal of the truceless war. Sometimes he was a prince, sometimes a Robin Hood. Now he was the hospitable feudal lord, dispensing a flowing hospitality to English and Irish alike, and anon the terror of the land, slaughtering and burning English and Irish without distinction, or a fugitive and an outlaw drinking water out of his shoe, and with a long stick toasting steaks cut from the loins of a stolen ox. Yet, the wife of this thief was first cousin to the Earl of Ormond, who, with the Earls of Leicester and Essex, kept the barriers in jousts before the Queen. Rory Ogue was in fact one of the first gentlemen of Ireland. Such was life then. Nor was there anything very peculiar in his career; it was only Irish and Elizabethan and quite *en régle*. Given a certain combination of circumstances, let Court breezes sit but for a while in a certain quarter, and the Earl of Ormond himself, playfellow of Edward VI., patron of Spenser, one of the greatest nobles of the Empire, would lead just such a life; to-day a pillar of the State, to-morrow a plunderer, passing through the land like a plague, his eye not sparing children; anon, a fugitive stealing one cow, and on a long stick broiling steaks cut from her side, just like Rory. A great western chief once led such a life, yet he married the widow of Sir Philip Sidney, who was also widow of Robert Earl of Essex. Rory must not be all mistaken for a rapparee. He was, as I have said, one of the great gentlemen of the realm. Great lords filed petitions of right against the Crown so, and not unfrequently, by sticking manfully to their work, carried off all the honours and profits of the controversy. Rory Ogue's western ally,

Shane of the Clover, and Shane's brother, Ulick, Earl of Clanricarde, wrung their own terms from the Government by downright war and rebellion; and the Earl of Ormond, too, in a manner and by deputy, played the same high game and won.

Who had the right in this controversy of Rory Ogue O'More *versus* Regina? Frankly, I cannot tell. It would require a volume adequately to set out the mere facts of the controversy, and the arguings *pro* and *con*, would fill another. Rory, at least, was perfectly certain that he was in the right. It was not for a claim in which he only half believed that the O'More, lord of many castles and rent-producing lands, converted himself into a demon of the pit, breathing flame and suffering himself as much pain as he inflicted. But he was O'More, had rights inherited from afar, nigh two thousand years old. These he would uphold against all men, and rather be rolled into his grave than surrender.

There is really something almost sublime in the manner in which these Elizabethan lords grappled with injurious governments, in the desperate resolution with which they on their side stripped for the duel, ready to endure all things and inflict all things. Such a stript chieftain, his own land first wasted and his own castles first broken, almost audibly addressed the ruling powers thus;—"Here, O injurious Viceroy, I stand and defy you. Death has no terrors for me, nor has cold or famine, nor the slaughter of my people, nor wakeful nights and laborious days. I defy you, Lord Deputy, and Hell at your back; and put me to the proof now, and you will find Hell going out of me."

We have seen landlords in our time rolled out of their estates much more ignobly. But these rebel lords of the Elizabethan age were a tough and stubborn breed. I sometimes feel as if such men as Rory Ogue had

THE OUTLAWED CHIEFTAIN

gathered into themselves the very strength of the elements, according to that strange pagan incantation which figures as one verse in St. Patrick's Hymn—

> I bind to myself to-day
> The swiftness of the wind,
> The power of the sea,
> The hardness of rocks,
> The endurance of the earth, &c., &c.

CHAPTER II

SIR HENRY SIDNEY ON THE SITUATION

SUCH was the enemy with whom young Harry Harrington was called upon by his uncle to contend. "It is the gap of danger, dear Harry,"—Sir Henry said as he gave the lad his last instructions,—"the gap of danger and a forlorn hope. Our sweet Saviour shield thee, my dear nephew, from the bullets and battle-axes of that bloody villain. Leix is the unbarred door of the fortress and the ingate of the Pale. If Rory drives us thence, all our many enemies in those regions have a free inroad into the heart of the settled country. The O'Conors of Ifaily, the O'Carrolls of Ely, the Foxes, M'Geoghegans, and Tyrrells of Westmeath, will confederate themselves under him as captain, and the O'Byrnes and O'Tooles on this side, joining hands with him, will raise again the discontented Geraldines of Kildare, for the Earl is not too well affected to the State, and he is led at will by his kinsmen. If Rory wins, the traitor Ormond will be at his old work again, playing Royalist at Court, while his bloody brethren and all his nation prey and burn the loyal subject. Don't trust a Butler, Harry, not the length of the lane. If Rory wins, Ormond wins, and the House of Sidney is disgraced and overthrown. But he will not win. I have sworn never again to make peace with him save on my own terms. He came to me in Kilkenny, and knelt before me in the Cathedral Church. He had a full advantage of my then distress and perplexities, harassed as I was by Ormond and his brute ally the Ox.[1] Such slaughterings and burnings as Rory's I thought that I never should forgive, but I was enforced, and now he is out again, and has overthrown the shire, and makes prey on the good subject over all the Midlands. There are a thousand pounds on his head by proclamation. That ought to serve well. Trust not the Englishmen over much. Even here, around Dublin, I know too well the false hearts of the Palesmen, and the new-comers are hardly a whit more reliable. Don't trust them over much, for by marriage or concubinage, or by interest and secret treaties, they are often closely allied with the rebels. Neither too much distrust the Irish. Amongst the worst of those rebel natives the Queen has staunch friends. No man in Ireland has been friendlier to myself, or more serviceable to the State, than Turlough Lynagh, The O'Neill, or a deadlier enemy to myself and to the State than Ormond. At the worst, dear Harry, warring in Leix and on Rory Ogue thou wilt learn what Irish war is like. An thou canst capture or kill that bloody villain Rory, or induce or compel him to accept decent terms, thy reputation is secured. For myself, why, Sidney will then unbuckle his harness with right goodwill and lay down his offices. Then for my gardens and my books, and a peaceful mug of home-brewed ale. Try this, Harry, good 'Saxon ale of bitterness,' lad, not the sweet stuff that these islanders delight in. My Irish friends, as thou knowest, have pleasantly nicknamed me Henri Mor na Beora, that is to say, 'Big Henry of the Beer.' Well

---

[1] *A private nickname of Sidney's for the Earl of Thomond.*

THE OUTLAWED CHIEFTAIN 603

they may; I love the liquor, and have made it serve me too. With beer I conquered the Butlers, and clipped the wings of high-flying Black Tom. Drink from the *mether*. Nay, lad, the corner, the corner! I shan't put on my sister's son, and a boy, the jest I played on some fine gentlemen at court. Be governed by circumstances, Harry, as they arise. Thy associate in the Government will be one who assuredly ought to understand his business, Alexander Cosby, son of Francis. How his father found the time to beget him passeth comprehension. If the stout captain Francis put but a tithe of himself into the lad he will do well, though I profess such butcherly soldiers art not much to my liking," &c., &c.

Sidney (Big Harry of the Beer), though not free from the criminality which characterized statesmen of that wicked age was, on the whole, a high-minded, generous and loyal sort of man, handsome, of a fine presence, huge and bulky in stature, merry and witty, and extremely courteous, a worthy father of that paragon of chivalry, Sir Philip. The story of how he conquered the Butlers with beer is amusing. When he invaded Tipperary, the Butlers' country, his army fell into a panic. They felt like boys entering a den full of "unpastured dragons." Sidney gathered them together, speeched them, and set a great many barrels of beer flowing. Under the mingled effect of oratory and strong ale the army plucked up its heart. The soldiers declared they would kill him if he did not lead them against the Butlers, and that night nothing was heard in camp but the singing of war-songs, whistling of war-tunes, sharpening of swords, and imprecations on the whole breed, seed, and generation of the Butlers.

CHAPTER III

Young Harry Harrington Goes North to War

So young Harrington, with troops provided by his uncle, full of young confidence and vainglory, went down to that burned and blasted country, associated himself with Alexander Cosby, and marched to and fro defending the country against Rory, who was at the time unable to make head against his enemies in the open field. For a while the Viceroy received good tidings. One day, however, came a pale messenger out of Leix and stood before Sir Henry. Such a face pulled Priam's curtains. "Your Honour, I bring bad news from Leix. Alexander Cosby and Harry Harrington are prisoners with Rory Ogue. He took them at a parley, and where they are now no one knows."

Here was an untoward revolution of fortune's wheel. Rory Ogue had now a hostage worth the pecuniary value of the whole of the blasted and burned territory, and was determined to utilize his advantage to the uttermost. On the heels of that doleful messenger came another, Rory's ambassador or pursuivant, stating the terms on which the outlawed chief would submit to the Government. But Sir Henry, though ready to pay every penny he could spare to save the life of his sister's son, would not as the Queen's Deputy consent to Rory's high territorial demands. He felt that concession here would be a blow to his honour and a serious injury to the prestige of the State. Rory permitted him to open communications with the prisoner, and young Harrington wrote to the Viceroy saying, "I will die rather than give my consent to those conditions. Never mind my worthless life."

I have always thought that Ireland is the richer for

THE OUTLAWED CHIEFTAIN 605

every brave and generous act performed by any one upon her soil, whether stranger or native. Sir Henry's loyalty to the State on this occasion and his nephew's submission to his fate, are quite in the early Roman style. Those noble historians, the Irish Four Masters, would have been quick enough to recognize, and that generously, the behaviour of these brave Englishmen.

In short, though Rory had his hostages he could make nothing out of them. Harrington was ready to die, and Sir Henry willing that he should die rather than see The O'More triumph at the expense of the State. Rory hesitated and pondered, and while he pondered the wheel of fortune took another turn disastrous to Rory. Rory keeping a firm grip on his valuable pair of hostages, lay for the time *perdu*. He had dismissed the bulk of his forces with orders to hold themselves in readiness at call. Of these hostages, the second, Alexander Cosby, was son to one of the remarkable men of the age. When the Queen's County was confiscated and made shire land by Philip and Mary, Francis Cosby, one of the bravest, and also one of the bloodiest and most ferocious men of his time, was appointed captain of the shire. Whether a hero or a ruffian, or, as is most probable, a mixture of both, he was certainly not a man to be despised, and fought his hot corner as well as any hot corner was ever fought before or since. Concerning him I excerpt the following anecdote from the pages of an old historian. From my knowledge of the condition of society prevailing then in Leix I have little doubt that the story is substantially true.

"Francis Cosby usually resided at Stradbally. Before his hall-door there grew a tree of great size with many wide-extending boughs. Upon this tree he used to hang not only men but women, and also male children. When women hanging from ropes dangled out of the tree, and when their babes hung beside them, throttled in tresses of their mother's hair, he used to experience an incredible satisfaction. On the other hand, when the tree had no suspended bodies, he used to address it in this wise: 'O, my tree, you seem to be affected by a great sorrow. No wonder, you are so long bare. But O tree I shall soon abate your grief; soon with bodies I shall adorn your boughs.'"

But there were barbarous reprisals upon Cosby's people too; of that we may be sure.

Attended by the most valiant and faithful of his men —Rory retired with Harrington and Cosby into the most secret of his fastnesses. It was in the depth of a forest somewhere on the borders of the County of Carlow. I don't find anywhere in Elizabethan Ireland that thorough loyalty of the clan to the chief which Sir Walter Scott so celebrates in his pictures of Highland society. In all the Irish clans there was a party in secret or open opposition to the elected chief, and the Queen had allies in every territory into which she sent her captains. On the other hand the faithfulness of the chieftain's personal retinue, of the men who lived at his board and had the charge of his person, was above reproach. Their honour was inviolate, and forms one of the most beautiful features of that strange period. Here in his forestine retreat The O'More kept watch over his hostages pending the issue. Along with him was his brother, a priest. Rory was a devout man in his own way. In feudal hall or under the greenwood tree this faithful brother said mass for Rory and shrived him. There was also with Rory a certain Cormac O'Conor, a gentleman who had been educated at the Court of England, but who, his claims on the adjoining King's County having been denied by the Government, had joined his fortunes with those of The O'More. Another unexpected sharer

THE OUTLAWED CHIEFTAIN

of the plunderer's wild existence was his wife. Rory, by way of clearing the decks for action, had first disposed of his children. They were intrusted to the secret keeping of friends beyond the limits of the war-theatre. A famous De Burgo chief at the other side of the Shannon, sheltered some of them. But Rory's faithful wife would not leave him. The Lady Margaret would taste the bitter with her lord as she had tasted the sweet. When Rory "went out" his wife went out with him, rode by him in his campaigns and forays, cowered low with him in the woods and mountains when his star was obscured. Elizabethan Ireland supplies many women of this heroic type.

CHAPTER IV

RORY CHASTISES HIS TRAPPER WITH RESULTS

Now in Rory's household there was a traitor. This person was by profession a trapper—*venator,* saith the historian—and in position, I suppose, a sort of slave. When plundered beef was not forthcoming he helped to stock the chieftain's larder with hares, rabbits, and an occasional deer. Amongst these proud men of war and gentlemen, he was a lonely and melancholy wight, a butt when they were merry, a thing to breathe themselves upon when enraged. He shared all the danger and none of the reward or the glory. Any day the branch of a Queen's County tree might bear his pendent body. Curious servile thoughts, much dumb discontent passed through his gloomy spirit as he sat watching his gins and toils waiting for the cry which told that some poor creature of the forest had come to grief. The glitter of gold, too, came and went in the dark places of his mind. There was a sum of £1,000 on the head of the man who ate his rabbits and perhaps never said "Thank you, *venator*." Rory thought as little of the trapper as of his foot-leather—serviceable stuff, his own. No one gave the sorry wight a thought or deemed that any danger could arise from such a slave. One day the trapper offended the chieftain; he was seen conversing with suspicious persons, or had been idle in his venatorial office or insolent to his superiors, or had committed some other breach of law or etiquette in the little company gathered there under the greenwood tree. The chief prescribed a flogging for the trapper, and thought no more of the matter. With aching sides and shoulders the servile man returned to his gins and toils, but there was a dangerous fire kindled in his breast. His name we don't know. Whenever our historians meet with a plebeian they withhold the name. Why should such fellows have a name at all? Nevertheless even in feudal Ireland they helped to make history.

CHAPTER V

CAPTAIN HARPOL AND THE TRAPPER

CAPTAIN HARPOL, commanding a detachment of the Royal army, lay in garrison in the Castle of Carlow, his thoughts much occupied with Rory Ogue. Indeed, it was hard for him to forget Rory, for Rory's mark was distinguishable wherever the Captain's eyes might turn. All around the castle were blackened ruins of houses, for Carlow, in spite of its castle and its strong walls, had been sacked and burnt by the terrible omnipresent Rory. Black gaunt ruins showed dolefully through the trees over the plains, the remains of country gentlemen's

THE OUTLAWED CHIEFTAIN

seats, of farmsteads and huts, destroyed by the same hand. Rory had left a dreadful mark upon five or six Irish counties. All the land around Carlow was waste and empty. The curse of Rory lay heavy along the shores of the Barrow. The peasantry had fled. Even Harpol's cattle fed only under the eye of Harpol's soldiers. Armed men watched them as they grazed, and at night drove them within the bawn of the castle, and locked and barred the gates. No one knew when or where Rory might next break out. From the Shannon to the Liffey all the midlands were a theatre for the vengeance of O'More. The fear of the great spoiler was over all the land.

Rory may have been thinking of Harpol this day, for, indeed, he was not far distant. Harpol most assuredly was thinking of Rory, and not pleasantly. Robert Harpol had an estate in Leix long since reduced to ashes and wilderness by the enraged chieftain; the charred ruins of Carlow lay under his eyes, perhaps the smoke of them in his nostrils. Yet Robert Harpol was a stout and brave man, as, indeed, were most of the Queen's captains at this time. If the chieftains were brave, the captains were equally brave. A soldier interrupted the meditations of Captain Harpol. "Your honour, there is a countryman below who hath tidings for your private ear—of great moment—of Rory Ogue."

In a moment the Constable was all alive.

"Yes, I will see him."

Enter now a rustical, shock-headed wight, indeed a very salvage man, with bright, small eyes peering through his matted glibb, and carrying nets upon his arm—in short, our friend the trapper, his loins and back still sore from Rory's punitory thong. The trapper's countenance, I fancy, was not comely at the best, nor could it have been improved by the passions which drove him thither—viz., revenge and the *auri sacra fames*. Yet to Harpol it was a face full of interest. Having louted low and glanced around him suspiciously, the salvage man drew nigh to the Captain, and unloaded himself of his secret, confidentially and familiarly, but in a fierce whisper, "Rory Ogue, with only thirty swords, is in the forest of ——, Harrington and Cosby with him. I know the place, your honour, and will bring you there and the sodgers—for a trifle." The delighted Constable did not haggle with the fellow about terms.

CHAPTER VI

CAPTAIN HARPOL'S MIDNIGHT SWOOP

As the shades of evening fell two hundred soldiers ranked themselves in the castle yard, silently without bugle call or other noise of preparation. Glad was the stout captain. This night's work, if successful, would bring to him great renown and also £1,000 in gold *minus* the trapper's stipulated fee: and remember, £1,000 then was worth possibly £15,000 now.

The night was wild, dark, and wet, *intempesta nox,* writes one historian. No moon or star lit Harpol upon his way, only the experienced mind of the trapper, who, guarded by soldiers for fear of treachery, plodded heavily forward in front of the column with his nets on his arm. With these he would not part. In his servile mind he had a purpose which will presently be disclosed. Through the moaning forest, under the tossing boughs, over soft and hard, in the teeming darkness all followed the trapper. At last he paused. The soldiers stood still, and Harpol stepped up to the guide. It was Rory's camp or fastnesse and consisted of a single good-sized house thatched with sods and bracken or rushes. It showed dimly through the night. All was wrapped in silence and slumber, the inmates dreaming such dreams as visit outlaws and plunderers.

CHAPTER VII

The Trapper's High Opinion of the Value of Traps

"This is the place," whispered the trapper. "See the house, Captain. Well, there he is. Rory is there, himself and his wife, and Cormac O'Conor, and the priest; and there in handlocks he has Harrington and Cosby. But whisper again," murmured the glibbed one. Harpol inclined helmet and martial ear. "Captain, you'll never kill him or take him less than I help you. Sure we all know Rory Ogue. He'll bang ye all hither and over around the door with his sword, and then he'll run this way down the bohareen into the wood. Captain, do you see this net?" It was dark, but probably the Captain did notice the tenacity with which the fellow stuck to his toils. "Well, Captain, I'll just spread the net here between the trees in the bohareen, and by the hand of O'More, but I'll hould him, nately, the same as I would a shtag." Even in the excitement of the moment Harpol and his friends could not forbear laughing: (*"cachinnos fecerunt,"*) under their breaths surely, at the venator's undisguised poor opinion of their prowess, and his confidence in his own art of venerie. Bidding the trapper, in some unrecorded Elizabethan phrase, "go to the deuce for a fool," Harpol prepared for the attack.

CHAPTER VIII

Rory Ogue Exhibits Terrible Sword Play

From the house two ways led into the forest. Both these Harpol beset, and with the rest of his men approached the house, marched up to the door, and bade his men break in. At the noise of the axes crashing through the door Rory awoke—all awoke. What an awakening! Seizing his sword, Rory sprang first at his captives where they lay, Harry Harrington and Alexander Cosby, and slashed at them four or five times in the dark. Calling loudly to his men, and bidding his wife and brother keep close behind him, Rory opened the door, and stepped out in the midst of his enemies, making terrible sword play as he went. The bright steel flashed this way and that, showering sparks into the night from the stricken armour of those who barred his path. The very sound of his voice, shouting the O'More war-cry, had terror in it. Men believed that Rory Ogue was superhuman, and even Sir John Harrington, the accomplished courtier and author, tells us he was an enchanter and wrought spells. Moreover, he was of great stature, and his slashings and cuttings must have been hard to endure. Stout Captain Harpol came to the aid of his men the more readily inasmuch as Rory was in his shirt, and he himself in complete steel, but soon reeled back from a tremendous blow which stunned, but did not kill him, for it alit upon his helmet. Slashing to right and left, *hinc et inde verberans*—one wishes that the trapper had caught one of them—Rory broke through the ranks of armed men, ran down the lane, and escaped into the forest. Had Harpol but taken the servile man's advice, and allowed him to spread his net in that bohareen, he would have netted not only the great spoiler, but £1,000 of good money, *minus* the trapper's fee, that night.

"Rory Ogue crept between our legs like a serpent," said Harpol's men afterwards in explanation of their poltroonery. "He sprang over our heads like a deer." "He practised magic against us and made our weapons softer than butter." What is certain is that The O'More through his strength and valour and sudden upbursting of Celtic battle-fury broke through Captain Harpol's company of well-armed men. Around Rory the ranks opened or were burst asunder by his sword-play, but closed again like stormy waters behind him. His heroic wife, the Lady Margaret O'More, was slain at his heels. So was his faithful brother. All the rest seeking to follow in the wake of the terrible Rory, were slain or driven back into the house. Harpol's men poured in pell-mell after them, and within there in the darkness a murder grim and great was committed, Harpol's men even killing each other in the wild mêlée.

When the bloody work was over and ignited torches shed a ghastly light upon the scene, the two prisoners were disengaged from the dead bodies. Alexander Cosby did not show a scratch; poor Harrington was a bleeding mass of cuts and wounds. Four or five of these were the work of Rory, the rest were given by Rory's men, and by Harpol's in the fierce mêlée in the dark. How happened it that Alexander Cosby had no wound, while young Harrington had fourteen? "An accident," said Cosby. "As I am a gentleman, a sheer accident." Nevertheless it turned out to be a bad accident for Cosby. Soon some ill-natured person suggested that he had sheltered himself under young Harrington's body, using it as a shield, which he could easily do if the first blow or two had made Harrington insensible. Whether this story was seriously believed or not, it ran round the island as a good military jest if nothing else, and Alexander Cosby never got the better of it. We can see him drop out of the saga without regret. The only other fact I remember about Alexander Cosby is that he had a wife named Dorcas.

Poor Harrington was conveyed away desperately wounded. He had fourteen wounds in all, as counted by his cousin, Sir John Harrington. His head was laid open. Sir Henry Sidney tells us that he could see his nephew's brain move. But all the fourteen wounds were found medicable save one. He lost for ever the little finger of his right hand.

Harrington lived for many years afterwards in the castle called New Castle, County Wicklow. Dublin cyclers are perpetually riding past the ruins of his castle, and past the little broken church hard by where he worshipped. Sir Philip Sidney was once here too, and prayed in the same little church. Our cyclers as they flit past might, with advantage, remember these things. Sir Harry Harrington was appointed Captain of Wicklow, and exercised a sort of command there over the O'Byrnes and O'Tooles. He and old Feagh Mac Hugh became good friends, but kept their friendship a secret.

CHAPTER IX

CONCLUSION

IN Sir Henry's household was a gentleman of a literary turn of mind called Derrick. He wrote a book, of which Sir Henry is the hero and Rory Ogue the villain, and adorned it with numerous plates, in most of which Rory Ogue is the central figure. It is called *The Image*

THE OUTLAWED CHIEFTAIN 615

of Ireland, and is a very curious and interesting monument of the times.

It was imagined that Rory could never lift up his head again after this business. Derrick was delighted. He had a plate made for his *Image in Ireland,* in which the great Rory, "whose thoughts did match the rolling sky," is represented utterly alone wandering through the forest. Behind him wolves are prowling around, expecting soon to sate their hunger on the flesh of the great spoiler. The book contains one long poem which is put into Rory's mouth, while in this woeful situation, "uttering the same most lamentably with brynishe salte tears, wolfishe tears." It begins—

"I Rori Ogge inhabitant of Leiske"

and is not such doggerel as one might expect. Such is Derrick's Rory Ogue. But such was not by any means the Rory of history. Even after this blow we find him in the field once more, with hundreds of warriors, foot and horse, and fighting pitched battles with his Irish and English enemies.

He was eventually slain in battle by the Chief of the MacGilla-Patricks or Fitz-Patricks, June 30, 1578. Sir Henry Sidney was not a little proud of this feat, which was performed under his auspices.

Rory's death is thus commemorated in the *Annals*—"Rory Ogue, son of Rory, son of Conall O'More, fell by the hand of Brian Ogue, son of Brian MacGilla Patrick, and that Rory was the chief spoiler and insurgent of the men of Ireland in his time, and no one was disposed to fire a shot against the Crown for a long time after that."

Rory's sons were scattered abroad over Ireland under the care of friendly lords and chieftains. Feagh Mac-

Hugh brought up the bravest of them, Owny. For years Feagh held this brave youth like a war-hound in the slips. Three years after Hugh Roe visited Glenmalure, Feagh slipped him, and like a hound gallant Owny flew straight upon his quarry. In short Rory's son conquered back the Queen's County, and held it for many years with a strong hand, and became more powerful and famous even than his father.

POETRY

JAMES CLARENCE MANGAN

Dark Rosaleen

O MY Dark Rosaleen,
    Do not sigh, do not weep!
The priests are on the ocean green,
    They march along the Deep.
There's wine . . . from the royal Pope
    Upon the ocean green;
And Spanish ale shall give you hope,
    My Dark Rosaleen!
    My own Rosaleen!
Shall glad your heart, shall give you hope,
Shall give you health, and help, and hope,
    My Dark Rosaleen.

Over hills and through dales
    Have I roamed for your sake;
All yesterday I sailed with sails
    On river and on lake.

The Erne . . . at its highest flood
    I dashed across unseen,
For there was lightning in my blood,
    My Dark Rosaleen!
    My own Rosaleen!
Oh! there was lightning in my blood,
Red lightning lightened through my blood,
    My Dark Rosaleen!

All day long in unrest
    To and fro do I move,
The very soul within my breast
    Is wasted for you, love!
The heart . . . in my bosom faints
    To think of you, my Queen,
My life of life, my saint of saints,
    My Dark Rosaleen!
    My own Rosaleen!
To hear your sweet and sad complaints,
My life, my love, my saint of saints,
    My Dark Rosaleen!

Woe and pain, pain and woe,
    Are my lot night and noon,
To see your bright face clouded so,
    Like to the mournful moon.
But yet . . . will I rear your throne
    Again in golden sheen;
'Tis you shall reign, shall reign alone,
    My Dark Rosaleen!
    My own Rosaleen!
'Tis you shall have the golden throne,
'Tis you shall reign, and reign alone,
    My Dark Rosaleen!

DARK ROSALEEN

Over dews, over sands
    Will I fly for your weal;
Your holy delicate white hands
    Shall girdle me with steel.
At home . . . in your emerald bowers,
    From morning's dawn till e'en,
You'll pray for me, my flower of flowers,
    My Dark Rosaleen!
    My fond Rosaleen!
You'll think of me through Daylight's hours,
My virgin flower, my flower of flowers,
    My Dark Rosaleen!

I could scale the blue air,
    I could plough the high hills,
Oh, I could kneel all night in prayer,
    To heal your many ills!
And one . . . beamy smile from you
    Would float like light between
My toils and me, my own, my true,
    My Dark Rosaleen!
    My fond Rosaleen!
Would give me life and soul anew,
A second life, a soul anew,
    My Dark Rosaleen!

O! the Erne shall run red
    With redundance of blood,
The earth shall rock beneath our tread,
    And flames wrap hill and wood,
And gun-peal, and slogan cry,
    Wake many a glen serene,
Ere you shall fade, ere you shall die,
    My Dark Rosaleen!
    My own Rosaleen!

The Judgment Hour must first be nigh,
Ere you can fade, ere you can die,
  My Dark Rosaleen!

(From the Irish of Costello.)

W. B. YEATS

Easter 1916

I HAVE met them at close of day
Coming with vivid faces
From counter or desk among grey
Eighteenth-century houses.
I have passed with a nod of the head
Or polite meaningless words,
Or have lingered awhile and said
Polite meaningless words,
And thought before I had done
Of a mocking tale or a gibe
To please a companion
Around the fire at the club,
Being certain that they and I
But lived where motley is worn:
All changed, changed utterly:
A terrible beauty is born.

That woman's days were spent
In ignorant good will,
Her nights in argument
Until her voice grew shrill.
What voice more sweet than hers
When young and beautiful,
She rode to harriers?

This man had kept a school
And rode our winged horse;
This other his helper and friend
Was coming into his force;
He might have won fame in the end,
So sensitive his nature seemed,
So daring and sweet his thought.
This other man I had dreamed
A drunken, vainglorious lout.
He had done most bitter wrong
To some who are near my heart,
Yet I number him in the song;
He, too, has resigned his part
In the casual comedy;
He, too, has been changed in his turn,
Transformed utterly:
A terrible beauty is born.

Hearts with one purpose alone
Through summer and winter seem
Enchanted to a stone
To trouble the living stream.
The horse that comes from the road,
The rider, the birds that range
From cloud to tumbling cloud,
Minute by minute they change;
A shadow of cloud on the stream
Changes minute by minute;
A horse-hoof slides on the brim,
And a horse plashes within it
Where long-legged moorhens dive,
And hens to moorcocks call.
Minute by minute they live:
The stone's in the midst of all.

Too long a sacrifice
Can make a stone of the heart.
O when may it suffice?
That is heaven's part, our part
To murmur name upon name,
As a mother names her child
When sleep at last has come
On limbs that had run wild.
What is it but nightfall?
No, no, not night but death;
Was it needless death after all?
For England may keep faith
For all that is done and said.
We know their dream; enough
To know they dreamed and are dead;
And what if excess of love
Bewildered them till they died?
I write it out in a verse—
MacDonagh and MacBride
And Connolly and Pearse
Now and in time to be,
Wherever green is worn,
Are changed, changed utterly:
A terrible beauty is born.

ANONYMOUS

By Memory Inspired

By memory inspired,
   And love of country fired,
The deeds of men I love to dwell upon;

BY MEMORY INSPIRED

      And the patriotic glow
      Of my spirit must bestow
A tribute to O'Connell that is gone, boys—gone:
Here's a memory to the friends that are gone!

      In October Ninety-seven—
      May his soul find rest in Heaven!—
William Orr to execution was led on:
      The jury, drunk, agreed
      That Irish was his creed;
For perjury and threats drove them on, boys—on:
Here's the memory of John Mitchell that is gone!

      In Ninety-eight—the month July—
      The informer's pay was high;
When Reynolds gave the gallows brave MacCann;
      But MacCann was Reynold's first—
      One could not allay his thirst;
So he brought up Bond and Byrne, that are gone, boys—gone:
Here's the memory of the friends that are gone!

      We saw a nation's tears
      Shed for John and Henry Shears;
Betrayed by Judas, Captain Armstrong;
      We may forgive, but yet
      We never can forget
The poisoning of Maguire that is gone, boys—gone:
Our high Star and true Apostle that is gone!

      How did Lord Edward die?
      Like a man, without a sigh;
But he left his handiwork on Major Swan!
      But Sirr, with steel-clad breast,
      And coward heart at best,

Left us cause to mourn Lord Edward that is gone, boys
   —gone:
Here's the memory of our friends that are gone!

> September Eighteen-three,
> Closed this cruel history,
When Emmet's blood the scaffold flowed upon:
> Oh, had their spirits been wise,
> They might then realize
Their freedom! But we drink to Mitchell that is gone,
   boys—gone:
Here's the memory of the friends that are gone!

JOHN KELLS INGRAM

The Memory of the Dead

> Who fears to speak of Ninety-eight?
> Who blushes at the name?
> When cowards mock the patriot's fate,
> Who hangs his head for shame?
> He's all a knave, or half a slave,
> Who slights his country thus;
> But a true man, like you, man,
> Will fill your glass with us.

> We drink the memory of the brave,
> The faithful and the few;
> Some lie far off beyond the wave,
> Some sleep in Ireland, too;
> All, all are gone; but still lives on
> The fame of those who died;
> All true men, like you, men,
> Remember them with pride.

THE MEMORY OF THE DEAD

Some on the shores of distant lands
Their weary hearts have laid,
And by the stranger's heedless hands
Their lonely graves were made;
But, though their clay be far away
Beyond the Atlantic foam,
In true men, like you, men,
Their spirit's still at home.

The dust of some is Irish earth,
Among their own they rest,
And the same land that gave them birth
Has caught them to her breast;
And we will pray that from their clay
Full many a race may start
Of true men, like you, men,
To act as brave a part.

They rose in dark and evil days
To right their native land;
They kindled here a living blaze
That nothing shall withstand.
Alas! that might can vanquish right—
They fell and passed away;
But true men, like you, men,
Are plenty here to-day.

Then here's their memory! may it be
For us a guiding light,
To cheer our strife for liberty,
And teach us to unite—
Through good and ill, be Ireland's still,
Though sad as theirs your fate,
And true men be you, men,
Like those of Ninety-eight.

JOHN TODHUNTER

Aghadoe

THERE's a glade in Aghadoe, Aghadoe, Aghadoe,
There's a green and silent glade in Aghadoe,
   Where we met, my Love and I, Love's fair planet in
     the sky,
O'er that sweet and silent glade in Aghadoe.

There's a glen in Aghadoe, Aghadoe, Aghadoe,
There's a deep and secret glen in Aghadoe,
   Where I hid him from the eyes of the red-coats and
     their spies
That year the trouble came to Aghadoe!

Oh! my curse on one black heart in Aghadoe, Aghadoe,
On Shaun Dhuv, my mother's son in Aghadoe,
   When your throat fries in hell's drouth salt the flame
     be in your mouth,
For the treachery you did in Aghadoe!

For they tracked me to that glen in Aghadoe, Aghadoe,
When the price was on his head in Aghadoe;
   O'er the mountain through the wood, as I stole to
     him with food,
When in hiding lone he lay in Aghadoe.

But they never took him living in Aghadoe, Aghadoe;
With the bullets in his heart in Aghadoe,
   There he lay, the head—my breast keeps the warmth
     where once 'twould rest—
Gone, to win the traitor's gold from Aghadoe!

I walked to Mallow Town from Aghadoe, Aghadoe,
Brought his head from the gaol's gate to Aghadoe,
   Then I covered him with fern, and I piled on him
      the cairn,
Like an Irish king he sleeps in Aghadoe.

Oh, to creep into that cairn in Aghadoe, Aghadoe!
There to rest upon his breast in Aghadoe!
   Sure your dog for you could die with no truer heart
      than I—
Your own love cold on your cairn in Aghadoe.

JAMES CLARENCE MANGAN

O'Hussey's Ode to the Maguire

WHERE is my Chief, my master, this bleak night,
    mavrone!
O, cold, cold, miserably cold is this bleak night for
    Hugh,
Its showery, arrowy, speary sleet pierceth one through
    and through,
Pierceth one to the very bone!

Rolls real thunder? Or was that red, livid light
Only a meteor? I scarce know; but through the midnight
    dim
The pitiless ice-wind streams. Except the hate that
    persecutes *him*
Nothing hath crueller venomy might.

An awful, a tremendous night is this, meseems!
The flood-gates of the rivers of heaven, I think, have
    been burst wide—
Down from the overcharged clouds, like unto headlong
    ocean's tide,
Descends grey rain in roaring streams.

Though he were even a wolf ranging the round green
    woods,
Though he were even a pleasant salmon in the unchain-
    able sea,
Though he were a wild mountain eagle, he could scarce
    bear, he,
This sharp, sore sleet, these howling floods.

O, mournful is my soul this night for Hugh Maguire!
Darkly, as in a dream, he strays! Before him and be-
    hind
Triumphs the tyrannous anger of the wounding wind,
The wounding wind, that burns as fire!

It is my bitter grief—it cuts me to the heart—
That in the country of Clan Darry this should be his
    fate!
O, woe is me, where is he? Wandering, houseless, deso-
    late,
Alone, without or guide or chart!

Medreams I see just now his face, the strawberry-bright,
Uplifted to the blackened heavens, while the tempestu-
    ous winds
Blow fiercely over and around him, and the smiting
    sleet-shower blinds
The hero of Galang to-night!

O'HUSSEY'S ODE TO THE MAGUIRE

Large, large affliction unto me and mine it is,
That one of his majestic bearing, his fair, stately form,
Should thus be tortured and o'erborne—that this unsparing storm
Should wreak its wrath on head like his!

That his great hand, so oft the avenger of the oppressed,
Should this chill, churlish night, perchance, be paralysed by frost—
While through some icicle-hung thicket—as one lorn and lost—
He walks and wanders without rest.

The tempest-driven torrent deluges the mead,
It overflows the low banks of the rivulets and ponds—
The lawns and pasture-grounds lie locked in icy bonds
So that the cattle cannot feed.

The pale bright margins of the streams are seen by none.
Rushes and sweeps along the untamable flood on every side—
It penetrates and fills the cottagers' dwellings far and wide—
Water and land are blent in one.

Through some dark woods, 'mid bones of monsters, Hugh now strays,
As he confronts the storm with anguished heart, but manly brow—
O! what a sword-wound to that tender heart of his were now
A backward glance at peaceful days.

But other thoughts are his—thoughts that can still in-
    spire
With joy and an onward-bounding hope the bosom of
    Mac-Nee—
Thoughts of his warriors charging like bright billows of
    the sea,
Borne on the wind's wings, flashing fire!

And though frost glaze to-night the clear dew of his
    eyes,
And white ice-gauntlets glove his noble fine fair fingers
    o'er,
A warm dress is to him that lightning-garb he ever wore,
The lightning of the soul, not skies.

AVRAN

Hugh marched forth to the fight—I grieved to see him
    so depart;
And lo! to-night he wanders frozen, rain-drenched, sad,
    betrayed—
*But the memory of the lime-white mansions his right
    hand hath laid*
In ashes warms the hero's heart!

(From the Irish of O'Hussey.)

JEREMIAH JOSEPH CALLANAN

Lament of O'Sullivan Bear

THE sun on Ivera
    No longer shines brightly;
The voice of her music
    No longer is sprightly;

LAMENT OF O'SULLIVAN BEAR

No more to her maidens
   The light dance is dear,
Since the death of our darling
   O'Sullivan Bear.

Scully! thou false one,
   You basely betrayed him,
In his strong hour of need,
   When thy right hand should aid him;
He fed thee—he clad thee—
   You had all could delight thee:
You left him—you sold him—
   May heaven requite thee!

Scully! may all kinds
   Of evil attend thee!
On thy dark road of life
   May no kind one befriend thee!
May fevers long burn thee,
   And agues long freeze thee!
May the strong hand of God
   In his red anger seize thee!

Had he died calmly,
   I would not deplore him;
Or if the wild strife
   Of the sea-war closed o'er him;
But with ropes round his white limbs
   Through ocean to trail him,
Like a fish after slaughter—
   'Tis therefore I wail him.

Long may the curse
   Of his people pursue them;
Scully, that sold him,
   And soldier that slew him!

One glimpse of heaven's light
  May they see never!
May the hearthstone of hell
  Be their best bed for ever!

In the hole which the vile hands
  Of soldiers had made thee,
Unhonoured, unshrouded,
  And headless they laid thee;
No sigh to regret thee,
  No eye to rain o'er thee,
No dirge to lament thee!
  No friend to deplore thee!

Dear head of my darling,
  How gory and pale,
These aged eyes see thee,
  High spiked on their gaol!
That cheek in the summer sun
  Ne'er shall grow warm;
Nor that eye e'er catch light,
  But the flash of the storm.

A curse, blessed ocean,
  Is on thy green water,
From the haven of Cork,
  To Ivera of slaughter:
Since thy billows were dyed
  With the red wounds of fear
Of Muiertach Oge
  Our O'Sullivan Bear.

(From the Irish.)

THOMAS OSBORNE DAVIS

Lament for the Death of Eoghan Ruadh O'Neill

"Did they dare, did they dare, to slay Owen Roe O'Neill?"
"Yes, they slew with poison him they feared to meet with steel."
"May God wither up their hearts! May their blood cease to flow!
May they walk in living death, who poisoned Owen Roe!

"Though it break my heart to hear, say again the bitter words."
"From Derry, against Cromwell, he marched to measure swords;
But the weapon of the Saxon met him on his way,
And he died at Cloc Uactair, upon Saint Leonard's day."

"Wail, wail ye for the Mighty One! Wail, wail ye for the Dead!
Quench the hearth, and hold the breath—with ashes strew the head!
How tenderly we loved him! How deeply we deplore!
Holy Saviour! but to think we shall never see him more!

"Sagest in the council was he, kindest in the hall:
Sure we never won a battle—'twas Owen won them all.
Had he lived, had he lived, our dear country had been free;
But he's dead, but he's dead, and 'tis slaves we'll ever be.

"O'Farell and Clanrickard, Preston and Red Hugh,
Audley and MacMahon, ye are valiant, wise, and true;
But what—what are ye all to our darling who is gone?
The rudder of our ship was he—our castle's corner-stone!

"Wail, wail him through the island! Weep, weep for our pride!
Would that on the battle-field our gallant chief had died!
Weep the victor of Beinn Burb—weep him, young men and old!
Weep for him, ye women—your Beautiful lies cold!

"We thought you would not die—we were sure you would not go,
And leave us in our utmost need to Cromwell's cruel blow—
Sheep without a shepherd, when the snow shuts out the sky—
Oh, why did you leave us, Owen? why did you die?

"Soft as woman's was your voice, O'Neill! bright was your eye!
Oh! why did you leave us, Owen? why did you die?
Your troubles are all over—you're at rest with God on high;
But we're slaves, and we're orphans, Owen!—why did you die?"

T. W. ROLLESTON

Clonmacnoise

In a quiet water'd land, a land of roses,
    Stands Saint Kieran's city fair;
And the warriors of Erin in their famous generations
    Slumber there.

There beneath the dewy hillside sleep the noblest
    Of the clan of Conn,
Each below his stone with name in branching Ogham
    And the sacred knot thereon.

There they laid to rest the seven Kings of Tara,
    There the sons of Cairbrè sleep—
Battle-banners of the Gael that in Kieran's plain of crosses
    Now their final hosting keep.

And in Clonmacnoise they laid the men of Teffia,
    And right many a lord of Breagh;
Deep the sod above Clan Creidè and Clan Conaill,
    Kind in hall and fierce in fray.

Many and many a son of Conn the Hundred-fighter
    In the red earth lies at rest;
Many a blue eye of Clan Colman the turf covers,
    Many a swan-white breast.

(From the Irish of Angus O'Gillan.)

JAMES STEPHENS

The County Mayo

Now with the coming in of the spring the days will stretch a bit,
And after the Feast of Brigid I shall hoist my flag and go,
For since the thought got into my head I can neither stand nor sit
Until I find myself in the middle of the County of Mayo.

In Claremorris I would stop a night and sleep with decent men,
And then go on to Balla just beyond and drink galore,
And next to Kiltimagh for a visit of about a month, and then
I would only be a couple of miles away from Ballymore.

I say and swear my heart lifts up like the lifting of a tide,
Rising up like the rising wind till fog or mist must go,
When I remember Carra and Gallen close beside,
And the Gap of the Two Bushes, and the wide plains of Mayo.

To Killaden then, to the place where everything grows that is best,
There are raspberries there and strawberries there and all that is good for men;
And if I were only there in the middle of my folk my heart could rest,
For age itself would leave me there and I'd be young again.

(From the Irish of Raftery.)

WILLIAM ALLINGHAM

Adieu to Belashanny

ADIEU to Belashanny! where I was bred and born;
Go where I may, I'll think of you, as sure as night and morn.
The kindly spot, the friendly town, where every one is known,
And not a face in all the place but partly seems my own;
There's not a house or window, there's not a field or hill,
But, east or west, in foreign lands, I'll recollect them still.
I leave my warm heart with you, tho' my back I'm forced to turn—
Adieu to Belashanny, and the winding banks of Erne!

No more on pleasant evenings we'll saunter down the Mall,
When the trout is rising to the fly, the salmon to the fall.
The boat comes straining on her net, and heavily she creeps,
Cast off, cast off—she feels the oars, and to her berth she sweeps;
Now fore and aft keep hauling, and gathering up the clew,
Till a silver wave of salmon rolls in among the crew.
Then they may sit, with pipes a-lit, and many a joke and "yarn";—
Adieu to Belashanny, and the winding banks of Erne!

The music of the waterfall, the mirror of the tide,
When all the green-hill'd harbour is full from side to side,
From Portnasun to Bulliebawns, and round the Abbey Bay,

From rocky Inis Saimer to Coolnargit sand-hills grey;
While far upon the southern line, to guard it like a wall,
The Leitrim mountains clothed in blue gaze calmly over all,
And watch the ship sail up or down, the red flag at her stern;—
Adieu to these, adieu to all the winding banks of Erne!

Farewell to you, Kildoney lads, and them that pull an oar,
A lug-sail set, or haul a net, from the Point to Mullaghmore;
From Killybegs to bold Slieve-League, that ocean-mountain steep,
Six hundred yards in air aloft, six hundred in the deep;
From Dooran to the Fairy Bridge, and round by Tullen strand,
Level and long, and white with waves, where gull and curlew stand;
Head out to sea when on your lee the breakers you discern!—
Adieu to all the billowy coast, and winding banks of Erne!

Farewell, Coolmore,—Bundoran! and your summer crowds that run
From inland homes to see with joy th' Atlantic-setting sun;
To breathe the buoyant salted air, and sport among the waves;
To gather shells on sandy beach, and tempt the gloomy caves;
To watch the flowing, ebbing tide, the boats, the crabs, the fish;

There you strike the golden ball and there you will be
    dancing.
  Who but you could foot it well? I have seen you many
      a time;
And there you rest by shining trees, where lights of
    heaven are glancing,
  Listening to the holy birds that sing the hours in
      chime.

Before our eyes, just like a flower, we saw your life un-
    folding
  As day by day you grew in bloom of early manhood's
      grace:
Ah, Death! to pluck the flower and to snatch from our
    beholding
  The head of rippled gold and the happy morning
      face.

W. B. YEATS

Meeting

HIDDEN by old age awhile
In masker's cloak and hood,
Each hating what the other loved,
Face to face we stood:
"That I have met with such," said he,
"Bodes me little good."

"Let others boast their fill," said I,
"But never dare to boast
That such as I had such a man
For lover in the past;

And I'm too poor to hinder you; but, by the cloak I'm
    wearing,
If I had but *four* cows myself, even though you were
    my spouse,
I'd thwack you well to cure your pride, my Woman of
    Three Cows!

(From the Irish.)

THOMAS BOYD

"Ballyvourney"

He came from Ballyvourney and we called him "Bally-
    vourney,"
  The sweetest name in Erinn that we know,
And they tell me he has taken now the last, the last
    long Journey,
  And it's young he is, it's young he is so very far to go.

He came from Ballyvourney, from the town set in the
    morning
  That has caught the lights, the lights of Dawn, we
    have waited for so long,
And he was Ballyvourney, the Child of Erinn's morning
  In his hope that shone before him, in his speech more
    sweet than song.

Where are you, Ballyvourney? God is good and will be
    giving
  Their own heaven, as they wish it, to the Gael:
In an island like our island there in joy you will be living
  Where the simple joys you loved will never fail.

Who knows in what abodes of want those youths were
driven to house?
Yet *you* can give yourself these airs, O Woman of Three
Cows!

O, think of Donnell of the Ships, the Chief whom nothing daunted—
See how he fell in distant Spain, unchronicled, un-
chanted!
He sleeps, the great O'Sullivan, where thunder cannot
rouse—
Then ask yourself, should *you* be proud, good Woman
of Three Cows!

O'Ruark, Maguire, those souls of fire, whose names are
shrined in story—
Think how their high achievements once made Erin's
highest glory—
Yet now their bones lie mouldering under weeds and
cypress boughs,
And so, for all your pride, will yours, O Woman of
Three Cows!

Your neighbour's poor, and you, it seems, are big with
vain ideas,
Because, *inagh,* you've got three cows—one more, I
see, than *she* has.
That tongue of yours wags more at times than Charity
allows,
But if you're strong, be merciful, great Woman of
Three Cows!

The Summing up

Now, there you go! You still, of course, keep up your
scornful bearing,

JAMES CLARENCE MANGAN

The Woman of Three Cows

O WOMAN of Three Cows, *agra!* don't let your tongue thus rattle!
O, don't be saucy, don't be stiff, because you may have cattle.
I have seen—and, here's my hand to you, I only say what's true—
A many a one with twice your stock not half so proud as you.

Good luck to you, don't scorn the poor, and don't be their despiser,
For worldly wealth soon melts away, and cheats the very miser,
And Death soon strips the proudest wreath from haughty human brows;
Then don't be stiff, and don't be proud, good Woman of Three Cows!

See where Momonia's heroes lie, proud Owen More's descendants,
'Tis they that won the glorious name, and had the grand attendants!
If *they* were forced to bow to Fate, as every mortal bows,
Can *you* be proud, can *you* be stiff, my Woman of Three Cows!

The brave sons of the Lord of Clare, they left the land to mourning;
Mavrone! for they were banished, with no hope of their returning—

As such I liked, as such caressed,
　　She still was constant when possessed,
　　　　She could do more for no man.

　　But oh, her thoughts on others ran,
　　　　And that you think a hard thing;
　　Perhaps she fancied you the man,
　　　　And what care I one farthing?
　　You think she's false, I'm sure she's kind;
　　I take her body, you her mind,
　　　　Who has the better bargain?

WILLIAM CONGREVE

False Though She Be

False though she be to me and love,
　　I'll ne'er pursue revenge;
For still the charmer I approve,
　　Though I deplore her change.

In hours of bliss we oft have met:
　　They could not always last;
And though the present I regret,
　　I'm grateful for the past.

I SHALL NOT DIE FOR THEE

Why should I expire
  For the fire of any eye,
Slender waist or swan-like limb,
  Is't for them that I should die?

The round breasts, the fresh skin,
  Cheeks crimson, hair so long and rich;
Indeed, indeed, I shall not die,
  Please God, not I, for any such.

The golden hair, the forehead thin,
  The chaste mien, the gracious ease,
The rounded heel, the languid tone,
  Fools alone find death from these.

Thy sharp wit, thy perfect calm,
  Thy thin palm like foam of sea;
Thy white neck, thy blue eye,
  I shall not die for thee.

Woman, graceful as the swan,
  A wise man did nurture me,
Little palm, white neck, bright eye,
  I shall not die for thee.

(From the Irish.)

WILLIAM CONGREVE

Song

Tell me no more I am deceived,
  That Chloe's false and common;
I always knew, at least believed,
  She was a very woman.

Alas! on that night when the horses I drove from the
    field,
That I was not near from terror my angel to shield.
She stretched forth her arms—her mantle she flung to
    the wind,
And swam o'er Loch Lene her outlawed lover to find.

Oh, would that a freezing, sleet-winged tempest did
    sweep,
And I and my love were alone, far off on the deep!
I'd ask not a ship, or a bark, or pinnace, to save,—
With her hand round my waist I'd fear not the wind or
    the wave.

'Tis down by the lake where the wild-tree fringes its
    sides
The maid of my heart, my fair one of Heaven resides;
I think as at eve she wanders its mazes along,
The birds go to sleep by the sweet, wild twist of her
    song.

(From the Irish.)

DOUGLAS HYDE

I Shall Not Die for Thee

For thee I shall not die,
    Woman high of fame and name;
Foolish men thou mayest slay,
    I and they are not the same.

JAMES STEPHENS

A Glass of Beer

THE lanky hank of a she in the inn over there
Nearly killed me for asking the loan of a glass of beer;
May the devil grip the whey-faced slut by the hair,
And beat bad manners out of her skin for a year.

That parboiled ape, with the toughest jaw you will see
On virtue's path, and a voice that would rasp the dead,
Came roaring and raging the minute she looked at me,
And threw me out of the house on the back of my head!

If I asked her master he'd give me a cask a day;
But she, with the beer at hand, not a gill would arrange!
May she marry a ghost and bear him a kitten, and may
The High King of Glory permit her to get the mange.

JEREMIAH JOSEPH CALLANAN

The Outlaw of Lough Lene

OH, many a day have I made good ale in the glen,
That came not of stream or malt—like the brewing of men.
My bed was the ground; my roof, the greenwood above,
And the wealth that I sought, one far kind glance from my love.

It's there you'll see the gamblers, the thimbles and the garters,
And the sporting Wheel of Fortune with the four and twenty quarters.
There was others without scruple pelting wattles at poor Maggy,
And her father well contented and he looking at his daughter.

It's there you'll see the pipers and fiddlers competing,
And the nimble-footed dancers and they tripping on the daisies.
There was others crying segars and lights, and bills of all the races,
With the colour of the jockeys, the prize and horses' ages.

It's there you'd see the jockeys and they mounted on most stately,
The pink and blue, the red and green, the Emblem of our nation.
When the bell was rung for starting, the horses seemed impatient,
Though they never stood on ground, their speed was so amazing.

There was half a million people there of all denominations,
The Catholic, the Protestant, the Jew and Prespetarian.
There was yet no animosity, no matter what persuasion,
But *failte* and hospitality, inducing fresh acquaintance.

THE RAKES OF MALLOW

When at home with dadda dying
Still for Mallow water crying;
But where there's good claret plying,
    Live the rakes of Mallow.

Living short, but merry lives;
Going where the devil drives;
Having sweethearts, but no wives,
    Live the rakes of Mallow.

Racking tenants, stewards teasing,
Swiftly spending, slowly raising,
Wishing to spend all their lives in
    Raking as in Mallow.

Then to end this raking life,
They get sober, take a wife,
Ever after live in strife,
    And wish again for Mallow.

ANONYMOUS

Galway Races

It's there you'll see confectioners with sugar sticks and dainties,
The lozenges and oranges, lemonade and the raisins;
The gingerbread and spices to accommodate the ladies.
And a big crubeen for threepence to be picking while you're able.

The Masque of Time ended,
Shall glow into one.
It shall be with thee for ever
Thy travel done.

PADRAIC COLUM

A Cradle Song

O, MEN from the fields!
Come gently within.
Tread softly, softly,
O! men coming in.

Mavourneen is going
From me and from you,
Where Mary will fold him
With mantle of blue!

From reek of the smoke
And cold of the floor,
And the peering of things
Across the half-door.

O, men from the fields!
Soft, softly come thro'.
Mary puts round him
Her mantle of blue.

A.E.

Promise

Be not so desolate
Because thy dreams have flown
And the hall of the heart is empty
And silent as stone,
As age left by children
Sad and alone.

Those delicate children,
Thy dreams, still endure:
All pure and lovely things
Wend to the Pure.
Sigh not: unto the fold
Their way was sure.

Thy gentlest dreams, thy frailest,
Even those that were
Born and lost in a heart-beat,
Shall meet thee there.
They are become immortal
In shining air.

The unattainable beauty
The thought of which was pain,
That flickered in eyes and on lips
And vanished again:
That fugitive beauty
Thou shalt attain.

The lights innumerable
That led thee on and on,

HERBERT TRENCH

She Comes Not When Noon Is on the Roses

She comes not when Noon is on the roses—
    Too bright is Day.
She comes not to the Soul till it reposes
    From work and play.

But when Night is on the hills, and the great Voices
    Roll in from sea,
By starlight and by candlelight and dreamlight
    She comes to me.

JOSEPH CAMPBELL

The Old Woman

As a white candle
In a holy place,
So is the beauty
Of an agèd face.

As the spent radiance
Of the winter sun,
So is a woman
With her travail done.

Her brood gone from her,
And her thoughts as still
As the waters
Under a ruined mill.

Each wave, that we danc'd on at morning, ebbs from us,
  And leaves us, at eve, on the bleak shore alone.

Ne'er tell me of glories, serenely adorning
  The close of our day, the calm eve of our night;—
Give me back, give me back the wild freshness of
    Morning,
  Her clouds and her tears are worth Evening's best
    light.

A.E.

Outcast

SOMETIMES when alone
At the dark close of day,
Men meet an outlawed majesty
And hurry away.

They come to the lighted house;
They talk to their dear;
They crucify the mystery
With words of good cheer.

When love and life are over,
And flight's at an end,
On the outcast majesty
They lean as a friend.

Yet we are the movers and shakers
　　　　Of the world for ever, it seems.

With wonderful deathless ditties
We build up the world's great cities,
　　And out of a fabulous story
　　We fashion an empire's glory:
One man with a dream, at pleasure,
　　Shall go forth and conquer a crown;
And three with a new song's measure
　　Can trample a kingdom down.

We, in the ages lying
　　In the buried past of the earth,
Built Nineveh with our sighing,
　　And Babel itself in our mirth;
And o'erthrew them with prophesying
　　To the old of the new world's worth;
For each age is a dream that is dying,
　　Or one that is coming to birth.

THOMAS MOORE

I Saw from the Beach

I SAW from the beach, when the morning was shining,
　　A bark o'er the waters move gloriously on;
I came when the sun from that beach was declining,
　　The bark was still there, but the waters were gone.

And such is the fate of our life's early promise,
　　So passing the spring-tide of joy we have known;

W. B. YEATS

The Meditation of the Old Fisherman

You waves, though you dance by my feet like children at play,
Though you glow and you glance, though you purr and you dart;
In the Junes that were warmer than these are, the waves were more gay,
When I was a boy with never a crack in my heart.

The herring are not in the tides as they were of old;
My sorrow! for many a creak gave the creel in the cart
That carried the take to Sligo town to be sold,
When I was a boy with never a crack in my heart.

And ah, you proud maiden, you are not so fair when his oar
Is heard on the water, as they were, the proud and apart,
Who paced in the eve by the nets on the pebbly shore,
When I was a boy with never a crack in my heart.

ARTHUR O'SHAUGHNESSY

Ode

We are the music-makers,
    And we are the dreamers of dreams,
Wandering by lone sea-breakers,
    And sitting by desolate streams;—
World-losers and world-forsakers,
    On whom the pale moon gleams:

Gleam for a moment,
And vanish away,
Of the white days
When we two together
Went in the evening,
Where the sheep lay:
We two together,
Went with slow feet
In the grey of the evening
Where the sheep lay.
Whitely they gleam
For a moment and vanish
Away in the dimness
Of sorrowful years:
Gleam for a moment,
All white, and go fading
Away in the greyness
Of sundering years.

WILLIAM ALLINGHAM

Four Ducks on a Pond

Four ducks on a pond,
A grass-bank beyond,
A blue sky of spring,
White clouds on the wing;
What a little thing
To remember for years—
To remember with tears!

EDWARD WALSH

My Hope, My Love

My hope, my love, we will go
Into the woods, scattering the dews,
Where we will behold the salmon, and the ousel in its
    nest,
The deer and the roe-buck calling,
The sweetest bird on the branches warbling,
The cuckoo on the summit of the green hill;
And death shall never approach us
In the bosom of the fragrant wood!

(From the Irish.)

SEUMAS O'SULLIVAN

The Sheep

SLOWLY they pass
In the grey of the evening
Over the wet road,
A flock of sheep.
Slowly they wend
In the grey of the gloaming,
Over the wet road
That winds through the town.
Slowly they pass,
And gleaming whitely
Vanish away
In the grey of the evening.
Ah, what memories
Loom for a moment,

On a green bed of rushes
   All last night I lay,
And I flung it abroad
   With the heat of the day.

And my love came behind me—
   He came from the South;
His breast to my bosom,
   His mouth to my mouth.

(From the Irish.)

SIR SAMUEL FERGUSON

Dear Dark Head

Put your head, darling, darling, darling,
   Your darling black head my heart above;
Oh, mouth of honey, with the thyme for fragrance,
   Who, with heart in breast, could deny you love?

Oh, many and many a young girl for me is pining,
   Letting her locks of gold to the cold wind free,
For me, the foremost of our gay young fellows;
   But I'd leave a hundred, pure love, for thee!

Then put your head, darling, darling, darling,
   Your darling black head my heart above;
Oh, mouth of honey, with the thyme for fragrance,
   Who, with heart in breast, could deny you love?

(From the Irish.)

Say that of living men I hate
Such a man the most."

"A loony'd boast of such a love,"
  He in his rage declared:
But such as he for such as me—
  Could we both discard
This beggarly habiliment—
  Had found a sweeter word.

DOUGLAS HYDE

My Grief on the Sea

My grief on the sea,
  How the waves of it roll!
For they heave between me
  And the love of my soul!

Abandoned, forsaken,
  To grief and to care,
Will the sea ever waken
  Relief from despair?

My grief, and my trouble!
  Would he and I were
In the province of Leinster
  Or County of Clare.

Were I and my darling—
  Oh, heart-bitter wound!—
On board of the ship
  For America bound.